BACK BEHIND ENEMY LINES

Chris Bridge

PEACH PUBLISHING

ISBN 978-1-78036-277-9

Published by
Peach Publishing

For my mother, Nora Bridge.

Yes, I too have a particular monster
a toad or worm curled in the belly
stirring, eating at times I cannot foretell, he
is the thing I can admit only once to anyone,
never to those who have not their own

Keith Douglas fragment

Prelude

July 2006. Northern France. A day hot enough to soften the tarmac; one of those rare days when clouds have been abolished and the sun is a brazier, edging the blue with purple and adding its own metallic tinge. It's not a day to be old.

Anna can see the glare through the window as she watches visitors queuing to go into the museum. A young girl, wearing a neat dress of blue and pink squares, is holding a small electric fan. The girl plays it round her own face in a series of circles, moving it too fast for it to be effective. Then Anna notices the small hands reach up briefly to cool her mother. When the mother smiles down at her and touches her daughter on the head, Anna experiences a tiny shard of jealousy. This is a new and strange feeling for Anna and it bothers her. The mother is wearing one of those straw hats that are to be found stacked in piles outside holiday shops; the kind of hat that protects but never looks stylish.

People move past her. Anna stays where she is, feeling disconnected, not for the first time in her life. They are outside. She is sitting in the air-conditioned chill of Memorial, the peace museum in Caen. When she left Normandy sixty one years ago she knew she could never go back. But here she is. When she was young she only wanted to forget. Now she is much older she needs to understand.

Monsieur Manchot comes into the room, greets her, opens his briefcase and takes out a thin green file which he places on the table in front of her. He performs the act like a conjuror and looks for her reaction as if she is an audience he is determined to wow.

Until that moment Anna has thought of him only as a fussy little Frenchman, rather pompous and long-winded, an exact man very careful to get things right. She notices that the moment he produces the file he places the briefcase back on the floor and lines it up with the side of the table.

She stares at the file. The people shuffling past outside cast their temporary shadows. In front of her is nothing more than a folded piece of green card. It has been much handled and in the process has lost its shine. The edges are fraying and the bottom corner of the fold is missing altogether. She can imagine how many times it has been pushed into a box or a filing cabinet and pulled out again. There is a name on the file. The name confuses her. It's not the right name and she wonders if there has been a mistake.

'Go on,' urges Monsieur Manchot, 'open it up. I've found it. I want you to read it.'

He's proud of himself, Anna thinks, and he has every right to be. She can see the excitement in his eyes. For him this is history coming to life, a rare affirmation that being an archivist matters.

But for Anna this battered green file is much too important to be hurried. She's reached the age when for whole months at a time nothing much happens. But this isn't nothing. The file might answer a question that has been snagging her thoughts for more than sixty years, irritating her like a torn nail, like someone knocking on the front door of her mind, a caller who refuses to give up and go away. This is important to her and she will take her time.

Sixty years ago she undertook an assessment, came to a conclusion, made a decision and killed a man. That moment became the turning point of her war, the tipping point of her whole life. This file may throw light on that incident. Anna has a daughter of her own but they never shared a moment like the one she has just witnessed through the glass. What happened, not far from where she now sits, cast a long shadow over her life, a shadow that has thinned but is still there.

She doesn't go to church any more, hasn't been for years. In spite of this, the language of her catholic upbringing has a hold over her still. She doesn't believe in a divine being or an after-life, but she longs to be forgiven.

She stares at the file, still reluctant to pick it up because there is another word left over from her days of faith. That word is redemption. She thinks of her life as a catalogue of mistakes. The folder may contradict this. Perhaps it will at last give her a reason to be proud of that wilful young woman who has unaccountably grown old and turned into her.

Is her German still up to this? She reaches forward, flicks open the cover and begins to read.

Part One

Normandy 1944

Chapter One

The plane rocked and shook itself, roaring through the February night.

When she remembers, Anna sees the plane differently. Unaccountably she finds she is looking down on it, as if she is in another plane, flying above the Halifax bomber, going with it to France. She sees the four engines growing out of the wings, their great propellers invisibly spinning, the Perspex turrets like bugs' eyes, alien and gleaming. Anna knows that hers is a borrowed view, purloined from a film or a photograph. The plane below her is fact. It happened, but she has never seen it like this. Her younger self was inside the plane, seeing little. It's sixty years since she lost the connection between them so remembering feels like watching a film about someone else's life, nothing to do with her.

Except there is no martial music, no film-score playing, and this isn't 2nd World War nostalgia, filling so many slots on the Yesterday Channel, programmes she has always avoided. It is a plane moving above the sea looking lonely and vulnerable, wave hopping, keeping low, monochrome in the moonlight.

All the way across, her younger self has been listening carefully to the Halifax engines, listening for a faltering, for a hiccup in the smooth endless blast of sound that was both a comfort and a threat. Now she heard a change which must mean they were gaining height. The engines sounded louder and their note was moving up the scale. The change made her look down the fuselage, past the front gunner. That confirmed her guess that they were already approaching the Normandy coast because she could no longer catch occasional glimpses of the moon-licked sea.

Gaining height was both a necessity and a danger. It was done so the navigator could look around for landmarks, something like the snail's trail of a river he could follow, or the engineered artificiality of a railway line. As soon as he found his bearings they would drop down again in case night fighters were around, in case the ack ack picked them out, silhouetted against the moonlight.

She sat very still on the narrow padded seating, leaning back on her parachute, conscious of both its softness and its flimsiness.

Fear and exhilaration. Before the war Anna had looked forward to love and marriage. The right marriage would cement her Englishness, make her belong. When the war broke out she had been twenty one, on the verge of true adulthood, ready to dive into life; believing that it would be like a placid lake on a summer's day, a surface she could splash through with a slick dive and cleave apart with her front crawl.

Liberation had been in the air. Fashions had changed, dances were modern, corsets had been abandoned. Exotic black singers sang new kinds of songs. People lived lives differently. There was a book called *Married Love*, even a Mothers' Clinic in Central London where you could get advice about contraception. 'There'll be no going back,' people said.

Her parents had tutted, thereby demonstrating a veneer of acquired Englishness. Bad things would follow, they prophesied. They looked over their shoulders at what was happening in Germany and Switzerland, the countries they had each abandoned, told her this mood couldn't last.

They had warned her and she hadn't listened. Tired of being spoken to as if she had no separate identity she had drowned out their voices. They talked of grim happenings while she dreamed of a different life, freer, more liberated. Would it never come?

Back then she'd had parents and a brother. By 1943 she found herself orphaned and alone. Her parents died in an air raid; her brother was killed in Norway. Then she hated her enemy, wanted to fight back, wished she was a man so that she could do her bit. 'I'm too weak, too short and much too female,' she'd fumed.

Shortly afterwards, out of the blue, she'd been contacted, followed by a fan dance of meetings in which she learnt of a new outfit called the Special Operations Executive (SOE) who needed people just like her, people with linguistic ability who could pass as native French speakers. Exhilaration and terror. There had been the exhilaration of being chosen and now the terror of her first assignment.

Why hadn't she made munitions, danced with soldiers, worked for the NAFFI serving sweetened tea while she waited for the war to end? She knew the answer. Because SOE had told her she was good, trained her, tested her and found no fault, had given her this assignment in what they said was a new kind of war. And she had been cocky, self-confident, taking each of their challenges in her stride, doing, they had told her, wonderfully well. So here she was: five feet four, physically weak, about to do what was only her second night time parachute jump, terrified.

Not long now and so much to remember. Over the Channel she had lost her real name, Anna Edith Julen. She would be Marie-Claire from now on, Marie-Claire Cardon. She was now a French national, wearing scratchy French knickers, her hair cut short and combed back in a French style, even her three fillings redone by a French dentist, using French amalgam. That had been a last minute thing and her mouth still felt sore from the drilling. There had been no anaesthetic. Pain was something you had to cope with, part of the training.

She felt horribly, wonderfully alone.

Other figures were in the plane but no one was sitting with her. The gunners were at their posts, helmeted and goggled. The legs of the mid gunner dangled not far from where she was sitting, turning this way and that as he continually searched the sky. The despatcher who, when the time came, would help to push out the containers and then assist her out, was somewhere up at the nose, sitting on the step, chatting to the navigator. The three containers lay on the floor of the plane just the other side of the seating area between her and the rectangular, bolted, metal hatch in the belly of the plane. The space was cramped. She'd had to step over the containers on the way in, difficult because of their bulkiness, and she knew she was too small to help push them out. They were packed with sten guns and grenades, everything the resistance group would need. The danger, she knew, was that the grenades might explode on impact, bringing the Germans to investigate. She hoped that this time it would be alright. The Special Operations Executive had learnt to pack them better, using endless layers of thin cardboard to cushion the shock.

There was so much that could still go wrong. Idly she wondered what it would be like if the plane was hit and she went down with it, if the parachute didn't open and she simply fell.

She was seated to one side facing the hatch, sitting in darkness, her back against the padded seat, her head occasionally falling against the skin of the plane. She was trying to keep warm. The pilot, navigator, dispatcher and front gunner were away to her right. The rear gunner was to her left, the mid gunner close by, above her head. Occasionally she heard them shout things to each other through the intercom system. In their terse, largely monosyllabic communication she recognised the shorthand of men who had worked together before, who were used to doing what they did.

Six of them: a team. She'd seen them at the base, standing by the enormous plane as she was driven towards it, talking, waiting, handing round cigarettes, looking at the sky, belonging to that masculine world she could never be part of, at ease with each other.

Ease, easy, tranquillité, au repos: words, states of mind she had now abandoned. There was no ease for the agent, no team, no individual she would ever be able to wholly trust.

The crew had watched her arrive and nodded towards her,

then gone back to their conversation, keeping an eye on their watches and the weather, smoking English cigarettes. She was loaded up with French cigarettes and chewing gum, things the French could no longer get hold of and so could be traded on the black market.

'Good luck, Miss,' her driver had said, then driven away. She wondered how many girls like her he had brought to the airport and how many were still alive. Was his good luck worth anything? She waited on the grass, standing apart from the others. The crew had taken no notice of her until it had been time to go. To them she was cargo, just another girl going to war.

The crates would go first and then she would jump. Usually it was the other way round, but not today. Was that because someone thought the equipment was more valuable to the war effort than she was? Or was it because the fields in the Bocage were so small that it was easy to be lost behind the high hedges, harder to hit the exact spot where her reception party was waiting? Anna had been instructed that they would locate the crates and then wait for her, get her safely away. She knew that once she had jumped the plane crew would breathe a sigh of relief, close the hatch and turn for home.

She was terrified. She was excited. Both states were dangerous. She was Marie-Claire Cardon. Her poem was Les pas from Charmes by Valéry. A French poem was better for coding the radio set, better because it kept you in the same language. From now on she must only speak one language: French. If anyone asked why her accent wasn't quite right for Normandy, she'd tell them that she had spent time in Switzerland, which is where her mother came from. For something to do she recited the poem in her head. There was no need. She knew it by heart, word for word, letter by letter, as she would need to.

Perhaps using only French was what she would find most difficult.

Her parents had always used two languages: French and German, sometimes keeping them separate, sometimes switching between them because they needed a different word or another concept. Sometimes, when they were angry with her or her brother, they slammed both languages together, swearing in both as if one was insufficient to express their anger. Which language had they died in, she wondered, when the bomb hit their London house, snuffing them both out at the same time. Had the inferno given them time to swear? She hoped not.

When the family came to England she'd had to learn another language: English. She'd bought sweets in English, gone to school in English, heard only English on the radio. Her brother (she mustn't think about him) had learnt English with her and it had become the language they shared, the one they could use to baffle their parents. English was also the language of her favourite songs: *More and more*, *It had to be you*, *That lovely weekend*.

She knew all the words. She loved singing them and now she mustn't. It was the kind of thing that could give you away. Where she was going everyone would be suspicious of her; everyone would be a potential informer.

The noise of the plane changed again. She thought this must be because they were going lower ready for the drop. She knew her landing spot wasn't far from the French coast. As if to confirm her thought, the dispatcher came slowly down the plane, climbed into the seating area and sat down opposite her, their knees close.

'Nearly there, Miss.'

It was horribly cold in the plane. They'd warned her about that and she'd had nothing to drink before clambering on board. Now she felt thirsty. When she touched her lips with her fingers they felt papery. They were stuck together in the middle and yet, in spite of having drunk nothing, she wanted to pee. There was a toilet in the plane. She could see it but it had no curtain, and even in the semi-darkness she hadn't wanted to sit there all exposed.

The plane was losing height. The lower they went the more it seemed to shiver and bump, as if the air had more holes in it the nearer the ground you got. She noticed the dispatcher was clipping himself on. She stood up and it was a mistake.

'Crates first this time. I'll tell you when we're ready for you, Miss.'

Bolts were drawn back. The hatch was lifted inwards and fixed. In the moonlight she could make out the silver lip as the darkness rushed past. The crates were readied, placed in a line across the floor, the two smaller crates first, the larger one at the back. One shove would send each of them spinning into the darkness. Every run was a danger for the crew: the fewer runs, the less danger.

The dispatcher readied himself. The navigator was shouting instructions, then just numbers, counting down from five.

'Now.'

Three crates were slid to the edge of the hatch and tipped out into the darkness. She watched as their parachute lines grew taut then went slack. Her radio was in one of those crates, sealed in its suitcase. She hoped it would land safely. She carried a spare set of crystals, just in case, strapped to her belt.

'Gone,' yelled the dispatcher.

Don't men love single words, she thought.

The plane was rising again and turning in a slow circle. Out of instinct she re-applied her lipstick. The dispatcher grimaced and she shrugged her shoulders, tried to smile.

'It's like a blind date,' she explained, savouring the last words she would speak in English for a long time. 'I need to look my best.'

The older Anna remembered the look on the dispatcher's face as the plane completed its turn, levelled out and went for the home run. It was the first time she had seen that grimness, that war-is-just-a-job look she would come to recognise in others and eventually find imprinted on her own features. He's been through three years of this already, she realised. He doesn't like the business he's in, sending little girls to war, feeding spy lines. Another thought hit her as she remembered. The top men at SOE already knew, didn't they? Normandy has already been chosen. The plans are being drawn up. But no one has told her younger self about the inferno that is coming.

'Now you, Miss,' the man said.

She must jump without showing any fear. She'd done her parachute drill at Ringway, on a rig, then from a balloon, then twice from a plane, once in daylight and only once at night. That night jump had been terrifying and the hatch had been bigger.

She clipped herself on, moved slowly to the edge of the black rushing hole and carefully sat on the silver strip, dangling her legs into the frozen air, feeling too big for this tiny space. The noise seemed louder and the plane jiggled around in the air. The hatch was so small she would have to duck her head and roll out sideways. How did bigger people manage? The dispatcher seemed to know what he was doing: he checked her parachute line and the clip, then made sure she was in the right position.

'A bit further, Miss. You're too far back.'

She shifted forward, holding onto the cold metal of the hatch edges which numbed her fingers. She mustn't overbalance. The plane was out of its long turn. It was straightening. Below her strange men waited to receive her. Were they French, might they be German? Some agents had fallen straight into enemy hands because they had been betrayed even before they touched French soil. Not every French person wanted the Allies to win.

She heard counting. She recognised at the same time that the dispatcher didn't trust her to jump, that he was getting ready to give her a push, so they didn't have to risk another run. She'd make absolutely sure that wasn't necessary.

'Now.'

She ducked her head and rolled quickly out into the silence, before he could help her out, before he could even wish her luck.

Years later Anna watches the black shape roll out of the plane and waits for the chute to open. How unbelievably brave of her younger self, how incomprehensible to her now. Alright, she thinks, I know I survived; my heart still pumps, my lungs draw in air. I am alive but I am not the same. The war made sure of that.

Chapter Two

It felt like being dead. It always did. One moment you were in a bucketing, straining, noise-ridden plane with the others and the next moment you were utterly alone, falling through silence. The transition was instant.

Her chute opened. She felt the jerk and then a new kind of stillness. For just a moment she seemed to have stopped falling.

She could see the whole of the moon now. She could make out fields and hedges below her, the Bocage, set out like a monochrome map. Just to her left there was an L shape made up of tiny points of light. The noise from the Halifax was already fading as it turned for home.

'Au revoir,' she whispered.

Looking down she focussed on the lights, saw the trees closing in on her and the hedges cutting her off from the wider view. Then the frosted grass was coming up to meet her. She had time to notice the snow patches on the north side before she was touching, knees jolted, rolling heavily onto her side, but still alive, bruised and exhilarated.

For a moment she lay still, giving her parachute time to settle. That would make it easier to roll up. Then she heard feet coming towards her, moving slowly, cautiously, looking for her between the hedges.

Had she already been betrayed? Were these feet German? Quickly she unclipped her parachute and moved away about thirty feet to the shelter of the hedge, out of the light of the moon, glad she was wearing dark clothes. Crouching there she used the chance of the darkness and of no one being close by to relieve herself copiously. That solved one problem. At the same time she reached for her pistol. She'd shoot from the hip if necessary. It was what she was best at, best in the whole training group and better than any of her instructors. She'd never done it with her knickers round her knees but she'd no doubt she could.

A minute went by, then three men were coming towards her like shadows moving across this unreal, moon-bright landscape. She stayed still. The moment they reached the parachute they began to roll it up. Not German, she thought. Germans would look for the person first. Only French would go straight to the parachute because silk was valuable.

So French. But Maquis or Milice? She'd been warned about the Milice: French nationals recruited into the Military police to do the Germans' dirty work for them, groups of thuggish Frenchmen, sadistic and without feeling. They were hated more than the Germans. If these were Milice they wouldn't know her name, couldn't ask for her.

'Marie-Claire Cardon?' Her new name came quietly across the field to where she hiding.

Yes, that was what she was now called. It was time to show herself.

'Here I am.'

'Welcome to France.'

Strangely there seemed to be no hurry. She expected them to move away from the drop zone as quickly as possible, locate the crates, call up the lorry, load them up and get away from here. Instead they began to question her. How many crates were there? Were there any packages? Did she have anything else for them?

'Like what?' she asked.

'Money.'

Said straight up. Another single word. Well, she was part of this male world now. She needed to fit in, to give as good as she got.

'Who are you?' she asked. She couldn't see his face very well. He was wearing a cap over his head so the moonlight, settling there, darkened his face. His voice was young and strong. She noticed that the other two men were hanging back, seeming to defer to him.

'Henri,' he told her. 'London calls me Racine'.

It was the right name. That anxious, wound-up part of her slowly released its tension.

'Yes, I've brought money.' She was carrying a million francs in several packages round her waist, near her precious crystals. Her landing had been good enough. She was sure they would be intact.

'Can I have?'

She was no longer frightened. Racine was the right name. She'd survived the jump. She was here.

'Sorry,' she said. 'Not now,' explaining, 'I'd have to undress first.'

'OK.' Henri spread his arms wide as he said it, stood his ground. 'Go ahead.'

She laughed. 'It's too cold.'

'It's never too cold,' countered Henri.

She threw back her head, 'Now I know I'm in France,' she told him, and stood quite still.

Other men came up to her. They asked for cigarettes and chewing gum. She gave each a pack. More figures crossed the field, asking for the same thing. Only when each had something from her did they move away. The process must have taken at least twenty minutes. What if the Germans had seen the plane and were even now on their way to intercept them, had already set up road blocks?

She listened and the night was silent. Only darkness surrounded them and the enduring cold of early spring.

The same trick is happening again. Anna finds she is looking down at heads in the moonlight, her new point of view hijacked from what it had been. How does memory work? The facts are true. She remembers both the cold and the euphoria. They had drummed it into her that this was the most dangerous point, the landing, the linking up, and they had warned her about euphoria because it took you off your guard. She even remembered that so much of what she had been told was guesswork. The Special Operations Executive was a brand new operation. It was staffed by enthusiastic amateurs. Much of the training was improvised. In all the months of hard work they had never met a real agent, for the simple reason that few if any had yet returned from active service.

Anna kept pace with Henri, walking beside him. Because she was small she had to part run to keep up but at least the exercise warmed her. He seemed aware of her but nothing else was said. Going through a gate she noticed that the three crates were already gathered there and that this gaggle of men seemed to know exactly what each person's role was. The crates, already stripped of their parachutes, were picked up without a word being spoken. The column, headed by Henri and herself, moved off towards another gate.

Beyond that gate was a lorry, waiting in a shadowed lane near cross roads, giving them several routes of escape down little roads they had probably known all their lives. She felt better still when she saw their positioning. This group knew what it was about. No one spoke. The back doors of the lorry were swung open. While the crates were loaded in, men quietly took their seats. One held out a hand to her and she was inside the lorry squeezed between two large Frenchmen, farmers she thought. Before the doors were shut she saw more figures coming from further away, emerging out of the darkness, each with a rifle. Her drop had been guarded, guarded all the way. Henri had posted lookouts in case of trouble. There was a professional feel to the whole operation.

They drove for about half an hour, going slowly without lights to avoid detection, relying on the moon to see the way. She was tired and suddenly very warm. The two men beside her radiated heat. She remembered the way she had squeezed up against her father when she was a little girl. His body had been so hot when you nestled against it. She wanted to sleep but knew she mustn't. Sleep would be seen as weakness and this group of men, mostly older, all more experienced than she was, would have to accept her authority. She would be their contact with London, receiving information, giving orders. She thought she could guess what they were all thinking. 'She's a woman, a mere slip of a girl, doesn't London know that there's a war on?' She mustn't sleep.

The lorry rocked. The men echoed the rhythm of the ride. It was hypnotic and it was one o'clock in the morning. Some of the others she noted were already sleeping, eyes closed, mouths open, heads nodding, too closely wedged to fall forward. All farmers, she thought, peasants who hate growing crops for the Germans, who resent being allowed to keep virtually nothing for themselves. They don't love us, she suddenly realised. They don't love England. We're simply the only friend they have, the only people who'll give them guns. They love the soil, this part of France. I mustn't forget that, she thought. I mustn't demand gratitude. They are the ones making the sacrifices.

The lorry turned sharply and stopped. Everyone who had been asleep woke up. From outside the lorry, doors were swung open and she had a chance to look out. They seemed to be in a large farmyard. Skilfully the crates were broken open and their contents checked as if this was a well-practised routine. Her two suitcases were set to one side. The rest was swiftly distributed among the men and then taken away to be hidden nearby. One moment the yard was full of bustling men and boxes, the next it was empty except for Henri, herself and her two cases. She checked their weight and opened the heavier one. The radio seemed intact. She wouldn't know until she used it and she couldn't use it near here. She would need to find somewhere where she could keep a look out for German tracker cars, somewhere where she put no one else into danger.

The men were coming back. Henri picked up one of her cases. She carried the radio case herself. Everyone went into the farmhouse where there was a fire and a woman standing by the stove, cooking what seemed to be a gigantic omelette.

Anna was astounded. She'd heard that the French were short of food. She asked Henri about it.

He shrugged contemptuously. 'The Germans aren't very good at what they do,' he explained. 'They're also frightened of the woods. They seem to think they might get shot if they go searching for hidden chicken coops or small clearings filled with maize. They come and they bluster but they don't find much. The shop keepers go hungry. We are okay.'

Unmarked bottles were brought out and opened. Wine was sloshed into tumblers and one of these was thrust into her hand.

'Drink.'

She would have preferred water but she drank the thin red liquid and thought, well here I am.

Someone found her a place to sit. A large plate, almost covered by an enormous triangular section of omelette, butter escaping from its edges, was plonked down in front of her. Someone gave her a fork. She wanted to say to them that she hadn't seen food like this for more than a year but she didn't. She found she was ravenously hungry and tucked in.

Round her everyone was now relaxed. The drop was a big operation for them and it had been a success. She could feel their satisfaction, could almost see it in the way their moustaches quivered. Soon they would be going back home to sleep. She felt she was amongst friendly and skilful people. The only disparate note had come from the woman who had done the cooking. Anna had distinctly heard her say to Henri, '...a girl and such a tiny one. What use can she be?'

After the meal they'd found her a bed in the farmhouse attic. She'd slept for twelve hours, woken in mid afternoon by a shout from downstairs. Her suitcases had gone, which meant no change of clothes. She dressed quickly. Although someone had clearly been in her room while she slept, no one had interfered with her belt. The money and spare crystals were still intact. Why hadn't she woken up? Had her alarm clock broken? She must make herself into a light sleeper if she was to survive. Without thinking too much about just who had been in her room and seen her sleeping she put the belt on and climbed down the ladder.

'We need to move soon,' Henri told her. 'German cars have been seen in the area. Last night's plane might have been spotted,' he explained.

All the 'packages' had already been moved. Her two cases were waiting for her in the place they'd take her to. He'd had to send them separately.

'Now what else do you have for me?' Henri asked, and held out his hand.

In the daylight she had a chance to look at him properly. He was not much older than she was. Mid thirties at the most, clean shaven, black haired, with blue eyes, young to be in command, she thought, but powerful. It wasn't only the way he held himself but the way he walked, the stillness in him. She sensed he was tense, wondered why she had been allowed to sleep for so long if she and he were in any danger. This time she didn't flirt but simply turned away from him, lifted her skirt quickly and took the money out of the hidden recess in the belt. Then she smoothed herself down and turned to face him, holding out the cash.

He took it straight to the window, holding up note after note, checking them and feeling the corners. She knew what he was looking for so she went to join him.

'The pin holes are there,' she told him, 'and the numbers aren't in sequence'.

'London's learning.'

She noticed he didn't take her word for it but continued to check, starting at several random points in the stack. The thumb of his right hand was deeply scarred as if someone had drawn a white line across his print and left it indented in the flesh.

'Right,' he said. 'Good.' He split the money into three piles, dealing it out like a pack of cards, moving backwards and forwards between the piles, never making a mistake. When he had finished he gave her one of the piles. 'I might need some of that back from you. We're getting more recruits and they need paying. Spend as little as you can. I'd keep it here but I don't want too much money in one place. Now we must get going.'

He was already moving across the floor of the kitchen towards the door. She wanted to shout at him, tell him she was thirsty and hungry, ask him about food for her. She noticed a jug of water. She picked it up before she followed him and tipped some of it into her mouth, swallowing and dribbling. There was a loaf of bread and a knife. She hacked off a chunk and followed him outside. When I get agents of my own, she thought, I'll take better care.

She didn't know what transport she expected, perhaps the lorry from last night, perhaps an old car. The yard was empty except for two cycles leaning against the barn. One was for him and the other was a girl's bike.

Henri was already astride his bike. 'You're a new farm worker,' he told her, 'taking the place of young men rounded up and sent to work in German factories. You're going to help my aunt with her farm. Her son has been sent away. You'll stay with her and do his work. If we are stopped that's the story we tell.'

'How far?' she asked.

'10, 15 kilometres.' He shrugged his shoulders.

It was more than five years since she had been on a bike. She gritted her teeth, determined she'd manage. She tried the seat and it was too low. So that's how tiny they thought she was. She'd be cycling with her knees hitting her chin and would look ridiculous, look suspicious. Henri was already out of the yard but she wasn't worried about that. I'm what matters to him, she reasoned. He wants to get rid of me. Well, I'll go better if I set the seat right to begin with.

There was a small black bag attached to the back of the seat. It had a tool kit inside it. She found the spanner and loosened the bolt, then made the adjustment, screwing the seat round to make it go higher. She was tightening it up when Henri came back.

'Quick,' he said. Back to single words. 'We must set off now.'

She didn't explain. She put the spanner back in the black pouch and mounted the bike. Much better, she thought. I might even get there.

She had to admit that he made allowances for her. Up hills especially he went slowly, even at one point getting off to walk when he was leaving her too far behind. Gradually they left the wooded areas and came out onto hill tops. Here the fields were wider and she guessed that they were given over to grazing rather than to growing crops. Her spirits soared. This was ideal radio country. If the aunt lived near here she'd be able to keep the aerial low, out of sight, let the hill do the work. She'd be able to keep a look out and stop transmitting when she had to.

They were coming towards a hamlet when Henri abruptly turned and ran his bike through a gap in the hedge. She followed and found herself in a small gravelled yard with a house on one side and a large barn next to it. Chickens strutted in the yard. A black and white dog went to the end of its chain and got ready to bark but seemed to change its mind when it saw Henri. It wagged its tail instead.

'Bikes in the shed.' Henri was off his bike and going towards the barn. Anna dismounted more carefully. She was sore and glad to be walking again. Her calves ached. She followed him into the darkness and saw that the barn had two storeys. The higher section ran for two thirds of the length of the barn and seemed to be used for storing hay. A wide, shallow raked ladder took you up there, its broad treads worn and sagging.

'Put your bike there and then follow me.'

She did as she was told, followed Henri's quick walk across the yard, noticed he didn't knock on the back door but lifted the latch and walked straight in. He didn't hold the door open for her either, just expected her to follow.

He's treating me like a man, she thought, as she passed from the last of the late winter sunshine into the darker interior. Does that mean he has accepted me as a comrade in arms? She rather doubted it.

His aunt, Madame Desaint, was over sixty, a tall woman, stooped with smart white hair tied in a bob. Her face seemed severe at first and deeply lined but Anna read something else in it as she came forward to be introduced. The woman looked tough and shrewd, unlikely to fuss over her, likely to take security seriously, the kind of person she might win over given time.

Madame Desaint's first words were not encouraging.

'Have you ever done any milking?'

She shook her head. 'No, I haven't,' she said, 'Will you teach me?'

Chapter Three

Sitting in her high-backed chair, sixty years later, Anna wonders if she could still milk, wonders if her fingers would find the rhythm, if the cows would still accept her. Perhaps it was the leaning forward which would be difficult for her old body, adopting and holding that semi-crouched position she had once slipped into so easily.

But what did it matter if she could or she couldn't? No one milked by hand anymore: it was all machines and mass production. Milking hadn't proved to be a useful skill. She'd learnt it completely, so that it had become second nature to her, something that she could do without thinking and yet, after France, she had never used it again.

But that wasn't quite true.

Now that she had given herself permission to remember, had opened the steel shutters she had so resolutely placed on her own past, the problem was that other memories too clamoured for her attention.

Whose idea had it been? It might have been her husband, Ronnie, but she thought it was her daughter, Heather. Heather's insistence, no doubt backed up by elongated sulking, had led them all to visit that farm near Princess Risborough. It was her low time, when she was left out of decisions, when it was as much as she could do to get up in the morning, manage the nanny, cook and crawl back to bed.

She remembered the five of them in the car, the way her second son, Colin, commandeered the front seat by claiming that sitting in the back made him feel sick. That meant that she was crammed in the middle at the back, keeping the peace between her eldest child, Alistair, who sulked because he felt he should have been in the front, and Heather who always sulked because she wasn't a boy.

What had the weather been like? Anna couldn't remember. No doubt they had paid money, tramped across fields, patted sheep and *peered into barns before they came round the corner and joined the milking demonstration which was about to start. A cow had been led in, an old docile cow, no doubt kept alive for this purpose.*

'Look, it's got shit stuck to its bottom,' Colin had said, loudly enough to turn several heads.

'That's enough, Colin.'

Colin had looked at her with derision. 'But it's true,' he said. 'I mean they could have wiped its bottom or even hosed it down.'

'Enough.' She had tried to insist, tried occasionally to be a mother to them, but they always treated her as a non-person, especially if their dad was nearby.

'It's a horrible, shitty old cow'.

Had she hit him, clouted him round the head in the way you weren't meant to any more, overcome by one of those periodic burst of anger? The details were suddenly blurred. Had she grabbed his hand and held onto him in a way he would hate? Perhaps she had. In either case he had clearly felt the need to get his own back because when the farmer's wife had asked for a volunteer Colin had resolutely volunteered her.

She'd shaken her head, tried not to budge from her place at the back, waited for enough time to pass so that someone else would have to do it. But then Heather and Alistair joined in and when she saw Ronnie nod she knew she had to step forward, had to accept their intended humiliation.

What was she to do, pretend she couldn't do it? Her hands wouldn't let her and besides, she found she was angry. She sat on the stool and without waiting for any instruction she patted the cow and talked to it, placed her face against its flank, reached for the warm squidgy udders and began to milk. She felt again that she was part of the pulse of something beyond her trapped, defeated present. She listened to the music of the pail and was transported, heard sounds and smelt smells that made her dizzy with longing, milked on until the pail was a third full. She was then so overcome by a sense of stumbling back into her own past that she stopped and got straight up from the stool.

'You've done this before,' said the farmer's wife.

'A little, in the war.' It was all the explanation she had been prepared to give.

Walking back to the car with her family they had made no comment, been quite uncurious, she remembered, but then it was a family thing, wasn't it, that they never asked about her past. She'd made quite sure of that.

But the thought hiccupped in her brain. Something had been said. The taboo on asking about her past had been broken. If she was to understand the life she had lived she must be truthful to herself. She was right that no immediate comments had been made; if anything her display of competence had surprised them, startled them, stunned her family into silence. No comment was made until they were back in the car, then Heather, who must have been no more than six at the time, had suddenly said, 'Mum, why were you talking those funny words?'

After the tension of her arrival came the anti-climax. Adopting her new identity, living it, seemed such a strange way to fight the war. She'd seen the east end of London with its broken houses and the gaps in the streets where houses should have been, like so many missing teeth in the city's jawbone. She knew allied armies were stuck half way up Italy, pinned down and losing men, however the newsreels liked to play it. All this was going on somewhere else. Her brother lay in a Norwegian grave, probably unmarked, and yet she lived this idyll pretending she was a milkmaid in rural France.

They gave her a house of her own, no bigger than a storage space. It was one up, one down. There was no running water. She'd have to make do with a toilet and a tap in the yard. The upstairs was no more than a deep shelf reached by a fixed ladder. In the autumn it must have been filled with hay and straw, piled up to the roof. By late February much of this had gone, although there was still more than enough to hide the radio.

Her house smelt of hay, scented with that slightly fermented, sweet echo of last summer. Bits of straw got everywhere. They hung in spiders' webs and clogged up the gaps between the stone slabs that lined the floor. They were light and bone-dry, so the small pieces that fell in a torrent when another bale was moved, skittered from her brush and preferred to jump over rather than into her dustpan. She'd begun by sleeping on the platform among the hay bales but it had been too cold so she'd been compelled to bring her bundled mattress down and sleep close to the fire.

The downstairs was draughty. She'd had to be ingenious with rags and even cow dung which she mixed with straw to block the gaps between the planks so the fire had a chance to warm the place. There was a bowl and a jug. She used the tap in the yard, bringing water that brimmed in the top of the jug and was to be poured into the bowl for washing.

Her village was on a ridge. Each morning when she came outside she looked across the valley to other hills. London had nothing like this. The openness thrilled her. Even before dawn, when she got up to do the first milking, it gave a sense of space. It was often star-dotted when she first came out, then striped with low light when the milking was done. She made a promise to herself that when the war was over she would always live in a house with a view.

Her days became routine. They each began with milking the cows, drinking a little of the warm milk, filling several churns. After that she rounded up the goats, milked them and boiled their milk to make cheese, adding rennet to make the mixture curdle. Then she separated the curds from the whey and wrapped the crumbling mixture in muslin before storing it in a small stone hut.

A good breakfast, then her delivery rounds.

Being a milkmaid meant that she could go anywhere, talk to anyone, learn as much as she could about the area. Petrol was difficult to get so she used Madame Desaint's horse and cart for her deliveries, visiting the town, keeping her eyes open, including Henri in her route so that she could pass on requests from London, ask London for anything Henri's group might need.

In the evening, after she had milked again and made her transmissions, Madame Desaint cooked for her and they ate together in the older woman's kitchen, talking about village life and farming, listing the latest inconveniences of occupation.

At night, tired out from the work and the worry, she slept well, huddled in blankets in front of what was left of the fire.

She was growing stronger, much fitter than she had ever been. Her body was changing, becoming more muscular, thinning. Was the shape of her face still oval as it said in the forged papers she carried everywhere with her?

The first time she had been stopped she was terrified. It was on the outskirts of Thury. There was a road block. A German soldier put up his hand to stop her cart while another soldier looked at her down the barrel of his gun. She was carrying nothing incriminating with her. The SOE silk maps of the area were still hidden in the loft. She hadn't yet started mapping. It was cold, mid March, one of those days that, even in France, slips back into winter. She was wearing a shawl over her head and thick woollen gloves.

She pulled on the reins and the horse stopped. She was ordered to get down, show her papers. The soldier's French accent was appalling but she understood him well enough. He didn't look at her as he spoke his commands and she tried desperately to make this into a matter of routine for her as well. She sat where she was, handed him the document and waited, looking in front of her, the very picture of a French peasant girl who wanted to be allowed to go on, thinking of the next delivery and not of interrogation and torture.

'Show me your face.'

She pretended that she hadn't heard him.

'Take the scarf off.'

She did as she was told, reluctantly, turning to look at him as she unwound the scarf, feeling the cold on her cheeks. He stared at her, looked back at the photo in her papers, looked up at her again and smiled.

She held out her hand for the documents but he seemed to be hesitating, reading the papers carefully, studying the words.

'Marie-Claire Cardon,' he said. 'I've not seen you before.'

'Then you've not been looking. I'm here three days a week. Can I have my papers?' She was pleased that her voice sounded assured even if she wasn't.

Now Anna understood. She remembered the incident, and what had seemed then to be a threat had transformed itself into something much more ordinary. She could still see the soldier's face with its close-shaven freshness, (why was the past more real than the present, so much more detailed than yesterday?). He must have been feeling lonely, stuck as he was on a cold road in a foreign country. The way she was dressed, he'd not noticed her as a woman until he saw the photo on the document. He'd probably only asked her to remove the shawl because he wanted to look at a pretty girl and she had once been pretty. Well, why not? It had been another time, another place.

He handed the papers over reluctantly. She flicked the reins and went on without speaking, relieved, triumphant. The identification papers were okay. They had been tested and she had got through.

She drew up outside the first house, a Maison de tolérance, got down and knocked on the door. She knew she'd have to knock twice. This was the brothel and the girls 'worked' late. At first she'd thought it bad-mannered to wake them at all, but then she'd got to know them and found that not only did they like to gossip but that they were excellent sources of information and such social outsiders that they could be no danger to her. It seemed that men couldn't drop their trousers without also dropping their guard.

From them she learnt about troop movements, key details

about which units were in the area, whose leave had been cancelled, what was happening with beach defences. Everyone was talking about an invasion but no one knew when or where it would happen. The French tarts both appalled and fascinated her. They talked about men as if they were a specialism, had so many words for them she didn't fully understand and didn't want to, seemed to be experts on size and shape and staying power. They mothered the younger men and felt sorry for some of the older ones, who took what seemed like forever to finish. Anna also picked up that their German bed fellows were no longer as confident as they had once been. These girls serviced the ranks. There was another brothel nearby for the officers. Sadly, it wasn't on her rounds.

Each evening she coded the vital nuggets of information, set up the aerial, opened up the case with the radio, arranged the copper coil, set the crystals. Using the radio was the most dangerous part of her day. All the time she was listening out for danger. She dreaded putting the headphones on, cutting herself off from her immediate surroundings. This too had been part of the training. Put your gun on the table just by your code pad. Take the safety catch off. You must be ready to shoot anyone who comes in through that door.

Once set she made contact, used her four checks, tapped out the code, at first letter by letter, then group by group, waited for a reply, signed off, then packed everything away. She destroyed the code sheets and swept up so there was no trace of footprints in the upstairs dust.

This way she became the part they had sent her to play. As her initial nervousness faded she began to pick up nuances. By listening intently to the responses, to the dialect of the Morse code, she could tell who was sending her messages, guessed which was a male and which a female hand, gave these unknown people names.

In spite of this familiarity she began to realise another

truth of her situation. Because the process of transmitting was dangerous and messages had to be kept short there was no warmth in the communication. Cold numbers and letters were sent and received. There was rarely any encouragement or praise, just more orders, so that she began to think of SOE as insatiable, and each of her Morse code contacts as cold-hearted. After each session, when the immediate danger of discovery was over, it would sink into her just how alone she really was.

Winter finally warmed into a secure spring and her farming duties changed. The cows went to the pasture daily now. It was her job to take them there. That first journey out of the barn she'd not forget. The cows were restless, tossing their heads and blowing out gales of air as they walked along the road. She had a stick in her hand but she didn't need to use it. The cows seemed to know where they were going, and when she opened the gate and let them into the field they ran and gambolled in ways she could scarcely believe. Rectangular galleons of cows jumped in the air, pawed at the ground and ran a little way as if they were calves again. By that afternoon, when she went to fetch them, they seemed to have forgotten their morning skittishness and gone back to just being dull, methodical, plodding, milk-making machines.

As spring warmed the landscape and she became a more familiar figure in the area she took to cycling round, taking the silk map of the area with her, carefully marking on it gun positions and guard posts. She was a stronger cyclist now and could manage the hills with greater ease, so she took to venturing further afield to satisfy her controllers' incessant demands for information.

Even with the extra risks she was taking, her own gleanings were deemed inadequate. Brutally, SOE demanded more details. To satisfy them she needed a network of her own.

Her first recruit was Franck, the son of her neighbour. He was seven, with dark hair that had a tendency to stick up as if he had recently received an electric shock. He was really skinny and he held his head high, tucking in his chin so that his head and neck looked elongated on his thin shoulders. He liked to be with the cows and, she suspected, with her. He used to run out of his house when she passed each morning on her way to pasture. She found Franck the right sized stick so that he could be her assistant in herding the cattle. He marched solemnly along at her side, occasionally prodding and shouting at a cow that had stopped to graze the new leaves on the hedge. He was one of those young lads no adult seemed to have time for, so she made a point of taking him seriously. She talked to him as an equal, and played a game with him spotting anything that changed in the village.

There was a good place for a lookout, a small knoll that commanded all approaches to the village, so she helped Franck build a den there, then suggested that he keep watch from that point every evening. He was to run and give her warning of strangers or different vehicles coming into the village, especially German cars with aerials. Evenings were her transmitting time. She bound him to secrecy, promised him chocolate which he had heard of but never tasted. He did everything she asked of him, seemed to worship her, even coming and telling her every evening after his two hour watch ended that he had seen nothing and the coast was clear.

The second recruit was Franck's grandfather. Apparently, Franck was telling everyone that he was doing something important now, something that he couldn't talk about. His mother never listened to her son's chatter but his grandfather, seeing the regular exits each evening and the new sense of purpose in the lad, had come to her with a guess about who she really was and asked if there was any way she could use him. He was a man of sixty five, white-haired, slender, stooped, too old for fighting. Because of his health (something to do with his waterworks, he once told her) he made regular visits to Caen, going fortnightly to the hospital, way beyond her cycling range. Once there he met lots of people coming in from other areas. He proved remarkably good at ferreting out information, sifting it and bringing it back to her.

Next she recruited Marcel. Madame Desaint had suggested him. Marcel was a farmer, had been one of the biggest landowners, farming the land that had been in his family for generations. Farmers hated the Germans. She knew that. They were forced to produce food for their occupiers who took most of it without paying. They were also compelled to beg for seeds and then had to work the land without the help of strong young men who had been sent to factories in other occupied lands. Farmers knew the landscape, all the hiding places, were loyal with the slow conservatism of their kind. But their limit was often the boundaries of their own land, that and the local market.

Marcel had real physical presence. He was an ex rugby player with one cauliflower ear, an upright bearing and a determined stride. He was also an astonishing worker. When a tree blew down and blocked the road he wielded the axe with such fervour that all the logs were chopped to firewood and stacked under the barn eves in a single day.

He was shrewd. When she had introduced herself and begun gradually to reveal who she was, she noticed the way his grey eyes thinned and his lips turned in on themselves. He'd listened and assessed, asked her questions and then suddenly held out his hand and smiled, told her his story. A year ago some of his pasture had been taken to build a barracks block, then more had been snatched for storage spaces. There had been no compensation. The Germans just marched in and commandeered his best fields. The new barracks not only sprouted ugly grey building where there should have been silky wheat but had made it impossible to access the next field without going the long way round. He proved admirable, strong in his hatred, security conscious and an excellent organiser. His farm had several outbuildings she ear-marked for storage when she had more equipment.

Even these three were not enough. SOE urged her to expand her area. To do this she needed people who travelled, people from the towns where she sold her cheeses. They were much more difficult and dangerous to recruit. Some worked closely with the Germans, which meant they either hated or loved them and it was difficult to tell which.

Anna held off further recruitment, balancing the gain against the risk. But as spring grew warmer the mood in the area changed. A few individuals began to seek her out. These were complete strangers from outside her own village who came straight up to her and volunteered. It put her on her guard. She told each of them as little as she could, never brought them together as a group, kept them well away from Henri and his band. Each of them she interrogated as best she could.

'Why?' she would ask. The single word was less incriminating if it remained unqualified by any detail.

'We listen to BBC,' a spruce, middle-aged dentist told her. 'It's true what they tell us isn't it? It's reliable?'

She nodded. For years the BBC had carried all the bad news.

'Well, the Germans are losing aren't they? The tide's turned hasn't it? I hear Novograd's fallen.'

She waited for more. He could be a German plant. He could be Milice.

'We know,' the dentist emphasised, 'about Anzio, about the raids on Hamburg.'

Was he genuine? He had a nice steady look and he seemed determined.

'Why are you telling me this?' she asked.

He hesitated. This is when she would know. If the reply was too gushing, if the offer was too strong, she would know and she would walk away.

'I feel guilty,' the dentist told her. 'The world is at war and

I just look after teeth. Can you use me?'

'German teeth?'

He nodded. 'All teeth,' he said as if it was a matter of sadness, 'What else can I do?'

'Encourage them to talk, ask questions,' she told him. 'Tell me the answers.'

His smile was right.

A week later when he brought information about the transfer of two key units to the Russian front she wanted to hug him.

But there must always be a gap, she reminded herself from her training; a gap between me and everyone else. They can listen in a group huddled round a hidden set. They can be a band of brothers, but because of the danger I put them in, the things SOE may make me ask of them, I have to keep myself separate. I can only survive, be useful, if I never lower my guard.

Three became seven, then nine. She loved these people for the risks they ran and she doubted them for the same reason. She often wondered if they had waited until they knew which side would win before volunteering, had waited because they wanted to be on the winning side, encouraged no doubt by de Gaulle's broadcasts. Or had they always hated the Germans but thought, until now, that the risks of fighting against them had been much too high? When she asked why one potential recruit had identified her as a British agent the old woman told her that she was far too pretty to be just a milkmaid, and much too knowing. This comment put her on her guard, made her more determined to live her cover.

But the change of mood persisted. Nine became eleven. SOE, in a rare moment of thoughtfulness, congratulated her. Henri, when she went to see him, was suffering from the same snowball effect. He was unfailingly courteous, taking his cap off and revealing a round line, high on his forehead where the weather-beaten face ended and the capped head began.

In spite of the new hopefulness he seemed to have aged over the last eight weeks. She sensed that he was strained. He complained to her, as if it was her fault, that he had too many men already, was running extra training sessions, wearing himself out. If she wanted to train these new volunteers in sabotage she must do it herself. He'd give her some sten guns and ammunition. He'd take her with them on the next raid and show her what they did but he couldn't run two groups. 'I'm sorry,' he told her. 'It's too much and the more men we have the more danger.'

She thanked him and he shrugged his shoulders, winked at her, put his cap back on, saluted her so she saw the scar on his thumb, then walked back into his farm. Even he is not my friend, she thought. I must stay friendless. In a way the thought gave her strength. She was truly independent now, way beyond her adolescent dreams. What is the final test of independence? That I can die and hurt no one by my dying. I can die and the world won't pause for an instant. I'm free from any emotional tie. Doesn't that make me the perfect soldier?

A few nights later she found herself crouching by a railway line on the edge of the track, nursing a sten gun, listening to the night sounds all round her. Just round the bend, Henri and his men were loosening bolts, removing track. It was cheaper than using explosives, much quieter and just as effective. Marcel was with the sabotage group, observing. She was standing guard. If anyone came she was to hold them up, Henri had told her. If they were Germans she must engage them. Her sten was fully loaded. She even had a spare magazine. If she started firing, others would join her. If she heard firing she was to make her way towards it.

'Engage them? Do you mean kill them?' she'd asked. She was a virgin in that sense too.

'If you have to,' Henri said, 'but only if you have to. Sometimes it's better not. Remember the reprisals.' He'd touched his cap in that curious way of his and walked back to his men.

The older Anna remembered the figure hanging from the lamppost in Tilly. She'd driven her cart towards the young man, whose arms now sagged from his shoulders as if his bones had been removed, like a straw man set to frighten people, not birds. His legs dangled like his limp arms, the toes dropping below the heels. As she came closer she'd noticed that the coated body swayed slightly in the breeze, moving backwards and forwards like an automaton.

She'd driven her cart underneath, glanced up and taken in the sliced up face and the open, glassed over, bulging eyes. He'd only hung there for a single day. As soon as night came someone had distracted the guard, while others had taken him down and buried him. Did he die and then they mutilated him? She hoped it had been that way round. She hoped he hadn't endured the deep slashes with several bayonets and then died from loss of blood. She had glimpsed his teeth through the leathery slits in his face, noticed the tongue was partly bitten through.

The younger Anna waited and no one appeared. Nothing moved. She could hear the men working, could pick out the noises made by spanners on steel, interspersed with the occasional hammer tap to loosen a nut that wouldn't budge. She knew there were other men round her, that she was part of a large protective circle.

Then she heard rustling and didn't know what to do. The wood was full of dried oak leaves. It could be a German patrol, stealthily moving forward. It could be a member of Henri's group checking on her. She turned slowly towards the noise and peered into the darkness as if she could change its opacity just with the force of her looking. She could see nothing. But the rustling continued, was getting louder, coming nearer. She looked at tree trunks, tried to make out the shapes of men or even of a rifle pointing round the edge, but she could see nothing. The noise seemed too careless to be a resistance person. It was constant, not intermittent. It wasn't made by someone darting from space to space, stopping, listening and setting off again. Whoever was making the noise didn't seem to mind being overheard. That meant it was probably Germans, carelessly carrying out a routine patrol.

Her mind stilled. Her fingers readied themselves along the frame of the sten gun. She found she wasn't frightened, just anxious to get it right. She'd much rather have been carrying her own pistol because she knew she was a crack shot. She'd spent less time with a sten gun and so there was more to think about. Ammunition was scarce. If she had to fire, she must fire in small bursts only. Single shots were best. She slipped off the safety catch.

As she waited for whatever was coming towards her she was convinced she could not be seen, she'd chosen her hiding place with such care. She could look along the track both ways but no one coming towards her from either direction would be able to pick her out because she'd made sure that the bushes included her in their darkness.

As the rustling moved towards her it seemed to be getting lower down. Perhaps it was someone moving along the ground, a man crawling? She saw the movement this time, watched the leaves being disturbed in the wind-made pile at the edge of the track. The tension emptied out of her along with the breath she quickly exhaled as a hedgehog emerged from the pile of leaves and, moving surprisingly quickly, trotted across the line, nose downwards, audibly snuffling. She started to laugh.

When she recounted this detail to Marcel he nodded, but again there was no smile. She sensed the strain in him.

Then, a few days later, her luck ran out.

Chapter Four

Two days later the sense of luck that had been with her since the landing in France was severely jolted.

She was on her bike, mapping, trying to record the German activity that she saw everywhere round her. It was mid April. Primroses and cowslips dotted the edges of fields and roadsides. New hawthorn leaves were a vivid green. You could smell the grass. The sky, as she cycled underneath its magnificence, seemed bluer than yesterday and wider than last weekend.

She'd heard of Rommel's new defences, of the concrete being slammed into sea-edged gun placements, of the barricades being strung along the coast. She'd heard of them but they were beyond her range. What she saw was increased numbers of troops everywhere. Thury seemed to be becoming something of a garrison town and, built into the hillsides some way back from the coasts, the Germans were placing guns, powerful artillery that pointed seawards.

Her habit, on mapping days, was to cycle by such places without seeming to be interested. She had trained her mind to remember. She'd appear uninterested in her surroundings but then take a single glance and look away at once, before starting to ask herself questions about what she had just seen to make the details stick: how many guns, how close to the wood's edge? How far from the road? Where were the men stationed? Could she spot where the shells were stored? In her brain she translated everything into an aerial view so that in the next woodland she could stop, pretend to need a pee, and add the detail to her map.

It was easier to do the mapping on hills when it might seem perfectly normal for a young woman to get off and walk. That gave her more time to look and check. By now Anna had no need to dismount. She could easily cycle straight up any hill in the area. Her leg muscles felt like warm iron when she washed herself. Last week she had cycled sixty kilometres in a single day.

Mapping was always dangerous. However hard she tried she couldn't recall all the detail in the evenings. That meant she had to take the silk map with her, neatly rolled up inside the handlebars, covered over by the rubber grip. It seemed to her such an obvious hiding place and if they found it they would know exactly who and what she was.

The radio and that map were the two fixed points of her life. The map was beautiful, the size of a headscarf, but with all the towns and villages printed on it as well as the physical details of hills and streams. It felt soft as only silk can, especially when there was no silk for stockings or blouses. Once she'd put it on like a headscarf to see if she could get away with that if she was caught. She looked at herself for a long time in the mirror. She could see the detail on the scarf however she tied it, but would anyone else realise? Then she looked at her face, was horrified to notice the way her eyes had sunk into her skull, the thinness of her features. She made a resolution there and then to eat more as she looked too unlike the photo in her papers. She must try to get more sleep too, but how could she when the best time for the radio was late at night and the cows had to be milked at dawn?

She also recognised something else about herself. The exhilaration was lessening and the fear was growing. Moments of relaxation became fewer. The early mornings were the best times. Then she walked her cows along the high trail, looked at the view and found time to repeat her promise to herself, that if she ever got through the war she would find the way to live in countryside like this, where you seemed to be able to look for ever.

She mapped assiduously, but however much information she transmitted, her controller, George, always wanted more.

She didn't understand George's insistence, the way he drove her. Surely the invasion couldn't come in Normandy. But in case it did she knew her duty: she was there to make as certain as she could that whichever young men were sent ashore under enemy fire, the casualties would be no heavier than they had to be.

Had someone else in a similar position been more careless with her brother's life?

Today she had come to investigate new building activity in what Marcel said had always been pasture land. It was on a hill. She slowed in case anyone was watching her and mimed tiredness, then stopped part way up the hill and began to push her bike. It was a warm afternoon. Every now and then she took a glance at what was happening. On her left a meadow used for pasture inclined away from the road. On her right the field sloped downwards, filled with already tall grass that would no doubt soon be cut for hay and used to feed the cattle next winter. The gun platforms were being built right on the edge of the field, nestling under the tree line where no plane could spot them. As she walked she kept her eyes on the road and took only occasional glances at the camouflaged gun placements, missing the bit in between, trying to get the positions fixed.

'What do you think you're up to?'

The German soldier was lying in the field under the fence. He'd been sunbathing in the long grass, taking a break. Now he was sitting up and looking at her intently. She didn't know how long he'd been watching her, didn't know what he might suspect.

'Going to see my aunt,' she told him and continued to walk, pushing her bike. She was near the top of the hill. Perhaps if she just got on the bike he'd let her ride away.

'No you don't. Stay where you are.'

She had been about to get on the bike. Obediently she stood where she was, looking sideways, across to the guns. The soldier was standing up and had climbed over the fence. Now he walked towards her. Tall, blond-haired without his cap, muscular but slightly fat, she thought.

'I've been watching you. More to the point you've been watching us.'

He was close to her. She put on her most dead-pan voice. 'Look, I'm on my way to see my aunt. I'm a milkmaid. I hate cycling up hills so I got off and walked. Of course I looked at the field, it's full of young men.'

She wasn't frightened. Fear was like an unreliable relation that vanished when you least expected it, perhaps when you most needed it.

'You didn't just gawp at our troops,' he told her. 'You were doing something funny with your eyes, looking and blinking.'

Blinking. In the intensity of her concentration she must have developed a mannerism that had given her away. She needed to distract him.

'I'm a milkmaid,' she repeated. 'Do you want to see my papers?'

It was a mistake. She realised that as soon as she said it. The French never co-operated, never offered anything. Wait until you are asked, then obey slowly and reluctantly. That was the rule and she'd broken it.

The soldier turned and shouted. She could almost feel the silk map wrapped up and stuffed inside her handlebars, a cylinder of thin metal away from her right hand. If they found it there would be nothing she could do. Two more soldiers got up from the grass, picked up rifles and pointed them at her.

'Lie the bike flat on the ground,' she was told. 'Now step away from it. Put your hands up.'

She did as she was told. One of the soldiers, a shorter man with dark hair, was already over the fence, picking up the bike, examining the tools, opening the puncture kit, taking the pump to pieces, as yet ignoring the handlebars. She stood quietly, waiting for the time to pass. They'd find it or they

44

wouldn't. They'd take her in or they'd let her go.

She could hear them talking amongst themselves, could understand the German they spoke. They thought she was a spy. They thought she was pretty, even if she had small tits. They'd all like to have her. In the experience of one of them the smaller girls were, the more they squirmed underneath you, the more they shouted. As she listened, without seeming to, she sensed that she might be alright after all. The soldier who had examined her bike was now riding it. His knees stuck out sideways and looked ridiculous with the saddle that low. Another was laughing at him. They were not much more than boys.

She was getting ready to explode with anger and demand that they give her bike back and let her go when she heard the vehicle coming along the top road and saw them leap to attention. She noticed that her bike was being carefully leant against the fence as the car drew up alongside them. She looked round slowly.

'Well.' A single word spat out, guttural, authoritative.

There were two figures in the car, a driver and an officer. The officer was smart, uniformed, grey haired and clearly Gestapo. She saw the twin lightening flashes on his lapels, took in the fineness of his coat, the kid gloves he carried in his left hand. His face was highly intelligent, the eyes dark blue and alert.

It was the eyes. She could see them still and physically winced at the memory.

'You!' He pointed at the soldier who had first stopped her. 'Tell me what you're doing.'

'I thought she might be a spy, Sir. I watched her get off her bike and walk up the hill. At first she wasn't watching the work and I thought that was odd. Then she was opening and shutting her eyes…' His voice trailed off as if he knew that he wasn't being convincing.

'And where did you watch from?'

'Sir?'

' It's an easy question. Where were you when she was walking up the hill, pushing her bike?'

The soldier stayed silent. The driver remained stony faced.

'Lying in the grass, Sir.'

'Shirking.'

'Observing.'

The officer blinked. His mouth hardened. He looked from one soldier to another and Anna saw that each of them was diminished by that stare. Then he was looking at her. She made herself into a picture of French intransigence. He continued to examine her closely, staring at her face. Then he appeared to make up his mind.

'Get in.'

She didn't move, continued to look at him dumbly.

'What are you waiting for?' he demanded.

'I need the bike. I can't leave it here.' It was rude but it was the right thing to do. No French girl would abandon a perfectly good cycle. Besides, the map was vital. It was the only one she had.

The older Anna wondered at her earlier self, at the danger and the calculation. Her younger self was risking a much more thorough search by the Gestapo and calculating that she would somehow get through it alive and go back to work. How had she been able to stay so calm? Were you born with only so much courage and when you used it up you couldn't generate any more?

'Put it in the back.'

The soldier who had been attempting to ride it quietly picked her bike up and put it in the luggage area at the back of the staff car, trying not to scratch anything.

'Now get in.'

She did as she was told.

The officer tapped his stick on the dashboard and the car moved forward.

She wanted to watch the soldiers, to observe their relief as the car swept away, but she kept her eyes fixed firmly in front of her and tried to remember the scene she had witnessed but not added to the map, fixing the details in case she ever got a chance to draw them. How many guns were there? How exactly had they fitted with the line of the wood?

The older Anna shook her head in disbelief.

They were heading back to the town. There was a Gestapo house there that she knew of, a place of terror, apparently chosen by the SS because its previous owner kept wine in especially deep cellars. She guessed that was where she would be taken for interrogation. Well, they had prepared her for this too. She had practised the lights and the questions in training, an awful experience following three days of sleep deprivation, but they always said that you never know how you will react to the reality until it wraps itself round you and puts its pliers to your front teeth. If they didn't want to shoot you in the back garden they hanged you from the meat hooks where no one would see your kick.

They were already close to the edge of the town. She stopped mapping in her head and wished the car was covered over. In case she couldn't resist interrogation she didn't want to be seen and recognised. She thought about the bike. A road check was always cursory. The soldiers hadn't looked inside the handlebars but the Gestapo certainly would. Okay, she couldn't have abandoned the bike without seeming to plead guilty. But, when the alternative had been to bring it with her, giving them time to examine it at leisure, shouldn't she perhaps have just climbed into the car without it?

Could she stand the pain? The trick, she had been told, was to anticipate so that it never took you by surprise, to tell yourself that pain didn't matter but that shame did. What condition would they leave her in? She knew she wasn't beautiful but her looks were alright, even with sunken eyes. Her teeth were good. Everyone had always said she had a lovely smile.

Get your story ready, she told herself, remember every detail. Your only chance is to prove that you have an aunt, that you sometimes do strange things with your eyes. If they found the map she would never grow old, but if she held to her will then others might. She suddenly saw Marcel's face with its earthy looks. I can silence all his doubts, she told herself. I can give nothing away. Then they will respect me as a comrade.

She had guessed correctly about where they were going. The car pulled up outside the Gestapo house in Thury. The officer waited for the driver to come round the car and open his door before getting out. She noticed that he did this without making a show. He was just a man stepping out of a car, leaving the door open for the driver to close. He didn't boss his driver and didn't thank him. He made no fuss over her either. 'Follow me,' was all he said.

Prudently she abandoned the bike and followed. Perhaps it would be there if she was released. It was more likely that she never would be released.

When she walked in she distracted herself by looking at the building, knowing that you can spend your courage before it's needed. She guessed that the house hadn't been much changed to suit its new inhabitants. The hallway was still the smart central space of a rich man's house. Where family portraits would once have been, two swastika banners hung from the ceiling. The hallway was big. Extra desks for clerks had been fitted into the space. Each had a phone and the necessary wires had been neatly tacked to the wall just below the dado rail. The officer walked straight across the hall and in through one of the doors. Anna followed. She guessed that this room had once been the dining room. When the officer sat down at the table she stood in front of it.

She was still in control, but she was becoming detached from herself as if reaching a different state of being. This new state didn't have time for fear. It was emotion-free and wholly focussed on trying to stay alive.

Then something so vivid, so unexpected. Anna remembered how she had recalled the faces of all those who had failed the training course, who were there one week and gone the next, who had wanted to be where she was now. If not for herself, for them, for those who never had the chance to stand where she was standing.

She had no plan for what she would do next apart from sticking to her original story, hoping, if it came to it, that this other relative of Henri's would vouch for her and say she was her niece. But before she mentioned anyone else's name she had to know that there was a chance. If there had to be death it should be in the singular: just her.

'Papers'.

The officer was holding out his hand. She gave him her identity card and watched him as he studied it. Much too old to be in the army, she thought. Perhaps he was called up because the war is going badly for them. He seemed to be wealthy, wore a ruby signet ring on his right hand, was that why he was in the SS? Had he used family links so that he had a better lifestyle with less possibility of being sent to the Eastern front? He seemed cultured, almost refined.

He held the card carefully and studied every detail.

Carte d'Identité

Nom
Prenom
Profession

Signalement

He read every word, looked at the signatures and then looked at her. She wondered if she should speak, decided to wait for him. He must see it was a fake, must know that one or other of the details SOE was at such pains to copy was wrong or already out of date. This wasn't a quick check at a road block. This was scrutiny. For the moment she'd act the cowed peasant girl, overawed at being in the presence of such a man. Soon she would get angry and bluster away at him but not yet.

His hands were very clean; his nails were cut in exact semi circles but the skin on the back of his hands was already well into middle age, becoming blotchy. In the gaps between his fingers she could see patches of eczema.

When he finished his examination of her documents he suddenly looked straight up at her. She recognised the look. It seemed that he might be trying to map her face, remembering the details. She was puzzled so she looked straight back at him, then remembered that a peasant girl wouldn't do that, would be too overawed, or if she did stare back would do it insolently. She had done neither. She had been studying his face as intently as he had studied hers, reading his tiredness, noticing how red his eyes were and how the lines on his forehead under the eyes were deep and square edged. In that moment he had ceased to be an enemy and was just a man.

That was how it must have started.

Quickly she dropped her gaze, but not before she saw a thin smile spread across his face.

She was instantly appalled. It hadn't needed threats and torture. He'd used her intelligence to trap her. Not a word had been spoken between them but she knew she had already revealed who and what she was.

Fuck, she thought. It was not a word she used, not a word that had ever passed her lips. She wasn't exactly sure what it meant but she'd heard the soldiers in the training camps use it continuously and it seemed suddenly appropriate. She got ready for whatever would happen next. It must be her death only. They would eventually shoot her so it didn't matter what they did to her face or her body, and in the meantime she must give nothing and nobody away. How many hours would she have to endure before the mercy of a bullet?

'Not bad,' he said and held the papers out to her, his elbow on the desk, his thumb clipped across the cardboard. The nails were minutely coruscated.

He knows, she thought, but he's giving me my identification card back. Why is he doing that? Instinctively she reached out for the document but he didn't let go. For a moment they held onto it from different ends and looked into each other's eyes. It's too late to pretend now, she thought. She felt immensely calm. The tension of pretending had evaporated.

He looked at her for a long time, his dark blue, reddened eyes darting across her features.

Then he appeared to make up his mind, repeated her address from the card without looking at it and said quietly. 'I'm letting you go. But you must go straight away.'

She didn't move. This was so unexpected. Was a dream taking over from reality?'

'My bicycle?' she had asked before she even thought to speak.

'Will be outside. Au revoir.'

Emphasised, not spoken louder, but the pause before it and the slowness of the French phrase registered with her.

He had pulled some papers towards him, picked up a pen and was starting to work through a pile of documents, moving the pen down the page as he read. No one outside the room took any notice when she turned to go and stepped through into the central space. She expected to be called back, but no one stopped her walking out of the front door and no one prevented her from pulling her bike away from the wall where it had been left unguarded. No one shouted after her when she cycled off into the suddenly cold, late spring day.

Only when she was back in her own house, Anna remembered, did she begin to shake. And that younger version of herself, that brave determined creature had no idea what had just happened or how much it would come to haunt her.

Chapter Five

The shaking went on for some time. Cycling back was difficult but when Anna got back into the familiar territory of her own room she found she couldn't pour water from the jug one handed, needed two hands to drink it. Making food was beyond her. She shook her clothes off and curled up in bed before the sun was down. Sometime long after midnight, she drifted into sleep.

In the morning the shaking had stopped, but the worry persisted. What had happened was too big for her to cope on her own. She needed to talk about what had happened. Could she tell SOE, ask George's advice, beg him to pull her out? During her training there had been rumours of escape routes, fishing boats slipping across the channel. Even as she asked herself the question, she knew the answer. SOE would simply pull the plug on her and leave her there. She had always known in theory that she was expendable. Now she experienced it as a fact. Even if she did try and tell George, what would she say? She couldn't tell him what had happened because she didn't understand it herself.

If not SOE then Henri. But once the words had passed her lips, what could he do but put his cap back on and walk away, stop all activity, tell everyone that they had been betrayed by a careless girl? To be arrested and immediately released marked you out as a double agent. It was what the Germans did with those they turned and those of their own agents who were arrested by mistake. Even Mrs Desaint, if she talked to her, would think of no other reason for her release except that she was now a double agent, working for the Germans. If she said a word to anyone no one would trust her again. She was stuck, learning what it is to be utterly alone.

The Gestapo man with the tired eyes knew where she lived.

He'd bothered to learn her address. He clearly suspected her. She was sure of that, but he had also let her go without the inconvenience of her having to answer a single question. Why had he said, 'Remember me'? Why had he said 'au revoir'? Did he expect there to be further meetings? Had he let her go because he knew where to send the radio direction cars, or because he would have her tailed and find her contacts, roll up her whole network rather than send a single young woman to be shot?

How she'd reasoned it all out, the older Anna remembered, reasoned it out and got nowhere near the truth.

For a while what had happened froze her. She retreated inside her own cover, milked and made cheeses, hid the silk map and missed her next two transmissions. Under the hot sun of April she waited for something to happen.

But nothing happened. If he was planning to roll up the whole network, why make it quite plain to her that he knew she was a spy? It made no sense.

She enjoyed the cows and the goats. Their pelts had become sleek with the plentiful grass. She made rich cheeses and when the soft skins formed she wrapped them up and sold them. For a whole week she stopped asking questions, kept herself away from all subversive activity, interrogated Franck so closely about who was and was not coming to the village that she could see she was frightening him.

'I'd tell you if anything was wrong,' he pleaded. 'I've been doing my job properly, don't you trust me?'

She'd looked down at him then, seen that he was fighting to keep his bottom lip from wobbling, wondered whether to hug him, decided not to.

'You're the best. Just the best,' she told him, and watched his face suffuse with pleasure.

Everything was normal when it shouldn't have been.

For a whole week in April 1944 she suspended her activities, then thought she would put matters to the test, risking herself but involving nobody else. She made a long transmission, giving SOE as much as she could remember about the gun positions. She told SOE she'd been ill, made the transmission longer than it needed to be so the Germans would have time to find her if they were listening. She waited, and when nothing happened realised that she was being absurd. He didn't need to home in on her transmissions. He knew where she lived.

She grew bolder, got some of her courage back. She carried on cycling without the silk map and looked to see if she was followed. She'd done tailing exercises in training. She was certain that no one was tailing her. No one at road blocks seemed at all knowing when they read her name on her papers. And it wasn't possible to keep herself to herself for long. SOE was asking questions with a new sense of urgency. Their sabotage grew ever more ingenious. When she made contacts with her group she heard of abrasive grease guns being used to disable railway trucks. They had new techniques for downing pylons. You put the explosives on each side at different heights so that the pylon toppled rather than settled when you blew it up. Different groups were cutting communications and power supplies each week. Whatever she was part of was growing in intensity. The invaders were rattled, strained, waiting for an event to happen, in the same way she was. You could sense that everywhere. The invasion was bound to take place soon, almost certainly at the pas de Calais, but no one could ignore Normandy. She abandoned caution, decided to think of herself as already dead and went back to work.

In response to her week of silence or because of the increase in activity they were now sending her another agent, code named Pierre. He would help run the burgeoning group she had built around her, help keep them organised and trained, leave her free to continue mapping the defences. He'd bring with him more weapons and money, more explosives.

It was her first drop in charge. She'd chosen the field. She'd transmitted the coordinates. Her group was, for the first time, going to provide the cover. The drop was like her own in that it involved a parachutist and crates, but this one also had the added complication of several smaller packages. It was May 10th 1944, two days after the full moon, when she found herself standing in the middle of a field staring up at the sky. An L shape of cycle lights was laid on the ground. She had an S-phone in her hand so that she could talk the plane in once it came into range. She kept thinking she could hear its engines but there was a lot of bomber activity these days. Rarely a night went by without the allies bombing somewhere nearby. Then she had contact, heard a voice on the set and the final arrangements were made.

Pierre would jump first. The crates and packages would follow. Now she could actually see the Halifax. The plane was a dark and growing shadow against the high moon-infused cloud. She watched it coming in, saw a small dark shape separate from it, then the grey parachute opened. Pierre swung down through the darkness before landing quite close to her. He seemed to be okay so she left him to others in her group. They would meet him and bring him to her. Meanwhile the plane was already turning for the next run. She watched carefully where all the packages fell and gave her orders. Packages could get widely scattered and it was important to collect them all in because they contained money and documents, even some names. Each one had to be collected. Luckily the spray pattern was good and everything had fallen on the field. She saw men and boys dash to pick them up before the last run, then skid away to the edges of the big field because they didn't want to be hit by what came next. The crate drop was more difficult. One of the parachutes didn't open. A big crate smashed into the turf on the edge of the field. Some grenades exploded. She heard the pilot swear as he turned for home.

Now they had to move fast. She had three transports. One group she piled into the lorry with the contents of the two crates that had already been collected. She sent them to drive into the wood with orders to wait there, wait for two hours in case the explosion had alerted the Germans to what was going on. Once they were sure it was safe they could drive away and hide everything as they had planned.

She rather thought there wouldn't be any reaction. Explosions happened most nights. The Germans couldn't check on them all. Soldiers who had been sent to investigate had recently sustained casualties. She guessed they would be left alone but couldn't ignore the possibility of an attack.

She asked another group to see what could be salvaged from the broken crate, then to clear the field, leaving no signs. She told them where to melt away if anyone came, gave them orders about how long to wait near the car and where and when she would see them the next day. The cycle lamps she collected in herself. Batteries were hard to get. The greatest difficulty about transmitting these days wasn't being discovered but getting batteries.

Only then did she turn to greet Pierre. He was trying to say something but she hushed him.

'Are you alright?'

'Yes, but I don't see…'

She interrupted him. 'Then we walk. This way through the wood.'

She set off at once. The field was already empty. 'I've two cycles waiting, hidden in the wood. You can ride a bike can't you?'

He stayed behind her. She walked as swiftly as she could. She had dreaded him coming. Her group was working well, but she knew how much they hated being led by a woman. He'd come and he'd take over. The men would be pleased. SOE had lost faith in her after her unexplained silence. So much was clear.

She had another dread too. Ever since the day she had been picked up by the Gestapo the strain on her was growing, beginning to affect her. Even now she knew she was on edge, that's why she had given Pierre no proper greeting, had been so rude. The terror was growing. She knew she had to stay in control.

Now they were walking through the woods, following a path she'd discovered, going uphill. The new grass made it soft underfoot. She was moving virtually silently, no longer worried by darkness, alert to every sound. She'd developed an affinity with this landscape. Pierre was keeping up but stumbling after her. How physically fit was he?

The bikes were leaning against the bank, hidden in moon shadow, in fact so well hidden she took a minute to locate them. Then she handed one to Pierre. 'Get the seat right. We've five kilometres to go.'

She heard him struggling with the bicycle seat, then they were off. She loved cycling at night without lights, swooping along the lanes with the trees on either side giving her a sense of speed, watching the shadows, squinting into the next bend. Going downhill was best of all. You seemed to glide above the road and the hum of your wheels against the tarmac or pebbles was a kind of music.

On the last climb up to her small house she had the impression that Pierre was struggling. She showed him where to put the bikes then led him into the house, found the lamp and lit it. Only then did she get a chance to look at him.

Oh God, thought the older Anna. God makes us young and he has only himself to blame.

Her young heart reacted before her head had a chance to reach any conclusions, even before her eyes had mapped him. He was beautiful, a very pretty young man, she thought. He was half a head taller than she was with sandy coloured hair and lots of it. He had brown eyes set in a wide face and a trim moustache. He was slender. She wanted to say thin, but he wasn't thin. His shoulders were wide and he seemed strong. His face cracked when he smiled, showing white teeth and crinkling the skin just under his eyes.

'Wow,' he said. 'That was some arrival.'

His French was good but the accent wasn't one she knew. She guessed at Canada and went into business mode immediately. It would give her time to think.

'You're staying here tonight,' she explained. 'We're going to move you often. You're very vulnerable. Because you're young they'll wonder why you haven't been sent to work in German factories. Your teeth are too good to pass as French. We'll have to keep you out of sight. You can't move round during the day like I can. There's no cover that will work for you.'

'A compliment, I think.'

She ignored him. What was this sense of warmth that was suddenly filling the room? The fire was virtually out. 'Tomorrow night I'll take you to your house. It's in the next village. The radio will be there waiting for you. You can get yourself set up. I expect you're tired. I slept for nearly twenty hours when I first arrived.'

She was conscious that she was talking fast, saying too much, but then she'd had no one to talk to for months.

'You wash in the yard. There's a pump. The toilet's in the yard too.'

She was covering everything but getting the order wrong. She was flustered.

'I've got you some food. I'm sorry it's cold.'

She uncovered a plate with bread, sausage and cheese on it, found a bottle of wine and poured him a glass. The night was cold so she poked up the fire and threw two more pieces of wood on to the red embers. They caught alight quickly, sending shadows dancing across the room.

'Sorry,' she said. 'I should have started with the food.'

He was eating carefully, neatly. He sipped the wine, didn't slurp it. She poured herself a glass. It would help her sleep. She'd made a bed for herself upstairs but it wouldn't be as comfortable as the one she was lending to him.

'Nice,' he said. 'The food in England isn't…'

'We don't talk about that, about home.' She sounded too shrill even to herself. 'We try to live just here, just in the moment.

The older Anna particularly remembered the way the fire light had flickered across his face adding its touch of mystery, noticed that with this memory there was no change of viewpoint. She was looking through her own younger eyes.

He seemed amused at her. 'Sorry.'

There was a pause in their conversation. He finished eating.

'Why am I really here?' he asked as he put the knife and fork down.

It was her question too and she had no answer to it so she said nothing.

'I mean that was one hell of a performance you put on back there. It left nothing for me to do.'

'There's lots more to do,' she told him, pleased by his compliment but trying not to show it. 'They've done very little sabotage training. I've learnt something while I have been here but I am sure there's much more that you can teach us.'

She'd put more logs on and the fire was much warmer now. The wine was warming her too, relaxing her, shaking some of the spy out of her. Could she trust Pierre? She wanted to. Could she talk to him frankly? It had always been a rule of hers to trust no one until she had to. She'd already organised to have him followed for two days during the next week, see where he went and what he did. It was what she organised for all new members of her group. Sometimes Marcel organised for them to follow her. She always spotted her followers. Why should Pierre be an exception?

'You need to find your feet, learn the people, learn the area.'

'Even if you won't let me move round in daylight.'

She looked at him. 'For your own safety.' Then she added, 'I kind of feel responsible for you.'

He looked down into the fire and breathed out heavily. 'SOE teaching,' he said, 'I see you were a good student.'

There was a note there, the older Anna realised, one she should have listened to.

She finished her wine, went outside to the toilet. The moon was free of the cloud now, bright and luminous above her, neutral in matters of warfare, powerful; chaste too, if legend was to be believed. She stood and looked at it for a moment, before stepping back inside.

'I'm sleeping upstairs. You take my bed for tonight,' she told Pierre. 'I'm up early in the morning to do the milking. It's part of my cover. I'll tiptoe round you. Sleep as long as you like. No one will move you before midday.'

She had to walk past him on her way to the ladder. He got up as she went past, touched her on the shoulder.

'Thanks,' he said. 'I feel safe.'

Two young people, surrounded by danger, seeing each other in the firelight and the lamp's soft glow.

She said nothing. The touch of his hand had been quite different from anything she had yet experienced. She could still feel it on her arm as if he had left a minute indentation in her skin. She wanted to hold on to that feeling when she climbed into bed, hold on to the shock of it and give herself time to work out what she would do.

Next morning she woke with the first light as her body was accustomed to and crept downstairs, feeling the cold from outside. The wood creaked in spite of her extreme care but Pierre didn't wake. He had thrown off some of her blankets. He was lying on his back, his head to one side, his moustache a dark smudge against the bolster. Half his front was exposed. She could see that strands of sandy coloured hair grew on his chest, linking his nipples together with a thick fuzz, lighter than the hair on his head, almost corn-coloured. It was exciting to see him there, although it felt indecent to be observing him while he slept. It would be easy, she thought, to wake him, watch as he sat up, talk to him, wait for him to smile. She found she was wondering what the rest of him looked like. She knew so little about things like that. Perhaps it was time to learn. Did morality really matter that much when tomorrow they could both be dead? Those songs from England, which had never been very far from her thoughts, now came back to her.

'*More and more this heart of mine confesses*'

She told herself not to be a fool. She really knew nothing about him. She needed to warm herself up by activity and the cows would be waiting. Later she'd find a reason to go and see him again. After all, she knew where they were moving him. It was she who had given the orders. She went outside and walked towards the barn. Everything looked the same as yesterday, but already it felt different.

She milked. She moved the cows to pasture. She collected the cheeses she made last week which had already formed soft shells and took them in a cart to the town. All the time she thought about Pierre. When she got back he was gone.

She knew he must be gone but it was still a shock. He'd left his bed unmade. Tonight she would strip herself and lie in the hollows his body had created. Until then she would leave it as it was. Perhaps his smell would still be there on the sheets. There'd be no harm in what she intended, she told herself. No one else would ever know. After her transmission she would go to bed straight away and lie down where he had lain. The next evening she'd get Marcel's report and if he was in the clear then she could call on him. That wouldn't be terribly forward of her would it?

Chapter Six

In fact it was three long days before she saw him again. In those three days he'd been less active than she would have been. Those who had tailed him said he had made no more than a cursory examination of railway lines and phone wires, working at night. In the daytime he slept and studied maps of the area, in the evenings and at night he went out on his bike or on foot getting to know the immediate vicinity, never travelling very far. He'd set his radio up and SOE had already reported to her that he was in communication with them, following the routines. The men of her group who had met him liked him. She could tell that. The French like rank and he had told them he was a captain in the British Army. Was he? Did it matter if he wasn't? Promoting himself to captain, if that is what he had done, would give him instant authority without him having to insist on it in the way she'd had to, forcing them to acknowledge that she brought the orders and that she was the paymaster.

She'd decided already that it would be wrong to share the command with Pierre. Groups need one leader. Pierre was the obvious choice but she found, when she thought about this, that she didn't want to hand over all authority to a stranger, however attractive he might be. It was as if she was separating herself out, making herself into two people just in case. There were enough volunteers now for them to split into two groups, she told herself, one based round her village and one to the west of Pierre's house. That way she could retain some authority even if SOE had lost confidence in her. Her brother's death still drove her to make sure that she landed as many punches as she could on the forces that had killed him. Her new arrangement would also be more secure.

That last argument had drifted into her mind only after

she had made the decision. It was by way of justification after the event, but when she explained her thinking to Pierre, she mentioned it first. They were at his house. She had cycled over after the curfew and knocked twice. He'd let her in at once, as if he expected it to be her. How could he have known? she asked herself. How could he have known that it wasn't one of the enemy? Perhaps he'd seen her cycling up the road. Perhaps he too was attracted.

He was alone, getting ready to go out. It was early May but the nights were still cold. He was wearing thick trousers and a dark jacket, the jacket roughly tied together with string. His chest, this time, was not on display.

She would use whatever authority she had left with him as soon as she got there. That was her plan. She'd only removed her gloves, and was stretching out her hands, stiff from holding the handlebars, when she announced to him, 'I've reached a key decision.'

'Okay.'

'I think we should split my group into two. I work with one half and you work with the other. With two groups we can do more, cause more havoc.'

He looked at her and smiled. 'You don't trust me do you?'

She brushed that aside, ignored the wide smile he used to say it.

'It's a matter of efficiency. It's the way the thing works,' she explained.

'But you don't.' He was being insistent.

Alright she'd tell him.

'I don't trust anyone. Sometimes I don't even trust myself.' He was forcing her into being the stern one, into sounding like a martinet which is why she added the last bit, to soften what she knew she must sound like.

'Okay. If that's the way you want it.'

He was already talking as if he was her equal. Soon, if she wasn't careful, he would make himself into her superior. He was a man, on his best behaviour for the moment, but quite capable of thinking he needed to take over.

She gave him some more reasons, piling them up. 'It'll be safer. If one group gets into trouble there's always the other one. It'll give you a chance to be in control,' she explained. 'You do see that don't you?'

He nodded. 'But we liaise?' he asked her.

She didn't liaise with Henri as a matter of routine, only when necessary, but then she didn't feel this way about Henri, did she?

'Of course we liaise, especially in the first few weeks,' she reassured him.

They divided the men by geography, assigning each person to the nearest group. It meant that she would lose Marcel, her most efficient member, but if that was alright with Marcel it would have to be alright with her. It was the natural consequence of what she wanted to make happen.

'When do we do this?' He was taking his cue from her, being businesslike.

She had won her point and that still mattered to her, but the moment she prevailed she wondered if she hadn't been a little abrupt. 'I'll get the word to them over the next two days,' she said. 'You can leave all that to me.'

'Then how do I call them together?' he asked.

It was a reasonable question. He was only being practical.

'You don't,' she told him. 'Marcel starts the process. That's the way we work.'

He was looking straight at her, weighing her up. 'So how do I contact Marcel?'

She hesitated then. It was as if there were two interactions happening in the room. One was about practicalities and could be described in words. The other was a feeling, a lilting counterpoint to what was being said. She was aware as she tried to boss him that she was attracted to him, against her reason, against her present will. Was this why they used the word 'falling' about love in both French and English?

She tried to concentrate. She'd made it a firm rule never to give the address and the method of contact to anyone. It was important that no one knew too much so no one could betray too many, only those next to them in the chain. To give this stranger Marcel's details felt like a betrayal, but wasn't it the inevitable consequence of her decision? She could say that Marcel would contact him. That would be the right way round, but then he'd know she didn't trust him. What should she do? SOE had trained her in none of this. As she pondered her problem, she knew she was only making matters worse by taking too long to say anything.

Pierre helped her out of her dilemma, by suddenly smiling at her. 'I shouldn't have asked that should I? You can't do that can you? It's against the rules.'

'That's right.' She knew she was smiling back, reacting to the way his smile made everything seem extraordinarily safe.

'Then you ask him to contact me. He can choose for himself.'

'I'm sorry,' she said. 'I'd like to say more. It's this war…'

He laughed at her then. 'There's no need to be sorry. You didn't start it.'

'No.'

She got up to go. The longer she had been with him the more certain she had become that such a good looking young man would have 'attachments', would have a fiancée or someone waiting for him back wherever home was. And even if he was free he was now in France, where the women had stayed at home and the young men were away somewhere else. If he was alone now, he wouldn't be alone for long. He wouldn't, couldn't, be interested in her. He'd put her to the test and she'd failed it. She'd chosen security over trusting him. Nothing could happen between them, she told herself.

'I'll see you in three days' time,' she was saying to him as she put her gloves back on. 'You're clearly on your way out now and I don't want to stop you doing what you must. This time you come to me, Thursday 8.30pm. Knock twice and then walk straight in. Okay?'

'Please stay for a drink.' He was holding out a bottle of brandy.

So he wasn't in so much of a hurry to go out after all, she thought.

'Where did you get that?' she asked him. Brandy was not available locally. The invaders had taken it all.

'Brought it with me. No one checked my luggage. Thought I might need it as a bribe.'

She'd tasted brandy only once, had been offered a sip by her father in the old days, in the house with the tall ceilings, the house they had lived in before coming to England.

'A small one, then. I mustn't stay long,' she added.

It's because we are both spies, because there is a war on that we can meet like this, she thought, meet without chaperones, without society's expectations. The social rules don't apply over here do they?

No, the older Anna thought, no, they didn't and the war was changing all that anyway. Soon the conventions would change back at home.

She took her gloves off again and sat down, even though she knew she shouldn't. He poured her what she thought was more than a small measure and sat down opposite her. Why didn't French houses ever have comfortable chairs? She noticed that he took a slug of his brandy while she took a sip. The brandy tasted of Christmas. She rolled its richness round her mouth while the silence grew between them. He was staring at his feet. Then she started laughing, explained the laugh by saying, 'You should be asking me about me and I should be asking you about you only we can't, because it's against the rules.'

'Try the weather,' he suggested.

'No,' she said, 'The French don't do that.'

'So what do we do?' His question to her.

'I don't know, sit and look at each other I suppose. Talk about the war like everyone else does?'

'That's work,' he said. 'Brandy and work don't mix.'

Was he still being followed? Had another member of the group seen her go into the house and was that person even now waiting to trail Pierre through his night's work? She didn't think so. Two days was the maximum they could find time for. No one would be outside. No one was tagging her movements.

Doing what she did brought terror at the same time as it gave her this wonderful freedom.

She looked across at Pierre and smiled at the thoughts going through her own head, took another sip and went to put the glass down on the floor, out of the way. It was warming her too quickly. She wasn't used to it.

Her glass never reached the ground. She found it was being taken from her. He'd moved very close, was holding her hand, lifting it slowly towards his face, kissing her knuckle just once and looking at her, smiling at her, saying, 'You're very pretty you know.' Then he looked at her more earnestly. 'You do know that don't you?' he asked, as if it wasn't just a matter of words but something that was really important to him.

She shook her head but didn't take her hand away.

'Well if there's nothing else that we can say to each other, you must let me tell you that.'

She closed her hand round his. He was warm and wonderful. When had she last touched a human being? In the combat lessons during training, before that when her brother had gone away. There'd been no one else.

His face was coming closer to hers. She closed her eyes, felt the warm, slightly wet touch of his lips on hers. Then he pulled away as if he was checking that what he was doing was okay. He was clearly a gentleman. She kept her eyes closed because she didn't want to look at him just now, was waiting for another touch of his lips, thinking that next time she'd kiss him back, next time she'd put her arms round him.

His lips touched her mouth again. This time she pushed back against the slight pressure, to let him know that she didn't mind, then opened her mouth slightly, amazed at the soft beauty of what she was feeling. Both her arms were now round him. When he stopped that kiss she reached up to the back of his neck and made him kiss her again.

She didn't want it to end, knew it must go no further. She pulled away from him then, reached for her gloves. 'I think we've already said goodnight,' she informed him and ran out of the room.

Time moved slowly until the Thursday night when he'd come to report to her at half past eight. That was the time they had arranged. She'd tidied the room, made up the bed, had food ready for him, some red wine. She'd dithered for ages about whether to light the fire or not. The days were now much warmer but the nights were still cold. She'd seen him first by firelight and it would save lighting the lamp. Wood was easier to get than paraffin.

They must talk business, check how he was getting on, had he got enough weapons, ammunition, money for his group? SOE hadn't sent as much money as they were going to need. Money mattered, it gave resistance fighters purchasing power in the black market, helped their families, persuaded the volunteers to carry on taking the risk. With more recruits they needed more money. There was a real danger that in the next month they were going to run out.

If they talked business first, then what would follow? What did she want to follow? Just to be kissed and held? Was that going to be enough? She thought of the words of the song.

> *More and more this heart of mine confesses*
> *More and more I'm caught in your caresses*

More and more I find it more than thrilling
To share the dream that I needed fulfilling'

Her body had begun to seem strange to her. First it had become slimmer and more muscular, now it was expressing needs she scarcely acknowledged. The situation was impossible. She mustn't get pregnant. What she wanted, she told herself, was courtship, but there might not be time. Is this what love is really like? she asked herself; not a long wallow in happiness, but a series of intense problems you have to solve.

She lit the fire. It would keep her warm in the night, she told herself, while her mind formed another picture altogether, of pink bodies embracing in firelight, half understood, like in a dream.

Pierre knocked twice at 8.30 and walked straight in. He left at about three in the morning, while it was still dark. As she lay in the cramped bed, already missing him, she realised they hadn't even talked about the money.

She'd fallen in love. She was a fallen woman. Sometime after the food and the wine she'd lost her balance, had discovered in herself a sense of longing so extreme that it simply took her over. The whole thing had been so joyous, so unexpectedly cheerful, and in a strange way, in spite of the fact that she knew very little and he seemed to know a great deal, she had taken control. It was as if all the sternness and the grief inside her had vanished and something else was bubbling up in its place. She'd pulled him to her and kissed him again, long pressured kisses that she could still feel on her lips.

'You won't make me pregnant will you?' she whispered, suddenly nervous and more than a little scared.

'No. I've got something to put on.'

'Okay,' she'd said and she'd closed her eyes.

The world as she came out of the house seemed new made.

All the colour was back on the trees now. Even the oak and the ash trees were stretching out with their new leaves. The countryside was a symphony of different greens. Blackthorn fumed into blossom along the edges of the woods, adding splodges of white. A blackbird pushed pure notes out into the still cold morning air, series after series, trill after trill. The war, which had never seemed very close since she came to France, was further away than ever. She sang out loud, oblivious to the danger.

> *More and more I'm less and less unwilling*
> *To give up wanting more and more of you.'*

But that same day she had to go back to work. The Germans were building ever more elaborate defences. SOE wanted to know about flooded areas and observation posts, needed to be sure they had the exact coordinates of any trenches where guns could be mounted. She had to cycle to do more mapping and the cycling wasn't quite as comfortable that afternoon. After curfew she met her group's latest recruits for sten gun training, deep in the wood. She explained the difference between firing a sten gun and a rifle, the way the sten pulled you forward while the rifle pushed you back. She took them through safety catches and how to change a magazine. She explained that you fired in short bursts, watched where the first bullet hit and then moved across to the target, told them not to panic but to stay in control. Only at the end did she let them fire a few rounds each. It was past three in the morning when she crept into bed to snatch a few hours' sleep before the milking began.

Her tarts were the ones who spotted the difference in her.

'Name?' they'd asked her. Then, when she said nothing, they commented on the blush which she knew had spread right across her face and down her neck, laughed at her confusion, offered her condoms so she could look after herself. 'I'm afraid they're German condoms. But they work well enough.'

She hadn't taken up their kindly meant offer. There had been a touch of jealousy, she thought, underlying the badinage, a shared understanding that she had found what they had agreed to manage without.

She met Pierre whenever she could, learnt the ways of his body and of her own, ran her fingers down his shoulder blades, rested her hands in the hollow of his back, leant against the corn-coloured chest hair and then traced with the tips of her fingers the way it reddened as it moved down to his sex. Soft and hard, the two states of him, the two feels of a man.

She knew she couldn't keep going at this pace. She needed more sleep than she was getting or something would give way. Her life had stopped feeling real, was more like a dream from which she didn't want to wake.

Chapter Seven

Hold it there. Savour the moment. Remember the completeness, the sense of riding on life rather than being dragged along by it. That was your moment. Just dwell on it and be glad.

But events had taken over. In the last week of May Pierre was called away to a liaison meeting. He would be gone for three days. SOE wanted more coordination between the resistance groups operating around or near the Cherbourg peninsular. Pierre gave her no details about the meeting and she asked for none. He couldn't even tell her when he would be back.

Now who doesn't trust whom, she wondered.

That night Marcel was arrested. His distraught wife came to see Anna the night after, told her that the Germans had arrived just at curfew time and taken him away in a car. She knew she shouldn't have come, but what was she to do? She was worried sick about what had happened to him. Anna calmed her down as best she could although they both feared the worst, advised her to go and stay with her mother. Reprisals were sometimes taken on families. The German soldiers, who were too frightened to go into the woods, could summon up the courage to round up a family and shoot them all.

The news snapped Anna out of dreamland. Questions flooded her. Might Marcel have talked, have given names to his interrogators? How did Marcel's wife know where Anna lived? Had Marcel been that indiscreet before his arrest? Where was Pierre when she needed him? Bone weary already she'd have to take over, get the message round Pierre's group at once, tell them to go into hiding and lie low. Most of the weapons must be moved immediately and hidden somewhere else. One lot should be left where it was to see if Marcel gave away its location. It was a check, the only one she could think of in the time she had. If the Germans came to collect it then she would know that Marcel had cracked.

Then she realised that this wasn't only about Marcel and Pierre's group. It also impacted on her. Marcel certainly knew about her, knew exactly where she lived. She must stop being the milk girl. Had she time to tell Madame Desaint or should she just go at once to her safe house, the old hut in the woods she had spotted on her travels, found to be uninhabited and a long way from anywhere else?

In the end she did tell Madame Desaint, promised to come back if she could, warned her to be on her guard, wondered if that grey haired Gestapo officer was orchestrating this chaos, had simply bided his time.

She moved at night, taking the radio in its case and a few clothes. Twilight came late in May and the wood was alive with noises. New leaves on the trees intensified the darkness and last year's leaves, dried to a crisp by the recent good weather, snapped and crackled under her feet. The trunks were grey as she passed them and she had to be careful to keep to the path. Her mapping skills came in useful. She pictured the gradients, checked them off one by one as she fled into the heart of the wood, was relieved when she saw the hut standing silver in the moonlight.

She set up the aerial at once in a field at the back of the hut and contacted SOE. The message they sent back took her some time to decode because her mind was racing to fill in the blanks and the flickering light from the candle made such close work difficult. When she looked at the decoded whole she couldn't believe it. Was this just a part of her dream state turning into nightmare? The message read:

Must warn you. Pierre contacted yesterday omitting checks. We fear arrest.

Radio messages sent from agents always had checks. It had been knocked into them during training that they must never

ever send a message without four checks: two bluff (in case someone else was listening) and two true checks. Radio sets were always vulnerable, and playing radios back when an agent was captured with his set was well worth the effort. It was what both sides did as they sought every possible advantage.

Marcel then Pierre. Now she could picture it all. Marcel in a prison cell, stripped, badly beaten, blood dripping from his mouth, injured but still alive, talking because of the pain and perhaps because of the threats made against his family. Pierre his first major victim, arrested because Marcel had betrayed him. Pierre's radio being played back against them. How long had they hung Marcel by the wrists before he broke? How many finger nails had they extracted before he couldn't stand the pain any longer and began to talk?

It had come to this. She was alone in a hut in a wood in a foreign country, cut off from all her contacts, unable to work, with no water and no food. No one knew where she was, so no one could betray her, but equally no one could come and find her if Marcel came back home, if it had all been an unnecessary flap. She might starve but she wouldn't be captured.

In fact she solved her food problem quite easily. SOE had ordered her to stay put and wait for instructions, to lie as low as possible and go nowhere. But that first night she ransacked her new place until she found a jug, washed it in the stream, then walked miles in a wide circle, looking for cows. Eventually she found some and began to milk, taking a little from each udder, making sure that no one would guess. Late May was a great time for milking. With the new grass all the udders would still seem full in spite of her pilfering. For another two days she lived on milk, desperate to find out what was happening, unable to contact anyone.

All this time agonising images filled her head. She knew what the Germans did. SOE had drummed that into them. For the occupiers, spies and resistance fighters were outside the Geneva convention, subject to summary justice. They could expect to be tortured and she had been trained how to resist interrogation. She guessed that whatever was left of Marcel had now been put up against a wall and shot or perhaps hanged, his body dumped somewhere as a warning to others. It was what was happening to Pierre that she couldn't get out of her mind, couldn't possibly come to terms with. His body belonged to her now, was her plaything. Part of her felt she might crack up under the strain of not knowing.

But forced isolation had its advantages. It made her rest. The weather was warm and then turned wet. She slept for long periods and when she wasn't sleeping and it was fine enough she sat outside the hut and watched the leaves fill out, the bluebells begin to wither, the last primroses fade. It was so incongruous. If there hadn't been a war this would have been like Swallows and Amazons, a magnificent adventure.

That evening SOE had news for her, wonderful news when she decoded it. Pierre had contacted them again, using his true checks. He'd had to go into hiding three days ago and had transmitted the last message too quickly, forgetting the checks. There had been a real hue and cry round him and no chance until yesterday to use the radio again. He was safe now and on his way back to her area. SOE had told him about Marcel. He would take extra precautions not to be caught.

Energy returned, surged through her. She danced in the old hut, kicking out her feet and hopping round the floor. As she danced she sang.

> 'When we meet again we'll be able to spend
> A lifetime as sweet as that lovely weekend.'

But how could she meet him? She couldn't go to his house. It was bound to be under surveillance. He would have to come to her. That's what he would do, come and look for her. He'd had a scare and his needs would be as great as hers. Not here, not in the hut. He didn't know about that. He would go to the little house she had run away from. She couldn't go home yet, but if she were waiting outside, keeping under cover, she could spot any danger, could even intercept him before he ran into trouble.

When would he come, she asked herself. The answer was simple. At night, after the curfew. It was the time of the full moon. There'd be plenty of light to spot him by. She could get there early and intercept him, see if anyone else was watching the house.

The weather was terrible, heavy rain squelched and splattered her walk through the wood. She was in position well before it went dark. She had requisitioned Franck's den for her vigil. Tomorrow she'd return it to him. Tonight it would enable her to watch all the approaches. She longed for Pierre's touch on her body. Marcel was forgotten, swept away by the great joy she had in Pierre's return. Soon he would approach her house and she could go and meet him. The very fact that it was a night of storm and rain, after all that fine weather, would help keep them out of danger.

The sky was empty of planes. The weather was much too bad for flying. She knew that any drop planned for tonight would have been abandoned before take-off because of the weather. She'd been glad of the wind and rain at first as they were a kind of cover for her, but they also made it much more difficult to hear if anyone else was approaching. Her shelter leaked. Soon water was finding its way down her neck and through the jacket she wore, spreading out across her shoulders. She hadn't eaten solid food for a week and was enormously hungry.

Nothing moved in the small hamlet so she had time to think about the rest of the message that SOE had sent her. The other two resistance leaders, the ones Pierre had gone to meet, had both been arrested. Only Pierre had got away, her clever Pierre. Luck was shining on him as it had always shone on her.

Then something was moving below her. She saw Franck's grandfather open his door and peer out into the wild night.

He seemed to be uncertain but he shut the door after himself and moved away down the road, heading for the crossroads just below her watching post. He might have information for her. He must know about the scare even if it hadn't involved their group. Quickly she slithered down to intercept him and learn what she could. Dripping wet with her hair plastered across her forehead, she must have seemed a strange sight, like a wolf-nursed child stumbling into civilisation.

Franck's grandfather wasn't at all fazed by her appearance. He reported no special interest in the village by the occupiers but lots of nervousness amongst the troops in Caen. Marcel had disappeared. No trace of him had been seen since his arrest and nothing else had happened.

'You mean the weapons that we didn't move haven't been touched?'

'No. They are still there.' He spoke in his usual pedantic way, clearly and distinctly. There could be no mistaking what he was telling her.

'Odd,' she said. 'What do you make of that?'

'Well, he said, 'They're either too busy chasing around, in too much of a flap, or Marcel has told them nothing. I wouldn't be surprised. He was always a stubborn man.'

They stood in silence, water cascading round them, now running down the path. 'I'm just going…'

She cut him off. 'Don't tell me. Stay safe.'

He turned and went on his way, then turned back. 'Did I see you here?' he asked her. 'Just in case anyone asks me.'

'Yes, you saw me.'

He was such a sweet, courageous man. She watched him walk off resolutely into the night then returned to her post. It was quite dark now and everyone was in bed.

Which way will he come? she asked herself. If she had been in his position she would have travelled across fields to the village, approaching from the other end because it was the highest point. She'd have avoided the main street and come to the house from the back, climbing the fence. But if she had been the one going to see him, she wouldn't have left it this late. She'd be there already.

Another cold, wet half hour passed before someone was walking down the main street, a dark figure wearing a jacket with the collar turned up, hands thrust into his pockets, walking quickly and straight towards her house. It was Pierre. She knew that walk now. If Pierre saw no danger and Franck's grandfather had sensed no danger either then why was she skulking up here when she longed to see him?

She stood up stiffly and scrambled down to the road. When she reached it she began to run, all the time watching the figure in front of her.

She saw that Pierre went straight up to her door, knocked twice and walked inside, obeying the instructions she had given him that first time. He didn't even turn round before he stepped into the house, didn't check if he was being followed, didn't see her hurtling towards him. He must be as anxious to see her as she was to see him.

As she rushed into the house following him he was lighting the lamp. She slammed the door shut to keep the night out, called his name and then stood back to look at him. His skin was glistening with the rain, his sandy hair matted and tinged with red because it was so wet, his mouth spread out in a wide smile, his eyes crinkled. His arms were already held out towards her.

'I thought you were dead,' she shouted at him. 'I thought I'd lost you.'

'No,' he assured her. 'Since you've come into my life I feel quite invincible. They were close but they never got me.'

She stood and stared, taking in the living reality of him.

'Come here,' he said. 'I want you so much.'

She walked towards him slowly, holding back the moment they would touch, making the most of the anticipation.

They kissed and the embrace was wet, cold and slippery;

only where their mouths joined was there any warmth.

'We need to get out of these clothes,' she said. 'I'll light a fire. We'll put the stuff to dry and crawl into bed.'

She found paper and kindling, bundled them together in the hearth. With one match she struck quick flames out of the heap then piled on top some thin logs, dry from being inside so long. Pierre was half undressed before she'd even started. He was untying and pulling off his boots, fumbling at his belt. She flung off her jacket and skirt, hung them to one side of the blaze, then unhitched her stockings and rolled them down her cold legs. When she turned round to look at Pierre he was already naked.

'Give me those,' he said.

Gently he hung them on the mantelpiece, making sure they stayed there by weighing them down with china ornaments. She handed him her blouse and her bra, slipped off her suspender belt and knickers, then dived into the bed and lay there shivering. He was quickly in beside her, wrapping her in his arms, cuddling her, trying to warm her.

He loves me, she thought. He needs me as much as I need him. For a moment they were still, listening to the wind and rain, watching the fire spread to the logs and catch them. Then she felt his hand moving to her breast and she was lost again.

Next time, she told herself, we'll take it slowly, or if not next time, when peace comes, when we can stay in bed for a whole week together. Now it's too urgent and I'm far too needy.

Afterwards he rolled over onto his back and she curled up under his arm.

'Are you hungry?' he asked her.

'Yes, I've eaten nothing but milk for three days.'

'Right, wait there. I've got something for you.'

He leant out of the bed and reached up to his jacket, pulled out two packages, gave one to her.

It was chocolate, a whole bar of chocolate. She began to eat it, filling her mouth with the hard lumps she broke from the bar.

'Wonderful,' she said, 'wonderful,' as the lumps began to melt and her mouth filled with sweetness. 'What's in the other package?'

He was watching her eat with enormous pleasure, was clearly pleased with himself, with still being alive and free.

'Just some money,' he told her. I knew we were running short.'

'You clever boy,' she told him. 'What more could any girl want?'

Soon they slept curled up together, satisfied, warm, dog-tired and at peace.

Yes, said the older Anna to herself, yes, I remember that moment. I always will.

She woke first. There was already daylight outside. More rain she thought too, no break in this sudden awful weather. She thought of the cows but Madame Desaint would have that covered, thinking Anna was still in hiding. She glanced at Pierre. He was still fast asleep, didn't even move when she rolled away from him and took herself outside to pee.

On her way back to him she saw the empty chocolate wrapper and the packet of money lying by the side of the bed. She wondered how much he'd been able to bring them, picked it up and unrolled it. Then she moved closer to the window, lifting each of the 1000 franc notes individually to the light.

It was like an instant eclipse. One moment she was in broad daylight, the next moment she had fallen into darkness. Horror, like a sudden towering wave, pushed her under and held her there, shocked, dismayed, even as her fingers continued to raffle through the corners and her eyes searched for what wasn't there.

These notes were unused, numbered in sequence, and they had no pin marks.

Real French francs always had pin marks. The banks always pinned 1000 franc notes together when they counted them. It was the way they did things. SOE had known that for a long time. She screwed her eyes up to shake any sleep out of them, checked again and put the money down, stuffing it back into the pack.

And he'd brought her chocolate. He'd been on the run and in that time of shortages he'd managed to find a bar of chocolate.

In an absent-minded way, almost without conscious thought, while one part of her reeled and lost balance, her training clicked in. Trust no one, they had repeated. Be alert at every moment to the possibility of betrayal. So as she stood there and physically shook, that trained, honed, doubting part of her brain was assembling a story about what was happening altogether different from the one she had been telling herself. Indeed, even as her heart struggled with its sudden desperation, this part of her brain was snapping all the links together. Pierre came directly into her house last night. He didn't take any of the back ways. He simply walked straight down the road, like anyone else who had nothing to fear. Why had he done that? She'd like to believe that he was so desperate to see her that he had thrown caution to the wind, but his speed had been constant. There had been no change of pace. Was it an act of bravado? No, he had no known audience. He couldn't know she was watching. He'd walked like anyone else would walk in a storm, head down, hunched, already wet and hoping not to get any wetter, as if there was no possibility of danger. Then she'd run in after him, slamming the door, and in spite of his recent escapade he'd not reached for his gun or whirled round to face her or reacted in any enemy-territory way. And that could only mean one thing. He knew he wasn't in any danger, knew that whoever came in after him, he would be quite safe.

How could he know that? It had to be because the Germans also thought he was working for them.

He'd been that careless before, she remembered. When she had gone round to his house that first time he'd let her in straightaway without precautions, without a gun at the ready, and he didn't know she was coming to see him that evening either. She'd given him no warning. But then, if it didn't matter who came to your door, if you can deal equally well with a member of the resistance or with a German platoon, why bother with safety?

More links, more despair. Marcel was arrested the day Pierre left, not the day before. It was as if the occupiers had waited for him to be out of the way. Had Pierre ordered that arrest? Had Marcel begun to suspect that something wasn't right? But why was Pierre's radio used without the checks? She wondered if Pierre had been arrested with the other resistance leaders by chance, by those who didn't know his double role. Had all three been held in the same cell so that at first he couldn't tell anyone who he was because they were always together? That was when the Germans must have used his radio without the checks. He'd have been furious about that. It must have been the day after, when he was interrogated alone, that he was able at last to identify himself as what he had always been - a double agent.

Her heart was struggling to be heard now, wailing its despair. But she wouldn't listen, even tried to switch her feelings off altogether as she continued the calculation.

It was because he was their agent that they had not only let him go, but given him his radio back. It was because he was their agent that they had also given him chocolate and money which had never been through a French bank. The Germans had kept the other two resistance leaders and let Pierre go. Marcel must have been arrested on Pierre's orders. The timing was too much of a coincidence. How had Marcel begun to suspect him? Marcel had said nothing under interrogation. That lovely courteous man had probably died without speaking, without even telling the Germans where the weapons were hidden.

Her brain didn't stop there. It ploughed onwards, taking what she had lived through and snapping more links together. She wouldn't share her command with him, had made sure he could only betray so much. That hadn't been in his plans. As a double agent he would have wanted to be part of a big group that he could inform on. He wanted names and addresses and she'd refused, wouldn't even give him Marcel's contact. That must have riled him. She'd thwarted his plans so... She must say it to herself. Her brain had already thought it, now her heart wouldn't stay silent. She must say it, say it loudly and slowly to herself...

It was because she had thwarted his plans that he had kissed her, undressed her and taken her to bed. His was a double betrayal, of her as a comrade, of her as a lover.

Song lines struggled to be heard in her overactive brain:

> *'I never gave my love away*
> *I kept it for the lucky day*
> *When I could give it all to you.'*

Suddenly she couldn't bear her own stupidity. Both parents dead in an air raid. Her brother dead by the side of a Norwegian Fjord. And what had she done by way of revenge? She'd made love to the enemy.

She turned round then to look at him sleeping, tried to fix this new picture onto the young man in the bed. She had to turn away and back into activity, so great was her sense of stupidity and of betrayal.

Could she prove his guilt? Each part of the story could be explained away. Marcel might have acted stupidly, calling attention to himself. The Cherbourg meeting might have been surprised and Pierre the only one to get away, so frightened that he forgot the checks. Had one of the other leaders before he was captured passed on old money sent to France before SOE knew about the pin holes? Pierre might have walked straight to see her because it was such a bad night that he thought the Germans would be inside and dry and because he loved her.

In a few minutes he would wake up and she must decide what to do. She knew she wouldn't be able to hide her doubts: they'd be written all over her face.

Somewhere soon an invasion was coming. Somewhere along the French coast young men like her brother would stumble ashore and run against the guns. Normandy must be a possible site. All the mapping, all the sabotage couldn't just be a diversion could it? If Pierre was a double agent he might yet jeopardise the lives of thousands.

What could, what should she do?

Let him go? No, if he was guilty he'd do far too much damage.

Hand him over to the others? No, that would leave her having to explain her part in all of this.

Ask SOE? What answer could they give that she hadn't already thought of?

Shoot Pierre and bury him herself, amalgamate the two groups and run them together? She'd never killed anything bigger than a wasp, didn't know if she had it in her. It was unthinkable.

And what if she was wrong?

Her clothes from last night were already dry. She dressed quickly, knowing Pierre could wake at any time, found her gun, took off the safety catch.

It's my decision, she told herself. I have to decide, then move on. But I must be sure.

Working desperately, quickly and silently now, she wrote him a note, told him to meet her at her hut after the curfew that night, explained how to get there. It was vital for what she planned that he didn't wake before she was out of the house.

If he woke to find her gone but read the note, why should he suspect anything? Of course he could bring a patrol with him when he came to see her, but then she would know.

Then she could be quite certain.

Her bike was where she had hidden it. She mounted it quickly and rode away through the rain and the wind, heading straight for his house, meaning to search it. She rode as fast as she could, anything to keep her feelings at bay, to hold off the pain.

The door was locked so she opened up a back window and climbed through. It didn't take her long to find the British-made radio or the crystals he used. They weren't exactly hidden, confirming her suspicions. Nearby were his coding pads and, quite unbelievably, the text of every message he had ever received from SOE. How dangerous, how stupidly careless. Unless… She put the crystals in her pocket. If he was innocent she would give them back. If he was guilty … well… he'd have no further use for them. Meanwhile he couldn't contact SOE and SOE couldn't tell him anything else that he would betray.

If he'd woken at once and walked straight here he could make it in 45 minutes. She'd cycled fast. That meant she had only another twenty minutes in which to complete a thorough search of his house.

She went about it methodically, knowing that if there was anything else hidden there it would be much harder to find. She was looking for another radio set, the one he used for his other masters. It had to be there. She reasoned that Pierre couldn't be seen talking to the enemy he was meant to be fighting so he had to have another way of contacting them, a way which didn't throw him open to suspicion. He could be using a dead letter box but that was cumbersome and took time. She was certain that if he was a double agent, Pierre would use a radio set, another one, working on German frequencies. But where would he keep it? It wouldn't be outside the house but inside, somewhere that was easy to get at and easier to put away in a hurry if the wrong person came to his door.

Her first rummaging turned up nothing. She began to breathe again, to believe that she might have got him wrong. She stood back against the wall and looked around her.

It was furnished like a typical French country room: a table, four high backed chairs, a heavy sideboard, crudely made, probably two hundred years old, a cast iron kitchen range with a small fire grate. There were logs to one side but no ash in the grate. The nights had been cold. Pierre must have lit a fire. If he had, and if he was as careless as she now thought him to be, then some ash would still be there. There was an ash bucket to one side but it was empty. The grate was swept clean. No soot had fallen in spite of the rain. It was even clean in the corners. What man, she thought, would be as house proud as that?

She knelt in front of the hearth as if she was praying. Part of her was. She had two futures. One was with Pierre, no longer alone, fighting, loving together, getting through the war. In the other she would be more alone than ever, cut off from normal human feelings, not the young woman, just the warrior, her only role. She stretched her arm up the chimney and felt for the recess she knew would be there, that section just above the mantle where the chimney widened.

Something was blocking it. She felt round. Time was running out. He could be here at any moment. Her hand touched a handle and she pulled. The case slipped out of its hiding place. She put it in front of her and clicked it open. German names, German marks, similar to her radio set but quite different. Now she knew.

She wanted to cry, to howl, but she mustn't. Quickly she closed the case up and shoved it back in its place. A small pile of soot had fallen. She left it where it was. The rain could easily have brought it down. She wanted to be as far away from there as possible.

She went out of the window the way she had come in, constantly looking around her. She cycled fast, just to get away and give herself time to think.

It was a desperate risk. If she ran into a patrol she had her gun and his radio crystals, not hidden but in her pockets. She had to take the gun with her. Later, grimly, she knew she'd need it. Better to walk though, she thought, better to go across the farm lands, avoiding roads, relying on the continuing bad weather to prevent her meeting another patrol. She ditched her bike as soon as she could, hid it well because she knew she'd need it again, then set off on foot.

It was broad daylight now, getting towards mid morning, and the rain seemed to be easing, the wind dropping. Everywhere round her she saw the storm damage, new leaves shredded from their branches, some branches, particularly from the ash trees, fallen to the ground, looking like arms pulled from their sockets. The ground was wet and heavy underfoot. Walking was slow and she needed to hurry.

It took her until early afternoon to reach the hut. She had still eaten nothing except the chocolate from last night. The hunger was slowing her down, making her light-headed. She approached carefully. The rain had changed the way it looked, turned the path into mud, but there were no footprints.

She'd take the risk. She'd tell SOE what she had learnt, alert them to what might have been betrayed, anything to keep active, to stop herself feeling. Using Valery's poem she coded her short message, *suspect Pierre is double agent, please advise*, got ready to send it.

She kept the gun by her side, set the aerial, started to transmit her identification, her four checks.

Instead of an acknowledgement and the signal to go ahead they began to send her messages. She didn't want this. She needed to warn them about Pierre but there was no way to cut them off. She listened to the Morse code, took down the letters, waited patiently. The messages went on and on. She'd filled two pages with groups of letters and was on to the third page when she began to understand just what it was that she was being told. A single 8 letter word was being repeated. Its first and sixth letters were the same, so were its second and last. It was the message she had been waiting for. The war which she had left behind in the bombed streets of London was about to catch up with her.

After five pages the message stopped. She broke the rules, didn't acknowledge and abandoned her own short coded message. No one would help her. She would have to act alone. She shut the set down at once, hid it as best she could. She had a lot of decoding to do.

Chapter Eight

Anna decoded the messages, made them into plans, spent a frantic afternoon walking and cycling round giving instructions. Everything was set for soon after midnight. Her groups knew what they had to do. She had told everyone to be extra careful, not an unnecessary word to anyone, friend or family, no one.

Now it was curfew time. She had a night of action in front of her: communications to be cut, a railway line to be dismantled. There'd be no rest the next day either. SOE wanted to know about tanks heading for the beaches, wanted to know about the movements of German soldiers inland.

At least she was no longer hungry. On her way back to the hut she'd come across a chicken coop hidden deep in the woodland, stolen six eggs from under a particularly broody hen, carried them home still warm inside her blouse, then made herself an omelette over a small open fire.

The weather had changed. A few hours ago the rain had stopped falling, the sky had cleared and the wind had dropped. Everything around her felt calm. There was just this short precursor, this little warm-up to all the action, then she'd be free to concentrate on the night's activity and whatever the next day might bring.

'Where do you hide a body?' Father Brown had asked in one of the stories her father loved so much.

'On a battlefield,' was the answer given by the priest's companion. It was a story that began with questions and answers. When she was old enough and she knew the story well but still liked to be read to, her father would ask the questions and let her give the answers. It was part of the closeness that had existed between them.

Soon there would be lots of bodies here. Normandy would

be full of bodies. One or even two more would make no difference, would cause no fuss. There would be no reprisals. That time was over, unless the invasion was a failure and the troops were flung back into the sea.

She was sitting in the wood just to one side of her hut, the darkness closing round her, cutting her off from the reality of what she was about to do. In the wood one world was settling down for the night just as another one began blinking its way into life. A fox had stalked past her. A blackbird had stumbled against her and sent out a shrill warning before roosting. Tawny owls were loosening up for the short summer night time. There had been no other noises, no stealthy sounds of an advancing patrol, no cars screeching to a stop over the hill.

Pierre was late. Her comrade, her lover, her double betrayer was keeping her waiting. Only yesterday she had sat in the rain expectantly, hoping he would come. Now she was waiting again, hoping perhaps that he wouldn't come at all.

What had he done when he woke up and found her gone and her note by the bed? Had he been relieved? Had he gone back to his house and tried to transmit to SOE? Yes, he must have done that by now. In which case he'd have looked for the crystals and found them to be missing. Surely that would make him wary, surely that would prevent him walking through the night to see her. Surely he must suspect that they had been stolen, not mislaid, and the thought must have crossed his mind that she had taken them. She'd given him plenty of time to contact both his masters. In that case they must know where she was waiting, must be coming for her either now or later while he kept out of the way.

Unless, that is, he was careless in many things, unless he thought he'd simply mislaid the crystals and needed her now for key information he could get from nowhere else, unless he was so confident in his seductive powers. Being a double agent took the danger away, made you careless. He might also come just to lie with her. That was her calculation. That was the wager she had made, the guess that would guarantee she had a future. He would come on his own as to an assignation, this man she now both loved and hated. None of the other thoughts would occur to him.

And if a German patrol came with him she'd slip away through the night, out of their clutches. She been trained in that too, making her way across Glen Lyon using scrub and heather to evade the watchers, getting through.

But if there was no patrol did that mean he thought he could deal with this slip of a lovesick girl without help?

When she saw him an hour later he was walking across the field alone, just as he had last night, wearing the same jacket, hands deep in his pockets, but this time with his head up. In an echo of yesterday her heart responded as if nothing had happened. She stayed where she was, watched him cross the open space, could see no other movement around him.

Why couldn't her heart understand what her head had calculated? Why did part of her long to run across and hug him to her, press her lips against his?

She let him come close, within range, a clear target in the diffused moonlight against the paleness of the field behind him.

'Why?' she suddenly called out into the night air, shouting louder than she needed to. She'd finally joined this male world of the single word sentence.

He came to an abrupt halt, looked straight at her even though she was certain he couldn't see her.

'Marie-Claire?'

'Stay where you are,' she commanded. 'Stay where I can see you.'

He did as he was told, stuck to the spot, fifteen feet from the hut, forty feet from where she was sitting, well within range. He kept his hands in his pocket too.

'The money you brought had no pin marks. I took your crystals,' she shouted at him. 'I found the other radio set.'

He was a shadow, a black smudge against the lighter background of the fields. She could see no detail on his face, had no idea what he was thinking, or how he was reacting to what she had just said.

She was a girl, wronged and hurt, about to break the most important commandment, the one from which there is no going back. Over their heads the sky was widening as the moon rose above the trees.

Then he was talking, shouting across the field. 'Of course. That's the game isn't it, Marie-Claire? I feed them the wrong stuff, send them away from everything that matters. SOE knows that. They've always known.'

Not true, she told herself. If SOE had known he was a double agent why did they warn her that he had been captured?

He waited for a reply, but perhaps because she didn't answer him he continued. 'You're angry because I didn't tell you. How could I tell you? You've done the training. You know the rules.'

His hands were out of his pockets and he took a step forward testing her resolve, then another, sliding his feet cautiously along the ground. There was something in his right hand that glinted even as he continued to talk to her.

'I'm a double agent,' he shouted, 'isn't that the only sensible thing to be? The Germans caught me and turned me in Poland, then let me go. It seemed to me so much better to cooperate than to die. What use would I be dead? The moment I could, I turned myself back. It was a two-way insurance, much easier to keep going until I fell in love with you.'

That sentence hung in the air between them. The wood heard it and wondered.

This scene doesn't matter at all to the world out there, she told herself. It's not about spying. It's not about winning the war. Tomorrow will happen anyway and if he lives or dies it will make no difference now. He can't betray an invasion he knows nothing about. I've made sure of that. This scene is only about us.

'And which side are you on now?' she asked, pushing the words out through the night-time air.

'Our side.' He was still inching forward. 'Our side. Why else would I walk so many miles to see you?'

The moon came clear of its cloud, lit up the scene, changed the shape of the wood so that the trees seemed to nod.

If she had heard that yesterday she would have believed him. But now she knew he was a liar.

He was still moving forward. Could he see her yet? Had the moon when it sailed clear of the wood shown him where she was crouching? She'd make it easier for him. She'd stand up.

She saw him hesitate in his movement, knew he had seen her now. Okay she thought, give me the last proof. Show me that this has nothing to do with love or I'll always have doubts and I may not be able to live with what I am about to do. Her hand was on her own gun. She'd been the fastest in the class, the fastest and the most accurate. Facing her was the man who had shown her a whole new world of love and intimacy then slammed the door in her face, the man who had proved to her that life could be magnificent and that betrayal was without limits. Her songs were wrong about love. She knew that now.

She kept her eyes on him, watched for the move she thought he would make. He hadn't said anything else about love, she noticed. Love had simply been a throw-away line he used to get closer to her.

Cloud swallowed up the moonlight again, darkening her world, making her less of a target.

When Pierre did move, he did it so quickly that it nearly took her by surprise. He must have been calculating how near he was to the edge of the wood, how far he had to run before he could find a tree to hide behind, to give him some protection. Suddenly he fired a single shot in her direction, presumably to make her duck, then sprinted to the edge of the darkness.

Training took over. Thinking was unnecessary. Now she

knew it all. Her first shot caught him in the chest and stopped him. The second one hit him in the middle of the face as he looked up towards her. It was quick and smart shooting; clinical, just like the exercises she had done in the training school, just like being out on that Scottish range with the sprung targets. She expected someone to say, 'Good shooting. Now put the safety catch back on, empty out your magazine, spare rounds on the table.'

But no one would say anything to her about this. She knew she was now the only living person there. Pierre was dead. His body wasn't moving. She made her way forward to make quite sure, stood in the darkness beside him, reached out and touched him with her foot.

She didn't cry, even though the wood was dreadfully silent.

When she had parachuted into France she had wondered if she was up to the job. Well now she had her answer. She was a good spy. She had done everything that had been asked of her, had given excellent service in the face of great personal danger. Tonight the groups she trained would do their bit to contribute to the massive tomorrow. They had their orders. She had warned them they might have to act without her. When faced with a choice between her own wants and the needs of her country she had made the correct decision.

She was no longer a virgin in love. She was no longer a virgin in war.

She sat for a long time at the side of his body, keeping vigil. At one point she reached out and touched Pierre's hair. The scalp was still warm. She sat on, and the night sky filled with planes. Loud explosions came from the north, long crumps of sound that reached her like so many echoes.

From her position high up, looking towards the coast, she could see dark planes flying in against the flak, seeding the sky with parachutes. Not just the single ones that brought people like her, but shape after shape, until the sky was filled with dainty parasols, fluttering almost gaily under the thin moon-infused clouds, showing pink and white against the explosions underneath.

Before she left him she reached out for a spray of wild white roses. The sappy spray was difficult to separate from the old wood. But she got it free and laid it on her lover. White for love? White for cowardice? A flower because what she had done needed closure, needed solemnity. She might have prayed, but what God would forgive her?

She stood in silence looking down at the body and the flower. Then she made herself move. Soon this area she'd grown to love would be churned into hell as war washed its insane way back into Europe.

If the front line was coming to her then she needed to be in the thick of things. It might take the Allies days to fight their way in from the coast to reach this point. They might never get this far. She must go back to Madame Desaint's spare house and take up her previous life. The risk was still there but there would be less time now. She needed to be nearer her set. If she was to make that move she must do it now, carrying her radio in its suitcase with her through this short chaotic night. Madame Desaint would be pleased to see her. Once she was back in her house she could take charge of both groups. She went back into the hut, picked up the radio and the aerial, then carried both past Pierre's body to where the bike was hidden. She couldn't disguise what she was carrying, so she fixed them onto the back of the cycle and began to pedal. It was a clear night but occasionally more cloud moved in and darkened the sky. If she was spotted there was nothing she could do. Tonight if she was caught there would be no torture. If she was caught she would simply be shot and that no longer frightened her. She had seen a man being shot and it seemed a relatively quick and easy thing to go through on the way to nothingness.

Noises were all round her but she met no one on the narrow lanes. The action was all to the south, enabling her to reach the house without any hindrance. Quickly she moved the radio and its aerial back into their previous positions. Then she slept in the bed they had shared together, wrapped in the same sheets that had cocooned them both only twenty four hours ago.

Noise woke her as the morning broke. It was the dull endless thud of heavy guns, hundreds and hundreds of them opening up to the north. She dressed and woke Madame Desaint, told her that she was back, that she would look after the cows and the goats again. Madame Desaint asked about the noise and Anna told her that she thought it might just be what they had all been waiting for. Excitement spread across the old woman's face.

'Here, in Normandy?' she said with a sense of pride. 'I'll have lived to see it.'

After dancing round the room for a few moments Madame Desaint fed her again with bread and cheese, fed her until she felt like going back to sleep. Why did bereavement feel like tiredness? She was yawning at the table when Madame Desaint suddenly said, 'Leave the cows today. Franck has been coping. I'll do the milking for one more day. It won't kill me. Go back to that bed of yours.'

As she lay in bed Anna realised that she hadn't cried. In all the churn of that day's horror she'd stayed resolutely dry eyed. Even when he was dead and she had sat with him, no tears had come. Had she killed something in herself with those two shots, she wondered. She'd like to cry now that the whirl of activity was over, just as she'd like to sleep. She suspected that tears helped, but instead she lay there, stubbornly awake and with obstinately dry eyes.

The older Anna shook her head. You'll wait a very long time for tears, she thought. The truth is that you've never cried since.

There was no let up and no time to think. She continued to

function as a spy and began to wonder about herself, about her coldness, about the way she simply coped with the aftermath of the invasion. It was as if Pierre was done with, as remote as yesterday's orders, something completed and over. She scarcely gave him a thought, welcomed the numbness, the anaesthetic of constant activity.

She learnt quickly that the invasion got so far and then stuck. The Allies hadn't taken Caen. She heard that Bayeux was uncertain. There were rumours of groups of parachutists who had got separated and were wandering around behind the German lines looking for a way back. SOE wanted reports, wanted to know about exact troop movements. She was to remember this as the time of her greatest danger. The front line was moving. French people were trying to get on with their lives. A girl on a bike could cross the battle lines and make her way back, could see what planes couldn't see and report everything she saw.

She pedalled and looked at everything she passed. It was as if she had made her pact with terror, had come to terms with death. In a strange way she had never felt so whole. She wasn't afraid and she wasn't exhilarated. She was in an altered state, living the job, becoming only Marie-Claire to the point where there was only one voice in her head.

She got on her cycle and made for the section SOE wanted to know more about. She passed the unburied bodies, noted their stillness, the way they seemed shrunken within their khaki or grey uniforms. She saw the blown up vehicles, metal crumpled and blackened by fire, breathed in the stench of cordite, mingled with heart blood and burnt flesh. Then there were the cows, upended, bloated out of all proportion, stinking, their now small legs sometimes sticking upwards in a way she could only describe as undignified. Occasionally groups of men huddled against the carcasses, taking cover, waving at her to go back. Then there were the noises. She learnt to distinguish the different noises made by the guns and mortars, learnt to fear the German mortars that sounded like a soft siffle, high in the air like a distant lark, or a small penny whistle, faint and elf-like, falling. But then with a spiral pulsing flutter it grew to a hissing whirr before exploding with ferocious blasts, followed by a whine of fragments that cut into the trees. And all the time she counted men, counted weapons, looked for artillery, blinked and mapped, making herself remember.

In the evening she transmitted coordinates and numbers, earning the praise of her controllers and feeling nothing at all. It seemed to her a stalemate. The towns and villages round her were taking a terrible pounding. Men she had worked with to bring this about shook their heads when she met them. She knew the meaning of the word expendable. She was expendable, French civilians were expendable, even the resistance. Only military movement mattered.

Then suddenly there was movement. The area round St Lo was bombed to hell and within two days the German front line had crumbled. Parts of it were now beyond the range of her bicycle. Many Germans were in full retreat, scrambling out of the area, shooting wildly because nothing mattered as much as their own safety. Other groups were determined to continue to resist. There were no more road blocks. She still went out each day, finding out what she could, knowing that what she reported on was so fluid that the situation on the ground would probably change before she could transmit the details. She went everywhere armed because she might need to defend herself. Once the front line had moved past her she would be redundant. Then they might let her go back home, as far away from all this as she could get.

Allied planes were doing terrible damage to the area. Each night she returned to her house, wondering if it would still be there. On the night of 28th July the automaton, the exhausted warrior that she had become, noticed that her front door was open. She approached the house cautiously, peered in.

The room wasn't empty as it should have been.

He was sitting on one of the chairs smoking, seemingly unaffected by the recent turn of events, his uniform still neat. The twin lightening flashes were clear on his lapels. His grey hair was thinner but neatly combed. She could see the ruby signet ring on his right hand. The old coat he had used to cover his uniform was hanging neatly over the chair back.

He turned towards her as she came in and said, 'Hello, Marie-Claire. Do you remember me? As you say, one good turn…'

Perhaps it was the tiredness and the effort at translation, the different word order. Well-known English phrases sounded so different in German, or had she by then simply stopped listening?

She shot him without thinking about it. Shot him the way she had been trained to. It was a close-range shot to the chest. She was never going to miss from that distance. He slumped forwards, but like with Pierre a single shot rarely kills.

His head lifted again, looked at her. 'I came to surrender to you.' The German words were faint but distinct. 'I saved your life.' Anna saw that blood was seeping through his uniform, staining its neatness. A look of mild surprise settled across his suddenly old face. Then he was still and the bleeding stopped.

She looked at him for a long time, sitting in the chair, his head now slumped across his chest. He was a man of her father's age, a man who spoke her father's language, a man just trying to stay alive. Now she understood why he had let her go. She was his insurance policy. She was the woman who could argue for him whatever he had done, the one who might protect him from any reprisals, make sure he reached the prison camp. He'd read caring in her face and that look had saved her, but not him…

She felt desperate. She wanted to cry but no tears would come. She must bury him because many Germans were still in the area. If a retreating group were to occupy the village, make a last stand here and find this dead body sitting in one of her chairs, then their reprisals would be terrible. She must protect her friends from that.

She had to tip his body forward to move him. He slurped out of the chair with a thud. She found that she couldn't lift him. He was much too heavy for her to manage. She'd have to drag him across the floor. First she cleared spaces so that she could get him to the door without hindrance. She tried to drag him by his feet but there was too much friction as his clothes rucked up. She changed tactics and made use of the rug, rolling him with great difficulty onto it then lifting the two ends and beginning to pull. The body shifted, the head rolled from side to side as she tugged him along. Once she was sure she could move him the rest of the way she left him there and went outside.

There was a shovel in the barn. She'd need a hole that was six feet long and two feet deep at least. Wherever she prodded the ground with her spade she met resistance. The ground was too stony. Someone would see the disturbed soil. She'd have to think again.

Then she saw the cattle trough, a heavy metal container settled into the soil. There was a plug and she emptied the water out, watched it run across the yard. Using a long piece of wood as a lever she flipped the trough over, forwards onto the gravel. She dug in its footprint. The soil had been left alone for years and was now sodden with the water she had emptied out. It was relatively easy digging and the sides seemed to hold together because of the wet. It took her an hour to make the right space. She wasn't used to digging. She had to keep stopping and taking a rest. By the time the body was in its grave there would be soil left over but that could be hidden behind the trough, out of sight, where she had already piled it.

Using the rug she dragged him outside, pulled him along the paving, his head banging with each tug. That was when she closed his eyes, not liking to touch him but unable to cope any longer with the way the dark blue eyes looked at her, mutely accusing. She knew she was making too much noise, kept expecting someone to ask what was going on, but her house had always been away from the others and no one disturbed her. She manoeuvred the dead Gestapo officer until his head was at one end of the hole. Then she had to lift him up and drag him along, before lying him flat again. It took her a long time. The mud helped, but each tug was at the very limit of her strength. Dawn was already streaking the sky by the time she had got him in and flattened him out, folded his arms over each other so that he lay like an ancient knight in one of those stone monuments. She owed him that…and more.

Then she covered him over with some of the soil, piling it up to use more of it and to make sure that the trough didn't eventually sink down too low in the ground. Then, using the same wooden levers, she slammed the trough back over the hole and walked around in it to make sure it settled.

She knew she should say a prayer but she no longer believed.

She returned the spade to the barn and walked back into the house.

She could hardly bear to be there anymore. It was where she had made love to Pierre. It was where she had shot the man who had saved her life. It stood as accusing counsel to all her misjudgments.

This had to be the end of her war. There was nothing else she could now do, nothing else she was prepared to do. She'd sleep for as long as anyone would let her and when she woke she'd find the nearest English soldier and hand herself in.

Chapter Nine

After disposing of the Gestapo officer's body Anna had slept for nearly twenty four hours. Noise and movement must have rocked the tiny house all night but she was beyond tiredness and had slept on. She always thought it was the change that had woken her. She'd gone to sleep to the noises of retreat, to the familiar sounds of German vehicles. She'd woken to lower cadences, more caution, running boots, shouted orders and silences. She'd woken and heard someone outside her window quite clearly ask, 'Have they gone?' English words, spoken by an English voice.

She'd shaken herself fully awake and dressed quickly, then stripped the cover off the bolster and tied it round a pitch fork before she peeped outside.

Her lane held a line of crouching men wearing khaki, keeping low, carrying the same rifles she'd last seen at the Scottish firing range. They seemed uncertain of themselves out in the open street as they waited for the order to take cover or to advance. She could sense the jitteriness in them. Their first battle, she had thought. I was once like that. But there was no pity in the thought, just a kind of recognition.

The voice of the warrior continued in her head. No one was in the yard. No one had rushed into her house and looked from the high window. How unprofessional! They'd have to sharpen up or they just wouldn't survive. If she was a sniper with a rifle she reckoned she could down six of them before they got her. If she had a sten gun she could get a whole lot more. Standing as far back as she could she cautiously opened the window and pushed the bolster cover out holding on to the very end of the handle, then waited.

She heard the argument below her, conducted in sharp whispers.

'They're surrendering.'

'It could be a trap.'

'You go and check.'

'Why me?'

'Go on, quick.'

She heard a man walk towards the door and stand outside, so she quickly went back down and opened it for him.

A British soldier was standing there, shaking so much she had to reassure him.

'I'm English,' she told him. 'I was waiting for you to arrive. It's not a trap.'

He cheered up then and smiled at her, put his rifle to the ground butt first and was about to lean on it when the warrior in her spoke again, 'I'd put the safety catch on first. We don't want accidents.'

'Oh,' he said, 'fair point,' and he bent down and clicked the safety catch.

Was it those words, their utter familiarity and safety, that had triggered the change? Was it the smile that went with the words? She didn't know, but the change was instant. Marie-Claire, the warrior, abandoned her, and Anna, the young woman she had once been, returned and was unable to cope. One moment she was reassuring him, in control and calm as she had been for months. The next moment she found that the sight of him in his familiar khaki uniform was doing terrible things to her. It was as if something inside her, wound taut from having to cope with too much, had finally snapped. She lost control of her legs and staggered against him, before leaning against the wall to support herself.

He was looking at her strangely.

'Excuse me,' she said, 'I think I'm going to be sick.'

She pushed past him, stumbled outside into the yard and lurched into the toilet, where she was copiously sick, retching on last night's food and then continuing to cough up phlegm which she had to spit out to clear her mouth. When she had cleaned her mouth as much as she could, she walked back into the room, went to the bowl and tried to wash herself and tidy up. She knew she must look ghastly. She noticed also that bits of earth were caked under her finger nails.

She thought the soldier might have gone but he was still there waiting for her. She looked in his direction and said, 'You don't have to wait. I'll be alright. You can rejoin the rest of the men.' Only it didn't sound convincing.

'But what about you? You don't look too good.'

He was a stocky man with a broad face and dark eyes. He was wearing a helmet which came down to the middle of his brow, hiding his hair. The khaki uniform was snug fitting and she guessed that he was a little too heavy to make an ideal soldier. His face wasn't clean shaven. He had several days of stubble and when she looked again at his eyes she saw they were supported by dark half moons of tiredness and fear.

'I'm fine,' she said, but she wasn't. This was safety, the moment she had been waiting for. Now barring ordinary accidents she could go back to England, leave the war and all its anarchy. She should have been smiling but instead she felt numb, empty, as if she was finished. Two people were dead because of her and the landscape she had grown to love was wrecked and blighted by war. She felt responsible; she felt as if she would never be 'fine' again.

'Excuse me,' he said to her, 'but you don't look as if you can cope.'

She shook her head. 'No I'm okay,' she assured him. 'You can rejoin the war. I'm just about to leave it.'

'Sit down,' he said.

Was it the kindness in his voice that started it all? Perhaps. But had it been kindness, she now wondered, or was it just his wish to escort her to safety because it would take him away from the front line and out of danger?

Heavy guns opened up nearby making conversation impossible, followed by a strained silence.

'If you're English,' he ventured, 'what are you doing here?'

After the last few days and weeks, after all her mistakes, she couldn't tell him, *had never told him*. She was determined to keep her failures to herself.

Instead she'd spread her arms out, made herself smile at him and simply said, 'I got stuck here. Thank God you've come.' She was sitting on the floor as she said it. Her legs seemed to have stopped working. He helped her to her feet and she didn't object when he kept hold of her, because she thought she might collapse again.

Her answer seemed to satisfy him. His obvious lack of curiosity suited her fine. She didn't want to talk about what she had been through to anyone.

But in the end that hadn't been possible. An officer had turned up and ordered the soldier to take her back to headquarters and then get back here on the double. And that had been it. No goodbyes, not to Franck or to Madame Desaint. The soldier absented himself from the rest of his platoon and took her back to headquarters, hitching a lift on a jeep to get her there. The roads they rushed down and the landscape they travelled through were so well known to her but were already becoming unrecognisable. There were new road signs and parked lorries. One of the hand-painted road signs, she remembered, pointed to Crapon, not Crépon. Because she was no longer working, observing, making her maps, she could see it all. She noted where fields had become lorry parks, where tank tracks bisected neat corn fields. Blackened buildings and shattered walls showed there had been fierce resistance. Burnt out, smouldering vehicles underlined that men had died. Was this what saving France looked and smelt like? Is this what she had helped to create? There were bodies in bags, bodies lying in the fields, ghastly charred outlines with outstretched arms and blackened fingers leaning out of still smouldering vehicles. And the bodies had a slightly sweet smell, the coagulated blood strangely, nauseatingly fragrant.

Like chocolate, Anna thought, not the finished product but the smell of making chocolate. Two smells had that power in her life. Tobacco, fresh out of the tin, made her see her father. The smell of a chocolate factory always took her back to the bloody fields of Normandy.

The soldier was solicitous. 'You don't have to look,' he told her. But she had continued to look, had taken it all in to add to the other images in her mind, had passed through it feeling a sense of sadness for the people and the landscape. It wasn't so much the soldiers that she pitied, but rather the dazed French people, trying to comprehend that this was what the longed for liberation actually looked like.

Then she hated what she had been part of. Her thirst to revenge the deaths of her parents and her brother, her need to do something to fight back, joining Britain's passionate cause had led not to glory but to carnage. It wasn't so much the bodies as the buildings. Had the people who bought that house on the hill done so because they liked the view? Didn't they know there was a war coming and their property would have strategic significance? The Germans had kicked them out and turned it into a fortress. The allies had shelled and bombed it to a ruin. She felt sorry for the French people she saw trying to put their lives back together. Slaughtered cattle lay round her like bloated punctuation marks. Generations had worked to build up those herds. What would they do now? Everywhere there was devastation, and when they passed French people on the road the faces looked back with incomprehension, not with victory.

Their jeep swooped between familiar and loved places, blackened, wrenched from themselves, changed in ways that would take years to repair. Her peace-time self couldn't bear it. Again no tears came, but instead a new kind of coldness invaded her as if she had conjured it. This was not the ruthlessness of the warrior. That had been a warm fiery feeling. This was a new sense of detachment that crept over her on that jeep-bounced journey, as if she knew she was separating out a part of her nature, jettisoning it into this vast conflagration she was passing through. She couldn't care for this country any more. It was too painful. She had been too much of a failure. Once she would have wanted to remain and help to put things right. Not anymore. She had no wish to stay and help its people, no wish ever to come back here. She had shivered with the strangeness of the feeling and with its great sense of release. Never again, she was saying to herself, never again. What I want to do now is hide.

That was when the soldier had put his arm round her.

'Are you cold?' he asked her, 'Do you want me to ask the driver to go a little more slowly?'

The last man who had put his arm round her was Pierre, six long weeks ago.

'No,' she said to the English soldier whose name she didn't yet know, 'let's get there. Let's get this done.'

She hadn't cried; she hadn't even sniffled. She travelled the rest of the way to the HQ with the arm of a strange man round her as if she knew she was about to cross a frontier and there would be no way back.

The headquarters turned out to be a selection of tents and two trailers. When they got there the soldier had treated her as if she was already his possession. She'd been waved past two sentries and taken in to meet a harassed colonel who was clearly far more interested in fighting the war than interviewing an English national trapped in the war zone.

'Yes?' was all he had said as they walked in.

'I found her in one of the villages, Sir.' The soldier had answered for her. 'She says she's English. We thought you might need to interview her, Sir.'

The man took a look at her companion and dismissed him. 'Very proper,' he said. 'Now you can go back to your unit.'

The soldier saluted, winked at her and left. Even before he was out of the room the man was talking. 'You'll need to be interrogated. You could be anyone. You could be a plant. If you go next door and find Corporal White he'll give you the forms. Fill them in and wait your turn.'

The colonel was going back to work, dismissing her, picking up his pen again and checking numbers against papers. He must be well over fifty, only a little younger than the Gestapo officer she had shot and buried. Now he was waving her away.

'I've been working for the Special Operations Executive,' she told him quietly. 'I was parachuted in nine months ago. I probably need to report.'

This time the colonel stopped writing, not only put his fountain pen down but closed it within its cap. She heard the click, saw him look at her. Then he picked up the phone.

'Name?' he asked her.

'Which one?'

'You'd better give me both.'

'Over here I'm Marie-Claire Cardon. My other name is Anna Edith Julen.' The English felt funny in her mouth, clumsy and different on her tongue.

'And who sent you over here?'

She looked at him then before saying, as quietly as possible, 'I'm not at liberty to say.'

She could see the annoyance spreading across his face as he asked whoever was on the end of the phone to get him Major Lustic. Then he waited, taking quick glances at her in ways he probably expected she wouldn't notice. Those looks were sceptical. She thought to herself, I don't think he believes me.

Then he was talking. 'Bill, it's Patrick. I think I've got one of your funnies. She says her name is Marie-Claire Cardon.' There was a long pause, then his face changed as he said, 'Really. You sure?' before he listened for nearly two minutes without responding.

When he put down the phone he looked at her quite differently. 'He's sending a jeep round for you. Meanwhile we are to hold you here.'

She was being processed. She was a bureaucratic detail. Well that was all she was fit for. She tried to stand upright and wait, but had to lean against the wall. She felt awful. Was that just tiredness?

'You look all in,' the officer said. 'Go and wait outside in the sunshine. Find somewhere to sit.'

She went out into the heat and gleaming bright light of that August day. The soldier who had brought her was still there. The moment he saw her he walked over, took her arm. 'They let you go then?'

'Yes.'

There was nowhere to sit so they stood together in silence. She wanted to be on her own, didn't feel up to talking.

'Don't you have to rejoin your unit?' she suggested after a short pause.

He smiled at her. 'Yes,' he said, 'but I don't think there's any hurry.'

She closed her eyes, saw the sun as bright pink through her shut lids, saw an image of the SS man's face imprinted there, could make out the grey hair, the horrified look when he realised he'd been shot. Instantly she opened her eyes again to get rid of the picture.

The English soldier was by her side, squinting into the sun. He seemed to feel the need to explain to her. 'It's like this. We've only gone thirty miles so far and we have to get to Berlin. I reckon if I catch up with them by the time they cross the border that'll be alright.'

She said nothing, just stood there. He expected her to laugh and she wouldn't.

There was another pause.

'What's your name?' he asked, 'I'm Ronnie, Ronnie Devonshire.'

'I'm not sure who I am anymore,' she heard herself say to him. 'I was Marie-Claire but I suspect I'm about to go back to being Anna.'

'Wow,' he said, 'you do need a bit of help if you're unsure of your own name.'

She was silent again, hoping he'd go away. She needed thinking time. What would she tell whoever debriefed her? She was still in the army, a member of FANY. She couldn't just walk away. She had to be properly demobbed, collect her pay. It was her only means of support. It wouldn't take her far. She'd need to work. They'd probably want the radio back and she'd left it in the loft. Her gun was there too.

Ronnie was talking, 'Can I do anything else for you?' he was asking.

'No, I'm alright. They're sending someone to pick me up.' She tried to make herself smile. 'Thanks for looking after me.'

'Well, I'm a bit hot standing here in the sun,' Ronnie said. 'Hope to see you again. I won't forget you.'

'Thanks,' she said, then added, shouting after him as he walked away, 'Good luck.'

Her de-brief had taken place in London. They'd found her a berth on one of the naval vessels going back from Normandy to Plymouth. From there she'd taken a train to Paddington because she had been ordered to report to the Baker Street office.

The day she reported the first signs of autumn were already noticeable. There was a softness in the air and the first few plane tree leaves scrunched underfoot as she walked up the street. She'd noticed too that tidying up was already happening, indeed there were even bits of rebuilding taking place. The cordite smell of the London she had left less than ten months ago was mostly gone. Fewer people carried gas masks through that sunny September morning. But they still looked anxiously upwards. Doodlebugs were the new horror.

She found she was longing for one to target her. I don't deserve to be alive. It would be merciful, wouldn't it, she thought, if that engine cut out and the bomb fell straight for me. After all her mistakes she felt she owed the world, needed to pay it back, and the only way she could do that would have been with her death. Here in daylight, in London, Normandy had ceased to exist.

Arriving at the building she gave her name as Marie-Claire and was asked to wait. It was already well past her appointed time when she was told that 'George' was ready to see her.

He stood up when she walked in. 'Hello Anna,' he said. 'Please take a seat.'

He was another man in his mid fifties sitting behind a desk. German or English, in uniform or dressed as 'George' was in his grey suit, what difference did it make?

There was a grey file on his desk which he must have been reading through while she waited. It had both her names on it. His first statement astonished her.

'Look,' he had said, 'I need to get one thing clear. There will be no other assignments for you. I am sorry but we won't be able to offer you another posting.'

She was about to tell him that she wanted nothing to do with spying ever again, when he carried on. 'The battle for France is almost over. The Falaise gap has been well and truly closed. Armies everywhere are moving too fast for spies to feed them anything that's useful. Thanks to the Americans the landing in the south went almost unopposed. So even if we wanted to use you there would be nothing for you to do.'

Even if they wanted to use her. She ran the words through her head, dissected them. So they thought she was a failure too. Her judgement, their judgement coinciding.

George's office was small and airless. There was a high window above the desk through which she could see the sky, as blue as forever, the same blue she'd seen as a child, the same blue as had often spread itself across the France she had just left. When she got outside again she thought, I will be free to walk for miles under its blueness, to gaze through its translucence, to see it reflected in the lakes and rivers of a country that is, I suppose, mine now; the only one I have, a country that is rejecting my service, even before I have the chance to tell it that I no longer want to serve.

'Right,' George said, 'now we have got that clear there are one or two questions I need to ask you, just for the records.'

She braced herself, got ready to confess her failings, hoped she would be able to paint the background for him before he leapt to judgement.

She gave him details of her service, probably only confirming what he already knew: the sabotage, the groups, what had happened since D-Day.

He took notes, prompted her when she went silent, when it seemed too much trouble to record it all. And when she finished he only had one question, but it was the one she had been dreading.

'We sent you Pierre.' George said. 'Do you know what happened to him?

'Pierre.' She repeated his name to give herself time to think, spoke it out loud in the way you talk of the dead, listed flatly like anything else that you hope has lost its power to hurt you.

'Yes,' said George, 'according to the record you worked with him over there. He stopped communicating with us on June 5th. We've heard nothing from him since.'

She began to talk, not knowing where she would stop. His was now one more body strewn across that battlefield. Clearly they hadn't found him or, if they had found him, they hadn't yet identified him. He was just another body with two bullets in it. Spies don't carry name tags.

She kept what she said to practical details, told him about the split in command, about the separate groups. She found she was describing it without feeling, with the same coldness that she had felt creep over her on that journey with the English soldier. She left out the loving, talked instead about the warning message from SOE, told George about the coincidence of Pierre's escape, about the thousand franc notes without pin holes in them, about the strain of deciding.

All the time she talked George wrote nothing, just looked at her. She was drying up, getting closer to what really happened, wondering still if she should stop and say, 'that's all I know'. Pierre had been her burden. Did she need to make George complicit in his murder? Oh what the hell, what did it matter? She was alone in a land that wasn't really hers. Her brother and both parents had died in and for an England that hadn't been theirs either. She felt as if she had sacrificed her youth on the same altar.

'I shot him,' she said and stopped talking.

George was very still, staring at her. 'That was a pity.' He made the comment flatly, as if he was stating a fact, made a note in what she thought must be her file. 'If you had told us he was working for the Germans we could have used that, fed him wrong information about troop movements within the beachhead, helped bring the break-out forward. A double agent was used from Spain in just the same way to make sure the southern landings were unopposed. Ironically this American double agent was also code named Pierre.'

'I am sorry,' Anna had said. 'I just didn't want him making a mess of the invasion.' She glanced up at the window and saw that it was now dull outside. The blue sky was slipping away from her.

George seemed to consider this point before asking, 'Have you told anyone else about this?'

'No.'

He continued to look at her so she added, speaking quietly, 'Why would I? I'm not proud of what I did.'

George was nodding as if he agreed with her conclusion. He was looking at her, sitting across the table, isolated in his own thoughts. Then he seemed to reach a decision.

'I'd like you to keep your secret a while longer. Do you think you can do that?'

She nodded fervently.

'In that case we can tell his wife something noble about him. She's pestering us for information. It goes without saying that we didn't know he was married or we would never have used him.'

The information seemed to bounce straight off her, leaving no bruise. Perhaps later she would feel another wave of betrayal sweeping over her but not now. How could she have got it all so wrong? Love was for fools. It wasn't just Pierre. Love was the real villain. Love had betrayed her.

George was becoming business-like. The time of her debrief was clearly coming to an end. He had other matters to move on to.

'You will, of course, be recommended for a medal.'

'No!' She said it at once, said it quite firmly.

He was looking at her again.

'No,' she repeated her refusal. The man who had saved her lay under a cattle trough. Her lover was crumpled up on a French hillside. The France she had fought for was pummelled and broken. A medal would mean questions, re-awakenings. She needed to forget.

'No.'

'Extraordinary.' He was shaking his head. 'You young women are quite extraordinary.'

He opened the file and checked something. 'You have back-pay to be collected. If you go down two floors and ask for Pauline she will sort that out for you. We did get everything back from you didn't we? Your radio? Your pistol?'

She nodded. Major Lustic had personally taken her back to her French house to get the radio set. He had told her to keep the gun as a souvenir. She would obey his order. If life continued to be this unbearable she would use it on herself. Major Lustic had waited while she said a strained goodbye to Madame Desaint. Franck had been nowhere around.

'Yes, everything,' she told George, making sure that she looked him straight in the eye as she said it.

'Well goodbye then.' He looked at her again, then made another note in her file. She felt him watching her as she went out of his room and down the stairs to find Pauline. When she finally got outside it had begun raining.

Chapter Ten

Her brother's flat was still there, unharmed. She could live there at small cost, eking out her back pay. She was free of all responsibilities. Safe. She had left her war behind.

But when she closed her eyes the war was still there. She saw the bodies, his eyes, accusing, heard the noise his head made bouncing along, smelled cordite, blood, had to snap her eyes open, shake her head. But the image of the flat was no stronger than these strange invading phantoms in her head. She looked at the Bakelite radio, the clock on the mantelpiece, the pair of china dogs her brother had bought as a symbol of Englishness, the Toby jug with the chip at the top of the handle.

These were objects to pin her in this place and this time. Only they didn't do that any more. It was as if everything she had tried to put to one side in France, to ignore so that she could function as a spy, now demanded that she take notice, that she remember.

It was quite unbearable. She was sure she was going mad.

She tried her best to cope. She stopped going to bed. She sat in the chair wrapped in a blanket, trying to read her way through the night and still get enough rest so that she could function the next day. She kept the light on, feeding coins into the meter, keeping it topped up because the shadows did strange things, took shapes, wore wonderfully neat coats with lightening flashes or hung from lampposts with split cheeks.

Then her voice stopped working. One morning she woke from a not-meant-to-happen sleep and found that her lips felt like clamps and her tongue seemed to have fixed itself to the top of her mouth.

The feeling faded with a cup of wartime tea, then came back when she went shopping. The greengrocer asked her what she wanted. He had a brown bag ready, stretched wide and balanced in the palm of his enormous hands. She opened her mouth and tried to form the words but nothing happened. He stared at her. She tried again, putting her lips together to form the 'p' of potatoes but couldn't do it. She was in a queue with others. She tried a third time but then, in a panic, she pointed. The greengrocer began to fill the bag, continually looking up at her face. She kept nodding as he threw in the huge, mud-encrusted Lincolnshire spuds. When she had enough she shook her head. He weighed the potatoes then threw the bag in the air to twist it closed.

She bought carrots and leeks in the same way.

When she got back home she tried to sing, thinking there is no one to hear me. If this is a kind of stage fright, here, with nobody around, I should be alright. She threw back her shoulders and opened her mouth.

Nothing. Nothing at all.

It felt as if something inside her had snapped and she would never be whole again. She panicked, found herself with the shakes, felt miserable but couldn't cry. The enforced silence went on for days then became intermittent.

If she couldn't speak she could clearly scream.

She woke one morning from the horror of being surrounded by great herds of bloated cows balancing on tiny legs, desperately mooing because they wanted to be milked. It wasn't a mooing sound most people would recognise as coming from cows. These dream animals sucked in gargantuan quantities of air and flung it out again from deep inside them giving it a hoarse, throaty quality that filled the valley and bounced back from the limestone cliffs. Their agony was immense and at first the sound they made drowned out the knocking.

But someone was pounding on the door of her apartment. She lay still listening to the noise, hoping it would stop. The call in the night was what you dreaded. She had to tell herself that she was back in England.

She went to the door and a young mother was standing there with her baby.

'Are you alright?'

She nodded.

'Only you were screaming so loud, I wondered.'

She tried to smile, to say she was sorry, but it came out like a shrug. The woman stared, waiting for an apology she could never have. Then she turned abruptly and walked away.

Anna didn't sit back down. Instead she poked the fire, threw on a bit more coal and stood leaning on the mantelpiece. She could scream but she couldn't speak. Was this what victory felt like? Did you survive only to find that you could never be whole again?

She tried praying but knew that she no longer believed. As a child she had been fervent. In adolescence God's hold over her weakened and she had become indifferent. The death of her family and what she had seen in France had moved her on from indifference towards dislike.

But because she was desperate she pushed all that to one side and went to a catholic church where she tried to ape the faith of her mother. She didn't attend a service but dropped in one evening, found a pew, crossed herself, knelt and began, in her mind only, to recite words she had learnt in childhood. It was an effort and it felt mechanical. She might as well be reciting her times tables. Then the rhythms returned and for a moment she was back in her childhood, feeling that she had only to open her eyes to find her mother kneeling at her side, saying the same words. She ducked her head and squeezed her eyes more tightly shut and carried on, doggedly, hopelessly, despairing.

Footsteps were walking quietly towards her along the aisle. She opened her eyes and her mother wasn't there. A young priest was asking her if she was alright.

She nodded.

He asked if he could be of any help and she shook her head.

He offered to hear her confession and she fled, clattering along the aisle, swinging open the heavy door and letting it slam behind her.

She knew she was exhausted, recognised that she had been pushed too far for too long. Often, mercifully only when she was on her own, the shakes came back and then she had to clasp her hands together, bring in her elbows and just hang on until the shaking stopped. It was strange to watch her hands oscillating of their own accord, sometimes moving so fast that they became a blur. What were they trying to do? Separate themselves? Shake themselves away from her? Her right hand shook more than her left. It was her gun hand. It was the one she had used to pull the trigger.

Time and place stopped functioning. The past was everywhere. Even in the middle of the day, in full daylight on the High Street, she found herself pulling along a body on a piece of carpet, the head rolling from side to side as she tugged at it. When she came to herself, people had surrounded her. She recognised their stares. She wanted to stay inside but that wasn't possible. She had to eat, pay bills, look for work.

After a time the symptoms diminished, leaving her able to ape normality. The trouble was that it didn't feel normal. She began to go out more, to walk around London, to get herself used to her new way of life. She found she didn't want to mix with other people much. Even on VE day she had kept inside and listened to the wireless, thought how satisfactory it was that they had finally won, then found she was mourning the loss of her parents, of her brother; mourning the death of a Gestapo officer who had saved her life and even mourning the loss of Pierre. If he had been different, this is the day they would have been waiting for.

There were no broad sunlit uplands now that the war was over, only a series of unsatisfactory short term jobs in offices, doing translations, following instructions, never having to think for herself. She knew she was drifting, couldn't seem to shake herself out of it. Men occasionally gravitated towards her but it would always, she later recognised, have taken someone remarkably thick-skinned to try and woo her.

It must have been more than a year after the war ended, around January 1947. She had never been very good at dates and since she disliked her own memory she could hardly recall any of them. It was bitterly cold. She couldn't seem to keep herself warm in that winter, even with the small fires she let herself burn, even crouched over the fire, forced to inhale the smell of coal dust because she needed the heat to warm her. The edges of rooms in those days were as cold as the fridges they didn't yet have.

She'd gone into the local library, was borrowing a book (she'd no idea which one) and was handing her ticket over for the card to be slotted inside it when a voice she didn't recognise said, 'Don't I know you?'

She'd looked up and hadn't recognised him at all. Without speaking she had shaken her head and prepared to walk away.

Ronnie had persisted. 'I'm sure it's you,' he said, 'the girl in the French village.'

She said nothing, was still trying to place him.

'You had two names,' he added. 'One was Marie-Claire but you didn't seem to use that one. I think the other one was Anne.'

'Anna.' She corrected him without realising that she was starting a lifetime's conversation.

'I'm Ronnie Devonshire.'

She had seen it then, seen the round face, remembered that he had kept his helmet on the whole time, even a long way behind the front line.

'Hello,' she had said.

'How extraordinary,' he commented. 'It is you. I mean, how extraordinary bumping into you like this.'

'Yes.' A third word uttered, building into a series.

'And are you alright now?'

What a question that had been, making her remember his previous kindness. And the answer was no, she wasn't alright. She still slept badly, had nightmares. How could she tell him what she felt? So she smiled.

'I say, let's celebrate.' Ronnie was always persistent. 'There's a pub round the corner, one with a real fire in the snug bar. We can warm up. Let me buy you a drink.'

She'd gone with him to the pub, had sipped a half pint of cider while he drank three pints and told her about his war. She'd listened and nodded in the right places. It had been warm in front of the fire. It was the first time she had been really warm for weeks. She supposed she must have begun to smile and to talk about how dull London was.

'Not at all dull, if you know the right places to go,' Ronnie had assured her.

He lived close to where she lived. They met again. It became a routine. He persisted with her. He never took no for an answer. And she noted, round the times with Ronnie, her symptoms lessened. Life became bearable. Perhaps he was all she deserved.

One day in February, after he walked her home, he kissed her and she let him. She tried her best to feel what she had felt before and the contact, just the not being alone, was pleasant enough. What I felt for Pierre only happens once in a lifetime, she told herself. It was just my bad luck that I chose the wrong man to love. This is as good as it will ever get.

The whole thing had gathered pace. Ronnie didn't have friends. He would have cronies all his life, work cronies and golf cronies, but he wouldn't have friends. So apart from his parents who were clearly delighted that Ronnie had 'found someone', as his mother had put it to her, there was no one else to meet and get to know.

When he asked her to marry him she said, 'Yes'. She'd been

on her own for too long, she told herself. Now at least she'd have a big part in someone else's life.

Marriage was going to be a kind of new beginning, a way of forgetting about France, the older Anna thought. It's not only spies who act a role. Was Ronnie a new kind of cover? He didn't deserve that, she thought. He didn't deserve me. He was always kind.

Part Two

England 2006

Chapter Eleven

These days Anna could put a name to what had happened to her. At that time there hadn't been a name, only that dull feeling of becoming detached from the people round her, of living in a fog, of watching herself as she talked, ate, walked, went through the motions of living. Now they called it Post Traumatic Stress Disorder, PTSD. It hits the headlines and everyone suffers from it. Then, because there was no name, there had been no treatment. She had always known she wasn't alone. She had seen its unnamed presence in many of the faces she met: returning soldiers who had risked everything for their children's futures and now found that those same children resented their coming home at all; older men who'd coped with fire-watching and driving ambulances but allowed the sheer adrenalin of it all to push them into permanent exhaustion; those whose dead eyes told you that they had seen one horrific sight too many and had lost the ability to hope. For some it had been the fighting, for others the letting go. The look was everywhere round her, held inwards and not to be talked about. You were still alive, so get on with it.

She was still alive. She had got on with it. She had abandoned Marie-Claire and become Mrs Devonshire. If only it had been that easy. Marie Claire had never really gone away.

Ronnie's photograph was three shelves down on the bookcase, across the other side of her sitting room, placed so that no one could imagine she had forgotten her dead husband. A stranger walking into the room would have noticed it at once. But from where Anna always sat it was hidden away behind the standard lamp. Poor Ronnie. He'd got the worst end of the deal when she took his surname and never quite lived up to his expectations. When Ronnie had died, with his disappointments intact, her married title had withered away and, as she had grown older, more and more of the strangers she came into contact with simply called her Anna.

As if she was a child again.

There were, however, exceptions to this general rule. Her taxi driver, James, always called her Mrs Devonshire; so did her gardener, Peter Garnett. The cleaning lady, Rosanna, contrived never to call her anything at all, but Anna suspected that if Rosanna ever needed to identify her employer to a third party then she would probably refer to her as Mrs Devonshire rather than just plain Anna. She was well aware, as she thought of this small group of respectful people, that what united them was the fact that she employed them directly and paid them money. That gave her status and, in their eyes, it made her somebody.

You both collected and shed names as you grew older. Her three children, Alistair, Colin and Heather called her Mum. Most of their children called her Grandma, although to Heather's children, who had two grandmas, she was Grandma Anna.

'Why can't I just call you Anna?' Heather's oldest child, who had inherited all her mother's gracelessness, had once asked her.

Anna had looked down on the small flaxen haired creature who, at three years old, spent her time testing and probing the boundaries, looking for weak spots in the adults who surrounded her.

'Because I'm not your friend, I'm your grandmother,' she'd told her.

'Why aren't you my friend?' the child had shot straight back at her. 'Is it because you don't like me?'

Anna knew she must let this child down carefully, not voice what was really in her mind. For years now she had put a muzzle on her thoughts, choosing instead to stick to soft platitudes that no one could object to. Even so, she sometimes said more than she meant to.

'No. It's nothing to do with liking you or not liking you. It's because grandmas can't be friends. Friends are very flimsy things. You can get rid of friends whenever you want to, but you can't get rid of grandmas.'

Anna was sitting in her high backed chair as she remembered the conversation. The small flaxen-haired creature was now a strapping, nearly six-foot-tall young woman, whose graduation photograph was somewhere in the house.

The room Anna sat in boasted a large open fireplace, its bent oak beam balanced across two chimney breasts. At the back of the fireplace was a big blackened, cast-iron fireback. The fire wasn't lit. Its metal fire box, balanced on four curved wrought-iron legs, spoke of the warmth it could bring to the room in winter. Except that she didn't use it any more. Getting the logs in from their pile in the garage had become too much of an effort, even after she had adapted the shopping trolley so that she could simply pull them through. Easier by far to reach down and switch on the electric fire. Besides, logs always discarded bits of themselves on the way through the hall. These bits seemed to stay there, totally ignored by Rosanna who liked cleaning the kitchen but hated vacuuming anywhere else in the house. If she wanted Rosanna to clean up all the bits of wood, Anna would have had to beg her to do it. Rosanna was nearly sixty herself and kept threatening to retire, so Anna could never ask too much of her.

She sat in the dim light of the sitting room with the electric fire on its lowest level. Early June pulsed against the three windows. Outside was blue sky, white clouds and a lifting wind. Bees and bluebottles tried to barge their way in, seeing the glass as no more than a sudden tightness in the air which would give way and let them through if they bounced against it one more time. Less and less light was finding its way into her sitting room. All those honeysuckles and pyracanthas that Ronnie had encouraged to grow up the sides of their house were dropping tendrils or throwing out side shoots as if they wanted to shut out her view completely, or even to bury her before her time. It was a nice afternoon. She knew she should get up, find the secateurs, pull back the heavy iron bolts of the back door, go outside and start pruning.

But she continued to sit where she was.

Getting up took real effort these days. She had to shuffle her bottom towards the edge of the chair and place both hands on the arms. Then she must rock herself forwards and backwards to gain momentum. Everything in her knees and her hips tried to resist. Standing up was like pushing open an old rusted door. It took so much effort that she had to pause once she was up, just to catch her breath.

Her phone was nearby, in reach, a phone with special amplification that her family had insisted on her having so that she could hear them when they spoke to her. Her hearing wasn't what it had been, but it also wasn't nearly as bad as she made it out to be. She liked to pretend that she couldn't hear because then she didn't have to listen for long. She could say rather quickly, 'Thank you so much for phoning but I'm afraid I can't hear you very well. I'm going to put the phone down now, goodbye.'

It was mostly her children who phoned, if she could call them hers.

She remembered Alistair's birth vividly. Labour had been long and painful. She could cope with that. The pain was deserved. It was when the baby was born, when she had felt the relief of this stuck thing slithering free and it had been wrapped and handed to her that it had happened. She saw its screwed up face, its perfection, its hopefulness. The midwife had handed her the bundle and she had refused to take it, had shaken her head. There had been somewhere a feeling of great joy but stronger and overpowering everything else was the knowledge that she didn't deserve this child. Pierre was dead. The Gestapo officer who had saved her life was dead.

Who was she to give birth, to have this miracle happen to her?

She'd turned away. For a whole day she refused to have anything to do with her child until Ronnie coaxed her round.

And after that she had never thought of them as her children, even though she had given birth to them. In her mind they were always Ronnie's children. She had done her duty by Ronnie. Three times her womb had filled and ripened. Three times she had felt the new life churn inside her. Three times she had hoped that this child would have something of her mother's grace, of her father's questioning mind. Three times she had given birth and seen at once that the child she was persuaded to feed not only looked like Ronnie but had attacked life just like Ronnie had: sucking greedily, taking in too much milk and then whining because it was full of wind. It wasn't like being a mother at all, she had thought; it was much more like being a human conveyor belt churning out clones of her husband. Two boys and one girl but even the girl, Heather, was another version of her father.

The worst thing was that it felt right. The children had become her punishment, for the two lives she had taken, for her wartime mistakes. She and Ronnie had had children quickly. Like so many others they set out to make up for the war years. Looking back she hadn't really been well enough. The nightmares were never far away. They advanced and retreated in waves. At the worst times her night time screaming woke the children. Then Ronnie's patience snapped. He'd made the arrangements. He'd hired the nanny, moved bedrooms round, arranged for the nanny to look after the children at nights. It was Ronnie who put their names down for boarding school.

So she survived by not letting herself feel very much. And they lived their lives round her.

The phone rang. Anna reached out for the handset and picked it up, found the green button and pressed it. Using the phone made her nervous. She didn't trust all this new technology. Phones used to have wires and chunky receivers that never slipped out of your hand. Phones used to have nice girls at the exchange who placed calls for you. Above all, phones used to be fully known and understood. When Alistair had introduced her to this new phone without wires, he had shown her so many different things it could do that she had become confused and dreaded pressing the wrong button. Alistair's son Roderick had then shown his dad lots more of what he called 'functions' which clearly even Alistair didn't understand. And she had no doubt that someone else, walking in off the street, could make it do even more wonderful things that Roddy wouldn't understand. Was that the ultimate function of a modern phone, to make everyone who used it feel inadequate? She hoped she'd pressed the right button as she took out her hearing aid and put the phone to what she now regarded as her better ear.

'Hello,' she said.

'Mrs Devonshire, it's James. How are you?'

One's health was a private matter. Why did everyone feel the need to pry into what you were feeling these days? In the old days you hadn't asked how people were. You simply expressed a hope that they were well, which was quite a different matter because it didn't necessitate any answer on their part. She was nearly ninety. How did anyone expect her to feel?

'Quite well, thank you,' she replied.

She had long understood that it was better at her age not to say exactly what you thought.

'And are you alright for tomorrow, Mrs Devonshire?'

Tomorrow was her weekly shop. These days doing any shopping was another enormous effort. She had to write a list. She had to be able to read it once she had written it. She had to push round a trolley which also acted as a walking frame. She couldn't afford to forget anything because this was the only chance she had to shop until next week.

'Yes, thank you. We said ten thirty didn't we?'

'Ten thirty, on the dot.'

This was the limit of their conversations. She always suspected that James was actually checking that she was still alive when he made these phone calls the day before their shopping trips. She got ready to say goodbye and to thank him for phoning her when, surprisingly, he started saying something else.

She listened to what he was saying and then she asked him to repeat it.

'I was asking you, Mrs Devonshire,' he explained, talking more slowly and a little more loudly, 'if you were looking forward to your ninetieth birthday party.'

That's what she thought he had said, but how could he know?

'Of course,' she said, 'I'll see you tomorrow. Thank you ever so much for phoning.'

She put the phone back in its cradle so that the battery wouldn't run out, then sat back in her chair and began to worry.

How did James know that it was nearly her birthday? She'd told no one in the area. She never celebrated her birthdays, simply ignored them. The fact that her children were all planning to come down and see her on her ninetieth birthday was a closely guarded secret. Beds had to be made up, but she had already successfully sneaked guest bed-making into Rosanna's routine without telling her why.

The whole point about living alone was that you didn't want fuss. You didn't want anyone else knowing your business.

But James knew and that meant someone had told him. The person who had told him could only be one of Ronnie's three children: Alistair, Colin or Heather. But why would any of them phone James? What possible reason could they have for doing that?

It worried her, gnawed at her, filled her with disquiet, made her push herself up from the chair and go through to the utility room. She put on her gloves, collected the secateurs, drew back the two bolts and stepped outside.

She wondered whether to take her stick, but it would only get in the way. She was only going as far as the windows. She moved carefully, holding onto the creepers. Then, when she was in position, she reached forward and began to cut.

It wasn't easy. She struggled to open the secateurs, then found that her hands hurt as she opened and closed them. The new growth was already so thick that for some pieces she had to use both hands in order to cut through. She didn't collect the pieces she cut, just let them drop onto the paving slabs.

And all the time she was thinking. Her brain still worked even if she had to crank it up sometimes to get it started. For so many years she had never really used it.

Why is one of Ronnie's children phoning James, telling him things about me, she asked herself.

The sun was warm on her back. She took frequent rests yet still it was slow going. She found that she couldn't reach very far up so that even if she kept at it she wouldn't be able to clear a whole window. The best she would be able to manage would be to clear the bottom two thirds. The honeysuckle was easier to cut through than the pyracantha, but the honeysuckle pieces didn't fall off when she cut them because they were inevitably wound round something else higher up and out of reach. At one time she would have pulled at them, but she couldn't do that now for fear of falling over and injuring herself.

Might one of the children have needed a taxi ride? she asked herself. Was one of them planning to come to her ninetieth by train, in which case it might be quite reasonable for them to phone James and book a taxi, casually throwing something about her birthday into the conversation? Heather lived only two hours away and had a 4x4 she was inordinately fond of using to bulldoze anyone else off the roads. She would definitely be driving herself. Alistair lived in central London and went everywhere by tube and taxi, but he was the proud owner of an over-large red Jaguar which he always complained spent most of the year in his garage. He too would be driving.

Colin was employed in the public sector, working, as he was proud of telling them, with 'real people'. This meant, as far as Anna could ascertain, that he hated all forms of public transport unless he could travel first class and someone else was paying. He was a very poor driver but Pamela would drive him down. From where they lived it was too much of a cross country route to use public transport. No. None of them had any reason to phone for a taxi driver.

She was getting into a rhythm now, cutting and dropping, keeping the secateurs square to the stem so that they didn't turn sideways and snag the blades. Her hands ached but she made herself keep going.

As far as she could remember she had never given James's number to any of her children. There were lots of taxi firms in the area. When Ronnie had become ill and Anna hadn't wanted to drive him everywhere, they had tried several of the companies before settling on James and using him regularly. If Ronnie's children had wanted a taxi driver the chance of them happening to phone the company James worked for was remote. Yet one of them had and the only place Anna could think of where they could have found his number was from her address book, the little one she kept by the phone. In that case one of her children had deliberately looked for his number, found it and written it down, had done all this while she was out of the room or she would have noticed.

There was a bird's nest just above the top of the second window. Was it this year's or last year's? Her eyesight wasn't wonderful. She peered at it to try to find out if it was freshly made or soggy with last winter's rain. She thought it was new. In that case it would provide her with an excuse for stopping. It was only June and the nest might still be being used. Even now the chicks could be cowering down in there waiting for her to go.

At one time no bird would have nested so near the house because she would have come in and out here several times every day as she walked and weeded and pruned, keeping it all neat. Now the birds were coming closer and closer as if this whole space was theirs. The birds were taking over the edges of the house in the same way that the rabbits had taken over her vegetable garden and the primroses had infiltrated the lawn. She couldn't manage it all any longer. At least she had cleared a bit of the windows but now she'd stop in case the adult birds were waiting to feed. She'd stop because she was tired anyway. She needed another sit down.

Before she closed the secateurs she turned and looked down the garden. The lawn was full of weeds and moss. Peter Garnett mowed it once a week but it needed more than that. It needed to be dug up and re-sown. The herbaceous border was a mess. The plants should have been divided years ago, properly spaced and fed. Now some of the thugs amongst them had run amok and strangled the more delicate plants and even the thugs were choked up with ground elder. This garden had once been hers, her pride and her joy, setting off the house she loved. Now she just couldn't cope with it any more and Peter was no gardener. He could mow lawns and clear pathways. That was all.

She looked at the garden and it accused her, accused her of being old and decrepit, of being unable to cope; accused her of being unfit to live there any longer.

But this was her house, the house she had chosen, the one she had persuaded Ronnie to buy against his wishes. She remembered when she first saw it and how something about the red brick, the sag in the red slate roof, something about the feel of the hill top and the look down into the escarpment had compelled her to snap out of normal passivity and insist. She'd played the coquette, told her husband how lovely it was, that it would have space for the children, suddenly thinking of them. 'They'll love its size. They'll have a bedroom each and I will have a garden.'

'But the windows are too small and it's too dark,' he'd said.

'I'm not sure it'll make money for us or even be worth its asking price when we come to sell.'

'I'd like to live here,' she told him, 'for the rest of my life, so the sale price doesn't matter, does it?'

He'd looked at her then, perhaps warmed to this improvement in her mood. Of course he'd shaved money off the asking price and used it to expand the sitting room, bring in more light.

And she had loved it, because it echoed the landscape of Normandy. It was high up with long views. Of all the things in her life it was the one to which she felt most attached, the first time she had let herself love anything after Pierre. Even in this decrepit state, it added continuous enjoyment to the unwilled act of staying alive.

That's why the phone call mattered. She continued to think about it as she carefully moved back inside the house, put the secateurs away, peeled off her gloves, and used the edges of the walls and even the corner of the water softener to support herself as she went back to her chair.

Before she jumped to conclusions she must eliminate every other possibility. Was it possible that James knew the date of her birthday without anyone telling him? Could he have remembered it from the days when Ronnie was alive and they went out for pub lunches? Ronnie always made a fuss of her birthday. Had James remembered the date from nearly ten years ago and worked out her age?

No. The idea was tempting but it didn't fit with what she knew. James had even forgotten his wife's birthday. He joked about it, never knew the ages of his grown up children, left all that for his 'missus', as he called her, to sort out and manage.

And anyway, even if his 'missus' had remembered from years ago, worked out her age and told James, it still didn't explain how he could possibly know about the proposed birthday party.

She hadn't wanted a party, would have preferred to forget

the whole thing. It was Heather who had suggested it, had clearly already talked it over with her brothers before she broached it with her mother. They wouldn't go out for a meal. (Were they embarrassed by the way she now ate and the slow way she moved between the tables?). Instead, ostensibly because it would be much more restful for her, they would all come and stay the night and cook her a fabulous meal, just her children, not the grandchildren because that would be too many. She didn't have to do the shopping. They would bring everything with them, including champagne.

Anna had looked at Heather while all this was being suggested, had recognised that her daughter thought she was being kind, but had deeply resented the way she was taking control. Alright, at her age she couldn't cook for all of them anymore. It was as much as she could do to cook for herself, but at least they could have begun by asking her what she wanted rather than doing her thinking for her.

She had tried to be gracious, had said a meal would be lovely and how thoughtful Heather was, yet all the time she had been thinking, I can get them all over within one day and one night. They'll sit there drinking too much and sparring so perhaps I won't have to say very much at all. If I turn my hearing aid off they'll just ignore me. Then the next day they'll all go and I shall have up to two months on my own.

Except she would never be on her own again. James knew about the birthday, she suspected, because at least one of her children regularly phoned him to ask how she was getting on. And there was only one reason for that: James must be reporting back to them about her growing frailty, keeping tabs on her, getting ready to tip them off that she wasn't coping.

She was under observation, just as she had been in the war. They were trying to take over her life, undermining her independence. They would say it was being done out of care and real concern but it was nothing of the sort. She was determined that she would be the one who made key decisions about her own life. She would let no one do it for her. In her paranoia she wondered whether, in addition to James, her children had a network of other people spying on her too.

Don't be ridiculous, she told herself. You have built a whole scenario out of a tiny suspicion. Wait until you have more facts.

Chapter Twelve

But was it so ridiculous?

Anna looked down at her hands as they rested on the chair arm. The skin was blotched and almost translucent, the flesh shrunk away. When they clutched her stick they were more like claws. She found it hard to associate them with her internal picture of herself. Surely they were somebody else's hands, not hers. In the winter or when it had rained for several days they ached persistently and she felt sorry for them.

The truth was that she wasn't coping physically. Her bedroom was upstairs and she crawled up to it each night. It was months since she had discovered that she couldn't get in and out of the bath, had started to wash herself all over standing up at the sink. Except there were places she couldn't reach any more, bits of herself she poked at with a wet flannel. Perhaps she had begun to smell a little, with that sour old lady's smell you could never quite remove. She hoped not.

Now she was back in her chair she was buoyed up to notice that the work she had done that afternoon had made a real difference. She could see through the window again, see the lawn sloping down to the bridleway, even make out the gate Ronnie had built her so that she could walk the back way through the woods when she went to the village. She could see the bench too, perched at the far end of the lawn commanding a view over the wide valley. Perhaps now it was summer she could walk there again, sit down in the sunshine and look across the river. The land sloped steeply away beyond the lane. It was where they should have built the house, she always thought.

She'd always loved high places.

She noticed that something was happening in her garden. It wasn't only the rabbits and the moss. Someone was opening the gate at the bottom of the garden and coming through it, trespassing. She peered out to see who it was and what he was doing. He seemed to be a young man, probably one of those yobbos she'd read about. He had long hair, unkempt, falling right down over the top of his collar. He didn't even glance at the house, just walked to her bench and sat down on it.

Wow, she thought, he knows about it, knows that you can't be seen from the lane if you sit there, that you can survey the world but not be surveyed in turn, except from this house. The lad settled himself on the bench quickly and got something out from his pocket, did something carefully with his hands, something fiddly that she just couldn't see. Then he reached into another pocket and took out something else. She thought it was silver because it caught the sun. He lifted it to his face and she understood. He's come for a smoke, where he can enjoy the view but where he can't be seen, she told herself. He's not a danger to me. He's just taking advantage.

She could phone for the police. They'd come straight away if she told them how old she was and said she was frightened. They'd come and remove the yobbo, give him a warning. She valued her privacy. If one lad came today perhaps others would come tomorrow. She didn't want her garden taken over. It would be better to nip it in the bud. She reached out for the phone. Was it still 999? They kept changing numbers but you still dialled 999 for emergencies didn't you?

Then she put the phone down. This wasn't an emergency. She wasn't being threatened and didn't want to get a reputation for calling unnecessarily, didn't want anyone coming to the house to ask if she was alright. They might look at the house she was living in and recommend that social services made an assessment. If she wanted her independence she must prove she could cope, must never ask for help.

She'd give it a while, watch what the lad did. He was just sitting there, sitting and smoking and looking at her view. How had he first seen the seat, she wondered. How had he known it was there?

She fell asleep watching the lad on the bench, just nodded off in her chair.

When she woke up he was gone and the bench was empty. She looked at her watch. It was past five o'clock, time to get her tea before it got too late.

What day was it?

Wednesday.

She made herself keep track of the days. It was one of her little challenges. Wednesday was baked beans on toast, easy and delicious and you could sit and eat it with the television on. She'd have a cup of tea at the same time, then she wouldn't have to get up again. It might be as well if she went to the toilet first. Those were three things she could do, all as part of the same journey.

It was always tricky getting the tin opener in the right position on the tin, but she could still turn the handle, lift the lid off, tip the beans into the pan and put it on the hob. She knew when she walked the tin over to the bin that it wasn't quite empty but then she couldn't eat a full tin of beans. They wouldn't all fit on her toast and it was too much effort to scrape out the last bits. Once it had been a sin to waste food; not any more.

She found the bread and put a slice in the toaster. She was slowing down and the beans were already bubbling. To stop them burning she pulled them partly off the hob and rested them on the wooden surround while she waited for the toaster to pop up.

Then she got a plate, scraped some butter over the toast and plopped the beans over. Carrying the plate carefully she went back to her chair and, turning on BBC 1 with the remote control, she began to eat.

She hadn't finished before she heard the high pitched whine of the fire alarm. Heaving herself up with force (she was sure she had pulled something inside her because there was a new, sharper pain), she shuffled off towards the kitchen. The siren was screaming. She could smell burning now and could see that the kitchen was filling with smoke.

The hob was still on, and the pan was still balanced half on the hob and half on the wooden surround which was now badly charred. The few beans left in the bottom of the pan were black and stinking. She found the right knob and turned the hob off. She picked the pan up by the handle and flung it into the sink. Then she filled her coffee mug with water and poured it over the blackened wooden edge. Finally she found the key, unlocked the back door and pushed it open to get some air.

The siren wailed for a bit longer, then went silent.

Damn it. The pan was ruined. The surround was ruined. The floor was a mess and she was exhausted.

You're an old stubborn woman, she told herself. If you can't manage better than this you can't continue to live here. She had to talk to herself like that, upbraid herself for her lack of competence. Giving in wasn't an option.

The clearing up could wait.

Why was life doing this to her for a second time? Back then it had been the fear of rape, of losing your finger nails one by one. Then it had been the short walk to the pock marked wall, hugging your badly mauled hands, no time for a blindfold, so you would be able to see the dark stains by your feet which told you that others had been there before you. The stains on the wall gave you more information, told you too that they didn't always shoot straight. Then it had been the hope of a quick bullet, so truly aimed that you never heard the shot that killed you.

But she had survived all that, and now she had another fear: the fear of being incarcerated in a home, of being locked up with the decrepit, with those who jabber and those who slobber. As she walked back to her chair, leaving the door open to get rid of the smell, images filled her mind like those in a

Hieronymus Bosch painting of hell, only this one was filled with the old, and this one was no vision. It was here. It was now. It was much more likely than capture had ever been.

She'd seen these people she would one day be sent to live with, seen them gathered together in expensive, beautifully furnished places. She'd seen the old man who was like a child playing with dinky toys on a table in front of him and telling everyone about the dog which had been run over when he was six; seen the woman spooning shepherd's pie into her toothless, drooling mouth; noticed the lady sleeping all day, every day because she didn't have much time left; spotted the one who cackled and had to be sedated. It was true that you had your own room but they kept encouraging you out into communal spaces. You were looked after by the well meaning and by the newly arrived, plonked down next to the woman in the incontinence knickers who had her skirt pulled up over her fat knees. And they wanted you to meet and have inane conversations. They wanted you to sing. They wanted you to have a weekly bath in a space like an operating theatre, lowered in, lifted out, washed because you couldn't wash yourself.

Once there she would be Anna, only Anna. No need for a prison number or a uniform. You went there when you couldn't run, you couldn't tunnel your way out, worse than Buchenwald, worse than death itself.

She knew she was being unreasonable to think like this. 'How else can you organise better care for the really old?' Colin had asked her.

'Little blue pills,' she'd told him. 'Give them little blue pills.'

Colin had laughed, nudged Alistair, 'So they can die happy,' he'd whispered to his elder brother.

She'd heard the whisper and been furious. What were they smirking about? Was that thing called Viagra blue? How could she be expected to know that? Why should she be laughed at for not knowing that? Blue pills had been issued to some SOE agents on particularly dangerous missions, given

142

to those who carried such vital information that it must not be risked. She was not at all impressed when Alistair joined in the light heartedness and said to his brother, 'I've no idea what you're talking about. I'm still functioning perfectly. Ask Lydia if you don't believe me.'

Ronnie's children. Ronnie's sense of humour.

James picked her up promptly at 10.30. She had cleared up as best she could and was waiting in the dining room when she saw him arrive. If she was quick she could get outside without him coming in, and if he didn't come in he wouldn't be able to smell the burnt wood from last night or see the mess in the kitchen. And if he didn't see it he wouldn't be able to report it.

It hurt like hell, and she knew she would suffer for it later, but she made herself walk quickly to the front door and had the door opened before James could ring the bell.

He seemed startled by her alacrity. 'Good morning Mrs Devonshire,' he said as he went round to open the car door for her. She followed him, still walking more quickly than she normally did. She wondered whether to try and throw herself into the front seat of the car, the way that able bodied people did, so that she could maintain this pace but decided, no, decorum was particularly necessary this morning because she had questions to ask.

He held the top of the car door and she adjusted her hand on the handle, lowering herself in slowly, trying not to exhale the air in her lungs when she finally sat down, then deciding it didn't matter. 'I'm in,' she said, pulling her skirt edges out of the way of the door.

He closed her door, then got in himself.

'Bank first please, James,' she said.

'Bank first, Mrs Devonshire. I thought it was a bank week. The truth is I couldn't remember if we went to the bank last week or not, but you obviously do remember.'

That gave her an opening. She'd use it straight away.

'Alistair says I have a hopeless memory. He tells me off for repeating myself.'

'Well that's not very polite if he does.'

James had clearly said this as a straight reaction, without thinking about what it would sound like. While Anna was concluding 'not Alistair then', James was trying to adjust his statement, perhaps realising that it could be misconstrued.

'That sounded all wrong,' he said. 'I don't mean to criticise him. He's your son after all. And I don't mean to imply that he might be right about you repeating yourself either. You don't do that with me.'

If not Alistair, then who?

She baited another hook. 'My children are always outspoken. They like telling me what I must do.'

'Outspoken or concerned?' he asked her.

She knew James hated confrontation, was always likely to appease. But the use of the word 'concerned' was interesting. She'd have to push harder.

'You don't know them like I do. It's outspoken. They're Ronnie's children. They don't do concern.'

She could see at once that she had shocked him. Ever since the war, the more she banned herself from remembering and saying what she thought, the more coruscating her brain had become. While Ronnie was alive she had been successful in keeping those thoughts inviolate but now her control was slipping.

She knew that James would mollify her at once. She'd ask for an instance and then she'd have the name.

'Oh I'm sure you're wrong about that, Mrs Devonshire. Take Heather for instance…'

She wouldn't have to ask for an example. The name was being given straight to her.

'…she is always concerned for you and about how you are getting on. She rings me regularly.'

Heather, with her father's round face and the pro-hunt

propaganda obliterating the back window of her 4x4. Heather was the one who was checking up on her. Or was it all of them?

'Okay,' she said to James. 'I might just have to give you Heather. She is a woman after all, but if you knew the other two …'

'I don't,' he said.

Just Heather then. But James was modifying his statement, being careful.

'That is, I don't know them yet, but Heather has kindly invited me to your birthday party. I'm hoping to meet them both there.'

She'd done what? Heather had told her mother it was just family but now others had clearly been invited as well, invited into what was her house, not theirs, not yet, perhaps not ever.

It *was* happening again. She was being spied on. Her family were checking up on her and not telling her. They were gathering information to use against her. She thought of the home that was waiting for her, of the slow death amongst the decrepit, which she would have to accelerate by refusing to eat. She knew her body was a mess but her brain was active. She was determined to stay where she was for as long as she could.

In the house with echoes of Normandy.

James had identified the enemy for her. He had also told her that he approved. Children should look after their parents, and by implication take over the caring and arranging of things when they could no longer do so for themselves. The world was on her children's side. Social Services had a duty to look after the vulnerable, which meant they could assess her needs and decide what should happen to her. All the polite, well-meaning world was ranged against her, and if they knew of the burnt cooker surround they would come running at her with their all pervasive, insidious brand of caring.

She was back behind enemy lines, without a radio and without a network. There was no one she could trust. They'd invited James to her ninetieth birthday party and hadn't told her.

What had her training taught her in that old rectory in Scotland? She remembered three to a room sleeping, eating meals on refectory tables, using the gents, with someone on guard, because there were too few female toilets. Their classroom must once have been the family drawing room. Some portraits still hung there but now competed with blackboards, charts and a rattling film projector.

'You'll be more on your own than you can ever imagine.' their teacher had re-iterated. He was a small man with a slight stammer that irritated at first, then you quickly forgot. They didn't know whether he was a soldier or a civilian. It had been a matter of speculation until they nicknamed him the Proffi Offi. He'd stood in front of the enormous picture windows with their view up to Ben More and spoken to them without barriers. 'You can either be afraid of your loneliness or you can see it as freedom. Knowing is what matters. Knowing and being sure. When you know your enemy you are free to act in any way you see fit. There are no rules where we are sending you.'

They completed the shopping and James brought her back home.

'Just leave the bags by the door, James,' she told him. 'I'm feeling good today. I can carry everything to the kitchen.'

James was doing what he always did and picking up her shopping bags from the boot, getting ready to carry them into the kitchen once she had unlocked the door and turned off the alarm.

'It's no trouble, Mrs Devonshire. You save your energy for something else.'

She couldn't insist. She'd have to let him walk into the kitchen. He'd see the scorch mark and he'd report it.

'There really is no need,' she repeated, but he was already

walking past her. She watched him put one bag down on the floor while he fiddled with the door handle. Even her old nose could smell the scorched wood.

She followed him into the kitchen, feeling like a naughty child. James was bending over the cooker. He had already put her shopping down and his fingers were tracing the burnt wood.

'I put it out,' she explained, 'so no harm's done.' She tried to sound bright and cheerful as she spoke.

But harm had been done because she could see the shock in James's eyes and she knew he would have to report it. How did Heather's network function? Would he phone Heather as soon as he got back home or wait for the next phone call from her? Did he have her mobile number so that he could always get in touch with her in an emergency?

Chapter Thirteen

Heather was the first to arrive on the morning of Anna's ninetieth birthday. Anna was in the sitting room when she heard the wheels of a car scrunch the gravel outside. The car's engine roared, then went silent. A car door was slammed shut and, at exactly the same moment, a woman's voice began giving detailed instructions to her husband.

Anna knew she should get up and get ready to answer the doorbell but she continued to listen, thinking all the time that this was only the start.

Heather seemed to be in particularly good form.

'No, Henry. Shopping first, then the cases.' There was a pause. 'Henry, you're not listening to me. We need the food first. The ducks and the cream have to go in the fridge. When we've done that, you can bring the cases in.'

Anna couldn't hear Henry's reply but guessed that it had been one of protest.

'Well put the cases down,' Heather was booming at him. 'Put the cases down on the gravel. It's not raining. They won't come to any harm there and find the shopping bags.'

Henry was obviously putting up stiff resistance because after a pause the boom continued. 'Look, you didn't have to do any of the planning. I did all the packing and all the shopping. I've got this thing organised. Just do it my way, without whining about it, please.'

That seemed to do the trick because footsteps were now crunching towards the front door. Two sets by the sound of things. Then the doorbell rang.

Anna got up and began, with stick in hand, to make her slow way to the front door, preparing to welcome the arrival of her only daughter in the same way that Caribbean islands welcome hurricanes.

She reached the door and they were both standing grinning at her. Heather, she noticed, was carrying nothing. Henry was struggling with three shopping bags. The bright sun made her blink as she stood inside her own front door looking from one to the other.

'Happy birthday, mother.' Anna felt herself embraced in a quick Heather hug. It took away the sunlight for a few seconds and then most of her breath. 'Ninety, actually reaching ninety. What a great age.'

The hug ended as suddenly and as violently as it had begun and Heather was pushing past her, moving into the house.

Have I said anything? thought Anna, have I said anything like, lovely to see you, do come in? I don't think I have and she is already past me, careering up my hallway and about, if my guess is right, to commandeer my kitchen.

She turned to her son-in-law. He was waiting patiently and politely. She had always shared a sneaking fellow feeling with her children-in-law. They were not Ronnie's progeny. Anna was about to say, 'Come on in, Henry,' when another boom from the kitchen told her that any words of invitation she uttered would be quite superfluous.

'Hurry up, Henry. I need that shopping.'

'Excuse me, Anna, I'm being summoned.'

She stepped aside and he scuttled past like the dapper solicitor he was.

She'd let them in. What should she do now? Go and help? Prove to them that she was quite capable of looking after herself?

As she made her way to the kitchen she heard a sudden hush and then whispering. They'd clearly found the burnt patch on the surround. She couldn't make out the words but it seemed to excite them both. As she passed the bottom of the stairs she began to hear fragments of what they were saying.

'…told you she wasn't coping…'

'…you may be right but I'd still say..'

'…if we find she's fallen and lain there all night…'

Anna was round the last corner by now. 'Excuse me,' she said to both of them, hoping that she was standing particularly straight as she did so, 'but you do realise you've left the car door open in the drive for anyone to see? There seem to be some cases by the side of it just waiting for someone to pinch them.' She looked up at their suddenly contrite faces. 'I left a pan on the side of the hob,' she explained to them, 'what's your excuse?'

'Henry!'

Heather's cry had been quite unnecessary. Henry was already moving, mumbling his apology in the way he always did, like someone saying his rosary, an act of such endless repetition that the individual words had long since been fused together into incoherence.

'Now, Heather, you can see that I have cleared a space in the fridge. I've given you the top two shelves. I hope that's enough. Would you both like a cup of coffee after your long journey?'

She knew she couldn't keep this act up for long. It's not that the brain stops working, she thought, it's that the body lacks energy and tiredness softens you up.

'Let me make the coffees,' said her daughter. As she turned to her mother she shook her hair to one side. At nearly sixty she still wore it in the fashion of a much younger woman, dressed like a younger woman too. Those trousers are far too tight round the bum, Anna thought. They may slim you down at the front but they do nothing for the rear view. Hasn't Henry told you?

She had no need to answer her own question.

Heather was saying to her, 'You go and sit down. You've got a big day in front of you. You need to get some rest before the others arrive.'

'Well, if you insist.'

'I do. Henry will bring you some coffee when he's finished

150

with the cases.

She's married a nonentity, Anna thought, as she made her way back to her recently vacated chair. But then, she thinks her father did exactly the same thing. I made myself into a nonentity because it suited everyone. Most of all, because back then it suited me and I simply wasn't capable of anything else.

The image of Proffi Offi slipped back into her mind. Had he really understood what he was sending those young naïve recruits into? Did he know what the war might do to them? She suspected he did. There had been something apologetic about his admonitions. What did it matter anyway? She couldn't confront him. He must have been dead for many years.

She sat down and watched the sunlight outside, the way it hit the lawn and spilled sideways through each blade of the poorly cut grass. There was someone else in the garden. That boy was there again, the one with the long hair and the smoking habit. She wanted to warn him that today wasn't a very good day, that there were other people round who might see him, but even as she thought that, a girl came to the back gate, a tall girl who stooped slightly and had her mousy coloured hair pulled severely back from her face and held together in a plait that fell over her right shoulder. She was calling to the boy and he seemed to take notice of her. He came down to the gate and they talked for a while, then he walked off with her. Not hand in hand, Anna noted. Was she his sister? She was taller than he was and the shapes of their faces were quite different.

Henry came in with her coffee and seemed to follow her eyes to see what she was watching. But he had missed her intruders. The two of them had gone. She could mention the boy who smoked on the seat but she knew she wouldn't. The old need secrets. It is all they have to fight back with, she thought.

'Sit down,' she told Henry when he had delivered her coffee and seemed at a loss as to what to do next. 'Sit down and keep me company.'

'Perhaps Heather…'

She interrupted him. 'Heather will love flying round my kitchen putting everything in the wrong place. She'll also enjoy shouting for you once she realises you have gone AWOL. Until that happens, tell me about work. Have you had any mad old women to deal with recently?'

Henry glanced sideways at the white painted door that led from the sitting room to the hallway and across to the kitchen. Then he sat down in what had been Ronnie's chair. 'Not mad,' he said. 'I did have one who wanted to change her will for the third time this month.'

'Tell me about her. She sounds interesting.'

'Well I mean I can do with the fees. Work is hard to get at the moment but I can't really change her will every time she has a whim.'

'So what happened?'

'I talked her out of it.'

She would ask how. Sitting, talking to one of her in-laws would be as good as the day got.

'How did you do that?'

She watched Henry as he explained that wills were vulnerable to challenge. Once you became deceased it was quite easy for the family to overturn your will. She noticed that he continually adjusted his tie knot while he talked, squeezing it and pulling it upwards. She wondered how often Heather had told him off for showing a shirt button. Apparently he had explained to his old lady client that the very number of changes she was making made it more likely that a challenge could successfully be brought against it, once she was deceased.

'Clever of you,' Anna said. 'Did you charge for that advice?'

'No, but don't tell…'

'Heather.' She was finishing his sentences for him, a thoroughly bad habit.

'I won't.'

The door opened, 'Henry, could you possibly spare me a moment?' whined Heather.

I didn't teach her that. I didn't show her how to insert so much martyrdom into a single question, Anna mused. But then I wouldn't have expected anyone to help. Martyrdom is the great English vice, she suddenly decided; it enables the English to pity themselves for doing exactly what they have chosen to do anyway.

'Can I send him along in a minute, Heather dear? He was just getting interesting.'

Henry, who had promptly got up and was half way to the door, had to come back and sit down. Heather was staring at her. When did she last call her Heather dear? Had she given her daughter more proof of her incapacity or shown something of the fight back? Then she ignored her daughter.

'What I wanted to know,' she said to Henry, 'is how your client could have got round that if she had wanted to carry on.'

Henry was taking her seriously. Heather tutted and left.

'Well, her best course of action might be to see two solicitors at the same time,' he explained, 'so there would always be another witness of her capability at that moment. That would make it almost impossible for a judge to overturn the will.'

'Thank you,' Anna said. 'Now duty calls.'

Henry got up and left. She had no idea what Heather needed other than the usual being taken notice of. Only a few minutes later she saw that Henry was outside. Heather had clearly noticed what Anna had not, that her gardener, Peter, was about to start mowing the lawn. Henry had been sent to find out more information no doubt. Heather's spy ring was clearly growing. Proffi Offi would have told her to be more discreet, to hide her intentions... *unless she saw no possible threat to herself.* Heather was formidable. Who else was she in touch with?

Two solicitors from different firms. She might need to

make use of that.

She watched the two men talking together, remembered what Proffi Offi had told them all those years before, that you didn't need to hear words to understand what was being said. Movements were enough. She saw Henry's reluctance, his hesitancy expressed in that intermittent frown whenever he asked anything, noticed that Peter constantly glanced towards the house, towards where she was sitting now, and that he often spread his arms out in a gesture that said - this isn't my fault.

They were talking about her. Peter was now pointing to the mower, as if to say, 'what can I be expected to do with that?'

A bad workman, Anna thought. Well he is the only workman I can get. I wonder if Henry understands that?

Then her reverie was interrupted. More noise was erupting into the hall. From the sound of it this was Colin, walking straight in through her front door, being greeted and welcomed by Heather, brother and sister filling the narrow hallway with the same excited noises they always made on seeing each other. Colin was talking about the roads, about what he would do if he was in government, how 'the sooner they had a series of toll roads so that those who needed to get to places fast could pay for the privilege and bloody get there, driving at any speed they liked, the better it would be for England.'

She didn't need to be there to see what he looked like this morning. He would be wearing an open necked shirt under some terribly loud coloured jacket. His blond, now slightly greying hair would be flying everywhere. The big face would be smiling broadly and his eyes would notice nothing around him until it was pointed out to him.

'Honestly,' she heard him say to his sister. 'You wonder sometimes what Dad fought for.'

He would be fatter than he had been last time and his wife, Pamela would be even thinner. She did his dieting for him, did his exercise for him, tried to compensate by cultivating

154

humility and quietness.

'Where's the birthday girl, then?' Anna heard Colin ask.

'In the sitting room, sitting down.'

'Well let me see her then.'

The door to her sitting room opened with a thump and Colin filled it as he began singing: 'Happy birthday to you, happy birthday to you, happy birthday...'

Dear God, I must stop this, thought Anna. He's going to sing the whole bloody thing, and I can't bear it.

'Hello Colin, how's your job going?' she asked him. 'Are you making everyone's lives better?'

He had stopped singing, was coming forward to give her a kiss and another child-of-Ronnie-hug when she suddenly had to exclaim, 'And exactly what have you done to your hair?'

It was blond again, not his usual mixture of blond and grey but just blond. 'You haven't dyed it, have you? Even your father wouldn't ....' She managed to stop herself just in time.

'The Borough's fine,' he told her. 'Actually it's thriving.' He had thrown himself now into the chair so recently vacated by Henry. He was sitting in it with one calf vertical and the other stuck out in front of him, slouching down as if he were mimicking the pose of a particularly recalcitrant teenager.

He'd recently become Assistant Director of Education after a life-time of doing the jobs that sound much better than they are. He had been Advisor on Behaviour, Leader for Learning and now he was Assistant Director. Now he was actually being entrusted with the whole works.

'I'm putting a rocket right through the Education Department. I'm stopping schools permanently excluding their most difficult pupils. The number of permanent exclusions is 50% down this year. We are being noticed in Whitehall. I've got the members eating out of my hand.'

'Hadn't you better tell your mother why that is?' Pamela had slid quietly into the room bearing two cups of coffee, one of which she handed to her husband. She's looking older, thought Anna, then she spotted why. As Colin had clearly started dying his hair she had stopped dying hers. It was now a really rather nice pepper and salt grey. Last time it had been an unnatural shade of purple.

'Hello, Pamela. What should he tell me? Is my son not being fully honest?'

Pamela snorted.

Anna remembered that when Roman generals were awarded a triumph a slave stood behind them and whispered all the time as the crowd cheered that fame never lasted, that triumph was illusory. Pamela had appointed herself to this role, would continually puncture her husband's pomposity.

'Pams isn't being very fair,' complained Colin.

Pamela snorted again. For such a thin woman with high cheek bones and too much powder on her face she could do a good snort. A terrible thought crossed Anna's mind. What if Colin begins to wear make up? Pamela will have to stop.

'It's a technical thing,' Pamela explained. 'All those who would have been permanently excluded are now being home educated which means they don't count on the figures. There aren't actually any more problem students in schools. But that's not the point apparently, the exclusion numbers look great and Colin will take the credit, won't you darling?'

It was water off a duck's back.

'That'll only be part of it,' Colin asserted. 'I've got the whole place working together. My speech to the conference was a wow. Did I tell you what I said, mother?'

It didn't need an answer. Colin began to recount his address and it gave Anna time to notice that Pamela was mouthing the words just to show how many times she had heard it before, time to notice that Henry had stopped talking to Peter, who was now mowing the lawn, going backwards and forwards at the most sedate of paces. By the time Peter had completed three sets of stripes Colin had reached his punch line and was laughing at it so heartily that no one else needed to join in.

The door opened and Heather appeared. She was now wearing Anna's cooking apron and a pair of Anna's blue plastic gloves. 'Enjoying yourselves you two?' she accused.

'Ah,' said Colin, 'is it family conference time?'

Heather lowered her voice (presumably so that I cannot hear, thought Anna). 'I want to show you something,' Heather said.

That will be my charred mark, thought Anna. She wants to show her brother just how incompetent I have become. I want to make a smart reply, but then they will know I can hear almost perfectly well and that will blow my cover on phone calls, so I had better just sit here. The same thing will happen when Alistair arrives. I'll bide my time.

'See you soon, birthday girl,' Colin cooed as he and Pamela left the room.

They've left their coffee cups behind, Anna thought. I could take those through, prove how competent I am. I could even borrow my own blue plastic gloves and do my own washing up. Is it worth it, she wondered, and then told herself that it was.

If only my central core worked better, she thought, as she heaved herself up and paused, stick in hand, before setting off on the walk of pain. Four steps and it will start to ease, six and I might just be able to smile while I walk.

She collected the three cups and slid them all into a plastic bag she kept down the side of her chair. Keeping the mugs upright was tricky but she could manage it. She went particularly silently across the hallway, arrived at the kitchen door and pushed it open.

Four sets of faces stared at her. Four sets of mouths stopped talking.

'What are you doing mother?' Heather asked. Trust her to recover first. The others were, for a moment, fully occupied with trying not to look guilty.

'Clearing up after you,' purred Anna. 'It's what I've done all

157

my life, isn't it?'

She marched her way to the sink.

'Gloves, Heather, please.' She began to run the hot water from the cistern into the bowl as she hoiked her stick over the edge of the basin and balanced herself against the sink, picking up the coffee cups one by one out of the plastic bag. 'Pamela, be a dear and pass me that washing-up liquid.'

They watched her wash up in virtual silence. No one offered to dry up for her. It's as if they are there to judge me and give me marks, she thought.

Half an hour later Alistair and Lydia arrived.

Alistair kept himself trim, ran marathons and did long walks. He still had his father's round face. His hair was white and he had grown a beard. He used the same setting on the cutters for both, so that hair and beard were of exactly the same length and consistency. His was nearly like one of those faces that could go either way up and still fail to be recognised as fully human.

Whichever way up his face went it had the look of the harassed. Anna didn't know exactly what Alistair did. It was something in the City, something to do with investments. She knew he was still hanging on in there, even though he was now past sixty and spent his time complaining that those round him got much, much younger.

Anna had heard the car and got to the front door first. The others were talking in the kitchen and she thought they had opened a bottle of wine and not offered her any. Their conversation was getting louder and under the cover it provided she made her way to the front door. She was able to open it even before they rang the bell.

Her eldest son seemed to be standing in the centre of the drive leaning against Heather's 4x4 and looking up at the house as if he was contemplating buying it. Lydia, wearing a well cut trouser suit in deep green, was locking the car.

'Hello,' said Anna, 'have you had a good journey?'

Lydia came straight towards her and gave her a kiss. 'Happy birthday, Mum.' She always said the 'Mum' as if she knew that Anna wasn't her real mother and that she shouldn't really be calling her this.

Alistair was still out in the middle of the drive, looking up at the roof.

'Is there a slate missing, Alistair?' Anna asked. 'Do I need to send for the builder?'

'Happy birthday, Mother.' Alistair stopped his survey of the house and moved towards her. 'You look…'

That bad, thought Anna. Which word is he struggling to find?

'…splendid.' His face actually lost its frown as he walked towards her but soon regained it. Having kissed her he absent-mindedly bent down and pulled a weed from out of the gravel.

A chill went through Anna in spite of the growing heat of the day. He's not looking at the house because he wants to buy it, she thought; he's wondering what it will make when they sell it.

The others had now heard the arrival and come rushing out. Anna was able to stand to one side and watch the usual greetings between them. Colin had made a bee line for Lydia and was flirting with her outrageously. Pamela had looked towards them and done another of her snorts. Heather greeted Lydia but then hugged her brother. They all ignored Henry and he clearly expected nothing else.

She waited until the greetings were over, then went across to her elder son. 'There's something I should show you both, follow me.'

She led the way into the kitchen and stood beside the burnt surround. 'There you are,' she explained. 'It's a patch of burnt wood. The others seem to find it very significant. I pulled a pan half way off the hob, then left the hob on and that's what happened. I dealt with it. Now I expect you will all want to get into a huddle and talk about me.'

She left them there, shocked into silence. I must be careful, she thought. I could be overdoing this. I must remember that they have all the cards, all the power, and the good spy should never show she is resisting. That is why I didn't challenge them about opening a bottle of wine and not offering me a glass.

She went and sat back down in the sitting room. After about thirty minutes of sitting by herself she was summoned through to lunch. They sent Lydia to fetch her and she came through graciously enough to what Heather called a simple lunch. It consisted of carton soup with crusty bread and great hunks of deli cheeses served on the flat Worcester serving platters she never used, the ones Ronnie's mother had given her for a wedding present.

The talk round the table was of jobs and responsibility. In spite of her recent sharp behaviour she noted that she was not required to join in and that she had been reallocated the role of nonentity, the one she had forged for herself all those years ago. Pamela had eventually found her a wine glass and filled it for her. Pamela had at least tried to engage her in conversation and asked her about what she had been doing recently. She congratulated herself on not saying, 'I have been brooding about my own frailty, about the past and the way it presses in on us, and above all I have been brooding on why I ever let myself marry your husband's father.' But she knew the answer, knew how unwell she had been at the time, how little hope and confidence she had been able to muster.

'Mother, are you alright?'

Heather was talking to her. She must have drifted into a reverie, detached herself again from the world round her. They were all looking at her.

'Absolutely,' she told them. 'Just a little tired. It's time for my nap.' She'd be gracious. 'Heather, that was a lovely lunch, but I really shouldn't drink at lunchtime. Now will you all excuse me?'

Get up as quickly as you can, she told herself, even if it

hurts. She pushed her chair back and swivelled round in it, grabbed tight hold of the handle of her stick, and got herself into position. Is no one going to offer to help me, she thought. Are they all going to sit there, toying with wine glasses, just watching me?

But they didn't watch her. There was a loud knock on the back door. When this had distracted them and Heather had gone to see who was knocking, Anna rocked herself upwards. Then she walked as quickly as possible out of the room. In spite of her effort she managed to get there last.

They were clustered round the back door. Peter was talking to Heather, showing her something, explaining that he had found these under the seat at the top of the garden, thought they should know. Colin was coming forward and sniffing whatever Peter was holding and explaining that he knew what these were.

Then he turned towards her and said, 'Mother, have you started smoking cannabis?'

Chapter Fourteen

Anna made herself dress for her birthday dinner. That meant she had to climb the stairs twice in one day, possibly with eyes watching her. She must do it upright, not crawling. It would be painful but it had to be done. She chose her moment when no one was around and began the climb, pulling herself hand over hand, ignoring the fact that her knees seemed fused together.

Once in her bedroom she sat on the bed to recover, then found the clothes she had chosen for the night. She knew they were clean and ironed. Leaning up against the bed, she put them on and set about tidying her hair which took her a long time: all the pins had to come out and be replaced. Her arm didn't want to be lifted above her shoulders any more. She could hear lots of noises around her as preparations were being made for the big dinner, lots of rushing up and down stairs with doors being opened and shut. She checked herself in the mirror before setting off to join them.

No one was watching. They all appeared to be in the sitting room with the door partly open. Anna came downstairs as quietly as she could and so she heard some of what they were saying. It intrigued her so much that she stopped to listen.

'…she deserves to have tonight…'

'…leave it for now…'

'…after the birthday…'

'…and are we all agreed? Pams, is this what you think too?'

Either Pamela didn't answer or she spoke so quietly that Anna couldn't hear what she said. Not that it mattered because Colin went on. His voice rose and fell but she heard the following phrases: 'What the neighbours think, God only knows… must seem careless to leave her living alone…give her three weeks then Heather and I will come back … check

162

up on her, start to make arrangements... will the Tuesday suit you Sis?'

Alistair seemed to take over at that moment. Perhaps it was that being-the-eldest-thing, not wanting a younger brother to dominate. '...must be worth a packet right now... she goes... we sell...'

Lydia's voice then drifted up the stairs: '...so run down... tea cups are badly stained...and that burnt patch...'

Anna let go of the banister, sat down on the stairs and quietly said to herself, 'It's my ninetieth birthday. Happy birthday Anna, happy birthday Marie Claire.' She looked around at the faded golden carpets, the long gleaming pine banister, the coffer chest in the hall with the big bronze plate that hadn't gleamed for years. She glanced out of the long window and saw that the chestnut tree had lost its white candles and was setting tiny conkers. Then she got up again and went down the rest of the stairs, banging her stick on each step so they would hear her coming.

The door was flung wide open. Heather, also dressed for the occasion, came to greet her. 'Mother, we wondered where you were. We're about to open the bubbly. You look wonderful.'

Even though it was June they had lit her fire. It was glowing nicely, long flames bending round the logs as if trying to measure the circumference, then at the last moment shooting upwards. As she went in through the door everyone stood and applauded. Anna noticed that James was already there, had listened to but not taken part in their conversation about her. The thought stopped her in her tracks, left her breathless. For once Heather appeared to notice her, actually took her arm and helped her to her chair. Alistair extracted the champagne cork and soon she had a glass in her hand. They all had full glasses and had begun to sing for her.

Take a photograph, she thought. Go on somebody, take a photograph of what's happening right now. You can print it and call it 'The Hypocrites'.

'Speech,' said Colin when the last notes ended - out of time and out of tune.

She waved him away, 'Not now, later. When have I ever had anything to say?...except that tonight, you do seem to have surpassed yourselves.'

She sipped her champagne and wondered if she had ever really liked the gassy stuff. Heather ran busily between the sitting room and kitchen, finally sending Henry to say that dinner was ready.

There were four bottles of red wine already opened on the table. Her family were clearly going to do some drinking tonight. They'd found and used Ronnie's large goblets which they each filled almost to the brim.

An hour later the bottles were empty, sitting interspersed between the greasy carcasses of three ducks, together forming a messy line along the centre of the table. Lethargy seemed to have settled over the group, so Anna did what she had done all day: got up to help clear things away. But she was firmly instructed to leave it to them because this was their treat.

After dinner they traipsed through to the sitting room, glasses still in hands. Colin had found the pudding wine that Ronnie must have stored somewhere in the house. Wasn't pudding wine meant to be sipped? Anna left most of hers and refused coffee. She didn't want to have to be up too often in the night.

'Birthday present,' Alistair announced.

He seemed very pleased with himself as he said it. Clearly they had all contributed because there was a small buzz of something like excitement. Lydia reached under her chair and pulled out a package. Anna noticed that it was flat but not square, a picture, if she guessed rightly. She looked round at the walls of the room, already covered with faded English watercolours, collected by her husband in that I'm-doing-culture-phase which had followed his retirement. Where would she put this latest offering when it had been unwrapped?

'Youngest, youngest,' Colin insisted. 'Dad always insisted that presents were handed round by the youngest. Heather, where are you? Just because you've cooked a meal, our kid, it doesn't mean you can relax.'

'Youngest, must be the youngest,' echoed Alistair, as if it were part of a chorus.

'I'm the youngest,' Pamela said quietly.

No one took any notice.

Lydia passed the package along to Heather. Heather got up and came swaying across the carpet towards Anna who distinctly heard Pamela repeat, 'But I *am* the youngest.'

Anna put her hands out to receive her present. Whatever this picture was like she would have to be grateful and find a place for it.

Her first impression was that it was very heavy. Her fingers had to tighten just to prevent it falling into her lap. She began to unwrap it, hoping no one would offer to do this for her. They didn't.

Her fingers found the joins in the wrapping paper, pushed sellotape to one side and in that way freed a whole edge. The paper surface in front of her now had a join in it, pinned together with another piece of sellotape. She peeled that off and opened up the wrapping paper, revealing that whatever it was had been double wrapped. The next layer was covered in folds of white tissue paper, several layers thick. These were sellotaped together.

The silence and the avid way they were watching was beginning to irritate Anna. Presents are weapons, she thought. Whatever this turns out to be, it won't really be for me. It is to make them feel good about themselves. She split the tissue paper and delved inside it to find the back of a solid silver frame. It wasn't a picture to be hung on the wall. It was one to stand up on a table.

She turned it over.

Now where had they got that from?

It was a photograph that she had never seen before. Black and white, grainy, easily recognisable. She could see that everyone was smiling at her. A glance at James told her that even he was in the know. They must have gone through military archives and then had the image enhanced. They had certainly taken some trouble.

It was Ronnie. It was the soldier in the helmet, round-faced, grinning at the camera, standing with his comrades, somewhere in France.

Now I could make a speech, she thought, but I won't. I may not like Ronnie's children but they are mine too, and a semblance must be maintained between us.

'Thank you, how very thoughtful of you all. You must have gone to so much trouble. Thank you very much indeed.'

She hoped that was enough and it was. They began to explain to her about who had come up with the idea, how Alistair's secretary had done the research, how wonderful some websites were. She let the talk flow over her while she looked at the face trapped under the glass, surrounded by silver.

I've lived ninety years of mistakes, she thought to herself, and they have framed for me the worst of all my blunders, a constant reminder of my lowest state. Staring at the photograph she dipped out of the conversation for a while and when she tapped back in they were all talking to James.

Alistair was saying, 'You see it's a photo of Dad when Mum first met him. He was dressed just like that. He had quite a war record. He was in the Normandy landings.'

'Several weeks after they first started,' Pamela added in a low voice, trying to insist on the truth. No one listened. She was immediately swotted aside by the power of the family legend.

Colin took up the story. 'Dad was on the front line when he first saw Mother. He was taking cover in this French village when he heard a noise in the house behind him and saw a white flag being waved out of the window.'

'He went in to see what was happening, being careful because it could have been a trap.' Heather's voice continued the story. 'He found this frightened girl, and do you know the first thing she said to him was, 'Excuse me I think I'm going to be sick.'

They laughed at that.

'Not very romantic,' Lydia commented, 'not one of the great first lines. What Alistair said to me when we first met was much sweeter.'

No one asked her what Alistair had said. Lydia wasn't family, just one of the in-laws. She might have a role away from the family, but when the siblings met she could always be discarded.

Alistair told the next bit. It was his speciality. 'Mother must have had a terrible time because she was all white and trembling. She tried to tidy herself up after being sick but he could see that she was in a real mess. Dad had to take charge of her, take her to safety.'

Heather turned to James, adding her bit of explanation, 'He was a very gallant man, my dad.'

'And why were you in Normandy, Mrs Devonshire? I mean, what had you been doing there?'

James's question had been asked directly of her but Anna was not given any chance to answer, even if she had wanted to. Colin immediately provided the official Devonshire family explanation.

'She told Dad that she had got stuck there. She doesn't remember anything else about it, do you Mother? Do you know that Dad even claimed that she had forgotten her own name? When he asked her what her name was, she gave him two. You were in a bad way weren't you?' He reached over to her and patted her on the knee.

The old have only two contributions to make, Anna thought: to be admired for growing so old and to leave money to others. Our memories are not reliable. Everything else about us is thought to be a nuisance. If you ask us questions somebody else will answer them.

James was still looking in her direction, so she felt the need to say something. 'I had a very difficult time in France during the war,' she said, speaking slowly. 'Shall we leave it at that?'

They had already left it altogether. Alistair was telling James that his parents had met again in London, just after the war. Dad had taken Mum under his wing and looked after her.

'How nice,' said James.

'And now we are looking after her,' Heather added, 'now that she has reached this great age.'

I am a trophy, Anna thought. I am something to brag about before they tidy me away.

Heather was back on her feet, walking just a little unsteadily. 'Shall I put the photograph up for you, Mother, where you can see it? How about over here?'

Anna hadn't relinquished the photograph. It had been taken from her, its weight removed from her knees. Heather had cleared the table at the other side of the fireplace and was positioning it carefully. 'There,' she said, giving it a wipe. 'You'll always see it if we put it there.'

'A toast,' suggested Colin. 'To Dad, war hero and Mother's protector.'

They all stood and raised their glasses. 'Our Dad.' Even the in-laws were calling him that, 'war hero and Mother's protector.' It was solemnly and seriously done, glasses raised towards the new photograph in its silver frame. They loved him, thought Anna. They loved him in a way they never loved me, but then he was so like them that they had to love him, didn't they, if they were to have any chance of liking themselves. But that wasn't it. She'd better tell herself the next bit too. And I didn't let anybody love me, did I? Nobody since Pierre. I was never very good at love.

The next morning she got up early and went quietly downstairs.

She had a battle to fight over the next few weeks and needed to win a little immediate victory so that what she planned to do later on wouldn't be so unexpected.

The kitchen was a mess. Plates were stacked everywhere, cutlery abandoned in waves across the table, pans thick with white grease. She would exhaust herself but that didn't matter. Once they had gone she could go back to bed and sleep for as long as she liked. She shut the door and filled the bowl with really hot water and began to wash. Glasses first, then silver, then plates. She repeatedly filled the draining board before seizing a fresh cloth and drying up. It didn't matter how many cloths she used. What did matter was that she could do all this quickly enough. She put everything away, bending and straightening painfully but keeping going. She felt the strength of her own determination.

She'd been up for more than an hour and there were no noises coming from above; not really surprising considering how much they had drunk the night before. The glasses were back in their places. The cutlery was in the drawer. The plates were all in the cupboard. It was just the tins now. She spread a newspaper on the table and shovelled onto it all the bones and as much of the grease as she could scrape, adding the few potatoes left over and a spoonful of cold cabbage. Each time she emptied a cooking pot she put it to soak, before starting to empty the next one. When she was done she scooped everything together in the newspaper and carried it out to the bin just beyond the back door.

It was 9.15. Back in the house she could hear movement starting upstairs. She brought the roasting dishes out one by one and fought them with a green plastic scourer, expecting any moment that the latch on the kitchen door would be lifted and one of her children or their partners would ask her what she was doing.

There were obstinate globules on the bottom of the roast potato pan. Never mind about that. No one would check if it was really clean. What mattered was that it was put away before anyone came down. She upended it onto the draining board and set about the broccoli pan. Then she dried both and put them away. Giving herself another lot of fresh water and yet more washing up liquid she began to swab surfaces. Her arms ached and her back was going into spasm but she refused to take any notice. As soon as the kitchen was cleared and cleaned she began to load breakfast pots onto the trolley.

She'd laid the table and put out cereal and bowls when she did hear somebody downstairs and moving about. Just in time. She'd offer them coffee. Whoever it was would be somewhat the worse for wear. Coffee was the antidote. She could become the mother again, administering cures.

She checked the table in the dining room before walking out into the hall. Whoever was up had already gone into the kitchen and closed the door. She lifted the latch and prepared to surprise them, then was shocked herself to see that it was Rosanna. Had she got the wrong day? Was this Rosanna's day? Thinking furiously she decided it wasn't.

'Hello,' Rosanna was explaining. 'I didn't think you'd be up yet. Colin phoned me, your son Colin. He asked me to come and do the washing up after last night. He must have forgotten he called me. They seem to have done it all themselves.'

So Rosanna too was being contacted. That meant James, Peter and Rosanna, all the people she paid to help her, were now recruited by the enemy.

What was it George had said when she told him she had shot Pierre for being a double agent? *That was a pity. If you had told us he was working for the Germans we could have used that, fed him wrong information about troop movements within the beachhead, helped bring the break-out forward.* Perhaps, now that she knew, Anna could do the same.

But for now Anna simply said, 'I've done all the washing up and clearing away. No one told me you were coming. I got up early and I've done the whole lot.' She knew she was letting her bitterness show; she also saw at once that Rosanna didn't believe her. Would her children believe her? Would Rosanna volunteer that she hadn't done the work herself? Wouldn't her children just presume Rosanna had done the work without even asking her?

In that case there would be no gain from her hard work and for the next three days she would be good for nothing, aching all over and unable to do much more than doze intermittently. What a waste. In spite of her training a bit of nastiness from somewhere inside her spoke for itself before she could censor it. Perhaps it was the strain of not voicing what she thought all yesterday, but she found herself saying, 'What I suggest you do next, Rosanna, is clear out the fire place and strip all the beds upstairs. If my children are still sleeping, so much the better. Tell them it's time they went. I have things to do.'

Rosanna looked shocked, so Anna added, 'And I'm not paying you for working this morning. Colin hired you and Colin can pay you.' A further thought occurred to her. 'If you don't know which one Colin is because you've only spoken to him on the phone, he's the fat one who dyes his hair.' Having off-loaded all that onto Rosanna, she went back into the kitchen to make herself a coffee and a piece of toast.

She knew she should feel guilty but she didn't. In a way she felt invigorated. It was time to fight back, time to do what she had once been trained for. If everyone was spying on her and threatening her independence she needed a network of her own, and she thought she knew where she would begin.

She sat at the dining room table to eat her breakfast and picked up a wash of whispered conversations at the foot of the stairs and in the hallway. It included some sobbing from Rosanna. She presumed that Colin was comforting her because when Pamela came downstairs she distinctly heard her say, 'I thought there was such a thing as safeguarding in local authorities, Colin. I'm sure it's somewhere in your job description. I presume it means that you can't put your arm round strange women and pat them on the back.'

No one came in to see Anna. Clearly her birthday was over. When other footsteps plodded down the stairs they were immediately ushered away from the dining room and the whispering continued. She could imagine it. They had thought her incapable before last night, now they must think her unbalanced and perhaps delusional. Who would they send to deal with her? Alistair because he was the eldest? Heather because she was the daughter? or Pamela because she was expendable? They must all be gathered round in the kitchen sipping coffee from mugs and discussing this latest turn of events.

Perhaps they were working out that she had actually done all the washing and clearing up on her own. But even if they reached that conclusion it would be overshadowed by the report of her outburst, its impact dented.

She'd nearly finished her toast and most of her coffee. Still no one came. It was like being a child again, like being sent up to your room and hearing others getting on with life when you were stuck on your own. If they stayed there much longer she would be completely finished and then she would feel like sleeping. That mustn't happen, not until they had gone. A bit of memory came to the forefront of her mind and played there. It was of an old woman with a zimmer frame, walking round and round the corridors of an old person's home, like a trapped animal, like a too confined zoo creature. She mustn't let that happen to her.

I've still got a brain, she thought. I'm still me.

There was a danger of course that her outburst might prompt them all into immediate action. Last night she had heard them say three weeks. She'd need all of three weeks for what she planned. She couldn't manage it any faster. Did she need to apologise?

No. It was monstrous what they had done, the way they had taken over her house, employed her cleaning lady without asking her, the way they were plotting against her.

But who would think it so? They had come down en masse for her birthday, cooked a meal, bought her a thoughtful present and made sure she had no clearing up to do afterwards. It would all be seen as kindness. You are allowed to do almost anything to the old under the guise of kindness, she realised.

It was time to take the initiative, to set the parameters. She picked up the toast plate and her coffee cup. The trouble was that she couldn't manage both and her stick. Leave the stick, she told herself, leave the stick and just see what you can do. It's time to take risks.

Moving slowly she walked out of the dining room and across the hall. The kitchen door wasn't on the latch so she simply opened it by walking into it, then took the three steps necessary to reach the sink. No one spoke. Nothing was said to her.

'Look, no stick,' she told them. They were all there, including Rosanna, nursing mugs of coffee, nursing hangovers, nursing their secrets. They didn't look guilty. If anything, they looked determined. There was something closed up and united about them. Only Henry seemed fidgety.

'Well,' Anna continued, finishing her survey, 'this is cosy. I laid breakfast for you all in the dining room, but if you prefer to have it standing up, crowded together in here, then so be it.'

She had placed the plate and the mug in the sink by now so she turned and leant against its edge, trying to stop her legs hurting so much.

Still no one spoke. That meant the floor was hers. She had better say something.

'Last night Alistair invited me to make a speech and I said 'later'. I think I added that I never had anything to say. Well now I have.'

They were watching her. This was unexpected. All the heads had come up. Colin, she noticed, was looking straight at her, his forehead lined with concentration under the too blond hair. Alistair had raised his chin and was jutting his face out from his ageing neck. Heather leant her head back against the cooker hood but she too was watching.

It was time to say it.

'I just thought there are some things you should all know about me. I want you all to know that I am quite capable of looking after myself in this house. I did the washing up. I laid breakfast for you all. I can cope.'

They stared at her. Incomprehension spread across their faces.

'I also want you to know that I like my independence. I do not like the fact that my children are taking over my life and organising those who work for me without asking my permission. When Rosanna turned up, unexpectedly, I gave her other work to do in place of what Colin had arranged. I think that is in order. It's my house. So Rosanna, I hope when you have finished your coffee that you will clean out the fire and strip the beds. Those are the things I find difficult. Perhaps you'd like to start that now.'

Rosanna looked doubtful.

'You can take your coffee with you,' Anna assured her.

Rosanna still looked towards Colin, who eventually nodded, so she left.

'Right, now we are just family. That means I can speak a little more openly.' She paused before continuing. 'Last night you all gave me a very thoughtful present. I know I thanked you then but let me do so again now. You'd worked hard to get that just right. You gave me a photo of your dad. You drank a toast to him. Well, can I just remind you that he bought this house for me. It's mine, and his will allows me to live in it for as long as I want to.' She thought she'd better repeat that bit, 'as long as I want to.'

She saw Lydia look sharply at Alistair, saw meaningful glances pass between them. These glances were more than just a reaction to the forthright way she was speaking. The looks told her of something vital to them that had just been thwarted. Alistair even reached out and held his wife's hand.

'I suspect I need to emphasise what I've just said so let me make it quite clear. I want to go on living here. Even if I begin to forget things, I still want to. Even if I find it difficult to move around, I still want to. Even if I might die because I have fallen down the stairs and no one will find me for several days, I still want to.'

They seemed shocked, sullen, rejected. They had been united before she came in to the room. Now they were looking at her as if she was losing it, as if she wasn't the mother they had grown up with.

She thought more carefully before she added the next bit, but as no one was saying anything she went on.

'Perhaps you don't know me very well, and I admit that is partly my fault. There are things about my past I have never told you. But I can be quite determined if I need to be.' She must stop soon. Her right leg felt as if it might give way and how she would get back to her stick she didn't know. 'I've been a bit lazy recently. I'll prove to you just how well I can cope. Now why don't you go through to the dining room? You'll be much more comfortable there. I'll put some toast on and bring it through.'

They left around midday. Alistair went first with a very concerned Lydia, followed soon after by Colin and a smirking Pam. 'Is that what she really said,' Pamela had asked her husband as they walked to the car, 'that you were the fat one who dyed his hair?'

Rosanna had left soon after Colin, which must have been almost immediately after she had been paid. There were traces of wood dust still in the hallway carpet, but at least the beds had been stripped.

Last of them all to go had been Heather. She and Henry had said goodbye to Anna and walked towards the 4x4. Anna had been ready to shut the front door and collapse into her chair when she saw that Henry was coming back, leaving Heather in the car. What's more, he was following her into the house.

'Have you forgotten something?' she asked him.

'Sorry to come back,' he explained when he was inside the house and presumably out of his wife's view. 'You must be dying for us all to get out of the way, but I just wanted to remind you that the house isn't actually yours, well not the whole of it. When Ronnie died you allowed me to alter his will, at Alistair's suggestion, so that each of the children owns a proportion of the house. It was a way of avoiding death duties. I forget the exact proportions but I think that between them they own about 30%. I just thought I should remind you because it makes everything so much more complicated…'

Henry was interrupted by Heather sounding the horn, clearly impatient to get going.

Henry stayed where he was. 'You do know that Alistair has lost a lot of money recently don't you?' he asked her. The horn sounded again: a single long blast. Henry grinned. 'I'm in trouble. I'd better go. I hope we weren't too awful.'

He was away, walking quickly towards his wife. As Anna watched from the hallway, Heather started the car into motion before Henry had even closed his door.

As Anna walked back to her chair ready to collapse, a few sentences of what they had been taught by Proffi Offi all that time ago came into her mind. 'Some of your network will always recruit themselves. To find the others you need to look amongst the natural enemies of those you are fighting.'

Chapter Fifteen

After her family went, Anna dozed through a couple of days, feeling good for nothing else. She had worn herself out with the worry and the washing up. She was back to using her stick, back to crawling up the stairs. Old age was like tiredness with added pain.

On the third day, feeling stronger, she walked round the house and tried to see it through the eyes of an outsider. The sink in the outhouse was a mess. Two African violets wilted on the windowsill. There was a light bulb stuck in the top of a bulb box. Was it a new one ready to be used or an old one on its way out, one that she had left there because she couldn't face the walk to the bin?

In the bright summer light she could see that the red towel was grimy and should have been washed weeks ago. Several rumpled pieces of cellophane littered the draining board. They must have once wrapped flowers or plants and had never been thrown away. There was a green and an orange piece of soap in a plastic soap holder from the fifties, its surface bleached and brittle. The window itself wasn't clean. The secondary glazing had come detached at one side and a spider had built its web between the two panes.

Walking back through the lounge she noticed the way that the carpet had long ago taken the pattern of the floor boards, showing long slightly indented lines. She needed new underlay, new carpets. The walls were overdue for a coat of paint.

That afternoon she went into her bathroom and for the first time in many years she pulled the net curtains to one side. The window was filthy. There was mould growing in the putty. Dead flies, each one lying on its back with its legs neatly folded up, cluttered the window sill. There was a desiccated queen wasp there too and a tortoiseshell butterfly.

She left the net curtains pulled back. In the extra light that flooded into the room she saw that the bath enamel was chipped and stained in a grey circle. Everything was old, the sink and the taps, even the bidet. The pink curtains had been the last thing to be added to the room but even they had lost shape and faded. Why hadn't she noticed this happening, put it right bit by bit? She went back downstairs.

The front drive needed re-laying. The gravel had kicked up into small dunes. Weeds cluttered the edges. The wooden greenhouse sagged and two of the panes were broken.

Her children were right. It was a mess. How was she ever going to get it all cleaned up? Perhaps she should move and buy something smaller and newer. But she didn't think she could cope with selling, house buying and house moving. Besides, even though it was messy she knew it and loved it. Whenever she walked or was driven back towards her house she noticed the sun dial on the front, above and slightly to the left of the front door. She enjoyed the way the white frontage shone under the dull patina of the weathered roof tiles. She even lifted her eyes to the tall brick chimneys. Her life might be nearly over but this was where she wanted to end it. Why shouldn't she?

Completing her survey she went out of the back door and stood on the overgrown paving that merged with the lawn. The boy with the long hair was there again, sitting on her seat at the bottom of the garden, admiring her view. She must have made a noise coming out of the house because he turned and saw her, but he didn't move away. Instead he lazily waved a hand towards her and then swept it in a great arc above his head before turning back to the view.

You'll do, thought Anna. You'll do for me.

She thought about going straight up the garden to talk to him, but she didn't want to frighten him off. Anyway, at that moment the front doorbell rang and she had to hurry if she was to reach the front door before whoever it was gave up and went away.

I am moving more easily, she thought, as she made her way down the hall. Perhaps I am coming back to life.

She opened the door. A young man was standing there with a clipboard.

'Yes?' she said, feeling foolish. Why hadn't she looked through the spy hole first ? Why hadn't she checked? This young man was quite capable of running past her into the house before she could shut the door.

'Hello and how are you today?' asked the young man.

She rounded on him. 'What's that to you? My health is my business. What do you want?'

He was smartly dressed and very sure of himself. 'Mr Devonshire asked me to call,' explained the young man, 'about the survey…'

He expected her to know and she didn't.

'What survey? My husband's dead. Unless you've been to a séance recently he can't have asked you to do anything.'

The young man consulted his clip board. 'Mr Alistair Devonshire.' He looked back at her. 'Is he still alive?' There was touch of insolence about the way he asked the question.

'Well he was earlier this week,' she confirmed. 'What's he asked you to do?'

'Make a preliminary survey,' the young man explained, 'give some idea as to price.'

'The price of what?' Anna asked this even though she had already made her own guess.

'The price of his house.'

She gripped her stick tightly. 'This house,' she explained to the smartly dressed young man, deliberately talking as if he was half-witted, 'is my house. I don't want to sell it. I have no intention of selling it. So no, you cannot do a survey. You cannot step into the hall. You cannot measure anything.' She'd noticed that he had a large tape measure clasped against his board. 'Is that clear?'

'This is his letter giving his consent.' The young man was quite unflustered by her defiance. 'You will see it mentions that by law he has the right to take requisite measures to determine the value of his assets.' The letter was waved in front of her. It glared in the sun. 'He does own part of the property doesn't he?'

I wish I was younger, she thought, taking the letter from him. If I was younger I could tear this up in front of him, but if I want to do that now I would first have to let go of my stick. If it falls to the ground I won't be able to pick it up, so it's too late for grand gestures.

Besides, she hadn't got her reading glasses. She needed time to think.

'Thank you,' she said. 'I'll let you know in due course. Goodbye.'

The young man didn't move. He dug his heels into her gravel and stood his ground. 'I've driven a long way to get here. You have to let me in. That letter explains it.'

She wasn't having this. For the last two days she had wondered if she was being unreasonable. Now she knew she wasn't. She took the letter and thrust it back at him. She'd take a risk. 'Show me where it says *now*' she insisted. 'Show me the word *immediate* or *instant*'.

He didn't move. 'Only I've not got my reading glasses and I'd hate to be wrong.'

She still held the letter out for him. He didn't take it.

'So it doesn't say I have to give you immediate access. In that case I won't. Goodbye.'

She turned to go back into the house but the young man didn't move. 'Your son warned me you might be difficult,' he said.

Anna turned back. 'Well then he was right. I will be difficult and for your information, since you have decided to take his side, he has never mentioned this matter to me, has never even asked me about having a valuation done. I'll weigh up the legality of your letter when I can read it. Would you like to weigh up my son's manners?'

This young man was tougher than she expected.

'I cannot challenge a client. It would be most unprofessional,' he asserted.

'Then take a piece of advice from me. If you are working for my son, invoice him regularly, refuse to continue working for him until he has paid the previous invoice. You've had a wasted journey but it could get a whole lot worse. Goodbye.'

He turned on his heels and he went. Watching him go she realised that she had been enjoying herself during the exchange, however threatened she felt.

Now I wait for the phone call, she thought. Alistair will phone me tonight. He'll have to.

She had money. What she didn't have was energy and strength. Well the money would have to compensate for her decrepitude.

She went to the sitting room and sat at the desk. Taking out a sheet of writing paper she composed and then wrote her letter. Once she had checked it over she put it into an envelope and addressed it to:

The Boy On The Bench.

There was still some sellotape left on the roll. She carefully cut a piece and then walked with the letter and the piece of sticky tape out to the kitchen.

There was a box of chocolates there which James had brought for her. She placed the envelope on the box of chocolates and stuck it down with the piece of tape. Tomorrow she would walk up the garden before breakfast and place it on the bench. Perhaps she would sit there and admire her own view before walking back. The boy came every afternoon at about four thirty. She'd have plenty of time.

That evening the phone rang and she picked it up, expecting

Alistair. It wasn't. It was Colin.

'Hello dear,' she said, the wind temporarily taken out of her sails. She had been ready for a verbal punch up. 'What can I do for you?'

There was a pause down the other end of the line.

'Well not really for me,' Colin said, 'actually it's for all of us.'

'What is?' She left her answer short and sharp, spat the two words down the phone.

There was another pause at the other end. 'Look, I know Alistair didn't warn you. The fact is that he told us he would and he forgot. I want to apologise for that. He really should have told you.'

'Warned me! Told me!' This wouldn't do at all. 'Don't you mean asked me?'

'Now, Mother, you have to be reasonable.'

'No, I don't.' She'd try to make him squirm. She'd challenge everything and see where it got her.

He tried another tack. 'Look, Mother, no one is trying to throw you out of that lovely house.'

'Put that in writing will you? I'll need all your signatures.'

Again he attempted to ignore her, ploughed on. 'All that we are asking for is an indication as to the value of our assets.'

'Then I am sure Alistair's young man can do that from the road, or even from a map reference and a photograph.'

This time the silence was longer. She let time drift, then added. 'When you were a little boy I could always tell when you weren't being truthful. I still can.'

There was no response. Had he heard? There seemed to be a verbal tussle at the other end of the line. She'd try another tack. 'Look, Colin, are you still there?' The tussle ended. She could hear him listening again.

'Let's start this again, shall we?' she suggested

He seemed relieved. 'I really think we should,' he said.

'How much money has Alistair lost?'

'Really, Mother, that is none of your business.'

'I see. Then my house is none of yours. Goodbye.'

She put the phone down, imagined Colin spluttering with anger, preparing to hit things like his father had. She wondered who he had been talking to. Was he having a tussle with Pamela or had Alistair gone round there? If he had, then he needed money badly. Should she offer him a loan? Did she have enough money to buy him out, buy them all out? Was that what the valuation was really for?

Then another thought struck her. They weren't about to charge her rent were they?

To take her mind off the problem she began to write a list. She'd start small. She'd start with bowls, mats, towels and that sort of thing. She'd get new ones and put them out. Every old cloth would be banished from the house. That would make a difference. Then she would need lots of cleaning materials and those smell dispensers she'd seen on TV. It all depends on the boy. I really need him, she thought. I can't use my others for this. In fact I may have to dispense with their services altogether if I want my independence back.

The next morning she took the chocolates and the letter and set off on her journey up the garden. She tried not to look at the lawn, kept her eyes on the far end of the garden where the view began. The first steps were the worst. Her whole body felt rusted up, as if she were having to continually free her joints from their inertia. Because of the effort involved she had to breathe through her mouth. Every now and then when the pain became too intense she rested; then gritted her teeth and continued.

She sat on the bench when she got there. Just in front of her the ground bunched and then fell steeply away. She looked out over the tops of trees at canopy height, then past them to sloping meadows, which at this time of year were a rich green, spotted with cows and sheep. Beyond the meadows the river glinted and small copses rubbed up against church spires.

Somewhere beyond that the land flattened but today there was a mist and she could see nothing further. No wonder he sits here, she thought. He has good taste.

She walked slowly back to the house, went back to the desk and got out the list she'd been working on. She'd thought of more quick wins. She was about to write them down when the phone rang.

'Hello.'

'Hello Mother,' she heard.

I wondered when you'd phone, she thought.

'Heather, what can I do for you?'

She knew it was a stupid phrase with which to begin a phone call but she had used it for years and she rather liked it.

There was another pause. It's the next phone call, she thought. They are phoning me in sequence.

'Where were you, Mother?' Heather asked.

'Where was I when?'

'I rang about half an hour ago. When you didn't reply I was so worried.'

'You didn't need to be. I'd walked down the garden. I wanted to look at my view.' Now who's avoiding the truth, she thought.

'Look, Mum, I know you'll think I'm interfering.'

'Then don't.'

'But I think you need to understand what the real situation is.'

'You mean about Alistair losing that money? Does he need a loan?'

'No, not Alistair.' Heather was already sounding irritated. Mind you, it had always been easy to irritate her. Both her brothers had at different times become experts in winding up their younger sister. All the same Anna noticed that there was no denial. Colin hadn't denied it either. Anna decided she wouldn't say anything else, would wait for whatever was coming next.

'It's about capacity.'

'Now what are you talking about? The only thing that has capacity round here is the septic tank, and unless you all had multiple baths last week it should be well within its capacity to cope.'

She could almost hear her daughter grinding her teeth.

'I'm not talking about the sceptic tank, Mother. I'm talking about your capacity to carry on living on your own.'

Now it was Anna's turn to stay silent. She hadn't expected such a bald statement so quickly. The chocolates had better work. That boy had better come and see her this afternoon. It was time to get angry. But Heather was talking.

'Don't you see that's what Alistair means to do, challenge your capacity to carry on living in that house? He'll do that to protect his investment. I mean, you did nearly burn the place down. You can't deny that. Have you continued to pay the insurance Dad set up?'

She stayed silent. Was that what the whispered conversation had really been about? She was back behind enemy lines with a vengeance, back on her own and fighting.

Heather, probably feeling she had the upper hand, ploughed on. 'So I wouldn't irritate him, Mother. Let the valuation happen. Agree to meet the man he sent and let him in. After all, you may have to prove that you can act reasonably and sensibly.'

Enough, she thought. It was time for both barrels. 'Let me play that back to you shall I, Heather? Shall we just make sure that I understand you correctly? Because Alistair has been stupid enough to lose what is obviously a large sum of money, no doubt through greed and incompetence, my capacity to manage my affairs is being questioned. He who patently cannot manage his own affairs is to take my house from me because I burnt about four square inches of the cooker surround. Have I got that right?'

She waited, loved the way her brain seemed to sharpen up

on an almost daily basis, focussed on the silence at the other end of the line.

'Right, I notice you don't deny any of that. So let's get the next bit straight too. I was persuaded to give each of you part of my house as a way of saving you from paying inheritance tax. It must be very frustrating for each of you that I have outlived your father by so many years. I suspect you have been waiting for me to die for such a long time and now Alistair has decided that he can't wait any longer.'

Anna heard the sigh, knew that Heather wasn't on her own. This too was a shared conversation. Was it Alistair or Colin who was with her? Might it be both? She heard a hiss and then the venom.

'God you've turned horrible, Mother. Just listen to yourself. What you said to poor Rosanna was unforgiveable. I mean, what is happening to you?'

'It's called capacity, dear,' Anna explained. She didn't add, it's also called waking up to the fact that I have spawned three ravening beasts in place of children.

Anna knew the conversation couldn't go on. The caustic side of her nature had become too dominant. It wouldn't be restrained or censored any longer.

'I don't think there is anything else to say is there? I clearly need legal advice. I think I'll get myself some. Goodbye.' She put the phone down.

In the silence that followed Anna found that her sense of exhilaration at having won the argument quickly gave way to despair. It was as if once the words had stopped flowing, once she could get over her own amazement at the way her brain was still sharp, still functioning, she became intensely aware that she was in a battle she couldn't win. She felt the extreme unfairness of the fact that she was having to fight the very people she should have been able to depend on.

It was like waking up again, but waking up too late to a battle that is all but over. What had the war done to her? No,

186

she told herself, don't think like that. The real question is, what did you allow to happen to yourself? And the answer came straight back. You lost faith. You lost faith in life because you decided you didn't trust in love. You allowed yourself to live loveless. No wonder your children are as they are.

Then something amazing began to happen, something that hadn't happened for years. A drop of moisture began to form in the corner of her right eye. She felt it like a tickle, then like a wet itch. It ballooned and began to slide. Another followed it. She knew her cheek must now be glistening and then that a tiny rivulet was widening and quickening as it annexed more ground, eventually reaching her chin. She was crying, crying at her own weakness and at the wasted years. She had driven dry-eyed through the aftermath of battle. Now she was suddenly overwhelmed by her sense of loneliness and isolation.

But I like loneliness, she reminded herself. I enjoy my own company. I do not want to live with others. I do not want to go into a home. Perhaps he likes loneliness too. He smokes a joint in my garden and only once has the girl come to see him there. I need both of them. Will he come?

He didn't come, or rather he didn't come to the house. She saw him sneak in through the back gate and sit on the bench. She knew that he had found the parcel because she saw him lean towards it, pick it up and stare at it. She couldn't see what he did next. She had hoped that he would come at once to the door, but she did half expect him to have his smoke first. She waited patiently, watching him from her seat, but when he dropped the stub, just where Peter had found the others, he took nothing with him and instead of turning towards the house he just walked out of the gate and vanished.

She was terribly disappointed. In spite of the effort involved she walked out of the back door and made her way to the end of the garden. Again, the more she walked the easier it got. It was warm, in spite of the sun being low. As she approached the bench she saw that the parcel was still there. The letter was unopened, but something had been written on it. She picked it up and turned it round so that she could read it. In neat letters that were almost like printing the boy had written,

'Thanks, but I don't eat chocolates.'

He hadn't even opened the letter.

She looked out across the view. The mist had gone. You could see for miles, could see the flat land beyond the villages. A low sun was rounding every contour, stretching every shadow, touching each part of the landscape with warm tones, like a benediction.

I must make myself come here every day and stare, she thought. Life, even at ninety, is worth living and I want to live mine here. It may be selfish, but ever since I first saw it I wanted this view. I pestered my husband to buy the house. I like to be high up and looking across a landscape. Like..

This time it was easier to remember. The two parts of her life were fitting together and the dreams had stopped.

Early the next morning before breakfast she found a hammer and a tack from the garage, then added a single sentence to the envelope and took it back down the garden. She placed the envelope on the bench then took out the two twenty pound notes and placed them on the edge of the envelope. Balancing the tack carefully she pinned everything to the bench, using the hammer. When she had done that she looked at it, hoping it would do the trick.

Underneath his comment she had written 'Do you eat these?'

There was a day to get through. She would cut more of the creepers away, let more light in. Then she would clear some surfaces. The African violets are beyond being saved. There are old wellingtons belonging to Ronnie. It's time to get rid of them.

She did it slowly, enjoying the fact that she was moving

better. She didn't want to be too tired.

This time he came. She saw him open the letter and pick up the two notes. This time he came straight to the house, sauntering, she thought, as if time was the least important dimension.

She went to the back door and opened it.

He was taller than she had thought, his height emphasised by that young man's special kind of slimness. His hair bobbed up and down as he walked. It was long and wavy, falling down to his collar so that his ears were two pink lines in the dark mass. She noticed too that the sauntering was a disguise and that, in spite of giving the appearance of not being bothered, he was crossing the lawn rather quickly.

She would have to get this right. A boy who had said thanks for the chocolates but left them there might be coming just to give her the money back and ask her to stop pestering him.

But he wasn't carrying the notes in his hand. He must have already put them in his pocket.

'Hello, my name's Anna Devonshire. Thanks for coming, I wanted to talk to you,' she said when he stopped about a yard away from her.

'I'm here.' It was all he said. Two words. He was a man.

Recruiting is an art, they had been told. *Spend time choosing who to recruit, do that on instinct but then check the facts, take some soundings. Once you have found the right person make your pitch. You may only have one meeting. You need to make it almost a matter of inevitability that they will work for you. You must also make them feel important.*

He was standing with both arms down by his side. His skin was wonderfully unlined and fresh, un-spotty too. He was clean shaven and very good looking. I bet his mother loves him, she thought. I think I also know why the girl came.

'Look,' Anna began, 'I suspect you might need some money because you have expensive habits and the times you choose to sit on my bench tell me that you are still at school.

Well, I have some money and I need some help. I find myself in a difficult situation and I suspect you are exactly the right person to help me. It would take very little of your time and I would be prepared to pay very well indeed.'

He stood there looking at her. Then he said, 'I knew you were watching me. It's why I waved. I hope you don't mind that I've been using your bench.'

He wasn't smiling as he spoke. She noticed that there was a sadness about his face but his eyes were assessing her. Her impression was that he was intelligent but there was something disjointed too, something that didn't add up.

'Not at all,' she said, then added, 'Look, can we go inside and sit down? I find it hard to stand for any length of time.'

She turned and presumed he would follow. He had begun his note with the word *thanks*. He had manners. 'You can smoke in the house,' she added. 'You must tell me what cannabis does for you.'

He had hesitated but he was following. She led the way into the sitting room. 'Why don't you sit over there?' She pointed out Ronnie's chair. 'Use the pottery dish as an ash tray.'

Then she sat down, desperate to get the weight off her legs, trying to make no noise at all, and again failing. She watched as he looked all the way round the room. He seemed to approve. 'This is some room. Are those paintings real?' he asked her.

'Do you mean are they originals? Yes they are.'

'It's like being in an art gallery.' His eyes were rotating, moving his head in circles, making her reassess her own room. How long was it since she had really looked at it? Funny the way art becomes wallpaper. The Ladbrooke would look much better with the lamp turned on underneath it. The John Crome was just in sunlight.

'Do you like paintings?' she asked him.

'No, not specially. It's just that I've never been in a room like this.'

'I meant what I said about smoking,' she told him. 'You

light up. I don't mind what you smoke. No one's going to bust you here and it'll get rid of the smell of old lady.'

He hesitated again.

'Go on, it's fine,' she told him.

He dug into his pockets and brought out three small packets. From one he took a small square of paper, into which he drizzled what she presumed was tobacco. Then, from the smallest package, he separated out several strands of what looked like dull green fibres and laid these on the paper. Returning the packages to his pockets he carefully pushed the materials to one edge of the paper and rolled it all together neatly, licking the edge and sealing the thin cigarette. When he lit it a sweet smell filled the room. As good as any air freshener, she thought.

He took a long drag and exhaled. The sweet smell intensified. 'Right,' he said, 'Just what kind of mess are you in, Mrs Devonshire?'

Chapter Sixteen

Tell him straight, she thought. Tell him how it is.

'My children think I'm too old to be living on my own,' she began. 'They think I live in squalor. They want to put me in a home, sell this house and pocket the money. I need someone to help me prove that I'm alright on my own, someone to help me tidy the place up and go shopping for me. I need someone I can trust, someone who is on my side.' He was listening. She took a deep breath and looked straight at him. 'I might also need someone who would be willing to hack into my son's emails so that I can see exactly what he is up to.'

A smile had spread over the young man's face. He took another drag, closed his eyes. 'You don't know me and yet you're telling me this stuff, no warm up, no slow introduction, you go straight in - cool.'

He wasn't fazed, just amused. She'd better explain. 'I know a little bit about you. I know you found my bench so you must have gone into several gardens looking for a place to smoke. I suspect that you chose my bench because you like the view. I know you smoke dope. I guess that you quite like your own company although the other week when a girl came round here you went straight off with her. I would hypothesise that you like her, because you told her about my bench, about the secret place you go to smoke which is hidden from the lane, where no one else has ever joined you.'

'Wow,' he said, 'You're not one of those old people who go quietly gaga are you?'

'I can go on. There is more.' She wanted to intrigue him. As she described what she wanted him to do it had seemed as if he might find much of it demeaning. That's why she had mentioned the emails. Talking to him was almost like flirting, absolutely ridiculous for someone of her age.

'What else do you know about me?' he asked. His face had become very serious.

'Not know, but guess,'

'Ok, what else do you guess?' He took another drag.

'You've got nice handwriting. That's rare. I'd guess you've always been good at school. You put the comma in after 'thanks' as well. Most people wouldn't have bothered with either the 'thanks' or the comma. I guess that you're honest. Most people would have taken the chocolates, shrugged their shoulders and walked off with them.'

She paused. Should she do the next bit? It might blow the whole recruitment strategy, but if you couldn't take risks at ninety when could you?

'I also think... although this really is more of a hunch... I also think you might be a bit lost.'

He didn't bridle, simply sat there looking at her intently.

'You saunter along but you have energy. You wave at me carelessly yet you write neatly, and you rolled that - whatever it is - with great skill.'

'Jesus,' he said. 'Are you a witch?'

'No.' She was slowing down. She could feel her own tiredness. 'I'm very frail and very old. It's the start of summer. I want a last summer in this house. When November comes I expect I will feel differently. Until then I want to stay here, and to do that I need your help.'

It was time to ask a direct question.

'Have you got a part time job? Might you be interested in earning some good money?'

He took another long drag and blew the smoke out into the room, seemingly enjoying letting it waft around her furniture and paintings.

'First answer, no, I haven't got a part time job.' He counted his answers on his fingers. 'Second answer, yes, I might be.'

'Good. So you'll want to know how much?'

She realised at once that the question was a mistake.

She saw him shake his head and look at her as if she wasn't understanding him. He was clearly his own person. She mustn't hurry this. Proffi Offi always insisted that recruitment was an art. Listening was the great skill. You should always give them time, let them do the talking.

'Let's not talk about the money.' Then he paused and added the word, 'yet.' He waited for a bit and she wondered whether to say something else, but training made her stay silent. Soon he continued, 'You do know, for all your guessing, that you might not fully understand me, just from watching me through your little window.' He paused, seemed uncertain what to say next. 'This is weird,' he suddenly announced, 'Do you know I've never smoked inside before? My parents don't know about this.' He held up the joint, then seemed to examine it, lost in his thoughts, staring straight at it. It was almost as if he was wondering why he was smoking it, as if the joint had already lost its importance.

'They wouldn't be able to cope if they knew.' He shook his head.

She wanted to say, 'How do you know?' Instead she again waited, waited for him to go on.

'Life keeps doing my head in, that's why.' His shoulders had tensed but now he let them drop and seemed, by an effort of will, to be making himself relax.

'I didn't ask. I don't mind,' she told him.

He looked at her again. 'Do you want a drag?'

He was holding the joint towards her. She was amused, pleased, hoped he wouldn't be offended by a refusal. 'I've never smoked,' she told him. 'Wouldn't it just make me cough?'

'Yeh, daft idea.' He took it back, held it away from the furniture so that any ash would fall straight onto the carpet.

She thought he was going to take another drag but he didn't; instead he hunched down as he suddenly began talking. 'They want me to do well. They've got their hopes all wound up. I mean, they never say anything but I can see it in their faces. It's like it's a theme, another dimension in the house.'

'Do well in what?'

'A Levels... University... life.'

He was looking at her and that long rusty training combined with an older person's patience told her to keep silent again and wait for some more.

'The thing is,' he went on, 'I'm what they call bright. I've no excuse. I can give them what they want.' Suddenly he moved and stubbed out the joint even though he hadn't finished it. With his hands freed up he ran them both through his hair. Then he got up and walked round, as if he no longer wanted the mood the joint was meant to provide. "Lost', you actually said 'lost'. I can't believe that.'

'Tell me about them,' she said quietly. Something else had come back from her training, something about understanding the heart of a person so that you would know what that member of your network might be prepared to do.

He didn't take her prompt. Instead he went off on another tack. 'Gemma's parents are quite different. They've split up and she kind of bounces between them. She seems to be alright about it. They split up when she was thirteen. First she blamed herself then realised it wasn't her, all that stuff.'

He was standing still now, one arm wrapped round himself. 'You see I always thought mine should have split up. I'm not sure they really like each other. I think they only stayed together for me and I have to live with that. I sometimes feel as if I am all their hopes, everything they dream about.'

He relapsed into another silence then suddenly sat down again and began to laugh. 'You are a witch,' he told her. 'I've never told anyone that stuff. You just know, don't you? You can see inside me.'

She'd find out more later but change the subject for now. 'What's your name?' she asked him.

'Nathan.'

'When do you take A Levels?'

'Four weeks.'

Her hopes fell. 'Then you won't have time will you?'

'A day a week. I can give you a day a week until they're over. Will that do?' He was talking decisively, no longer being introspective.

'Are you sure, Nathan?'

He looked at her. 'I need the money. I owe my dealer.'

'And after A Levels?'

'I'll give you more time. I'll have a whole summer to fill before Uni.' He looked at his watch.

'Saturday. I'll see you Saturday, Mrs Devonshire.'

'I told you my name was Anna.'

'Yeh, but I can't call you that. What time will you want me?'

'Nine o'clock. Bring Gemma if you want to. I can find work for both of you.'

He went and she watched him go, striding up the lawn and out through the gate. She thought she had better get herself some food before she was too tired to eat. She collected crackers and some cheese and brought them back to the sitting room.

Will he come, she wondered to herself, or will he think better of it? He didn't seem to be the kind of lad who would break his word. If he didn't come she had no way of contacting him. If he didn't come there was nothing she could do, and she would have lost her £40. It was only Wednesday. She had two full days to wait.

The two days, as it happened, didn't pass as uneventfully as she expected them to. At ten the next morning she heard the front doorbell ring. When she looked through the peephole she saw that Colin and Pamela were standing outside. Only when she opened the door did she see that there were two cars in the drive, not one. The young man was back, confined to his car for the moment and no doubt nursing his clipboard.

'Mother,' Colin said, speaking very quickly, 'I know this is an imposition, but I happen to be making the key-note speech in Aylesbury which means I need to be in Buckingham by 11.15, so I haven't got very long. They are paying me rather a lot of money and I don't want to be late.' In just these two sentences he had walked in through her front door, taken her elbow and was leading her back into her own house. He was a big man and she couldn't physically resist him. She noted that his hair was even more blond than last time. How often does he dye it, she wondered, as she tried to keep up with his pace.

'Now this won't take very long, and I've brought Pams to sit with you while it happens. She'll stay with you until I get back so you needn't be frightened or anxious about having a strange man in the house.' He turned round to look for his wife. 'Pams, where are you?' he called.

'Waiting to be invited to come in.'

'Whatever for?'

'It's called manners,' Pamela explained. 'It's what you were born without.'

Good for her, Anna thought, and felt a wave of sympathy for Colin's wife. But then the wave of sympathy carried her too far because she found that she was inviting Pamela to come in and Pamela was saying that she didn't mind if she did and wiping her shoes on the mat even though they weren't dirty.

She came in and stood beside her husband: the fat and the thin, the tall and the small, Ronnie's child and Pamela, a fellow sufferer and another woman who had made the mistake of marrying a Devonshire. Colin was still holding onto her elbow and was now steering her into the sitting room. The front door was left wide open.

She had to keep moving; he wasn't giving her an option. She wondered whether to dig her stick into his foot and bring him to a halt. He might even have to limp onto whatever platform he was due to show off from later that morning.

What she did was to push her stick forward and jam it into the corner of the maroon chair. It brought them both to a halt although he nearly pulled her over in the process.

'Stop,' she was saying. 'Stop man-handling me in my own house. I won't be intimidated like this.'

She looked up into his face, the face she had once washed and from which she had wiped away tears. In it she could read no possible feeling for her. It was suffused with a glow of self-love and self-belief. It was the face of a certain kind of evangelical preacher, the face of a man who has found, after not very much prayer, that God thinks exactly as he does.

'Pamela,' she asked, 'will you please go and shut the front door? I don't want anyone else coming into the house.'

Pamela went to shut the door, which left them alone just for a moment. Anna expected that Colin would at least pick up her stick which had fallen from her hand, but he didn't. It was as if he knew what she had done and why she had done it. She had made him angry. Was that why he put his hand under her arm and led her to her chair?

Is he going to push me down into it, she wondered. But he didn't. He simply left her there, standing by her chair, separated from her stick. Sod him, she thought. He knows I can't stand for long, that I can walk only short distances unaided, that I need to lever myself up. If I sit down I'm stuck for the day.

Colin had gone out of the room to find his wife. She heard whispered conversation, then the door was being opened and Colin was shouting to the man outside, no doubt inviting him in.

To be this helpless, to be this dependent.

Footsteps were returning. Colin was bringing the young man into the house without her permission. No doubt he would smirk and feel triumphant. Perhaps he would drum his fingers on his clipboard. She could hear them getting nearer. Had she emptied the commode this morning? Such routine actions were difficult to remember when you reached her age. Colin would let the young man walk all round the house and she didn't want him to see it if it wasn't clean.

She reached the maroon chair and leant against it, then

pushed forwards reaching out for the stick. The carpet was a long way down so she decided to use the chair arm to lower herself so that she could kneel on the floor, reach for the stick and use both the stick and the arm to get back up.

She got one knee down then the chair began to move away. The force of her leaning must have freed the castors from their deep ruts in the carpet. She was falling forwards. As she fell she was aware that at least two people were coming in through the sitting room door and watching her fall. What a triumph for the young man, she thought. I send him packing one day and a few days later he has the satisfaction of watching me fall literally and metaphorically flat on my face.

It seemed to her, as she fell, that no one rushed to help her. Perhaps what was happening so slowly to her was speeded up for them, giving them no time to react.

Her knee gave way. Her face hit the carpet, then there was no more movement, only stillness. She raised her head and looked towards the door and saw them standing there: the dyed blond and the clip board man. They were standing there watching her, not moving.

She wasn't in pain. Her fury at herself for giving them this show of incompetence was so overwhelming that it gave pain no chance to register. She mustn't lie there. She must move.

Slowly she turned onto her side. Only then did hands reach out to help her up. She heard Pamela asking if she was alright, heard herself answer, 'Yes, of course, this is part of my daily exercise routine. I was about to start my usual two hours of yoga.'

Nothing seemed to be broken. She was bruised and jarred but she was in one piece. Pamela had her standing now and had given her the stick, gently turning it so that the handle was towards her hand. Anna turned her back on them and went to her chair. Now she would have to sit down.

Colin glanced twice at his watch. He didn't seem to have moved at all, just watched as his wife looked after her. Without a word of sympathy he began to talk.

'Mum, this is Alan Hazell. He's come to value the house. I must dash now but I'll leave Pams with you so that you aren't on your own. When I've done my stuff and answered some questions I'll be right back.'

And he was gone, banging the front door shut, crunching across the gravel, starting his car and spinning the wheels as if he was trying to be the same age as his own children.

Alan Hazell stood in the doorway. Then he said, 'Well I'd better get on. I'll try to keep right out of your way.' He had a clipboard and a tape measure. 'I'll make a start upstairs.'

Could she make him go away? If she tried to force the issue, which side would Pamela come down on? She wondered whether to phone the police and have him ejected but decided against it. She could hear the conversation now with its repeated phrases about just how difficult old people can be.

Pamela was standing over her, clearly uncertain about what to do next. She'd better say something.

'I'm sorry about what I said. Thank you for helping me up.'

She realised she didn't know her daughter-in-law very well. Perhaps this was a chance. Pamela was always direct in the way she talked to people. Why not ask her a direct question?

'Why are they doing this to me?' she asked. She could feel the ache in her body now. The more she calmed down the more the pain was able to register. Tomorrow she'd be lucky if she could move at all.

Pamela was standing up, still wearing her coat. Perhaps she was waiting to be invited to sit down.

'Take your coat off, and sit down,' said Anna. 'Colin won't be back for ages yet. I don't expect any of this was your idea.'

Pamela seemed to make up her mind. She took her duffle coat off and folded it neatly along the back of the settee, then went across the room and sat down in what had been Ronnie's chair. Her face, Anna noticed, was heavily made up, contrasting oddly with the greying hair. She was neatly turned out, as always, her hair tied up in a careful bun. Every network needs an insider, someone close to the heart of the enemy. Could she turn Pamela, persuade her to change sides?

'Do you need a cup of coffee?' Anna suggested. 'You must have been travelling for hours. I'd offer to make you one but I'm a bit shaken. Why don't you help yourself?'

When Pamela came back in she seemed to have made up her mind to speak.

'We're not doing this to you. Please don't think that... Mum...'

The word was hesitantly used. I'm not your Mum, Anna thought, although I wouldn't mind if I were. You do have something about you.

'...Look,' Pamela was saying, 'this is just the consequence of those changes Alistair made to Ronnie's will. I mean it makes sense, doesn't it, that we try to save some of the money from the taxman?'

Anna wasn't going to let her off that lightly. 'But why now? You all own a bit of the house so why can't you wait until I'm dead, find out what it's worth then? I mean you can't make any use of it while I'm alive, can you?'

Anna watched her daughter-in-law hesitate again.

'Well, I might as well tell you. I always thought you would have to know some time. It's for a loan.'

Anna waited. She was sure there was more to be said. Having said so much Pamela was bound to say more.

'Alistair needs a loan. He's lost a lot of money and he risks losing his house.'

'So he needs my home as collateral.'

Pamela nodded.

'Then I don't understand why Colin and Heather have become so involved.'

Pamela laughed. 'They stick together, don't they, the Devonshire children? They've always been close and this crisis has brought them even closer. They know that what they are doing is what their father would have wanted. That's why they think it's okay.'

'And if Alistair is to get a loan, they must have an up to date evaluation.'

She was thinking out loud but she saw Pamela nod.

Should she ask how much Alistair had lost? Probably not. Time to change the subject.

'So what's Colin talking about at the conference?'

'Himself, of course.'

Anna laughed. 'Which particular aspect of himself?'

Pamela shrugged. 'Colin doesn't have aspects, he just is. But then you know that don't you?'

Now she must be careful. To nod would be to reveal that she knew more than she had ever let on. She mustn't do that. She must hide her new feisty self and revert to the part she'd played for sixty years.

'I sometimes feel I don't know my children very well at all.' If she wanted to learn more she must give something back. 'You know, when they were younger, I never thought of them as my children. I wasn't very well at the time, had to have a nanny to help, but I expect you know that. And when I began to recover it always felt as if I was bringing them up for their father.'

'Yes, Colin loved his father.' Pamela looked across at her mother-in-law. 'Colin has only ever loved two people in his life: he loved his father and he loves himself. You and I never stood a chance.'

'Doesn't that make you unhappy? Anna had asked the question instinctively, before she had a chance to censor herself.

Pamela looked across at her, clearly surprised at the directness of the question. 'It did once, but not anymore,' she said. 'I always liked my own company and when you are with Colin you can always be on your own. He doesn't need you to listen to what he says because he isn't talking to you.

He doesn't need reassurance.' She paused again, then said, 'I shouldn't really be telling you this, but as you don't know anything about computers I'm sure I can. You see, when you set a password you need at least five letters and a number. Colin's password is Greatest1. Can you believe that?'

Anna not only believed it but would make sure she remembered it.

She must have nodded off and Pamela must have left her there because when she opened her eyes her sitting room was empty.

What time was it? Before she looked at her watch she heard talking, two sets of voices out in the hall. One was Pamela, the other was clearly attached to the clipboard.

'So is it worth spending money on? I mean, the kitchen's a disgrace.'

'Not on the kitchen. Whoever buys it will want to put their own stamp on it.'

'The carpets then?'

'No, the same applies.'

'So we just leave it as it is then?'

'Well, there is one thing that would make a difference. Tidy up the front. Re-do the drive. Get the house painted outside. That'll show a potential buyer what's possible.'

'And how much do you think we can expect to get for it?'

Alan Hazell hesitated. It was the pause of a man who values his own professionalism. 'I need to go back to the office and make some comparisons. I need to consult my partner.'

'Okay, Alan. You'll e-mail us later then.'

The voices went silent. Pamela was clearly ushering him out of the house. Anna heard footsteps on the gravel.

And then they will usher me out, she thought. Pamela wasn't here to look after me, she was here to protect the clipboard man.

And she was lying to me, lying about the loan. It isn't a loan they want. They are still planning to sell my home. Greatest1.

She'd better write that down, tell Nathan, see what he could do.

When Pamela came back into the room she let her make a cup of tea and pretended that they were again the best of friends. If she couldn't recruit Pamela she wouldn't give her any information that might be used against her. When Colin came back to pick his wife up he didn't even come into the house, just sounded his horn from outside.

Then the house was hers again.

There was very little time. A week had already gone by. In another two weeks Colin and Heather would come to inspect the house and today she had proved how vulnerable she was by toppling over right in front of Colin. How far was she willing to go in order to save her home? The gun Major Lustic had persuaded her to keep as a souvenir was somewhere in the house. Had she kept some bullets? She couldn't remember. Perhaps it was time to check.

Chapter Seventeen

On Saturday morning Anna was up early. She had her list. She had her plan. She had her card ready with the pin number written down. If this was war, she had to take risks.

Just before nine she heard a knock on the back door. It took her some time to turn the key and pull back the bolts. She'd expected him to use the front door, had already taken it off the latch. Perhaps Nathan didn't know what the front of the house looked like. She was aware that she was moving stiffly after the fall, but she soon had the door open and some summer air, newly rinsed and already heating up, jumped into her tired house.

Nathan and the girl were standing back from the door with the sun behind them. It's because they don't want to startle me, she thought.

'Come in,' she said. 'I've put the kettle on.'

They came towards the door. Gemma was as tall as Nathan. At first glance Anna thought she looked severe. It's the hair, she thought. She's got a thin face, why does she accentuate its thinness? She's got lots of hair. It would look so pretty if she just took it out of that absurd plait and let it really frame her face.

'Mrs Devonshire, this is Gemma.'

He'd got good manners. Someone had brought him up well.

'Hello, Gemma.' Should she shake hands? Would Gemma want to shake her hand or even to touch her? I'll learn a lot by trying, she thought.

She pushed one hand forward and Gemma took it, held it firmly enough without squashing her, didn't let it go straight away like some people did, as if they couldn't bear the touch of an older person.

'Nice to meet you,' she said.

Did she mean that? These days, they all said it.

Anna looked at Nathan and thought, he isn't certain about her. He's brought her because he likes her but he doesn't know how much he likes her or perhaps he brought her simply because I asked him to.

'Come in,' she said. 'It's coffee. I don't do tea. How many sugars will you each have?

They let her make the coffee and stayed out of her way. This was such a relief from Heather pushing past her, banning her from her own kitchen. She could hear them in the sitting room. Nathan seemed to be talking about her paintings.

When the coffees were ready she called them into the kitchen. There was no way she could carry three full cups. Then she led them back into the sitting room.

They sat side by side on the gold coloured settee, side by side but not touching.

'Right,' she began, and told them what she wanted. Shopping first then a clean-up. She suggested they catch the bus there and get a taxi back, but when Nathan looked at the list he told her he'd borrow his parents' car. They wouldn't mind. They trusted him. He was a good driver.

'Okay,' she said, 'if you're sure that is alright.'

'I'm a good driver,' he repeated. 'I've been driving for more than a year. No accidents.'

Then this was her card. This was her pin number. They were to go to a cash point and get out £300. Half of it was for them as wages. The other half was because she needed cash. They were to use the card to pay for the things they bought. She'd written them a letter about that, in case anyone asked. Nathan took the letter from her and glanced at it.

'So I'm your grandson am I?'

'Well you might be.'

He laughed at that but Anna noticed that Gemma didn't join in with the laughter, seemed uncomfortable.

206

'And here's £20. It was going to be for bus and taxis but you can give it to your parents to cover their petrol costs.'

She went through the list with Gemma, explained that she wanted bright colours, that she needed to make a show. She told them they were to spend lots because spending was part of the proof that she could cope. John Lewis was the place. They could get it all there, except perhaps the cleaning materials. Gemma nodded, but didn't say anything except, 'Right, Mrs Devonshire,' a phrase she repeated like a mantra, but the eyes, set deeply to either side of her elegant face, never brightened.

It's just a job for her, Anna thought. She's not going to get involved. Why should she?

Then they were gone. With my card and with my money, Anna thought. Okay, now I must do my bit.

She picked up her phone book and slowly turned the pages until she found Colin's number. Then she sat and dialled it, hoping it would be Colin, not Pamela, who answered. She could fool Colin. She wasn't so sure about Pamela. Pamela would be more suspicious. She must remember to act the fool, to sound as stupid and as old as she could.

The phone was picked up at once. 'Colin Devonshire.'

'Hello Colin.'

'And what can I do for you today, Mother?' Her phrase parroted back to her.

She heard only his usual cheerfulness. There was no consciousness of his appalling rudeness the other day, no contrition in his voice.

'Well not for me. It's for James actually.'

'For James?'

'I don't know why dear, but apparently he wants to send you something, send you something by what's it called? That computer thing where you send messages through the air.' She paused. She hoped she wasn't overdoing this pretence at stupidity.

'Emails, Mother. I think you mean emails.' She could sense

207

that Colin was already bored with her.

'Well where does he send it to? I mean, what is your address, not your house, your computer's address.'

'Have you got a pen, Mother?' Now she could hear the exasperation in his voice.

The pen was in her hand and the note pad was ready. 'I think there's one somewhere.' If he thought she was gaga she'd better play up to his beliefs. She made some shuffling noises and then announced. 'Found one.'

'Write this down then, it's all in lower case and you mustn't leave any gaps. Ready?'

'I'm ready.'

He dictated and she wrote colin.devonshire@blueyonder. Perhaps he was feeling guilty because he explained about the 'at' bit, told her it wasn't the two letter word but the a in the nearly closed circle, told her James would understand.

She wrote it down and then, so that he mightn't be suspicious later on and discuss this with his 'Pams', she explained that the real reason for her phoning was to ask him how his speech had gone.

The boredom left his voice immediately as he told her about his reception.

When she had congratulated him and put the phone down she wrote underneath the email address: *Password: Greatest1*. She didn't know if the password was in lower case or not. Knowing Colin it might be all capitals. She'd see what Nathan could do with that. She wondered whether to ask him in front of Gemma or to keep it just between them. She decided that secrecy might be better.

The young things were back soon after 11.30. This time the front doorbell rang and when she opened it Gemma was already surrounded by bags. She could see different shades of red spilling out between the handles. Nathan was emptying the boot. They put all their purchases inside the house then Nathan said he had to return the car and Gemma went with him.

The moment they got back she set them to clean bathrooms and toilets, then the kitchen. She noticed they divided the work between them, rather than working side by side. Scrub everything, she told them, then throw out the old towels and flannels and washing cloths and bring in the new. Nathan asked her about the secondary glazing. 'Take it off,' she told him. 'Stack it in the garage.' The room looked much better at once, much lighter too. She showed them both where the bin was and together they moved it to the front door and then filled it up. She was being ruthless. Things she had kept 'in case' were all thrown away. Windowsills became less cluttered. Surfaces were cleared. The house seemed to lift off its haunches. Infected with their energy, she went into the utility room with a black polythene bag and filled it with wilted plants and hardened split bits of soap. Then she threw in the cellophane from the flowers someone had once bought her. She opened a cupboard and it was full of Ronnie's old gardening clothes. She had to hold the bag carefully to get them all in. Then she called for Nathan and he came and threw it into the bin for her, squashing it down.

Gemma, who happened to be passing, said, 'You could re-cycle some of that.'

'After your A Levels we'll do lots of recycling,' Anna reassured her, 'but for now I don't have time.'

It was four o'clock when they both began to tackle the utility room. Anna went outside again and tried to continue pruning, snipping off more of the tendrils that still covered too much of the window. Nathan followed her out and watched her working.

'Got any shears?'

'In the garage,' she told him. 'The back door's open.'

He came back and simply cut a long straight line above the windows, snipping cleanly, giving the house a fringe. It took him hardly any time at all. When it was done he went back into the garage and came out with a yard broom and swept everything up into a pile.

'It's addictive, this cleaning lark,' he commented.

She told him where the rubbish heap was and he scooped the stuff up and walked away down the path. She walked part way to meet him so that they were a little further from the house.

Fishing the piece of paper out of her pocket she gave it to him.

'Um,' he said when he'd read it. 'What exactly do you want me to do with this?'

'They've had the house valued,' she explained. 'I want to know what it's worth and what they are planning for me. Nothing else.'

'You sure? Hacking into an email is illegal.'

'So is smoking dope,' she told him.

He smiled at her. 'Just don't let Gemma find out.' He put the piece of paper in his pocket.

'Okay.'

Gemma was down on her knees scrubbing at the floor, sloshing water about. She scowled at Nathan when he stepped towards the door. Nathan immediately backed away, offered to go round and in through the front. Anna said that was alright with her too. She needed a walk.

Just before 5pm Nathan fixed two fragrance machines, one in the lounge and one in the hall. Anna noticed that he called Gemma to help him when he couldn't make them work and that she laughed at him for his incompetence. When both machines were functioning they came to say goodbye.

She paid them £75 each. Nathan thanked her. Gemma said it was far too much, but when Anna refused to take any back she took twenty pounds for herself and gave the rest to Nathan. He seemed puzzled.

'You need it more that I do right now,' was all Gemma said. She wasn't smiling.

They went together out of the back door, walked down the garden and sat on the bench. Anna watched them through her wonderfully clear windows. Nathan didn't roll a joint and Gemma sat very close to him. He put his arm round her and she let it stay there. They might have been talking. They were looking straight ahead of them but they didn't kiss. In a little while Gemma walked away and Nathan waited, presumably until he was sure she was out of sight, before rolling himself a joint.

She had a week before she would see them again, a week to get used to the different way her house looked, felt and smelled. But early on Wednesday evening Nathan was back, appearing suddenly by the bench and walking down the garden.

'Shouldn't you be revising?' she said when she had successfully struggled with the back door.

He shook his head at her. 'You're not one of my parents, Mrs Devonshire. That isn't you speaking. You're different.'

'Sorry,' she said, 'none of my business.'

He held up a piece of paper. 'I've got some stuff for you. I've been on your son's emails. I'm afraid it's bad news.'

'Isn't the house worth very much?' she asked.

'No, the house is worth a fortune. That Alan Hazell says there aren't many like it, not of this size, that they rarely come on the market. When they do, people live in them for forty years. He values it at just under £850,000.' He paused. 'Did you know you were worth that much?'

She made no reply. 'So what's the bad news?' she asked.

'You have a daughter called Heather, haven't you?'

'Yes.'

'And a son called Alistair?'

She nodded.

'Well he's in trouble. His emails read as if he's desperate. He's lost a packet. There are strings of emails between him and his brother and sister. They're both supporting him but they're arguing about whether to take a loan out against the value of the house or whether to sell it.'

'But it's my house.'

'Yeh, most of it seems to be,' he said.

'So they can't do anything about it while I'm alive, can they?' The words betrayed more worry than she had meant them to. She could see that Nathan was concerned and it touched her.

He hesitated. 'Well maybe they can and maybe they can't.'

He seemed to be changing in front of her eyes. The young man she was looking at was a serious person, not a wastrel, not a druggie. She wondered if Gemma ever saw this side of him and what she would think if she did.

'Did you ever sign a piece of paper saying that others could do things for you if it was necessary?' Nathan asked her.

There had been something, something arranged when Ronnie was still alive, something that she had agreed to because Ronnie had wanted her to, to give her peace of mind. (Peace of Mind, what a stultifying thing to wish on anyone.) It was done so that the family could help her if she needed it, if she was left on her own. The compliant person she had been in those days had signed and they had smiled at her.

'They think you did,' Nathan explained, full of concern. 'They think that you have given Power of Attorney to Alistair. That means he can agree things for you, sign cheques for you, do all that stuff.'

Her memory was sharpening. There had been a form, a form she had signed because it was referring to a time way in the future, so far away that there had been no reason not to sign it.

'What can I do?' she asked him.

'I don't know. I'll try and find something out.'

She didn't respond.

'Look, I'm sorry,' Nathan said, 'I've got to go. I must do some of that revision you were talking about.'

'You get back,' she said at once, 'Thanks for coming.'

He didn't move. He seemed to be looking at her intently. He was young, absolutely in his prime, and yet he seemed genuinely concerned about her. 'Are you sure you'll be alright?' he asked.

'Yes,' she said, not feeling it, touched by his concern so that she felt the hint of tears.

He didn't go at once. 'I can ask Gemma to come and sit with you if you want.'

'Hasn't she got revision?'

'Her subjects are mostly coursework, it's not the same,' he explained.

'No.' She made herself sound confident. She didn't want Nathan to have to explain anything to Gemma and anyway, the whole point she was trying to prove was that she could cope on her own.

'No, I'm actually quite tough. You go along.'

'I'll see you Saturday then.'

And he was off, striding quickly down the garden. Anna shivered although it was still warm and crept back into the house. She needed to sit down.

They won't do it, she told herself. Even Ronnie's children won't treat me that badly. But she knew, even as she thought it, that they would, that they would be able to fashion it as doing what was best for her. Family trust was a delusion. They'd say she couldn't manage on her own. They'd invite her to come and live with one of them, knowing she would refuse. She imagined being patronised every day by Heather, being herded like one of her dogs. When she'd turned down their self-sacrificial invitations they'd think that was because she would be happier in a home. They'd sell the house and take what was their share, perhaps each lend some to Alistair to get him out of trouble, and all along they'd know it was what Ronnie wanted and that meant it was alright. They would be looking after her in the same way Ronnie had, just as they had no doubt promised him before he died.

And what about her share? She was worth about £600,000, plus the other bits and pieces. What would they want her to do with that? She knew the answer already. They would suggest that she pass much of it on to them now so that, if she lived a bit longer, no one would have to pay death duties on Ronnie's hard earned money.

And worse still they had no need to ask her about any of this. They could just arrange it amongst themselves. They could do so because they had a piece of paper she had signed which gave them the power to do anything in her name. Even if she passed their inspection next week, how could she resist the overwhelming force of what they could do to her in the name of caring?

She felt helpless. Once I was something, she reminded herself. Once I had a part in controlling the fate of young men running across a beach in Normandy. Even in the war the odds had not been so fiercely stacked against her as they were now. I'm alone, she thought. I'm ninety. The feral child, the convicted murderer, both have more rights than I have.

She had reached rock-bottom. This was her situation. This was her danger. Her post-war, married-to-Ronnie self would have been overwhelmed.

But she didn't feel overwhelmed. Somewhere inside her she found that she was still alive and fighting. War clarifies everything, turns complexity into something simple. If her family were prepared to treat her that badly then she, in her turn, could abandon the niceties of family life and fight them back.

If her family were to be defeated then they must get no hint of what she was really up to. They mustn't ever find out about Nathan and Gemma. That meant she had to cut her children off from their sources of information. What was the phrase Proffi Offi had used? It came to her immediately. It was called de-coupling.

The first problem was James. He would insist on carrying things in for her, which gave him access to the house. He was bound to notice its new neatness and report on what was happening. She couldn't sack him because she needed someone to take her shopping. She might be able to get rid of his services later when and if Nathan and Gemma could take over, but that wasn't yet.

She bustled out into the garage, stiffly turned the long key, then pulled open the white door and heard its restrainer dragging musically across the concrete. She found the old shopping trolley which she had used for logs and pulled it out into the daylight. It was a mess but it still pulled on its wheels. Rummaging round on what had been Ronnie's work bench she found an old dried up cloth which she poked around the shopping trolley, dislodging bits of bark and two years of dust. It began to look better. She'd put it by the front door, then ask James to put the shopping into it. She'd tell him that she must do more for herself. She simply wouldn't unlock the front door until he was back in his car. That would solve the James problem.

The next problem was Rosanna. Friday was Rosanna's cleaning day. First thing Friday morning Rosanna would use her back door key to walk into the house and she would immediately see how clean it all was. The surprise Anna had planned for would be spoilt. How was she to manage this?

There was always the bolt on the back door. She never bolted this particular door on a Thursday night and she took her own key out of the lock so that Rosanna could let herself in. If she were to leave the bolt on and the key in the door Rosanna would effectively be shut out.

But how would Rosanna react?

She'd have to go round to the front door and ring the bell. Anna could be there to meet her, dispense with her services and that would be Rosanna dealt with. She'd get the key back and give her £100 in lieu of notice.

But the more she thought about it the more she disliked the idea. It was too sudden, too deliberate on her part. Even if it prevented her family from hearing of the big clear-up it was bound to raise their suspicions and make them wonder what she was up to.

Perhaps she could play Rosanna's reluctance to do any hard work against her. What if she was to phone up and ask her to do three days a week instead of one morning? She could lay it on thick, say she wanted floors washing and a cycle of thorough carpet cleaning, that she had decided to light fires every night so the grate would need regular cleaning and fresh logs bringing in. She played the conversation through in her mind. Rosanna would be bound to retreat and say she couldn't do it. Anna would say what a pity that was because this was what she now needed. If Rosanna couldn't see her way to doing the extra hours then she would have to find someone else who could.

It was a good solution. Anna decided she'd try it and looked for the number in her book.

'Hello,' she said when she got through. 'It's Mrs Devonshire.'

She heard hesitation on the other end of the line. 'Oh,' said Rosanna. 'How strange. I mean I was going to phone you.'

Instinct told Anna that she should listen before she spoke, should wait to hear what Rosanna had to say. She waited.

Rosanna went on, talking as if it needed a little courage to say what had to be said. 'Only I'm not well. I've been to the doctor and he says that I need a rest. I was going to phone and ask you if you could cope without me for the next two Fridays.'

Anna listened and understood. She felt like asking what was wrong with her. She wondered if she should be solicitous and sympathetic in the hope of learning something more or at least of confirming what she suspected.

Instead she found herself saying, 'No that's fine. I'm sure I can cope for two weeks.

'Thank you, Mrs Devonshire,' said a relieved voice. 'I'll see you Friday fortnight then.'

When she put the phone down she knew at once that she should have added, 'And once you are fully well we can talk about the extra hours I'll be needing.'

She sat very still in her chair and said very quietly to the room, 'They've set me a test they haven't told me about and taken away, as far as they know, any means I have of passing their inspection. They've told Rosanna to make her excuses and left me to do all the tidying and cleaning on my own. They are determined to condemn me.'

Chapter Eighteen

Gemma didn't know why she was standing outside a rather posh house early on a Saturday morning by herself. She had rung the doorbell and could hear the old lady making her slow way down the hallway. It would take her some time to get to the door, then the bolts would have to be drawn back before she could be let in.

Why was she here? The old lady wasn't her problem. If it had been her gran or even Nathan's gran she could have understood. But this was a complete stranger, an old lady that Nathan had somehow picked up and agreed to do things for.

Come and help, Nathan had said. It'll be a laugh, he'd said, and she'll pay well.

Exam time was just horrible. She'd finished every assignment, done and re-done them so often she was dizzy with it. The teacher had promised A grades but there might always be a problem with the moderator. The moderator's word was final and Gemma knew of problems last year and the year before. Both those year groups had been disappointed. She hoped she would be alright. She had to trust the school, but she still worried. Another week and there would be nothing else that she could do about it, only wait until August for the results.

Soon she'd be free of it all. Soon she could turn her attention away from school work. Soon she would be able to spend time solving her biggest problem of the moment: Nathan.

He should be with her now, listening to the pantomime behind the doors, putting that silly fixed grin on his face, getting ready to say hello.

Where was he? He'd said he must do something for the old lady first, something that she needed done. He'd been mysterious, hadn't given her any details and she'd thought, no.

He's after something for himself. He'll be finding Risco to get more dope or he'll be having a lie-in and sending me to get the day started for him. He was so inconsistent, so all over the place, so much the wrong person for her.

Everyone said so. Her friends had warned her. They'd agreed he was good looking but had told her he was right out of her league. Okay, his face was kind of nice and he'd got a lovely smile but he was a druggie and an oddball. He was bright too. Look at those A Levels he was taking and didn't he want to be a lawyer?

She'd looked at him then, had stared at him across the common room, seen the way he sat on the broken settee, almost as if he was lying flat, doing his best to be horizontal, on his own, not talking to anyone. She'd got straight up to go to her lesson when the bell went, but he hadn't moved. That might mean he hadn't got a lesson but he probably had. What had her dad said? Something about brains not being everything, how you needed drive and determination. The two Ds. Her dad would take one look and tell her not to bother.

Then Nathan asked her out, told her he knew of a seat in someone else's garden with a wonderful view.

'A seat,' she'd said. 'Is that it? Why not the cinema or a pub or a party?'

'I don't do those,' he had told her. 'I do seats. I just want to show you a view I happen to know about.'

She hadn't believed the 'just'. No boy she had been out with ever did 'just'.

Why had she agreed? She'd done so on the spur of the moment, intrigued perhaps? No that wasn't it. She wasn't intrigued. She'd looked into his eyes when he'd asked her out and seen something in them, something that was in direct contradiction to the offhandedness of his invitation, something that didn't fit with his reputation, so she'd said yes.

I can always push him away if he tries anything, she'd thought. He won't take much pushing.

The old lady had got the door open at last and was standing blinking in the sunshine, looking round for Nathan. Join the club, Gemma thought, and immediately explained that he'd be along later.

The old lady looked so disappointed it was almost funny. Gemma followed her into the hall. At least this week it didn't smell. Last week it had been horrible, last week she had wanted to gag. They'd had to sit there and drink coffee made in that dirty kitchen. Well, at least this week the surfaces would still be clean.

'I'll make some coffee,' the old lady said. 'Your first task today is to talk to me and brighten me up.'

Gemma wondered if she could stand watching her make the coffee. Just filling the kettle was such an effort. The old lady had to hug it to her because of the weight, then carry it back over to seat it on the base. That took her two goes to get it right. Then she had to peer at the light just to check it was on.

The cups were nearly clean. There was a tiny tide mark of coffee on the inside of one of them just under the handle, but she'd seen worse in her own house. She could cope. If the water was properly boiling she shouldn't catch anything.

On their first 'date' Nathan had been punctual. That surprised her. He also seemed to have dressed himself better than he sometimes did. The jeans were clean and so was his striped shirt. They'd met by the war memorial. He hadn't said she looked nice or anything like that, even though she had tried on and discarded several outfits because she wanted to get it right. He hadn't reached out to hold her hand. All he'd said was, 'Hi. You came. Follow me.' He led her down the road and along a lane she vaguely remembered from childhood walks with her father. It had been a warm evening and he had walked quite fast, but she'd had no problem keeping up. Suddenly he had stopped and said, 'We go through here.'

Here was a small gate clearly marked 'Private.'

'Are you sure about this?' she'd asked.

'Yeh, it's fine.'

In spite of herself she had followed him through and found herself on the edge of someone's tatty lawn. There was a house about a hundred yards away, two storeys of red brick under a sloping tiled roof. It looked like the castle in The Sleeping Beauty, its windows nearly covered with creepers, like a place waiting for a prince to call and wake everyone up.

'Are you sure it's alright, Nathan?' she'd asked.

'Yeh, the old lady knows I sit here. She doesn't mind.'

So they'd both sat there. She'd expected him to sit close, to hold her hand, perhaps to attempt to kiss her, but he had done none of these things. 'Just look,' he'd said, and she had looked.

How had he found it, she wondered. Sitting on the bench, you were level with the tops of the trees. It gave a quite different perspective, but the trees didn't block everything out. You could see beyond them over meadows down to the river.

She'd sat on the bench and she'd looked, not just at the view but stealing glances at Nathan at the same time. He seemed absorbed, his eyes tracking from side to side, his nose moving up and down, just looking, saying nothing.

Any moment now he'll try to touch me, she thought. Any moment now I'll have to decide if I want him to kiss me. Actually she knew she did. Why else was she here? But he made no move at all.

'Great view,' she told him when the silence began to weigh on her.

'That's why I wanted you to see it.'

Now, she thought. Now he'll start to talk to me. Now I'll find out why he asked me out. But he said nothing else for a time which left his last sentence echoing. There had been no inflection. If he'd said, 'That's why I wanted *you* to see it,' she would have known where she stood.

Then she gave up on the riddle and thought, here I am. It's not what I expected but it's okay. She sat back a little further in the seat, watched the light thicken and gradually drain out detail from the scene. She became aware as she sat that the air was filled with song, that little birds were everywhere. She breathed out deeply and something shook loose inside her. She stopped asking questions; her eyes glazed. She thought she could smell the river, smell its wetness even from up here. She let herself drift.

'I want to ask you something,' the old lady was saying, now that they were back in the lounge with their coffees.

'Ask away.' Well she had to say it didn't she? Even if Nathan didn't come she'd be able to escape from here by five.

'Do I smell clean?'

God, what a question. Straight up, no messing. What the hell should she say?

The old lady was looking at her, pleading, defenceless. She had this posh house and all these things and yet she needed to know if she smelled all right.

'Course you do,' Gemma told her, and made herself smile at the old dear.

'No,' the old lady was saying, 'it's a serious question. When you get to my age it's difficult to know. I can't really tell if my clothes are clean. There isn't a good light in my bedroom. My son put in one of those new kinds of bulbs so I wouldn't have to keep changing it and they're not bright enough. I can't ask Nathan these questions; it has to be you.'

You could do Health and Social Care and study these things in theory, but this was the reality. This was what it was really all about. What did Mrs Devonshire expect now, that she'd walk over and give her a sniff? The old lady had dropped something down her blouse. Gemma could see that from where she was. There was a yellow stain stretching between two buttons. Come on Nathan, where are you? Why aren't you here?

'I didn't ask to be old.' The old lady was explaining. 'It just crept up on me. I need to be at my best on Tuesday. It's no good getting the house tidy if I'm a mess. I'm sorry to ask but I'd be so grateful.'

Fuck this. She didn't have a choice. Where the hell was Nathan? It was time to dump him. She hated not having a choice. She put down her mug and walked over. She breathed out first then sniffed the air above the old lady's head, expecting to smell something unpleasant, something incontinent. Actually it wasn't like that at all. There was a bit of a smell of old skin but nothing worse. She stepped back. 'You're fine,' she said. 'But your blouse isn't clean. Shall we see if we can find a better one?'

'I'll have to show you.'

The old lady could get up the stairs but only just. She had to pull herself up by the rails on the banister. Several times she stopped to take a breather. Gemma gritted her teeth and moved up slowly behind her. Reaching the top was clearly some kind of achievement. 'I'm up,' she said, and smiled.

Gemma had carried her stick up but then realised she didn't need to. There was another stick waiting there. The old lady had two, one for upstairs and one for downstairs.

'This way.'

Gemma followed her into the room. It wasn't one they had done last week. The light was awful. She had to do something about that. 'Wait there,' she said, 'sit on the bed and get your breath back. Where do you keep spare bulbs?'

It was great to rush down the stairs, great to move at her own pace. She found the drawer in what the old lady called 'the dog house' and there was a spare 100 watt bulb. She took it upstairs, found a chair that would hold her weight, stood on it and made the swap.

The room was now brighter. It was better to be doing something rather than nothing, much better. The old lady looked wacked. 'Shall I sort out stuff that needs washing and anything that needs dry cleaning? Then I can put some washing on for you. I might even get it all dry and ironed before tonight.'

'I'd be so grateful. I'm sorry to ask.'

'Your daughter should be doing this for you,' Gemma said, as she rummaged in the drawers. Most of the blouses weren't quite clean. She gathered them up and ran downstairs. Whites at 40°. There was plenty of washing liquid and softener. She set it all going then went back upstairs.

The old lady was still sitting on the bed. 'I wonder,' she said, 'is there one clean blouse? I need to change out of this one.'

There was. Gemma carried it over. 'Shall I go?' she asked.

'No need, unless you want to.'

Her face was the oldest thing about her, her face and her hands. Her shoulders were still rounded, almost plump, although the biceps sagged into long knotted lines when she dropped her arms. The bra seemed too big, not quite filled out. Gemma turned to the wardrobes, picked out some dresses to take to the dry cleaners. When she turned back the old lady was doing up her top button. She looked better now that she was dressed.

The bell rang. Thank God for that. Now where the hell had Nathan been?

'Go and let him in,' the old lady said. 'I can make my way downstairs.'

Gemma ran downstairs and tugged the door open. 'Where the hell have you been?' she asked, 'You'd better have the most fantastic excuse.'

A glance at his face told her that he was extremely pleased with himself.

'Solving a problem,' he told her and he held up a large brown envelope.

'Leaving me here on my own, more like,' she reminded him. She wasn't certain enough of him to nag him like this. She must make herself stop. She knew he'd hate being nagged.

He came in past her and began to explain. 'It's that family of hers. They want her to go into a home. She gave them

Power of Attorney and now she wants it back. I looked it up on the internet and I've got the forms.' He held up the envelope again.

'Meanwhile you left me here, having to do all sorts of personal stuff.' She couldn't stop herself.

Nathan looked crestfallen. 'I'm sorry, but this matters too.'

He hadn't been having a lie-in. He hadn't been meeting his dealer. He'd been rushing round trying to sort things out, helping.

'But perhaps she needs to be in a home.' This thought had been growing on Gemma all morning. 'Are you're sure we're right to be doing all this for her?'

'I like her, Gem. I think she should make her own choices. I just think that about everyone.'

He'd not called her Gem before. He'd neither held her hand nor kissed her, although he had put his arm round her last Saturday.

They had to stop talking because the old lady was coming down the stairs, holding herself upright, risking each step. She looked better in the clean blouse and Gemma had to admit that there was something plucky about her.

She set them to work. By the end of the day the house was clean, its surfaces as close to sparkling as slightly tired paintwork can get. Nathan showed the old lady the dining room table and the way it now shone. He seemed to need her approval.

He'd also helped Anna with the forms, explaining clearly what had to go where. Gemma had listened and been impressed with the care he took. This lad who seemed so wrapped up in himself that there was no room for her, was taking time with someone he hardly knew, explaining clearly, telling her where to sign. She crept up and listened, then rested her hand on his shoulder for just a couple of seconds. He didn't appear to notice.

She thought back to their date. She'd let the scene absorb

her, had let a flood of bird song take her over simply because there was nothing else to do, wondering how long they would sit there for. Then Nathan had said the most surprising thing, suddenly, out of the blue, as the light fell further.

'So my guess was right.'

'What guess?' she'd asked him.

'My guess that you would sit here with me and not need to talk. I get so fed up with this constant need to talk to everyone about everything. I thought you might be like me in that way.'

Was she? She hadn't been unhappy. Of all the dates she had ever been on it was the strangest. She'd decided then and there that she wouldn't tell her friends anything about it and that wasn't only because there was nothing to tell.

It had been raining when the two young things had left so they didn't go and sit on the bench as they had the previous week. Anna had wanted to watch them together from the window, wondering if there was any further softening between them. Gemma had seemed so jumpy without him but had performed all those personal services and never complained. The revocation papers had been completed. Anna had noticed the way Gemma had listened. She'd seen the touch and hoped it was the start of something between them. Perhaps they would have the chance that she had squandered. The papers were still lying on the table. Had Nathan meant to take them with him? He'd said something about them needing to go to a notary. Never mind. Things were going well. She had some freshly-ironed, clean blouses for Tuesday. Gemma had packed up some of her other clothes to go to the cleaners. Getting the papers to a notary could wait until next week.

Chapter Nineteen

Tuesday came. Reinvigorated by the way the house looked Anna had even cut some blue delphinium spikes from the garden and stuck them into the tall white vase on the coffer chest.

Quite *Homes and Gardens*, she thought.

She intended to enjoy her little victory but was wondering what part she should play. She could go back to seeming like the submissive mother they had grown up with, or she could make herself into something just a little more threatening, remind them of that outburst on the morning after her ninetieth. Should she tell them her secret or dangle it in front of them like a mystery? Perhaps she'd claim she did everything herself.

They are coming to persuade me to go into a home, she reminded herself. They'll be coming with brochures. They'll be recommending that I go on a series of visits to look round places with names like Rivermead and Sunrise. If I know Colin he will already have booked a visit for later today. They will be thinking they have to spend a short time looking around the house, tut tutting to each other about the mess they expect to find. All the time they will be steeling themselves to sit me down and talk to me before they take me to see one of those places. They will have it all planned because they think I live in a slum. Only now, thanks to Nathan and Gemma, that slum is in nearly immaculate condition. What will they do when they walk round it? They should be pleased to find it like this. But I expect they will be hugely disappointed.

They will feel like that because I am in the way. In all the world there is not a single person who wants me still to be here. The thought sobered her. She dismissed any possibility that they would ever leave her alone.

Take it a day at a time, she told herself, and today is your day. You can win a skirmish.

The doorbell rang.

Anna had been careful to have nothing ready, no mugs with coffee, no biscuits already on a plate. If the visit was meant to be unannounced then she must not betray that she had heard their conversation, that she was aware of their intentions.

She walked slowly towards the door, turned the key, pulled back the bolts, then stared at them. Heather was dressed mostly in black, looking very severe. Colin was wearing a blue striped shirt that was now much too small for him. One of the buttons on the curve of his stomach looked to be under serious strain. He was holding his hands behind his back, hiding something from her.

'Hello,' she said, 'what are you two doing here?'

She stood in the doorway blocking their access to the house. She noticed that a red kite was perched in the chestnut tree behind her children, quite a young bird because it had no white on its head. Three scavengers, she thought, how fitting. It was mid morning. The sun had already moved round to this side of the house. She could see their faces clearly.

'We've been concerned…' Heather began.

'You could almost say that we felt neglectful…' Colin interjected. Their round Ronnie-like faces were sudden masks of sympathy.

Heather bent down towards her. 'Look Mother, can we possibly just come in and talk to you?'

She made up her mind then which part she would play. She would not be the submissive mother. She would take them on.

'No,' she said, making it sound as final as she could. 'I don't want you in the house. I'm not prepared. You see, I've got nothing ready for you and Rosanna's ill. Why didn't you tell me you were coming?'

It was warm in the sun. She found she was thinking that she really must get outside more. Walking mattered. It would

228

keep her fit. She should be doing two or even three turns around the garden every day while the weather was like this.

They were staring at her. She had propped herself against the side of the door and was holding her stick in one hand. She was quite comfortable like that looking into her children's faces.

It was, of course, Heather who recovered first, seizing what she thought was an opening. 'But that is the point, Mother, isn't it?' You can only really cope, can't you, when you know people are coming to help you? At other times, at your age, you just have to let things go.'

Colin was nodding, his blond hair bouncing a little. 'It's quite understandable at your age. I mean, you have been managing heroically.' The hair bounced some more. Anna wondered if he was now using conditioner.

'We must confess,' Colin added, 'that's precisely why we didn't warn you we were coming. You put on a brave front. We know that. We admire you for it. You want us to believe that you can cope and so Heather and I thought...'

If they were to understand who she now was then she mustn't just listen. She interrupted her son. 'Is that what you think?' she asked him directly, 'that I can't cope on my own?'

He hesitated. She could see that he wanted to suggest, to persuade, to get her to say the hard things for him. Direct questions had always worried him.

'Cope is perhaps the wrong word,' Colin backtracked. 'Cope makes it sound too final. Heather and I want you to be comfortable, comfortably able to manage without having to worry when anyone comes to see you. I mean it must be an intense pressure, a real strain.'

She interrupted him again. 'I don't understand. I think that's just words you're saying. Why can't you answer my question, Colin? Do you think I can't cope living on my own? Is that what you think?'

It was Heather who answered for both of them, her no

nonsense approach sweeping away her brother's sophism. 'Yes, Mother,' she said. 'If you want it spelled out, then yes, we do think you're not coping any more. We think this house is now much too big for you. It's such a strain that it's making you snappy. That's why we've given up our time to come and talk to you. Now will you stop all this nonsense and let us in?'

Anna looked at her daughter but Heather wasn't waiting any longer. She was already walking straight towards her as if she was determined not to waste any more time.

Anna held on to the door handle with one hand and continued to lean against the door frame, effectively blocking Heather's entrance. Her daughter seemed to tower above her. She'd hold them up for a while longer.

'And what if the house is spotless?' she asked. 'Will that prove to you that I can cope? What if my house is actually cleaner than yours?'

Clearly Heather wouldn't even consider the possibility. 'What are you talking about, Mother? You're becoming delusional. I don't know what's happening to you these days. You used to be sensible. You used to have a sense of dignity about you.' She paused for just a moment and lifted Anna's hand off the door handle and pushed past her. Colin shrugged his shoulders but followed his sister into the house.

Anna gave them a couple of minutes. There had been no point in resisting any more. She couldn't have held onto the handle and defied her daughter. Nevertheless, the sense of physical assault had shocked her. She needed to collect herself. She looked up at the red kite. It was still there in the branches, partly hidden by leaves and newly formed tiny conkers. What was it waiting for? Then it gave one of its eerie calls as another kite swooped overhead. She turned away from the sunshine and went inside. There was no point in going round the house with her children so she made her way back to the sitting room and her own chair. She was about to sit down in it and wait for their verdict when she thought no, it's time to walk down the garden. She'd sit on the bench and wait for them there.

She pulled open the back door and stepped down onto the path that Nathan had swept. She felt alive. She felt inviolate. As she took each slow step down the lawn she saw the view move out from behind the edge of the garden and stretch itself far away. The light was clear. Later there would be a heat haze. It was only mid morning but she hoped that the bench would be dry. In case anyone was watching from an upstairs window she kept her pace regular and didn't pause until she had reached the seat. Then she sat down and placed her stick carefully to one side, right against the arm rest where it couldn't slip out of her reach.

The river glinted. A pleasure boat was making its way against the current. The greens, which only a month ago had been many different shades, had now all merged together into their midsummer massiveness. Somewhere quite far away a bird rode up in the air, turning circles. Was it a buzzard? There had been buzzards in Normandy. Now they seemed to be spreading across England.

She sat and soaked up the splendour of it all and noticed that she was stretching her old hands out to absorb the sunshine, turning like all living things towards the warmth. She wouldn't close her eyes. She mustn't go to sleep. There was a fragrance of lush grass and the sweet smell of drying soil. She watched an orange-tip butterfly working along the bank, moving westwards.

Sometime later she was conscious of footsteps coming along the lawn towards her. She waited. The bench was long. There was room for all of them.

'Sit down and enjoy the view,' she told them. 'I'm sorry you've had a wasted journey.'

She could sense the frustrated anger in each of them. It was like being close to a fire alarm that is about to go off. She felt it like an enforced silence as if they had lots to say but weren't prepared to say it. She continued to look in front of her, to watch the view. They didn't sit down so she picked up her stick and swept it slowly across the scene in front of her. 'This is why I want to keep living here. I love this house. I love this view.'

There was another silence. If they weren't going to say anything she would continue. 'I've decided to dispense with Rosanna's services you know. I think it was just laziness on my part to keep her on. It prevented me from doing the cleaning that I should have been doing for myself all these years. I suppose it is a pity from her point of view that it took her illness to show me what I should have recognised long years ago.' She needed to involve them, pull them in. 'Now what should I pay her in lieu of notice, Heather? I wonder if you could give me some advice?'

When Heather said nothing Anna continued, 'I thought that three months' pay was about right. What do you think? I don't want to end up at an industrial tribunal do I?'

'Mother, you've become impossible. I mean really impossible.' Heather moved round in front of her, hissing the words so that the s sounds became snake-like and threatening.

'Whatever do you mean?' Anna asked.

Heather was clearly beside herself and Colin, who had also moved round in front of her, seemed scarcely more in control. The shirt button on his stomach was, if anything, tighter. Could it suddenly come off and hit her in the eye, she wondered.

'Okay I haven't the slightest idea how you have pulled this stunt,' said Heather, 'and I don't want to know. We came here to help and we're clearly just wasting our time.'

'Have I passed then?' Anna asked, looking up at them. 'Did I pass your inspection?'

'What inspection? Colin suddenly asked. 'Who said anything about an inspection?'

'I take it that's a yes,' Anna said, 'I take it that means you both realise that I can cope perfectly well on my own so that we can stop all this nonsense.'

She waited a few more moments and then added, 'Will you both be telling Alistair or shall I phone him myself?'

No one said anything else so they walked back to the house together. She offered them coffee and Heather made it. She heard a whispered conversation with Heather admitting to Colin that there was no point in doing that today. While Anna was trying to listen to their conversation she noticed that there was a pile of Care Home brochures on the coffee table. She poked at them with her stick.

'I won't be needing those,' she said. 'You can take them with you.'

Colin snatched up the pile in one of those great gestures of his and marched out of the house.

The moment they were left alone Anna found that Heather had a speech ready. 'Okay, Mother,' she said, 'you've made your point. Now let me make mine. If you are so sure you can cope, then cope. Cope whatever happens. Cope with Alistair on your own. Neither Colin nor I will be coming back to look after you. We're washing our hands.'

They left soon afterwards. Anna chuckled to herself, then glanced down at the table where the brochures had been. Alarmed, she realised that Nathan's envelope was no longer there. It must have been under Colin's brochures. He must have snatched it up with his handful of Care Home propaganda. Would he realise, or just throw the whole lot into the back of the car and then sweep them into the bin? If he opened the envelope he would know at once what she was trying to do. She could hear the phone call telling Alistair that if he was going to act he needed to do it at once, while he still had the power.

She'd won a skirmish but at the cost of severely damaging her chances of winning the war.

Chapter Twenty

Was Nathan gay?

Gemma was sitting in the Sports Hall on a truly hot summer's day. The room smelt of fresh chalk and old sweat. High above her head the cricket nets hung in dusty swathes, festooned with shuttlecocks. She was sitting in the third row from the left, six desks from the back in a hall full of eighteen year olds ready to take the General Studies paper.

She had her lucky teddy on the desk in front of her, two spare biros, two sharpened pencils, a bottle of water and a packet of softmints. The papers were also on the desk but turned face down so that nothing could be read. At the front of the hall, clocks were being checked and hasty whispered conversations were taking place about absentees. A door banged at the back as a late comer rushed in.

She could see Nathan in front of her, his long hair over his shirt collar as he sat, throwing his head partly back, staring upwards. She knew that nothing would happen for at least five minutes. They got you in early, told you late comers would not be admitted but then they let them in anyway, and you were always waiting to start. Someone was fiddling with a window pole, trying to let in more air.

Was he gay? Was she only a form of camouflage? After she had touched him on the shoulder and they had finished the long day with the old lady he had walked her home in the rain, both of them getting steadily soaked. In films a walk in the rain is always passionate: rain falls, faces smile, hands interlock, the two people lean together, then kiss.

They'd walked and talked. Talked about the old lady, and Gemma had been surprised by how much Nathan seemed to like her and to be on her side. She'd told him about the sniff, about the checking of clothes. At one point she had turned to him and made him stop by standing in front of him on the pavement while she said, 'But don't you think she should be in a home? Don't you think she'd be better off being properly cared for?'

The rain had made his hair lose its bulk. She could see how thin his face really was. He'd shaken his head like a dog coming out of a pond. 'She's alright,' was what he said. 'She's okay.'

Then he'd added, 'Stop being so Health and Social Care.'

What did he mean by that? She'd said nothing, just walked at his side. Why doesn't he hold my hand? Why doesn't he use this chance to put his arm round me? What's wrong with him?

Then she had begun to think differently. Perhaps it's not him. Perhaps it's something about me. What does he think is wrong with me? she wondered.

She was too tall. Her hips were much too wide and her breasts too small. When she looked in the mirror she couldn't describe herself as pretty. Perhaps he simply didn't fancy her.

Someone was talking at the front of the Hall. 'Now remember you have to answer all of the multiple choice questions and then do one question from each section. The time is seven minutes past nine. You have three hours. I'll warn you when there is half an hour left. You may start.'

The three hours had swum by. They had to leave row by row. She never knew why. It was simply the way things were always done at their school. Nathan had left long before her row got a chance to move. It was all over. She had nothing else to do that afternoon. She supposed she would go home and talk to her mum. She had some washing to do and she needed to start tidying away her notes and files, deciding what to keep in case it was useful at Uni. and what to chuck.

She was one of the last out. She expected that everyone else would have gone home or at least gone to the common room, but then she saw him standing at the end of the short corridor as if he might be waiting for her. 'I don't suppose you fancy coming into town for a coffee?' he said as she came up alongside him. Perhaps he didn't touch her because he didn't know if she wanted to be touched or not. She made herself smile.

'I'd love that,' she said.

It was hot. The road had a dustiness to it as if the last morsels of moisture had been sucked away by the surprising heat, leaving the remaining little bits of dirt weightless and free to dance around.

'Well?' he said.

'The exam's over. That's all I care about,' she told him. 'And for me that was the last one. All over, all done. Now the waiting begins. What about you?'

'Three more. Another week.'

'Ah,' she said and, coming to a quick decision, she reached out for his hand at the same time as she said, 'That's what you get for being brainy. Stay thick like me and you'd be finished.'

He didn't let go of her hand but he appeared to be surprised. Then she felt him return her grasp. For a moment it was as it should be, then he was lifting her hand. She thought he might swing their arms together just to seal matters but instead he was shifting his grip, lifting her arm over her head and holding it up as if she were a prize fighter.

'Gemma Braithwaite, champion thicky,' he announced to the road and a passing Tesco's van.

She'd counter that at once. Keeping her hand straight up in the air and gripping his fingers so that he was unable to drop his own arm she shouted out, 'Nathan, who knows everything except his own mind.'

She turned to face him as she let his hand go and saw it drop to his side. A cyclist with sweat patches under the arms sniggered as she glided past them, her wheels leaving faint snake-like tracks in the grey-brown dust that had collected at the edge of the road.

Then there was silence.

He was standing straight in front of her now. She looked up expecting to find him laughing but saw at once that he wasn't. His hair was casting a shadow over his face, but even in the shade of its luxuriance she could see that he was frowning, sucking his mouth in and pushing his brows forward so that his eyes were lost in canyons of unhappiness.

'That's what she said.'

'Who?' Gemma asked him. 'Who said what?'

'The old lady, not exactly your words but the same thought. She said I was lost.'

Lost….it was the right word. That would stick. It would become her word for him from now on.

'When…when did she say that?'

'When we first met. It's why I like her. I felt she saw straight through me… as if she was a witch.'

Gemma could see that he was upset, not about the comment but about the truth of it, the being lost.

They were standing on the pavement. She'd take another risk, take him over and take charge just as she had when he couldn't fix the perfume machines.

'Come on, let's get that coffee.'

This time she took his hand as they turned, took it, squeezed it, and then let it go. She'd wait for whatever happened next.

What happened next took place only at the periphery of her vision. They were crossing the road heading for Costa when she became aware of a figure running down the square in their direction. Seemingly, as soon as it was in range, the figure stopped and bellowed, 'Nathan.'

She turned and recognised Risco. He'd been at their school, although he was much older. He'd owned the corridors until he had been thrown out and now he was acting as if he owned the street. He was standing with one hand on his hips and the other hand thrust out, beckoning with his index finger. Something had happened to his skin since Gemma had seen him last. It had become leathery as if he spent long hours looking into the eye of a storm. He'd always had a sneer but now it was swallowing his face, twisting it. He'd grown more thick-set as if he worked out. His hair was black and gelled so that it added to his height.

'Nathan, leave your tart and come here. I want a little word.' It was shouted deliberately loudly to make heads turn.

'I thought you'd paid him,' she hissed.

'It seems not quite,' he said, then he was walking away from her and towards Risco, making her the 'tart' who was being left.

She knew she should turn and go, then stay away, have nothing more to do with him, turn now and go home. Nathan wasn't lost, he was stupid. She had files that needed sorting. Mum would be wanting to know how the exam had gone. Her school days were finally over. She'd make phone calls, find someone else who wanted to celebrate, get drunk. But her legs were acting differently, they were striding out to catch Nathan up, pushing past him to get there first.

Up close Risco looked more like the bully he'd always been. He'd shaved but his skin was too uneven to let any blade slide neatly across it.

'How much?' she asked.

Risco pushed her away. 'I don't deal with third parties, only directly with clients.'

Nathan had caught her up and was promising Risco the rest on Saturday evening once he'd been paid. He'd pay the rest and that would be it. He was holding both hands up, fingers stretched wide in compliance. Gemma stayed close, determined to listen.

She watched as Risco stretched a hand out and grabbed Nathan's chin. 'Two payments,' he said, 'remember the terms. There's a payment for the goods and another for the knowledge…'

Nathan wasn't fighting. Perhaps he couldn't. She could see where Risco's fingers were digging into his chin.

'…and I have lots of knowledge about you,' Risco continued. 'I know where you live. I know that you've been seen with a credit card by the cash machine, not checking a statement before you take money out but withdrawing big sums and…' he let his voice drop as if this was the real accusation, 'I know you've stopped buying.' He let Nathan go. 'I'm a good business man, me. I don't like losing customers. I like my clients to stay loyal, so here's your next purchase.'

Deftly Risco removed a small package from his sleeve and thrust it into Nathan's trouser pocket. 'You can pay for that one the week after.' Then he stepped back. 'Good day Nathan. Good day Nathan's tart. Always a pleasure.'

It should be a day of celebration. The last of her exams was over. Nathan had invited her for a coffee. But now this. She couldn't abandon him, just leave him there, in the small square, in the tall heat. She put her arm through his and walked him to the coffee shop, pushed him down into a chair at an empty table as far away from anyone else as possible and went to get the coffees herself.

She'd never been as grateful for the slowness of counter service. She could think and she could watch. Nathan was just sitting where she had plonked him down, seemingly inert. What was he thinking? Why hadn't he given the package back? Why hadn't he stood up for himself? The queue jerked forward as another customer paid and moved towards the drinks pick up point.

She ordered Americanos with milk on the side, scooped up several sugars and two wooden stirrers, then carried them over to Nathan.

'Okay,' she said as she sat down, 'We've got to stop this.'

He gave her a sad smile. 'I didn't think you'd want anything to do with me if you knew.'

For a moment she was puzzled. 'No, I mean Risco. We've got to stop Risco. I didn't know you owed him. I thought you'd paid.'

' I thought so too, but there is no such thing as paying Risco. How does he know about the old lady's card? Now he does, he'll just want more. I haven't been able... I can't see a way out. It's why...' He tailed off and only later would she wonder what the why had been about and whether it had anything to do with her.

'We go to the police,' she said. 'I mean, he planted drugs on you. He blackmailed you and I heard.' She was thinking this through. 'I'll go with you.'

He turned and looked at her. 'One, my parents would have to know.'

She didn't wait for number two. 'Tell them,' she said. 'Just tell them and get it all straight. Then he can't touch you. Then you'll be free of him.'

He shook his head. 'Would I?' he said. 'He's losing customers. He'll keep giving me stuff I don't want any more and making me pay and....' Suddenly he seemed on the verge of tears. 'I couldn't bear my parents' disappointment. They'd say nothing, not a single word. They'd just look. You don't know what that's like. And even if I told them it still wouldn't stop.'

She didn't want this despair. She wanted action, to do something now. 'But the police would have to act, wouldn't they? They would have to lock him up if I went with you.'

He looked straight at her. 'He'd be charged and he'd be bailed. A trial date would be set for a few months' time. Meanwhile he'd be out there. Do you want that?' He shook his head as if he was answering his own question. 'I'm not worth that, am I? I couldn't let you.'

He hadn't touched his coffee. He hadn't put milk in or added sugar.

Then he said, as if it were a final statement, 'You need to stay away from me. I'm such a waste of space.'

She never knew why she said what she said next. 'Okay, if not your parents then ask Anna what to do. I sometimes get the sense that she knows some strange things. Besides, she likes you.'

He made no response. 'Now drink your coffee. Revise hard. Get to Uni. and you're away from all this. I've got some files to sort.' She'd finished her coffee and she got up to go. 'See you Saturday then?'

She said it as if it were a question and waited until he nodded. Then she walked away.

Anna waited for something to happen but nothing did. Were the papers still on the back seat of the car? Had they been read? Might Alistair even now be signing away her house on her behalf?

She wanted to contact Nathan but knew that she mustn't, at least not until after his final exam. Until then, until Saturday, there was nothing to be done.

She found herself really looking forward to Saturday. She'd heard nothing further from Colin and Heather. She was enjoying the clean house. Peter had been and cut the lawn but the rest of the garden was a mess. She wondered if she could give the young things some weeding to do. First they must get some more papers for her to sign. Then they could begin on the garden.

She was waiting for them in the dining room where she could sit at the table and look out of the window. It was cool there. She must remember to ask Gemma to check her summer clothes if the weather was going to stay like this. Perhaps she should start them working on the front garden even though she rarely went out there. No, the back garden was what mattered. She'd been walking down to the bench every day and sitting there until she became uncomfortable. Perhaps they could buy her a waterproof cushion, one she could leave out there, one that wouldn't matter.

She saw them walking along the road and then turning into her drive. As a couple they weren't any closer. She could see that at once. If anything they seemed to have been arguing. Perhaps their exams had been going badly. She couldn't study them any more closely. She had to be up and moving, ready to let them in.

When she got the door open she looked at them both and said, 'Come in. Whatever's wrong? You'd better tell me.'

They seemed to have swapped roles. Gemma was more certain, Nathan more remote... more lost. Gemma was offering to make the coffee and, seeing the look on Nathan's face, Anna accepted at once.

The moment Gemma was out of the room Nathan began to talk. He told her he had a problem, told her quietly, full of resignation, exuding hopelessness. Then Gemma was bringing the coffees in. 'So what do we do, Mrs Devonshire? Do we go to the police?'

To be asked, to have her opinion sought. She'd listened to the story and it had exhilarated her in a way that was quite extraordinary. She'd also seen what they hadn't, because the story fell into her area of expertise: how to make things happen when the law may not be very helpful.

'No,' she said. 'I suspect to Risco the threat of the police is worse than you actually going to them. If you go he's going to be horrible to both of you because he has nothing further to lose. If you hint that you might go then I suspect he may leave you alone. For him the police will be an inconvenience. He'll have had lots of history with them.'

'So we do nothing then?' Gemma asked.

'No,' she said. 'You must do something. If you do nothing he'll see you as an easy source of money, wait for a bit and then come back more fiercely.'

'So what do we do?'

'You do just enough to make Risco realise that to keep trying to get money from you is no longer worth the risk to him. That's the tipping point you have to find.'

'So he stays out there.' Gemma seemed horrified. 'He carries on being able to do this to others.'

Anna nodded. She was suddenly thinking of a bullet moving in a straight line through the night air, of a chest jerking backwards, of a face looking up at her.

'Justice takes longer and is not within your power,' she told Gemma. 'But remember that one defeat will weaken him. You told me how much he hates losing clients.'

'You're good,' Nathan said. 'You're a witch. I told you that before, but what do we do?'

'Where's the stuff he gave you that you didn't want?'

'Here,' Nathan took it out of his pocket.

'Right, you give that to me.'

She held out her hand. Nathan seemed reluctant. She'd better explain.

'Well first, you mustn't be stopped and searched. No one must find this on you. This is the safest place isn't it? Who would suspect such an old lady?'

Nathan gave her the small package. It was warm from his trouser pocket. She put it on the table.

'Now we work out the right amount of pressure to apply,' Anna said. 'How much do you actually owe him?'

'Nothing. I paid up last Saturday.'

'Then you mustn't pay him a bonus. I don't think you can buy him off. If you pay him anything extra he'll be back. I think we must make it very clear that he can get nothing else from you and that you won't be pushed around.'

Gemma picked up the pronoun at once. 'We?' she asked.

'Yes,' Anna said. 'I think I've got to become Nathan's grandmother again.' She ignored the look on Gemma's face.

'Involving me does two things. It persuades Risco that your family already knows, so he has no use he can make of that knowledge he talks about. It also tells him that three people know about today's threats, not just two. It might just make him start to think that the police will have to take the word of an old lady. If I give this little package back to him and tell him there'll be no more money I think he'll leave you alone.'

Gemma was clearly the one doing the thinking. 'How do we arrange that?'

'I'd have thought that was obvious,' said Anna. 'I can hardly go to him so you will have to bring him round here.'

'No way,' said Gemma. 'No way at all. This is Nathan's problem, not yours.' Her eyes were fierce, her mouth set.

Anna was enjoying herself, being of service, being listened to.

'Why not?' she asked.

'He might attack you. Once you let him into this house you'd be so vulnerable. It's a kind thought but we can't involve you.'

She was binding them into her network. She needed them for her last summer. Their problem was perfect for her. It was time to take another risk.

'Before you decide to leave me out, Gemma, I want you to go over to the desk in the corner there. Somewhere at the back of the top drawer you will find something that might surprise you and might convince you that I am not quite defenceless. When you have found it, can you bring it over here?'

Nothing frees you up so much as the imminence of death. She would only use the gun in self-defence, but a thought was beginning to intrigue her. If she shot Risco she might go to prison. How would prison compare with an old folks' home? In both you were locked up. In both you had occasional visitors. The meal times were about the same too. But prison was not full of the decrepit. Prison would give her the company of young people. It would guarantee her the medical care she needed and free her from anyone making a fuss. It would shock her family in ways from which they would never recover. Above all it wouldn't be called Rivermead or Sunrise and, once in there, no one would put her in a room with other people of her own great age and make her sing.

But first, before prison, there would be the trial. She would enjoy that enormously, provided she could stay awake for long enough. She would stop being a nobody. She would become a sensation. Crime was perhaps the answer to her problem. If she could perform well in court, Alistair's having Power of Attorney would no longer matter.

Gemma had found what she was looking for and was carrying the cloth bag over with great care.

'Is this what I think it is?' she asked. She put it on Anna's lap.

Anna fumbled at the drawstring, gradually loosening the end of the bag, then she reached inside and pulled out her wartime pistol by its barrel, still oiled, still gleaming, just as she remembered it. Only the weight surprised her.

'Wow,' said Nathan.

'I was meant to hand it in, but Major Lustic let me keep it.'

'Is it loaded?' Gemma asked.

'No.' She wouldn't tell them about the bullets. They were hidden in another drawer. She put the barrel down and picked it up by the butt. It was heavier, but once she had it rising in the air it seemed to become a part of her again. That unity of purpose between hand and eye which had already cost the lives of two men was waiting to be called into action.

'I mean, but really,' said Nathan. 'Have you ever used it? I mean have you shot anyone?'

'I'm afraid so,' she told him.

'No,' Nathan said. 'No. Great advice but I have to handle this myself. I'll give the stuff back and refuse to pay him. I'll let him knock me around.'

'It won't be loaded but he won't know that. I'll only use it if he threatens me. Otherwise I'll keep it out of sight. Why not?'

She saw Nathan look towards Gemma.

'You don't have to decide now. Get some work done, then decide.'

She made her confession about the missing papers. She knew that when she sent them out to fetch another set she'd find the bullets, make sure the gun was loaded when Risco came. She felt more alive than she had at any time in the last sixty years.

Gemma had decided that Nathan wasn't gay. She had come to the conclusion that he hadn't held her hand or kissed her because he didn't like himself enough to feel that he could. She didn't know how she felt about this discovery. It raised the question of why he had sought her out; why he, with all his cleverness, was going round with a girl who did BTECs. He'd been so awful with Risco, so submissive. He had collapsed afterwards, white flag and defeat spinning in both his eyes.

Now she was nervous about being back in the square with Nathan, on the way to the notary. She expected a shout at any moment, more threats, more intimidation. She kept close to him, kept her eyes down because she didn't want to know if Risco was watching them.

They'd reached no conclusion about Risco. She could see that Nathan was keen on the old lady's answer, but seeing her sitting there, as wrinkled as the apple she'd left at the back of the curtain, looking at them through watery eyes and with hands shaped more by the bones than by the muscles, Gemma couldn't see it working. And how did they get Risco there? They couldn't just suggest going for a walk, happening to turn up at the old lady's house, inviting him in for coffee.

But if it did work, it might solve their problems, and the old lady was entitled to take risks if she wanted to. She's had her life. They were on the brink. There was that to add to the considerations.

Going to the notary wasn't quite straightforward. Nathan had unwisely explained that he needed another set of papers because his grandmother had lost the first set. This prompted the question as to whether she really was a competent person if she was so forgetful. The solicitor's clerk even suggested that Nathan might be doing his grandmother a disservice by helping her to revoke the arrangement. After all, he didn't know when she might suddenly need help, and if Power of Attorney was already in place, it made everything so much easier to arrange.

Gemma found she was listening not just to the words but to the tone. She noticed how much Nathan was reacting to this picture of Anna as a problem to be sorted. She thought of Anna's gun and found herself wondering if the bland solutions to the problem of old age offered by her Health and Social Care course were the best that society could come up with. Perhaps you should arm the old, issue them all with guns.

Nathan dealt with it by simply insisting on being given another set of papers and saying nothing, saying that the decision was Mrs Devonshire's and he would pass on their concerns.

They went next to the cash machine to take out £300. Nathan put in the card and Gemma turned round out of instinct to watch the square.

Risco was standing in the shade of the hornbeam, watching them both. Is that where he did his dealing? Or was Saturday a collection day? He was some way away and because of the shade she couldn't be sure if he had seen them. She nudged Nathan.

'We're being watched.'

Nathan was busy at the machine, punching in the numbers, committed to the process. No one else was queuing up. They needed someone to come along, to provide a measure of protection. There was often a queue at the machine, but not today. If Risco chose to come over he could be there as the money was dispensed, could snatch it from them. If he got a move-on he could get the card too.

What had the old lady said about balancing risks? That's why Risco was staying where he was. If he crossed the square now someone would see what was going on. Perhaps if it was only Nathan he might come over because Nathan wouldn't resist, but it occurred to her that she had challenged Risco the other day and that might well be holding him back.

She turned to face him now, stared at him, folded one arm over the other and just looked at him.

Risco didn't move but now she was sure he was watching her. Gemma listened to the noises made by the machine, heard the card being ejected, the money being disgorged. Only when she was sure that Nathan had everything put away did she break the connection. Then she told him to wait where he was and not to follow her.

As she walked towards Risco she hoped she'd got the calculation right. He would know she didn't have the money and she didn't have the card. This was still a square at midday on Saturday. There were lots of people round. There was no risk to her because there was too much risk to him. She was beginning to think like the old lady. She quickened her pace. He was smaller than she was. She could look down on him. She'd enjoy that.

'Nathan's tart, to what do I owe this pleasure?'

She had her words ready. 'We'll pay you a final instalment of £100 this afternoon and we'll return the last package. If you want it you have to come and collect it. Then that will be that. You'll get nothing more out of either of us. If you don't come then that's it anyway. Nathan's paying you nothing else and we'll chuck the stuff away. Okay?'

'I set the deals. I do the collection.'

She ignored that and gave him the address. 'Four o'clock on the dot or no deal, and if you give either of us any trouble after that we'll both go to the police.'

She turned away and walked towards where Nathan was waiting. Is he worth all this, she asked herself, when she looked at him from across the square.

'What did you say?' he asked her when she reached him.

She didn't give him any details.

'I gave him an invitation,' was all she said. 'The plan is on. I think he'll come.'

Chapter Twenty-One

'Right,' said Anna, when Gemma told her what had happened. I'd better have a sleep this afternoon. I must make sure I'm ready for this.'

She abandoned the plans for weeding and got them to continue clearing the paths. She found hoes, rakes and a thin trowel to get between the cracks in the paving. She showed them where the wheelbarrow was. She opened up the coolness of the garage and found the yard brush.

'You get on; I'll sleep. At three o'clock we'll get ready for our visitor.'

In fact it was hard to sleep. She had the gun down the side of the chair. She'd found the bullets and the chamber was full. Would they work? Did bullets have use-by dates? She had to remind herself that the intention was only to use the gun if Risco made threats.

She lay her head back against the chair and closed her eyes. Life was no longer a slow slide of inactivity into the arms of death. She was back in action and it felt tremendous.

What if she did have to use the gun? It had been such a long time. Surely she had forgotten so much. She went back over the drill, could hear again the words barked across the firing range, made herself visualise taking off the safety catch. Where would she aim?

Go for the shoulder. She didn't need to kill, just to wound. The shoulder was a bigger target than the arm. Go for the shoulder. Make sure he had the use of his legs so that he could get away. He could then make up his mind whether to report it. They might have to call an ambulance. When they had just got the carpets clean it would be a pity if there was too much blood.

What would happen to her next? Would she be sleeping

here tonight? She'd just got the house right. The paths would soon be clear again. She'd forgotten to ask about the waterproof cushion. Well, perhaps that didn't matter. She might never walk down and sit on the seat again if the police came round and took her into custody.

You're being a stupid woman, she told herself. No one will shoot anyone. Risco will do as he is told because I've set the risk barrier too high. Because Gemma mentioned £100 we will have to pay that. I need to sleep, she told herself, or I will be good for nothing later, and she closed her eyes again.

It was 3.15pm and the old lady was still asleep. Gemma and Nathan had come in from the back garden and wondered whether to wake her or not. Eventually it was Nathan who decided that they had to.

'It'll take her some time to come round,' he'd said. 'We need to wake her straight away.'

They were both nervous now that the time was approaching. Gemma had felt the tension rising in Nathan all afternoon until he seemed stretched out on it. It was in the way he stood. It was in his voice. His sentences were shorter and more high-pitched, like a plucked violin string.

'She'll need time to go to the toilet and time for a cup of tea,' Nathan added.

Gemma tried to wake the old lady with her voice alone, but there was no response. She had to resort to shaking her until she jerked awake suddenly, startled and a bit confused.

'Oh dear,' she said, 'have I slept for too long?' and she blinked at them through watery pale eyes. Then to Gemma's relief she seemed to remember everything that was planned. 'What time is it?' she asked, pushing herself upright in the chair.

When Gemma told her it was only 3.15pm, she unaccountably said, 'Good, I don't want to miss anything. First I was worried I wouldn't sleep, then I was worried I would oversleep.'

Asked if she wanted a cup of tea, the old lady shook her head. 'No, I think that can wait until afterwards.'

While they waited they told her what they had done in the garden and, perhaps to clear her head, the old lady walked to the window where she could see the path that stretched back along the side of the garden. Even to Gemma it looked freshly scraped and clean.

Anna seemed pleased with their work but she quickly went and sat back down. Gemma noticed that her eyes continually strayed to the small package and the pile of £20 notes.

You can wait for a front doorbell to ring, you can be entirely focussed on listening out for it, and it will still startle you.

When the bell rang Gemma jumped. She glanced at Nathan. He was pale-faced, steeling himself for whatever would happen. Hearing the bell he immediately got up to go and open the door, but she didn't let him.

'Not you,' she told him. 'I was the one who invited him here.'

She walked alone down the golden carpeted corridor to the front door and opened it.

Risco was there, on his own, the same look on his face, the same hunched shoulders, his arms slightly bent at the elbows as if life was something you might need to punch.

'I'll get the stuff,' she told him. 'I'll get the stuff and the money.' She'd handle it herself. She'd seen how shaken Nathan was. She'd avoid the other two being involved. 'Stay there,' she told him, and turned away to go back to the lounge.

'Whoa,' he said. 'Slow down, Nathan's tart. My time costs money. £100 isn't enough now I've had to get myself out here, especially now that I know where you live.'

He said it all with a kind of awful self-assured sneer. Suddenly she found she despised him.

'£100 and the dope returned. That was the deal,' she said again.

'I'm not playing your game. You and Nathan have to play my way. It was £100. Now it's £200. If you keep me waiting out here any longer it'll go up further, Nathan's tart. Where's your manners? Aren't you going to invite me in?'

He was refusing to deal with her and so he must take whatever happened next. They must play the grandmother card after all. Her own presence hadn't been enough, but at least she'd shown him she wasn't afraid.

'£100 is all you're getting,' she told him. 'Come in and collect it or fuck off now, empty handed. Which will it be?'

She turned and walked into the lounge, leaving the front door open. She knew he was following her so she walked straight into the room. She would be the hostess. She would do the introductions. She'd show him manners.

'You know Nathan,' she announced as he came into the room. 'This is his grandmother, Mrs Devonshire.'

Risco seemed momentarily taken aback by the sight of the old lady, then his acquisitive streak seemed to take over. 'Nice place you've got, dear,' he said, surveying the room and the view. 'Got lots of money have you? Is it your card Nathan keeps feeding into that cash machine? Right, well your grandson owes me loads. Are you going to pay up like a goodun?'

Gemma had walked through the room and was now leaning against the mantelpiece. It gave her a good view of Risco strutting around. She watched as he walked straight to Mrs Devonshire's chair and lent over her. She saw Nathan stiffen as he got ready to protect her, to physically pull Risco away if that proved necessary. Mostly she looked at the old lady's face and saw how serene she was.

Gemma heard Anna say, 'Nathan has told me everything about his dealings with you. I don't think he owes you anything at all. But a deal's a deal so there's the package and there's the money for your trouble. It's the last money you'll ever have from any of us. I suggest you take it.'

Gemma heard Risco roar with mock laughter, watched

him fling himself on the settee.

'Naw,' he said. 'It doesn't work like that.'

'I think you'll find it does,' Anna continued, talking sweetly and reasonably. 'Nathan's told his family. You can't blackmail him. He's given up that stuff you used to supply him with. I'd take your money and the package and leave us alone.'

Risco sat on the settee, both arms flung behind him, and shook his head.

'Two hundred,' he said. 'That's the hundred I was promised and the hundred for walking up here. Look at all this,' he said, gesturing around the room with one arm. 'You can afford it.'

Gemma watched as Anna reached out with her left hand, took the pile of money and put it down the side of the chair.

'I'm withdrawing the money,' Anna said. 'You've lost your chance of that. You should never have had it anyway. I believe my grandson when he tells me he has paid you in full. Now take the package and go.'

She's loving this, Gemma thought. She isn't in the slightest bit afraid. Gemma stared at her. Cool, she thought, really cool. We don't know the meaning of the word.

The sneer was back on Risco's face. Gemma had the distinct impression that he had been in such situations before.

'Naw,' he said, and he got up from the chair and walked over to the side table, picking up a fancy jug with a high pouring lip and a gold painted handle. He seemed to look at it as if he loved beautiful things. Gemma wondered if he was going to take it with him instead of the money. It was beautifully painted with a spray of flowers in yellow, pink and blue.

'The thing is, I've watched Antiques Roadshow,' Risco was saying, for all the world as if he didn't want them to despise him for lack of knowledge. 'This is a lovely thing but it's only got a value if it's in one piece.' Then he hurled it at the hearth just under where Gemma was standing where it shattered, one piece hitting her on the leg.

'Whoops, how clumsy of me,' he added by way of

unnecessary commentary, 'now what shall I pick up next?'

Because she had been watching the jug and listening to Risco, Gemma missed the moment when the gun appeared. But suddenly there it was, in the old lady's hand, and she was doing something to one side of it, switching something that seemed a little stiff, but which she managed to make move. What was she doing? The gun was only to be used as a threat, wasn't it?

'Get out.' The old lady said, pointing the gun from her lap. 'I'm bored with you being here. I suggest you go before I ring for the police.'

Risco was surprised. This clearly wasn't in his plan, but he didn't seem about to back down. He looked at the old lady as if he found her comic, like a figure from a pantomime.

'Hey Gran,' he shouted, 'do yourself a favour.'

Whether it was the words, the way he called her 'Gran' when she wasn't his gran, or the fact that he began to walk towards the old lady as he spoke, Gemma never knew, but before the noise shocked her she saw the old lady smile, saw the gun come up as if it knew what it was doing, noticed that Risco was suddenly unsure. Then he was reeling backwards at the same time as a loud noise filled the room and seemed to hold them all in its reverberations.

She'd seen it but she couldn't take it in. It had happened in front of her eyes and she could recount the details but, in spite of that, she found herself fighting to understand what she had actually witnessed.

Of the four people in the room only Anna was in total control. Gemma watched as she snapped open the revolver and shook out the bullets, turning the chamber vertically to check it was empty before closing it up again. Then she was talking. 'Gemma,' she was saying, 'as you invited this young man round perhaps you would be good enough to ask him if he wants you to call him an ambulance.'

Risco was sitting on the settee, his left hand grasping his

right shoulder. He was looking at the old lady as if he too didn't believe what had just happened.

'You shot me,' was all he said.

Gemma shook herself into action. It was like walking across the room in slow motion. 'Do you want me to get you an ambulance?' she asked. There was blood under Risco's fingers where he clutched his shoulder, blood beginning to drip down his arm. 'Only we don't want any unnecessary mess on the settee,' she added.

Nathan too was now reacting. He came over to the settee and peered at the shoulder. 'You're going to need that seeing to,' he said. 'I'll call an ambulance anyway,' and he picked up the phone.

At first Gemma didn't understand why Risco got up from where he was sitting and ran out of the house. Then suddenly she did. How could he ever let anyone know that he had been shot by an old lady? What would that do to his image? How could he threaten and swagger once it became common knowledge that he had been bested by a pensioner? Perhaps it was the release of tension after the action, perhaps it was her understanding that there would be no repercussions, but suddenly she found she was laughing, holding onto the back of the settee and laughing in a way that shook her whole body.

Then another thought hit her. With the threat of Risco removed, at least until his shoulder healed, she could perhaps now find out what Nathan was really like.

'I'll have that cup of tea now, if it's alright with you,' Anna was saying. Gemma saw her fiddle with her skirt and pick up five rounds that had fallen into her lap.

Her hand had still worked. Her eye was still true. They had remembered how good they were together. One shot and she had hit his shoulder. The fact that he had been very close to her and had been standing in front of the window made him into as clear a target as you ever get, but at ninety she had still

256

done it. Three targets, four bullets, two men dead and another the walking wounded.

The room stank of cordite, drowning out the feeble attempts of the Febreeze machine to convince her that the world was all summer scents and skipping lambs. Once the whole landscape of Normandy had seemed impregnated with its after-note: that human-made, low-register, metallic stench that clung to everything, even in the open air. Here in the room it was concentrated, made powerful, like the gas the dentist used to use before injections came along.

She was breathing, she noticed, in short bursts through her mouth, as if her own body could scarcely cope with what she had put it through. When she closed her mouth and tried to breathe only through her nose the smell intensified, but she was getting enough air. She needed the cup of tea. She needed to sit down, but first there was something she must check.

For in the moment of the shot itself she had felt intensely alive, almost as if she were young again. Eye, hand and hearing had been so acute that she had registered both the noise of the shot and the thud of the impact. But there had also been another sound, a fraction of a second later, the noise of something hard hitting something solid.

In spite of her breathing problem she made herself get up and walk slowly across the room to peer at the wall next to the window and then at the picture above the desk. There she found what she was looking for. It was in the top corner, in her least favourite part of the oil painting, the place where a brown leafed tree had been added by the artist, probably at the last moment, to balance and contrast with the light spilling over the hill behind the torrent. To her mind it had always spoiled the painting. There in the corner just inside the golden frame was a hole that had split the board, opening up the hint of a yellowish line that snaked down between the poorly painted leaves. Nestling in the hole, so gently that it seemed to have been placed there, was a bullet. She'd missed the bone and gone through the flesh only. It would be sore for weeks but it would heal and leave him as he had been before, unless he failed to get it properly dressed.

'Look,' she said, when the young things came back into the room. 'Look at this.' She lifted her stick to point more clearly. 'The bullet went straight through him. He only has a flesh wound. There'll be no damage to the bone so he should heal quickly.'

Anna went back to her chair, lowered herself down and began to drink her tea, taking little sips, using it to calm her breathing.

There was silence in the room in the aftermath of such activity. Nathan broke it. 'Now where did you learn to do that?' he asked her.

Should she tell him? The temptation was there. This was her chance to break the silence of sixty years. But then there would be more questions and where would those end?

'A misspent youth,' she told them. 'When I was your age there was a war on.'

Nathan was staring at her. 'You have to tell me,' he said. 'You have to let me know. Was that a lucky hit or are you are good shot? I mean, straight through the shoulder!'

She didn't answer him because she didn't want to tell him everything. Instead she found herself thinking about the Gestapo officer. If she had been a poor shot he might still have been alive. He'd come to the house because he was surrendering to her. He would have been her prisoner and she would have got him back to the nearest army unit somehow, would have pleaded his case. She wondered how it would have gone. She'd have had to find him some clothes. Stepping outside in that uniform would have been far too risky.

Yet it would have been worth it. He might have held the answers to the questions she needed answering. What had happened to Maurice? Which side had Pierre really been on? If only she had waited. If only she had missed. Her whole life

258

might have been different.

She could have got him safely handed over. She would have called up the group, asked them to guard him.

Anna took another sip of tea. Was he still there? Had anyone moved the trough and dug him up? Had they found the dog tags and did his family know what had happened to him?

How could they? She was the only one who knew how his life ended. The same smells were round her now: cordite enveloping a room, that sickly sweet smell of blood seeping out from underneath a punctured skin. Then it had been like a curtain falling on her youth, bringing it to an end, closing it off without applause. Now…what did it matter?

She became aware that Gemma was leaning over her. 'We have to go now. Nathan has to do some revision. Are you alright?'

Did the SS Major have grandchildren?

'Yes, I'm fine. I'll put this away.' She pointed to the gun. 'Thank you for what you've done.' She fished out the money from the side of the chair. 'I owe you a bit more, but will this do on account? You will be here next week, won't you?'

She looked into their faces and saw in both of them that they were still shocked.

Nathan was saying something that she must listen to. He was pushing a piece of paper at her. She took it but had to ask him to repeat what he was saying.

'This is my number, if the police come round. I want to be involved. Will you phone me?'

She agreed and they went, not out of the front door but out of the back. She watched them cross the lawn, saw the hands reach out and touch, then stay together. It was good when those in your network liked each other. When they reached the seat, the young things sat down together. She saw Nathan's arm go round Gemma's shoulder. It was then that she looked down at the table and saw the dope was still there.

Had Nathan left it because he had forgotten it, or did he no longer need or want it? Should she throw it away? The police mustn't find it there. Perhaps when Gemma had gone Nathan would come back for it. They were sitting together for a long time, seemingly talking, still not kissing.

She got up and, taking the gun, went to put it back in the drawer. She picked up the bullets and the dope to hide them in the same place. When she got back to her chair she looked out across the lawn and saw that the seat was empty.

Chapter Twenty-Two

When Anna's phone rang three days later she was sure it would be the police. She glanced at the clock. It was just after nine and she was still in bed. Sitting up first she carefully picked up the phone.

'Hello,' she said nervously, wishing she was up and dressed so that she would feel less vulnerable.

'You can't revoke Power of Attorney because you have to accept that you are in fact no longer competent,' said the male voice. 'I don't know who's put you up to this, but…'

'Who is this?' Anna asked, recognising the voice but disliking the way he had launched straight into the conversation without any preliminaries.

'There, that proves it,' said the man on the phone. 'How can you claim to be competent when you don't even recognise the voice of your own son?'

So like Ronnie, to launch straight in without the preliminaries, not to ask anything about her.

'I've not felt as well as this for years,' she said.

There was a short silence. The voice when it started again was louder. 'What are you talking about, Mother? I didn't ask you anything.'

'No, Alistair, you didn't. You didn't start by checking that I was okay, so I thought I'd tell you that I'm more than okay. In fact I'm good.' Being with Nathan and Gemma was changing her language. She heard the sudden in-drawn breath but went on before he could launch again. 'I gather Colin must have read the private papers he snatched up from my table and informed you of the contents. You needn't worry, I have already filled in another set. It'll be properly done and once it has been witnessed I'll send you the copy. I'm simply taking away your Power of Attorney. I intend to run my own affairs.'

There was silence down the line so she carried on talking because she remembered what Nathan had told her. 'Can I presume that you have the form in front of you, that Colin has sent it on to you? It's properly filled in. It clearly shows my intentions. It may not even need to be witnessed.'

There was a further silence, then the voice said, 'But *you* didn't fill this form in did you? Someone did this for you or with you. You've got to be careful, Mother, when you get to your age. People can take advantage.'

She wondered whether to ask it, then decided she had nothing to lose. She would never rely on her family again. If necessary she'd make sure of that. 'Now Alistair,' she said, 'I'm glad you phoned. I hear you've lost some money recently. I wondered if I could help you out by giving you a loan.'

She thought he might have put the phone down since there was such an intense silence on the other end of the line.

'Alistair,' she said, 'are you still there? Did you hear my question?'

She remembered him as a child, the way in which he had given way to others when he had to, particularly to his younger brother, and how he had seethed with resentment for days afterwards.

'Alistair?' she said again.

'I'm still here.'

She could hear it in his voice, that resignation before he had to give way. 'How much I've lost is none of your business, but I doubt if you have enough to help me out. I think I may lose the house.'

'How on earth…?' she began to ask.

'You wouldn't understand, but it is serious. Still,' he said, 'it may solve one of your problems.'

There was something jaunty about the last sentence, a rising cadence at the end of it that made her uneasy.

'I wasn't aware that I had any problems,' she challenged. 'What do you mean?'

'If I lose my house,' the voice on the end of the line said, in a resigned but still antagonistic tone, 'at least I'll be able to move back in with you, into what is, partly at least, my house. I'll have to bring the family of course and the Jaguar. Then we'll be able to look after you. Won't that be fun?'

Could he do that? What could she say? Suddenly her network seemed inadequate. She'd need another recruit, someone who understood the law. 'You may own a small proportion but I'm sure you haven't the right to move in during my lifetime.'

'We'll see about that,' said Alistair. 'Goodbye Mother.'

The phone went dead. She put it back in its slot then began to get up. An idea was forming in her head, another way of fighting back and perhaps of doing something else as well. If nothing else happened before the weekend she'd put it to Nathan and Gemma. It might also give her the only chance she would ever have to answer her questions.

With BTECs completed and Nathan's debt problem solved, at least for the time being, Gemma gave herself permission to think about love and sex. According to the films both of these things picked you up, transformed you and swept you away. In the depth of longing they created, and in the passionate grunting that invariably followed, the most important thing seemed to be that you lost your sense of self and moved into another dimension, into one in which you felt completely fulfilled.

If that was so then perhaps Nathan wasn't the man for her after all. At first she had felt chosen by him and in some ways the flattery of that choice had been the most important part of the coming together. A sense of exasperation had quickly followed as she realised how lost he was, how much he drifted. This, in turn, had been followed by uncertainty about exactly what he wanted from her. The boys she had been out with up to now had quickly moved from holding hands to groping her.

Nathan's hands had never strayed and having been quite ready to fend him off until she was ready, she then found herself regretting that he seemed so self controlled.

Even last night, after the cosiness of sitting on the bench and talking about the extraordinary shooting they had witnessed, he had walked her home, pecked her on the cheek and gone straight back to his revision. She'd wanted to sit with him for longer, to speculate about just what Anna meant when she said her youth was misspent. What could she have done in the war that involved shooting people? Part of her was glad that Nathan was revising. She dreaded him messing up his exams. But another part of her felt that she deserved just a little more attention.

And what did any of this have to do with love? She didn't think she was in love. If love was about losing your sense of self then she couldn't remember having ever been so self-aware. As she had done her hair that morning, brushing the long tresses then pulling them to one side so that she could plait them, she wondered if she made herself too plain for Nathan. Friends slapped on make-up, reddened lips, highlighted eyes, made their hair thick and wavy. Should she, now school was over, change her appearance? Might Nathan find her more appealing if she signalled her willingness more clearly? Was the plait she hung over her right shoulder too old-fashioned, even if it kept her hair tidy for the whole day so that she never had to carry a brush?

She'd loosened the plait, shaken out her hair, run her fingers through it to give it body, peered at herself through the resulting waterfall. Should she have it cut short, dye it purple or green? At least with the plait she could still make use of single earrings when she had lost one. The girl in the mirror, the one with the masses of hair, looked less individual and somehow signalled that she was conventional. Quickly she had redone the plait, sealing the end with the simple elastic band. She had looked like this when Nathan had chosen her and if he ever did invite her to go to bed with him, that was when she could shake her hair out.

Mind you, the only plan Nathan had made was to see her on Saturday at Anna's house. His last exam was on Thursday. He hadn't told her that. She'd had to look it up on the exam timetable. So just what was she expected to do with this, her first week of freedom? Would he come and find her on Thursday night? She'd heard there was going to be a massive sixth form party on the Saturday. Would he go? Would he ask her to go with him?

She'd walk into town. She was bound to bump into someone there. She had fifty pounds from the old lady. Perhaps she'd buy herself something.

She was never certain why she changed her mind. Perhaps it was because the long summer before Uni meant that everything could be infinitely postponed. Maybe it was just curiosity that made her decide instead to walk to Anna's house, just to check if she was alright. Gemma needed to know if the police had called, if there had been any follow up from the shooting. The idea that she might learn something that would need to be communicated to Nathan before the weekend had flitted into her mind, but she wouldn't have admitted it as a sole or even as a particularly important motivation.

Anna was glad to see her. She learnt at once that there had been no repercussions from the shooting but became aware that something else had happened. She seemed upset, agitated, quite in contrast to her calmness when facing Risco last weekend. At first her agitation made her seem confused. She'd asked if it was Saturday and whether Nathan was coming, then seemed to recover herself. But she'd let Gemma make the coffee, hadn't even supervised. Instead she had remained in her chair.

They'd sat in silence for a while and then she'd started to talk, to answer the question Gemma hadn't even asked, as if she read her mind.

'I learnt to shoot during the war,' she explained. 'My parents had been killed. My brother had died in Norway. I needed to do something so I volunteered for service. They taught me how to shoot, how to trust your instincts. There were strict rules. You had to empty out the magazine after each shot. They were terrified of accidents. I always suspected that someone had recently been killed in training and that death had left them wary.'

It didn't seem right to ask questions so Gemma waited.

'I hope I didn't shock you. You thought it was bluff and I thought I might have to do it for real. The moment I saw him I knew I'd have to use the gun.'

The old lady seemed to be inviting questions and only through asking could Gemma find info for Nathan. 'How did you know?'

'They taught us to read people. Because our lives might depend on it they gave us lessons in psychology. It was in the way he walked. The moment I saw his strut I didn't think he'd back down. You were quite safe. I was always a good shot.' Gemma, wondering if it was alright to probe further, pushed another question into the room. 'Who?' she asked. 'Who trained you in judging people?'

'We never used real names so I can't answer your question,' Anna explained. 'Secrecy was the point. We were paired off for interrogations. One had to ask questions and the other to hide information. It's funny,' she suddenly added, 'the secret to hiding information is to completely forget it. If you once think about it, you find that it fills your mind.'

Why is she telling me this, Gemma wondered. On Saturday, when we wanted to know, she would tell us nothing.

'And were you ever interrogated?' Gemma risked, just in case Anna really wanted to talk.

'We took turns. I was better at being interrogated. I wasn't very good at playing the role of the interrogator. You see, I never really saw the point.'

Gemma tried again. 'I mean for real. Were you ever interrogated for real?'

She was watching and this time she saw a flicker in the old eyes.

'Never for real,' she said. 'I'm sorry to disappoint you. There were real heroines then, but I wasn't one of them.' She smiled at Gemma then said, 'I know it's not Saturday but could you do something for me?'

A few tantalising glimpses then nothing more. Gemma found herself wondering what the old lady had looked like when she was young, when her skin was plump and not blotchy, when she could walk without thinking about it.

'Yes, of course,' said Gemma.

Walking into town, an hour later than she had intended, Gemma realised that she had stopped thinking about Anna as merely being old. It had been difficult to do anything at first but be fixated by the wrinkles, the slowness and the disability. Walking behind her was a drag. She was so slow. You had to hold back just to be polite, but all the time you wanted to run past, or tell her to stay where she was while you fetched whatever she needed. It was quite different from dealing with her own young nephew where it was a pleasure to watch him try something he couldn't yet manage. Then it was easy to be patient.

Her dad cursed old drivers for slowing the traffic. It was as if you got to a certain age and then you were just a nuisance; you became a Saturday job, or a family duty. The old were no use to anyone. They clogged up the NHS and spent too much tax payers' money. But Anna, as she now thought of her, was emerging from her wrinkles. Gemma found herself musing as to whether this was because she knew her better or because the old lady was doing more and trying more.

It was the shooting that had brought about this change. Gemma still didn't know what to think about it. Was it just a lucky shot? From the shoulder to the heart or to the head isn't far. What if she had killed him? Instead of innocent victims of a thug they would have become witnesses to a murder.

She reached the square and went into the travel agents. There were brochures everywhere. She couldn't work out the order. Was it alphabetical or geographical? Her real problem was that she didn't know where Normandy was.

Luckily the staff left her alone. But when she had browsed without success for some time, their lack of interest began to annoy her. They were studying screens, not really busy, just pretending. Did they think she was too young to book a holiday? Did they think she was simply wasting their time?

She concentrated on France. Why else would Anna want cross-channel ferry timetables? But the only France brochure she could find was full of gites and Anna had said hotels with en-suite facilities. She'd have to ask.

She wanted Nathan to be there. He would know. He'd do the asking for her.

The girl at the counter was only a little older than she was. She made herself walk towards her and ask.

She left the shop with everything she wanted, timetables and brochures. She looked at T-shirts in M&S but didn't buy any in case there were better ones in other shops, then walked over to Bates's.

Bates's was a dying shop. Its windows were tired. People used it just for the odd item if they happened to be in town. If they wanted to make a serious do-it-yourself purchase they got in the car and went to B&Q. But Anna had asked for Bates's and it did say over the door that Mr Bates was a locksmith. There must be hundreds of better places on the internet but then Anna didn't have a computer.

The shop was laid out in areas: gardening, household, tools, ladders, buckets. It was empty of customers and cold. There was a girl on the till; she was wearing a green fleece.

'Is Mr Bates in?' Gemma asked.

'I'll fetch him.'

She walked off, leaving Gemma in possession of the shop. There was plenty of time to steal anything and casually walk out. She looked around for a camera and couldn't see one. The power drill on display was £99. She could easily pick it up and walk away.

Mr Bates was as old as she feared he would be and no, he didn't change locks any more. He was sorry. It was a job he had liked doing but he couldn't keep up to date. Often changing locks these days meant changing doors. There was someone he knew who'd do the job in a day. He wrote down a name and a mobile number for her.

Another old person, she thought, at sea in the present day, clinging to the wreckage of what they've always known.

She thanked him and went back out into the heat.

Anna asked Gemma to phone the number for her. The man at the other end was already on a job. There were noises in the background. She found herself having to answer a number of questions. Was it an emergency? Had the house been broken into? Was it a separation case? Gemma wasn't sure what he meant. 'Have you had a bust up with your partner and you need the locks changed before he comes back?' the man asked.

'No, nothing like that.'

'Okay, I'll do it on Friday,' the voice said and asked for the postcode.

Friday was Nathan's first day of freedom, but she couldn't leave the old lady on her own.

'Would you like me to come round and just be here?' Gemma asked. 'I mean, if that makes you feel more comfortable.'

It sounded patronising, the moment she'd said it. 'I mean, I know you can cope and all that,' she added.

'You intend to prevent me shooting anyone else, don't you?'

'Something like that.'

Anna smiled. 'Yes, that would be nice.' Then she hesitated before saying, 'I hate to be a nuisance but now I shall need a solicitor, or rather two solicitors. Can you find Yellow Pages? Look in the hall under the phone. We need people who are prepared to come round here.'

Gemma found the book and brought it over. The type was too small and Anna was defeated by it, so she passed it back.

'Read out the names for me will you? I'd like someone local, not one of these big companies.'

They found a local firm and again Anna asked Gemma to make the call. Yes, the firm could send someone out to the house. They had a slot on Friday.

'What's it for?' Gemma had to ask.

'I need to make another will,' Anna told her.

That evening, after her tea, Gemma went round to Nathan's. She knew she could phone or text him but she wanted to see him again, to try to sense if there was anything between them.

Nathan's mum answered the door and stood in the middle of it with her arms folded.

'He's got his exams, you know,' she said. 'He's revising hard. I don't really want him disturbed.'

A few weeks ago she would have just accepted that and meekly turned away, but she had faced down Risco and she could face down Nathan's mum.

'Fifteen minutes,' she told the woman in front of her. 'I'll be his break.' She raised her voice so that if he was listening Nathan would hear her. 'It's about the job we both do,' she added. 'This week the day's changed.'

The woman turned in the doorway. 'Nathan,' she called.

But the call was unnecessary. Gemma saw that he was already at the top of the stairs and coming down. He was holding his hands up to his mother as if to placate her. 'I need a break. I need some fresh air, Mum, I won't be long.'

Then he was shutting his mother into her own house,

promising to be back soon.

When the door stayed closed he said, 'Let's go and sit on that bench,' and he put his hand on her shoulder.

She felt it alight there, warm and alive. She put a hand up to meet it. Their fingers touched and there was something different.

'I was putting off calling you,' he explained. 'I wanted to get to Thursday afternoon and finish this part of my life first.'

'First' meant something would follow. First was full of promise. She let go of his fingers and walked at his side.

'Have you heard about Risco?' he asked her as they made their way down the summer shrouded lane.

'No, nothing. The police haven't called on Anna either.'

'They won't. Risco is telling everyone that he was walking in the countryside, on his own, when he was suddenly shot at. He's no idea who did it. He thinks it must be a case of mistaken identity.'

Part Three

Normandy 2006

Chapter Twenty-Three

Gemma found herself caught up in the whirlwind of their planning: the rush to renew Anna's passport, the buying of a second hand car, taxing it, insuring it, finding the right stick-ons to dip the headlights, getting a GB sign. They had also bought a light folding wheelchair. 'So that I won't slow you down,' Anna had said.

And if those were the public faces of going on holiday there had also been the private arrangements to be made. She bought T-shirts and knee-length shorts. She bought a pack of new knickers and a lighter bra. Determinedly she had also walked into the chemist, where she picked up and paid for two packets of condoms and some sun lotion. The girl at the till probably thought her a right tart, hoping to get laid on holiday.

Well perhaps she was. The condoms might be necessary. She and Nathan would be sharing a bedroom and she didn't trust his planning abilities.

She wasn't quite sure, at first, how the idea of the double room had come about. After all, it wasn't to save money. Anna clearly had plenty of funds if she could buy a wheelchair and a car big enough to take it, just to go on holiday. They could easily have had separate rooms.

Anna had broached it with her, had said one afternoon, 'We've met a snag. We're booking very much at the last minute and the hotel with ground floor rooms north of Caen only has two rooms spare. Two of us will have to share and I'm sure you'd rather share a room with Nathan than with me.'

Something inside her had leapt and jiggled about but she kept her face straight and asked if it was a twin-bedded room.

'I very much doubt it. This is France. It's only for three nights.'

Then Anna had looked hard at her, peered at her through the powder-flecked glasses. 'If it's not alright we can try somewhere else. I owe you a lot. I don't want to make a mistake about this but I thought you wouldn't mind.'

'We haven't as yet,' Gemma told her, speaking simply, letting her secret out.

'I rather thought not.' Anna was still peering at her. 'He needs time. He's a great lad, Nathan. He also needs to get away from home.'

'How do you know all this?' Gemma wanted suddenly to take a short cut, to slice through the uncertainty and fumbling round of being young and jump clean into decisions that would settle her life, get it all sorted. 'I mean, what should I do about Nathan?'

Anna put her hand up. 'I'm the wrong person to ask about that. I…' She was hesitating. Gemma could see that she was thinking about what to say. 'I fell completely in love for my first time and then fell out of love with life itself. There were extenuating circumstances. There was a war on.'

Wow. This was new. Anna talking about herself, talking in a voice full of regret. Gemma wanted to know more and she was wondering what to ask when Anna went on. 'There's no right, no wrong about these things. At least your generation is able to make mistakes and move on. We were less lucky.'

'Have you asked Nathan whether he minds sharing a room with me?' Gemma found herself suddenly asking.

Anna looked straight at her. 'You want me to tell you that he suggested it, don't you? You want it to have been his choice.' Anna was smiling as she said this and Gemma tried hard not to nod. 'Nathan isn't like that, is he? If you want to know what happened, he made the phone call for me and then asked me to check with you to see if you minded.'

'He's a coward isn't he?' Gemma suddenly blurted out. 'Why couldn't he ask me himself?'

'Because if he'd asked you it would have been different,

wouldn't it? He'd have been asking you to let him fuck you, or whatever you call it these days.'

Anna's use of the word shocked Gemma. It was as brutal as the shot had been. Not the word itself. She was used to the word. What shocked was the word in the mouth of an old woman.

Then Anna was reaching out to touch her arm. 'If I ask you, I'm only asking you to share a room. Don't you see that he doesn't want to rush you either? Maybe he doesn't know what you want, or what he wants. Take the summer, get to know him. Share a room and see what happens. The room is en-suite. You can always bring pyjamas. If you want to warn him off, why don't you borrow some striped ones from your dad?'

Without thinking about it Gemma had reached forward and hugged Anna gently, then said, 'You're so open about it. I couldn't have had this conversation with either of my parents.'

'Well at my age there isn't time to pretend.'

The hug had surprised Anna. No one hugs the old, she thought. There are dutiful kisses but no hugs. It's as if they think old age is contagious. Well, perhaps any age is contagious. Is that why I put myself in the way of the young?

She was sitting in the ferry's lounge, listening to the announcements in two languages and finding she could still understand them both.

They had brought her up in the lift from the car deck and parked her here, with a view across the shipping lanes. Then they had gone off to stand on the deck and watch England slip away through a wind-blown lace of swooping gulls.

What was she doing here, she asked herself, and immediately she answered her own question. I'm staying alive. I'm having a holiday. I've re-done my will. I've changed the locks on the house. I've told no one I'm going. I slipped away once before and now I'm doing it again.

It was a great relief to be on the move again. In a burst

of suppressed feeling she realised how much she resented the constraints of her room, the limits of her chair.

Back to France. She'd left it more than sixty years ago. It would, no doubt, all be changed. She was readying herself for disappointment, uncertain as to why she had come. She knew that others went back often, men in uniforms clanking medals, but they were recalling success, remembering a time when they had done something well, enjoying the adulation as the only antidote to the process of ageing. Ronnie had returned for several reunions. She would be going back to the scene of her failures, of her great misjudgments. She thought suddenly of the bloated cows with their ridiculously short legs sticking in the air. At least it will all be cleaned away, she thought… as I am about to be.

She shook off the morbidity. Even in this modern craft she could feel the swell now they were outside the harbour wall and there was something exhilarating about being on the move again. This feeling had begun on the harbour front, waiting in the line of cars, watching the way they were sorted, listening to the gulls. In age you had to grab at such moments and she had felt lighter because of the holiday atmosphere that surrounded her. When you spent most of your life stuck in a chair it was wonderful to drive into the open mouth of the ship and hear the double clank of the steel ramps. Even having to get out in a very tight space with Gemma holding the door so that it didn't scratch had been fun.

She felt that she was letting go of her middle life, returning to her youth, more daybreak than candle-end.

And she would see what she would see, go back to the village and the small town, look again at the house the SS had commandeered. Perhaps it would all be so different that she would recognise nothing and come away disappointed. The past was a closed book wasn't it? You couldn't ever go back there, could you?

They were clear of the coast now and people who had stood

outside to see the land draw back were coming in and finding places to sit, filling up the spaces round her. Should she save room for the young things? She decided it wasn't necessary.

They were leaning together on the rail. It was getting colder because the ferry had gathered speed and was heading out towards the middle of the channel. At first they had been crowded out there. Now most other people had gone. Summer clothes were no match for this sudden onset of a cold, sea-borne wind.

England was a line on the horizon, a smudged thick line that moved up and down. Gemma leaned into Nathan and snuggled closer.

'Put your arm round me. Keep me warm. I don't want to go in yet.'

He was wearing a coat, she noticed. Had he been on a ferry before? Did he know that it got this cold?

She waited for his arm to go round her but in fact he was moving away. What did that mean? She looked at him and saw that he was taking his coat off, chivalrously handing it to her. 'Here, put this on,' he said. 'I'll be alright.'

The wind was whipping his shirt round him, pushing it against his rib cage. She noticed how thin he was, not much waist and a skinny bottom.

'No,' she replied. 'We can do better than that.' She took the coat from him and put his left arm back into the left sleeve, then put her right arm into the right sleeve. She tried to pull the front of the coat together to close them in but it wouldn't join up and it was flapping round them like a sail.

'Now put your arm round me.' It was an instruction and he did as he was told. 'Here, grab hold of that.'

She slid her arm round him inside the coat and together, holding one side of the zip they just about got it closed.

'There,' she told him. 'Now we can both stay warm and stay out here. It's a good job we are the same height.'

She could feel his warmth now she was holding him close. His body was hot against her. She looked around her. Other women who were still on deck were having trouble with their hair, having to continually push it away from their eyes. Her plait kept hers under control.

They were closer together and yet nothing was happening. She looked again. They had this part of the deck virtually to themselves. Two small boys were running everywhere but taking no notice of them.

She looked at Nathan. He was staring out from the edge of the boat, not at her but at the sea, his eyes fixed on the horizon. She tried to follow his eyes but she could make out nothing special, just the long swell of the sea. 'What are you looking at?' she asked him.

She felt his reaction before he spoke, felt his body register his disappointment. 'That's what she'd say.'

'She?' Gemma asked, hearing the complaint in the words.

'My mum. When he takes no notice of her she asks my dad what he's looking at. She even asks him what he's thinking. He hates it. I know he hates it but he says nothing.'

Gemma soaked up his bitterness, his words falling from him and running away like the spray on the side of the ship.

'Don't you remember,' he continued, 'when I invited you to come and sit on the bench, that I thought you'd be able to sit there, look at the view and say nothing?'

She remembered and she tried to placate him. She tightened the arm that was round him. 'It's enough being close to you,' she said. 'Go back to your watching.' She stuck her face forwards and looked at the line that was England. Another ferry was already setting out behind them. She could see it as a shape that stayed the same size when the land moved backwards.

'Sorry,' Nathan was saying, 'I know you want more from me. I just don't know what else I can give you right now. I'm a mess. I thought you knew that.'

Instinct told her how hard he had found it to say that. She determined to treasure the words, make as much of them as she could.

'In your own time,' she told him. 'I can wait.' She reached sideways and pecked him on the cheek. 'Sometime, when you are ready, you can tell me what else your parents do and say, then I'll know what to avoid.'

She thought he laughed at that, but in the squall that was now blowing round them she couldn't be certain. His arm round her was placed not pressured. She'd have liked him to squeeze her at least once. She needed to know that he might be worth waiting for.

That night, in the first hotel not far from the ferry terminal, they had separate rooms. Only tomorrow when they moved inland would they be sharing. Anna had gone to bed early. She had tried to stay awake but was in danger of nodding off before she had finished her coffee. 'It's all that sea air,' she explained. Gemma had walked with her to her room, checked that she could open the door, and said goodnight. All Anna had said was, 'Make sure you finish the wine before you turn in. It's a good bottle. I don't like waste.'

'How is she?' Nathan had asked when she returned to the table and he'd refilled her glass.

'Staggering,' in both senses of the word.

'Here's to Anna,' he said, raising his glass.

She joined in the toast. 'You really like her, don't you?' she found herself saying.

'Yes. I do.' It was stated as if he hadn't realised that he did. 'Did you hear her French? I couldn't keep up with it. She spoke like a native. I'm sure they…' he swept his glass round in the air to include the dining room … thought she was French.'

'Can I ask why you like her?'

'She's her own person. She's decisive. She knows what she wants from life.'

'Or what she doesn't want?'

'What do you mean?' His movements were becoming looser. She wondered how much of the wine he had drunk.

She'd tell him. They were having a conversation. 'I agree with everything you've said. Her French is fantastic. She's a crack shot, unless she was trying to kill Risco, but when I look into her eyes I see fear. She doesn't want to go into a home. She's terrified of that.'

'Yes,' he said.

'But be practical. One day she'll have to. We can't look after her. We have our lives and Uni.'

'She hates her family.'

Gemma realised that Nathan was still listing the reasons he liked Anna and wasn't really listening to her.

'And you hate yours?' she demanded of him.

He put the glass down, perhaps because it was nearly empty.

'Not hate,' he said. 'Hate would be simple.' He stopped talking for a moment then suddenly started again. 'We're both only-children, no brothers or sisters. Your parents had to let you go because they split up.' He took a long, deep breath as if it was necessary to fill his lungs to their capacity in order to carry on. 'Mine dislike each other intensely but they have stayed together for my sake. They limit their lives because they want to do what's right by me. And I have to carry that. It's as if they have loaded all their disappointment in each other and stuck it on my shoulders. It's as if every time they look at me they want me to be grateful for their sacrifice.'

'Wow,' Gemma said. She couldn't think of anything to add. She reached for her glass and drank some more wine. Then she stretched out and laid her hand on his for a moment, not daring to leave it there.

He turned and looked at her and she saw how torn and wounded he was. An idea struck her. She let it grow in her mind, checked it out before she spoke it. She would ignore

Anna's advice. The dining room was emptying. Guests were leaving the detritus of their meal on every table and wandering away. Waiters were tidying up, laying for breakfast. She felt tired herself but she was also determined.

She picked up the bottle and shared what was left of it between them.

'Okay, I don't know what to say,' she told him. 'But I'm glad you told me. That makes me feel special.' She paused. This was it. 'If you want to know what I think, and what I've thought for some time,' she continued, 'it is that all this means you're frightened of having a relationship. Well, sex isn't a relationship. It can be just sex. Let's finish this bottle then I want you to come back to my room for some simple no-strings sex. You look as if you need it. Besides, it'll save all that heavy worry tomorrow night when we have to share a room.'

She'd said it. He looked at her. In his startled face she couldn't tell what he was thinking, couldn't read what he was feeling. 'Come on,' she said, smiling for both of them and downing the rest of her glass. 'I promise I won't talk. At the very least you can enjoy another view. I promise that I'm worth looking at.'

Anna heard the knock on her door the next morning and heard her name being called. She walked towards the door and opened it. She'd slept well and woken late, dressed in a hurry so as not to keep them waiting.

Gemma was outside the door. 'We wondered if you were ready for breakfast,' she said.

'Quite ready.' Then she looked at Gemma again, noted the different look, the more relaxed mouth, something shining in the eyes. She wondered whether to say anything but decided not to until she was sure. Instead she picked up her key and began to walk slowly down the hotel corridor. I can't ask them if they slept well, she thought as she inched forwards, pressing hard on her stick. Yesterday had taken it out of her. Today would be a struggle.

'Where's Nathan?' she asked, and noticed the slight blush on Gemma's face, confirming her suspicions. 'Gone to the restaurant. He said it was to get us a table but I think he was just hungry.'

Again Anna told herself to make no comment, remembering how hungry she had been the morning after, so close to where they now were and so long ago.

They went into the dining room and Nathan was waving to them. 'It's a buffet. You sit down, Anna, and I'll fetch you some croissants. They bring the coffee round.'

Anna sat, happy to be waited on. She watched them both at the buffet, Gemma getting herself some fruit in a bowl, Nathan stacking croissants on a plate. They leant together more, had a unity about them, came back together. Well, she thought to herself, this holiday has achieved something.

'Where are we going today?' Nathan asked when they'd put the plates full of food on the table and a waiter had poured them coffee.

'Caen,' she said. 'There's a place I've heard about. I think it's called The Memorial Museum.

'Memorial, no 'the' and it doesn't call itself a museum. I've heard of it too. There's a leaflet in reception,' Nathan told her. 'I'll fetch it for us.' He got up immediately, taking a half-eaten, strawberry-jam-laden croissant with him before dashing away. His absence gave Anna the chance to look at Gemma and say simply, 'You look happy. Whatever happens, remember how you feel right now.'

'I don't know what you mean,' Gemma began, then giggled and added, 'Nathan always said you were a witch.'

Nathan came back and sat down with two leaflets, one in English which Anna noticed he gave to Gemma, and one in French that he passed across to her.

'I've been so slow, haven't I?' he suddenly said to her. 'You were here weren't you, here in Normandy? That's why we've come, isn't it?'

She had been finishing the last crumbs of a croissant when the question hit her. She looked up to see the two of them staring at her, faces eager, like children again, far too young to be having sex.

She took her time. It wasn't a question you could answer in a single sentence. Once she said yes there would be more questions and she would have to tell them about her mistakes, about her misjudgments. Could she do that? Could she let others in on what she had done: those two men dead?

But if not them, who? She wondered, as she thought all this, whether that was why she had really come. Not to get away from Risco, not to stop Alistair moving into her house, those were simply excuses. She had come because she had questions that might have answers, and because the body she buried might actually still be there.

'Yes, I was here.'

'When?' Nathan's single word question. Before she answered it she must put a limit on what she was willing to tell them, set some parameters, dampen their curiosity.

'Only from February to August 1944. It was a short period and I didn't do that much. And before you ask me anything else, I should tell you that there are things which happened to me then that I am not willing to talk about, even now.'

She saw their faces fall, realised they felt patronised, wondered if Gemma understood about 1944, knew at once that Nathan did.

He said, 'You were here in Normandy on D-Day, behind the lines. You're English and you speak perfect French. You're also a crack shot. How old did you say you were?'

'Ninety.'

She watched as he did the calculation quickly. 'You'd have been 26,' he said, 'and only three years older than we are now when the war broke out.'

She waited for the next question, drank a little coffee, not too much as she didn't want to have to make them spend the whole morning finding toilets.

'How did you arrive? I presume you weren't living in France at the time?'

She could answer Nathan's question. 'By parachute, on a moonlit night in February, with some snow still on the ground.'

She saw his eyes widen, didn't want his adoration.

'You were an agent weren't you?' It wasn't really a question. 'You were one of those spies who worked with the resistance.'

Now she realised that Gemma understood too.

Anna nodded. 'Yes,' she said. It was a simple statement of fact.

Chapter Twenty-Four

The museum was approached through a line of flags. Nathan was right. It called itself Memorial, thought of itself as more than a museum. It was also, she noticed, a place that worked to promote peace. They'd had to park a little way off so she agreed to be put in the wheelchair and pushed. It confined her but they could then move faster and she could save energy. The problem, she realised, as soon as she got into the museum, was that neither of them had pushed a wheelchair before. As their eyes flitted round the exhibits they tended to leave her facing the wrong way and she had to repeatedly turn her head to look at what she wanted to see.

She realised too that she was tired after yesterday, with that awful residual tiredness of old age, the kind that takes days to shake off. She looked at maps and saw lines moving across landscapes, picked out the names of towns and villages she had known, tried to match sepia or black and white photographs to places she remembered, but simply felt dizzy. It was well displayed, neatly arranged, and yet to her it seemed utterly false, totally irrelevant to what she had been through. The reality had been chaotic; this was ordered and controlled.

Could you have a museum that demonstrated the chaotic nature of war and what a battlefield looked, smelt and felt like? The D-Day section told her it couldn't be done.

Then they moved into an area that dealt with The Resistance. She saw a photograph at once that called to her through her tiredness and she asked Nathan to stop and turn her round so she could take another look. It was of a girl with proper French hair, wearing the same clothes she had worn, the ones they had all kept mending, her ankles beautiful and her shoes nearly worn through. This was apparent because the photograph allowed you to look underneath the shoes and see the black mark on the soles with just a strip of lighter coloured unworn leather round the edges. They were good shoes. They must once have been a prized possession and loved, as the girl too would once have been loved. The shoes, pointing downwards, reminded Anna of ballet lessons, but this girl was not on her points. The toes were pointing to the unswept floor, pointing to it but not reaching it. How long, Anna wondered, had she danced from the end of her rope? Had the others been strung up first? Had she watched them die before it was her turn? They were all hanging in a room, dangling from meat hooks attached to the ceiling, almost certainly in a cellar. Perhaps Anna had even known the house where it had happened.

It was a photograph of her greatest terror and he had saved her.

'Did you know any of them?' Gemma's voice was full of concern. The hanging girl's face was turned away from her. She looked at the other faces and shook her head.

Nathan swivelled her chair round to push her to look at other things. In doing so he brought her close up against a section that dealt with Rivalries and Reprisals and suddenly there he was. Her chair was moving, moving her away. She must look again. She must read the label.

'Can you go back? Back there.'

She pointed at the photograph, at the trees on the skyline, at the sloping meadow at the edge of the wood, with the just visible hut in the top right hand corner. The picture was small, no more than eight by ten inches. It looked like a poor quality, family snap.

'There,' she explained. 'That photograph. I need to see it.'

Nathan jerked her to a stop, then pulled her slowly backwards until she came in line with it.

'Is that right?' he asked.

She leant forward and read the label, first in French and then in English.

The body of a British Agent. This photograph was taken by a local man who stumbled across the corpse on the morning of D-Day. The place in the photograph is well away from any action of the previous night. Was this an example of deadly rivalry played out between different resistance groups?

The tears startled her. It was only the second time she had cried. She didn't want them to be there. Not in public. It was the shock, she told herself, the shock of suddenly seeing his body, crumpled up the way she had left it. A battlefield had been the right place to hide a body, but where she had left him hadn't been a battlefield, hadn't been touched by the war. Her flowers were clearly visible.

The tears wouldn't stop. She wrestled her handkerchief out of her sleeve and dabbed at herself fiercely, raising her glasses with her finger. She tried to stem the flow, but she continued to cry and there was nothing she could do about it. She was conscious that Gemma was kneeling by her side, asking if she was alright. Her throat wasn't working properly and she couldn't answer.

Then there was someone else at the other side, speaking to her in French, trying to find out what the matter was. She made a great effort to pull herself together and become again the unfeeling person the war had made her.

'The caption is wrong,' she told them, saying each word as clearly as she could. 'He was someone I knew, someone I worked with. Then I found out that he was a double agent, so I had to eliminate him. He didn't die because of rivalry.'

The effort of speaking had stemmed the flow of tears. She was winning back. She looked to both sides of her and saw startled faces. Then Gemma's hand was on her knee, offering her another handkerchief. The moment she took it they began to wheel her away.

She was conscious as they went of a whispered conversation taking place above her head, conducted in French between

Nathan and the stranger. She heard Nathan explain that she had been there, had been an agent. She caught the excitement in the voice of the museum attendant, then something about needing to know more. A Staff Only sign was being moved away from in front of her and she was wheeled down a corridor into a room with chairs and a rectangular table. She looked round, glad to see that Gemma was still with her.

Then the museum attendant was leaning over her and asking if she would like a coffee. She got up out of the wheelchair before she answered, not wanting to appear any more disabled than was necessary, took Gemma's arm, walked over to the table and sat down on one of the chairs. 'Thank you,' she said, 'I am a little thirsty.'

The three of them were left alone. It gave her time to dab again at her eyes. 'Do I look alright?' she asked Gemma.

Gemma scrutinised her. 'Not bad, but don't let anyone take your picture.'

Anna thought she should explain a little. 'I'm sorry about all that back there. I don't know why I cried. The man in the photograph was the man I told you about,' she said to Gemma, 'the one I fell in love with.'

'Fell in love with, you said, then eliminated!' Gemma's incredulous voice was like a judgement on her. It echoed with an unspoken, *How could you?*

What could she say? 'I suspect that's what they want to ask me about and, the trouble is, I don't know how much I am prepared to tell them.'

'We can just go,' Nathan suddenly said. 'We don't have to talk to them unless you want to. I can say you are getting forgetful, that you made a mistake.'

Anna looked up at him. At least he appeared to be on her side.

'I could even say that you just wanted a bit of recognition and have made the whole thing up.'

She didn't have to say anything by way of reply. It was

Gemma who intervened. 'I don't think they would believe you. Those tears came from somewhere.'

'It's too late anyway,' said Nathan. 'They're coming back.'

The young woman from the museum had brought with her an older man whom she introduced as Monsieur Manchot, a senior researcher. He was a lean, small individual with thinning grey hair and shoulders that looked as if he had spent too long studying.

'Madame,' he said to her as he came forward to shake her hand. 'Meeting women like you is one of the privileges of my life.' His English was accented but impeccable. She wouldn't need to use French; that made things easier because Gemma would be able to understand.

'Coffee is on its way. Now, please can I take some details?' He was carrying a small attaché case from which he withdrew a large notebook held together by a band. He unwrapped it and took out a proper fountain pen from inside his jacket.

'Your name please.' He had the pen ready, holding it over the blank page with great intensity.

It was all too fast. She hadn't worked out what she would tell him. 'Wait,' she said. 'I need to know what use you may make of any information I give you. It's not just my story, others were involved.'

He didn't seem at all put out. 'Quite right,' he said. 'I'm an academic historian, not a journalist,' he explained. 'But some of what we discover does find its way into the press particularly, if I may say so, on your side of the channel. I cannot always control the uses that others make of my research.'

'Then use my code name only,' she told him. 'I don't see that doing any harm. My real name is Anna but my code name was Marie-Claire Cardon.' She let him write it down, approving of his neatness. Nathan and Gemma were sitting to either side of her. For them, she thought, this must be so embarrassing. What must they think of her?

'And where are you staying, please, whilst you are in France?'

'Oh goodness knows,' she told him. 'Nathan has done the arrangements.'

'Monsieur Nathan?' he asked.

Nathan gave him the name of the hotel and the town which he wrote down.

'I need that in case, when I cross check, I can give you any information about your previous contacts. Now I presume you were working for SOE?'

She gave him the details, remembered her serial number: 27-land-23AJ 43, told him the name of her controllers. When he had a page of information he put his pen away and, diving again into the case, brought out a small recorder. 'I hope you do not mind if I record what you have to tell me. It is quicker than writing every word.' Fussily he leant forward and recorded an introductory section, then switched it off.

The coffee came and was handed out. 'Right,' he told her when she had her cup. 'I understand you have information about a British agent who was killed around D-Day. Perhaps you would like to tell us what happened.

She began by leaving out the love, feeling it was none of their business, but as she launched into her story she realised it would make no sense without, so she asked if she could begin again.

She told it as simply as she could, sticking to the horror of her discovery of his betrayal, detailing the checks she made, talking about the eve of invasion instructions. She tried not to look at anyone as she spoke, simply made this a thing between herself and the little machine in the middle of the table. She said more about the choice she had to make between the singularity of her love and the multiple lives of those already embarked. She left out the sitting by his body watching the parachutes falling. When she'd finished she asked him to switch off the machine. She must ask her question, the one she had long suppressed, must ask it not least because Gemma and Nathan were sitting beside her. She hadn't looked at them yet, hadn't dared to in case there was disapproval written across both their faces, but the closer she came to death the more truth seemed to matter.

Because of her embarrassment she kept her head down as she spoke. 'My controller said it was a pity I had killed him. At my de-brief he told me that I should have let them know he was a double agent, then they could have played him back against the Germans. Apparently something similar happened at the invasion in the south which meant the Germans were waiting at the wrong place.' She stopped talking and looked straight at this man from the museum, this disinterested academic. 'I want to know whether you will keep that photograph in the exhibition now you know what I have told you and if you do, what will the new label say?... I also want to know... what you think of the choice I made.'

He looked back at her with clear grey eyes. 'Madame, I am not God, only a historian. I judge no one. My job is simply to tidy up the past. I always arrive after the battles are over.'

'You see,' she went on, ignoring his equivocation, still not looking at the young things, needing certainty, 'even to this day I don't know if I was right to kill him. That night he shouted up to where I was concealed, that being a double agent was the only way to be.' Now that she had started she had better put all her thoughts into words. There would never be a better time. 'I realised later that my proofs were incomplete. Even the fact that he shot at me proves nothing. Perhaps it was a shot to keep my head down. I have asked myself so many times whether he only wanted to disarm me so that he could have another chance to explain. He wasn't to know I was a crack shot, was he?'

Her question brought only silence so she added the final bit, for the first time using his name. 'The thing that has haunted me for sixty years is this: if Pierre betrayed Marcel, he never betrayed me. I have wondered ever since whether I killed a man who had made me an exception to his double dealing and let me live… perhaps because he also loved me.'

Gemma was to remember particularly the slow hesitant way in which Anna had spoken. She'd been both thrilled by the story and disbelieving. How could someone so slow and old have once been pivotal to a moment in history? She kept glancing at her whilst she talked, looking for the tough-as-nails young woman who'd had to face such a dilemma quite alone, but all she could see was a tired old lady leaning on the table, some of her make-up now missing, somewhat red around the eyes.

The sheer horror of that choice shocked Gemma and made her look at Nathan. She wondered, particularly after last night, if she could ever kill him, whatever he had done. She felt suddenly in the presence of greatness, but was at the same time appalled at the extent of Anna's hurt. She found she was hoping that the museum man would excuse her and make it all right, even after all this time. But she knew he couldn't.

She reached out and held the old woman's hand. It felt cold to the touch and the skin had a kind of plastic feel to it, more like a false limb than another human being. She squeezed the hand as she put her arm round the shoulders. The silence was pressing at her. She felt she needed to speak.

But before she could think of any words she heard Nathan say to Anna, 'Wow, I knew there was something special about you. To have been there…to have had to make that choice… at that moment. Whatever happens to me will always be tiny by comparison. And the thing is that you didn't crumble into indecision. You made up your mind… you made a choice. Even at that hideous moment…you coped.'

Monsieur Manchot rose and packed away his machine. He closed the notebook and wrapped its elastic band round it.

'It has been a privilege meeting you, Marie-Claire Cardon. If I find anything out I'll be in touch.'

Anna got back in the wheelchair. The museum attendant opened the door and led them back out, with Nathan pushing.

It was lunchtime. Anna was clearly exhausted and they had a short way to go to where they were staying that night. The room might not be ready until 3pm, so whilst Gemma took Anna to the toilet, Nathan scouted out the café and the restaurant.

Gemma and Nathan ate whilst Anna pushed food around a plate. Nathan had bought Anna a glass of wine. 'I think you need this; at least it will help you sleep in the car,' he told her. They didn't speak much, and when they reached the car Anna insisted on Gemma sitting in the front so that she could map-read for Nathan. They were hardly out of the car park before Gemma noticed, looking behind her, that Anna's eyes had closed.

Gemma kept one finger on the map as the car sped along. Nathan was a good driver. He was coping well with driving on the right. He seemed to be enjoying himself. Their route was straightforward but because she was thinking so hard she didn't want to lose her place on the map. As they headed north and west she kept her finger moving across the page. She thought about being Anna, being here and being alone. She thought about the enormity of what Anna had been part of. Everywhere you looked there were signs to battlefields and memorials. She'd noticed smaller signs as well, pointing out the graveyards. 'Do you think,' she whispered to Nathan, 'Do you think we could pull off at the next cemetery? She's fast asleep and we can leave the windows open. I just want to have a look.'

They parked the car under a tree, opened the doors quietly and pushed them shut. Anna hadn't woken. Then they were walking together down the neat pathways and over the clean-cut grass. The graves were British. Gemma stood in front of the first one and read:

6023857 PRIVATE
G J DRAPER
THE LEICESTERSHIRE REGT.

7TH AUGUST 1944 AGE 26.

Anna's age at the time. Another young person with a serial number, the number bigger because there had been so many soldiers. Initials. No first name.

Each grave was set in a narrow line of neatly planted earth. There were trimmed roses, curled daffodil leaves, blue iris. Gemma walked on and read more names and ages. Then she began to notice the messages. These were often at the bottom of the gravestones and sometimes hidden by the plants.

> AT THE GOING DOWN OF THE SUN
> AND IN THE MORNING
> WE WILL REMEMBER THEM

Had anyone remembered them, she wondered. Did family come and visit?

> HE LIVES FOR EVER
> IN THE HEARTS OF THOSE
> WHO LOVE HIM

She wouldn't cry. These weren't her family. To cry about strangers who had died so long ago was an indulgence and she wouldn't be part of that. She walked on, not reading every one, the sun on her back. She felt herself to be full of life, as if she could feel the blood running through her, and was aware of the intense wonder of just being alive. She turned the corner, began the next row.

> TO A BEAUTIFUL LIFE
> CAME A SUDDEN END
> HE DIED AS HE LIVED
> EVERYONE'S FRIEND

Of course they felt like that about him.

NOR TIME NOR SPACE NOR HUMAN POWERS
YOUR GOD LIKE SPIRIT CAN CONFINE

She was thinking of Nathan, suddenly aware that he was no longer walking at her side. He had slowed down, hadn't yet turned the first corner. She was ahead of him again. He didn't seem to have a God like spirit, but he did have something. Perhaps as a couple they also had something. It wasn't just sex, was it, or the fact that they had to share a room?

She was aware that the grave she was standing in front of was different even before she began to read it.

A SOLDIER
OF THE
1939 TO 1945
WAR

KNOWN UNTO GOD

In spite of herself she found that she was crying. Perhaps she had been crying for some time. It wasn't over, was it? History had echoes and whatever had happened here, before even her parents were born, wasn't over for Anna. As she stared at the stone Gemma thought she heard something of the sound of guns and imagined a body so destroyed it could not be recognised.

She wandered away to calm herself down. There was an area she could see over the other side with many fewer, different, chunkier stones, set apart. She'd go and look at those, give herself time to recover. The grass was springy under her feet. The sky was blue. School was over. She was on holiday. If she hadn't been here in this place she might have wanted to skip and dance.

This time there were no messages, just names and ranks. Some graves had three men in them.

'Germans,' Nathan explained. He had followed her over.

'In the same graveyard?' she asked.

'Why not?'

And when she thought about it she couldn't see why not. Hatred passes. The blue sky days like this one keep coming round. The cemetery was a place of healing. But not for Anna. Pierre must be somewhere in one of these cemeteries, Gemma thought, but not under his real name. Even at Memorial they didn't seem to know who he was.

Suddenly she had had enough. She felt she was growing older the longer she stayed there. Besides, they mustn't leave Anna too long.

She reached out a hand to Nathan and this time he clasped her hand back, locking his fingers through her own

'Have you seen the ages, Gem. Some of them are no older than we are.'

She looked up, saw that he had tears in his eyes.

'Come on,' she said, suddenly pleased that he had been so moved by what he had seen. 'We need to be getting back.'

There was no message at the hotel. Anna went off to her room for a longer sleep. She'd see them for dinner. The afternoon was their own.

Their bedroom was at the end of the corridor. Shyly Gemma led the way, pulling the case her dad had lent her. Nathan had the swipe card key and he couldn't make it work. 'Give it here,' she said suddenly, taking it from him and hearing the click the first time she tried.

It was a double bed.

'You're trapped now,' she told him, 'trapped for the whole night. Last night you could always have got away, sneaked out and gone back to your own room, but not tonight.'

He was lying on the bed, testing the mattress.

'But I didn't go, did I?' he reminded her. 'And I do have the car keys. I can always creep out and sleep in the car if you get too demanding.'

Gemma kicked off her shoes and lay down on the bed beside him. They held hands and stared at the ceiling. Nathan was right, she thought. There are times when you need someone you can just be silent with.

Chapter Twenty-Five

When Nathan asked her, at breakfast the next morning, what the plan was, Anna already knew where she wanted to go.

'I'll take you to the village where I lived. I expect it is still there but it must be changed out of all recognition. First we must go to Thury.'

'Why Thury?' Nathan asked.

'It's on the way. It's also the town where I sold milk and cheeses. It's where the Germans used to have a road block.'

She was feeling much better. She had slept all afternoon, woken in the evening for dinner, and then gone back to bed soon afterwards.

'It's also where I chatted to some of my best informants.... at the Maison de tolérance or what you would call the brothel.'

Gemma choked on her coffee.

'Why do the young,' Anna asked them, 'always presume that the old know nothing about life?'

It wasn't only that she felt rested. Asking her question yesterday at the museum had been a relief. She felt somehow lighter and more detached from herself.

'As it happens, the girls who worked there gave me some of my best information. Men are apparently more likely to talk once they have been .... I won't finish the sentence. It is only breakfast time.'

Gemma, she noticed, was caught between shock and the need to giggle. It came out of her like a kind of forced splutter.

'Ladies, please,' said Nathan. 'Some of us have sensibilities.'

The waiter was hovering. Did they want more coffee?

Gemma was dabbing at her saucer with her paper napkin, trying to wipe it clean before proffering it to the waiter.

'Thury is also where the Gestapo had a house. I was only taken there once. But that is another story.'

And now I have started talking I may not be able to stop, she thought. I mustn't get to be a war bore. This is their holiday too.

'Tomorrow,' she announced, 'we will go to the coast. I can sit whilst you two swim. You'll have had quite enough of my memories by then.'

Thury was much bigger. She'd noticed bungalows on the way in that hadn't been there before and some new industrial units down by the railway line. Much of the building was recent, she thought, and she recognised none of it. Only when they reached the square did it begin to come back to her.

They parked under the church, its slate covered spire pointing at a God somewhere up in the blue sky that stretched above them. Its solid, without frills architecture reminded her of the local people she had got to know.

She got out and looked round her, recognising little of it. Shop fronts change over time. Bistros open and close. It looked neat. Tubs of flowers fronted the steps up to the west end of the church. When she had been here it had all been shabby, and then in the last days much of it had been destroyed. She'd heard that the retreating Germans had set fire to the château, seeking to destroy what they could no longer own. She remembered the man hanging, the deep slits in his face.

Then there it was, confronting her, the house across the square with the two sets of steps leading up to the front door, leaving room for cellars underneath. Today it had window boxes with trailing geraniums. Today it seemed to have reverted to being just somebody's home.

'Come on,' she said, and started walking across the square, glad not to be in the wheelchair any more but moving, however slowly, under her own steam. The house was cleaned up, spruced. As she got closer she noticed not just window boxes but freshly painted shutters and curtains. It slept in the morning sun, quite unmoved by its own history.

'You see', she told them when they stood together, puzzled.

'History finishes with things and moves on. It's a nice house, grand in its way, and during the war people died in its cellars. I don't know where yesterday's photograph was taken, but probably in the cellars of a house like the one you are staring at.'

'There should be a plaque,' Gemma suggested.

'You can't have plaques everywhere. You need to leave room for the living. Time moves on,' she told them, sounding pompous even to herself. 'It's part of the deal. Didn't you read the small print?'

They got back in the car and she gave directions. She was glad the two young things were happy together and so content to be tourists.

Now she recognised the landscape and asked Nathan to slow down. She felt herself becoming animated. 'I used to cycle all this,' she told them, 'on a bike with no gears.'

The car was climbing. Thury was behind them, nestling as it always had in its shallow dish of hills. The land was becoming more sparse and now she could pick out the newly built barns attached to the same houses she had previously known. At the entrance to the village itself she asked Nathan to park the car. 'I'm sorry if you are bored, but please indulge me and allow me to walk in. This place once meant everything to me and I don't want to rush it.'

They parked and got out. For a time the young things kept pace with her then seemed to want to lag behind, looking at the view. That suited her fine. Perhaps when she reached the end of the village she'd send them back for the car. It was further than she had remembered. Until then she'd just soak it all up.

She'd seen it first on that cycle ride, swooping in as evening fell with the cold early spring stinging her face. Now it was hot sun and sixty years later. The doors were different and there were more aerials, satellite dishes and cars. The odd gap between houses had been filled in but the shape of the long village was the same. She picked out Madame Desaint's house. Its door was open and filled with one of those swinging metal curtains that were once a fashionable way of keeping out insects.

She walked on and there it was, her own place, now with an extension and noticeably smartened up but still next to the farm.

The yard door was partly open and she peeped inside, looking first at the new double-glazed back door. Children now lived in the place. She could see a plastic trolley and a scooter on its side. There were plastic figures too in the edge of the drive: a doll with blonde hair and a thick set plastic creature with an enormous chest and the face of a wolf. The outside privy had been demolished to make way for the extension. She guessed at three upstairs rooms now, probably two bedrooms and a bathroom. She could make out where old tiles met new ones. Trust the people here to waste nothing, she thought.

Then she turned her head and looked for what she hoped would be different, but it wasn't. There was the drinking trough, still in the same spot, the soil behind slightly raised. It clearly wasn't used as a drinking trough any more. Someone had filled it with those ubiquitous red geraniums.

She looked at the house and it looked back at her, as if it had quite forgotten the girl who dragged the body across the yard. She looked again at the trough and wondered at her younger self, at what she'd done.

The young things had caught her up. 'Is this the place?' Nathan asked.

'It was smaller then, just one up and one down with open stairs to a loft area where they stored hay and straw. It's been extended,' she explained. 'It had an outside loo.'

She must have raised her voice because a young woman came out of the house and walked into the yard, carrying a child.

'Excuse me,' she said. 'Can I help you?'

The child was doing what children do when they meet strangers: nestling his head into his mother's shoulders for protection at the same time as he stared at the old lady in the yard. He was hot and tetchy. Perhaps he had only recently woken up.

'I'm sorry to disturb you,' Anna said. 'I used to live here during the war. I was just having a look.'

The woman hitched the baby up to make herself more comfortable. She stuck the other arm out in a gesture of welcome. 'Come in. Look round. The house isn't tidy.'

'It never was,' Anna reassured her. 'Are you sure this is alright?'

A small girl now came out of the house and at first clung to her mother's leg. Then, plucking up courage, she picked up the scooter and began to move in circles round the yard.

'Tell me,' said Anna, 'how long have you lived here?'

'Only five years. We had it converted when we knew I was pregnant.'

'And before that?' Anna nudged her into giving more information

'It was derelict. No one had done anything with it for years. The house had been used to store hay and the yard was strewn with broken machinery. The upstairs hadn't been touched for a long time. It was full of junk. We made a hole in the roof and flung it all out into the yard.'

The child was getting fidgety. Gemma came up and held out her arms. The child gave her a sideways look and then allowed himself to be picked up. Freed from the child, the woman tidied her hair by pulling it back into its pony tail. 'Come in. Please come in.'

Anna walked towards the door, went into the extension and then through to the old room. It had been modernised out of recognition, not so much an extension as a rebuilding. Even the fireplace she had lived in front of had been replaced by a wood-burning stove. Everywhere was right angled corners

304

and white paint. Even the stairs seemed to have been moved.

No plaques. The world has to move on. She felt for a moment the bitterness of her own words. She looked at the spot where she had made love for the first time, the place where she had killed the Gestapo officer. There was only a polished wood floor and more children's toys spilled across it.

'Lovely,' she made herself say. 'You've changed everything and made it lovely. When I lived here it was quite different.'

She could see the young woman was pleased with what she had said.

Gemma and Nathan had remained outside. 'Your grandchildren?' the woman asked her.'

'Yes.' To tell her anything else would take too long.

'The trough outside in the yard. I remember the trough,' Anna said, leading the way back out into the sunlight. 'Did the builders move it?'

'I don't think so,' she said.

'Is there anyone who would know?' Anna asked.

The woman frowned at her as if she was now becoming tiresome.

'I'm sorry to be a nuisance,' said Anna, 'but it is important. In 1944 I hid something underneath that trough. It might still be there.'

'What did you hide?' Anna could see the woman's eagerness, the sudden excitement that had wandered into her child-intensive days.

Nathan and Gemma were standing close to her. She'd say it in French and then in English so that Gemma understood.

'Nothing valuable,' she said twice. 'I hid a body there.'

A look of horror spread across the young features of the woman. Sharply she took the child back from Gemma and called her little girl, taking them into the house.

The three of them were left in the yard.

'Oh dear,' said Anna. 'I seem to have upset her.'

'Whose body?' Nathan asked her. 'The more I get to know

you, the more alarming you become.'

She'd have to tell them.

Another day, thought Gemma, another story. Was there no end to this old lady's past? It was such a strange holiday, the fumbling sweetness of the nights with Nathan contrasting with the blackness of Anna's history. Sometimes a thin layer of cloud takes all the heat out of the sun. It had happened yesterday and it was happening again today. She listened to the story Anna was telling and wondered if what she was hearing was possible. Even if you stripped off the years, could such a small person, on her own, have done all that?

Then, in the middle of the story, the young woman at the house had re-appeared. 'J'ai téléphoné et quelqu'un qui était là pendant la guerre va venir,' she told them. Nathan had translated it one way then Anna had corrected him and translated it another, so that Gemma understood they were to wait where they were.

They had waited. Anna finished her tale and eventually a tall, very upright, white-haired individual with a long straight neck came into the yard. He looked at Anna casually, did a perfect double-take, then walked towards her as if he was transfixed. He said her name without being told it, called her Marie-Claire as if he was trying the name out to see if it fitted. Anna nodded and suddenly he was all over her, kissing her on both cheeks, then hugging her, standing back to take a good long look and shaking his head as he did so.

Then he started shouting into the house. Although she didn't understand what he shouted, the young woman appeared with two chairs and plonked them down, then stood nervously whilst the old man introduced her to 'Marie-Claire'. Gemma picked out the words 'résistance' and 'héroïne', noticed that the young woman did a kind of curtsey before she went back into the house. Two more chairs were brought out and they were gestured to come over. Coffee was mentioned somewhere in a stream of incessant French.

'This is Franck,' Anna said suddenly, turning round and breaking back into English. 'He was one of my network. I've told him that you are my new network. He said I always did pick them young.'

Then Anna turned back to Franck and began asking him questions. The young woman and the children reappeared. There was fresh coffee in great white cups.

Gemma heard the name Marcel. It was said and repeated, then the tone of their reunion changed and became dipped in sadness, but she didn't understand and she didn't want to ask. Every now and then she glanced at Nathan. He was listening intently but losing the flow. 'It's too fast,' he whispered to her. 'I'm trying, but I can't keep up.'

There had come a time when Franck put down his coffee, walked over to the trough and shook it. He got hold of the edge and tried to move it. Gemma saw Anna go and join him, gesturing towards the back, miming the fact that she had tipped it forwards. More words were exchanged and Anna was nodding furiously.

She came back and sat down. 'We're going to lift it out of the way. See if he is still there,' she explained to them. Then she added casually, 'Because it is a body the police will have to be involved.'

Sixty years. If it was there, it had been in the ground for sixty years. Was that time to make it a skeleton or would they be seeing a still rotting corpse? Anna realised she had no idea how long a body took to decay.

'I'm afraid it'll mean more waiting, but they are going to get us some lunch. Why don't you two go for a walk? This must be so dull for you. Tomorrow we go to the seaside.'

She looked across at Nathan and he nodded. 'If you carry on walking down that way you'll get to my look-out post,' Anna instructed. 'There's a great view and I know you like views.'

Then she was back to talking French and they were walking out of the yard.

'Do you think it's true?' Gemma asked Nathan as soon as they were out of hearing. 'I keep looking at her and thinking she's making all this up. She's so small and frail now. Even when she was younger she can't have been any size at all.'

They were walking slowly uphill. There were houses on their left and open fields on the right. The fields sloped upwards and there was no view to be had.

'It's the truth. It has to be,' Nathan said. 'Franck is real. Franck recognised her at once.'

'Then who is she?' Gemma asked. 'I hated history at school, dropped it as soon as I could and did Child Care instead. Now history's coming to life around me. I mean, she must have been someone.'

'She's haunted by it,' Nathan said.

It was the right word. It was the word that fitted Anna. For sixty years she had felt a failure, Gemma realised. She'd killed two men, one an enemy who had been her friend and one her lover who had also been her enemy. No wonder she had told nobody at all. No wonder that Nathan liked her. They were two of a kind.

They walked in silence. The houses thinned, the fields grew messier.

'I can't help thinking,' Nathan said eventually, 'that she is the most remarkable person I've ever met.'

She squeezed his hand. It was no longer strange to be holding hands with him. Their hands, she realised, had come together of their own accord as soon as they started walking. And it wasn't just sex that he liked her for, although he had what she considered to be a considerable appetite, finishing quickly and then ready to start again far too soon for her. He hadn't said he loved her, and she had never mentioned the word, banishing it entirely from her thinking so that she didn't mess up with him. Instead, what she was conscious of was just how much he was relaxing, letting go of the strains that she had always felt were twisting him. There were silences like now but they were different, and words really felt unnecessary.

The road was about to make a turn and as it lurched to the right the land fell suddenly away on the left. There was a small path that led up to a high point. Without discussion they took it, following Anna's instruction. It took them quickly to a kind of grassy platform from which you could see everything. It was exactly chosen. You could watch both roads, see vehicles coming from far away.

'It's where she stationed Franck,' Nathan explained. 'I could follow that bit. He was only seven when she recruited him. She put him here as look-out whilst she used the radio transmitter.'

'What a view!' Gemma said. She looked around her and knew that Anna was right. There was a body under the drinking trough.

'Look!' She stuck out her arm and pointed. A car was coming up the road. It had stripes and a siren. 'It's the police car. We had better get back.'

It took Franck and Anna some time to convince the police. Gemma noticed many sideways glances and much shaking of heads. Eventually another man from the village had carefully driven his tractor into the yard. He extended the arm and with two spikes lifted the trough, pulling it clear and taking it out of the yard. Later she was to see it dumped on the other side of the road, its geraniums leaning at a crazy angle.

Franck found a spade and gingerly began to scrape the soil away. Gemma held back, didn't want to watch. The others were there, Nathan peering into the rectangular space, even Anna standing with her stick and watching. Heaven knows what she was feeling.

The moment they found him all the heads tilted forward. The young woman herself came for a look, then covered her mouth. Okay, Gemma had said to herself. I'm part of this. It's an exhumation and I'm part of it. I need to see what they see.

She walked over and Nathan made way for her. At one end of the rectangle was a shallow indentation. It held the curve of the side of the spade that had made it, of the long sweeps Franck had made as he searched. Then there were finger marks because the spade must have struck something and then, unmistakeable, the open nose of a skull shining white and moist, just poking through the black earth.

Gemma held Anna's hand and looked. 'Are you alright?' she whispered, and the hand responded.

'I needed to do this,' Anna told her. 'He deserves a decent burial.'

More phone calls and then a magnificent al-fresco lunch with baguettes, cheese, tapenade and a tub of richly scented pâté. There was wine and coke. The wine just sloshed into tumblers.

It lasted for more than an hour. Other people from the village arrived and introductions were made until the yard was full.

Then two official looking men came and pushed their way through to peek at the exposed nostrils before ordering everyone back and putting on white coats. Their arrival pulled the gendarmes away from the food and back to their duty.

That's it, Gemma thought. Now he will be exhumed. They'll put up a screen. The remains will be dug up, put into a bag and taken away. There'll be nothing to see and we can go back to the hotel. It's late afternoon. When will Anna get her sleep?

But it didn't end like that. Other figures began to arrive. She saw a man in denim carrying a camera and another with a microphone. They commandeered a space on the edge of the yard and began to set up, checking levels, counting in that ridiculous way of theirs. The reporter was talking to Franck, meeting Anna, making notes. Then he seemed to vanish for a while before suddenly reappearing and speaking into a camera that was close to his nose. He stood still when he had finished until someone gave him a signal and he moved away. The crew then took the camera over to Anna, but she put up her hand. 'Non,' she was saying. 'Non.'

They had built a kind of tent over the place where the trough had been. Gemma had been standing on the edges of the scene, now she went over to Anna and suggested that they make a move.

'Are you needed here?' she asked

But she found the old lady resolute. 'I owe it,' she said. 'I owe it to the man I shot. I'd like to wait a little longer. I hope you're not too bored.'

Gemma left the yard and looked down the road. What had been so empty when they arrived was now lined with cars, including two great white vans with satellite dishes. She went back in and told Nathan, then together they warned Anna. 'They have outside broadcast units already. What if the BBC gets here? Everyone will want an interview. If we go now, we can vanish.'

Anna shook her head. A kind of determination had spread across her features. 'I'll hate it, but I'll do it. It gives me a chance to apologise for what I did. Perhaps someone from his family will see the piece. He may have had grandchildren.'

They got back to the hotel at 7pm, only after Gemma had insisted on tearing Anna away from the yard. She had brooked no arguments. 'She is an old lady,' she told them in English. 'She's been here all day. She needs rest.'

They'd let her go. Nathan had gone for the car and Gemma had walked Anna to the edge of the road to wait, holding her arm, conscious they were being filmed, that nearby someone was doing a piece to camera. When Nathan arrived she helped Anna into the car as quickly as she could, making sure her skirt wasn't trapped in the door before closing it. She'd seen such things so many times on TV but she couldn't believe that she was part of it, that as they slowed to pass the gates someone was reaching out a camera to Anna's window, trying to get that final photograph.

'Well, they'll remember your visit,' Gemma told her, leaning forward to do so. But Anna made no response. She was sitting in the front seat, staring ahead of her, her shoulders hunched, her stick clasped in her hand.

Chapter Twenty-Six

Anna looked out of the windscreen at the horizontal evening light spilling across the landscape and felt a sense of release. They were driving downhill. Soon they would be leaving the bocage country and crossing the plain, heading back to the hotel. She'd walked this way, cycled this way, driven a horse and cart up and down this same road. Once she'd been young; once that young self had been unreachable. Now she was joining herself up, like Humpty Dumpty, putting the pieces back together, becoming whole.

There were still regrets. If only she had paused before she shot him. If only she had looked at her Gestapo officer first and let him speak. She should have known he wasn't there to harm her, that he was no threat. If he was finally rounding her up, knowing what she was, he would surely have sent someone else to fetch her in. She should have thought first, shot later.

When she had been younger still, before she took her first communion, the priest had talked about sins without forgiveness. She'd wondered what they were, who had the list. She'd been for a time frightened that she had already committed one of these sins without knowing it.

How innocent I was, she thought. How innocent we all were. Now I know what the priest meant. But it's not about God. It's about us, and even today I cannot wholly forgive myself for what I did to him.

It felt right to have been there in the village, right to have had the body exhumed, right to have said what she said in the TV interview. It had been an act of contrition on her part, forced against the grain of the questions, insisted on in the face of an interviewer who had wanted to glorify in the act.

Tomorrow they would go to the beach and put all this behind them. It was a promise she had made and she wanted to keep it. But first she had to get through the rest of today.

The light was forensically clear as the sun sank lower. It had been good meeting Franck again, but she hadn't liked all that praise. He had always admired her with that small boy's adoration of anyone who treats him as an adult and takes him seriously. But if she was pleased to have kept faith with the man she killed, why at this moment did she feel such a sense of emptiness inside her?

She wondered if, quite unconsciously, she had just done the one thing that she had been meaning to do ever since: make amends, pay the visit, make sure he got the burial he deserved. And beyond that? What was beyond that? Was there anything else that needed her to do it?

She asked herself the question and no immediate answer came to her, but there was something else. It was as if a new voice was calling to her, one she hadn't heard before, an insistent voice that she might have to listen to one day. But not now. She was too tired. She pushed it away.

They had already turned. They were going back to the channel and soon they would be going home, back to her family, back to a house that was too big for her, back to the real possibility of being put into a home. Even if she hadn't known it was a mission, it had now been accomplished. Even if she hadn't known, in all the years of self-contempt and denial, that this was what she wanted to do, the thing was now done. It had been put right as far as it was within her power to do so. *Mission accomplished.* Were there any sadder words in the English language?

She'd heard Gemma's question but didn't want to talk because there was nothing to say. She felt empty and she would keep that feeling to herself. She also felt her own tiredness, wanted to sleep.

But sleep hadn't been possible.

The hotel knew about it. The man on reception, when she collected her key, congratulated her. People in the dining room peered at her then whispered to their neighbours. Someone sent over a bottle of wine. She scanned round to see who it was and saw a startlingly young man bow his head to her and raise a glass. She raised her glass back.

She ate because she was hungry, ate with an appetite she didn't know she had, first scallops, then bœuf bourguignon, after that a slice of lemon tart. Nathan was keeping her glass full, urging her to drink so that she would sleep, explaining that it would be bad manners to leave any of a bottle of wine that had been so kindly sent to their table.

Then the waiter came over and excused himself but they had come up with a name for the man in the grave. Did Madame know that he had been a certain Major Hans-Peter Wagner?

Hans-Peter, such a small boy's name. A picture of a mother bending over her tiny baby and crooning his name came into her mind. She shook it away, reflected that if he had been in the Gestapo he almost certainly had committed many sins without forgiveness. The thought somehow cheered her up. Perhaps the man with the slits in his face, the girl with the shoes pointing downwards, perhaps Maurice. She ordered coffee.

The two young things were quiet but at one point Nathan suddenly said, 'I've been working it out. He may have saved your life but he was trying to use you simply to stay alive. No one can blame you. Franck certainly didn't.'

At the end of the meal she pushed her wine glass away.

'Finish the bottle between you,' she ordered, 'That's me done. I need my sleep. Tomorrow,' she reminded them, 'we go to the beach.'

She'd been glad when Gemma had immediately got up and walked with her. She felt unsteady, was grateful for the attention.

Before she put her nightie on and got into bed she looked at herself, naked, in the bathroom mirror, looked at what age had done to her, noted her sagging breasts, the way her stomach had developed folds, saw the way the muscles in her arms had turned to knotted string. Only her pubic hair was white-flecked and strangely luxuriant.

Major Hans-Peter Wagner, I always thought you must have fancied me a little. Well, you should see me now.

The next morning she had woken to a knock on the door. It had pulled her from dreams that had seemed so real. Their horror was vivid, their detail immediately forgotten. The knocking was insistent and there was Gemma's voice to go with it, saying something about breakfast and not much time. She must have been sleeping deeply, sleeping later than she would at home. She shouted at the door and staggered out of her bed, got ready as quickly as she could which wasn't quickly at all.

There was no one outside the door when she finally opened it. They hadn't waited for her. She made sure that her door was locked and set off along the corridor.

They were in the dining room, sitting to one side. The moment they saw her they waved her over. Only one other couple lingered over their breakfast. Was she too late? She hoped someone would bring her coffee. Her mouth was dry after the gift of wine.

She sat down and immediately a waiter came over. She apologised for being late and he said nothing was too much trouble. He'd made a fresh pot of coffee when he'd see her coming into the room. He bustled away and came back with the morning papers.

'I thought you might like to see,' he explained. 'If I know them they will soon trace you to this hotel.'

She flicked one of the front pages over and found a photograph of herself. Was she really second page news? Nathan picked up another. Gemma leafed through a third and gasped when she found a picture of herself and Anna crossing the road.

'You are everywhere. On the front and the inside pages. I wonder if they covered this back in England?' she asked.

'So much fuss.' Anna pushed the papers away, not wanting to read any of it. 'There can't be that much real news. Anyway, it's all over. Major Wagner will be properly buried and we can go to the seaside. Nathan,' she asked. 'could you get me a croissant and a bowl of fruit salad if there is any left?'

She was determined to go to the coast. She needed to think, to interrogate her own feelings, and there was something comforting and timeless about sitting on a beach watching the waves, listening to their eternal conversation.

She ate the croissant and accepted more coffee. Then she was conscious that the receptionist was hovering. She looked up at him.

'Madame, a Monsieur Manchot has been in touch. He was wondering if you could call in at the museum. He says he has information that will interest you.'

She looked out of the window. The sun was shining. It was another hot day. She wouldn't be put off. 'Tomorrow,' she said. 'Ask him if we can come tomorrow.'

She wanted the smell of the sea in her nostrils. She wanted a reminder of childhood summer holidays, of a time before responsibility. Monsieur Manchot could wait.

'Get your togs,' she told Gemma and Nathan. 'We'll make a dash for it.'

They'd gone to Arromanches where they could look across at the remnants of the Mulberry Harbour. Gemma had suggested she sit on a towel but Nathan had borrowed some euros and come back to the car with a single deck chair and a stick-it-in-the-sand sunshade which he carried onto the beach. Anna followed with her stick, Gemma brought up the rear with a pile of towels. Nathan found a place for Anna on the stretch of dry sand under the wall, made sure she was comfortable, then changed and ran to the edge of the sea.

Anna sat under the sunshade and looked across the sloping surface of the sand to the horizontal line of the sea. Nathan had out-run Gemma and reached the water first, but then he had hesitated whilst Gemma had ploughed straight in. It was a shallow beach and she had to wade out a long way before she could start to swim. Anna noticed that Nathan lifted his body as he went in deeper, jumping clear of the little waves, then he too was swimming, overtaking Gemma, heading out in a straight line until he was out of sight.

Anna looked round her. The schools hadn't yet broken up for the summer. There were only pre-school children, shrieking round the curled up water as it rushed in, mothers standing close, watching for too big waves. Most of the beach was occupied by the recently retired, the silver-headed, heavy-waisted brigade. The men were in baggy shorts, the women in full swimsuits, hair tied back. A few swam, most didn't. Nathan, she noticed, was coming back in, standing up in the water and holding something imaginary above his head, his eyes on the shoreline, wading in as quickly as he could go. She could see that he was finding it hard work, pushing against the water, and wondered if anything was wrong. But then when he reached the shore he suddenly went to ground, lay flat on the beach and looked along an imaginary rifle. She knew that he was seeing what it must have been like on the beaches for the men wading in against the guns the morning after she had shot Pierre.

Nathan rolled over, got himself up and went back into the water to wash off the sand. Gemma was quickly at his side and Anna watched them coming up the beach, leaning in together, talking. Nathan's face was pulled thinner by the mass of his wet hair and Gemma's plait, still intact, was being squeezed to get rid of the water. Anna felt a surge of affection for her companions.

And there it was again, this new voice fighting for her attention, as irritating as a memory you can't quite place.

Perhaps it had been there for a long time, unable to be heard above the cacophony of her guilt. It was still indistinct, uncertain, like the fluttering of her own heart. Again she pushed it away.

They came up to her, found towels and flopped on the sand, their young bodies such a contrast to her own. She let her eyes linger along Nathan's legs where the wetness had matted the fine leg-hairs, pulling them into little dark arrows that pointed to his feet. Even as she watched, the sun began to dry them out and snap them apart. His skin was smooth. He was more muscular than she had imagined. Gemma was pale skinned in her bikini, more likely to burn.

The sea was moving away from them, exposing some mud banks and a rash of small rocks. It seemed like a message.

The next day she presented herself at Memorial's information desk. Nathan and Gemma had dropped her off and gone into the city. They had arranged to meet her in two hours' time. The moment she gave her name she sensed a flurry of excitement, a quickening of the pace as Monsieur Manchot was sent for. He came quickly, fussily, holding his attaché case and gesturing.

'Well,' he said, the moment he reached her. 'I had rather thought you wanted to stay anonymous, but your picture is everywhere and I have had so many requests for information about you.'

He was walking at her side, seemingly impatient at her slowness.

'I hope you haven't told them anything,' she said.

'What could I tell them? What have you told me?' he asked by way of an answer. 'Your code name, and your real first name, that is all. And so far I have denied all knowledge of you. They are much more likely to find out from the hotel. When I phoned last night and described you, the man on reception said he thought I must mean Mrs Devonshire.'

'How did you describe me?'

He suddenly seemed flustered.

'Was it my beauty or my age you focussed on?' She stopped herself in time. 'Don't answer that,' she told him. 'I am conspicuous because I am travelling with two young people. Let's leave it at that.'

They had reached the same room as before. Coffee was waiting. Monsieur Manchot sat down and opened his case, doing everything slowly and deliberately, taking papers out and arranging them on the desk in front of him.

'You have information?' Anna said, prompting him.

He cleared his throat and referred to a page of notes before beginning. 'I have been through the SOE files. We have some duplicates here. It is an arrangement that we find very convenient, although it took some negotiating, I can tell you. By reading the files I have been able to trace the histories of some of those you were in contact with.'

He looked up from his notes. 'Okay so far?'

He is seeing only my age and going slowly because he thinks I cannot follow what he's saying, she thought. She wanted to hurry him up. Fear was growing somewhere inside her. Did she really want to know the truth about Pierre?

'Henri. Let's start with Henri, code named Racine,' said Monsieur Manchot. 'He survived the war, became a Mayor. He died in 1987. He had two children, one of whom lives in New York.'

She nodded, wondered about his indomitable aunt.

'Marcel, I think you knew a man called Marcel.' Monsieur Manchot looked up at her and she nodded, preparing herself. 'He was not so fortunate. He disappeared before D-Day. His wife never saw him again.'

'So what happened to him?' she asked.

Monsieur Manchot shrugged his shoulders. 'We do not know. The supposition is that he was betrayed and killed but they never found a body. His name is on the resistance memorial. You can draw your own conclusions.'

320

She nodded. It was as she expected. Had he betrayed himself or had he been betrayed?

'Which brings us to the man you knew as Pierre.'

This was it.

'We have to admit that when we labelled the photograph you saw we were basing our assumptions on local information. The corpse had no dog tags and the finding of his body was something of a sensation. One of his group identified him, told us he was a British agent, but called him simply 'The Captain'. He could give us no other name for him. Until I spoke to you we had not successfully cross-checked identification from the SOE records. You gave us that link, told us he was code named Pierre, and we have followed up that information.'

His eyes were shining. This is what his life is like, she thought. He searches for information, follows patterns, dryly seeks out truth.

'With your information we found his file. Did you know that Pierre was originally from Canada, from near Quebec?'

'What was his name?' Anna suddenly asked, 'I mean his real name.'

Monsieur Manchot looked up from his notes. 'Well it appears he had more than one, even before he joined SOE.'

She was shocked. She found herself repeating the words, 'More than one?'

'He had married twice, once in Canada under the name of Pierre Laval and once in England under the name of Peter Levy. Both wives survived him.'

She absorbed this startling information. Pierre must be his real name, in which case he had broken every rule by using it as a code name. But, against that, in calling himself Pierre he had at least told her something that was true. Oh God, she thought, I made two women into widows!

This sudden deluge of information after a silence of sixty years was too much for Anna, but Monsieur Manchot wasn't finished.

'With your information I have also found his German file,' he announced. She watched as he opened his briefcase and took out a thin green file which he placed on the table in front of her. He performed the act like a conjuror and looked for her reaction as if she was an audience he was determined to wow.

She sensed that this was his last trick because the moment he had produced the file he placed the briefcase back on the floor and lined it up with the side of the table.

She stared at the file. It was nothing more than a folded piece of green card. It had been much handled and in the process had lost its shine. The edges had frayed, and the bottom corner on the fold was missing. She could imagine how many times it had been pushed into a box or a filing cabinet and pulled out again. There was a name on the file and that confused her because it wasn't the right name.

'Go on,' urged Monsieur Manchot, 'open it up. I've found it. I want you to read it.'

He's proud of himself, Anna thought, and he has every right to be. She saw the excitement in his eyes. For him this was history coming to life, a rare affirmation that what he did as an archivist mattered.

But for Anna this battered green file was too important to be hurried. It was just possible that its contents could vindicate that awful decision forced on her because thousands of paratroopers were already on their way. It had been the turning point of her war, the tipping point of her whole life.

Was her German up to this? She reached forward, flicked open the cover and began to read.

But making the translation was too much for her. She found her head was reeling so she pushed the file away.

'Tell me, please,' she asked. 'I need to know.'

Monsieur Manchot nodded. He was clearly pleased to be asked. He looked down at his notes.

'The Germans called him by a third name.'

She was listening again. So he was a double agent. Might

her judgement, after all, prove to have been correct?

'They called him Paul Laput. They caught him in Poland when they heard his transmissions. I must tell you that I do like the German files, they always kept such meticulous records. They caught him and interrogated him. The record is quite clear that he promised to spy for them if they let him go.'

'So I was right,' she said. 'He was spying for the enemy.'

Monsieur Manchot frowned. 'In a way,' he said. 'In his way.'

'What do you mean?'

'As I was saying, the German records are excellent and, amongst other things, they record his controller's frustration. Pierre, I will call him that to save any confusion, only passed them very little information and he is full of excuses: he has trouble with his radio set; he mislays a crystal; he becomes ill. It's all in the file.'

Pierre had told her about Poland, shouting it through the night. So that part of his story was true as well. He had allowed himself to be turned because it was better than dying. Perhaps everything else he had told her that night was correct. Perhaps SOE did know all about his double role. Perhaps he had been playing a dangerous double game of disinformation.

No, that couldn't be true or George would have been known, wouldn't have made that comment. Her mind was running away with itself. She needed to keep to the facts.

'And his English records. What do they say about him?' she asked quickly.

Monsieur Manchot smiled. 'About the same really. They had real doubts about using him in France because he had been so ineffective in Poland. In the end it was just a matter of the volume of the work that had to be done. Do you know they only sent him out because they had such confidence in you and in your ability to manage him?'

She had to ask him to repeat the last sentence. Even then she didn't take it in.

So Pierre was neither wholly truthful nor completely

dishonest, neither hero agent nor sinister double. He was a beautiful young man who didn't even try to be whole. Two wives and herself! There were probably more women as well. Who did he spend time with in Poland? Whilst she had grafted, he had played at it. Did that mean he was harmless? He was careless with women, careless with information, careless with money. He was a clever linguist with a liking for danger, a man born to deceive, quite unprincipled – no wonder he had passed all those SOE tests that came with the training.

She looked around the room, trying to clear her head of all that she had heard. It was too much, too overwhelming. She had fallen for the kind of man every part of her upbringing had warned her against. Because she was so passionate about her work she had presumed that Pierre would be the same, fighting for his masters as fiercely as she had fought for hers. Even if he had heard the D-day information, she realised, he wouldn't have been particularly interested, would never have informed the Germans. She could have let him live and it wouldn't have mattered.

She had killed two people and in each case it had been unnecessary.

Monsieur Manchot cleared his throat. 'You asked me two days ago if I thought you had made the right choice.'

She waved the question away. She was already ashamed of it.

'And I wouldn't answer. Well now I must.'

She stared at him.

'D-day was a close run thing. Had Pierre been the active, convinced, double-agent you thought he was, had he betrayed the invasion, had the Panzers been brought up earlier, the consequences would have been extreme. Certainly, you did the right thing. The only possible action in the circumstances.'

She looked away. The tears were starting again. She was being exonerated.

Monsieur Manchot was saying something else and she

knew she must concentrate, but her mind was elsewhere.

'I'm sorry,' she said, 'you will have to repeat that.'

'I am sorry to say that we have no copy of your own file. If you give me your address in England I will try to send you a copy. Would you like that?'

She nodded and thought, why not? She could imagine what it would say.

They got back to Anna's house late in the afternoon two days later. It had started raining in France and anyway, Anna had nothing left to do there. 'Why can't she spend a day in bed recovering, getting up for dinner and spending the rest of the day sleeping?' Nathan had asked.

'So that we can do the same? Is that what you're thinking?' Gemma had laughed back at him.

Nathan looked hurt, then laughed it off. 'Of course,' he'd said. 'Why not?'

Why not indeed?

He'd changed whilst they had been in France and Gemma liked him better. He seemed less strained but had in fact had grown more serious, reading and re-reading everything about Anna in the French papers, ordering a book about the SOE from Amazon. The bond between him and Anna was stronger. Then there had been that charge through the water with his imaginary rifle, the flinging himself down in the sand. 'It doesn't seem real, any of this,' he said to Gemma. 'I don't seem real.'

On the ferry he bought all the English papers, pointed out they were also carrying Anna's story.

Would he revert now that they were back home? Gemma hoped not.

They reached Anna's house at two o'clock. It was the last time that the wall-mounted sundial could show before the sun left the front of the house.

Nathan parked the car in front of the garage and Anna got slowly out of the front seat and looked around her. Gemma was worried about her. She had been silent for much of the journey and whilst they had gloried in her war history she had seemed bored – no, that wasn't the right word – seemed saddened by it. She also seemed weaker. She gave Gemma the key and let her turn off the house alarm, a job she had always done herself. When she reached her sitting room she just sat down in the chair and didn't move.

'Are you glad to be back?' Gemma had asked. She received no answer. Perhaps the old lady hadn't heard the question.

Nathan went out and bought everything Anna needed and then they left her on her own. They enjoyed walking away at their own pace, first to Nathan's house and then to her own. When Nathan made a show of leaving her she told him that wasn't necessary and that her mother would understand.

The next day Anna seemed brighter. Whilst Nathan mowed the lawn Gemma opened windows to let some air into the house and picked yellow roses to go on the chest in the hall. Until they went to University they were the old lady's carers. She'd offered them a bedroom in the house whenever they wanted to stay over.

Gemma was standing in the dining room when she saw two vehicles pull into the drive, following each other in as if they had been driving in convoy. One was a 4x4 with pro-hunting propaganda clearly visible through the back window. The other was a wide, red, old Jaguar. Gemma recognised it from the Morse series her mother watched religiously whenever it was repeated.

Three people got out. They were clearly siblings. They had the same round faces, the same assured way of standing. Gemma recognised them at once. She'd dusted their father's photograph often enough. These were Anna's children. One of her sons was thin, the other fat. Their sister was taller than either of the boys. They walked towards the front door as if it was theirs. They rang the bell fiercely.

Anna's voice came through from the sitting room. 'Gemma, will you see who that is, please?'

She went slowly to the front door, pulled back the bolt and opened it.

Seeing her there was doing something to their faces. They weren't surprised so much as disgusted. A kind of joint sneer went round the group. It gave her time to ask what they wanted, but before she had completed the sentence they were pushing past her. How rude, Gemma thought. They are just as I imagined them.

She wondered if she should follow them into the sitting room but they had closed the door, leaving her in the corridor. She wondered what she should do now. Was Anna safe with them? What pretext could she use to follow them in? She knew none of them lived close by so they must have been on the road for some time. Perhaps they would like a drink. She knocked on the door and opened it without waiting for an answer, walked into the room she had cleaned that morning. It was looking smart. They could have no complaints.

Anna was sitting upright in her chair and looking rather restrained. Her daughter was standing over her, blocking one of the windows. The thin brother was in the tall chair and the larger one sprawled on the settee.

They all turned round and looked at her as soon as she walked in. She had the impression that someone had been talking and had immediately stopped. There was a hint of tension in the room.

'Ah, Gemma,' said Anna. 'Come and meet my family.' She introduced them in turn. 'This is Alistair (thin one), that's Colin (fat one), and here is my daughter, Heather.'

Gemma looked at each of them in turn and made an effort to smile. 'Hello,' she said, then added by way of explanation, 'Nathan's out in the garden. Shall I fetch him in to meet you all? I actually came in to see if you wanted any coffee.'

The overweight son Colin sat up and looked at her. 'Yes to coffee. No to Nathan,' he said. 'If you would bring us some coffee that would be lovely but then we would like to be left on our own.' He finished his orders with a smile that he switched on and off almost instantly. It was meant to be endearing but only succeeded in being patronising.

Gemma stood her ground, looked towards Anna, realised that by walking into the room she had put her into a bind, forced her to make a choice.

'Fetch Nathan please, Gemma, and then make coffee for six,' Anna said.

As Gemma left the room she heard Anna say quietly but firmly to her son, 'Colin, most of this is still my house. I will say who comes into my room and who does not.'

Gemma closed the door and knew she must fetch Nathan soon, but she didn't move away at once and so heard Heather say, 'They're gold diggers. Can't you see that, Mother? They're after your fortune. You're getting weaker. They've virtually kidnapped you, taken you to France on a holiday they no doubt demanded. Can't you see you are being used?'

'They look after me. And what precisely are you three after,' Gemma heard Anna ask, 'if not my money?'

'Your dignity, your respect…' It must be Alistair talking. It was a different voice. Gemma filled the kettle, switched it on, then hurried off to fetch Nathan.

She found him in the top corner emptying the grass. The moment she told him what had happened and what she had overheard he switched the lawnmower off and followed her into the house. 'We have no part in this,' he told her as she made the coffee. 'It's up to Anna if she wants us there.'

'But gold diggers!' the label had horrified Gemma. She put everything on the tray and carried it across the hall. Nathan opened the door and she went through towards the still cluttered central table. It was within Colin's reach but he did nothing to help her find room for the tray. Nathan had to follow her in and move the magazines to one side.

The room was full of a hostile silence. Gemma poured the coffee, passed round milk and sugar, got ready to leave. She was determined not to give the impression of being anything but what she was: a girl doing a holiday job. Nathan was about to follow her out when she turned in the doorway and said, 'This, by the way, is Nathan. I'm sorry, I should have introduced him when we came in.'

They looked up at her then.

Colin said, 'We guessed as much. You must be the dope smoker.'

Gemma took Nathan's arm in case he reacted. He didn't.

Heather had clearly been waiting for them to be gone but the effort of staying silent was too much. She turned to face them and said slowly, 'I don't know what you were both thinking about, swanning off to France with an old lady. When I phoned and couldn't get an answer I thought Mother must have fallen over in the house. For all I knew she could have been dying. I was worried sick until I saw all that in the papers. Don't you think you should have let us know?'

Gemma felt Nathan grow tense at her side and, nervous about what his love of the old lady might lead him to say, she spoke herself.

'I'm sorry you were worried,' she said, 'but Mrs Devonshire made the plans. I knew she had just changed the locks. I rather thought she didn't want you to know what she was doing. It was up to her.'

'For Christ's sake, she's an old lady,' Colin exploded. 'She needs looking after. If either of you had the slightest capacity to think, you would have seen that.'

Gemma gripped more tightly on to Nathan to stop him reacting, but it was too late.

'She's a bit more than an old lady,' Nathan said very quietly. 'I wish you had seen the respect she was accorded over there, in France. What she did in the war was remarkable. If you'd read it all properly you wouldn't be saying these things. Now we'll leave you to talk. Come on Gem.'

They turned to leave the room.

But Colin interrupted their leaving. 'I read it,' he said. 'It was faked, wasn't it, and you and our undistinguished press fell for it. If you'd known our mother when she was younger you'd know she could never have lifted that trough on her own, let alone dragged the body in the way described. She's been filling your head with stories, trying to impress you. She watched that Gestapo man being buried. She can't possibly have buried him herself.'

Immediately Colin stopped Alistair began talking, as if he was trying to top what his younger brother had said. 'Our dad was the real war hero. That's his photo over there. Normandy to Berlin without a scratch on him.' He paused. 'You say you're her carers but I imagine in September you'll be off. In my day you wouldn't have got to University but now everyone goes, so I expect you'll both scrape in.' He let that gibe settle then added, 'Who'll look after her when you disappear? It'll be back to us.'

Then there was another voice: Heather's. Only this time it sounded different, less bombastic, more hurt. 'My brothers are wrong,' she said slowly. 'I think what the papers said is true. I think Mum did do all those things.'

Gemma was astonished. Heather had turned to face her brothers, as if to prevent any interruptions. 'When we were little she never claimed anything about her time in the war. There was only that extraordinary incident of the milking, do you remember? She had plenty of opportunity. Why start to invent a glorious past now? It doesn't make any sense.'

Then she turned back to look at Gemma. 'She left us out,' Heather continued. 'She told you everything about this fascinating and important part of her life but not us, her own children. She left us out completely. Just think about that. Just imagine how that makes me feel.'

Gemma had heard every word, but standing by the door she could both watch Heather and look past her, to where Anna sat in her chair by the fire place. And she saw a sudden change in the old lady's face, a grimace, as if she was in pain. Was all this too much for her? She seemed more frail, less alive. No one else was looking at Anna. Gemma took a step forward, then the face relaxed and went back to normal, so she stayed where she was.

Heather was talking again. 'And there is something else you need to know,' she added, reverting to type. 'On one of my trips to the house I bumped into a lad called Risco. He told me all about how you two overused her credit card, robbing her blind, and about how my mother shot him. At first he didn't want anyone else to know, but now you have made my mother famous he's telling everyone. He's even been to the police. I expect they will have a say in whatever happens next.'

Chapter Twenty-Seven

Heather supporting her, standing up against her brothers and stating that what was in the papers had been true. Heather talking of her own hurt. At that moment Anna heard the voice that had been whispering to her, heard it loudly and clearly, like tuning in one of the old radios. At last she understood what the voice had been trying to tell her.

All this time she had been looking the wrong way. It hadn't been about Pierre and Major Wagner. Her guilt must have attached itself to them and her terrible sense of wrongness had prevented her from seeing more important things. The resolution of her past in Normandy had only made room for other regrets. Edith Piaf was wrong, so was Sinatra. You could regret for ever.

Pierre and Major Wagner belonged to wartime, were excusable because of the war. The rest of the world had already absolved her of culpability. She had even begun to forgive herself.

Now there was this new, painful thought. She wasn't the only woman to marry the wrong man, to have difficulties in her life. In spite of that, every mother's first duty is to love her children. Every child needs to feel loved. Perhaps that was her real culpability: not to have loved them. The excuses crowded in but she pushed them to one side. I was too concerned with myself and I never found a way to make real contact with them, she thought. If they act as they do now, whose fault is that?

Heather's hurt had been a way of reaching out. Anna knew she should have said something at that moment, but the shock of her own realisation had been too great, and later on there had been no chance. The three of them had left soon afterwards, arguing amongst themselves.

Instead she had talked to Gemma and, strangely, Gemma had understood. She had an old head, that one. When Nathan was finishing the lawn and Gemma was collecting coffee cups Anna had put her thoughts into words.

'I was wrong not to have told them,' she said. 'I thought it was embarrassment. It wasn't. It was a kind of vanity. I should have talked about my past. Perhaps then they might have told me things about themselves. We might have been closer.'

Gemma nodded.

Two days later the police came to the house.

Anna gave them the gun at once, and the rest of the bullets. She told them she would plead guilty to not having a licence. They were so young the pair of them, no more than Gemma's age. They seemed to her like a boy and a girl, dressed up in summer uniform with all kinds of equipment that clanked when they stood up. Yet they handled her gun with a kind of reverence.

'Is this the gun you used in France?' the girl asked her.

'Yes.'

They put it in a polythene bag.

'Didn't I merit an armed response unit?' she asked them.

'Not if you're over eighty,' they told her. 'It's a question of resources.'

They asked her about Risco and she described his visit and what had led up to it. In the middle of the story she remembered the dope, went and fetched it and handed that over too. It merited another polythene bag. She told them the gun had been hidden from Nathan and Gemma, took full responsibility.

They wrote down every word and then read it back to her. She signed the statement.

'Do I come now?' she asked them.

'No, but don't leave the country in the meantime.'

She waited weeks and nothing happened. She was sorry to

have lost the gun. It could have been her way out when going into a home was next threatened.

The two young things worked on the garden, collected their A Level results and brought them to show her. The grades were good enough and they confirmed their University places.

Throughout the summer they often slept over at her house using the spare bedroom. She asked no questions, was glad of the company. Then the police returned and told her there would be no prosecution.

'But I shot him,' she said, not understanding.

It was the young man who answered. 'It was decided that it wasn't in the public interest to put you in court,' he explained.

They went away and Anna had to confess that she was relieved. She'd had enough of publicity. And she had another plan in place, one that would leave Gemma and Nathan in the clear. Everything was still in her hands, just. She was determined that it would stay that way, but the timing had to be right.

Two days later a large envelope with a French stamp arrived. In it Anna found a thin brown file. Monsieur Manchot had been as good as his word and sent her records. Anna picked up the file. She opened the brown cover and counted five sheets of paper.

She read slowly. The file held details about her recruitment, about her training, about the decision to deploy her. As she read she picked up from it all the sense of desperate men trying to make something work, taking risks by using women as agents and arguing about it. Then she came to the last page, the summary written by the man who had debriefed her, the man she had called George.

Agent Marie-Claire Cardon was landed in Normandy, France, by plane in February 1944 to work alongside local resistance groups as a radio operator, collecting information about gun placements and troop movements as well as taking part in acts of sabotage. She carried out her duties for seven months with outstanding courage and devotion to duty. Her work involved extensive travelling in the area. She had to pass numerous enemy controls, sometimes on a bicycle with maps hidden in her handlebars. She personally organised a number of receptions in the area. She also took part in a sabotage operation against the Caen to Bayeux railway. In all this time she maintained the integrity of her network and personally eliminated an operative she had good reason to suspect might compromise their activities. Her unit took part in key preparation work for the Normandy landings and afterwards, until the breakout, she continued to map and report on troop movements, often cycling alone through areas of intense military activity. She was one of our most reliable and effective operatives. She was offered a military decoration but she refused, preferring to retire with anonymity into civilian life.

She put the piece of paper down and closed the file. She found she was wondering more and more about her state of mind when she left France. The amateurs who ran the SOE were trying to defeat Hitler. They'd had no duty of care for those who had been pushed too hard, had seen too much. She had survived when others hadn't, was still alive. That had been enough for them. They knew about shell-shock, didn't understand Post Traumatic Stress Disorder.

She flipped the file open again and re-read the summary. In re-reading it she realised that she had just enough vanity to wish the young things to see it. She might send a copy to Heather by way of an apology.

and personally eliminated an operative she had good reason to suspect might compromise their activities

It was very close to absolution.

She had a month until the young things would leave.

She knew she must make the most of it but sensed that they were already drifting away, wrapped up in each other and in thoughts of University. Then they would go with many promises she knew they meant to keep.

Her family phoned her and paid her visits, but never singly. She wondered if she should say something to them, but there was no opening and the basic situation hadn't changed. Any softening by her and the moves to put her into a home would start immediately. She saw the way they looked at the house and its quick deterioration now that she did all the cleaning herself. No doubt they got reports from James who once again took her shopping and to the bank. He would say she was slowing down. What were they waiting for? Alistair still needed money. They knew she couldn't cope on her own for long. She suspected it was the stories in the paper. They didn't want headlines when they made her go into a home. They needed to allow enough time to go by so that people had forgotten. My past, she often thought, has come unexpectedly to save my present. What it cannot do is give me a future.

Then autumn flamed the topmost leaves of the red oak tree on the small green space just beyond Anna's front gate. Day by day she watched the colour spread downwards until the small tree glowed orange in the clotted October air. One night a wind plucked at the tiles on her roof. The next morning when she looked out she saw stripped dark branches and thin metallic twigs sticking out above grass that was coloured like sunset with fallen leaves. Gemma and Nathan had gone to University and Anna knew that she could no longer manage to live in her wonderful house. She was slowing down with the cold and the inactivity. She was feeling even older.

Throughout the rest of October she did very little. When Gemma and Nathan came back home for a weekend to get their washing done, she saw in their faces that they were no longer quite the same people they had been in the summer. University was taking them over, giving them fresh horizons, pulling them further away from her. But they bustled round and put the house back into order, buying her a little more time.

November started off unseasonably warm. The roses put out another flush of flowers. Weeds sprouted everywhere in the borders Nathan had cleared so assiduously during the summer. Fallen leaves curled up and dried in the thin persistent sunshine, so that the light breeze rattled them across the steps and the paving slabs. Lying in her bed, resting the many aches in her body, she could hear the sound like a far off murmur, a kind of incantation, calling her. Two deaths were waiting for a third. She just hoped her family would leave her alone until the right moment came.

She had made her preparations. The bottle of brandy was already by the pond, just tucked in against the stalks of Black Eyed Susan. She had searched for and found the green mattress which had once been part of the hammock; had pulled it out of the summer house, fighting to get it free from the tangle of deck chairs. Afterwards she had been so exhausted from the struggle that she had left it overnight on the grass. Only two days later had she felt up to dragging it across the lawn and lining it up against the wet slabs, just within reach of the brandy, out of view from the house. When the time came for her to lie down, she wanted to be as comfortable as possible.

She worried about putting it off much longer, but conditions had to be right. If it was to be her last act she must be able to carry it out. A fall would be fatal now, not if it killed her but if it didn't. If she broke her hip she would have to go to hospital, be mended and then be assessed. No assessment of her needs would let her go back home and live on her own. Her children would return to see her with triumphant 'told you so' looks splattered across their Ronnie-like faces. She couldn't bear that. The waiting began to make her impatient.

She had always meant to write something down: a few thoughts, an explanation about her will, even perhaps an account of what happened to her in the war and afterwards. Several times she had come close to starting her written statement but each time she had desisted before beginning. I want to tell them everything or nothing, she had thought. There isn't time to tell everything and anyway, who are 'they'? We like to imagine we are so important, she thought, but once we die we are only papers to be tidied away, and no one has time to read anything we write. If I am not going to be there to watch them read it, what good is a statement to me? She was standing at her window with these thoughts, watching the blackbirds in the crab apple tree, noticing that the grass was still growing.

In the end she'd written her children a letter, explaining her wish to keep her destiny absolutely under her control. She'd stated clearly that in no way had they driven her to this final act. She'd apologised for not having been a better mother.

Then the change happened as the weather man had predicted. The next wind would come from the Arctic. England would have a cold snap. Frost was guaranteed. There was a danger of icy roads in the morning.

It was time. She'd keep her independence to the last.

She had already eaten her supper when she heard the weather forecast, and she had a strange tussle with herself about whether to wash up afterwards or just to leave the plate and cup where they were on the table by her chair. In the end she carried them through to the kitchen but didn't wash them up, just left them by the sink for someone else, whoever that might be.

Her nightie was already downstairs. It was the one that Heather had given her two years previously, unworn, sufficiently opaque and sufficiently thin. She took it, still in its wrapping paper, from the drawer in her desk.

She put the note for her children on the chest in the hall,

propping it up against the brass dish.

It had to be dark. It had to be cold enough. At nine o'clock, which was normally her bedtime, she made sure that the front door was unlocked, then took a last look round before switching off the light and walking outside. She didn't close the back door behind her but marched incredibly slowly straight up the dark garden, wheeling her walking frame across the frost-tinted grass until she reached the pond. There she paused. Her last walk and she was badly out of breath.

Before she took off her clothes she reached down carefully for the bottle of brandy, still clutching her walking frame. Then, when she had located the liquor amongst the now blackened stems, she painfully straightened herself up. She was already cold and would soon be colder. Lifting the bottle to her mouth she took a long swig of the brandy, allowing it to glug right down her throat. It wasn't what Ronnie would have called good brandy but at least it made her feel warm inside. She wondered whether to put the cap back on but decided not to. Instead she balanced the bottle on the wall before she began to strip.

It was difficult, standing up and keeping balanced, especially difficult in the darkness. She part leant against the low wall as she took off her jersey, unbuttoning it and slipping it off her arms, shaking herself to make sure it fell. Her skirt she simply unhitched and stepped out of, vaguely pushing it to one side with her foot. The cold was biting into her already. She felt it like a pain, like a recent bruise, and hoped that she had been right in her calculations about its limited ability to hurt her. She knew about hypothermia. It had been part of her training. The cold was her friend; it would take her kindly, sting, then the warmth would spread as all feeling left her extremities. That was what they had warned her about. The brandy would help and accelerate the process. She felt for the bottle, took another long swig, found the wall again and balanced the bottle back there.

Next she took off her vest and unpeeled her tights. The moon was rising, close to the full. In its light she could make out her white skinny legs still holding her above the earth. She freed one foot by leaning back against the wall. Her tights were still stuck to the other foot. It would be nice to take them right off, for when someone found her, but it didn't really matter.

Another swig, more warmth inside her as the cold continued to fasten onto her skin. She knew her fingers were beginning to stiffen. She must carry out the next part of the plan or the process of dying would take too long and be unbearable. To make herself carry on she conjured up the faces of the decrepit, heard the murmur of shrill voices saying to her, 'You have to go into a home. There is no escape. Dying with dignity is a myth. Give up, stay warm, hope your mind founders.'

She moved the brandy bottle down onto the grass and propped it up there. Holding onto the frame she took the nightie out of its package and held it out over the pond so that it touched the water. At first it was light in her hands, then grew heavier as the water pulled it down. Holding it by the neck she dipped it in as far she could, then lifted it up and slipped it over her head. The soggy mass of the nylon slapped onto her shoulders and chilled her again so that she was gasping for breath and finding it very difficult to push her arms through against the wet chaffing of the material. As she moved the material down her body the water stung into her already icy skin. Her fingers were now quite numb and the wetness made it all the more difficult to pull the nightie down over her breasts and her bottom.

She had never been so cold, but now at least she was decently clad. It was time to lie down on the mattress.

She let go of the walking frame and pushed it away from her. Then she knelt, making sure her head was near to the brandy bottle. Once she was kneeling she pushed her legs out behind her and lay down on her front.

Funny that she had thought of the mattress. Why had she needed to be comfortable when her skin was shrieking at her, the pain of the cold intensifying? She wondered how long it would take, and when the hurt would reach its own crescendo. Pierre had known what it felt like to die. Major Wagner had experienced it too. Now it was her turn. She shifted round to make herself more comfortable, realised that the mattress itself would insulate her and might slow the process down. Well, it was too late. She reached out again for the brandy bottle and took another mouthful. This time she found it hard to swallow.

To keep her mind off the intense cold she tried to think clearly about what death would be like.

She didn't believe in an afterlife so there would be no glowing line of well-remembered faces waiting to greet her, no walking down a long corridor of light while music played and a choir sang her home. Instead she would simply stop breathing, her heart would stall, her brain, once it was starved of blood and oxygen, would shut down. In that moment the conscious part of her would cease to exist.

The mattress was very thin. She could feel the ground underneath her, so she shifted a little to one side to avoid a stone.

Because there was no God, there would be no judgement. There would be no chance either to apologise again for Major Wagner's death or to seek more details about Pierre. She now felt that human transactions were so complex that notions of right and wrong were only intermittent signs in a shifting, fractured landscape. Failures were passed on. She had been hurt by the war and had therefore failed as a mother. Now her children were as they were.

She would die and there would be nothing, except for that great silence which she would no longer be there to hear. But even as she thought all this she understood that death itself

341

was not an end, that every part of her body had already died many times and been replaced, dissolved to molecules, drifted away, become just another fragment of everything that is.

She was already both seed and stalk, both fresh leaf and autumn coloured fall. She would become the wet soil under the tree and the fox that left its footprint there. She would be in the rain that crumbled the prints' sharpness and in the frost that preserved what was left. She was a part of that great energy that can neither be created nor destroyed.

She had been there when the world began, been gas and matter. She had travelled through space, been frozen deep and magma-heated many times, had attended the birth pangs of her universe and would be there again at its demise, would survive that and be an infinitesimal part of whatever happened next.

What did it matter, ceasing to be Anna? What did it matter that there never was a Marie-Claire? Everything that she had been was already being recycled, taking many forms, just occasionally drifting close to consciousness. When they found her they would cremate her worn out wreck of a body, returning it quickly to the wind. In a few days' time her bodily incarnation could be anywhere.

Either the thinking was successfully distracting her or she was already dying. Her sense of being cold was losing its intensity. Her rigid hands could hardly clutch the bottle as she heaved herself up and took a last drink through numbed lips. Then the bottle slipped out of her hands and fell away from her. She could hear it emptying itself into the grass.

I was a wreck when I came out of the war, she thought, a kind of nothing, hibernating through my middle age. I'm glad right at the end that I came back to life and found my other self. I have learnt too late that life means fighting, that we are meant to struggle. In spite of my decrepitude I've actually enjoyed this summer as much as any other.

When she had lost all feeling in her toes and fingers a

strange illusion of warmth began to spread through her as if the ground she was lying on was suddenly warmer, as if winter had passed in a few hours and summer was back. More time went by in a kind of suspension. She felt better, wonderfully warm, almost too hot, and she wondered whether to take off her nightie to cool herself down. But she remembered that she needed to be decent when they found her, and decided in a vague far-off kind of way that she was too tired and needed to sleep.

The last thing she saw before she closed her eyes and finally let the blackness take her was a full moon wreathed in cloud, sailing across the sky, part of another rhythm, another cycle, always moving, on and onwards...

Coda

Nathan and Gemma weren't invited to Anna's funeral. Indeed, they only heard of her death through Nathan's mother who had read about it in the local paper. Being neither notified nor invited didn't surprise them very much. The family were clearly claiming Anna back as one of their own. During the Christmas holidays, as a mark of respect, they went and sat on her bench and held their own minute of silence, looking out over the view she had loved.

That, they thought, was that. So they were surprised in April to be invited to visit the offices of Wending and Parlow, Solicitors, where they found themselves sitting opposite a man who introduced himself as David Snowden.

'I wonder,' he began, 'if either of you remembers Anna Devonshire?'

'Our old lady,' Gemma said, 'of course we remember.' She leant forward and touched Nathan's hands. Anna's death had shocked him more than it had shocked her. The moment Nathan had found out he had come to visit her at Uni, seemingly distraught.

'She was a great lady,' said Nathan. 'How could we forget?'

'Well,' said the junior partner, 'it seems that she didn't forget you either. Perhaps it would be best,' he explained, 'if I read it in her own words.'

The large mahogany desk in his oak panelled room boasted a leather edged blotter. David Snowden smiled as he extracted a thick brown envelope from underneath the maroon leather and then shook from the envelope a small number of A4 pages folded lengthways. They fell heavily and resisted his fingers as he opened them out. He found the place and coughed before he began to read.

' 'My husband Ronnie's money must go to my children, but

the little money I brought into the marriage, that I inherited from my parents and from my brother, I would like to be shared equally between Gemma Braithwaite and Nathan Bourne.''

Gemma suddenly thought of Heather, knew she must have been furious.

'That means,' David Snowden explained, that once you have given me your details I will be transferring £24,673.19 into each of your accounts.'

'She paid us well for what we did,' Nathan said. 'I never expected anything else.'

'There is more.' David Snowden found another place in the will. "There is also one painting that I particularly care for. It's neither terribly good nor terribly valuable but I want to leave it to Nathan Bourne, as a momento."

David Snowden paused in his reading. 'The painting is over there,' he explained. 'I took it out of the safe and propped it against the wall.'

Nathan was already standing up and moving towards the parcel. Gemma watched as he picked it up and brought it back to the table. Then he quickly peeled off the paper and the bubble wrap before lifting it free. There it was with its foreground of rocks and the great swollen stream pouring between them. There were four trees on the left and one on the right, a blue sky and the wonderful swirl of mountain that faded into pure light as the evening sun began to dip below the horizon, gilding the leaves.

On the left a figure you couldn't quite make out climbed over a stile. In the top right hand corner, snug against the elaborate gilded frame and still lodged there, was the bullet that had gone right through Risco's shoulder.

'That was her trouble, wasn't it?' Nathan said. 'She always was too good a shot.'

Acknowledgements

I must acknowledge my debt to so many people and sources.

I learnt about the activities of those extraordinarily brave women of the SOE from Marcus Binney's book: *The Women Who Lived for Danger* and about what it was like to be a spy from *The Spy Wore Red* by Aline Countess of Romanones. To find out more about Post Traumatic Stress Disorder I read *A War of Nerves* by Ben Shephard.

Phil Kemp from the Yorkshire Air Museum kindly allowed me to clamber around inside the only reconstructed Halifax Bomber in the World. He told me the lipstick story.

An ex-soldier who had served in Bosnia gave me more intimate details about suffering from PTSD.

More and More was sung by Vera Lynn; *That Lovely Weekend* by Dorothy Carless. I heard both songs on a CD called *We'll Meet Again* (Romantic songs of the war years) under the Gift of Music Label.

Then there are those who read early versions of the book and gave me useful feedback. I am indebted to Patrick, Bob, Awen and in particular Jane Austin, as well as to members of the Guppy's Tuesday night group.

Finally there is my wife, Sheila, who corrected every version with a vivid and invariably accurate red pen.

About the Author

Chris Bridge was born in Hull, England in 1947. He studied English and Philosophy at Nottingham University and became a teacher after graduating. He eventually became Headteacher of Huntington School, York, and finished his school career as a National Leader of Education. He has been a regular contributor to poetry magazines and his poems have featured in the winning lists of *Hippocrates* and *Stanza* poetry competitions. *Back Behind Enemy Lines* is his first novel. He lives in North Yorkshire.

Printed in Great Britain
by Amazon.co.uk, Ltd.,
Marston Gate.

Personal Effectiveness for Teachers

Val Rowland & Ken Birkett

SIMON & SCHUSTER
EDUCATION

Text © Val Rowland & Ken Birkett 1992
Illustrations © Simon & Schuster Education

First published in 1992 in Great Britain by
Simon & Schuster Education
Campus 400, Maylands Avenue
Hemel Hempstead, Herts HP2 7EZ

British Library Cataloguing in Publication Data
Available on request from the British Library

ISBN 0 7501 0185 7

Cartoons by Rodney Sutton
Typeset in 10/12 pt Plantin by Photo·graphics, Honiton, Devon
Printed in Great Britain by T. J. Press (Padstow) Ltd

Contents

Acknowledgements

We should like to thank everyone who has contributed to this book, in particular Tom Williams (ex-headteacher) for his invaluable comments and Mal Rivers (headteacher) for her constructive feedback. Finally, special thanks to John and Laura Rowland and Claire Harmer for their patience and tolerance.

Introduction

Who is this book for?

This book aims to help anybody in the teaching profession who wishes to improve their personal effectiveness, and interpersonal skills. It doesn't matter at what stage in your career you might be. The quality of your relationships in terms of influencing and interacting with others is always crucial, whether it be how you are treated and respond as a subordinate; or how you manage others. Personal effectiveness has to be worked at on an on-going basis. People at all levels can always learn something new which will impact on their work or social life.

Undergraduate and graduating teachers

You may be preparing to launch into a teaching career and be reasonably confident about the curriculum and teaching methods. But only now are you turning your mind to the realities of liaising with the wide range of personalities that you will meet in the classroom, in the staffroom and at parents' evenings.

For you, this book can act as an interpersonal skills learning manual.

Teachers in mid-career

You may have a number of years of demonstrable success in the classroom and now wish to work on developing successful relationships with pupils, colleagues and parents.

Personal Effectiveness for Teachers can help you analyse your feelings and behaviour, and suggests areas to work on for improvement.

Teachers in managerial positions

In a managerial role you need to use a distinct set of behavioural skills if you are to be effective in influencing the performance of other people towards achieving goals.

Personal Effectiveness for Teachers outlines various ways to motivate and influence others to best effect.

Another key aspect of your role is that of assisting the development of your staff. This implies that you should be able to help them to assess their career needs and aspirations in some structured way, and hence support their endeavours towards professional success.

This book will assist you in considering the various attributes of your staff and ways in which you may guide their development. You will be able to help build on strengths and minimise weaknesses.

Why are interpersonal skills important?

Success at work and in our social life depends on the impression we make on others. We are constantly being judged by other people on the basis of the way we look and behave. Sometimes we are not good at picking up the clues from other people's behaviour about how we are being perceived.

Interpersonal skills are important because we can learn to be much more sensitive to how others see us. We can maximise the impact we have on others if we know what the important elements of behaviour are. *Personal Effectiveness for Teachers* aims to give readers guidelines by which they can develop successful relationships. It outlines how they can understand and modify their own behaviour to suit particular situations and different personalities.

The professional role of teacher involves many forms of communication in different types of interpersonal relationship. Teachers who are able to develop effective interpersonal skills will stand a greater chance of maintaining job satisfaction in situations of change and turbulence. To be a successful teacher you need to understand how to communicate well, how to recognise and understand the needs of everyone around you, how to relate this to your own needs and, of course, how to develop your career to your own satisfaction. In short, personal effectiveness is the key-stone to success.

Using the book

The main premise of the book is that **YOU** have to take on the responsibility for resolving problems. No-one knows more about you than you do yourself. But sometimes you need guidance on taking time out to reflect and focus on problems and potential means of solution. It is, therefore, very much a 'how to' approach that is used in this book, which focuses on how you can influence situations to help yourself.

Throughout the book there are case studies which illustrate situations and practical exercises for you to try. By working through these you will gain the confidence to behave in an appropriate and effective way. At the end of the book there is a series of exercises which may be used for group training sessions with relevant colleagues. We have included trainer's notes to show how the exercises might be used and what the objectives are.

The contents of this book relate to three broad areas:

General self-development, covered in chapters on:

- Achieving effective interpersonal skills·
- Managing yourself
- Moving up the ladder
- Coping with stress.

Coping with others and situations, covered in chapters on:

- Working with colleagues
- Succeeding in the classroom
- Managing your boss
- Meeting parents.

Developing specific work skills, covered in chapters on:

- Chairing work meetings
- Developing interview skills
- Handling appraisals and staff development.

You may wish to follow the sequence as set out in the contents or work through the book as your own needs dictate. To gain greater insight it may be useful to work with a colleague, friend or partner.

By opening *Personal Effectiveness for Teachers* and reading this far you have indicated a wish to discover more about personal effectiveness. We hope you find the book useful and wish you every success in future interpersonal communications.

Val Rowland & Ken Birkett 1992

1 Achieving effective interpersonal skills

In schools and other organisations, approximately 80 per cent of the problems that arise are those concerning people. As a result, many organisations are increasingly providing interpersonal skills training for employees to help them manage both themselves and others. Communications, problem solving, influencing, motivation, effective teamwork and many other skills are included in such programmes. One theme running through all these courses is the benefit of being assertive. Yet many people misunderstand assertiveness and often mistake it for aggression.

Types of behaviour

We may look at behaviour in terms of three main types; aggression, passivity and assertiveness. Most of us move from one type of behaviour to another, depending on the situation and with whom we are dealing.

When asked what sort of words describe these three types of behaviour people commonly include those listed below:

Aggression	Passivity	Assertiveness
angry	timid	confident
dominant	meek	knowledgeable
volatile	put upon	firm
hot	lacking confidence	fair
out of control	mild	in control
violent	accepting	considered

The benefits of assertion can easily be seen. It is much better to feel confident and in control than put upon or angry and volatile when dealing with others. Keeping behaviour under control is a skill that can be developed and improved.

Aggressive and passive behaviour seem to be much more innate than assertiveness, relating to the 'fight, flight' sort of behaviour we can identify when under threat. From earliest days, human beings have been helped by nature to deal with threatening situations by either standing ground and 'fighting' or 'running away' from the problem. Physical changes take place in the body to help us meet these needs. As civilisation has progressed, a third option (that of remaining and dealing with the situation) has emerged. Assertive behaviour, by which we can deal constructively and confidently with such problems, has to be learned.

Passive and aggressive behaviour may be grouped together and called non-assertive behaviour. In general, assertive behaviour will encourage assertive responses, and non-assertive behaviour will prompt non-assertive responses.

Some examples from everyday life help to illustrate the point.

(a) In a supermarket queue someone says 'you don't mind if I go first do you, I haven't got much and I am in a rush?' and you say OK when really it isn't.

(b) A colleague asks you to stay late to help with something and you angrily refuse or passively agree.

(c) You buy a suit you are unsure of because the assistant says it looks good.

In cases like these we are often the losers because we feel bad at the time or later and cause other people to feel bad and react in a negative way towards us. Assertive behaviour can help us to react in a positive way and with constructive outcomes.

As we have said, non-assertive behaviour tends to come more naturally but at certain times we need to be assertive. Assertive behaviour can be developed. We all have the ability to learn and develop skills which will help in our work and personal lives.

Assertiveness

Being assertive means taking responsibility for our behaviour, having respect for ourselves and others, and being honest. It allows us to say what we want or feel but **not** at other people's expense. It means understanding the point of view of other people, and being self-confident and positive. It is not about winning come what may or getting your own way all of the time. Assertiveness is about handling conflict and coming to an acceptable compromise.

Aggressiveness

Being aggressive means getting your own way at the expense of others, making them feel worthless, incompetent or small. It doesn't necessarily have to involve conflict. Humour and sarcasm can also be very aggressive.

Passivity

Being passive means ignoring your interests and allowing others to manipulate you. It often means denying how you *really* think or feel. Passivity means **not** being active, **not** recognising your own needs and goals and **not** doing something about them.

Exercise 1

1 On three sheets of paper, brainstorm all the words you associate with:
(a) assertiveness,
(b) aggression,
(c) passivity.
Place them in order of priority.
Consider how the words make you feel. What are the benefits of

assertiveness in specific situations, eg dealing with your headteacher or handling a difficult pupil?

2 Consider how you might respond assertively, aggressively and passively to the following situations.

(a) Your headteacher asks you to take a group of pupils on a school journey during the Easter holidays. You don't want to go this year but you did go last year.

(b) A parent asks you to give extra attention to a pupil who has done badly in a mock exam. You feel this would be unfair on the rest of the class.

(c) As a favour, you allow a colleague to use your classroom every Wednesday morning. When you arrive in the afternoon the board has not been cleaned and the furniture has been left in an untidy state. This is the third week running that this has happened and you are beginning to feel annoyed.

Assertive rights

We may express our own needs *and* take account of others. This may be formalised in a bill of assertive rights. The following statements outline some of our rights:

- the right to have and express feelings and opinions
- the right to be listened to and taken seriously
- the right to set priorities
- the right to say 'no' without feeling guilty
- the right to ask for what we want
- the right to get what we pay for
- the right to ask for information from professionals
- the right to make mistakes sometimes
- the right to choose not to be assertive.

By believing in these basic rights we are empowered to demand and give proper treatment. As the final statement shows, there may be occasions when we choose not to be assertive. For example, your partner doesn't like an outfit which you are particularly keen on, and you decide not to buy it because you want to please the other person. By choosing not to be assertive, you are deciding to bide your time on something and let things pass for the moment. Developing techniques of assertiveness does not mean that you **have** to be assertive all the time if you don't want to.

Before continuing let us summarise the benefits of being assertive.

Advantages of being assertive

1 One of the most often voiced advantages is that personally it makes us feel better about ourselves – it gives us confidence and prevents us from feeling powerless.
2 In terms of career development, a more positive image is communicated to others. It is more likely that potential will be rewarded.
3 If we take responsibility for our own behaviour, we are much less likely to blame others and make excuses for our mistakes. In the long term this will save time and energy.

An assertive script

The following steps outline how an assertive script is generally conducted. We shall then apply it to the examples in Exercise 1.2.

1	**Describe**	the behaviour that created the problem; for example, 'When this happened, . . .' 'When you said . . .' Avoid emotive or evaluative comments about the behaviour – just say what the behaviour was.
2	**Express**	how you feel, **not** how you think the other person feels; for example, 'I feel . . .' **not** 'You make me feel . . .'.
3	**Explain**	concisely and clearly how you feel.
4	**Empathise**	with the other person's situation, interest and possible or expressed views.
5	**Specify**	what you would like the other person to do and what you would be willing to do to reach a solution; for example, 'I would prefer . . .' 'I would like . . .'.
6	**Choose**	your response; for example, 'If you do . . ., then . . .' 'If you do not . . ., then . . .'. This information should be used to clarify your position but not threaten the other person.

You will not always need to use all the steps but whatever is appropriate to the situation. With practice you will find that this rather mechanistic approach will come more naturally.

Now let us look at the examples in Exercise 1.2.

2(a) Your headteacher asks you to take a group of pupils on a school journey during the Easter holidays. You don't want to go this year but you did go last year.

Describe	When you asked me to take Class 3 on the school trip,
Express	I felt this would create an unfair burden on me–
Explain	especially as I took Class 4 last year.
Empathise	I realise that you are short-staffed at the moment, but
Specify	I would prefer to leave it for a year.
Choose	If you do insist on this, I should like you to consider allowing me to have time off in lieu.

2(b) A parent asks you to give extra attention to a pupil who has done badly in a mock exam. You feel this would be unfair on the rest of the class.

Describe	When I received your letter asking for extra attention for Jim,
Express	I felt this would be unfair to the rest of the class.
Explain	I do have 32 other children doing this subject.
Empathise	I understand that you are concerned about Jim's future,
Specify	but I really don't feel that I can spend any extra time with him. If you wish, I could see if any of my colleagues would be prepared to give him extra tuition, or I could give you the telephone number of a tutoring agency.
Choose	If you don't accept this then I could see the headteacher.

2(c) As a favour, you allow a colleague to use your classroom every Wednesday morning. When you arrive in the afternoon the board has not been cleaned and the furniture has been left in an untidy state. This is the third week running this has happened and you are feeling annoyed.

Describe	When I got to my classroom yesterday,
Express	I felt very cross.
Explain	The room was in a hell of a mess and the blackboard was not cleaned.
Empathise	I understand that you are in a rush to get to meetings on Wednesday afternoons,
Specify	but I would prefer you to leave the room clean and tidy.
Choose	If you don't agree then I would prefer you not to use the room.

You will have noticed that 'I' is used a great deal in these scripts. This is something many of us are not used to. We are brought up to put others before ourselves, and so using 'I' so much can seem a little strange until you get used to it. It is important to realise that you are not saying 'I' in a selfish way but in a way that allows others to know your feelings. It is in fact a much better type of expression than 'You make me . . .', etc. To illustrate, let us consider Exercise 1.2 again and possible aggressive and passive responses.

	Aggressive	**Passive**
2(a)	Why do you always ask me? Just because no-one else will do it, don't think I will. I've quite enough on my plate without any more. You never seem to think we have a private life. All you think of is this school!	Yes of course I'd love to. When exactly is it?
2(b)	Don't you realise I've got 32 others to teach? Jim will have to take his turn with the rest.	When I can I'll try and make time for a bit of extra tuition.
2(c)	Do you think I've got time to start clearing up after you every Wednesday? It really is too much.	Avoid the confrontation and accept the situation.

No doubt in reading through these you are imagining the manner in which these words might be said and the tone of voice. This brings us to another important aspect of assertion – body language.

Body language

Much has been written about body language in recent years. Although we should not take too much notice of the supposed meaning of individual gestures (eg, rubbing the ear means someone is lying or folding the arms is defensive), we do pick up clusters of signals and interpret them.

Observing people allows us to pick up clues about how they may be feeling from the way their body moves, from their posture and facial expression. Airports and railway stations are good places to observe body language.

When we want to be assertive and use the right script it is important to use appropriate body language to reinforce the message. Realising the impact of body language and using it to positive effect is something we can develop.

Body posture

How do you normally stand? Is it upright or slouched? Do you balance on one leg and then the other when talking to people? How do you walk into a room full of people? Do you sidle in hoping no-one will notice you, storm in creating disruption or do you walk tall and straight and in a dignified way?

Assertive body posture is firm, balanced on both feet, straight, head held high giving an aura of confidence. If you are sitting and someone comes to talk to you, you will be at a disadvantage if you stay seated. If you get up, stand firm and talk to the other person on equal terms you are much more likely to be able to stand your ground and be taken seriously.

Teachers who stand while pupils are sitting in class are reinforcing the dominance and power of their position. A difficult discussion with a worried parent may require a different approach altogether, possibly sitting in easy chairs to encourage the parent to relax and explain the problem.

Voice

The tone of voice, volume and pace also give signals to those with whom we are communicating. A firm, clear and steady voice which is also warm and sincere is appropriate to assertive behaviour. Dull, monotonous and quiet speech can often be irritating to the listener and will not accord with an assertive script. On the other hand the loud, strident tones we associate with aggressiveness are also likely to convey the wrong message when we want to be assertive.

Speech pattern

Fluent, unhesitating speech which emphasises key words will reinforce the assertive message. Hesitation or an over-fast pace will be unlikely to convince the listener that you have confidence and are in control.

Eye contact

Maintaining eye contact but not staring at someone is important when we want to be assertive. Staring someone out can be most off-putting and signals dominance. Avoiding eye contact, looking down or looking away will not convince the other person that you are wanting to be taken seriously.

Facial expression

Quite often, we smile unknowingly when we are in a difficult or threatening situation. This is often because of embarrassment. We don't want to be considered unfriendly even when we are using words which are designed to let the other person know we are displeased. This type of reaction is quite confusing to others and can be taken as aggression or sarcasm. If you want your message to have maximum impact then facial expression has to be consistent with the words and other body language which you are using.

A tight mouth or firmly set jaw are likely to convey signs of aggression and tension.

General

All of these factors together are sometimes called **gesture clusters**. When they are all giving out the same message the effect can be very powerful. Sometimes people talk about 'personal presence' – an indefinable quality. However, if you analyse the behaviour of a person with 'presence', using the aspects we have just been considering, you will probably find that they correspond with confident, assertive behaviour.

Exercise 2

Watch the television with the sound turned down and try to identify the feelings, mood and context of the situation. See if you are right by video-recording the programme and playing it back with the volume turned up. You could also listen to a radio play, paying particular attention to the tone, volume and pace of voice of the characters.

Being aware of the impact of these variables on your own behaviour will make an enormous impact on your success in inter-relating with others.

Assertiveness techniques

We will now look at some specific techniques which you may use, bearing in mind the points about body language just discussed.

Positive assertiveness

We often find it extremely difficult to accept genuine compliments in a way that is positive. For example, if you are complimented on a new outfit you may say 'Oh I only got it in the sale' or 'I've had it for years.' The assertive way to reply is to agree in a simple and direct way; for example, 'Thank you – I was pleased with it myself.' Another example might be if you have been praised for a job well done. An assertive response would be 'Thank you – I was pleased with the way I did that too.' By responding assertively you are positively acknowledging the thoughts and behaviour of the other person. In other words you are agreeing with them. If you say 'Oh it was nothing', for example, then you are denying the other person's view.

Praising others for genuine good work is one of the most neglected forms of managerial behaviour. Possibly one of the reasons why managers find it so difficult is because of the negative responses they receive. By behaving assertively you will be helping your manager to behave in a mutually beneficial way.

Negative assertiveness

This technique will help you to cope when you are being legitimately criticised for a mistake. The most important aspect here is the understanding that, as discussed earlier in the assertive bill of rights, everyone has a right to make a mistake sometimes.

By taking this on board you will avoid being manipulated by others, through feelings of guilt or anxiety, into either seeking forgiveness and trying to make up for your mistake, or denying the mistake and making excuses. You won't feel good about yourself if you behave in either of these ways.

Using this technique, you assertively accept those things which are negative about yourself. In a simple and direct way you verbally cope with your errors as if they are exactly that, no more and no less.

The technique can also help you cope more effectively when you receive valid criticism about the way you have done something. For example;

'You didn't handle that parent very well.'
'You're absolutely right. I did lose my temper, didn't I?'

The aim of negative assertiveness is to stop you from being manipulated into feeling guilty. It doesn't mean you don't have to try to sort out the result. What's happened is past, the thing to focus on is what to do about it.

Negative enquiry

By asking for more information about what is negative you are aiming to break the manipulative cycle. You are allowing the person you are coping with to be more assertive.

You do this by actively prompting further criticism about yourself or by pre-empting more information from the critical person in an unemotional way. What you are in fact saying is 'Let's look at what I am doing that may be wrong or that you don't like.' You behave as though criticism offers the opportunity to get some information about what has prompted it in the first place.

An example might be:

Colleague	'You really have been acting strangely lately.'
You (calmly)	'What exactly do you mean when you say that?'
Colleague	'You don't seem to have the time to discuss problems any more.'
You	'What sort of problems do you mean?', etc.

Fogging

Fogging can be used in situations when you want to stop the other person from nagging or trying to manipulate you. As the name implies, fogging creates a temporary barrier or cloud for the other person, slows them down and forces them to think a bit more about what they are saying. For example, if a colleague says something like 'You were really on the warpath in the meeting today', a 'fog' response might be 'Yes, I can understand why you thought that.' By answering like this, you are not agreeing with the criticism but only that you can see why they feel it themselves. By agreeing in principle you are assertively coping with the situation by offering no resistance for them to strike against.

Some examples of fogging statements are given below.

1 You can agree with the truth in any statement. 'Yes, I did get home late for supper.'
2 You can agree with any possible truth in someone's criticism.
'Perhaps you're right – I should budget for emergencies.'
3 You can agree with the general truth in logical statements.
'You're absolutely right, Alan. What you say about budgeting makes sense. When I feel I need to review my financial affairs I will.'

You are in fact going through a process of acknowledging what the other person has to say and 'fogging' can allow them to give you the space to voice your own thoughts and feelings.

Broken record

The broken record, as the name implies, is a technique whereby you keep on repeating in a straightforward and calm way the message you are trying to get across. Children are extremely good at this as you will no doubt have discovered.

The broken record technique is particularly useful in conflict situations – when saying no, when asking questions for clarification, when correcting someone who is in a position of authority, when being taken advantage of and when expressing feelings or opinions when the other person isn't listening. For example, when you don't want another drink, you simply repeat the core phrase, 'I don't want another drink, thank you.'

Broken records eventually get a response because it is uncomfortable to listen to the repetition for too long. Do not be side-tracked by irrelevancies, just keep saying in a calm and repetitive way what you want to say.

For example:

You 'I can't stay behind this evening.'
Other 'But the point is . . .'
You 'I'm sorry, I can't stay this evening.'
Other 'Jeremy stayed last week and he lives farther away than you.'
(This is an attempt to side-track.)
You 'That's irrelevant, I can't stay tonight.'
Other 'You are usually much more co-operative than this.'
You 'Let me say it again . . .' etc, etc.

You have to stop the other person from bringing in irrelevant trivia which will confuse you and try to influence you against your wishes. You also have to be aware (as in all assertive situations) of your body language. Once again, your body language should be consistent with what you are saying.

If an important side issue comes up you can agree to discuss it when, and only when, you have finished with the main issue. You could try asking for feedback if you don't think the other person is understanding or hearing you. For example, you might say something like 'What do you think I'm saying?' or 'What do you see as my position?'

By being persistent in this way you will stand a much better chance of achieving your objective than if you lose your temper. Once again, it will take practice to become successful with this technique.

Using empathy

Sometimes, the distinction becomes blurred between saying 'no' to a request and saying 'no' to the person. By understanding and empathising with the other person's position you are showing that you have listened carefully and appreciate how they feel, but your answer is still 'no'. You might say something like 'I understand that you have a deadline to meet and I'm sorry but I really can't stay this evening'. In this way, you are softening the 'no' and not rejecting the person themselves.

Try Exercises 3 and 4 – they may be done individually, in pairs or in small groups.

Exercise 3

1 Identify a situation (which can be either from your personal or work life) where you felt your behaviour had not been as you would have liked. Think about what went wrong and how you would behave in a similar situation in the future. The following outline may help.

Your problem scene

- When did it happen?

- With whom did it occur?

- What were you talking about?

- Where did it take place?

- Was there anyone else present?

- What did the other person say or do?
  (Their problem behaviour)

- How did you react?
  (Your problem behaviour)

A similar scene in the future
You should consider the following:
- the setting
- the time
- who will be there

- what will be your core phrase
- develop an assertive response around the core phrase
- memorise and use
- make sure your body language is consistent with your speech.

Exercise 4

Recognising assertiveness

Decide whether the following are submissive, assertive or aggressive behaviours.

1 One of your staff is leaving the school at 5:00 pm. You ask her to hang on for a moment to discuss a problem. She responds, 'I've got to go . . ., can we discuss it tomorrow?'
2 Several candidates are being interviewed for the post of deputy head. You ask one of your staff if they will show them round the school. They respond 'I haven't been here long and don't know everything, but if you really want me to take them round, I suppose I can – if you're sure . . .?'
3 A parent rings up to complain that Johnny is always coming home with torn trousers. The response from one of the teachers is 'What do you mean – torn trousers. It's nothing to do with me – I don't teach Johnny – You're speaking to the wrong person.'

   Another response from a different member of staff is 'I'd like to help, but I've been off sick for the last two weeks – this is my first day back – I'll go and find someone who knows the position. They will be able to talk to you, hold on a moment.'
4 You're holding a staff meeting to discuss the proposed re-structuring of the department. Everyone seems to approve of your ideas except three people who haven't said anything one way or the other. You invite their views:

   A 'I'm sorry I'm not sure I understood how it will work, but if you think it's a good idea . . . well . . . I agree.'

   B 'I believe that the proposal is too rigid in structure. I cannot therefore go along with the re-structuring plan.'

   C 'It's a load of bunkum. Totally unworkable – typical management idea. The union will be on to this in no time.'

Using inner dialogues

We all talk to ourselves quite frequently. Obviously, what we say to ourselves influences how we behave. You often see tennis stars at

Wimbledon openly talking to themselves to get psyched up during the game and telling themselves they can do it and so on. We have to develop means by which we can talk to ourselves positively rather than always thinking the worst (the worst will probably come true if we wish it hard enough). We must learn to look at the positive side.

For example, instead of thinking, 'I've got this dreadful parent to meet, she's going to blame me for the fact that Sally is not achieving. She threatened to report me to the governors last time, perhaps I should have put her in a different class with the ten-year-olds . . .'; we should be thinking, 'I'm meeting Mrs X tomorrow. I have done my best for Sally – I did take advice from the special needs co-ordinator. If the governors get involved, I can show them what I have done and what I've achieved . . .'

Coping with anger

In many situations you have to deal with another person's anger. Typical situations may occur with a boss, a parent, a child or a friend. What you should try to do is reduce their feelings of anger so that you can achieve more effective communication.

The first step is to recognise and acknowledge the anger you are picking up. For example,

'I can tell that you are very angry about this.'

Then you can demonstrate that you are prepared to try to solve the problem. For example,

'Let me hear what you have to say. Why don't we talk about what happened.'

Use active listening to hear all the points before moving on to trying to solve the problem. For example,

'From what you say, this must have been a problem for a long time.'
'I can understand that this seemed like the last straw.'

If you have genuinely created all or part of the problem then it would help to admit this at the beginning. For example,
'Maybe I should have booked another car.'

In handling anger in this way you are showing that you are prepared to try to resolve the conflict. In other words, you are showing that you are able and willing to deal with problem solving. You are not just trying to fob off the other person, which would probably lead to more problems in the long term.

Exercise 5

1 Assertion exercise

This exercise has been adopted from *The Assertive Woman* by Phelps and Austin (Impact, 1976).

Consider the following situations and think about your ability to behave in the way outlined. It may be helpful to think about how your behaviour alters when you are with different types of people; for example, at school, with family, with friends.

(a) Speaking up at meetings and asking questions.
(b) Commenting about being interrupted at the time it happens.
(c) Stating your views to an authority figure.
(d) Entering and leaving a room full of people.
(e) Speaking in front of a group.
(f) Maintaining eye contact when in conversation.
(g) Being competent and using your authority without labelling yourself impolite, bossy, aggressive, etc.
(h) Asking for a service you expect/have paid for when you haven't received it.
(i) Being expected to apologise for something you are not responsible for, and not doing so since you are right.
(j) Requesting the return of borrowed items without apology.
(k) Receiving a compliment and acknowledging that you agree.
(l) Accepting a rejection.
(m) Not getting the approval of a significant other person.
(n) Discussing another person's criticism of you openly with them.
(o) Telling someone that they are doing something that is bothering you.
(p) Refusing to do a favour when you don't want to do it.
(q) Turning down a request for a meeting.
(r) Telling a person when you think they are trying to manipulate you.
(s) Expressing anger when you are angry.
(t) Arguing with another person.
(u) Responding appropriately when someone tries to put you down.
(v) Talking about mistakes you have made.

2 Scenarios

For both of the following scenarios, write down how you would respond, and what you consider to be passive, aggressive and assertive responses.

(a) Hi – can I ask you a favour? I've got 3B on Wednesday and would appreciate having room 6. I know you normally have 6 on a Wednesday, but do you think we could swap? (You have planned a specific activity and don't want to swap.)

Your reply:

Passive:

Aggressive:

Assertive:

(b) You are attending a regular team meeting. A new member of staff sits next to you and starts smoking. You find this very annoying. When lighting another cigarette they say, 'You don't mind if I smoke do you?'

Your reply:

Passive:

Aggressive:

Assertive:

Communication

Communication may be thought of as the sharing of information, attitudes and feelings by words, tones and behaviour. Reasons for communicating include: gaining or passing on knowledge, getting or giving help, learning or teaching, changing ideas, persuading and negotiating. Sometimes people talk about effective communication, but that would seem to be a misnomer. Communication involves the receiver of a message understanding it in the way the sender meant. If the message is not received in this way then there has not been communication or, as some would say, effective communication. The problem with communication is that there are many barriers. For example, people's perceptions, their ability to make judgements, noise, interruptions and the inability to write clearly, etc, all affect the process of communication.

We can make a distinction between direct and indirect, and non-verbal and verbal communication. In direct verbal communication the sender is in direct one-to-one verbal communication with the receiver. This gives the opportunity for feedback. For example, clarifying questions might be asked, or the receiver may say 'I don't understand what you mean.' Feedback may suggest that you have to change your approach. You can prompt feedback in various ways. For example, you could ask someone how they are going to complete a task you have just asked them to do. You could ask if the meaning is clear. You could ask for their opinions on the subject. Another way is simply to offer the chance to ask questions.

Direct non-verbal communication gives different problems because the feedback process is more difficult, if not impossible. Receiving a written instruction from someone in a different geographical location doesn't give much room for instant feedback and clarification.

Indirect communication of both types increases the potential for errors and misunderstanding to creep in. Many situation comedies are written like this. The characters often engage in communications where one thing is sent and something completely different is received.

In your own communication with others it is helpful to realise the value of feedback, either asking for it yourself or volunteering it if you are on the receiving end.

Exercise 6

1 Consider situations where you have been the communicator and have received feedback in some way. Think about how this helped the situation.
2 Can you think of any situations where asking for feedback would have improved matters?

Oral or written communication?

Speech allows for instant feedback and is therefore more useful than written communication. The written word, however, may be more appropriate if a record is needed later. Some managers become obsessed with writing memos because this is seen as a way of covering themselves against questions later. In some cases, a memo may be needed but often it is too time-consuming. It is important to use the most appropriate communication methods for the circumstances, remembering the inherent flaws in all types.

The relevance of body language was discussed earlier in this chapter. When communicating orally, body language gives out a very clear message. If the body language is inconsistent with the speech, confusion and misunderstandings may result.

Exercise 7

Choosing the appropriate method of communication

'Right then, it's up to you how you organise the change in your own departments.'

James Greenfield, the headteacher of a large secondary school, brought the meeting of his department heads to a close. He had just told them that the school was to introduce an appraisal system in line with local authority requirements. A pilot scheme had been operating in several schools in the country and there had been a mixed reception about the results.

Julie Rivers is the recently appointed head of English. As she walked back to her room she was thinking, 'How do I get this across? Do I talk to them or put it in writing?'

Put yourself in Julie's position and list the advantages and disadvantages of communicating this message (a) orally and (b) in writing.

Exercise 8

Communication exercise

Think of a situation in which you have recently had a 'communication problem'. The situation could be at home, work, or socially. In particular consider the following points:

(a) With whom did the problem arise?
(b) What was the communication about? Were you trying to:
   • receive information
   • give information
   • express a point of view
   • persuade someone
   • other?
(c) Where did the problem lie? Be honest. Was it with:
   • you

- the other party
- both
- neither (ie the fault of someone outside the situation)?
(d) On reflection what was the cause of the problem? Was it:
- physical; for example, external noise
- in the language used
- body language
- attitude expressed
- other?
(e) How do you think you could behave to avoid a similar thing happening again?

Barriers to communication

There are three main areas where barriers to communication may arise:

(a) the manner in which a message is sent;
(b) the message itself;
(c) the manner in which the message is received.

The manner of communication

Plan your communication by asking the questions:

- **what** do I want to get across?
- **who** needs to receive the message?
- **why** do I have to communicate?
- **when** do I have to send the message?
- **how** can I best put the message across?

By asking these sorts of questions you should come up with an appropriate way to communicate the message.

The message itself

Two of the main barriers here are ambiguity and the use of jargon.

(a) **Ambiguity**. When language can be interpreted in more than one way, misunderstandings can occur. Try keeping communication simple using direct and clear language. For example, saying 'Mr Jones rang and said the meeting's on', may relate to a whole host of different situations and meanings.

(b) **Jargon**. This may refer to the use of technical vocabulary or language which is pretentious or obscure. If you have to use technical vocabulary, consider whether or not the receiver will know what you mean or whether some form of explanation may be necessary. Try to avoid using pretentious language. The message should be kept simple with easy-to-understand words. No doubt you could give examples of messages where the meaning is hidden amongst flowery language. This impresses no-one.

Receiving messages

Poor listening skills, distortion and an unreceptive atmosphere all threaten the communication process.

(a) **Listening**. Effective listening is an activity that takes a lot of practice and care. We often do not listen giving full attention to the person conveying the message. Our minds may be elsewhere. Try to ensure that your listening skills are fully developed by concentrating exclusively on the person and the message that is being sent. If you are the sender, feedback is one way of trying to make sure that other people are listening to you. Also be aware of the fact that people tend to listen selectively: they hear what they want to hear. When a listener does not 'hear', they tend to fill in the gaps in what they receive from previous experiences, or form ideas which correspond to their stereotypes. People interpret behaviour on the basis of their culture. This is obvious when we consider people from different countries. But it is also apparent when gender intervenes, for example, or between managers and subordinates.

Avoiding listening may be indicated by argument, interruption and ridicule. This has to be countered by assertive listening: let the other person know that you hear what they are saying.

Some useful tips for maintaining effective listening are given below.

1 Create a pleasant but business-like atmosphere.
2 Focus your complete attention on the speaker.
3 Demonstrate interest in what is being said.
4 Minimise interruptions.
5 Time the meeting carefully; Friday afternoon is *not* usually a good time.
6 Seek clarification if the meaning is not clear.
7 Provide information when appropriate.
8 Use verbal reinforcers such as 'I see' and 'yes', when appropriate.
9 Use consistent body language; for example, maintain eye contact and nod occasionally.

10 Show respect for the speaker and his or her viewpoint.

11 Try to empathise.

12 Do not pre-judge the speaker's topic as routine or dull. A poor listener often makes a judgement and tunes out.

13 Do not evaluate the speaker's remarks in advance. Poor listeners often react too quickly because of their own attitudes and biases.

14 Try to concentrate on the content rather than the delivery of the message.

15 Avoid taking too many notes. If necessary, note down key points.

16 Avoid over-confidence that might be produced by the difference in listening or speaking speeds. Most people talk at a rate of approximately 125 words per minute, and can listen and think easily at about four times this rate. Utilise the time between speaking and listening speeds to evaluate what the speaker is saying.

(b) **Distortion**. Messages alter and are embellished as they pass from one person to another. This can be dangerous. Consider the following example:

Anna Roberts, a primary headteacher, was talking to her staff. 'The tidiness of the school is becoming a problem. A neat and tidy environment gives a good impression to visitors and improves the response of the children. Make sure that you are watchful of the situation.'

Alan Jones went home and told his wife that the head had been criticising them all for having an untidy and disorderly school.

Jim Reynolds told his mother, 'The head was on the war-path. She thinks the school is a filthy mess. I reckon she's got an inspection visit sometime soon. Either that or she's trying to get some money out of the governors!'

This type of situation happens all too often and can ultimately lead to mistrust and bad personal relations. To avoid distortion, think of ways whereby you can make sure the message was correctly understood. Think about the best method of communication.

(c) **Unreceptive atmosphere**. Timing is an important consideration when communicating. If the receiver is preoccupied or it is the end of a particularly hard day, or an unpleasant occurrence has happened, then the message is not likely to be received well. Also, if the sender is not credible, then communication is unlikely to happen properly. Encouraging an atmosphere of trust and belief is essential to communication.

Why is communication difficult?

A few potential problems of communication are outlined below.

(a) Understanding the facts.
- time might be needed to absorb and reflect
- the concept might be difficult to understand
- the facts may conflict with preconceptions
- some words may be misinterpreted
- listeners are often selective in what they hear and what they reject
- the message may be rejected as boring or unreliable.

(b) Feelings.
- what does the speaker *want* the receiver to hear?
- what impression is required?
- the speaker may be frightened or embarrassed
- the speaker may feel stupid
- the speaker may consider saying nothing.

(c) Attitudes.
- the receiver may consider that being persuaded shows weakness
- the receiver may consider that new information will confuse
- the receiver may worry about what is expected
- the receiver may not want to change.

Questioning

In many situations, questions are a useful form of communication. However, in some instances they may have a negative effect. The difficulty with questions is two-sided: how questions are *intended* and how they are *perceived*. For example, the type of question that begins with 'Do you mean to say that . . .?', may be intentionally destructive. The tone of voice in conjunction with these words may be used to put down an idea. It places the onus of 'proof' of an idea's value on the contributor of that idea, with no apparent participation by the questioner.

The other difficulty with questions involves perception. Individuals may freeze or cringe in response to a question, and especially to a barrage of questions. Educationalists use questions to sharpen the competitive environment as well as to reinforce learning. The result of this type of conditioning may lead to a 'need not to fail' attitude, where individuals feel they must make the answer the right one. The effect is that individuals may hesitate in responding. They may even spend energy to discover the answer that the questioner wishes to hear. In these situations, pleasing the questioner (boss, teacher, parent, etc) becomes more important than an honest joint search for new and useful information, ideas and solutions. Another perceived effect of questions is that they may limit thinking. Questions are helpful where an individual wishes to focus upon a particular point and unhelpful where speculation is required.

Written communication

This form of communication often proves difficult for many people. With written communication, it is important to get the message across as unambiguously as possible. Unlike verbal communication, there is no opportunity to elicit feedback and understanding. The following tips may be useful.

1 Structure the communication so that it has an identifiable beginning, middle and end.
2 Be brief and to the point.
3 Organise your thoughts before you start writing.
4 Try to capture the reader's immediate interest.
5 Make the tone of the writing appropriate, eg friendly or formal.
6 Be positive. Where appropriate, quote action steps, eg 'Information on school training days will be sent out on 23 March'.
7 Avoid jargon.
8 Keep it simple. Some examples of simple and complex words are given below:
   - make   – fabricate
   - begin   – initiate
   - end   – terminate
   - large   – substantial
   - correct   – right and proper.

9 Aim for clarity of content through word economy. Often, one word achieves the meaning of three or four; for example,
   - now   – at the present time
   - because – in view of the fact that
   - while   – during such time as
   - yes   – in the affirmative
   - urgent   – for your immediate attention.

10 Vary the structure and length of your sentences to produce a clear message.
11 Each sentence should include only one central idea or theme.
12 Write concise paragraphs – not more than four or five sentences usually.

The following list of questions will help you to evaluate the effectiveness of your written communication.

1 Are my words correct for the intended message?
2 Is my sentence structure clear?
3 Are my sentences and paragraphs logically arranged to promote understanding?
4 Have I given all the necessary information?
5 Have I answered all the likely questions?
6 Is it too wordy?
7 Is my language natural and sincere?

Summary

There are positive advantages to being assertive. In particular, feeling good about yourself generally enables you to behave more confidently in all types of situations. By using the various techniques of assertiveness as outlined, and being aware of the importance of body language and communication methods, more effective behaviour can be developed.

We shall be referring to these techniques as we go through the book, either directly or indirectly, to help you deal with some of the issues involved in personal effectiveness.

Assertiveness is based on a philosophy of personal responsibility and an awareness of the rights of other people. It means behaving in a rational and adult way in order to be able to reach workable compromises.

In subsequent chapters we shall be building on this, by looking at specific relationships and problem areas, and outlining how you might apply assertiveness skills.

2 Working with colleagues

This chapter aims to develop the work on assertiveness in the specific context of working with colleagues. How do you handle conflict, for example? What happens when there is a personality clash? How can you contribute most effectively in group situations and gain effective contributions from others?

Conflict

Consider the following situations and how you would respond to them.

1 You want to introduce a new learning scheme. You are assured of support from one of your colleagues. When you go to the meeting your colleague does not give you the expected co-operation.
2 You write a report on school management and some of the key issues you feel should be looked at. Your boss uses all your ideas for a document of his own.
3 A difficult pupil is causing you problems, you arrange to meet the parents after school at a time to suit them rather than you. They arrive half-an-hour late and you have another meeting scheduled.

Did you respond in the same way to all three situations? What are the other possible alternative responses? The more possible alternatives you can see to these situations, the more likely it is that you will be able to achieve a successful outcome.

Figure 2.1 on page 30 shows five conflict-resolving styles using a matrix of level of assertiveness and level of co-operation.

Think back to some of the conflict situations you have been in and how the parties handled it. What were your reactions to the other person? How did they respond to you? Did the encounter have a successful outcome? By reflecting on these types of situation you will gain greater insight into your own personal style and the ability to evaluate its appropriateness. The questionnaire on p. 30 is designed to

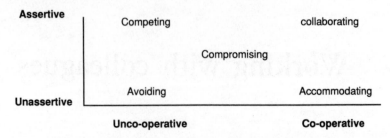

Figure 2.1 (From *A Managers Guide to Self-development* by Mike Pedler, John Burgoyne and Tom Boydell. McGraw Hill, 1986)

help you assess your preferred style of handling conflict. If you feel it appropriate, you could try to get a group of colleagues to complete the questionnaire and then have a discussion on the results.

Conflict management questionnaire

(From *A Manager's Guide to Self-Development* by Mike Pedlar, John Burgoyne and Tom Boydell. McGraw Hill, 1986.)

Choose from the 30 pairs of statements the one in each case which best fits your preferred style of handling differences between you and others:

1(a) I am usually firm in pursuing my goals.

(b) I attempt to get all concerns and issues immediately set out in the open.

2(a) I put my cards on the table and invite the other person to do the same.

(b) When conflicts arise I try to win my case.

3(a) Once I adopt a position I defend it strongly.

(b) I prefer not to argue but to look for the best solution possible.

4(a) I sometimes sacrifice my own wishes for the wishes of the other person.

(b) I feel that differences are not always worth worrying about.

5(a) I accept the views of the other person, rather than rock the boat.

(b) I avoid people with strong views.

6(a) I like to co-operate with others and follow their ideas.

(b) I feel that most things are not worth arguing about. I stick to my own views.

7(a) I try to find some compromise situation.

(b) I am usually firm in pursuing my goals.

8(a) When conflicts arise I try to win my case.

(b) I propose a middle ground.

9(a) I like to meet the other person half-way.

(b) Once I adopt a position I defend it strongly.

10(a) I feel that differences are not always worth worrying about.

(b) I try to find a compromise solution.

11(a) I propose a middle ground.

(b) I avoid people with strong views.

12(a) I feel that most things are not worth arguing about. I stick to my own views.

(b) I like to meet the other person half-way.

13(a) I am usually firm in pursuing my goals.

(b) I sometimes sacrifice my own wishes for the wishes of the other person.

14(a) I accept the views of the other person, rather than rock the boat.

(b) When conflicts arise I try to win my case.

15(a) Once I adopt a position I defend it strongly.

(b) I like to co-operate with others and follow their ideas.

16(a) I try to find a compromise solution.

(b) I sometimes sacrifice my own wishes for the wishes of the other person.

17(a) I accept the views of the other person, rather than rock the boat.

(b) I propose a middle ground.

18(a) I like to meet the other person half-way.

(b) I like to co-operate with others and follow their ideas.

19(a) I feel that differences are not always worth worrying about.

(b) I am usually firm in pursuing my goals.

20(a) When conflicts arise I try to win my case.

(b) I avoid people with strong views.

21(a) I feel that most things are not worth arguing about. I stick to my own views.

(b) Once I adopt a position I defend it strongly.

22(a) I attempt to get all concerns and issues immediately out in the open.

(b) I feel that differences are not always worth worrying about.

23(a) I avoid people with strong views.

(b) I put my cards on the table and invite the other person to do likewise.

24(a) I prefer not to argue but to look for the best solution possible.

(b) I feel that most things are not worth arguing about. I stick to my own views.

25(a) I attempt to get all concerns and issues immediately out in the open.

(b) I try to find a compromise solution.

26(a) I put my cards on the table and invite the other person to do likewise.

(b) I propose a middle ground.

27(a) I prefer not to argue but to look for the best solution possible.

(b) I like to meet the other person half-way.

28(a) I sometimes sacrifice my own wishes for the wishes of the other person.

(b) I attempt to get all concerns and issues immediately out in the open.

29(a) I put my cards on the table and invite the other person to do likewise.

(b) I accept the views of the other person, rather than rock the boat.

30(a) I like to co-operate with others and follow their ideas.

(b) I prefer not to argue but to look for the best possible solution.

Circle the letters below which you circled on each item of the questionnaire.

Statement pair	I	II	III	IV	V
1				a	b
2				b	a
3				a	b
4	b	a			
5	b	a			
6	b	a			
7			a	b	
8			b	a	
9			a	b	
10	a		b		
11	b		a		
12	a		b		
13		b		a	
14		a		b	
15		b		a	
16		b	a		
17		a	b		
18		b	a		
19	a			b	
20	b			a	
21	a			b	
22	b				a
23	a				b
24	b				a
25			b		a
26			b		a
27			b		a
28		a			b
29		b			a
30		a			b

Total number of
items circled

I = Avoiding, II = Accommodating, III = Compromising, IV = Competing, V = Collaborating
The highest number shows your preferred means of resolving conflict. More equal scores show a flexible approach.

Avoiding behaviour is unassertive and unco-operative. The individual does not tackle the conflict. This may involve waiting for a better time or withdrawing from a potentially threatening situation. Typical responses include:

- 'I'd prefer not to discuss that now'
- 'That is outside my brief'
- 'Let's talk about that later'.

Accommodating behaviour is unassertive and co-operative. An individual neglects his concerns to satisfy those of other people. It may take the form of obeying when you don't want to, selfless generosity or giving in to someone else's point of view. Typical responses include:

- 'I agree with you there'
- 'I concede that point'
- 'You have convinced me'.

Compromising behaviour is intermediate in both assertiveness and co-operation. The object is to find a means of going some way to satisfy both parties. It falls mid-way between competing and accommodating. It might mean splitting the difference or exchanging concessions. Typical responses include:

- 'I'll give you . . . if you give me'
- 'I suggest we meet halfway'
- 'Let's find a quick solution'.

Competing behaviour is assertive and unco-operative. An individual pursues his own concerns by using his own power and expertise. It may mean simply attempting to win, defending a position or standing up for your rights. Typical responses include:

- 'I must make my position quite clear'
- 'My view is clearly the most rational'
- 'If you don't do this I'll . . .'.

Collaborating behaviour is both assertive and co-operative. This represents a problem-solving approach. The aim is to try and reach a solution which satisfies both persons. It may mean exploring the issues on interpersonal problems or resolving a resource problem. It requires honesty and openness and the willingness to listen to the other's point of view. Typical responses include:

- 'Let's work together on this'
- 'My position is . . . what's yours?'
- 'How can we solve this?'

Interpretation

We are all capable of operating within all these types, although we are better at using some than others. A realistic assessment of this will enable you to think about more appropriate conflict resolution modes in different situations. The effectiveness will depend on individual skill and the specific requirements of the situation.

In general terms, conflict is an inevitable part of life in modern organisations. Clashes of interests abound in virtually every area that you can think of. Developing effective interpersonal skills will give you the insight and confidence to try to resolve conflict in a productive way.

Giving and receiving criticism

Whatever your role in the organisation there will be occasions when you have to criticise a colleague. There are several points to consider when trying to criticise constructively.

1 The person giving the criticism (you) should speak for him or herself and express his or her own feelings and opinions clearly. For example,
   'I think that you . . .'
   'I get upset when you . . .'.
   (Notice the use of 'I' again here.)
2 The criticism should be directed at something said or done. It should not take the form of a personal attack.
3 Through criticism a person wants to be told exactly, and in concrete terms, what has been done and what have been the consequences.
4 The criticism should be directed at something which the person has the possibility of changing in the future.
5 Criticism should be given as near to the event as possible and hopefully when the person is in a receptive mood.
6 The person needs to be able to show what they feel about the criticism and know that those feelings are accepted.
7 The person also needs to have the chance to explain what they did and why.

A step-by-step approach might go something like this.

1 **Introduce the topic** (Choose a suitable time and make sure your conversation will be private.)	'Jean, I'd like to talk to you about class 4b.'
2 **Make your criticism specific**	'Jean, I've noticed that you always leave class 4b ten minutes early on Wednesdays.'
3 **Get a response to the criticism** (Your aim is to get agreement.)	'Do you agree?' 'Is that the way you see it?' 'Why is this happening?' 'Have you noticed this?'
4 **Ask for suggestions about the changes you want**	'What changes can you/we make?' 'How can you go about making an improvement?'
5 **Summarise and clarify the suggestions**	'So let's agree in future that you will . . .'

Exercise 9

Consider another situation and outline how you would handle it using the previous step-by-step approach. You can probably think of many examples, but to help you, here are a couple of suggestions.

1 A colleague on a working party which you chair has failed to turn up on the last three occasions.
2 You notice that a colleague's standards of dress and personal hygiene have slipped. You have had complaints about the smell from your subordinates.

Remember the discussion on communication skills in Chapter 1. By using effective listening skills we may discover there is a good reason for the personal behaviour. By approaching the criticism in a constructive way you will leave yourself room to accept genuine reasons.

Feedback

When giving feedback on an individual's performance it is important to allow the person to preserve their dignity and self-respect. You also need to make sure that real communication takes place. This can be achieved effectively in the following ways.

1 Focus on the behaviour of the person and not the person themselves.
2 Describe events, rather than making judgements about them.
3 Provide information and share ideas with the person rather than just giving advice.
4 Explore and discuss possible alternatives, rather than providing a solution.

If you are the object of feedback from someone else, the above guidelines will help you as well. Try to get the person on an objective track by, for example, pointing out that they are being judgemental or that there may be other possible solutions that haven't yet been explored. By coping with the situation assertively you are in a good position to move forward positively. If the criticism is justified, remember to accept it assertively and bear in mind the discussion earlier about making mistakes.

Teamwork

We spend a great deal of time within groups of one sort or another. We may describe a team as a group who feel energised by their ability to work together. Teams work together to make maximum use of the experience and ability of each member in order to reach the team's goals.

Teamwork consists of the tasks that members of the group perform to meet group goals.

Team roles are the behaviour patterns which must be shown by team members. These are needed for getting the work done and maintaining the group as a cohesive unit. Within any group there will be several different team roles required for the group to achieve its objectives. If these team roles are not acknowledged and accepted then the effectiveness of the group will be diminished.

Dr R Meredith Belbin (M Belbin, *Management Teams*, Heinemann) of the Henley School of Management has identified several key roles of successful groups. He believes that a balanced team, in terms of these roles, can be considerably more productive than teams which are imbalanced.

Team implementor

The implementor tends to be conservative and practical, and have a high degree of organising ability, together with strong self-discipline. Another positive feature of this type is that they are not easily discouraged. The weaknesses of the role are inflexibility and a blinkered approach.

Chairperson/co-ordinator

The chairperson tends to be confident and trusting, and his or her personality is characterised by calmness, self-control and self-confidence. A strong sense of objectives is felt and all potential contributors are dealt with fairly. An allowable weakness is that this type tends to hog the floor, compete with other members and be rather rigid in outlook.

Shaper

The shaper has a high need for achievement and tends to be anxious, outgoing and dynamic. Other qualities include a readiness to challenge complacency, ineffectiveness or self-deception. On the negative side,

this type is prone to impatience, irritation and provocation. There may be a tendency to 'steamroll' others.

Plant

Individuality, serious-mindedness, unorthodoxy and self-sufficiency are the features of the plant. They tend to have high levels of imagination, intellect and knowledge. They are open to new ideas and approaches and are highly creative. Some may be at the genius end of the spectrum. A problem with plants is that they tend to have their heads in the clouds and disregard convention and practical details.

Specialist

The specialist is a single-minded, self-starting person who provides knowledge of technical skills in rare supply. A potential drawback is that he or she may only contribute on a narrow front.

Resource investigator

Enthusiasm, curiosity, extroversion and communication are characteristic of this type of person. They have a capacity for contacting people and exploiting anything new, and are well able to respond to a challenge. Unfortunately, they tend to be unreliable and lose interest once the initial fascination has gone.

Monitor/evaluator

This type tends to be the critic; the sober, objective and prudent judge. The monitor can also be tactless and demotivating, however.

Team worker

As the name implies, this type is the team builder; socially oriented and sensitive. The team worker promotes team spirit and trust. On the other hand, he or she may be indecisive and take the team's side unrealistically.

Completer

The completer is characterised by a painstaking, orderly and conscientious approach. There is a high degree of perfectionism and everything is thoroughly checked. The negative side of this type is the worrier who is reluctant to let go.

Role preference

Dr Belbin has devised a test to ascertain individual role preference. Some organisations use this test in selection or in training programmes to try to get a balanced work team. It may be useful to use the test in your school so that project teams, for example, are as evenly balanced as possible. The test may be found in his book referred to earlier.

Can you identify some of the roles otlined above from your experience of working within groups?

Exercise 10

Working with a colleague, think back over your careers and identify the most effective work group with which you have been involved (either as leader or member). Try to identify the characteristics of the group that made it so effective. Be as specific as possible.

Now do the same with the least effective group you have been involved with.

What lessons can you learn from this that will influence your behaviour in the future?

The following checklist will help you to evaluate the success of individuals working in teams.

Barriers to effective team working

The following types of behaviours have been shown to impede the work of a team.

1 Failure to listen to points made by other team members.
2 Constant reiteration of one's own point of view.
3 Raising irrelevant and unhelpful points.
4 Concentrating on the impression one is making oneself rather than on completing the task.
5 Constantly restating arguments instead of recognising them as alternatives.
6 Failure to participate.
7 Failure to check how people are feeling about the discussion.
8 Failure to be aware of the reactions to one's own contributions from other team members.
9 Failure to take notice of time.

10 Failure to clarify objectives.
11 Failure to be clear about what has been decided.
12 Trying to go back and re-open a question which has already been decided.
13 Avoidance of particular issues.
14 Lack of creativity and 'sparkle'.

Influencing skills

There are various ways of influencing others, including:

- rewards and punishments
- assertive persuasion
- participation and trust
- common vision.

Your use of these will depend on your own personal style and position.

Rewards and punishments

In general, punishment is not effective as a long-term strategy. Describing goals and expectations and their consequent benefits is much more likely to produce results. If you are able to offer meaningful incentives then you are in a stronger position.

Assertive persuasion

Proposing ideas and arguing the pros and cons in an assertive way will help you to present ideas in an open, honest and fair manner. Several research studies have shown that people are motivated first by habit, then by emotion and then by reason. By understanding this you can develop appropriate methods of influencing.

Participation and trust

By acknowledging your own feelings and allowing others to express theirs without feeling threatened, you will encourage feelings of trust in those with whom you are dealing.

You need to test their understanding and reactions by encouraging feedback and listening to their point of view.

Common vision

Find common ground between you when discussing proposals. Identify common hopes and aspirations. What are your common value systems? Try to generate a shared view of the problem or the proposed change. If possible, identify any exciting possibilities that may arise if you can get agreement.

Some practical suggestions

The ability to influence others will assist you in many aspects of life. It is important, however, to distinguish between influencing and being dishonest or unfair. The following are some suggestions for influencing others to your point of view.

- set objectives for your talk, report, etc.
- carry out careful research: you need to be able to field questions and present various sides of the problem
- be clear and precise about what you want
- know about the perceptions and knowledge of your audience
- start by using arguments that you think you can get agreement on
- try to promote harmony rather than conflict, by presenting a compromise
- if possible, link your communication to other more familiar and acceptable areas
- develop good presentation skills: remember, non-verbal messages are extremely revealing
- be seen to be fair and honest: fairness is valued more than expertise and knowledge.

Force field analysis

Force field analysis is used to identify forces for and against change, so that the restraining forces can be removed and the changes accepted.

For example, the offer of a new job may pose you some problems. Force field analysis could help, as Figure 2.2 shows.

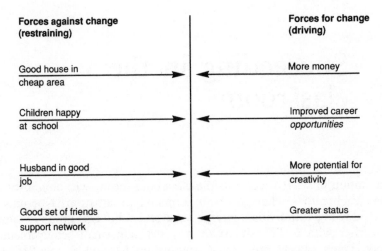

Forces against change (restraining)	Forces for change (driving)

Good house in cheap area — More money

Children happy at school — Improved career *opportunities*

Husband in good job — More potential for creativity

Good set of friends support network — Greater status

Figure 2.2

Exercise 11

Use force field analysis on a current problem area. Discuss with a colleague how you might minimise the forces against change and develop those that are working for change.

Summary

Potential conflict situations are encountered virtually every day. By understanding how you can respond more effectively when working with others, you can learn to behave in a more effective manner. In giving and receiving criticism, for example, you can gain a more positive outcome.

Contributing to the development of effective teams is going to become even more important in schools in the coming years. Understanding different team roles and how well a balanced team can perform will help enormously, particularly in situations of change.

Developing good working relations with colleagues needs time and effort. However, a co-operative and collaborative working atmosphere will enable you to cope more readily with the stresses and strains of modern teaching life. By using positive influencing skills you will be able to establish positive and supportive working relations with others.

3 Succeeding in the classroom

The notion of what success in the classroom means will obviously vary from teacher to teacher and from situation to situation. Not only are we talking about individual interpersonal skills, but also group dynamics. A teacher with a difficult group may evaluate small achievements as major events. On the other hand, another teacher will be able to achieve more. By using some of the reflective techniques discussed earlier, you will be able to make realistic assessments of your own performance and areas for improvement. Everybody, whatever their sphere of activity, should be engaged in a continuous search for improvement. The Japanese word *kaizan* embodies this philosophy. Basically it means that nothing is ever perfect. Everything can be improved upon. So when we talk of improvement this is not meant to be interpreted in a derogatory, but in a positive way.

Success may also be thought of in terms of examination results, few absentees, and so on. We are particularly interested in what we may call the 'behavioural' aspects of success. Creating an environment where the teacher is in control of a group of interested and contributing pupils may be called success in these terms.

Preparation

Some people would argue that this contributes to at least 90 per cent of all teachers' success rates. Good preparation will give you confidence. This not only refers to preparation for a session or day, but also to a term or an academic year. You should be aiming to prepare a meaningful sequence of learning activities. Controlling a class of children is made easier by a carefully prepared programme which provides interest, variation of pace, and stimulating teaching and learning methods.

Be prepared for pupils who finish first. Alleviate potential boredom by having back-up materials, worksheets, etc, so that they can continue working on their own. Have reinforcement materials pleasantly and attractively displayed in the classroom. Develop ideas for games using the topics and themes that have just been taught. In this way, you should be able to maintain a high interest level for all pupils.

Punctuality is also very important. Being late will mean you are flustered, appear ill-prepared and result in your lack of confidence. You expect pupils to turn up on time and so should you.

Presentation

Some of the techniques of presentation have already been discussed in the section on communication in Chapter 1. In this specific context, being able to explain clearly, asking probing questions and leading pupils on to solutions are all relevant interpersonal skills which are needed for success. In a survey of pupils one of the main reasons for assessment of a 'bad teacher' was the inability to explain the subject well. It is interesting to note that the willingness of pupils to learn often gets eroded because of poor explanation or presentation methods. Using the communication techniques of probing and feedback will enable you to assess pupils' levels of understanding. You may wish to evaluate your own performance and the appropriateness of the technique you have used (see Exercise 12).

Exercise 12

After one of your classes, evaluate how well it went on the basis of the following criteria:

- perceived level of pupil interest
- disruption level
- responses to questions
- other methods which may have been used to encourage learning.

Presentation also involves your own personal style of appearance. This should reflect your professional status, and reflect pride in the way you look. As a role model for pupils you have tremendous influence.

Classroom management

The classroom should be arranged in a way that enables pupils to behave as independently as possible. Equipment should be clearly available and easily accessible. Care of equipment by both teacher and pupils must be emphasised. Respect for the learning environment needs to be generated. The teacher must show that he or she values the pupils' work by, for example, displaying it around the room. In this way the pupils' feeling of worth will be enhanced. Pot plants and drapes in a consistently used room add to the aesthetic value. This encourages pupils to realise that the teacher is respecting and improving the learning environment.

Consider whether you need a teacher's desk. If you sit behind a desk you are erecting a physical barrier between you and your pupils which will hinder communication. If you do feel a desk is essential, consider its position: try to minimise the barrier effect. Other furniture in the classroom should be arranged to encourage free-flowing, two-way communication.

Activity

All pupils of whatever age must be active, either mentally or physically or both, during all the lesson. Obviously the subject matter will determine the type of activity to a large extent, but means must be used to achieve this type and level of activity.

At the same time, to reinforce this, the teacher must also be active throughout the lesson, always interacting with one or more of the pupils. Interest and enthusiasm will be picked up by all types of pupils. Similarly, lack of interest will quickly be communicated, with consequent results.

Discipline

Control and discipline should not be seen as negative and 'fire-fighting' activities. The exercise of discipline should be a habit in the classroom. Constant monitoring and vigilance using consistent tone of voice, words and body language will engender respect from pupils. Without such respect, a disciplined class becomes much more difficult to achieve. Any chink in the teacher's approach is likely to be mercilessly exploited by pupils.

Using assertiveness techniques can be of enormous help in maintaining discipline and control in the classroom. Keeping a calm outward appearance and using the broken record technique, for example, has often proved successful with a difficult pupil or group. For instance, Alex found that when she had a particularly bad group she started to get angry and behave aggressively towards them. The situation deteriorated and she began to dread Tuesday and Thursday mornings. During an assertiveness training course she was able to practise assertive

responses using role-play situations with a group of teachers. She started to use these in the classroom, quite tentatively at first, but within five weeks she was noticing changes in pupil behaviour. The most important thing she discovered was that behaving aggressively had been exacerbating the situation; previously, she had thought it would be more controlling.

Timing

An experienced teacher will know the importance of the timing of their intervention in the learning process. Knowing when to explain, when to allow discovery, when to be involved, and when to stand aside is all part of the teacher's professional role. The techniques on interpersonal skills discussed in Chapter 1 will reinforce these ideas. Assertive responses can be used; for example, consider using positive assertion. Praise and recognition at the right time will have an impact but it is surprising how often this is overlooked.

Atmosphere

Developing good interpersonal relationships in the classroom will also depend on how the teacher behaves outside it. The pupil survey referred to earlier also revealed the importance of the interest taken by the teacher during the hustle and bustle of the school day. Some teachers were reported as 'ignoring you when they pass in the corridor' or 'not being available to discuss problems.' Pupils gain an overall impression of teacher behaviour and this has a direct influence on the atmosphere inside the classroom. There is a delicate balance to be achieved between care and understanding, and discipline and control. The ideas of fair and honest treatment of people in general, as discussed in Chapter 1, have specific relevance in establishing a positive atmosphere. Pupils in the secondary phase also reported the need to be treated as adults. Once again, behaving assertively will help towards achieving an atmosphere of mutual trust and respect.

Listening skills are also important in establishing a positive atmosphere. Teachers who are willing to listen to pupils' comments and incorporate their ideas tend to be more successful in generating interest and getting a response.

Where possible, giving pupils a choice of activity will engender feelings of control. For example, a choice of essay title or which books to read will increase the feelings of participation, responsibility and being treated like an adult.

In the primary phase, negotiations can also take place between pupils and teachers on the type of tasks to be carried out and so on. Similarly, the teacher may discuss expected levels of performance and when tasks should be completed with individual pupils. By doing this, pupils should feel constantly challenged. Laziness has to be consistently monitored, with no slack allowed. This is sometimes called running 'a tight ship'. Leniency will eventually result in problems which will be much more time-consuming than keeping constantly alert to what is happening.

Problem pupils

Inevitably there will be some pupils who bring more problems than others. The most direct way of trying to resolve this is to talk in private to the pupil on an individual basis. Discuss what you find unacceptable, strive for agreement about the behaviour and then try to move on to improvement. Outline what you both might do to bring about such an improvement. If possible, check pupils' records for clues to past and present problems. This will give you discussion points about which to probe for reasons.

Individuals who are repeatedly problematic may need to be referred to someone else. You should not feel this is failure on your part. The skill is in knowing when you need to refer without undermining your credibility with other pupils and colleagues. Some problems may not be within your power to resolve. You may have to talk to the parents, a pastoral tutor, or other teachers of the particular pupil. The problems should then be managed and monitored by everyone concerned, working as a team. Chapter 6 on meeting parents will give you further ideas.

Summary

Various aspects of classroom management have been discussed. The ability to create an active, participating, disciplined and interested class is an obvious characteristic of a good teacher.

Using the skills of assertiveness and effective communication, success can be achieved. By adopting the view that everything is capable of improvement, you can be constantly searching for better ways of doing things for the benefit of both pupils and teachers.

One of the variables which we haven't mentioned yet is how you manage yourself. This obviously has an impact on how you manage in the classroom and is the subject of the next chapter.

4 Managing yourself

People start off in life with a basic set of skills and aptitudes, together with a complementary level of intelligence. By dint of circumstance, fortune and endeavour, these are deployed to varying effect throughout a lifetime of experiences. Some people seem to maximise their resources; others, however, never seem to fulfil their potential.

One explanation for the different outcomes may be that the more successful, or effective people, organise themselves so as to maintain a high level of everyday performance, in a manner which enables them to exploit the frequent new opportunities which life presents. This chapter discusses ways of making better use of some of the resources at our disposal, so that we may 'raise our game' to this more effective level.

Time management

Time is a finite resource. When we feel that there isn't sufficient time to do what we want to do, we have to either reduce our demands of it or use it more efficiently. Improving our utilisation of the time available is a major step towards career and life success. There are several techniques for achieving effective time management.

- a week comprises 168 hours
- you may sleep eight hours a night = 56 hours
- hence there remain 112 hours which you can utilise.

An improvement of 5 per cent in the effective use of this time wins you 5.6 hours!

In other words, three minutes saved, or better utilised, in every hour is worth over five hours a week to you.

We will start by concentrating on your working week. This might comprise up to, say, 35 hours pupil contact and a further 10 hours in associated activities. How can you maximise this?

Key tasks

The starting point is to set out for a typical four-week period what you intend (or are required?) to achieve. Classify these tasks under, say, a maximum of eight–ten key task areas. For example:

- essential reading/study
- preparation of syllabus material
- classroom teaching
- dealing with homework
- individual teaching (tutorials, etc)
- pastoral matters
- non-classroom teaching (field trips, etc)
- administration.

Having developed the key task areas, possibly by subject or level, you need to set down the time that you are supposed to (or need to) allocate to each of these commitments. You can describe these in units of hours, or percentages, as you wish. Exercise 13 will help you to work through these steps.

Exercise 13

Make a start by mapping out your key task areas and then expand these by adding the appropriate key tasks. Do this initially for a week's work to get the feel of it. Then assign the desired number of hours to each task.

You could use the following format.

Work activity   **Estimated hours required**

Key task area 1 – Preparation of syllabus material

reading		1
drafting	key	2
collecting materials	tasks	1
arranging and timing		$\frac{1}{2}$

Then proceed to work your way through each key task area, expanding them out into their associated key tasks.

At the conclusion of the exercise, you can then summarise the hours by day or week, according to your need for clarity or control.

Having worked your way through Exercise 13, you then need to gather data about what actually happens in practice. This is usually best tackled by setting up and maintaining a **time log**.

Time logs

A time log is simply a record of what actually occurred over a selected period. The first time you keep one, you will very likely be shocked by the result! What actually occurs over a period often varies significantly from the intended apportionment of time. Perhaps, importantly, what actually happened often varies from the unrecorded recollection of what happened! This insight alone more than justifies the time and discipline required to carry out the recording exercise over a period of some days or weeks.

The following examples show two approaches to logging work activities.

Typical time log – Format 1

Date:

9.00	**Target**	Teach maths modules 11 and 12 (60 min)
	Actual	Prompt start. Interrupted by colleague (5 min)
		Fruitless argument with two pupils (5 min)
		Didn't complete module 12

10.00	**Target**	Free period – preparing short test (30 min)
	Actual	Interrupted by Head of Year (5 min)
		Finished preparing test (3 mins late)

10.30	**Target**	Administer test to second year (30 min)
	Actual	Overran slightly – test finished
		Next teacher slightly put out – pupils noisy

This log would continue throughout the day and then on through the month of the trial. On the evidence so far the teacher is either not coping with interruptions, or not planning for them. Hence each of the three periods had an unsatisfactory outcome.

Typical time log – Format 2

An alternative approach is to just keep a narrative record of events as they unfold through each day, for a working month.

Date: Key Objective: 10.30 Plan school visit

9.00   Session went well. Completed the subject matter.
       Pupils co-operative. Developed idea for project.

9.45   Misplaced a page of notes. Felt irritable. Pupils troublesome.
       Gave them balance of work for homework. Intend to speak to
       Head of Maths about work overload.

10.30 Preparing idea for school visit to local computer company.
       Colleague from Physics not very helpful. Work not completed
       – have to finish it this evening.

The log continues to record successes, disappointments, reasons, influencing factors and feelings, patterns and explanations, throughout the day.

Exercise 14

Build on the earlier work by thoroughly working out your Key Task Areas and your Key Tasks. Decide what log format would best suit you in your circumstances. Keep a daily log for a period of four working weeks.

Analysing the log

At the end of the trial period, the next step is to correlate the various events and outcomes under headings which shed light on the pattern of your performance. For instance, the best headings for you might be:

- number of satisfactory work-period outcomes in each day
- reasons for satisfactory outcomes:
  good preparation?
  your mastery of subject?
  no interruptions?
  you felt on top form?
  you like the class?
- number of unsatisfactory work-period outcomes in each day
- reasons for unsatisfactory outcomes:
  poor preparation?
  uncertain subject area?
  interruptions?
  you felt below par?
  you dislike the class?
  you are overloaded?

You then need to write a figure against the heading summarising the number of times each of these items was a feature of your month's work. Distinct patterns will emerge – the predominance of successes, interruptions, and so on.

Working your way through a detailed record of your working life will not only provide you with indications of areas for improved time-management, it will also give you a further fascinating insight of yourself:

- Are you less well organised than you thought?
- Are you too accommodating? Can you say, 'Sorry, no'?
- Do you dislike more pupils than you realised?
- Does the log show that you work more evening hours than you realised – if so, what is the **exact** reason for this?

- Does your work rely to a greater extent than you realised on the co-operation of others? Are they co-operating? Can you handle this?
- How often do you feel irritated, and what most causes this?
- Do you tend to put things off?
- Are you being too perfectionist in the time available?

All of these perceptions about work outcomes and feelings are valuable if you are to build a plan for effective time management.

Exercise 15

Having compiled your time log (Exercise 14), refer to the two lists in the section on 'Analysing the log' and assess which items would apply to you.

Planning the better use of your time

Having looked through the unsatisfactory outcomes, from the results of Exercise 15, and considered these against the insights of yourself which relate to these, you will want to take action. Start with the areas of greatest potential gain. There are a number of possible actions:

(a) Assign priority numbers to the things that really should count for you and your pupils. Priority 1 items must be achieved at all costs. Priority 2 items must receive extra attention. Everything else must meet normal expected standards. Time must be devoted from leisure if necessary to meet the deadlines for Priority 1 items.
(b) Decide if you need to change your behaviour with others to preserve your precious time (eg, refuse to be interrupted).
(c) Be absolutely single-minded when a task is important to you.
(d) Learn to read faster. There are plenty of books on the subject of speed reading for you to refer to.
(e) Learn to write quicker and more effectively.

Suggestions (a)–(c) can be implemented instantly. Do so and then keep a log for a further suitable period and observe the improvement. You could try to evaluate the gain in terms of time. Give yourself some positive reinforcement!

Time-planning stationery

Any large stationer will stock a variety of time-planning pages for insertion into covers of various price ranges. Acquire a selection that suits your personal style and needs. To an extent, if it isn't already so, time planning needs to become a habit for you.

Time planners are a briefcase equivalent of the wall charts supplied by companies like Sasco. You can use them in a similar way to record events, targets, projected meetings, periods reserved for research, study and so on. In addition, you may feel the need to maintain a conventional diary. There are various trade-offs to consider. Once you have more than one time-planning system you need to keep them aligned. On the other hand, pocket diaries showing one month per page are easy to carry with you.

Special considerations for school managers

Managers may spend less time in the classroom and have other more diverse demands on their time. Potentially and paradoxically, those who manage are less free agents than those who are managed. Certainly, they are more prone to having other people consume their time allocation. Time-consuming activities to watch out for and control, but which nevertheless may be important to you, could include:

- operating an 'open-door' policy
- allowing time for unscheduled crises
- allowing time for staff relations
- dealing with external relationships
- arranging for professional updating
- liaising with the world of business
- telephoning
- prioritising
- liaising with administrative staff and delegating.

Time, people, money, competence: these are the principal things which exercise the ingenuity of managers. Savings in the 'time' area will directly benefit the remaining three.

Writing effectively

Writing is another area of activity where it is possible to gain notable increases in efficiency to your great advantage. Essentially, when writing to somebody you are seeking to impart information, acquire information, or initiate action. You wish to achieve your aim with clarity and with as few words as is reasonable in the circumstance. All of this must consume as little of your time as possible and yet build on your relationship with the recipient. To achieve this will usually require thought, practice and continuing vigilance.

Within the context of school life you can consider writing under two main headings:

- letter writing, including brief notes and memoranda
- report writing (not the *pro-forma* approach to communicating with parents about their children's performance, but rather the business assessment type, analytical report).

Letters, and their equivalents, will usually be written on a one-to-one basis, perhaps with copies to other parties. Reports will be more heavily structured, formal, and intended to aid discussion/decisions.

Letter writing

The starting point for writing a good letter is to ask 'Why am I writing this? What do I want to achieve?' Further useful questions could be 'Who am I writing it to? How would he or she like me to regard him or her?' Another useful way of preparing to write a comprehensive letter is to work your way through the following question list of potential points to be addressed:

- Who?
- What?
- Why?
- When?
- Where?
- How?

Having decided your purpose and the points to be covered it is vital to select the most effective order of writing.

Structure

People who work in advertising, and very often earn their living with words, are quite sure that the first and last paragraphs of a letter are the ones which make the most impact. Moreover, the first paragraph is the place to tell the reader something to his or her advantage. The last paragraph is a good place to summarise some action that you would like taken, or propose to take. This approach ensures that the letter is read in the first place, and that your requirements/intentions are noted.

Exercise 16

Read through the following two letters.

Proposed letter
Dear Head

You will be very pleased to hear that the Newtown Round Table group has decided to donate £300 towards the costs of the fourth-year visits to the car factory. This should leave us with a small surplus on the venture. (Note: This is good news for the Head.)

My contact at the group advises that his colleagues would welcome a written invitation from you for two of them to join one of the trips. The date of the first visit is Monday 12th July, in six weeks' time. Can you please oblige, and would you also provide me with a copy of the letter. (Note: This clarifies the action the Head must take.)

Alternative letter (not recommended)
Dear Head

I would like you to help me by inviting some of the people at the Newtown Round Table . . . etc (Note: This letter starts off by specifying another demand on the Head's time.)

Refer to a recent letter, either to you or from you, and restructure it to better effect.

Style

In his book, *Writing to Win*, Mel Lewis advocates 'Short words in short sentences, in short paragraphs' for the most effective communication. To an extent this might be modified by the character and preferences of the intended recipient. You will have to be the judge of that.

Another prescription along the Mel Lewis lines is:

- sentences to remain within a maximum of 15 words
- paragraphs to have a maximum of five sentences.

Our own preference is to have sentences which can go to around 30 words if necessary; and paragraphs which never exceed five sentences in number. But you should also try to achieve a mixture of actual sentence and paragraph length so as to introduce variety. Hence, for example, if you have a one-liner which is really important, then that can constitute a paragraph by itself.

Your preferred style might be curtailed by the 'house style' adhered to by your school. Our preference, for example, is to write memos and letters as if speaking to the recipient. In that event one uses contractions such as you'll, we'll, doesn't, they've, and so on. If the house style discourages this, then you will need to conform. But writing as you would speak makes easy reading.

Watch out for jargon and acronyms

Key Stage Three or KS3 will be common parlance when discussing the National Curriculum in school. However, it may be totally without meaning for a friendly local employer you are writing to. The same goes for ATs (Attainment Targets), and so on.

Old-fashioned language

Some people use words and phrases in letters that they would never utter in conversation. Dorothy Stewart, in *Handbook of Management Skills*, cites the following examples:

- with all due despatch   –   as quick as possible
- endeavour to ascertain   –   try to find out
- customary channels   –   in the normal way.

Mel Lewis gives us the following examples:

- pertaining to   –   relate to
- we are of the opinion that   –   I think
- advise us as to   –   tell me
- ultimo   –   of last month
- proximo   –   of next month

Archaic language in letters is, at the least, a turn-off!

Vocabulary

One's powers of expression are dictated by the number of words at one's command, the imagination with which they are used, and one's capacity for caring about the quality of the message.

If you feel the need to augment your own wordpower then have to hand not only a dictionary, but also a thesaurus and, possibly, a dictionary of synonyms and antonyms. On our bookshelves we also have *The Oxford Writers' Dictionary*, *Room's Dictionary of Confusibles*, the Penguin book *Usage and Abusage*, and Chambers *Words*. One homespun technique for keeping in 'wordwise' condition is to have a go at a crossword puzzle at any level, however lowly, on a daily basis.

Spelling

If you are one of those people who has problems with spelling then work at becoming really expert in using the books above. In recent years, due to advances in technology, there is also a whole range of further help. Look in any mail order catalogue and you will see electronic versions of a dictionary and thesaurus. These are similar in appearance to a calculator. Word processors, of course, include a spell-check facility – as used on the draft of this book!

Report writing

Reports are usually much more meaty than letters and memos, etc. This results in the need for greater emphasis on structure. You may well have encountered this discipline if you produced a thesis or dissertation at college.

In the world of business, companies often publish rules for the layout of reports so that all departments produce them to the same pattern. Typical report-structure contents might include a selection from the following:

- introduction/summary
- data
- commentary
- request for authority
- case studies

- background
- analysis
- costs
- conclusion
- acknowledgements

- research method
- findings
- recommendations
- appendices
- bibliography.

If you are not constrained by a published format then the essentials are the introduction (some explanation of what you have done and why) and the conclusions (executive summary). Some organisations prefer to print the conclusions first. Then, if your judgement is trusted, and your recommendations are sound, there is no need to waste everyone's time by discussing the matter further. There is a need to be extremely disciplined about the content of a report – as you see, it can soon grow to a novel!

Finally, Mel Lewis makes the useful suggestion that you should always include a covering letter or note with a report. He believes that this is the equivalent of the handshake when you enter a business meeting.

The letter gives you a chance, in a few chosen words, to sell the report. It also reminds the boss why it has been written. The recommendations for letter writing discussed earlier therefore apply. For example, you start off by telling the recipient some good news for him or herself.

Exercise 17

Analyse the quality of your last six letters/reports. What shortcomings can you now see in them? Were the contents in the best order – jargon-free, interestingly written, and so on?

Speaking effectively

From time to time you may be faced with an occasion when you need to address an audience which is not comprised of pupils. You may, instead, be speaking to colleagues, parents, local employers, or perhaps governors. To the uninitiated, perhaps unpractised, such an event might be fraught with tension and be viewed as an unwelcome ordeal. This is unfortunate, because the reality is that you are being presented with an opportunity to get across some message about a topic where you are very likely a key player. Moreover, so long as you are a reasonably competent speaker, you will have the undivided attention of that audience. Public speaking is a further opportunity to show yourself to good advantage.

This section is concerned with hints on how to make your presentations interesting, informative and, perhaps, memorable. The subject matter is divided under four sections:

- preparing the talk
- delivering the talk
- using visual aids and microphones
- handling questions.

The bulk of the work is in good preparation. Most of the potential stress is related to competent delivery.

The headings presuppose that you might be speaking for up to an hour and that you have had a couple of weeks notice of the event. Even so, much of the advice is relevant under the circumstances of shorter talks and shorter notice.

If, however, you are only given ten minutes notice, then the best you can do is to write down six or seven key words and order them on the back of an envelope! In this situation, try to limit your talk to a maximum of five minutes. Start off with a joke if you can; for example, 'I've heard of impromptu performances, but this is ridiculous!'

Preparing the talk

As with the practice of most career skills, success is proportional to the effort you put into effective planning. The planning in this case starts with answering the following questions:

(a) What is the purpose of my talk? Am I aiming to advise, inform, instruct, educate, influence, enthuse, etc?
(b) Who are the members of my audience? Bosses, peers, juniors, experts, novices, parents, employers, a mixture, etc?
(c) How long is my session? for example, 45 min + 15 min for questions?

In addition to answering these questions, you should visit the room or auditorium, or at least get a reliable description of it, if it is new territory to you. You will want to know about power points, projector, screen, a lectern, the need for and availability of a microphone, and so on.

The material

No doubt you have a well-established routine for generating lecture and teaching material. For talks, this needs to result in a standard structure – introduction, the body of the talk, conclusion. This relates to the well-known maxim 'Tell them what you're going to tell them. Then tell them in detail. Then summarise by telling them what you've told them.'

The body of a 45-minute talk should, according to your topic, have a maximum of six to eight main headings. Even if you deliver a 'masterclass standard' talk to an enlightened audience they won't retain more than this number of messages!

The order in which you arrange these headings will be determined by two considerations, the first of which is obvious and the second of which is vital, if you are to be regarded as a 'good' speaker:

- the need to proceed in a logical, helpful sequence
- the need to create interest, entertain and give a performance.

One way to create this interest from the start is to sequence one or two of your most important headings early on. If you do this, though, you must make sure that the audience understands the context of what you are saying. However, try to save your most interesting points for the final part of your talk.

Writing the conclusions

It is often useful to write the conclusions before the introduction or the main body of the talk. This is where you will reiterate the key messages and weave them all together. Quite often, it is useful to have an OHP slide which shows how the various 'boxes' of information inter-relate. If you can think of one or two colourful similes to describe the concepts and notions in your talk, so much the better. This is a trick which writers use to make their work interesting and entertaining. For example, 'Forgetting to make a budgetary return would be about as popular as deposing a Prime Minister!' If you can work in the occasional joke, and if you can tell them effectively, these usually help you to be remembered by an audience, but don't get carried away from your main purpose! However, don't joke if you can't carry it off.

Writing the introduction

You are now in a position to write this, since you now know 'What you are going to tell them'. When you actually deliver the introduction, your talk will just be beginning, so keep it simple.

Preparing your speaker's notes for the day

Speakers who make the best impact **never** stand at the front and read from voluminous notes. The act of prolonged reading takes too much concentration in itself, and contact with the audience is lost. They would wonder why you didn't just send them the notes to read themselves.

Good speakers use one of these three techniques:

(a) They have a little batch of index cards with key words and messages written on them. These are often punched through in one corner and loosely tied together (so that it doesn't matter if they are dropped).

(b) They have a paper copy of their slides on the lectern, and they build words around these as they go along.

(c) They use no notes at all – being much better gifted than the rest of us!

You will develop your own preference. Many use method (a).

The text so far has been devoted to the preparation of material, and some final general points are:

- try to marshal your facts in simple building blocks
- try to describe them in a colourful way: anecdotes help, too.

Giving the talk

From the audience's point of view, you are potentially very interesting. If they are strangers, they won't yet know any more than they can see. If they know you, they will be interested to see how you come across. Your task, if you are to be anything other than a talking book, is to project your personality to them.

Personality, in this context, is projected by clothes, stance, voice, word content, gestures and eye contact. You can deploy most of these to your advantage.

(a) **Clothes**. You will obviously wear what convention dictates. It is quite common and perfectly acceptable for a speaker to remove a jacket. Wear clothes which will let you move about comfortably.

(b) **Stance**. If you are feeling stressed, this is likely to be reflected in your stance. You need to stand, or sit, fairly erect, but at ease. If you don't, your breathing will be inhibited and you will speak unnaturally, and feel uptight.

(c) **Voice**. Unpractised public speakers tend to speak too quickly. This makes for stuttering and incomprehension. It is much better to speak slower than normal, rather than quicker. The audience will feel that this is a measured and thoughtful form of delivery. Leave a gap of a few seconds occasionally.

(d) **Word content**. You will be building up the word content around the key words on your cards. Try to deliver them with varying emphasis. Raise and lower your voice a little. Avoid jargon, unless everyone present will understand. Some words are quite hard to say out aloud; for example, 'statistician'. One trick for dealing with such words is to unnaturally emphasise the first vowel; for example, STAtistician. Sort difficult words out beforehand. If you can't say the word on the actual day when you are giving your talk, then make a joke of your trouble. Wave your arms in despair!

(e) **Gestures**. Gestures are very helpful in creating powerful images. (Watch any political party conference on television.) But if you do use them, then move quite noticeably. Don't just move your wrist; point with your whole arm.

(f) **Eye contact**. This should vary with the size of the audience. If there are less than 20 people, be sure to let your eye come to rest on each person present from time to time. (Note: come to rest means let it stay there for a second or two. This has the useful effect of persuading everyone present that you are speaking quite often to them in person.) If your audience is larger, then look at a point about two-thirds of the way to the back. Occasionally look to the left and right ends of the front rows. Whatever you do, don't scan each row from left to right in turn throughout your talk – this is known as searchlighting. It becomes quite comical for the audience! At the very least it will destroy the illusion of relaxed normalcy you have created.

Exercise 18

Map out and then prepare a 15-minute talk on the relevance to society of your specialist subject. Try to incorporate all the preparatory steps discussed so far. Imagine you will be speaking to an audience of 25 people.

Using visual aids and microphones

Visual aids, in the context of a talk, usually take one of four forms:

(a) flip charts.
(b) overhead projector (OHP) slides.
(c) film slides.
(d) videos.

Unless you have relatively sophisticated facilities and back-up you are most likely to be using the first two of these. Probably the best compromise from all of them is the overhead projector slide.

If you are portraying words, then try to keep within a maximum of six or seven lines. If these are typed, then use capital letters throughout. Leave at least four spaces between each line. Make sure you have a good typewriter ribbon. If you are using a word processor, then use the 'bold' facility throughout.

Slides are excellent for portraying trends in the form of graphs and histograms, etc. The occasional cartoon is a very popular way of emphasising key points. If you are not an artist, you can cut suitable figures from periodicals and paste them onto a sheet of A4 paper. Additionally, when you have your slide printed, you will bring in an extra dimension by colouring it as appropriate with crayons or special ink pens (obtainable from any decent stationer).

Do make sure you 'shine a light' through your slides to see the general effect when they are finished. On the day, and in the hall or classroom, you may find yourself lumbered with an antiquated projector in a neglected state. You can often improve the projection by using a tissue and some water from the speaker's glass, applied to the lens, the mirror and the surface you put your slide on.

Decide beforehand what you will do if something (eg, power failure) prevents you from using your slides (eg, you could use a flip chart instead).

Using the slides on the day

The following gives a few pointers about using your slides.

(a) Try to arrange the siting of the equipment so that you and it are never between any of the audience and the screen. It is surprising how often these things happen. If it is a square room, a good place for the screen is across one corner.

(b) Do not lose eye contact by talking to the screen.

(c) You need to give the audience time to comprehend the slide. It may be difficult for them, initially, to understand the messages and listen to you at the same time.

(d) Sometimes it helps to uncover portions of the slide as you progress through the points.

(e) If it is an important occasion, you may find it helpful to get someone to put your slides on for you, leaving you to concentrate solely on performing.

(f) Too many slides can give the effect of a crammed session.

(g) You will have been monitoring your schedule by propping up your wristwatch in front of you. If you find you are slipping behind, then rapidly decide if there are a couple of slides you can omit, rather than trying to cover them all quickly.

Microphones

Microphones come in two main varieties:

(a) those which are attached to a stand or lectern.

(b) those which are fixed to you – clipped to your shirt, blouse, jacket or tie.

With the former, you need to experiment to see just how far away you can stand or turn your head without your voice fading. With the latter, you need to remember that you are attached to an amplifier by a piece of wire throughout your performance.

A microphone will only project what you put into it. If you speak in a flat colourless way, it will make sure that everyone present can properly hear your flat, colourless delivery! But there is no doubt about it, the larger the room the greater its benefit. A microphone will save you 45 minutes of strenuous effort and allow you to concentrate on your real task.

Handling questions

Question time is the last opportunity you have to get really understood. It is a very welcome chance to end on a high note of rapport with your audience. You may have allowed one or two pressing questions as you proceeded, but make sure it is only one or two. The following will give you some pointers for handling questions.

(a) Questions should be answered briefly and to the point.
(b) At some time, somebody will ask you a question to which you do not know the answer. Don't try and bluff it out; say you don't know and ask if anyone else present does. If not, offer to find out the answer and report back. Advise them of possible sources of further information.
(c) If there is any doubt about the meaning of a question, then ask for clarification.
(d) Don't let any one person hog the question period (this quite often happens). Make sure that you select a representative sample from the questioners. For instance, don't just take questions from the men, or the women, or seniors, etc.
(e) If anyone is hostile, make very sure that you remain courteous. The audience will then remain sympathetic to you. If the person continues, tell him or her that you will meet them in the interval to discuss their issue.
(f) When time is running out, say you will take three more questions.
(g) Finish the session on some upbeat message and thank the audience for listening to you.

Rapid reading

Teachers, along with people in many other occupations, find it necessary to read a large quantity of written material. They spend many hours carrying out essential reading. In a chapter which is devoted to managing yourself we felt it desirable to point readers towards a way of reclaiming some of this valuable time by speeding up their reading process. There are proven techniques for achieving this improvement.

This book should be regarded as an introductory summary. There are a number of excellent books on the subject, which include: *Rapid Reading Made Simple*, G. R. Wainright, W. H. Allen, London; *Rapid Reading*, Janis Grummitt, The Industrial Society, London. Each of these books includes instruction, advice and exercises on learning and applying the steps to more efficient reading.

Reading speeds

An average person, on average material, will read at around 250 words per minute and could expect between 60 and 70 per cent comprehension. With knowledge of the techniques and some determined practice this speed figure can be improved by several hundred per cent – a striking improvement!

Some basic theory

Most people learned to read by reading aloud to somebody. This process required the written word to be recognised and then pronounced. Later, we learned to read inside our heads (ie, do it silently), and we still followed the same procedure outlined above. But pronunciation is not necessary if we are not speaking audibly. Dispensing with the redundant step is one of the early lessons in becoming a rapid reader.

Another key point is that reading is seen as a passive process where it is not required to expend much energy. The notion is that the writer has done the work; 'all we have to do is to read it'. To read more quickly requires a change of viewpoint about this. An efficient reader has to put in some applied endeavour; a conscious effort to proceed in a certain manner.

Thirdly, the nature of the reader's eye movements is crucial to the speed of reading. Slow readers fix on every word in turn. Faster readers focus on fewer words (they jump some words). They still see those words but do not focus on each one individually (instead, they fix on groups of words). Slow readers also 'regress' (ie, go back to words from time to time and also wander).

To bring about change requires the desire to do so and the belief that success is possible. Improved concentration is also necessary.

Some techniques for improvement

Reading speed can be adjusted to suit the material being read. Janis Grummitt speaks of 'reading gears':

- study reading – up to 200 words per minute
- slow reading – 200–300 words per minute
- rapid reading – 300–800 words per minute
- skimming – 600–60 000 (!) words per minute!

The choice of gear, she suggests, is related to:

- the nature of the material
- our purpose in reading
- external factors (eg, environment) and also how we feel.

Sometimes it is useful to deliberately read things several times at different speeds. It is almost always more efficient to read something quickly twice than to read it slowly once. Some possible reading strategies are:

- preview (at skimming speed), then read
- preview, read, review
- read, then review.

To assist with comprehension and recollection:

- read things critically in order to understand better
- reinforce key points for better retention
- associate ideas with other ideas for better recollection
- develop confidence in your improved abilities.

Some general hints

The books on the subject of speed reading appear to unite in stressing that the old (bad) habits must first be eliminated. Words must not be pronounced in the mind. The number of eye fixations per printed line must be reduced. Regressing to earlier words must be eliminated. Faster and faster reading must be practised. Note, this activity in itself helps you stop pronouncing words mentally (because there isn't then the time!).

Because a high rate of comprehension is still required, despite increased speed of input, it is necessary to read critically to ensure initial comprehension. It is also necessary to accentuate key points in the mind for the sake of better retention. A system whereby you can associate really important messages with some other item of information is the way that many people with a 'good' memory actually recall important things that they have read.

Summary

In this chapter we have concentrated on four self-management activity areas, where a conscious effort to attain improvement will produce a virtually instantaneous personal benefit.

Time management

Whilst time itself is immutable, the way in which we utilise it is subject to a wide range of skill. There are just three steps to take towards an improved personal deployment.

(a) Set down in writing what you need to achieve and by when. If necessary, allocate priority categories.
(b) Record what actually takes place over a set period of time.
(c) Analyse the record and produce a plan for improvement.

In conclusion, it will be clear to you that you can do this for your leisure time, as well as your work time. And of course you can combine them if you choose.

Writing effectively

Communicating by the written word is a vital skill for the serious careerist. Doing it well has the effect of promoting a good image of yourself. With practice you can drastically reduce the time required to write high quality, effective letters and reports.

Speaking effectively

A speaking opportunity is a further chance to project your ideas; to communicate effectively; to improve your confidence. It is also a way of bringing your merits to people's attention.

Rapid reading

Anyone whose occupation implies large volumes of reading, with high degrees of absorption, should increase their reading efficiency.

5 Managing your boss*

One of the most often quoted sources of dissatisfaction at work involves relationships with the boss. Managing your boss means enabling you to minimise the negative aspects of the relationship and enhance the positive aspects. It means influencing the way you are perceived by your boss to your own advantage.

Common problem areas

Do you recognise any of the following problem areas?

- my boss is never there when I want to see him
- my boss doesn't show me how to do things properly
- my boss doesn't understand what I'm trying to achieve
- my boss doesn't show appreciation
- the better I am, the more work my boss gives me to do
- my boss finds it impossible to delegate
- my boss often criticises me
- my boss doesn't back me up
- my boss feels threatened by me
- my boss is indecisive
- my boss interferes with what I'm doing
- my boss is disorganised
- my boss excludes me from important meetings and information
- my boss is a perfectionist
- my boss rejects my ideas
- my boss is unpredictable
- my boss usually blames someone other than himself
- I don't feel I can tell my boss when I've made a mistake
- my boss has a terrible temper
- my boss takes the credit for work I have done.

---

* We have assumed that the boss is male to avoid writing his or her throughout. Statistically, there are more male bosses in education than female.

One of the main players in this relationship of course is you. What can you do to minimise these negative aspects? Let us have a look at each of these in turn.

My boss is never there when I want to see him

Quite often, the relationship initially works out OK, but gradually a change may be noticed. What might be happening here is that you are taking up the boss's time in a way that is unproductive or unrewarding from the boss's point of view. You may be taking up time by asking too many questions, interfering at the wrong time, bringing up less important issues, possibly in an unclear way. From your point of view you need information to do the job, from his point of view you are wasting time.

An immediate method of trying to improve the situation is to make your boss view time with you as time well spent. Try to highlight areas where his time will be saved in the long term. You want to try to present solutions rather than problems. Use your meetings with your boss to tell of accomplishments and decisions made. Don't ask your boss for information that you can easily get from someone else. By using other communication channels you will be able to maintain an image of being well-informed and on top of things.

John, a headteacher in a large secondary school, was confronted by Alan every Monday after assembly. Alan was head of the pastoral care unit. He gave a detailed run-down of problems encountered in the previous week. Eventually John began to avoid him. Not only was the information often routine and unnecessary for John to know in detail, but it also came at an inappropriate time. Alan needed to talk things through, but he didn't *need* to do it with the boss. He might have established a network of colleagues with whom he could have got things off his chest. In this way, he could have established the position of seeing John only when necessary and also fulfilling his own needs for talking things through.

If a boss becomes so switched off by this type of behaviour he is much less likely to listen when there are crucial issues to be discussed.

My boss doesn't show me how to do things properly

Many people in subordinate roles look for direction from their bosses. Your value to your boss lies in the extent to which you can and do direct yourself and achieve results.

Once you have been given the go ahead for a project it is up to you to see it through. If you become dependent on your boss that is your problem, not his. So clarify the constraints within which you are operating and then go ahead to complete your project without becoming over-dependent.

You may say that the boss's job is to manage. This is a negative and limited view which will not get you anywhere. You have to show that you can take the initiative and keep on working independently. If you do not, someone else will show such qualities and they will get noticed, rather than you.

It will help if you develop an effective network of resources. This will take time and effort but the rewards can be well worthwhile and will illustrate to your boss that you are a person who learns the ropes quickly and effectively.

Julie was appointed by her headteacher, Brenda, to take charge of the school library. She was given a special allowance to do the job. Julie constantly asked Brenda how she should do all the routine jobs as and when they cropped up. Brenda became increasingly impatient and suggested that Julie should use her own initiative more. Julie felt that Brenda was deliberately refusing to show her how she wanted the library organised. Eventually, Julie asked if she could be relieved of the post and give up the special allowance. Brenda agreed with relief and appointed someone else who was prepared to take initiative.

If Julie had been able to work on her own and bring forward new ideas about running the library, her own standing and status would have been enhanced. As it was, by becoming over-dependent on her boss, she significantly contributed to the deterioration in their relationship.

My boss doesn't understand what I'm trying to achieve

One may ask in response to this, why should he? A boss cannot know everything that is going on without feedback from you. What you are really saying is that the boss should know and understand all the aspects of your job. In reality, your boss will only take in those aspects of your job which he needs to know in order to make judgements and decisions. If you really feel the need to communicate about this, keep it short and simple with the salient points mentioned. Going into minute detail will switch your boss off and create more problems for you.

Lynda, the teacher of the reception class in an infants school, had many good ideas about how four- and five-year-olds should progress and just how important their place was in the school. She went to see the headteacher frequently about her ideas and plans. She became upset when the head showed little interest and refused to allocate her extra resources. She felt that the head failed to understand her aspirations, and she began to feel personally affronted.

Fortunately, at around this time, Lynda went on an assertiveness training course. The result was that she reflected on both her role and that of the head, and assertively asked for a meeting of limited duration once a month with the express purpose of discussing the aims, needs and targets for the reception class. This was agreed to and Lynda felt that her views were being listened to. The head was happy to plan a limited time into his schedule for these discussions.

My boss doesn't show appreciation

It would seem that one of the hardest things for a boss to do is give praise for a job well done. In your own job you will often give praise and encouragement to pupils and expect the same yourself. Our socialisation process, from birth onwards, encourages us to rely on external praise.

You have to learn to minimise the need for external approval and appreciate your own worth. Try evaluating your own performance: are you learning and growing? Do you feel you are improving on what you were doing a month, six months ago?

If your boss doesn't give positive feedback, assume he values your work in the same way that you are learning to do. Highlight your achievements: praise doesn't have to come from the boss. It is just as valuable when it comes from you, assuming of course that the evaluation is realistic.

If your boss doesn't give praise because he feels threatened, try to include him in your achievements. Give him credit for your success. Emphasise the importance of his contribution.

The better I am, the more work my boss gives me to do

Here is a classic case where the ability to say 'no' without feeling guilty is crucial. By not saying 'no' you are, in fact, under-estimating your own value and down-grading yourself. The normal pattern goes something like this.

- you perform well
- you are appreciated and given more work
- you feel needed and good about this
- you are now creating a self-image of indispensability and your boss has expectations of compliance.

If at this point you do start to say 'no', expectations are not fulfilled and your boss views you with disapproval. It is quite likely that you will now get into a spiral of doing more and more work because of the fear of his disapproval and the desire to be valued.

You need to be clear about how you value yourself – then you can negotiate acceptable arrangements about work. When you are saying 'No', say it in a way that represents positive elements rather than negative. For example, say 'I will take on the extra responsibility, but project X will be delayed!' rather than 'If I do that I shan't be able to cope with anything else!' By phrasing your response in this way you are showing co-operation, but not over-loading yourself with too much work.

Janice, a primary school teacher, found it very difficult to say 'No'. 'Oh! Janice will do that', was often heard. She was very keen and committed but gradually her workload grew so much that it started to affect her health. She had quite a lot of time off with various minor ailments. This, of course, caused severe disruption to the school. When a new headteacher was appointed he assessed the situation for what it was and talked to all the staff. His talk with Janice outlined his understanding of her commitment and enthusiasm, but also made clear that he didn't want her to take on too much.

Janice was lucky she had a change of boss. However, she could have prevented much of this situation by sometimes saying 'No'.

My boss finds it impossible to delegate

Delegation is one of the most difficult things to do. One of the reasons is the feeling of losing control. If your boss delegates work, how does he know that he will get a good job done? You have to behave in a way that will convince him that you are professional and competent, and that he can have confidence in you.

Show him that you are in control of your work and that you can function independently. He won't know that you can do these things unless you show him you can. He may lack confidence in himself and you can bolster up his ego by demonstrating your ability, but in a way that won't undermine his confidence and make him feel threatened. You have to read the situation carefully; show him that you can cope with the responsibility, but that you are also on his side.

Also recognise that there may be situations where the boss feels that he is the better person to do it: for example, talking to an irate parent or telephoning to fix a meeting with the chair of governors. The personal touch may be what is needed in such situations. You will have to weigh up the reasons why your boss does not delegate.

Your boss may also be unable to delegate because of bad past experiences. If he has had a subordinate in the past who was incompetent and created problems for him, he is likely to have developed a management style that is non-trusting. You have to wean him out of this by showing him (and quite often this means actually pointing out to him) that you can be trusted to do the job well. Let him know when you have done something well or if you have received positive feedback. In this way, he will gradually build up the confidence to trust you.

As already mentioned in Chapter 1, you have a right to make mistakes. In fact, all managers should see their mistakes as important learning events. Sir John Harvey Jones (ex-Chairman of ICI) has gone so far as to say that he would fire a manager who did not make mistakes. He believes that if a manager is not making mistakes, he is not taking risks. So if you do make a mistake, assertively accept it and show to your boss the learning points you have gained from the experience and how you can improve things in the future. You will need to build up his confidence and trust again.

Joyce, in her first year of teaching music in a primary school, was asked by her headteacher to take charge of the preparations for the annual school play. She accepted eagerly but found throughout the rehearsals that the headteacher made frequent appearances. He made many suggestions for alterations and additions, and eventually took over the directing. Joyce, young and newly qualified, put up with all this without complaining, feeling too inexperienced to make a stand. The following year, with more experience and confidence, Joyce was again asked to produce the play. She was able to accept on condition that she would be left alone to do the job in her own way. She reminded the head of the part she played in last year's success and he was happy to leave her to it.

My boss often criticises me

If you have to endure constant criticism your confidence will eventually be undermined. It is important to get the matter under control (see Chapter 1 on how to cope with criticism, for some ideas). You may have to cope with the fact that you either conform to the way the boss wants things done, or move on elsewhere. Sometimes, a positive approach to learning from the criticism rather than rebelling against it, will enable your boss to view you in a different light.

My boss doesn't back me up

This type of behaviour soon undermines your authority and you quickly become regarded as the underling with no power. There are many possible reasons for this type of behaviour. Your boss may not realise what he is doing, he may feel threatened, he may need to feel in control, or there may be new information which changes the situation.

Objectively, his reasons for not supporting you may be valid, but if it causes embarrassment and undermines your position then you need to take action. You need to find strategies that will put the boss on your side, so that you can work as a team. In this way you will be controlling his behaviour. He will be much less likely to by-pass you if you are an integral part of an authoritative team. Personal power can be a very potent weapon. Your lower position in the hierarchy can be minimised by your own personal power.

When your boss doesn't back you up you need to address the issue in an assertive way. Don't let it pass or he will see you as a pushover and so will other people. State your case clearly and tell him why you are displeased and what you would like to happen in the future. Explain why it was important that you had his backing and when you had agreement to it. Always make sure that you present your case in a reasoned way. Don't minimise the power of the opposition's argument. Tell your boss what the argument is, but why it should be done your way. When your opponent then presents his arguments, your boss will already have heard them and your counter proposal.

Tracy, an experienced teacher of infants, was making plans as she always did to meet the parents of her pupils at separate times in the evening after school. She learned that the father of one of her pupils, a notoriously violent man, had just been released from prison and was planning to accompany his wife to the interview. This situation had occurred before with another parent. When she had asked the headteacher to be there he had refused and made light of the matter. The interview with the parents on that occasion had turned out disastrously. Fearing for her safety and a repeated performance, Tracy approached the head and asked for his backing. He gave his full support. He took part in the interview and escorted the parents out of school afterwards.

This case highlights the need for realistic assessment of a situation. If you feel you need help or backing do not be afraid to ask.

My boss feels threatened by me

If you feel this then you need to analyse the situation carefully. Does the boss fear that you have greater knowledge, more ability or more political 'nous'? Does he feel that his relationship with you is too competitive and forces him into win/lose behaviour?

Unless you are really trying to oust your boss from his position (a high-risk strategy), you are much better off working alongside him as a team. When someone feels threatened they begin to engage in extremely defensive behaviour and a vicious spiral starts. This often results in a complete breakdown of the relationship.

Try to minimise his feeling of threat. Be aware of your own secret agendas and the impact that this is having on your own behaviour. Try to see things from his point of view.

Tony, a young teacher in a comprehensive school, was keen to make a contribution towards the out-of-school activities – an important part of the school's curriculum. Bill, the deputy headteacher, was justly proud of the school's reputation and had always taken the lead in organising the school camping trip. Tony suggested a change to a more rigorous activity, which would be more appealing to pupils. They were very enthusiastic and voted against the old-style camp.

Although Tony was pleased about this he realised that his relationship with Bill was suffering. He analysed the situation and came to the conclusion that Bill was feeling left out, a situation he could understand. He decided to talk to Bill directly, and asked him to lead the expedition – at the same time emphasising the pupils' wish for this. He offered to do all the preparatory organisation himself. Bill, now feeling that his power position had been restored, began to treat Tony more as a friend and colleague, rather than as a threat.

This case shows once again how you as an individual have to take responsibility for trying to resolve a situation. If Tony had behaved in a competitive way then it is likely that this relationship would have gone from bad to worse. In the long run, it would be you who would be expending a lot of time and energy trying to recoup a worsening situation.

My boss is indecisive

You complete assignments promptly and you are on top of the work, but your boss sits on the information and doesn't make a decision. This can be really frustrating, but before blaming the boss too much, think about what you could do to alter his behaviour. How much effort does he have to put in to reach a decision on what you have presented? Make it as easy for him as possible to take in the salient points and come to a conclusion.

If you do this and you still have problems, think about why he is behaving like this. One reason could be fear. Survival strategy has often been seen as keeping your head down and not sticking your neck out. Your boss may simply be afraid of making decisions. One way to counter this is to present a 'what if' analysis – what is likely to happen if we don't do this and what are the implications if we do? By presenting possible consequences you are allowing your boss to evaluate the case more easily.

The boss who leaves decision-making till the last minute is also frustrating but he may have good reasons. He may want to get more information or allow his own thought processes time to consider the problem. Or he may simply be suffering from work overload. He may, however, think the problem will go away on its own. If you have this problem try to keep your boss informed of deadlines, operate independently, keep him informed and see if he stops you. If you have established a good track record he is more likely to let you carry on. Finally, try to show him that his own self-image will be enhanced by acting promptly and being decisive.

Bob, a newly appointed geography teacher at a Lancashire school, was sure that some of the less able and, in many cases, less well-behaved pupils would gain from going on a field trip. In the past, this had been felt to be a waste of time and money. He had made a lot of enquiries at other schools, consulted some of his old college friends and finally presented the headteacher with a list of suggestions for approval. The head did nothing, partly because he wasn't sure of the LEA's response and partly because he felt it might be a disaster. As time passed, Bob became increasingly anxious for a decision. He needed time to plan and organise the trip if it were to go ahead. Eventually, he went to the head and said 'What if we are the only school who discriminates among pupils – allowing some to go on field trips and others not? If we can go ahead we can gain a lot of good publicity for the school out of this.' By using this approach, Bob eventually got his way and the trip went ahead.

My boss interferes with what I'm doing

Your boss might be interfering with your work because he hasn't been getting the results he wants. Check out whether or not you have anything to learn about the way you do things. He will maintain control as long as he thinks things are not going to be done the way he wants them to be.

If you are doing things well, getting results, and he is still looking over your shoulder, then he's over-controlling. This acts as a de-motivator for you. You could make a stand on this one. Point out that you are getting the results he wants and your methods are appropriate. Work out carefully why he is behaving like this. Once again, he is probably afraid to let go. Find out why he feels he has to watch your every move and then try to allay his fears.

Withholding information from your boss, which is quite a common response, is actually counter-productive. The more information you give a controlling person the more he will feel in control and the less he will interfere.

Charles is the headteacher of a comprehensive school which had had consistently good examination results until the previous year. Although the results were good they were below those of two other comprehensives in the town, whereas before they had always been better. Sue, a relatively new teacher of 'A' level biology, became increasingly irritated with Charles who was constantly in and out of her classroom checking her pupils' progress and her teaching methods. This was also happening to other teachers. Sue realised why Charles was behaving in this way and made a point of providing information on the pupils and the work they were doing at regular intervals, emphasising the high standards that were being achieved. Although Sue found this a hassle it was preferable to Charles's constant interference. She didn't completely succeed in keeping him away from her classes, but the frequency of his visits diminished.

My boss is disorganised

The disorganised boss is a common problem. Chaos and disorder impact on everyone. The more dependent you are on your boss the worse this will be. So first of all, lessen your dependency. Assigning blame to your boss won't help either: this is very unproductive. You need to be creative and find solutions to the problem. Assigning blame won't change his behaviour but will damage your relationship.

You can even make his disorganisation work to your advantage. Take on more responsibility and he will be relieved that you are doing some of his work. You may feel this is unfair but it may be the only way to deal with this sort of boss.

Take copies of everything you prepare for your boss. When you go into a meeting with him, take extra copies with you. Don't expect him to remember things – double-check everything and remind the boss of important appointments. Do this in a way to highlight your own level of organisation and not his level of disorganisation. If he forgets to turn up, carry on without him. Don't give the impression that you think the most important person isn't there! If you adopt this sort of attitude you will eventually learn to work with it, rather than resenting your boss's weakness. Don't try to make him feel guilty, just supply what he is lacking in order for you to do your job properly. Although your boss's methods are irritating to you, if they work for him he will be quite happy with the way he operates. So avoid trying to organise him, it probably won't work.

My boss excludes me from important meetings and information

Once again, you have to reflect on why your boss is behaving in this way. Is it a question of cost? Does he feel that you have enough on your plate? Does he worry that if you know too much you will become more of a threat?

Make out a good case as to why you should attend the meetings you want to, or receive the information you feel you need. Phrase the points in such a way that he will see how *he* benefits from this. If you do succeed, reinforce the point by highlighting the benefits of your attending; for example in further work that you were able to do.

Another aspect of this type of behaviour involves status. Being in possession of classified information is seen as self-enhancing. If you are allowed to possess restricted information, you are in fact diluting your boss's feeling of power. Being allowed to attend important meetings also has an impact on other members of the meeting. Your boss may come under pressure or be criticised for allowing you to attend when members of other sections and departments are excluded.

If you develop a reputation of being a storehouse of relevant information then people will start to want you to attend meetings. In meetings, make sure that what you have to say is presented clearly and succinctly. Practise this so that your contributions are seen in a positive way: this will make people want to listen to what you have to say. Chapter 7, on handling meetings, gives many more hints on this.

John, a teacher in a large comprehensive school, was put in charge of careers. He thought this was a good promotion opportunity and readily accepted. He worked hard to build up the department but was a bit put out when he was not invited to meetings concerned with pupils' progress. John had devised a questionnaire for pupils. The results of this gave him a good idea of appropriate career paths each pupil might follow. Armed with this information, John was able to persuade the headteacher that it would be to his advantage if John was present at the progress meetings to give out the information he had. Once John had gained access to these meetings, he rapidly gained the respect of other members of staff. In this way, he was able to highlight his qualities to a much wider audience. His job satisfaction was also higher because he felt he was able to make a meaningful contribution.

My boss is a perfectionist

To deal with this problem, you first have to decide whether you consider your boss to be successful or not. If his behaviour is generally succeeding then you haven't much cause for complaint. If his perfectionism is causing you problems, then you have to analyse why. Does he think you are not doing your job to his standard? Examine what you do, and try to see it through his eyes. Is there room for improvement? If you feel you are doing a good job, reassure him. Let him know of your successes, new ideas and so on. This will allay his anxiety and diminish his need to perfect every little defect. If your boss does find a genuine error, don't confront him and be defensive, learn to accept criticism and learn from your mistakes (see Chapter 1).

George is the headteacher of a junior school which has an excellent reputation. He expects a high standard from his staff, not only in the classroom but also in administrative work. He expects registers to be without mistakes, record books to be precise and detailed, and reports to be models of perfection. Alice, a teacher of middle juniors, never seems to quite meet the requirements of George. One day, George noticed a spelling error on her blackboard and asked Alice to see him after school. During the discussion Alice could feel herself becoming more and more defensive and the meeting ended with her feeling very upset and humiliated.

Twenty four hours later she realised she should have admitted the mistake and not try to get out of it or justify it. Although she felt that George was slightly over the top in his approach she wasn't critical of the way he had handled the meeting, but of her own response. On reflection later, she realised that George was held in high esteem by parents, governors and officials and that she was lucky to be working in that type of school. This overall perspective enabled her to cope more easily with some of George's 'nit-picking' behaviour.

My boss rejects my ideas

You come up with an idea which you think is good, but your boss takes little notice of it. Your feelings for your boss diminish and relationships can become strained. Remember that your boss probably hears many good ideas. What matters to him is how implementable your idea is and how it fits into the total picture. Implementing an idea means allocating resources; and resources are often stretched. He has to practise ideas to achieve his overall objective.

If your suggestions are backed up by practical cost-effective means of making them work and an assessment of the benefits, you are more likely to be successful.

Organisation policies often stand in the way of good ideas. Your idea may involve the co-operation of other people for implementation. Your boss may be in dispute with one of these people or he may be going through a power struggle. He won't communicate this directly to you: you will have to work it out for yourself. There are many other reasons why bosses reject ideas. He may have been asked to cut costs, for example. Your idea, in the short term at least, will cost money. Although you can see the benefit for the school as a whole in the long term, it isn't necessarily good for your boss at the moment. If you are not getting support for your ideas – stop and work out why they are being rejected.

Peter teaches in a comprehensive school in Surrey. He volunteered to take part in running the school's sporting activities. Peter is a cricket enthusiast and was surprised to find cricket was not one of the sports offered by the school. He approached the headteacher about including cricket in the sports curriculum. The head, conscious of cost and the difficulty of introducing a new sport from scratch, rejected the idea. Peter realised that he could have brought up the idea in a more positive way. He explored the possibility of fixtures with other schools, the cost of equipment, how it would fit into the curriculum and so on. The following year, Peter put concrete proposals to the head who was able to evaluate the idea much more effectively and agreed to start a pilot scheme in the summer term.

My boss is unpredictable

Is your boss the moody type who blames everyone else for his problems? Does his behaviour towards you blow hot and cold? One explanation may be that he is not satisfied with your performance. But on the other hand, he may be a person with regular mood swings. When he thinks things are going well he is on a high, but when things are going wrong he sees himself as worthless and he sinks.

The cool silent treatment may mean he thinks you are not doing a sound job. There are clues to this. First, the mood swings are reserved for you; the cool treatment doesn't happen to the others. Second, verbal criticism occurs around the same time as you get the cold treatment. On the other hand, when you perform well, the boss's behaviour towards you warms up. If this is the case, you know he is reacting to you and not something in his personal situation. You can then start to work out what to do about it.

While your boss's opinion of himself may change, your opinion of him may be constant. The danger, as far as you are concerned, is keying your moods to his. You don't have to be trapped in his distorted self-appraisal. Try to be objective. Maintain a constant stance towards him based on the needs of the job.

Constancy of your behaviour is easier said than done. Many of us take on responsibility for other people's moods; if you get out of this habit you won't panic when the boss is cold towards you. Try to gauge his moods day by day, and when he is in a bad mood don't put him on the spot by asking what's wrong. Even if he wanted to tell you, it is inappropriate to ask.

My boss usually blames someone other than himself

It is very difficult for a lot of people to admit to making a mistake, so they blame others. In doing this, they are attempting to preserve their own self-worth, however deluded this may be.

If you have a boss like this it is pointless to argue about the issues, because he is worrying about something else – his worth. Showing that it was he and not you who caused the problem will get you nowhere. However, neither should you accept the blame placed on you.

The technique for dealing with this is to deflect the matter of blame and move on to action which will rectify the error. Action allows you both to come away with undamaged egos. One teacher reported that her boss called her in one day and said, 'Where are the reports for 3b?' The teacher defended herself by saying 'You said those had to wait until the first and second years were in'. The boss took issue with her and said, 'No, I told you I wanted those reports by Friday'. The teacher knew she was right and her boss wrong. She felt unjustly accused and they got into a heated argument about who was to blame. What she should have done in this situation was to say, 'I don't remember you telling me but maybe you're right. Why don't I go and do them now?'

In this way any question of blame is put aside in favour of action which will try to rectify the situation.

If the blamer still can't get into problem-solving gear, take things further. While putting aside the question of blame, you can acknowledge and analyse the error in detail (and disastrous consequences if necessary) and then take on the responsibility for improving the situation.

I don't feel I can tell my boss when I've made a mistake

We all have the right to make mistakes (see Chapter 1). If we don't make mistakes we are not taking risks. It could be argued that if we are not taking risks then we are not growing and developing. The main point about mistakes is that we should learn from them rather than see them as negative occurrences. Once we can take this idea on board then we can feel more able to admit mistakes.

Not being able to admit mistakes often means that we panic and put off dealing with the problem. This often makes matters worse. Rachel had asked her headteacher if she could order some new equipment. He agreed, providing the price was kept under £200. When the bill came it was for £50 more because one of the items was separately priced. She dreaded sending the invoice to the head and kept putting it off, all the while increasing her own level of anxiety. What she could have done was to try to negotiate a discount with the supplier, or failing that, discuss a fund-raising idea with her boss that would raise the additional £50. In this way, the problem would have been solved more quickly.

If you don't deal with a mistake at once, the solution is to act non-defensively as if the delay had never occurred. Don't let your panic and fear cause you to delay one more day. Act now and you will probably find that the problem has appeared much greater than is really the case.

My boss has a terrible temper

Quite often this situation occurs with a boss who feels insecure, especially with people he relies on. He may worry about things not being achieved in the way that they should be and so shouts and screams to get the message across.

If your boss is like this, instead of running away and avoiding him, let him know that you hear what he is saying. If you can, be one step ahead. Raise issues first which gives him no time to develop rage and aggression. Stand your ground and don't become defensive. Defensiveness implies weakness; this will only exacerbate his lack of confidence in your ability.

When your boss gets so angry that you can't get a word in edgeways, it may be appropriate to withdraw from the situation. You could say something like, 'I can't discuss this with you while you're shouting so I'm leaving. But I would like a chance to discuss this problem with you later.' This is not turning away from the problem, but is allowing for a calming-down period after which the discussion may be more rational. Also, if you make the first move you are more in control.

My boss takes the credit for work I have done

This tends to be a fact of working life. Some bosses are more prone than others. The boss who gives credit where it is due is usually one who feels secure and confident. Good managers realise that giving credit encourages and motivates people to do more.

But if your boss is of the kind who doesn't give credit, look for ways to highlight your achievements to others. If you take time to develop professional relationships you will have many opportunities to keep them up-to-date with what you are doing. You can do this in a subtle way. Just by a mention here and there you can indicate what your contribution has really been, rather than the image which your boss is trying to portray. For example, you could say 'I couldn't call yesterday, I was busy writing the head's speech for speech day.'

It's up to you

We have been emphasising throughout this chapter the kind of actions you can take to remedy some of the problems of boss's behaviour. This may seem unbalanced because it is you who has to make the effort. Unfortunately, this is the case. Only *you* can act to create an acceptable situation for *you*. If you blame others and do nothing yourself you will achieve very little. You will gain more if you analyse a situation, both in terms of others and how you contribute to that situation. This process of self-reflection will stand you in good stead in relationships in all areas of your life.

Exercise 19

Using some of the problems that have just been discussed, think of situations from your own working life where you may have seen better results if you had acted differently. In particular, try to identify instances where you have 'blamed' the boss and griped about it, rather than considered the influence *you* had on the situation. If you accept the premise that it is only you who can change things, this will help you to assess where changed behaviour on your part would have been valuable.

The question of power

By its very nature your relationship with your boss is one of superior–subordinate. Your boss has power because of his position but there are other sources of power besides this. Where does power come from and what can you do to increase your own power which will help in your relationship with your boss?

Position power

This comes from your role within the organisation and as we have said, gives you less authority than your boss.

Resource power

You have this power if you have control over resources. These may be money, time, equipment or anything else that people need and which they can only obtain by your agreement. How much of this type of power do you have? Do you control a budget, for example? Are you responsible for allocating timetables? Volunteering for tasks and activities that give you access to more resources or powerful people may be appropriate. Each piece of work you do potentially gives you more power. How can you use this increase of power to gain more power? For example, if you go on a course and gain expertise, can you join a higher-level working party within the county or area?

Information power

Information that other people don't have, or don't have yet, is an important source of power. Knowing what is going on inside the LEA, at national level or within your area, can give you an enormous advantage. It allows you to make better informed decisions and to act more effectively. One way of gaining access to this type of power is to join local or national committees, put your name forward for working parties, consultancy groups and so on. In this way you can join networks of information.

Expert power

If you can convince people that you know more than they do then you will have this type of power. An obvious example is the expertise which comes from your specialist, professional training. Parents will be in a much less powerful position than you because they haven't had the same training. Other examples are doctors and lawyers. They are in possession of knowledge and skills which we don't have; they can, therefore, create an air of mystique about their work. This gives an enormous amount of power.

Consider ways in which it may be beneficial for you to create greater expert power. Attending a special needs course may be one example.

Person power

The sheer force of your personality can be a source of power. Do you influence people with your sense of enthusiasm? Do you get on well with people?

Getting more power

In order to resist the power of other people, you can develop a greater power base for yourself. Start by drawing a power net (see Figure 5.1) with you in the middle and the relationships which are important around you. Assess the various power aspects of these relationships. How much does the relationship impact on your lifestyle? How much power do these people actually have? What type of power is it? Can you do anything to match it?

For example, a school caretaker has position power. The headteacher relies on a good service from the caretaker to help in the smooth running of the school. Establishing a good relationship where the power base of both is recognised is necessary for harmonious relations. It is interesting, in this example, that while the status positions of these roles is easy to assess, the dependency needs are more complex.

It is important, therefore, not to dismiss anyone as being of low status, or of little account. By assessing the power structure in more detail you will see that nearly everyone has some sort of power. It is also worth remembering the old saying, 'Be nice to people on your way up; you may meet them again on your way down'.

Another effective way of gaining more power is by collaborating with your colleagues. The power of collective action may win your boss round to a point of view when individually he has been able to resist it.

Finally, the purpose of gaining more power is to get a **fair** share. Don't be greedy. Let people see that you use the power you have in a responsible way, and not for your own individual gain.

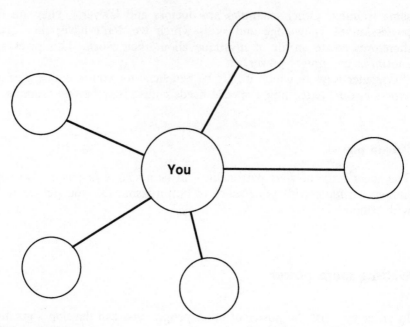

Figure 5.1 Power net

Summary

Although people often complain of problems with their boss, we have shown that quite often the solution is in your own behavioural response. By analysing the problem carefully and evaluating your own contribution to it, you can start to work on improvements. In most cases, alterations in your own behaviour will minimise your negative feelings towards your boss.

Developing power positions will also help you to control situations which affect you and, in so doing, minimise the control of your boss. Additional power can be gained by such things as taking on more responsibility, becoming an expert in a particular field and joining appropriate committees and working parties.

6 Meeting parents

Teachers can regard parents from a number of viewpoints. At some time or another, parents will behave and respond in accordance with each of the following roles:

- **prime customers** — send their children to you for the benefit of their education
- **collaborators** — share with you the responsibility for their children's education
- **critical evaluators** — assess the quality of the results of your professional endeavours
- **help-seekers** — seek your insight into the various traits exhibited by their children
- **input-providers** — bring information to your attention which you need, or they feel you need.

As a professional you are expected to assess which of these roles is predominating in the parents with whom you are dealing at any time and, having done so, then to react to their needs and satisfy them accordingly. This chapter discusses ways in which you can establish and maintain satisfactory working relationships with parents.

What do parents want of teachers?

Following on in detail from the list above, parents want:

- success in educating their children
- even-handed, equitable treatment for their children
- progress reports
- opportunity for discussion about progress and the future
- advice on matters of concern about their children.

What do teachers want of parents?

Teachers want:

- responsible co-operation, in general
- interest in their children's education, in particular.

Teacher/parent contact can be divided into two categories for the purpose of this text:

(a)	**Parents' evenings/open days**	– Prearranged set pieces, with a timetable and anticipated range of topics.
(b)	**All other meetings with parents**	– Sometimes by appointment, sometimes at short notice, sometimes spontaneous.

In category (a), the emphasis for success will rest on planning, and in category (b), on careful thought and conduct.

Parents' evenings/open days

In this kind of scenario you are in the 'chair'. Some of the advice given in Chapter 7 on chairing work meetings will help you towards achieving your objectives. For maximum success you need to carry out the same thoughtful planning activities. You need to assemble the following in advance:

(a)	**Facts**	– results, figures, dates, trends – at least for your own use. Are you able or prepared to give copies?
(b)	**Reasons**	– observations, deductions, opinions – at least for your own understanding. Are you able, or is it politic, to explain all these to all parents?
(c)	**Explanations**	– from your reasoning, what will you actually say and do to help parents assimilate exactly where their children have reached, educationally?
(d)	**Forecasts**	– what is likely to happen in the short and medium term, on the assumption of the past rate of progress by the pupil? To what extent are you able to report this?
(e)	**Advice**	– what counsel are you able to offer?

Parents' evenings usually represent the main programmed opportunities in the school year for parents to discuss progress and, possibly, to express their concerns or seek your advice. If you have adhered to a preparation structure similar to that recommended above, you will very likely be well-organised to help most of them. On the other hand, your thinking will have spanned all those pupils within your responsibility. The interest of individual parents will, naturally, be sharply focused on their own offspring.

Somehow or other, you will want to convey your strong sense of personal interest in every one of your pupils, to every one of their parents. There are a number of ways in which you can demonstrate this concern and dedication:

- you can have all the information to hand that everyone might expect of a conscientious expert (ie, facts, reasons, explanations, forecasts and advice – as suggested above)
- you can prepare a brief summary of pluses and minuses with respect to every child (note: start with the pluses!); this can be augmented with an opinion of what the pluses could produce – as long as the minuses are subordinated
- you could practise both the above against a projection of yourself as someone dedicated to the success of all pupils.

Awkward parents or situations

Sometimes, despite meticulous preparation, boundless dedication and endless goodwill on your part, you meet hostility or disbelief or sheer ill-manners! What do you do about it?

1   You decide in advance what you would do if it arises!
2   You find out the exact cause of the trouble.
3   You aim to deal with **that** point, rationally.
4   You don't present your response as an argument.
5   You never lose your temper.
6   You decide whether to involve anyone else.
7   You defer a really serious situation to another day.
8   You make every reasonable effort to end up 'friends'.

Exercise 20

Recollect your last parents' evening, and answer the following questions.

1 To what extent did you assemble the facts and interpret them?
2 Did you have all necessary information to hand on the night?
3 If not, why not? (eg, time pressures)
4 How many of the parents seemed dissatisfied?
5 What were the causes of the dissatisfaction?
6 Do you feel that you responded satisfactorily on all occasions?
7 If not, what should you have done differently?

All other meetings with parents

At meetings other than parents' evenings, there is likely to be a much wider variety of circumstance dictating the need for a get-together. At parents' evenings you could reasonably anticipate the topics and, according to pupil ability, forecast the way in which a discussion might proceed. With the meetings we will now discuss, there is potentially a much wider divergence in subject, direction, manner discussed, and outcome.

Some typical reasons for special meetings with parents are:

• to voice concern
• to report some circumstance

- to give information
- to express annoyance
- to express support
- to seek information
- to seek advice
- to express an opinion
- to negotiate
- to persuade
- to warn
- to deter.

(Note: This list is representative and not necessarily conclusive.)

If you analyse this short list of reasons, and can infer the circumstances which might have prompted some of them, a number of thoughts will come to mind.

First, some of such meetings will be either at short notice, or, perhaps, spontaneous. There may be little, or no, time for preparing your response (on the assumption that you were not the one who instigated the meeting). So, just how urgent is the subject? The answer to this question may have a bearing on the timescale of your response. You will clearly need to make an assessment.

Second, a full consideration and reply can only be given in response to all of the facts (and their dates and occasions), feelings and, possibly, consequences. Chapter 8 on interview skills gives you a great deal of advice about gleaning information from others. You will note that people communicate not only by words, but with their eyes, posture, movements, facial expressions and mode of dress.

Very careful and disciplined listening and observation are always advisable to obtain a comprehensive sense of the other party's true message to you. Allowing someone, particularly someone with a grievance, the chance to reiterate is a valuable tip. All of this applies equally well to giving either an instant response, or a more leisurely reply.

Third, having thoroughly understood the facts, the feelings and the intent associated with the meeting; is there any other information that you require from any other source, such as details of precedents, opinions from colleagues, reference to records, the school rules on such matters, before you can give a complete response?

Fourth, to what extent are you empowered to deal, completely, with the particular circumstance which has arisen? Do you need to refer to a senior? Are there forms to sign? Are there other authorities or agencies which are required to be involved?

Coping with people who are concerned or agitated

Occasionally, we all have to cope with someone who is not behaving within the bounds of normal convention. Due to some sense of stress they may shout, bluster, threaten, profane, cry, retreat into silence, become inarticulate, make false accusations, become hysterical, or act in some other unusual way. On such an occasion your objective will be to encourage a return to normal behaviour as soon as possible. There are a number of ways of achieving this. Some general steps are outlined below:

- listen attentively and show that you are doing so
- listen openmindedly; this comes through to the other party
- keep control of your own features, smile when you can
- show that you appreciate the importance of the issue
- use the other person's name quite often
- be courteous and friendly
- let the other person see that you expect normal behaviour.

These seven tactics, carefully practised, will deal with all but the most serious disturbances. We can now consider how to deal with some particularly difficult circumstances.

Emotional outbursts

These either result from a loss of control, or an intention of the parent to emphasise their feelings. They might also be deployed to intimidate. Alternatively, they could be used to obtain greater sympathy. Emotional actions often prompt emotional reactions; it is remarkably easy to join in and abandon justice, logic and even-handed rational assessments.

Because one person can never completely deduce another person's motivation, we usually need to remain slightly sceptical if we are to deal with displayed emotion (this does not mean that we should display our scepticism). We need to remain inwardly dispassionate so that we can continue to listen and act fairly.

Recognising emotional distress and displaying sympathy can show that you care, but it can also distort your sense of fair play.

Personal attacks

In this context we are speaking of verbal abuse. If you work in an area where there is a likelihood of physical attack, then no doubt the school has a well-understood procedure to deploy in that situation.

When someone launches a tirade of personal verbal abuse it may stem from two sources. They have either lost their temper – in which case it can be regarded as an emotional outburst (see above), or it is a tactic to undermine your ego. If you have a relatively weak ego, then under attack you will take a passive role (give in). In the latter case, it is an attempt to bully you into a course of action.

Two responses are possible, and in the order given:

(a) Try to keep calm, use their name, and remain courteous and friendly.
(b) If that doesn't quickly work then you must terminate the interview. This shows the aggressor something about you. You will start off better next time.

If you are impelled to take this action and the person is still in full flood, it is very likely that he or she will immediately go to a third person. You had better quickly report the situation to your boss.

Asking and answering questions

Much of human communication rests upon the practice of asking and being asked questions, and giving and receiving answers. Most of your meetings with parents may be conducted in exactly this manner. As with all social skills there are ways of going about this process which produce the most effective results. Here are some pointers for you to consider:

1 Watch out for provocative questions, they provoke hostility.
2 People will often stop listening whilst they are composing their next question. This is disadvantageous because it deprives one of valuable input from the other person.
3 Some questions are very much more effective if asked at exactly the right moment. However, really searching questions might need advance preparation.
4 People sometimes ask questions in order to demonstrate their own cleverness. These questions are not, therefore, aimed at building relationships or dealing with concerns.
5 It is always a sound discipline to cease talking immediately after having asked a question – many of us have difficulties in actually doing this!
6 Direct questions tend to compel the recipient towards direct answers. For example, if you ask, 'Does your son, John, have regular weekly pocket-money from you?', you will receive a more direct answer than to the more general question, 'Does your son, John, receive any money?'

7 General questions allow the answerer a wider scope in response – they do not pin people down. Conversely, general questions allow the possibility of a much more comprehensive response. Which type of question you ask will depend upon your judgement of your requirements at the particular moment.

8 People often ask ambiguous questions which could have a number of different interpretations. Mostly this derives from lack of thought, although occasionally it is deliberate. In either case, a re-statement is called for.

9 Rhetorical questions are asked for the effect they make, not in anticipation of an answer; for example, 'Do you really want me to believe that?' Occasionally, this is a valid tactic, but it doesn't do much towards creating a rational dialogue.

10 Some people habitually answer a question by asking one in reply. This may be necessary if the original question was ambiguous; but it is often used as an evasive tactic. The habitual counter-questioner often sounds evasive, or appears as someone wishing to seem clever. Occasionally, people fall into this habit from sheer unwillingness to contemplate seriously what their answer truly is. You will have to decide why somebody is actually doing this, or else point out to them that this is no way to make progress in the matter under discussion.

Exercise 21

Rate yourself with marks out of ten for each of the following. (Note: 1 = poor, 5 = average, 10 = perfect.)

1 I never ask provocative questions.
2 I always listen carefully.
3 I always ask questions at the right moment.
4 I never ask questions to demonstrate my cleverness.
5 I always stop speaking, having asked a question.
6 I choose between asking direct or general questions.
7 I never ask ambiguous questions.
8 I never ask rhetorical questions.
9 I only answer a question with a question in order to clarify.

A good questioner would be better than average for all nine.

Dealing with parents (and others) by telephone

The telephone can be a great blessing in support of a busy work-schedule. Making, or receiving, a five-minute call can ostensibly save a 30-minute, or more, meeting, so long as both parties achieve entirely satisfactory communication! This condition is often not met. Here are some reasons why:

- unless a telephone call is prearranged, the caller has an element of surprise – this may unbalance the outcome
- because telephone calls are costed against time, there may be felt a pressure to make decisions in a hurry
- important things may be omitted, or hurried over
- it is harder to maintain concentration on the telephone – the mind tends to drift
- you cannot observe a person's reaction to your words, hence you are deprived of input
- it is easier for misunderstandings to arise, because the aural messages are not reinforced
- if the call is not prearranged, it may come at a time, for example, when you will be interrupted, or when it is noisy.

Some pointers for receiving telephone calls are given below:

- listen very carefully, take notes, and undertake to call back rather than half-deal with something instantly
- expand your notes and file a copy, immediately – it is amazing how many people let something important go unrecorded
- if the matter is important, talk less: this will have the effect of making the other party talk more, hence increasing the input to you
- if you think you have reached an agreement, be sure to restate it in your own words – also include that in your notes
- never push yourself into a quick decision by telephone
- have a ready excuse for terminating the call if desirable.

The following gives some advice on making successful telephone calls:

- make out a checklist of points you intend to cover, and in which order, before you call; tick them off as you progress
- never, ever, be afraid to call back if you subsequently find you have made a mistake
- if the topic is really important, between you and a parent, try not to handle it by telephone

- on the other hand, if it is vital that you exchange words, and you just cannot meet the person face to face, then the telephone is more personal than a letter
- telephone calls are, in any event, often best followed up with, at the least, a short note of confirmation.

The telephone can sometimes be very helpful:

- it is easier to say 'no' on the telephone
- it is easier to sound really determined
- you can quite easily cut-off further discussion
- you can limit and control the flow of information
- you can save a great deal of time if you are properly prepared for the occasion.

The telephone and its efficient use by you responds to a bit of disciplined practice. Others sometimes use it to put you at a disadvantage, but you can also learn how to deal with that.

Successful parent liaison

Meeting and dealing with parents is clearly an important activity in the working life of a teacher. Such occasions can sometimes be prompted by a sensitive circumstance. You can build a reputation for being 'good with parents' by conducting yourself according to certain behaviour patterns. The following may be of use:

1 Don't try too hard to be liked. Attempting to be more than normally pleasant often comes across as strained or defensive.
2 Always be a good listener. This is invaluable.
3 As well as listening intently, observe closely. Try hard to develop a sensitivity to other people's motivations and wants.
4 Try to be open-minded in the face of complaint or criticism.
5 On the other hand, retain a little personal scepticism when faced with emotion.
6 Never threaten someone, even in an implied way.
7 Try not to feel uncomfortable when facing conflict. Analyse what you are receiving and deal with the reasons behind it.
8 It is particularly important to try to think clearly under pressure. If you just can't do this, then slow things down or defer the topic until you are better prepared.
9 Commit yourself to trying to give reasonable satisfaction.

Exercise 22

Having worked your way through this chapter, how well do you feel you cope (or could cope) with parents who were temporarily acting in an irrational manner?

How do you, or would you, respond to someone who is clearly displaying, to you, an emotional state of mind?

How do you, or would you, respond to strong personal verbal aggression?

Set down on paper the outline of your responding strategies for managing these circumstances. Then expand the work by setting down the detailed steps you would take.

Summary

At the opening of this chapter we expressed the view that you could regard parents as 'prime customers', 'collaborators', 'critical evaluators', 'help-seekers' and 'input-providers'. No doubt many will just regard themselves as 'caring parents'. Occasionally, some of them will have an almost obsessional concern for some facet of their children's welfare. Equally, from time to time, some teachers will focus unreasonably sharply on some aspect of school-life.

Effective working relationships between the two parties obviously depend upon a measure of sensitive understanding of each other's viewpoint. However, in times of stress, one party or the other may not have the presence of mind to recognise this fact. Much of the content of this chapter has been devoted to ensuring that you are able to maintain the quality of your parent–teacher liaison performance.

The material covered in Chapter 7 will reinforce the various messages and techniques which we have just been considering.

7 Chairing work meetings

Communication is generally considered to be a vital element in the management process; and meetings between various groupings of people are a common way of implementing communication. Effectively organised and conducted, meetings can be a tremendous force for channelling the energies and thoughts of those present towards the achievement of collective goals. On the other hand, an unnecessary, ill-organised, poorly controlled meeting can set a project back for months, if not forever!

In your school-life you may have already established these views for yourself. You may already 'chair' work meetings and wonder how you can improve their effectiveness. Alternatively, you may still be waiting to control your first committee or work group. In that event you will need to decide how to achieve a good result, when you do start.

This chapter sets out some practical guidelines for success in either circumstance. Get into the good habits suggested herein and your meetings will always be effective!

(Note: due to equal opportunity considerations, it is commonplace to refer to the chairman role as 'chair', and to address the holder of that role as 'chair'. This convention has been adopted here.)

Exercise 23

Cast your mind back to a recent meeting which you attended.

1 How effective was it?
2 On what basis are you judging its effectiveness?
3 If it was successful, why was that?
4 Could it have been even better? How?
5 If it was unsuccessful, why was that?
6 In retrospect, what should have been done to ensure a more desirable outcome?
7 Was that action outside the chair's powers or, perhaps, abilities? How so?

8 On the day, would you have produced a better result if you had been in the chair?

Reasons for meetings

Potentially there is a wide variety of circumstances where bringing people together for a meeting might be desirable, for example:

- to generate ideas for solving a problem
- to counteract an undesirable trend
- to make a plan of action
- to reach a decision
- to announce a decision
- to reach a compromise or consensus
- to practise democracy
- to demonstrate the principle of joint involvement
- to explain some circumstance
- to hear reactions to some circumstance
- to authorise something or somebody
- to practise team-building
- to observe a rule, ie to conform to some constitution (eg conduct a board of governors meeting).

Whether or not you decide to hold a meeting on the basis of any, or all, of those reasons will depend upon the importance and immediacy of the actual topic in your mind. So, before deciding to call people together you need to ensure that sufficient advantage will ensue from that action!

Exercise 24

1 On the basis of the checklist given above, draw up a short-list of three circumstances where a meeting would be desirable.
2 Draw up a further short-list of three circumstances where the communications objective could be achieved without a meeting. In these cases what alternative device would you use?

Who should attend?

Assuming you have got some input in the question of who should attend, perhaps you can answer by using the following sub-categories:

- who **must** attend (their presence is **essential** for some reason)?
- who else could contribute greatly if present?

Again, you can make your choice against the list of reasons for meetings.

In general, smaller groups often produce quicker answers and hence are conducive to immediate action. On the other hand, larger groups may be helpful for wider communications about a problem, and also, ostensibly, for the democratic process!

Whether or not a meeting is small or large, you always need to take the view that people's time is valuable and that there is a cost associated with their attendance. An unnecessary requirement upon someone to attend a meeting is both unprofessional and wasteful of resources. It is also probably detrimental to the quality of the outcome.

Another variation is that, as chair, you may often find that colleagues ask to attend on particular occasions, when their presence is not really needed. This situation, too, requires a discriminating approach from you. One way or another you will have to work hard to limit the attendance and draw it only from members of the two sub-categories given.

Exercise 25

In Exercise 24 you short-listed three circumstances where you would call a meeting. Who would you summon to attend each? Give your reasons for your selection.

Roles at formal meetings

As mentioned in the list of reasons for meetings, there are sometimes formal meetings held in accordance with a written constitution, or at least conducted in a set, structured pattern. A board of school governors conducts its business in this way. The following explanation will help you if you should ever become involved in 'councils' of this kind.

   (a) **Chair**. Controls the meeting. May occupy the role on the basis of his or her work position, or because they have been appointed by somebody, or by the vote of the committee members.

   (b) **Vice-chair**. May occupy the role for any of the same reasons as given for the chair.

   (c) **Secretary**. Compiles the agenda, arranges meetings, produces and circulates minutes, monitors the actions placed on members by the chair. Usually appointed because of his or her job, or by the chair.

(d) **Member**. May be voted onto the 'council' or 'board' as the representative of a work group, etc, or be appointed by the chair or vice-chair.

(e) **Substitute**. Someone who stands in for a member and has the same voting rights.

(f) **Co-opted member**. Someone who can attend and make some specialist contribution. Will not usually have voting rights.

In meetings of the kind implied by the roles described above there is sometimes a need for considerable tactical skill from the chair, vice-chair and, perhaps, the secretary. It is advisable for a newcomer to serve as a member for a year or two before taking up a higher office.

The chair and vice-chair are in actual command of events. The secretary is often the one who works behind the scene to 'oil the wheels' and progress the business.

Informal meetings

Most committees, work groups, working parties, etc, are of the informal variety; often called together on an *ad hoc* basis for a specific purpose.

At most, there will usually be just three roles:

- chair
- secretary
- member.

Decisions may be made on the basis of:

- chair's view – after group discussion
- vote of members – after group discussion.

The meeting could be recorded in a number of ways:

- everybody takes their own notes
- the chair issues a list of points for action
- the secretary circulates formal minutes.

In this type of gathering, the chair's role is paramount. The secretary, if there is one, may well just be one of those present who has volunteered (!) to keep notes of any decisions made.

Preparation for meetings

Preparation is an essential ingredient of success. If you want to earn the reputation of being an effective chair you need to invest time and effort in preparing the ground first. Take into consideration the following points.

1 Think carefully about where and when the meeting should take place . . . location, timing, convenience, general suitability.
2 Ensure that you understand what you and your committee are empowered to do. For example, are you intended to produce some recommendations, or do you have the authority to make a decision and then implement it? Are you speaking for yourselves or are you representing the interests of others?
3 Before the meeting, find out the opinions, wishes and needs of other interested parties. This will help you to understand thoroughly the context of the purpose for the meeting.
4 Assess whether there is a need to talk through the issues, in advance of the meeting, with any key personalities. Do you need to give anybody a thorough briefing on an important issue? Are there 'seeds to be sown', so to speak? Is there a need to marshal support on some unavoidable, thorny issue?
5 Compile an agenda for yourself. You need to clarify, in your own mind, what is to be discussed and why. You also need to map out a few potential choices of action or solutions. There may be an advantage in identifying unacceptable answers or courses of action, together with your reasoning. You may, or may not, in any particular circumstance need to circulate a written agenda. But you **always** need to have prepared one for yourself!
6 Prepare, or have prepared, any supporting paperwork that is necessary to explain and amplify an agenda item. For example, is there recent correspondence which lends weight and urgency to the deliberations?
7 Circulate any information in good time, to enable committee or group members to comprehend the content. Some people seem to take a delight in announcing that they were not given sufficient time to prepare themselves properly!
8 Consider whether there might be a need to send courtesy copies of any paperwork to people who are not committee members, but who nevertheless ought to be kept informed. This step can often be overlooked, and yet could be a crucial omission – especially if it's your boss you leave out!
9 Having gone through as many of the preceding steps as you feel necessary, decide what you will do if unsatisfactory outcomes start

to emerge during the meeting. How will you forestall trouble? Will you, perhaps, make it clear that you have the casting vote? Will you, perhaps, defer final resolution until another day? Will you seek the help of another key person present?

10 Finally, arrange your own forthcoming work-schedule so as to ensure that you can arrive at the meeting venue a little early. Ask the person who will act as note-taker to do the same, so that you can start the business the minute the last delegate arrives.

Exercise 26

You are a form teacher and your pupils are in the age-range of 14–15 years. The headteacher has asked you to liaise with a local employer who would like to co-operate with providing work experience, in accordance with the National Curriculum.

Your contact is the personnel manager of the company. You are to develop some initial ideas for consideration. You may invite some colleagues to help as appropriate. How will you prepare?

Behaviour at meetings

As with most activities in life, different people respond in different ways at meetings. Some people are more forthcoming than others; some act imaginatively; others are less assertive than their fellows; and so on. Since you, as chair, are 'conducting' the meeting, you need to detect these different patterns in order to 'orchestrate' the best possible outcome from your group. You need to observe who contributes what and then utilise that knowledge.

Putting this in context you will find that there may be people present who:

- propose ideas – 'What if we did this?', or 'How about writing to Mr X?', or 'Could we merge with so and so?'
- say nothing – perhaps an habitually quiet person who will only respond to a direct question, unless brought out by the chair
- support other speakers – 'I think that's a good idea.', or 'Yes, let's do that and also write.'
- constructively criticise – 'I like that plan but we need to make sure we publicise it better than last time.'
- monopolise the meeting – would speak most of the time, if allowed by the chair

- destructively criticise – 'That idea won't work.', or 'That sounds fine, but . . .', or 'You've got a lot to learn.'
- volunteer – often offer to undertake further action
- adopt an 'anti' stance – express a lack of faith in the meeting; negative in general attitude; unwilling to accept responsibility for further action; resent the chair.

Clearly, if the group members are properly selected, the chair will expect all present to contribute as best they can, and to be as helpful and as constructive as possible.

After 15–30 minutes, who is contributing what will become apparent; with practice, who needs encouraging and who needs controlling becomes clear. Appreciating this and then acting upon it is one of the key skills involved in running successful meetings.

How you decide to act on any particular occasion will depend upon your goals in calling the meeting, the relative importance of the agenda items, and, to an extent, the mix of people and talents at your disposal.

If you, as chair, need ideas and consensus then you have to encourage participation from all and then guide group conclusions towards the desired aims. If, on the other hand, your main aim is to spread understanding of a decision already taken, then you need to make a major, personal, contribution on the subject. You will also aim to encourage those who appear supportive, to endorse the policy, and you will probably seek to minimise negative comment.

In either event, or for that matter for any other desired outcome, spending some effort on classifying the various contributors as specified in the list will help you to control the meeting towards producing good results.

However, you should welcome the finding that your committee is comprised of a variety of contributing types. There is considerable research by Dr Meredith Belbin to suggest that the best results ensue from a team containing a mix of attributes and associated behaviour (see Chapter 2). For an effective meeting:

- you want someone to produce ideas, but not everyone
- you want someone to evaluate and constructively criticise those ideas
- you need someone who has a very good understanding of the subject, and so on.

As indicated at the start of this chapter, your task is to orchestrate these diverse responses towards a satisfactory conclusion.

Exercise 27

Think of six or seven characters that you sometimes meet in a group situation, perhaps in the staffroom. Reflect on their habitual interpersonal behaviour. Now classify them according to how you would expect them to behave at a committee meeting. You can devise your own classifications if you so choose.

Take it a step further and decide how you would utilise each of them if they were members of a committee meeting under your chairship, to produce ideas on the topic of 'How to make pupil field trips more educationally effective.'

Chairing the meeting on the day

If you have followed the steps described in the text, when the day actually arrives you will already have:

- decided that there is a sound reason for the meeting (rather than called it just because it seemed a good idea)
- carefully selected the membership (rather than just chosen the instantly available)
- appointed the most suitable person as secretary (taking notes may be a minor part of the role)
- prepared, for yourself at least, an agenda; alternatively, you may have sought from others some suggested items to be included in an agenda to be circulated in advance of the meeting
- taken soundings of various viewpoints and lobbied support (rather than rely upon good fortune and instincts on the day)
- alerted yourself to watch for particular behaviour patterns, assuming you have not previously sat in committees with all these people already.

In terms of running the meeting itself you need to take the following into consideration.

1 **Introduce each agenda item** as it arises. You can either do this yourself, or get the person with the most specialist interest or knowledge to give the background. Alternatively, you might ask the secretary to refer to any key correspondence or other documentation. One of you needs to say what the committee is required to achieve in the matter.

2 **Encourage contributions** from all present. This need often applies

to the more junior, or sometimes younger, people in attendance. On a topic-by-topic basis you will not expect an **equal** contribution from all, but you will aim for **some** input from most.

3 **Take clear control of the meeting**, regardless of any relative status between you and others present, outside the meeting. By becoming chair of the group, you have accepted the final responsibility for the outcome and quality of the work of the group. As long as you have prepared yourself thoroughly, your authority is unlikely to be challenged.

4 **Remain polite, calm and businesslike**, particularly under any provocation which might arise. In general, most of those present will sympathise with the task of the chair, and be helpful.

5 **Look out for 'hidden agendas'**. At some time, you will almost certainly come to realise that one or more of those present will have aims that differ from those of the committee. They may discuss a topic in such a way as to achieve another objective, perhaps elsewhere. In such circumstances you have a number of options open to you:

(a) Fall back on your pre-meeting preparation, perhaps by quoting a view you received from some influential person.

(b) If the person is clearly speaking against what is an emerging consensus, then you can seek support from those present.

(c) If you do suspect a hidden agenda then you can say words to the effect that 'We are discussing *this* issue, on *this* occasion, within *this* context.'

(d) As a last resort, if an unfruitful or unacceptable outcome is looming, and if there is no support for you in evidence, then defer any decision until another occasion. In other words, if it is important that you win your way on an issue, and you can't see how to do it on the day, then defer the issue to make sure that, at least, you don't lose on the day.

6 **Keep the committee's aims in mind**. It is virtually impossible to prevent various speakers from digressing from time to time. In such circumstances, you need to bring the meeting back on course, in a fairly light-handed way if possible!

7 **Keep the business moving**. When everyone has made an initial contribution, then ask for further **brief** contributions. If you feel that people are beginning to go over the same ground again, then say so.

8 **Keep the peace** between any different factions. This is one of your responsibilities. You can always suggest that philosophical arguments, and the like, can best be aired outside the meeting. If necessary, call a brief recess.

9 **Recognise that members are sometimes restricted**. Sometimes people come to meetings as the representative of a group. In that circumstance they may well have been briefed as to the outcome they are to try to achieve. If their brief turns out to contradict the consensus of opinion at the meeting, then clearly there may be difficulty. In extreme cases the representative may feel obliged to ask that the minutes record his or her minority vote against the consensus. Obviously, it is better to have total accord, but sometimes a minority vote can be dealt with later, outside the meeting.

10 **Listen carefully!** This is crucial (but probably very difficult for us all). If a meeting goes on for more than half an hour, listening properly calls for a disciplined and sustained effort. As well as ensuring that someone keeps notes of the business as conducted, the chair needs to at least jot down key words and who said them. The chair would be wise to also record decisions and actions, together with responsibilities.

11 **Ensure action**. Placing a responsibility on somebody present for taking further action is another duty of the chair. A popular way of recording these is to have an 'action' column down the right-hand side of each page of minutes. This will display the person's initials and the date by which they are required to complete something.

12 **Help the note-taker**. It is usual for the person taking notes to precis what they hear and then, if there are to be minutes issued, produce

these from the notes after the meeting. There are, however, occasions when some part of the business is resolved by everyone agreeing to a particular phrase or sentence (and no other!): for example, 'The committee agreed that, on this occasion only, members would travel to the new site. This agreement will not be regarded as a precedent for future cases.' The chair would have dictated this minute.

13 **Conclude the meeting** in a methodical manner. Just as you opened the meeting by introducing the first agenda item, so you should close proceedings by a sensible, business-like, routine.

You will usually find that it pays you to summarise aloud the decisions reached and to remind the members of the actions agreed. This activity is one of the reasons that made it advisable for you to keep brief personal notes of key outcomes as the meeting proceeded.

If there is need for a further meeting, then now is the time for everyone to consult their diaries and agree when it will take place. Thank people for their attendance and help, then close the meeting. Finally, agree with the note-taker a date by which you will be given the transcript for your agreement, before circulation.

If, in your meetings, you manage to consider all, or most of the points raised above, then you are likely to earn a deserved reputation for effective chairship. Good meetings rarely ensue from good fortune or goodwill; they arise from careful, effective and disciplined chairship!

Exercise 28

The section 'Chairing the meeting on the day' was summarised under thirteen headings.

1 Which particular activities might be difficult for you? Why is that in each case?
2 Is there a common theme running through these activities? What is it?

Sometimes people have difficulty with the activities which require the chair to 'confront' committee members. Examples of these are: 'take clear control of the meeting', 'keep the peace', 'look out for hidden agendas', and so on.

Work out your strategy for dealing with your 'block', if you have one.

After the meeting

The final step in the sequence is for the chair to ensure that, as a consequence of the meeting and the decisions taken, something actually happens. Otherwise there was little practical point in holding it.

Inform

All interested parties should be advised of the decisions reached and the actions agreed. This may just require that minutes are sent, and perhaps a set published on a notice-board.

If you found it necessary to have a pre-meeting discussion with some key figure, then you may be advised to report back. This step has the advantage of continuing to hold that person's interest, or perhaps commitment.

Monitor

You should 'keep your finger on the pulse' by regularly checking on the progress of the actions which you placed on people. Virtually nothing is more inclined to convince people that meetings are a waste of time, than when subsequently nothing happens.

Once someone has left the meeting room, then your requirements may become just one of many tasks jostling for priority in their life. You will need to be single-minded in continuing to compete for some of their time.

Support

One effective way to ensure continued application to the agreed actions is to regard yourself as a general purpose resource, to be utilised as necessary. Make your committee members realise that they may call upon you to help clear away obstacles, provide assistance, help them think further, get authority to do something, and so on. This attitude will demonstrate your continuing commitment and also maintain the 'team' concept of the meeting.

Broadcast progress

Another way of maintaining the impetus is to report progress as it occurs. Committee members and other interested parties will benefit from the positive reinforcement of knowing that things are moving forward: that the committee's strategy is being implemented.

Your role as chair

Post-meeting activity is as vital as the pre-meeting tasks discussed earlier. After the meeting you, too, return to the melée of a busy worklife. However, as chair, your reputation is to an extent related to achieving the purpose which made you call the meeting in the first place. This means that you probably will need to allocate a higher priority to continuing involvement than any other participant.

Once you took the first step of calling the meeting, you committed yourself to see the whole thing through to a successful conclusion. It is rather like taking a ride on a roller-coaster. Once the carriage starts moving you have to stay on until the end of the ride.

Exercise 29

Have you been to a recent meeting where there was less follow-up activity than there should have been? Were all interested parties subsequently informed? Did progress appear to have been monitored? Was continuing support available to those required to take action? Has progress been broadcast? If not, what wasn't done and how did this lessen the effectiveness of the meeting?

The total process of chairship

In this chapter we have worked in detail through a process which can be summarised by Figure 7.1. Most of these steps and their sequence represent a commonsense approach to a number of managerial activities. This is not surprising. After all, chairship is a managerial activity. To

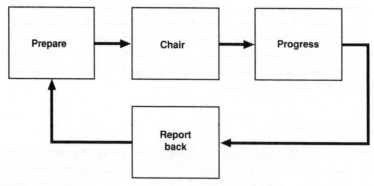

Figure 7.1

master this particular skill, you just need to apply, in a determined manner, the principles discussed.

Summary

In general, meetings have someone who acts in a chairing capacity. The role may not necessarily be called chair. It may be called facilitator, convenor, group leader, etc. There seems a need for someone to co-ordinate, prompt, mediate, facilitate and generally 'oil the wheels' for the sake of good progress.

It follows from this that considerable advantage can accrue to the person who can carry off this role effectively. If that person needs to get something done which requires a group input, they can harness the collective talents to that end.

On the other hand, if 'senior management' want somebody to figurehead a collective responsibility, an effective chair is an obvious choice. Hence, a career might be considerably enhanced by the possession of such skills!

8 Developing interview skills

Within the workplace, interviews are of two varieties:

1 Interviews for employment selection, where a candidate will be invited to discuss his or her application with a panel.
2 Face-to-face, often one-to-one, meetings where one party can be regarded as the interviewer and the other party as the interviewee. Such meetings might take place for:
- giving information (receiving information)
- giving counsel (receiving counsel)
- stating a grievance (hearing a grievance)
- giving feedback (receiving feedback)
- administering discipline (receiving discipline)
- making an offer (receiving an offer).

The topics are presented in pairs to emphasise the two-way nature of interviews. A common cause of breakdown in situation 2 is that the imparter of the information to be exchanged, tends to assume a **dominant** role (as opposed to the **principal** role). This hinders the communication activity which is supposed to be occurring, by limiting any contribution from the other party. The latter assumes a **minor** role (as opposed to a **contributor** role) in what is intended to be a two-way process.

The nature of the interview topics listed, highlights the importance of becoming skilled as both an interviewer and an interviewee.

This chapter suggests ways in which you can sharpen up your performance in interview situations, to the benefit of your career and to the satisfaction of your colleagues.

Exercise 30

To check just how important interviews might already be to you, note down the occasions during the last six months when you have been involved, on a one-to-one basis, in any of the following situations:

advising, counselling, discussing a grievance, feedback, disciplinary activity, or just giving and receiving important information.

The practical essentials of successful interviewing

The following should be taken into consideration.

(a) **Preparation.** What do you need to impart, receive and achieve? What, in general, do you anticipate is going to occur? How will you deal with that? How will you achieve your purposes?

(b) **Behaviour at interviews.** Speaking/listening/interjections; questioning techniques; behaviour patterns; selective use of language; body language and micro-signals.

(c) **Action after interviews.** Recording facts and opinions; confirming agreements; maintaining normal relationships.

Exercise 31

Think back to the last important, one-to-one, meeting in which you took either the principal or the contributor role.

1 What preparations did you make?
2 Did you achieve your purposes?
3 What happened afterwards?
4 If you did not achieve your purposes, why was that? Was it due to inadequate preparation? Did you somehow get diverted during the meeting?
5 Do you anticipate a more satisfactory result next time?

Preparation

The essential starting point is setting out what you need to achieve. After that, it is only a short step to deciding what information you need to impart. An often neglected step, though, is the further need to decide what you should receive in return.

We are, perhaps, all prone to believe that once we have spoken, then the desired communication is complete. But how do we know that our message has been understood in the way we intended? The answer is, only by arranging things so that the recipient has to demonstrate that this is so. In other words, not only must the recipient be given ample opportunity to participate, but also *you* must analyse what you are hearing and seeing. You need to take careful account of this requirement in your planning.

The discussion so far has been as appropriate for somebody who is summoned to attend an interview, as it is for the person who has instigated the meeting: this is a general truth that applies no matter what the meeting's purpose!

It is often a wise precaution to try to anticipate the other party's reaction to receiving information; and then to decide how you would (and should) react to that.

Finally, although there may be some occasions when you need an element of surprise, which leads you to give no advance warning of an intended interview and its purpose, the general rule must be that you do give as much notice as possible or desirable. Otherwise, you will often not get a considered response to your endeavours.

Behaviour at interviews

Most of the time during an encounter between two people at the workplace, either one or the other party will be speaking. How much each person speaks will depend on the purpose of the meeting. For example, during a job interview, the interviewer will encourage the interviewee to speak for **at least** 60 per cent of the time. If, on the other hand, you have arranged the interview for the purpose of giving information, then it is likely that you will speak for the major portion of the time.

If it is your meeting, then the starting point is for you to say, very clearly, what you wish to achieve from the interview. You may also, depending upon the purpose, give the other party the opportunity to express his or her aims.

Listening

In the communication process, **listening** properly is just as important as **speaking** efficiently. Whereas careerists and would-be communicators often attend training courses to become proficient speakers, how many of us look for training material to enable us to become competent listeners?

Having taken our turn at speaking, it is very tempting to start writing key words on our notepad which will form the basis of what we will say when it is our turn to speak next. Obviously, in so doing, we are giving less than our undivided attention to the other party's contribution. The result will be that we shall not receive some potentially valuable input. To communicate to best effect, you actually need the other person's input, be you interviewer or interviewee. Only by receiving this can you best frame your further responses.

There is good evidence to suggest that the best one-to-one communication is achieved when each party matches the other party's information needs in a manner which suggests that each understands the other's situation. G. Laborde's book, *Influencing with Integrity*, covers this in good detail.

Interjections

Even though we have resolved to listen as well as speak, this doesn't mean that we never interrupt. If you can hear that someone is digressing, or unnecessarily repeating himself, or is over-emphasising some relatively unimportant aspect of the business at hand, then interject.

Interjections are useful in that, carefully chosen, they can bring someone to a halt, but still let you sound positive. You can stop the other person in full-flow without putting them down. For example:

'That's an interesting point, could you tell me about that in particular?'

'Yes I understand you, let's consider doing . . .'

'Does that mean that specifically we must . . .?'

'When exactly would we write that?'

'I see what you mean, how could we implement it?'

All of these interjections have the additional advantage of indicating that you are listening and are considering the possibility of building on the other person's thinking.

Exercise 32

Imagine that you are interviewing a senior colleague for the purpose of obtaining important information about a new syllabus. He or she digresses and rambles, and is a little short on patience, too. Work out about six or seven interjections, similar to those given, which will retrieve the situation, and which nevertheless will still leave you on excellent terms with that person.

Behaviour patterns

When you meet someone in an interview situation, you are, instinctively, hoping for behaviour which corresponds with the acceptable norm in your school, and no doubt this is how you anticipate that you will come across to the other party.

However, quite often an interview for, say, job selection, stating a grievance, administering discipline, or giving counsel, is far removed from everyday experience. There may be tension, emotion, embarrassment, fear, or excitement present which will influence both of you. What can be done to negate these?

(a) **If you are the interviewer**, interviewing across your desk, in your room, is not helpful to effective communication. (It will certainly emphasise your status, though, if that is your intention.) To facilitate communication:
   - adopt a relaxed posture and friendly form of speech
   - plenty of eye contact and a tendency to smile demonstrates an open approach
   - use the other person's name quite frequently
   - watch out for negative emotion creeping into your speech; on the other hand, positive emotions, such as high enthusiasm, will help.

(b) **If you are the interviewee,**
   - consciously relax yourself before you walk in the door – after all you are only going to meet another human being!
   - remember you have done your homework in preparation for the interview (whatever its purpose)
   - smile from time to time, use the other person's name when you can and maintain frequent eye contact
   - demonstrate that you are listening when the interviewer is speaking by nodding, and indicate that you are interested by inclining your head towards them
   - when it is your speaking turn, speak slightly slower than your normal rate, don't hurry and keep your thoughts marshalled
   - remember that sometimes interviewers, too, are embarrassed and that you should make an effort to help them to feel at ease; emotion often clutters up the process of transferring information.

Selective use of language

An interview is usually held because one of the parties wishes to either give or receive some message or information. Sometimes, as in employee development counselling, it is much more of a two-way process. In either case, noting the nature of the words and phrases chosen, and the order in which they are used, will yield valuable, additional information.

Nierenberg and Calero in their book *Meta-talk (Guide to Hidden*

Meanings in Conversations), Simon and Schuster, New York, have cited the following instructive set of classifications:

(a) **Softeners**. Prefaces which attempt to influence the listener in a positive manner. For example,
'You'll like what I'm about to tell you.'

(b) **Foreboders**. Attempts to put the listener in an anxious frame of mind. For example,
'It really doesn't matter.'

(c) **Continuers**. Attempts to get the listener to disclose his thoughts. For example,
'Go on – now you're talking.'

(d) **Interesters**. Attempts to arouse the listener's interest. For example,
'Do you know what happened next?'

(e) **Downers**. Attempts to put the listener in a defensive frame of mind. For example,
'Don't be ridiculous.'

(f) **Convincers**. Attempts at apparently logical reasoning to persuade the listener. For example,
'Everyone else believes this.'

(g) **Strokers**. Attempts to persuade by fulfilling the believed needs of the listener. For example,
'Someone who's had your amount of experience will see that I'm right.'

(h) **Pleaders**. Attempts to deal with one's own emotions, (eg, uncertainty). For example,
'I'll try.'

We live in an age where the eloquent use of English is declining; people often use clichés in an attempt to add colour to their conversation. Even so, if you listen carefully, you can often hear some colleagues drawing from the sample classifications given above, in an endeavour to achieve their purposes in an oblique manner. Listen carefully!

Body language

Body language, as described in Chapter 1, is now widely recognised as being important in one-to-one situations. To an extent, people may take a somewhat blasé view of its value. This is probably because of a proliferation of articles on the subject in popular magazines. The argument would go 'If we all know that crossing your arms signifies rejection, or opposition, then we'll take care not to do this – especially when it's important to us.' This negates the value of interpreting body-language signals. However, this is a gross over-simplification of non-verbal behaviour.

In reality, as well as by speaking, we communicate with:

- our eyes
- our posture
- our movements
- our facial expressions
- our mode of dress
- extensions of ourselves (glasses, cigarettes, handbags, our office arrangements, etc.)
- the distance we choose to keep between ourselves and others.

A further crucial point is that we use all these in clusters, rather than singly; and we do this constantly.

You can use this knowledge in a constructive way to reinforce your verbal communications. You can also observe whether another person's words are consistent with their non-verbal communication. An interesting book on the subject is *Body Language* by Allan Pease, Sheldon Press, London, 1984.

Micro-signals

Some experts use this term to describe a range of signals that are just as revealing as the more physically obvious gestures, but which require much closer attention for their detection:

- eye pupil contractions or dilations
- blink rate
- small movements around the mouth
- changes in facial and neck skin colour
- twitches and other involuntary movements.

Any of these may be evident when something is said, or implied, which causes stress of some kind. They can occur because of one's own words (eg, you may have just told a lie) or the words of the other person (eg, they have just embarrassed you). Allan Pease's book also covers such non-verbal information.

Behaviour at interviews

As you have seen, there is a strong need to be interventionist and proactive in interview situations. If you just let whatever will happen,

happen, then you are wasting an opportunity to influence the quality of the outcome. In other words, you may have attended the interview hoping or intending to achieve something to your advantage. If you leave it to chance then there is a fifty-fifty possibility that this will happen. If you remain alert, watchful, and use the techniques and knowledge described, then the odds of achieving your purpose will increase dramatically.

In interview situations, communication can be made much more efficient by:

• consciously deciding when to speak, when to listen, and when to interrupt
• disciplining yourself to listen carefully
• making positive interjections in order to save time and offer valuable encouragement
• adjusting your behaviour to put the other person at ease
• consciously analysing speech to assess someone's purpose
• consciously arranging your non-verbal signals to help reinforce your verbal message
• consciously analysing someone else's non-verbals to see if they are congruent with what they are saying
• watching out for micro-signals which reveal further useful information about the other person.

Exercise 33

Look back to p. 121 to remind yourself of the eight classifications of influencing tactics.

Think now of someone you know who has a noticeable tendency to use such language and structure of phrase. Why does he or she do that? Is it accidental? Laziness? Deliberate? Why so?

Also, as an experiment, listen to conversations in the staffroom to spot the general prevalence of influencing tactics.

Action after interviews

What, exactly, you do after the interview will to an extent be dictated by the purpose of the meeting. For example, if it was a job interview, then there will be forms to complete, letters to write and a number of administrative procedures dictated by 'the system'. In other circumstances, say after a counselling interview, any further activity may be entirely at the discretion of either, or both, parties.

We suggest that, regardless of any dictat from the system, you always carry out, as a minimum, the following routine.

1 If you have followed the recommendations about the need to listen, then you will only have made the scantiest notes during the interview. You are advised to expand these to the necessary level of detail as soon as the meeting concludes. Make sure that you record anything of significance; something which surprised you, for instance.

  These notes are an *aide-memoire* for you and can be used to prepare if necessary for any further meetings. So you may adopt your own style. Anything that needs recording for other parties will require a different note.

2 If you have agreed to do something significant, or the other party has given some undertaking, then confirm this to him or her in writing (unless it has been specifically agreed between you that this is a verbal understanding only).

3 Consider whether there is anyone else who needs to be informed of progress or outcomes . . . do this whilst it is fresh in your mind. Consider whether this is best done verbally or in writing.

4 Carry out any actions you have promised to do, and let it be known that you have done so.

Interviews with particular purposes

Now that we have considered the total interview process, it is appropriate to look at the different types of activities which might be required for particular interview situations.

Employment selection interviews

These are the most prevalent form of formal interview. The selection, about to be made, could result in the payment of hundreds of thousands of pounds in salary alone over a working lifetime! Maximum efficiency is required from this expenditure, for the sake of the pupils and the tax-payers. Furthermore, the interviewee is about to make a crucial career decision.

(a) **Key activities on the part of the interviewer.** Pre-interview activities should include acquiring a thorough understanding of the needs of the job, plus a consideration of what the ideal candidate would bring to that job. Furthermore, the interviewer should make an objective assessment of the colleagues that the successful candidate will then work with, so that they all might complement each other as far as is practicable.

In some business sectors, and many schools, information about the job would be embodied in a **job description**. Information about the ideal type of candidate would be contained in a **person specification**. If these do not exist in your school then you should generate drafts for yourself and then confirm their aptness with a knowledgeable colleague. Do ensure that you are not describing parts of a job that only exist in your imagination. Also, make sure that you are not requiring, of the ideal candidate, a totally unnecessary qualification or tranche of experience (do you really need a successful channel-swimmer with a PhD to teach pupils to swim 25 metres?). Although we are making light of this point, it is a fact that employers miss endless opportunities of making satisfactory appointments, because of pursuing a woolly notion of the real requirements of the job and the qualities required of a good applicant. This practice also negates 'equal opportunities'.

The Institute of Personnel Management, Wimbledon, London will send you a free leaflet on 'Codes of Practice' for all these matters in response to a telephone call (081-946-9100).

At the interview, the interviewer should start the ball rolling by describing the school's particular needs in respect of this appointment. He or she should also advise the candidate what the panel hope to achieve 'today'.

Having set the scene, the major part of the proceedings should be

WE LIKE TO MAINTAIN AN INFORMAL APPROACH HERE.

devoted to the candidate answering questions which are aimed at assessing his or her suitability for the job. If you have followed the pattern already given in this chapter you will have prepared a brief, which works towards fulfilling your aims. Don't waste much time on generalities. This encourages the interviewee to digress. Use all your available time to probe their suitability. Make sure that the candidate speaks, or has the opportunity to speak, for at least 60 per cent of the time. You want lots of input!

Allow a short, but reasonable, period at the end of the interview – when you have got the information you need – for the candidate to ask you questions related to the school, its style of operation and anything else that is cogent. If necessary, have someone else available to complete this at length after the interview.

After the candidate leaves the room, expand your notes.

(b) Key activities on the part of the interviewee. Pre-interview activities should include acquiring a thorough understanding of the needs of the job (see Chapter 10). Also, you need to glean as much information as possible about the school, its catchment area and, if possible, any of the key members of staff. All this gives you the context within which your specialism will be deployed. It may help you to frame better answers to the forthcoming questions.

If the interviewers are experienced, you will find that you are the main speaker during the interview. You will have every opportunity to shine, and this is the way to regard the session.

You have already received in this chapter a lot of information about how to communicate to best effect; now deploy that knowledge. If you find, as often happens at selection interviews, that the questioner digresses, you need to deal with this. He or she is wasting some of the time that you need to demonstrate your competence. However, this is one circumstance where you can't interject many times. Instead, you will have to answer the unnecessary question, but make your reply lead back into the area of your experience and expertise. Bring them back on course! If you manage to do this, and the other candidates don't, you will end up as more of a known quantity than they will.

Don't stack up a long list of questions about the school, to ask towards the end of the interview. On the other hand, you will be expected to ask some, so have two or three ready. These questions should have answers that you could not obtain elsewhere. You can indicate that you have already researched the answers to other important queries.

At the conclusion of the interview, try to make sure that you shake hands with the person who chaired the panel. Retain their hand just a little longer than you normally might. (Touching is also part of the communication process, and handshakes are one of the few socially acceptable ways of achieving this between strangers in this country.) Maintain eye contact throughout the handshake, and thank them personally for their time.

Finally, if somebody has consumed alcohol within a few hours of the interview and the other party hasn't, then it is detectable and, possibly, offensive. Additionally, alcohol often slows down the thought processes.

If, after all this, you do not get the job, then take the philosophic view that it was good interview experience. Job interviews, as a practice, look as if they will be here for some time. Conducting them and attending them is, at the least, a good learning experience. Each time you take part in an interview you will improve.

Grievance and disciplinary interviews

From time to time, situations arise where somebody raises a grievance: for example, about their situation, about a colleague, about their boss or about a subordinate. There are various degrees of formality assigned to these matters.

If somebody just needs to 'let off steam' because of continuing frustration with, for example, their work schedule, then this may result in a serious, but relatively informal, chat with the boss. On the other hand, if a head of department has been physically attacked by one of his or her subject teachers then there will be procedures to follow and these will take cognisance of employment law and its associated Codes of Practice. This is particularly so wherever there is the prospect of disciplinary action being taken against an employee.

(a) **Informal interviews**. Conducting and dealing with informal interviews is, really, just a matter of common-sense. There is a need to create the appropriate atmosphere for rational discussion and a requirement to bring out all relevant facts. There is also the advisability of devising measures to deal with the problem.

Some such grievances can be dealt with by merely providing the aggrieved party with a sympathetic ear. Usually, though, this would be regarded as a short-term palliative measure. If someone has reached the stage of wanting to discuss their grievance with somebody in the management chain, then serious consideration is required. However, these situations should not be confused with those discussed in (b).

(b) **Formal grievance and disciplinary interviews**. Occasionally, in most organisations, situations arise where acceptable standards of treatment, or conduct, are breached. The following examples illustrate the point:

- employee believes that the employer has breached his contract, and registers a grievance to obtain redress
- employee feels that he or she is being sexually harassed, and registers a grievance to obtain assistance
- employee believes that, as a member of an ethnic minority, he or she is being subjected to unfair discrimination.

You will note that none of the examples involves the employer raising a grievance. This is because, in the event of dissatisfaction, employers will institute disciplinary action.

Organisations usually have a set procedure for dealing with formal grievances. This often results in the grievance being heard in the first place by somebody in the management chain (eg, head of department). The following advice applies in such circumstances.

Seriously consider whether you should have a witness present. If you decide to, then he or she should not take part in the proceedings, but should sit to the side and take comprehensive notes. This will leave you free to concentrate on hearing the evidence and extracting essential information. It will also give you the opportunity, later, to exchange assessments with your witness. If you are the aggrieved party, on the other hand, you too should consider taking along a witness, on the same basis (probably a friendly colleague).

In either circumstance, remember that this may be the first step in a chain of events that may next include a panel of people, and ultimately be heard before an industrial tribunal. So at this first step, be as careful, factual and as non-emotional as you can.

If you are the interviewer, you are seeking to resolve such grievances as are within your power and competence. If you are the aggrieved, you have come to the meeting seeking redress. These two aims should be kept in mind, and should dictate the behaviour and actions of the parties present.

Turning now to the other kind of formal interview: disciplinary interviews. The following examples might represent typical situations for disciplinary action:

- teacher is felt to be incompetent and the head invokes disciplinary proceedings
- teacher is involved in unacceptable conduct (eg, abuses his or her boss) and the head invokes disciplinary proceedings
- teacher is charged in criminal proceedings, and the head invokes disciplinary proceedings.

Handling the disciplinary interview might imply a clear step-up in interview competence, when compared with hearing and dealing with grievances.

Reaching the correct decision depends on eliciting the appropriate facts; this might depend upon some background knowledge of the law. After all, at the end of the day, somebody may be dismissed.

If you are given the task of conducting a disciplinary interview, you will need to be provided with two kinds of brief beforehand:

- the evidence in support of the allegations, and if there is one, the response to those allegations
- expert opinion about the legal implications of the matter.

At the hearing itself, the school's formal procedure may allow for the introduction of participating witnesses, and also for the party to be represented by a colleague, or a trade union officer. On the basis of what has been said in this book, you can see that these proceedings will not be left in the hands of an inexperienced or junior person. You may find the advice contained in Chapter 7 helpful when it comes to keeping control and achieving a just, and politically acceptable, outcome.

If you should, on the other hand, find yourself on the receiving end at a disciplinary interview, there are a number of steps you should take if you are to defend your position properly. Your main aim, of course, will to be to present yourself in the best possible way. Your secondary aim will be to minimise any punishment. To achieve these aims you need to take the following action:

- gather as much relevant information as possible and then produce an edited document which includes all material which is favourable to your position
- bring sympathetic witnesses to speak up for you on the day
- if you are a member of a union, get the union to find you an advocate to speak your part at the hearing
- if you are to speak for yourself, work your way through your prepared brief, which **must** include some difficult questions for your accusers to answer
- be professional, polite and as incisive as possible on the day. But note, if you are clearly 'guilty' you have to express contrition, and point to your previous record, your achievements, your qualifications, and anything else that is remotely helpful (even domestic and social circumstances).

In conclusion, apart from perhaps pay-bargaining interviews, disciplinary interviews are often felt to be the most testing of meetings. The reality is that the same rules of conduct and the same techniques apply to all types of interviews and they will stand you in good stead.

Counselling interviews

Most people, at some point in their life, find themselves faced with a worrying and perhaps difficult circumstance. This may be related to either their work situation or their domestic scene. In any event, it is often the case that the effect of one impinges on the other. In the majority of cases, people ultimately provide their own solution to the problem by somehow deploying the resources available to them. Occasionally, however, a problem is especially severe in the eyes of the sufferer and the difficulties linger on; work performance and relationships may suffer and it becomes obvious that help is needed. One way of bringing assistance to bear is to provide counselling.

(a) **What is counselling?** At its simplest, counselling occurs when a person with a problem together with another person, preferably with counselling skills, talk through a situation for the assistance of the person with the problem. A fundamental belief, on the part of those who counsel, is that the person with the problem is the expert on that problem. The aim is to encourage the sufferer to talk about, explore further, understand better and, ultimately, conceive a plan of action to use the resources to hand to resolve the situation. Support continues through this action.

(b) **Counselling skills**. A number of organisations offer courses on counselling procedures and techniques. If you are seriously going to consider offering counselling help, you may wish to attend such a programme. The remainder of this section gives an overview of the topic.

(c) **Application areas**. People may experience stress and distress because of a wide range of circumstances (see Chapter 11). Typical examples are associated with bereavement, debt, ill-health, workload, children, advancing age, substance abuse, marital discord, change of house, personal relationships, and so on.

These concerns can manifest themselves by modifying the person's normal behaviour pattern. Typical manifestations could include deteriorated memory, apathy, emotional outbursts, slow thinking, reduced judgement, absenteeism, deteriorating time-keeping, unacceptable appearance, and so on. Some of these effects could result in the onset of disciplinary proceedings against the person and, hence, instigate a further need for counselling.

(d) **Counselling stages**. Initially, the need is to create an appropriate rapport between the two parties and this should be in a sympathetic environment away from noise, people and interruptions; ideally without time pressures. Subsequently, the counsellor will need to:

- be an effective listener
- draw inferences from what is said and how it is said
- not interrupt the flow
- be empathetic
- continue to create an atmosphere of confidence and trust
- display a non-critical acceptance of the person's difficulty
- be prepared for periods of silence
- give opportunity for the expression of emotion.

Ultimately the counsellor will aim to:

- guide the person towards the desired action
- help identify attainable goals
- help the person appreciate their own strengths
- assist in identifying further resources needed
- arrange for any essential other support
- encourage the person to be responsible for the solution.

(e) Some concluding points. Counselling brings with it some special responsibilities which need to be kept clearly in mind. For example, once started as a form of aid to a person it can't be suddenly withdrawn, leaving the problem-experiencer in mid-air, so to speak.

You need to remain aware of your own limitations. The person with the problem mustn't be allowed to push you beyond these bounds. Further specialist help is sometimes necessary.

You must not allow the problem-experiencer to develop unrealistic expectations. You must avoid him or her becoming dependent upon you.

You must make clear the limits of confidentiality which will apply, and be authorised if necessary to set these.

You need to ascertain the extent to which any desired extra resources might be available to you.

Summary

As you will have now realised, good interview skills are an important career activity. Furthermore, face-to-face communication can improve immeasurably with a bit of dedicated practice.

The absolute fundamentals of preparation, behaviour at interviews, and subsequent action represent a pattern common to many career and managerial activities. It is really about producing a plan, putting that plan into action and then following through until you see a conclusion.

But, above all, interviews are an exercise in communications. And to communicate well, it is essential to appreciate the other party's needs.

9 Handling appraisals and staff development

Many organisations, within a wide variety of business sectors in the UK, practise a form of staff appraisal. This is not a new technique, but it has enjoyed an upsurge of renewed interest since the early 1980s. From that time, there has been keen interest in finding ways of getting employees committed to the aims of the organisation: techniques that will encourage employees to develop themselves for the sake of the efficiency of the enterprise, and also in order that they may maximise their work enjoyment and personal career success.

Within a properly constructed and carefully implemented appraisal scheme there are concepts and procedures which go some way towards assisting the achievement of these aims.

Appraisal in the education sector

The Government took steps towards the introduction of appraisal for teachers and this led to a dispute. Subsequently, this dispute was referred to ACAS (Advisory Conciliation and Arbitration Service). An Appraisal and Training Working Group was formed and delivered its report in June 1986.

Following on from this report, the School Teacher Appraisal Pilot Study began in January 1987. The study involved six LEAs, each of which developed schemes based on the principles set out in the ACAS report. The pilot study was overseen by a National Steering Group and this body met on numerous occasions to assess and record progress. After its final meeting in July 1989, a comprehensive report *School Teacher Appraisal: A National Framework* was produced by the Department of Education and Science and published in 1989 by HMSO.

There are many varieties of appraisal scheme, each with some differences of emphasis. However, because of the obvious relevance to all schools of all that has been described above, this chapter relates, where advantageous to you, to comments, observations and notes on the ACAS philosophy on appraisal. Wherever it seemed helpful, or appropriate, we have quoted from the report (as allowed for in the report).

Development appraisal – a definition

Development appraisal is a process where a person (appraisee) and a practised observer (appraiser) work together to assess the appraisee within the context of his or her job. Together, they seek to establish strengths and also to identify areas where improvement is desirable. Targets of competence and knowledge for the appraisee are set down, these are related to career aims and a coherent career strategy is planned.

Once the system is introduced, it becomes a continuous and systematic process. This sense of continuity is an important aspect of the method. Without it, appraisal merely becomes likened to an occasional personal competence audit, rather than a joint initiative to achieve mutual aims and lasting benefits.

Agreed principles

For teachers, an appraisal system might take into account the following matters:

● planning teachers' in-service training
● helping teachers, and their headteachers, to see when a new assignment would help their professional development
● identifying teachers' potential
● recognising when teachers are experiencing performance difficulties, resulting in appropriate assistance
● helping staff appointment procedures, by facilitating better information for references (by using appraisal documents as a data-source).

As you can see, the emphasis is on raising the quality of education in schools by providing positive help to teachers with their careers. All of this helps to facilitate better directed training, leading to proficiency and job-satisfaction.

Benefits of appraisal

There are many claimed benefits of appraisal and in the education sector, these could include:

- greater confidence and morale for individuals
- better professional relations and communications within schools
- wider participation in and better targeting of in-service training
- better career planning
- better informed references.

However, since there are around 30 000 schools and 415 000 full-time teachers, these benefits might be difficult to assess, on a nationwide basis, for some time to come.

Organisations in other business sectors perceive benefits in addition to those mentioned as follows:

(a) Appraisal is seen as an aid to workforce planning. Workforce planning can be defined as a process by which an organisation's workforce needs are compared with the anticipated workforce available. This comparison is carried out in terms of specialisms and levels of expertise.

(b) Appraisal is seen as a valuable training tool for managers. This is because the proper operation of the method requires that effective interpersonal relationships are created. Some managers have to work hard to achieve this competence.

(c) Appraisal is seen as a way of measuring personal performance levels and consequently as a way of deducing a person's relative worth to the organisation – this is then reflected in an individual reward.

(**Note**: The latter application is **not** in any way included in the agreed principles for the ACAS scheme to be applied in the education sector.)

Equal opportunities

Practisers of appraisal are often at pains to express the need for equal opportunity principles to hold sway. It seems particularly appropriate to guard against developing and acting upon a stereotyped notion of what a person might be, rather than progressing on the basis of careful observation and rational assessment of the facts. Particular groups of people who frequently experience discrimination include women, married women, ethnic minorities and people with disabilities.

Who should be included in the appraisal process?

In commercial organisations, once a system is introduced, it is common practice to appraise all permanent staff. Indeed, it is felt necessary to do so in order to gain many of the advantages cited.

In schools, it would be likely for all teaching staff to be included.

Who appraises whom?

The general rule is that the appraiser of a person should be his or her immediate supervisor. In education, though, this could be either the headteacher or another experienced teacher designated by the head. In general, the appraiser should be a person with management responsibility for the appraisee.

These two approaches, immediate boss or a designated senior, are the ones commonly adopted by most organisations. You need to consider what are the advantages and disadvantages associated with either choice. If the appraisee's immediate boss is to conduct the appraisal, then the key points for consideration are:

- the immediate boss should know best about a subordinate's strengths and weaknesses – because he or she is paid to know!
- the immediate boss should have the closest interest in the performance and welfare of a subordinate, because these are reflected within the performance of his or her group
- the immediate boss should be the one to reap the benefit of closer interpersonal relationships which appraisal can bring.

On the other hand:

- the immediate boss may well have a very wide span of responsibility. There may be so many subordinates that the appraiser role would impose too large an extra workload to perform properly
- the immediate boss may not have sufficient authority to ensure that the agreed or desired actions are followed to a successful conclusion
- there might, on occasion, be a situation where the appraisee anticipates unfair discrimination from a particular appraiser; in that circumstance, a variation might be permitted from the general rule, or the headteacher's initial choice.

There are strong reasons for attempting to adhere to a general rule which places the responsibility for appraisal on someone's immediate boss. This is because the immediate boss is the person charged with obtaining and maintaining a group performance.

What should be appraised?

Appraisal should be related to a person's job description. For teachers, this should reflect the balance between his or her teaching load and other responsibilities outside the classroom. Up-to-date job descriptions are essential and central to the whole exercise. This is a commonly held view of organisations which have implemented an appraisal system.

If a job, such as a headteacher's, has wide managerial responsibilities, specific areas of focus need to be agreed on, so that the whole job need not be covered. This parallels the practice for senior jobs in other sectors.

A key issue concerns the level of detail to which the job description goes. If it is too general, then there are not sufficient reference points to form the context within which the appraisee needs to consider both performance and competence levels. If it is too detailed, this welter of detail can obscure the main focuses of the job. Some organisations attempt to bring clarity by adding statistical data to the duties; for example, number of hours per day, or frequency per annum, etc.

Another important aspect of job descriptions relates to the adoption of a uniform approach to expressing job content within an organisation. In other words, job descriptions should be written to a standard pattern across the school.

Frequency of formal appraisals

In organisations in other business sectors, the following practices are typically found:

- trainees and new entrants are appraised more frequently than most staff
- recently promoted staff and people who are experiencing obvious difficulty may be appraised more frequently than other staff
- a one-year cycle prevails for most, on a continuing basis.

The ACAS group considered that the frequency of appraisals should vary in accord with the stage in a teacher's career. The pilot study group, however, recommended that at this stage of the introduction of the appraisal method into the field of education, a two-year cycle seemed an appropriate standard. Their points of consideration were to produce a framework which gave maximum benefit to teachers and to schools, but did not allocate an additional unmanageable workload to all concerned.

The components of the appraisal programme

An appropriate sequence for schools might be:

- an initial meeting between appraiser and appraisee

- self-appraisal by the appraisee
- classroom observation
- collection of data from other sources, agreed with appraisee
- an appraisal interview, in which professional targets for action are agreed
- the preparation of an appraisal statement, to be agreed by both parties
- follow-up, including a formal review meeting.

For comparison, the following is a collection of additional practices sometimes found in other business sectors:

- appraisee considers and assesses whether their job description truly reflects the role that he or she is expected to achieve
- peers are given the opportunity to assess colleagues
- subordinates are invited to comment on boss's traits
- boss relates target achievements to salary recommendation.

Figure 9.1 on page 139 depicts the pilot group's recommendations for the components of an appraisal system and their relationships within a biennial cycle.

The initial meeting

This is a scene-setter, an occasion where understandings are made and agreements reached on what is to be the best way to proceed. The pilot study group envisaged a number of purposes, which are listed and commented upon below.

(a) **To confirm the purpose and clarify the context of the appraisal.** It is clearly very important that teachers who are new to appraisal use this opportunity to confirm their understanding and discuss any concerns.

(b) **To consider the teacher's job description.** It is quite often the case, in some organisations, that an appraisee and the manager start off with a different perception of the relative emphasis which might be placed on the various duties.

(c) **To agree the scope of the appraisal, identifying areas of the appraisee's job on which the appraisal might usefully focus.** This particular step sometimes calls for sensitivity by the appraiser who is the appraisee's boss. He or she may already know quite well that improvement is needed in some specific areas. However, it is desirable that appraisees identify these for themselves and hence become more committed to subsequent targets.

(d) **To agree the arrangements for, and scope of, self-appraisal**

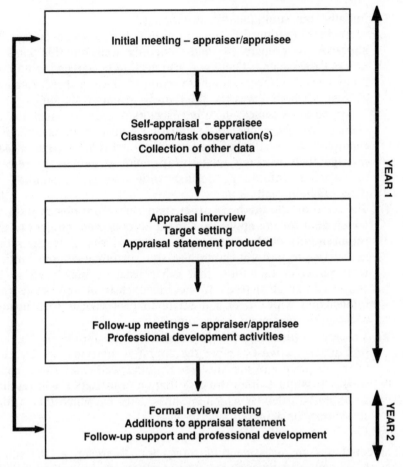

Figure 9.1 Frequency of appraisal reports and the appraisal cycle

and its relationship to the other components of the programme.
The inclusion of an element of self-appraisal in a scheme is
currently considered to be an enlightened practice. Self-appraisal
gives the appraisee a right to a structured and visible input, on
the basis of formal self-analysis. The appraiser must ensure that
the appraisee realises that the amount of attention given to this
activity may well determine how much benefit he or she actually
gets out of appraisal.

(e) **To agree arrangements for classroom observation, subject to
the requirements of the scheme.** This is a key part of the
information-gathering process. This should be very helpful to
teachers as it will cause them to reflect on the feedback
subsequently given. Some teachers may find the prospect daunting

initially, but subsequently stimulating.

At the initial meeting the appraiser will need to encourage the appraisee to prepare for and hopefully welcome this kind of rational assessment. There will also need to be agreement on how many periods of observation are required. Two or three, totalling at least 1.5 hours, was the pilot study recommendation.

Appraisal schemes in other sectors sometimes include an element of observing and evaluating someone in action. For example, banks and building societies assess how counter-staff manage their working relationships with customers in respect of advising, informing, dealing with queries, responding to dissatisfaction, and so on.

(f) **To agree on the methods other than classroom observation by which data for the appraisal should be collected, subject to the requirements of the scheme.** For the majority of teachers this may relate to pastoral duties and administrative responsibilities. It is possible, therefore, that other teachers may need to be consulted. It also needs to be made clear at this stage that information which does not relate to professional performance will neither be sought nor accepted.

(g) **To agree a timetable for the conduct of the appraisal.** The key preliminary activities before the appraisal interview, as depicted in the diagram and just discussed, might well extend over some weeks. It is quite often the case that an organisation will publish an appraisal calendar which specifies dates by which the various steps must be achieved.

That concludes an assessment of topics for discussion at the initial meeting. As you can infer from the subject matter, for both the appraiser and appraisee, this represents the opportunity to create a positive and energetic onset to the partnership.

Self-appraisal

Having considered at length the initial meeting, we turn now to the next component part in the chain: self-appraisal. How can this best be carried out? The ACAS report, at Annex B, published a check-list, which we believe would assist all self-appraisers. It included the following questions:

- What are the main tasks and responsibilities of your post?
- What parts of your job, recently, have given most satisfaction and how could these be used to best advantage?

- What parts of your job have given least satisfaction and what might be done to overcome this?
- Were there any problems or difficulties which prevented you from achieving something you intended or hoped to do?
- Are they still a cause for concern?
- If so, could they be eliminated?
- What changes in the school organisation would be beneficial to help you improve your performance?
- What additional things might be done by your headteacher?
  - or your head of department?
  - or you?
  - or anyone else?
- What do you think should be your main targets/goals for the next year?
- How would you like to see your career developing?

As you can see, all these questions are framed to encourage the appraisee to take the responsibility for identifying and dealing with factors which may be inhibiting further job-efficiency and career satisfaction.

Classroom observation

This step is an appraiser activity. The ACAS report, at Annex C, published a useful checklist to assist classroom observation. It included a series of questions to be addressed; these were framed in the following format:

- Preparation –   Was there a planned programme?
                    Was the aim of the activity clear?
                    Were adequate resources available?
                    Had the learning environment been considered?
- Teaching skills – Was the material well presented?
                    Was mastery of the subject displayed?
                    Were the pupils involved?
                    Was there awareness of individuals' needs?
- Follow-up –   Is homework set regularly?
                    Is pupils' work marked and recorded regularly?
                    Do pupils get feedback?
                    Are parents informed of pupils' work and progress?
                    Does the teacher evaluate the success of his or her teaching?

Some of these questions make it desirable for the observer to be briefed in advance by the appraisee. For example, there will be a need to explain the context in which the lesson will be given, and its aims and purposes.

Finally, it is very desirable that there is an early exchange of impressions of the teaching which has been observed – normally within two days, whilst the impressions are still strong. Furthermore, since there will be a number of observation sessions, each successive feedback should comment on any common strands which emerge.

Collection of other data

This activity will tend to involve other people. As a result, the pilot study group has been particularly careful to record views on how to carry it out in a manner which safeguards the integrity of the system. Consequently, Appendix 4 to their report comprises 'Guidance and Code of Practice on the Collection of Information for Teacher and Head Teacher Appraisal'. Some of the essentials are discussed below.

(a) **The teacher's appraiser must be familiar with relevant national and LEA policies and requirements.** This is an essential part of the information needed for a contextual assessment of the appraisee's professional performance.

(b) **The appraiser needs to acquire background information** – on the appraisee's wider professional responsibilities, the school's aims, pastoral arrangements, departmental policies, and so on. Again this is contextual, but this time more directly related to the appraisee.

(c) **The appraiser needs the previous appraisal statement.** Careers typically cover a long time-span. Reference points and trends give powerful indications towards personal development.

(d) **For the appraisers of headteachers, additional data is required – curricular policies, the organisation and deployment of the staff, links with outside bodies, financial and management systems, and so on.** These potential needs tend to emphasise the requirement to focus on some selected areas when headteachers are appraised. This is comparable to the practice in commerce where directors may be assessed against a few key business indicators; for example, profitability, business growth, cash-flow, company image, and so on.

(e) **When interviewing people, appraisers need to be careful to explain the purpose of the information and the way in which it will be treated.** Any misunderstanding may tend to produce distorted inputs, to the disadvantage of the appraisee and to the discredit of the system.

(f) **Written submissions should remain confidential to the author, the appraiser and the appraisee.** To achieve confidentiality on a continuing basis probably implies that the written input is destroyed after its use for the forthcoming appraisal.

(g) **Those offering significantly critical comments should be asked to discuss them directly with the appraisee before they are used for appraisal information.** (The substance of grievance or disciplinary proceedings should never be used in the appraisal process.) These recommendations are vital for the open and developmental philosophy of the scheme as envisaged for the education sector.

(h) **Those giving information should not be put under any pressure, save that of relevance and accuracy.** This does not mean that someone with some important information (perhaps being the only one with that information) can opt out of giving it. It means that the contributor has a right to decide the content of that information.

(i) **General comments should be supported by specific examples.** This tends to accentuate facts as opposed to opinions.

(j) **Any information received anonymously should not be used.** The interesting question arises here as to whether the appraiser should inform the appraisee of such information, since it may be difficult for the appraiser to forget it. Probably, the most practical answer is to say that the appraiser must decide according to the nature of the information and on the likely effect of telling the appraisee.

Exercise 34

On the basis of your present job, carry out a self-appraisal as if you were preparing for a forthcoming appraisal interview. It is suggested that you work your way through the self-appraisal questions quoted on pp. 140–141.

Exercise 35

Imagine that you are soon to be observed in a classroom session by your appraiser. The observation will be based on the format suggested on p. 141. Choose a suitable lesson in the forthcoming week as the occasion and then go ahead and perform on the day as normal. Subsequently, award yourself marks out of ten for each of the points in the checklist.

Do the same again for a lesson in the following week about which you feel some professional dissatisfaction.

Exercise 36

Imagine your appraiser will now collect other data. What are the key messages that he or she may derive about your pastoral duties performance and your administrative duties performance?

The appraisal interview, target setting and appraisal statements

The appraisal interview is central to the whole process. It is the occasion when the results of earlier steps – the initial meeting, the self-appraisal, the classroom observations and the other collected data – are brought together, considered and acted upon by the appraiser and the appraisee. The dialogue in the meeting can now focus on specific areas of interest within the context of the appraisee's role.

To be of maximum value, the appraisal interview needs to be conducted in a suitable atmosphere and in the right spirit. An

interruption-free location is desirable, and both parties will have to contribute a positive approach to the business at hand. The appraisee may be uneasy about discussing some aspects of his or her work. The appraiser may find the prospect of suggesting some development targets, daunting. Both parties will need to remind themselves of the benefits which can ensue, and also remember to appreciate each other's point of view.

The ACAS report suggested a structured approach to the discussion which includes the identification of development targets, and also forms the basis for the format of the appraisal statement. This can be found in Annex D to the ACAS Report. In fact, the various elements suggested are included in similar form in a wide variety of appraisal schemes.

The discussion commences with consideration of the appraisee in his or her present role and across its constituent parts. For a teacher this could be:

- in the classroom – preparation, teaching, follow-up
- in the school/community – pastoral care, cooperation/teamwork, curriculum involvement
- as a manager – management skills, leadership, self-determined professional development.

The discussion would continue with consideration of the appraisee in potential future roles. For teachers and others this would imply:

- further training – type and duration
- further experience – type and duration
- potential – for what and when
- career aspirations – to what and by when.

These two discussion groupings lead naturally to the consideration of professional targets:

- What are the aims? By when? What resources will be needed?
- How will all this be brought about and progress monitored?
- How are subsequent attainments to be measured?

If there has been a previous appraisal cycle, targets already attained need consideration and remark. In some appraisal schemes, this would be the first topic at the meeting.

Finally, the essence of the entire meeting will be drawn into a summary note of the occasion. The appraisal statement, in its entirety, is the responsibility of the appraiser. However, both parties will, ideally, signify their agreement to everything within it. This is usually brought about by the appraiser producing a first draft of the intended entries, for discussion with the appraisee. Most often, a few word changes and a minor difference of emphasis here and there are sufficient to produce an accord.

Appraisal schemes usually incorporate strategies to cope with the comparatively rare situations when serious disagreement remains. These strategies take one of three forms:

(a) The appraisee has the right to seek the intervention of the next person higher up the management chain.
(b) The appraisee has the right to ask for a further appraisal from a different appraiser.
(c) The appraisee has the right to 'appeal' to some party(s).

Such action is usually a rare occurrence, if an appraisal interview is characterised by mutual goodwill.

Once the appraisal statement is completed to the satisfaction of both parties, action to implement the agreed arrangements would normally commence. The statement itself would be placed in the appraisee's file, which would have a very restricted list of approved accessees. Typically these might include the appraisee, the appraiser, somebody who was responsible for personnel matters, and the headteacher. Supporting papers are often destroyed once their original purpose has been served.

Follow-up meetings

Follow-up monitoring and action are usually considered essential to maximise the benefits of appraisal. Some commercial organisations go so far as to institute an across-the-board 'appraisal-recommendations audit' after three and then six months. At the least, managers are generally expected to keep in regular and timely contact with the progress of training and development activities; and also with the rate of achievement of targets. Such activities may, or may not, result in the formality of an appraisal follow-up meeting where sheets are initialled to signify progress.

If the appraisal cycle extends to two years, then it would probably be essential to make provision for a formal review meeting at the half-way point, that is after a year.

Formal review meeting, additions to statement, follow-up support and professional development

Most appraisal schemes practised in the UK operate on an annual cycle. In that event, all the activities in the cycle occur yearly. However, a two-year cycle might sometimes be chosen because of economic considerations.

In the latter case, the essentials to be achieved are:

- to establish and continue a trend of positive progress
- to demonstrate continued interest in, and recognition of, achievements
- to amend plans to reflect altered needs
- to review potential and career aims.

This implies a review of performance and possibly some observation within the cycle. Of necessity there will need to be joint further consideration of the current career status and the likely way ahead. Some further targets may need to be established and planned. All of this will require additions to the appraisal statement.

When the appraisal cycle is complete, the whole process recommences. Organisations usually find that the practice becomes markedly easier on this and subsequent occasions.

Exercise 37

Following on from the work in Exercises 34–6, imagine that you are now at the subsequent appraisal meeting.

1 What training/development will you now propose for yourself:
   (a) to benefit your performance in your present job?
   (b) to prepare yourself for a different role in the future?
2 What, in particular, has prompted proposals 1 and 2?
3 What will be the aim of training for your present job?

General comments

1 Most organisations, in many business sectors, insist that a manager's duties include the assessment and development of all the staff within their control. Sometimes these activities are carried out within the structure of an appraisal scheme, sometimes not. In either event, there should be a continuing, all-year-round interest devoted to this aim.
2 One advantage of carrying this out within the aegis of appraisal is that a uniform and considered method of procedure is imposed upon what might well be a diverse set of approaches practised by a cross-section of managers.

3 On approaching their first appraisal cycle, many staff may experience concern. This may arise from:
  • doubts about their own competence
  • concerns about being compared with others
  • potential embarrassment about the frank discussion which characterises the appraisal meeting
  • apprehensions about the competence of the appraiser
  • fear of the unknown.
The fact is that there is nothing new about being assessed, compared and counselled, by people of varying standards of competence, it is just that these things become more 'visible' within the context of appraisal. Furthermore, since all staff are appraised, there is no comparative disadvantage arising from the system itself (everybody is in the same boat).

4 If a scheme includes the facility of a self-appraisal, and probably the majority in the UK at this time do not, then that is an important and enlightened precursor to an 'open' style of management. Some appraisal schemes merely provide an opportunity for management to formulate their views on the performance and development needs of their staff. Some schemes do not even require the manager to make these views known to the appraisee.

The opportunity of carrying out a self-appraisal, and then discussing with the appraiser creates a self-generated yardstick which helps point the way to the best interests of the appraisee.

5 Schemes which require both parties, the manager and the managed, to establish development targets with timescales, resource requirements, progress monitoring agreements and success-indicators, strongly reinforce an employee learning within an organisation's development culture.

6 The process of operating a scheme is a powerful management-training tool for the appraisers. Many of the activities are entirely concerned with human resource management. Since they are obligatory, the manager quickly becomes involved in a great deal of practice, which prior to the introduction of the scheme might never have been undertaken.

7 Most organisations which operate appraisals find it essential to establish appraiser-training courses. Such courses will often include some role-play practice sessions.

Summary

Appraisal is not new in the UK, but it is enjoying a resurgence of interest and adoption. Appraisal is, at heart, a communication tool, and prior to the 1980s organisations were often somewhat tardy about establishing good communications.

With the onset of a much greater push towards economic efficiency in the 1980s, organisations have been obliged to find ways of increasing the efficient use of their workforces. This has included a search for a means of broadcasting the organisations' aims and encouraging each individual to adopt them and strive towards meeting them. In its turn, this has resulted in the need to assess the extent to which each individual has succeeded in doing so. Having established comparative levels of performance, it becomes necessary to address the reasons for any shortfall. Often this results in the detection of training needs.

From the individual's point of view, a job is very often the access point to a lifelong career. This implies development activity, which is a close neighbour of the training needs discussed above. It then becomes advantageous to both employer and employee to combine these concepts – as indeed they are within the development appraisal philosophy.

10 Moving up the ladder

Some people embark on a particular career because they have a strong feeling that it is a calling for which they are well-suited; a role where they can make a maximum contribution to society. Others follow an occupational path because of family precedents; the job may possibly be a traditional family interest.

It is likely, however, that the majority of people today drift into careers and occupations, often as a consequence of:

- the encouragement, or example, of a friend or relative
- a particular series of examination or test results
- influence by some branch of the media.

The likelihood is that you, personally, were impressed by a combination of factors en route to the job you now have. This explanation may imply that you require some job satisfaction in addition to that of seeing your pupils do well.

Exercise 38

What is it that YOU need from your job now and in the future?
You need to answer this question before you can seriously consider the direction you wish your career to take. Look at the items below, and prioritise them for yourself by writing a comment, or a number, against each one. Do you require:

1 The satisfaction of a job well done?
2 Status?
3 Enough money to live well on?
4 Power?
5 Interaction with others?
6 Opportunity to learn more about your specialism?
7 Opportunity to administrate a school?

8 An engrossing occupation?
9 The pleasure of shaping someone's life?
10 To work with other institutions, like employers, to benefit society?
11 Anything else?

Can we influence the future?

Career planning can help to focus your ideas on where you want to be in the future and how to get there within some defined timescale. Many of life's experiences do not 'just happen'. Life goals, or pulling motivators, serve as sources of energy which pull one into the future in varying but identifiable ways. A colourful, but apt, analogy is: You are adrift in an open boat in the vicinity of a shoreline (this is you in life!). There are various rocks about and you are in possession of an anchor on the end of a rope. You select a series of the most suitable rocks and, using the anchor as a grappling iron, you gradually pull yourself towards your ultimate, desired, destination.

Obviously, the apparently fortuitous possession of the rope and anchor is analogous to the acquisition of valuable knowledge, or skills, or a

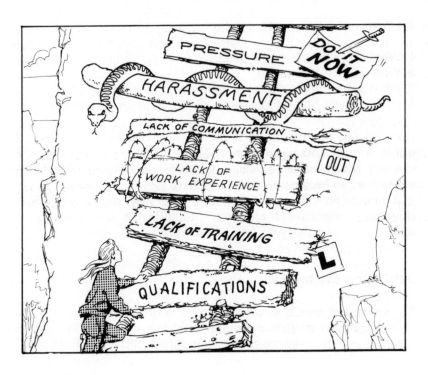

prudent pattern of behaviour, and so on. Furthermore, you will have to choose the rocks which are within your own, personal, casting distance!

Finally, at each stage along the way, you will review the remainder of your journey from your current viewpoint. The further opportunities presented will relate to the particular position which you then occupy and, indeed, **planned to occupy**.

The practical essentials of career planning

    (a) **Targets**. Where or what do you want to be?
    (b) **Appropriate attributes**. You must either have, or be able to develop, the knowledge and skills to get from your present to your desired future position.
    (c) **Coherency**. Some integrated notion of how most of the important things which you do, can be used to take you towards the next step, or in the right direction.

Exercise 39

Jot down your existing career plan.

1 What are your career targets?
2 What is their timescale?
3 What will you need to become in order to reach them?
4 How will you bring about the required changes in yourself?

How did you get on with Exercise 39? Were you able to say, instantly, where you are going, and how you will get there? Alternatively, did you only have a single target in mind, and no detailed idea of what you might need to become in order to achieve it?

If you are already organised, then we will help you develop a useful alternative perspective. If you hadn't really thought it through then you will develop, shortly, your first career plan!

Setting career targets

An effective approach to charting out a desired future is to project it from a recorded past. It is helpful to do this in respect of your total life, and not just with regard to your career. Take a holistic view of your life, where everything you have experienced relates in some way to where you are now.

Charting your personal/professional lifeline

Tape together, side-by-side, two sheets of A4 paper. Draw a straight line from the lower left-hand corner of one sheet to the upper right-hand corner of the other. This represents your 'lifeline' (see Figure 10.1).

Write your present age at the top right corner. Divide that figure by two and write in that number halfway along the line. Then put in the appropriate figures at the quarter and the three-quarter points.

Now, start to add event data to the chart. Write the age you were, for each recorded event, at the appropriate distance along the line and add a few words somewhere convenient on the chart with an arrow pointing to that age. What you are seeking to recall are happenings which have had an influence on where you are now. Also, include activities which indicate your preferences. For example:

- 'O' levels achieved
- charismatic characters who influenced your way of thinking
- some particular childhood success

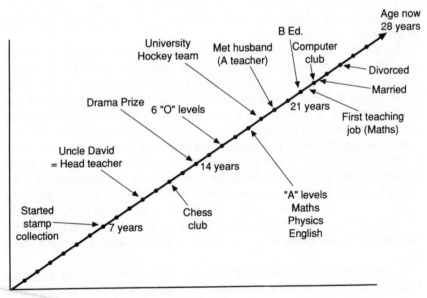

Figure 10.1 Personal professional lifeline

- what your parents said of your future
- hobbies and interests throughout your life
- advice from your own teachers.

Also add data from your current domestic scene. For example

- how you met your partner
- the influence that he or she has had
- your involvement in community activities.

Don't let the paper size limit you; if necessary, make a larger sheet. You want patterns to emerge, even if it is only to indicate apparent randomness (this will be extremely unlikely!). This process can be very important to you, so it is worth spending some effort on it. If you have got a partner at home, then it is likely that he or she will have a good insight of you to augment your own. (Maybe you could construct a chart for each of you.) Otherwise, ask a good friend to assist.

You will quite likely fill the sheets with events, names and recollections. You will almost certainly detect themes which indicate the nature of the activities that you find satisfying, even though these may have apparently different emphases. For example, you may have been a boy scout (girl guide), a member of a cricket team (hockey team), a member of the Conservative Club, and a chorister. A common strand here could be that you are by nature, affiliative; that is, you get pleasure from being one of a group. In that event, you might find being a headteacher very unsatisfying. The point of the exercise is to identify and question your needs.

The people in life who have the most satisfying careers, are those who get paid for doing the same sort of activities (*in detail*) at work, that they pursue for nothing in their leisure time. Various jobs may imply a high element of talking, listening, telling, or being told. Others may imply a lot of administration, control or co-ordination. Yet others may rest on political acumen, etc.

By constructing your professional lifeline, you are assessing your true preferences. This will help you to identify an appropriate career target; the kind of job that would be rewarding for you in every sense of the word. It is worth noting at this point, that to a certain extent, different people can carry out the same job with different emphases. Although this latitude may be somewhat limited in some cases, there might well be scope for minimising some of the potentially irksome aspects of some roles.

Before continuing to select a career target, it is necessary to think hard about your personal preferences. Having thought, and having made a provisional selection, you can now move on to the next phase. This comprises producing a supporting plan of how to get from where you are now, to where you want to be.

Outlining a five-year plan

One sheet of A4 is sufficient for this exercise. The format of the plan will look like that in Figure 10.2. This first attempt is a provisional trial to get used to the idea of the exercise.

You are actually portraying a few milestones to take into consideration. Five years is long enough to allow for a significant change (for the better) and short enough to allow for a constant feel of progress.

At each of the intermediate age points you should indicate what you intend to achieve that will take you the next step towards your chosen career target.

Examples for career targets might be senior teacher, head of year, head of history, office technology teacher, and so on. In each case, the intermediate milestones might depict the acquisition of a necessary qualification, or an essential tranche of experience.

You have now completed steps 1, 2, 3 shown in Figure 10.3.

Let's consider step number 4 – what is the job that you selected, and then supported with a five-year plan?

- How have you analysed it?
- Is there a job description, or outline, available?
- Do you know someone well who occupies such a job?
- Do you work in close proximity so that you have had all the

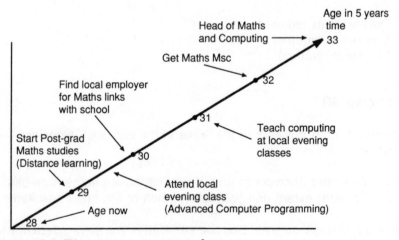

Figure 10.2 Five-year career target plan

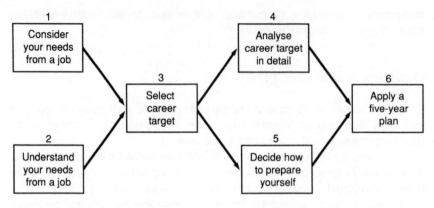

Figure 10.3 shows the overall process you are working through

opportunity you need to observe *and understand* the implications of holding that role?

A summary checklist of the features that you will need to understand about a job might look like this:

- Duties
- Responsibilities
- Activities
- Work pattern
- Principal characteristics
- Location
- Salary
- Qualifications required
- Experience required
- Behaviour required

Exercise 40

Attempt to draft answers to the items in the checklist. Consider your answers.

1   Were the answers to any of the first seven items 'turn-offs'?
2   To what extent can you satisfy each of the last three items?

How did you get on with Exercise 40? Unless you have selected a job role which was absolutely 'made for you', there will have been one or two aspects about the first batch of items which caused you to reflect a while. This is usually the case.

As with most things in life there are both upside and downside aspects to jobs. You are looking for a role which has predominantly favourable, or attractive, characteristics. This ought to relate to more than merely a higher salary. If, on detailed examination, there are just too many negative aspects associated with the job that you thought you desired, then you clearly need to think again.

On the assumption that you have now selected a particular career target, and that you have analysed this in some detail, we will now look at what you have to achieve to make yourself worthy of the job, or at least an acceptable candidate for it.

Qualifications, experience and behaviour

We have now reached step 5 in Figure 10.3. Planning how to combat any apparent shortfalls in your personal profile, is the key to access to a different future. Implementing that plan requires some work; but it mostly requires persistence and a measure of single-mindedness.

Qualifications

On the assumption that you are already a teacher, or studying to be one, this book is not going to dwell on the topic of how to acquire formal qualifications.

There is just one aspect that may be worth drawing to your attention, though. Distance-learning materials can be a great aid. The Materials And Resources Information Service (MARIS) directory is a useful reference source. You can inspect a computerised version of this at many public libraries and Jobcentres via a Training Access Point (TAP) terminal. You can telephone MARIS direct on Ely (Cambs) 661284.

The directory of materials available is relatively cheaply priced (reasonably within the range of all but the most severely strained school budgets). Some of the actual learning materials are more costly, but you may be able to collaborate with other users. Furthermore, if you can regard what you buy as essential to your work, it is tax-relievable.

However, one way or another (distance learning, part-time study, or programmed reading), you will have to get any essential qualification required for your target.

Accreditation and the gaining of formal certificates of competence, diplomas and degrees, etc, looks as if it will continue to feature large in the practices of the various professional institutes. In that event, if you want to maximise your career choice, you have to join in!

Experience

Schools, colleges and other institutions tend to specify the 'experience required' for a job in one of two ways. They either ask that you have a number of years exposure to some circumstance, or they call for you to have practised something over an unspecified time-scale. You will need to bear this in mind when planning to build up the required experience.

There appears to be a number of interesting possibilities for teachers when it comes to actually gaining experience.

(a) Secondment. This is probably the least easy to arrange, but is also the most effective provider of practice. Apart from being seconded on some basis to another department, faculty or school, the possibilities also include local employers and industrial training centres.

(b) Job rotation. In many organisations, it is common practice for two, or more, people to exchange roles for six months or so. This is done for personal development purposes. It implies, initially, a basic competence on the part of each participant. People who have experienced this process generally vouch for its efficacy as a training tool.

(c) Teaching at night school. Colleges which provide evening classes for students often have difficulty in finding lecturers of an appropriate standard who are prepared to commit themselves for one or two evenings a week, for the 36–39 weeks of the night school 'season'.

(d) Substitution. There are many occasions when somebody is planned to be absent (eg, maternity leave) when it would be most helpful to the head of department to have a willing substitute to 'act-upwards'. This may well be the easiest of the options to arrange. Broadcast your availability!

(e) Summer schools. The Open University runs summer schools to give distance learners the opportunity of tutorials and face-to-face discussion. You may have the opportunity to offer your skills.

(f) Private tuition. There has always been a steady market for special coaching. This may not be the most desirable way of gaining experience of teaching a new subject, but it will be effective.

(g) Social talks. Throughout the autumn, winter and spring, there are many societies which have regular meetings. (Note: There are 9100 Women's Institutes and 2200 Townswomen's Guilds, alone.) A typical meeting format is to listen to a speaker, have a question-and-answer session, then round off with cheese and biscuits. Your subject may interest a society's secretary.

Behaviour and appearance

An often neglected, but absolutely vital consideration for people pursuing a planned career path is the manner in which they act, and the associated aspect of personal appearance.

Exercise 41

Before reading on, think about your next career step, or perhaps the one which might follow that. What sort of style of behaviour will be required for the job? What sort of general appearance might be expected of the job-holder? Jot down your initial thoughts and a few key words.

You might be influenced by the behaviour and appearance of someone you know in such a job. Is the person the perfect role model? Or are you a little surprised at an element of what you regard as non-conformity? In either case, how is the person generally regarded, in that respect?

(a) **Behaviour**. The list below gives a few classifications which might categorise prescribed behaviour patterns in various job situations:

- appropriate to status – for example, how should a head of department act?
- appropriate to role – for example, do you expect a PE teacher to smoke?
- conforming to the style of the organisation – for example, does the school have a reputation for involvement with the community and social ventures?
- supportive of that which has been adopted by one's seniors and peer colleagues – for example, work ethic, parent communications, general discipline, pupil welfare
- an example to one's junior colleagues – for example, positive attitudes, expertise.

You should bear in mind that selection panels have expectations in these matters.

(b) **Appearance**. Style, manner and quality of appearance is a very personal and individual matter. Our general pattern may often have evolved from what we experienced at home in our childhood. Many of us may perpetuate a particular standard and broad style, throughout our lives.

On the other hand, many organisations, particularly commercial entities, have developed a style of dress and appearance which all employees are expected to adopt. This becomes the corporate uniform.

In all professions, including teaching, there are some individuals whose standard of appearance makes them noticed by all, or most. This may well be an important career-success influencer.

Exercise 42

What is the desired mode of dress in your school/college, or in the organisation in which you plan to work?
Here are some broad categorisations to help your classification:

- formal and smart
- casual and smart
- socially acceptable
- reflecting one's age
- reflecting one's job
- other?

1 In which category would you place yourself?
2 Where would you place heads of departments in general?
3 Where **should** they be, in your opinion?
4 Do you consider any differences you have detected of sufficient career importance to warrant you considering making a change?

Role models

One important and valuable way, particularly for the younger person, to learn successful behaviour (and perhaps successful appearance) is to study someone in the organisation who is already a success.

- What are his or her strengths?
- How does he or she actually achieve results?
- Why is he or she in that job?
- Is there any visible area of weakness? If so, why has that not stopped him or her? Or do you think that they would have gone further without that fault?
- What do others think of him or her?

A study of this kind would proceed, largely on the basis of observation, over some period of time. The role model need never know about it. The study can serve a number of purposes:

- it can illustrate someone's successful style
- it can confirm that success can be achieved from a composite of attributes
- it can, by comparison, give you a further insight of yourself (this is of great value at any age!)
- it might show you a price you are *not* prepared to pay for success of this type.

Probably most of us, at some point in our life, have adopted an admired characteristic observed in someone else. Role modelling is doing just that, with a sharp focus on career patterns.

Senior people in the teaching profession, on reading this, might well consider acting as role models – unknown to the recipients! They could do this, for instance, by taking care to explain the reasons for taking particular courses of action; hence giving insight into essential organisation behaviour.

Utilising personal and job power

By deciding to read this chapter you may have declared an interest in further developing your career. You have already seen that there is a systematic way of going about this. There is also a need to get some driving force behind your endeavours; a need for harnessing some power to them.

Dictionary definitions of 'power' are 'ability to do or act'; 'influence'; 'vigour'. These words are particularly apposite in our context.

There are many sources of power:

- knowledge, expertise, skills, experience, aptitudes
- job authority and responsibility
- stewardship for a budget
- information
- personal attributes (leadership, presence, etc)
- patronage (contacts, goodwill, support, etc).

It is fairly clear that we all have a measure of these sources available to shape daily and on-going events; be they work, domestic or career-related.

Complementary to a decision to plan a successful career, there is also a requirement for a decision to utilise the power sources available to you, towards that end. These sources may be job-related, or they may spring from personal traits. Together with physical and mental capabilities, personal traits also include emotional and social characteristics. Emotional capabilities, to an extent, determine our expectations from life. Quite often, *what we expect to get is what we then actually get.*

You must nurture a strong expectation of achieving your chosen career target. By adopting this attitude you will, automatically, align your power sources to your task. Focus your working life on your career aim.

People who specialise in giving occupational guidance often feel the need to give particular counsel to women. This is cogent for those making their way up a professional ladder.

Special considerations about women careerists

There is often a preponderance of men in senior management positions. Many researchers have sought to explain this phenomenon, and the following gives some of the findings:

Role conflict

It is sometimes said that the imbalance between men and women in terms of career success, reflects an imbalance of duties and responsibilities in life. This is particularly so in the domestic situation. It is sometimes said that if male partners were to take an equal share in the domestic role, then women would be able to make a career commitment which would equal men's.

Much of the basis of the division, between the sexes, of domestic responsibilities is nothing more than a perpetuation of stereotypes that might have been valid 50 years ago. In the 1990s, only child-bearing need be the exclusive province of females!

Child-rearing can be a shared responsibility; as can the acquisition of food and its preparation; and the care of clothes, and the cleaning of the home.

Aspiring female careerists, who intend success, may need to address the matter of achieving an equitable division of domestic responsibility.

Some attitudinal and behavioural patterns: male/female differences

The following are quoted from *Career Structures for Women in the Water Industry*, K. F. Birkett, 1988. Women tend to embroider their statements and qualify them with caveats, thus introducing signals of modesty, deference, possibly ingratiation, and conditionals. (This may actually make them nicer people.) However, men seem to feel no need or desire to do this. A selection panel, mostly men perhaps, may interpret a female response of this sort as weak, hesitant, unsure and un-managerial. If you feel that this applies to you, decide whether you need to take account of this possibility.

Women are said to find it difficult to work with people they do not like. Men seem to have learned to tolerate one another in the workplace, and to work effectively with people they may dislike. Managers find it irksome to have subordinates who work less than well together.

Women tend to focus on their own concept of themselves. Men are more attuned to what bosses and others in the workplace expect of them.

Women tend to suppress their own achievement and leadership needs by slipping into supportive roles. Males do not have this tendency to the same degree.

A woman likes to be sure that she has all the qualities mentioned in a job advertisement. Most men, if they have a few, will apply on the assumption that they can pick up the rest 'on the job'.

Men and women have differing approaches to career planning. Women ascribe paramount importance to doing the present job well and proving one's ability by that. They also believe that hard work is the other key determinant. This could be summarised as a 'here and now' approach to career success. Men subscribe to the notion of continuously developing new skills for future use. They also believe in the critical importance of human relations skills for career success. Paradoxically, women seem better naturally endowed with these skills.

Mentors

Another way to boost a career, for aspiring men or women, is to acquire a **mentor**; someone who will agree to giving career counsel. There is enormous advantage in a mentor/protégé arrangement. There was an upsurge of interest in such developmental arrangements in the UK in the 1980s, but recently media interest seems to have abated. The device, however, remains effective.

The ideal mentor is:

- successful
- knowledgeable
- a good communicator
- interested in people

- probably senior to you
- probably older than you.

Ideally, you are aiming at an on-going series of informal, personal, career tutorials. Your mentor can give you professional, political and business insights of your organisation.

If you are already in a senior position you could, with considerable personal advantage, offer to act as mentor to some of your younger staff-members. The gain to you comprises additional managerial experience, and, of course, greater competence by them in their duties.

Understanding the organisation

There is just one remaining area of potential shortfall, to be addressed by all who aspire to progress within any organisation. If you do not already have a **thorough** grasp of the functioning of your school, you **must** devote some time to this aspect. The following questions illustrate the point:

- What is the theoretical remit of each department?
- Is the *actual* responsibility different from the *theoretical*?
- Which departments really control what, and are all equal?
- What control information is published by, and for, whom? (If you, personally, do not receive this, can you take any steps to get sight of it?)
- Which are the key job roles (in teaching and in management)?
- Who are the key figures?
- Are they key figures because of their role alone, or also because of their personal attributes?
- What style of behaviour and appearance is adopted by key figures?
- Where does your job fit into the scheme of things?
- Are you quite well-known to all, or most, of the key figures?
- What could you do to become better known to them?
- What does one have to do, and in what way, to achieve good results?

Hopefully, on looking through these questions, the vital importance of the answers to your career will become self-evident.

In summary, one needs to understand what is supposed to happen, who makes it happen, and where in all this you are aiming to be.

Applying your five-year plan

The steps in the procedure up to now have been:

- you analysed your needs from a job
- you analysed your path through life to where you are now
- you selected a desired and appropriate career target
- you analysed that selected target in some detail
- you have considered, at length, what you might need to do in order to ensure success in your ambition.

The remaining activity (step 6 in Figure 10.3) is to draw up a weekly, or perhaps monthly, programme of mini-achievements to support the annual milestones on your five-year plan. For example, if you need to study, you will draw up a work programme. If you want to get some experience by acting as someone's substitute, then you will need to start negotiating this at the appropriate time. If you are seeking a mentor, this will need arranging.

Your programme of mini-achievements may just be a hand-written schedule of, say, ten activities to achieve each milestone. You may also feel the need to draw up a simple bar chart to show the respective time-scales.

Now that the potential steps along the way from here to wherever you wish to be, have been pointed out, achieving your aim may just be a matter of single-minded application.

On the other hand, having considered, in depth, your career in teaching, you may have come to the view that you are in the wrong profession. If that is the case you will want to consider the available alternatives. One good starting point is *Careers A to Z*, published in association with *The Daily Telegraph*. This is a careers encyclopedia which is updated every few years and there will almost certainly be a copy in your local library. *Careers A to Z* covers career opportunities from a wide range of perspectives, and will almost certainly provide you with some initial inspirations.

Summary

Successful progress with a career requires more than aptitude and hard work. It benefits from you developing a coherent plan of action and keeping this in mind over the years. Sometimes, fate seems to smile, sometimes not. Good luck can be described as occurring when opportunity meets preparation.

11 Coping with stress

What is stress?

Stress has been defined as a misfit between the individual and his or her environment. An external event, such as a row with a colleague, being on a tight time deadline at work, dealing with a difficult pupil problem, attending a governors' meeting, or an interview with an aggressive parent, may all be examples of stressful situations. Stress also creates internal responses, such as sleepless nights, sweaty hands or an emotive response, such as an aggressive outburst. Stress, therefore, creates both internal and external consequences.

It has to be emphasised, however, that stress is not necessarily a bad

thing. We all need a certain amount of stress to get up in the morning and to motivate us. Too much stress is what is of concern. This happens when the demands on us become too great. Each individual has a different way of coping with too much stress, and many people differ in their ability to cope at different times.

Definition

The state of affairs which exists when the way people attempt to manage problems, taxes or exceeds their coping resources.

Causes of stress

We briefly discussed the flight/fight response in Chapter 1. Faced with an external threat, our ancestors would either stand their ground and fight, or run away from the danger. Bodily responses took place to enable them to react as effectively as possible in both situations. Blood was pumped around the body faster, to increase the oxygen supply to such organs as the heart, muscles and brain. Adrenalin was produced; this chemical sends messages to the brain to help the body respond. The caveman was thus primed to either fight or run away. The survival of the caveman depended on these responses.

Modern humans still respond physically in this way when a threat or a stressful situation is encountered. Adrenalin flows, the heart beats faster, sugar is broken down for energy, and so on. Some typical examples of stressful situations are: you are suddenly awakened by a noise in the middle of the night; someone jumps out into the road in front of you; or you may have a sharp exchange with your head of department. Whatever the cause, as soon as the message reaches the brain and is perceived as threatening, several changes take place in the body.

The pituitary gland is activated. Nerve impulses from the brain reach the pituitary gland and small quantities of hormone are released into the blood. Blood circulates around the body relatively quickly and is, therefore, an efficient medium for communicating with different parts of the body as quickly as possible.

The hormone from the pituitary gland reaches the adrenal glands, and the production of adrenalin is stimulated. Further physiological changes are put in action by this release. Up to this point you won't really have noticed anything happening, but the release of adrenalin soon brings about detectable changes. The major purpose of the changes is survival.

Some of these noticeable changes, together with their purposes, are given in Table 11.1.

The changes in Table 11.1 are normal healthy responses aimed at ensuring survival in a threatening situation. When our ancestors lived in caves the responses were very effective for priming the body to fight or run away. What is different now, however, is that we don't normally

Table 11.1 Physical changes that may take place in a stressful situation

Change	Purpose
pupils of eyes enlarge	to allow more light to enter the eyes so that any potential source of danger can be seen quickly and more clearly
hearing may become more acute	to enable the detection of danger from a further distance; this gives more time to think about what action can be taken
breathing becomes faster	to increase the amount of oxygen in the blood; which is like fuel for action
the heart pumps faster and harder	to speed up the flow of fuel, and to carry away waste products quickly
the face may go pale	to minimise loss of blood if wounded, it is taken away from outside the body; also a clotting agent secreted into the blood ensures that the blood will clot quicker and similarly reduce the blood loss
sickness or diarrhoea may occur	to get rid of surplus weight if one has to run away quickly
fuel-rich blood is sent to the muscles	to enable the muscles to be used more effectively
increase in sweating	to enable you to lose the heat generated, as effectively as possible; the human body can only work efficiently over quite a small internal temperature range
shaking or trembling may occur	to warm you up if the cooling system has come on but you haven't done anything physical to actually generate any heat

release this physical energy by hitting out or running away at speed. Our bodies, therefore, have no automatic outlet for the tension. It is this build up of tension which can result in unpleasant symptoms in the short term, or serious conditions in the long term. Stress management involves finding harmless ways of discharging all this potential energy.

Recognising symptoms of stress

The first stage of being able to cope with stress is to identify the symptoms. The following checklist may help you to identify some of your own symptoms. It is possible, however, that these symptoms may be due to some other cause.

- increased pulse level
- higher blood pressure
- palpitations
- cold hands and feet
- aches and pains
- change in appetite
- diarrhoea
- constipation
- queasiness
- frequent colds
- migraine
- blurred vision
- skin eruptions
- frequent urination
- getting irritable more frequently
- feeling anxious for no apparent reason
- going on the defensive
- being more critical
- feeling depressed
- crying more than usual
- being more aggressive
- being unable to concentrate
- vacillating in decision making
- making more mistakes
- being more forgetful
- being irrational
- being unreasonably negative
- being less able to make realistic judgements
- changing work habits
- changing personal habits
- neglecting personal appearance
- being unable to sleep
- being more lethargic
- drinking more alcohol
- smoking more
- changing eating habits
- a reduced sex drive
- increase in absenteeism
- being more accident prone
- relying more on medication.

Fatigue is the body's warning signal which tries to prevent us from carrying on until total exhaustion. Unfortunately, people are often not aware that their work performance is declining at the point where fatigue becomes exhaustion, as Figure 11.1 shows. People's reactions to stress vary. Some can take extreme levels of stress for longer than others, but eventually bodily health will suffer.

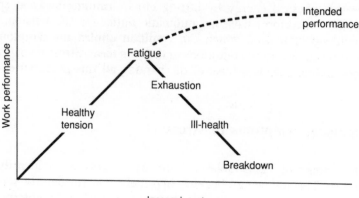

Figure 11.1

Depression

An extreme consequence of stress can be depression. Depression means permanent feelings of dejection and apathy, and can be caused by things other than stress. It is important, therefore, to try to understand the reasons and what can be done.

Work-related depression may be caused by external factors, such as failure to meet a deadline or being passed over for promotion, or by factors internal to the individual such as innate feelings of hopelessness, inability to cope and personal inadequacy. Often the result of depression is social isolation which, of course, makes the problem more difficult to solve.

Depression is made worse, in a work context, by the feelings of perceived lack of control. Headteachers can try to alleviate this by allowing participation in decision making, developing team working activities and supporting the training and development of staff. It may be useful to evaluate the way of working in your school to see if improvements can be made. Possibly you could suggest different methods to your headteacher for consideration.

As discussed earlier, individuals react differently to the same type of events. For example, when someone fails to get a promotion it may be perceived in different ways. One person may feel it is unfair, possibly get angry and think they will never be promoted: despair may be the result. Another person may consider it a trial run, evaluate what they can do well and what they need to do to minimise weaknesses. A third may be greatly relieved that they don't have to assume extra responsibility. Talking to a respected colleague, who will help you clarify the issues involved, may be all that is needed to allay feelings of despair.

Severe mental depression is, of course, an illness requiring specialist medical attention. Unfortunately, depressed people withdraw and avoid social contact. Often an outsider can perceive someone else's depression, for example, by recognising links between particular events and types of behaviour. By listening and offering support in moments of crisis you can be an invaluable asset to a friend or colleague. You can help yourself by developing a support network of friends and colleagues who will be able to help you in times of trouble.

Finally, it should be stressed that depression is not something you should be ashamed of but something which can be relieved by taking positive steps.

Sources of stress

For many years Dr Thomas H. Holmes, Professor of Psychiatry at the School of Medicine, University of Washington, has been involved in stress research. As a result, he and his colleagues have developed a social readjustment rating scale for evaluating the impact of various life events (see Table 11.2).

The research confirmed that if an individual accumulates 300 or more points (life crisis units or LCUs) during a two-year period, he or she is likely to have stress-related problems. Eighty per cent of those with 300 LCUs or more, experience serious illness within twelve months, between 200 and 299 LCUs, about 50 per cent of people have serious illness; between 150 and 199 LCUs, about 33 per cent suffer ill-health.

Exercise 43

Using the social readjustment rating scale, evaluate the number of LCUs you have accumulated over the last two years. Do you have a high score? We shall look at some of the ways of dealing with unacceptable levels of stress later on in this chapter. Although you may have an acceptable score now, it may be useful to repeat the exercise every six months or so.

One way of trying to minimise the effect of stress is to try to keep other areas of life stable when experiencing change. For example, if you change job it helps if you can postpone a planned house move. Of course, this may not be possible if a job promotion occurs in a different location. Being aware of the potential stress, however, may help you deal with it more effectively. The message is to look after yourself by developing coping strategies.

Table 11.2 Holmes and Rahe's social readjustment rating scale

Life event	Life crisis units (LCUs)
Death of spouse	100
Divorce	73
Marital separation	65
Jail term	63
Death of close family member	63
Personal illness or injury	53
Marriage	50
Fired at work	47
Marital reconciliation	45
Retirement	45
Change in health of family member	44
Pregnancy	40
Sex difficulties	39
Gain of new family member	39
Business readjustment	39
Change in financial state	38
Death of close friend	37
Change to a different line of work	36
Change in number of arguments with spouse	35
A large mortgage or loan	30
Foreclosure of mortgage or loan	30
Change in responsibilities at work	29
Son or daughter leaving home	29
Trouble with in-laws	29
Outstanding personal achievement	28
Spouse begins or stops work	26
Begin or end school or college	26
Change in living conditions	25
Change in personal habits	24
Trouble with the boss	23
Change in work hours or conditions	20
Change in residence	20
Change in school or college	20
Change in recreation	19
Change in church activities	19
Change in social activities	18
A moderate mortgage or loan	17
Change in sleeping habits	16
Change in number of family get-togethers	15
Change in eating habits	15
Holiday	13
Christmas	12
Minor violations of the law	11

Demands

Another common cause of stress is having too much to do and not enough time to do it. The working wife and mother is a classic example. Since the Education Reform Act, the demands on teachers have increased enormously and stress-related problems are increasing at an alarming rate.

One way of trying to deal with this is to work out effective ways of managing your time. Try to define clearly what your priorities are both at school and in your personal life. Take proper breaks from the pressure – this may be going to a yoga class, taking up a hobby, or going on holiday. Whatever suits you will help. Inappropriate breaks will make matters worse. There is no use trying to force yourself to jog for half an hour every day if you don't like doing it!

Stimulation

At the opposite extreme, having too little to do can also create stress. A boring and uninteresting job may produce the same symptoms as one which is too demanding. People who become depressed because they have a boring or lonely lifestyle often find it extremely difficult to get out and make social contacts.

People

Other people are a prime source of stress. Is there a particular work colleague who often annoys you? Is your boss reasonable or does he or she make unrealistic demands on you? Do you get on with the people you live with? Do you have particularly difficult pupils to deal with on a regular basis? Are there contacts with governors which you find a problem? Do you find parents become aggressive during discussions with you? It may help to identify the part you play in creating these reactions in others.

You

How much pressure do you put on yourself which is unrealistic or unreasonable? Do you always expect to have the perfect job? Do you expect the house or car to be gleaming even though you have a heavy workload? Do you try to live up to the ideal image of teacher, wife, head of department, mother, husband or father? Do you always expect your classroom to look attractive and well-organised when it is unrealistic to do so?

Many of us put unnecessary pressures on ourselves. Often we pick these up in childhood and we never question them. As we discussed in Chapter 1, the ability to say no without feeling guilty can reduce a lot of pressure on us.

Work stressors checklist

The following checklist sets out the types of stressors that may occur in your work situation. Evaluate your own role by identifying those items which apply to you.

Job

- too much (or too little) work
- keeping up with new developments
- changes in procedures or policies
- changes in working hours
- physical working conditions
- time pressures and deadlines.

Role

- lack of relevant information/support/advice
- no clear objectives
- unclear expectations from DES, LEA, governors, boss and colleagues
- being caught between different groups.

Responsibilities

- people (pupils/colleagues)
- budgets
- equipment.

Relationships

- poor relationships with pupils/boss/colleague/subordinate
- difficulties in delegating/accepting delegated responsibilities
- lack of peer group support.

Career development

- under-promotion, frustration and status incongruity
- over-promotion (promoted beyond abilities)
- lack of job security (eg, potential school closure or merger)
- no career development plan

- no prospects of career development in current situation.

School climate

- pressures from central government policies
- pressures from senior management
- restrictions on behaviour 'politics'
- low autonomy
- financial problems
- demands from parents, governors, etc.

The symptoms that are likely to develop from these types of work stressors are high blood pressure, high cholesterol levels and ulcers, and also, low motivation, job dissatisfaction and low morale. The result of the latter creates organisational symptoms such as low performance, low academic results, and so on.

Personality and stress

There has been much research in the USA and Sweden into the predisposition of certain people to stress. Two distinctive types have been identified, 'type A' and 'type B' people.

Type A people seem to be at higher risk. They are more likely to suffer from coronary heart disease. Characteristically they are competitive, aggressive, striving for achievement, irritable, hasty in speech, time-conscious, always having a feeling of being under pressure. They tend to be so involved in their work that other aspects of their lives are relatively neglected.

Type B people are more relaxed, less competitive, less work-orientated and less prone to coronary heart disease.

Exercise 44 may help you assess your level of concern for work.

Exercise 44 Are you a workaholic?

1 Do you often not have time to get your hair cut?
2 Do you frequently try to do two things at a time?
3 Do you 'talk shop' on social occasions?
4 Are most of your friends associated with your work?

5 Do you wake up worrying about school problems?
6 Do you dream about school or school-related situations?
7 Do you frequently keep people waiting?
8 Do you find it difficult to relax on Saturday mornings?
9 Do you take work home at weekends?
10 Do you feel that if you can only get over this patch everything will be all right?

If you answered 'yes' to more than half of these questions, you might wish to consider how important work itself really is to you and if that is really the way you want it to be.

Draw a circle and divide it into sectors to show the relative importance of these factors to you in terms of time, impact on your life and so on. There is no 'ideal' answer but the example in Figure 11.2 might indicate that work and finance are taking up too much time.

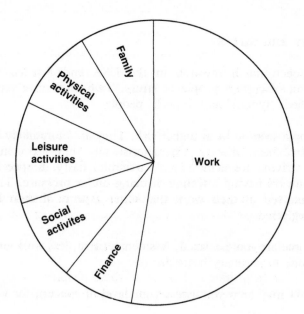

Figure 11.2

Managing stress

The following factors have been identified as helping individuals to cope with stress.

(a) Time perspective. Stressed and depressed people tend to be orientated in the past:

- don't live in the past, look to the future
- don't resist inevitable change – be positive and go with the force.

Stressed people also tend to be preoccupied with short-term goals, rather than planning constructively for the long-term future:

- plan ahead.

(b) Social support.

- try to keep work in perspective, develop a healthy social life, outside interests, etc
- try to share problems with others
- identify colleagues with whom relaxation times in school can be shared and enjoyed

(c) Be in control. Know your strengths and limitations – you need to feel that the focus of interest in life is yourself and not external events: encourage feedback on how you are doing and attempt to work on areas of weakness

- list the strengths and positive aspects of your current situation
- list all positive elements of your job in the previous week/month/year
- list the negative elements and ways of dealing with them or changing them.

(d) Personal identity. Develop a healthy and positive self-image:

- identify people you get on with and who you feel have respect for you
- consider your behaviour in relation to these people
- try to find ways of improving or changing those aspects which you are not happy about.

(e) Coping mechanism.

- develop the ability to anticipate problems
- take preventative measures if possible to buffer, protect your feelings and above all to manage the crisis constructively
- meet the crisis head on and deal with it: denying the problem and repressing feelings can only lead to further trouble.

Coping with stress at work

Some practical suggestions for coping with stress at work are given below:

- actively listen to what others are saying
- before speaking up at a meeting or to a work colleague ask yourself three questions:
  - Do I have something important to say?
  - Does anyone want to hear it?
  - Is this the time to say it?
- be positive about current changes – look for aspects which will (even eventually) improve working life
- study other people's coping systems and, if appropriate, put them into operation for yourself; eg, assessment of pupils for the National Curriculum or recording pupil progress
- make a personal development plan: highlight one area to deal with at a time
- when getting frustrated or irritable (eg in a motorway hold-up), ask yourself why you are allowing it to annoy you: use the time to relax and think positively
- when you are really feeling pressured STOP! Ask yourself:
  - will this matter in five days (five months) time?
  - must I do it now or can it wait until I have time to think properly?
  - what is the worst thing that would happen if I didn't do it?
  focus on one small part of the pressure that can be isolated and dealt with immediately to give yourself confidence
- learn to say 'no' – don't over-commit yourself (eg, cut out irrelevant courses and meetings)
- be realistic about deadlines; if you are not, you will only let people down later. Make a time schedule and stick to it
- try to build in 'breathing spaces' during the day; for example, take a short walk, take a lunch break and don't work while eating
- do one thing at a time: spreading your attention will increase stress and lower performance in everything. Keep a checklist of urgent tasks and eliminate them when dealt with
- find an escape valve
- keep an element of detachment in your job
- check on the following; do you:
  - eat a balanced diet and not drink too much alcohol?
  - have enough sleep?
  - have regular, vigorous exercise?
  - smoke too much?
  - have regular health check-ups?

It may be useful to record what is happening in your life on a daily basis. Figure 11.3 is an example of how you might record events and details.

Inputs   Date : _____

Meals	Quality
Breakfast	
Mid-day	
Tea	
Evening	
Alcohol	**Amount**
Type :	
Tobacco	**Amount**
Sleep / rest	**Amount / hours**
Type :	
Recreation	**Amount / hours**
Type :	
Medicine	**Amount**
Type :	

Figure 11.3 Daily record of lifestyle

Outputs

Hours	Worked	Fun	Active recreation :
Achievements			
Things delayed or put off			
Things I really wanted to do			
Times of tension		Relieved by :	
Times of depression		Relieved by :	

Figure 11.3 Continued

Stress diary

It may be helpful to keep a stress diary for a few weeks, noting on a day-to-day basis what the stressful events were on that day and how you dealt with them. This will help you to develop an action plan for dealing with potential stress situations in successive weeks. For example, if you have to see a difficult parent you may wish to write down and rehearse what you intend to say. The following outline may help.

Think back over occasions or situations that were stressful for you. Recall in particular what you did, or tried to do, to help you cope. The format in Figure 11.4 may be helpful. Recalling what you actually do in stressful situations will help you to devise action plans for the future.

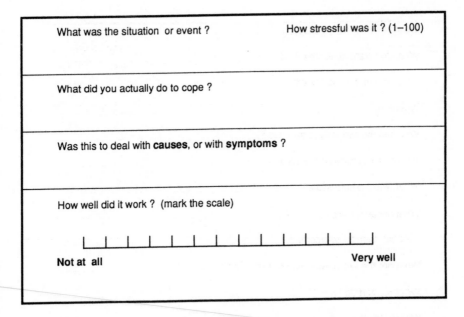

What was the situation or event ?	How stressful was it ? (1–100)
What did you actually do to cope ?	
Was this to deal with **causes**, or with **symptoms** ?	
How well did it work ? (mark the scale)	

Not at all   Very well

Figure 11.4

Figure 11.5 puts forward an action plan for stress management at work. The aim of this process is for you to end up with a clear outline of how you can pursue a less-stressful lifestyle. It is useful to have a separate action plan for each initiative.

Relaxation

It is impossible to be both tense and relaxed at the same time. Developing relaxation techniques will help to minimise stress. Once again, the techniques you use will be personal to you but here is a list of possibilities:

- reading
- listening to music
- watching a favourite TV programme
- making love
- taking a leisurely bath
- prayer or meditation
- yoga
- dancing
- playing sport

Initiative identified _____

What do I want to achieve? _____

What information do I need? _____

Where from? _____

Who has the authority to approve? _____

Who else needs to be involved? _____

What was the time-scale? _____

What obstacles are in the way? _____

How can they be overcome? _____

What are the likely positive/negative effects? _____

What support do I need? _____

Where from? _____

Other factors to consider _____

_____

_____

Review date _____

Figure 11.5 Action plan

- breathing exercises
- listening to audio tapes of relaxation techniques.

Exercise 45

1 Find a quiet, comfortable place where you won't be disturbed. If you are using an office, close the door and take the phone off the hook.
2 Take off your coat, and loosen anything tight such as a belt or tie. Sit in a comfortable chair, preferably one with arms so that your

arms don't have to dangle, then wriggle around until you are really comfortable.

3 Close your eyes and create a mental image of a small, well-lit, familiar object, which you have just been looking at, a pen, a watch-buckle, a button, nothing too complicated. Imagine it against a neutral background.

4 See it in detail, keeping it still – don't let it rotate or have anything else enter the picture. Try to hold the image in place for three minutes or so, longer if you can. If need be, open your eyes and look at the real thing again to improve your mental image. Then concentrate on seeing more detail.

Exercise 45 will produce the following physiological effects if done properly.

- your oxygen intake will go down, so your breathing will slow
- your blood pressure will reduce slightly, and the amount of oxyhaemoglobin in the blood will be reduced
- the production of fatigue chemicals in the muscle tissues (especially lactic acid) will reduce
- electrical conductivity in the large muscle groups will change and they will tend to relax.

The mental effects produced are much harder to measure accurately, but are likely to include:

- lower level of anxiety
- a more relaxed, calmer feeling
- reduced frequency of irritation
- increased ability to think logically and rapidly.

Summary

We all undergo different levels of stress at various stages in our lives and have different capacities for coping. Methods for coping also vary from individual to individual. Awareness of potential problems is the first step in alleviating stress. Various individual exercises may be used. For example, studying the sort of life style you have, how you spend your time, whether or not you feel a sense of achievement and the demands that are made on you.

By then addressing the *importance* of these demands, imposed upon you by others, you can appraise the relevance of your behaviour. In particular, stress at work can be re-evaluated by looking at such aspects as the job, your role, responsibilities, relationships, career development and school climate. Action plans may then be developed to make improvements in problem areas. For example, in some areas you may be setting too high a standard whereas in others you may be able to delegate some of the work.

Finally, a good way of alleviating stress is to do relaxation exercises or other appropriate activities.

12 Practising

Case study 1 – Chairing work meetings

A week ago, the headteacher advised a meeting of all staff that the entire school would transfer next year to new premises, two miles distant. This news came as a complete surprise.

You are Brenda (Bill) Smith, head of fourth year. You have now been asked by the headteacher to hold a meeting with your teaching staff to get their initial reactions.

Additional information: One of your six staff-members, Harry Johnson, always tends to oppose change, and he always has a lot to say. Another of your staff, Mary Jenkins, is a very clear thinker, a good speaker, and is prepared to consider suggestions on their merits.

Spend a short while roughing out a list of the topics that you believe might be raised during the meeting. How will you ensure that you achieve the objective set for you by your headteacher when you meet your six staff-members?

Case study 1 – Trainer's notes

1 This exercise could be operated as a role-play. If you do so, then you could brief Harry to be 'difficult' and Mary to counter his arguments and attitude.
2 Brenda/Bill should initially produce not only a list of topics but also one or two thoughts to go with each item. This is so that the 'chair' is tuned-in from the start.
   There might be questions and comments on: changes in teaching duties, change in size of the pupil population, assistance to teachers with transport, how the move will be carried out, etc.
3 Brenda/Bill might be wise to attempt to discuss possible issues with both Harry and Mary in advance of the meeting, thus giving her/himself an advance insight.

4 At the meeting the chair should appoint a note-taker. After the meeting they should, together, produce a short report.
5 The chair **must** extract contributions from all present.
6 The chair should keep a balance of contribution and watch for over- and under-contribution.

Case study 2 – Meeting parents

Wayne, a 12-year-old in your class, is the middle-school chess champion. His mother commented on this with much pride at a recent parents' evening. She went on to voice the view that he would follow his older brother into a career as a computer programmer. She also said that he would need to achieve a degree in mathematics (as did his brother) for a successful career.

The difficulty for you is that his continuing performance in all numerate subjects is, at best, moderate. You have diplomatically pointed this out to this mother.

She has now made an emotional telephone call to you, asking to see you together with the head of middle school. How will you deal with this situation?

Case study 2 – Trainer's notes

1 This exercise could be operated as a role-play. You could assign three delegates to the active roles and any others present would either be silent observers, or play minor roles as developed in the script.
2 The situation would probably best benefit from holding the three-way meeting as requested by Wayne's mother. At that meeting she must be encouraged, by her son's teacher, to act in a non-emotional manner (however, you might brief her, privately, to make things difficult).
3 Wayne's track-record in all subjects must be commented upon and this could involve consulting his other teachers, if you choose.
4 The school's careers-teacher could be consulted on the question of the kind of personal characteristics and also academic prowess required of a computer-programmer.
5 If Wayne's brother attended the same school, it might be helpful to see if records exist of his early progress.
6 Some further information from Wayne's mother, on the day, might be helpful. For example, how does Wayne feel about the school in general? What does he do as hobbies? Does *he* want to be a programmer?

7 Wayne's mother must be told the facts as they have emerged and been interpreted.

Case study 3 – Managing yourself

Mark, an excellent subject teacher, was promoted 12 months ago to head of third year. He is having great difficulty in coping with the workload. The school's professional tutor is helping him to understand and remedy the difficulties. One of the tools the tutor has used is the procrastination questionnaire (Figure 12.1). This has been completed by Mark.

Study the responses, consider the steps advocated in Chapter 4 on 'managing yourself', and produce a brief report specifying the actions and their sequence which Mark could take to get on top of his new job.

		Strongly agree	Mildly agree	Mildly disagree	Strongly disagree
1	I invent reasons and look for excuses for not acting on a tough problem.			X	
2	It takes pressure to get on with a difficult assignment.	X			
3	I take half measures which will avoid or delay unpleasant or difficult action.			X	
4	There are too many interruptions and crises that interfere with my accomplishing the big jobs.	X			
5	I avoid forthright answers when pressed for an unpleasant decision.				X
6	I have been guilty of neglecting follow-up aspects of important action plans.			X	
7	I try to get other people to do unpleasant assignments for me.				X
8	I schedule big jobs late in the day, or take them home to do in the evening or weekends.	X			
9	I've been too tired (nervous, upset, hungover) to do the difficult tasks that face me.		X		
10	I like to get everything cleared off my desk before commencing a tough job.	X			

Figure 12.1 Procrastination questionnaire

Case study 3 – Trainer's notes

1 Mark has some good points; your delegates should notice these and see if they can be utilised to deal with the weaknesses. Essentially, his troubles spring from not prioritising and also allowing interruptions. He also has trouble delegating (this is another interpretation of answer number 7 in the questionnaire).
2 The delegates have the opportunity here to develop a key task area and a key task analysis as described in Chapter 4.
3 There is also scope for designing the layout of a time log to suit Mark's circumstance, so that he can understand exactly where his time is going.

Case study 4 – Orlingbury Comprehensive School

Orlingbury Comprehensive School is an 11–18 school situated in a market town in the East Midlands. It has 1250 students, of which 150 are in Form Six. The school admits 220 students each year: two primary schools in the town each send 40 pupils annually, and the additional 140 pupils come from eight nearby village schools. The school has generally enjoyed a good relationship with the local college of further education, to which a considerable number of pupils transfer at 16. In the last few years, about 16 per cent of pupils have achieved five 'GCSE' level passes or equivalent: this compares poorly with the county rate (20.3 per cent) which, in turn, compares poorly with the national average of 23.4 per cent. Approximately 40 per cent of students are staying on into the Sixth Form: in addition to 'A' levels, the school offers a variety of courses, many of which are for one year only. The overall pass rate at 'A' level is encouraging (80 per cent) and about 25 students each year are proceeding to university, polytechnic or colleges of higher education.

The senior management team (see the organisation chart in Figure 12.2) consists of the head, first deputy, second deputy, and three senior teachers: one senior teacher is responsible for the Sixth Form, one for examinations, and one for resources. The main school is organised on a year basis with a head of year responsible for each year group in years one to five. The heads of year go through the school with their groups, so that after a year as head of fifth year, a year head becomes head of first year. The heads of year are assisted by deputies who remain in the same year group. The academic work of the school is organised through five faculties, each with a head of faculty and a deputy head of faculty. Each faculty contains a number of related subjects (eg languages), and

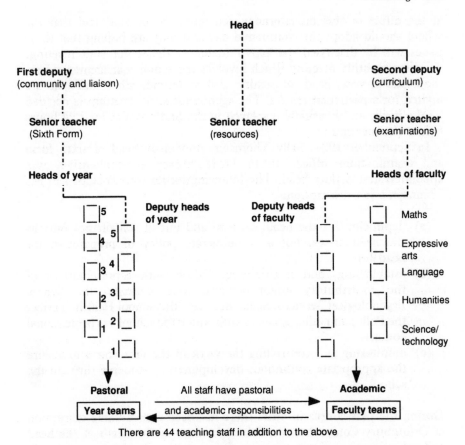

Head

First deputy
(community and liaison)

Second deputy
(curriculum)

Senior teacher
(Sixth Form)

Senior teacher
(resources)

Senior teacher
(examinations)

Heads of year

Heads of faculty

☐5
☐4 5☐
☐3 4☐
☐2 3☐
☐1 2☐
     1☐

Deputy heads of year

Deputy heads of faculty

☐ Maths
☐ Expressive arts
☐ Language
☐ Humanities
☐ Science/ technology

Pastoral   All staff have pastoral   **Academic**
Year teams   and academic responsibilities   **Faculty teams**

There are 44 teaching staff in addition to the above

Figure 12.2 Orlingbury Comprehensive School: Existing staffing structure

the heads of faculty are expected to develop the curriculum, allocate resources, and organise all aspects of teaching and learning. The job description for a head of faculty has not been reviewed since the school opened in 1974. The heads of year are expected to be responsible for the overall care, and progress, of all students in their year group. They do not have any job description, and complain constantly that they are seen almost solely as agents of school discipline.

There is now serious concern among some staff over school discipline. Two members of staff have been physically assaulted on school premises in the last year: the pupils involved were suspended for six weeks but then re-admitted by the governors: at present, ten pupils are actually suspended officially, and a number of others have been excluded for short periods. There have been a number of unpleasant incidents in the neighbourhood over the lunchtime period, and staff are very concerned at the effect of this on afternoon schooling. Some staff feel that the school should adopt the continental day and they are hoping that these issues will be discussed, perhaps initially, at the senior staff meeting. This is a monthly meeting which involves the senior management team, the heads of year, heads of faculty, and sometimes other staff who are invited for a particular reason. The agenda for such meetings is decided by the head, and is usually displayed in the Staffroom at least 24 hours before the meeting.

In September 1984, Sally Thomson, previously head of sixth form and examinations officer at an 11–18 Surrey comprehensive, was appointed first deputy head. The following duties were included in Ms Thomson's job description:

(a) deputising for the head, both in and out of school, not only as the need arises, but as a deliberate policy of preparation for headship.

(b) establishing, and maintaining, liaison with representatives of the contributory junior schools, local colleges, the School Psychological Services, Social Services, the School Health Service, the Police and other agencies with which the school has professional contact.

(c) monitoring and controlling the work of the year teams to ensure the appropriate continuous development of students through the school.

During the past couple of years there has been considerable disruption at Orlingbury Comprehensive School because of the death of the head and delay in appointing a new one. Because the school has a very wide catchment area, the problems of excluding pupils from the school at lunchtimes, and of sending them home at short notice were exacerbated. Parents in some of the villages are beginning to look towards the Manor School, a smaller school in a neighbouring town. As a result of the disruption, the school's links with the local college have also been rather unsatisfactory lately. Throughout this period, Ms Thomson has been unable to create any sort of professional relationship with either the local schools or the supporting services with which the school usually co-operates.

The senior management team in the school has been aware of the need to improve all aspects of liaison, and this was the reason for delegating this responsibility to the first deputy. At the start of the new school year, the team is meeting to decide on what steps can be taken to improve the situation. Ms Thomson is most anxious to be given a clear brief as she feels strongly that she has not yet established herself either in the school or in the local community.

Questions

1 What should Sally Thomson do to ensure an improvement in the situation?
2 What are the implications?

Case study 4 – Trainer's notes

This case is designed to integrate much of the material in the book. After reading through the case study, the trainer can then start a discussion on the implications. Some of the items that might arise are:

- **Handling meetings** – Sally Thomson should make sure that she has included relevant agenda items; she might have discussed with the Head her wish to handle that part of the meeting herself.
- **Effective interpersonal skills** – Sally needs to behave assertively at the meeting. She also has to gain support and co-operation for whatever is decided. She has to maintain that support and co-operation during the following months of action.
- **Managing yourself** – Objectives should have been set before the meeting so that Sally can present the meeting with a clear idea of what she is trying to achieve.
- **Managing your boss** – When the meeting is held, Sally needs to have the support of her boss. She also needs freedom to act without over-supervision when she is putting the agreed ideas into action.
- **Developing interview skills** – Sally will be meeting many different people while carrying out her community and liaison role. The ability to find out the answers to questions from these people and gain their commitment and support using effective questioning techniques will be very important.
- **Moving up the ladder** – Sally can greatly improve her professional image by achieving success in this particular area.

Possibly other areas might be raised such as coping with stress and meeting parents. The aim of the case study is to try to show how all the topics discussed in the book are inter-linked.

Case study 5 – A problem colleague

Consider a problem with a colleague you have experienced recently. Analyse the problem. The following guidelines may be helpful.

- What was the problem?

- What action did you take?
- What was the outcome?
- Did you need to take any further action?

Discussion points

- How effectively was the problem dealt with?
- Were other approaches considered?
- Were there any difficulties with your approach?
- How could you have prevented the problem from occurring?
- How did you think the other person perceived the situation?

Case study 5 – Trainer's notes

Encourage the individuals to assess the problem as outlined. Then, using pairs or small groups, each problem can be discussed, using the discussion points as a guide. This technique can be used for other similar exercises, where sharing experiences can be of immense benefit.

The trainer can then highlight all the learning points at the end in a plenary session.

In addition, some of the experiences may be used as a basis for role-play. Form the group into pairs and allocate roles using the material which has been presented. One person can play the role of the problem colleague and the other can role-play the situation which they had previously experienced. After the role-play the group can jointly work through an evaluation. The following structure is offered as a guide.

- Did the discussion start in an appropriate way? Was the nature of the problem outlined?
- Did effective communication take place?
- Did the individual control the discussion?
- Were potential solutions outlined?
- Did the discussion end with both people feeling a solution was possible?
- Did both parties agree on what was to happen in the future?

Case study 6 – Responding assertively

Suggest assertive responses to the following situations which have arisen at work:

1 You have been asked to lead an inter-departmental working party of

ten people. You find that one member, the head of maths, continually tries to take over the leadership from you.

2 You have been asked to take on some different work, but it is not the sort of work which interests you. There have been hints that co-operative people 'get on' in your school.

3 You have discovered that a female member of staff, but not someone for whom you are directly responsible, is being sexually harassed by a male colleague.

4 You have been head of English and drama in a large comprehensive school for a year, but find that it does not provide you with the opportunities you were seeking, and which were promised, when you took it on. In particular you were hoping to be able to develop drama across all age-groups.

5 You are a teacher in the science department. You have put forward several progressive ideas but constantly find them blocked by your head who seems insecure.

Now compare these responses to passive and aggressive responses in each case. What are the likely outcomes? Can you identify the benefits of behaving assertively?

Case study 6 – Trainer's notes

These incidents are becoming all too common in the workplace. There are no definitive answers. The objective is to get the group to discuss the advantages, disadvantages and consequences of various responses. Assertive responses can be identified along with the consequent benefits.

Case study 7 – Sharing experiences

Each member of a small syndicate group contributes experiences of particular situations that have been important for them. For example, when was it felt that a situation was handled well? What did the individual do that made it work? By contrast, when was it felt that things could have been handled better? What were the circumstances? What could have been done to improve the situation?

Case study 7 – Trainer's notes

The shared experiences may be used for group discussions and analysis. The trainer needs to start the discussion and ensure that everyone has a fair amount of time to express themselves.

After the group has considered their own examples, note down on a flip-chart all the learning points that have emerged from the exercise.

Typical responses when things have gone wrong include:

- 'Lost my temper.'
- 'Knew I should have waited till I had all the facts.'
- 'Started behaving defensively and couldn't stop myself arguing with him.'
- 'I was so angry I couldn't help shouting.'
- 'This had been boiling up for weeks.'

Typical responses when things have gone well include:

- 'I was so pleased I kept calm.'
- 'I practised what I was going to say the night before and stuck to my script.'
- 'I waited till I knew I'd get his complete attention.'
- 'I was conscious of giving out consistent body language, type of voice and so on. I knew I could be credible if I could just project a powerful image. I was shaking like a leaf afterwards though!'
- 'I didn't let her bamboozle me with irrelevant issues. I stuck to the point and wouldn't let go.'

Bibliography

Allen, R. E. *The Oxford Writer's Dictionary*, Oxford University Press.

Belbin, R. M. *Management Teams*, Heinemann.

Birkett, K. F. *Career Structures for Women in the Water Industry*, Unpublished research.

The Daily Telegraph, *Careers A–Z*.

Department of Education and Science, *School Teacher Appraisal: A National Framework*. HMSO.

Grumitt, J. *Rapid Reading*, The Industrial Society.

Holmes, T. H., Rahe, R. H. 1967, 'The social re-adjustment rating scale', *Journal of Psychomatic Research*, 11.

Laborde, G. Z. *Influencing with Integrity*, California, Syntony Publishing.

Lewis, M. *Writing to Win*, McGraw-Hill.

Materials and Resources Information Service, *MARIS Directory*, Ely, Cambridge.

Meta-Talk (Guide to Hidden Meanings in Conversations), New York, Simon & Schuster.

Muir, F. *Chambers Word*, W. & R. Chambers.

Partridge, E. *Usage and Abusage*, Penguin Books.

Pease, A. *Body Language*, Sheldon Press.

Pedlar, M., Burgoyne, J., Boydell, T. *A Manager's Guide to Self-Development*, McGraw-Hill.

Phelps, Austin *The Assertive Woman*, Impact.

Room, A. *Room's Dictionary of Confusibles*, Routledge & Kegan Paul.

Wainright, G. R. *Rapid Reading Made Simple*, W. H. Allen.

Further reading

Adair, J. *Developing Leaders*, Talbot Adair Press.
Courtis, J. *Recruiting for Profit*, IPM.
Cox, G. Dainow, S., *Making the Most of Yourself*, Sheldon Press.
Sargent, A. *Turning People On – The Motivation Challenge*, IPM.
Stechert, K. *The Credibility Gap*, Thorsens Publishing.

NIGHT OF
THE SHIFTER

NIGHT OF THE SHIFTER

Caridad Piñeiro
Megan Hart
Linda O. Johnston
Doranna Durgin
Katie Reus

MILLS & BOON

Published in Great Britain 2014
by Mills & Boon, an imprint of Harlequin (UK) Limited,
Eton House, 18-24 Paradise Road, Richmond, Surrey, TW9 1SR

NIGHT OF THE SHIFTER © 2014 Harlequin Books S.A.

The Shifter's Kiss © 2013 Caridad Piñeiro Scordato
The Darkest Embrace © 2013 Megan Hart
Cougar's Conquest © 2011 Linda O. Johnston
Night of the Tiger © 2011 Doranna Durgin
Tempting the Jaguar © 2013 Katie Reus

ISBN: 978-0-263-91398-9

89-0614

Harlequin (UK) Limited's policy is to use papers that are natural, renewable and recyclable products and made from wood grown in sustainable forests. The logging and manufacturing processes conform to the legal environmental regulations of the country of origin.

Printed and bound
by CPI Group (UK) Ltd, Croydon, CR0 4YY

THE SHIFTER'S KISS

CARIDAD PIÑEIRO

Caridad Piñeiro is a multi-published and award-winning author whose love of the written word developed when her fifth grade teacher assigned a project—to write a book that would be placed in a class lending library. She has been hooked on writing ever since.

When not writing, Caridad teaches workshops on various topics related to writing and heads a writing group. Caridad is also an attorney, wife and mother.

Chapter 1

The ocean was the only place where Victor felt truly free.

He did a scissors kick with his fins and pushed toward the great swath of coral reef teeming with life.

For the past week he had been riding out with his cameras and other equipment and dropping beneath the calm surface of the Caribbean to the unique world below. As he approached the reef, he caught sight of an immense shark circling around the lowermost edges of the coral. The large female cut through the water with ease, her powerful body graceful. Her deep charcoal skin, far darker than that of a normal reef shark, was a shock against the pink–white coral and cerulean blue of the waters.

All around her teemed yet more reef sharks, both male and female, but none as big or as imposing. It was almost as if she was the queen of the school, not that this species of sharks normally engaged in that kind of behavior. But with her unique size and coloring, he could picture the natives warning him that she was one of the shark gods who protected the many islands along the Kuna Yala, telling him not to anger her by defiling her precious reefs.

He smiled against the mouthpiece of his scuba gear as he thought of the native legends and, for a moment, allowed himself the fantasy of it. He imagined that big beautiful beast patrolling the waters to keep the area safe. Shifting into human form for a short respite on land before returning to guard the sea around the smattering of islands.

Pulling up his underwater camera by the leash attached to his weight belt, he snapped several pictures of the school of predators. Only hammerheads were known to swim in groups, and identifying yet another species with this behavior would be an important discovery for his research paper.

He was so intent on recording the shark's behavior that he didn't realize he had let himself drift down into the midst of the school until the softness of sand beneath his feet and the bump of a fin against his side warned of danger. Instinctively he jerked in a breath and held it, a mix of primal fear and intense joy racing through him at the thought of being among such magnificent creatures.

Slowly he settled to the bottom and kept his movements small and nonthreatening. The lesser sharks surrounded him, their dark, glassy eyes vigilant as they kept up the constant movement they needed to survive. Suddenly the sizeable, darker shape of the queen shark slipped into his peripheral vision as she approached.

Sleek muscles powered her near, but he kept his position, watchful but unafraid. Nothing in the sharks' behavior was threatening. If anything, they seemed inquisitive, especially the unique specimen who inched ever closer with each pass of her formidable body. He guessed her to be almost eight feet in length, far larger than the other nearby reef sharks. Combined with her shadowy charcoal coloring, he wondered if he wasn't misidentifying her species until she turned and approached him. She had the familiar broad snout that all the other reef sharks in the school possessed, confirming that he had been correct with his identification.

As she swam toward him slowly, he braced himself and kept his breathing smooth. She swung away from him at the last second, but she was so close he could touch her. Had to touch her.

He ran his hand along her deeply muscled flank and the skin was sandpaper rough beneath his fingers. She quickly shifted away but then began that almost lazy inquiring circle around him again. This time, as she passed his gaze caught hers and shock traveled over him.

Nothing was dead or flat about that gaze. If anything, it radiated human-like intelligence and interest.

Impossible.

He shook his head to drive away that thought and checked his dive watch to see if he had been down for far too long. Then he checked his pressure gauge for good measure.

All good. It was just his imagination getting the best of him, but maybe it was time to go in. He already had a load of photographs and data to analyze from the various monitoring stations he had set up at spots along the reef. It would take some time to start the generator, boot up the computer and download the data from the wireless stations.

Time for him to go and get some work done.

He went top side and hauled himself up onto the platform on the back of the boat. His arm and shoulder protested the movement, sending shards of pain throughout his upper body. He released his mouthpiece and pulled off his mask, his teeth gritting against the hurt. All along his arm and shoulder, the scarred skin pulled tightly against more pliant flesh as he bent to remove his fins and tossed them onboard. He sucked in a breath then, taking a moment to fight back the discomfort. When he did, awareness of the fin slicing through the water just a few feet away registered.

The sickle-shaped, charcoal-grey fin cut through the water as the shark approached, and this time fear won the battle. He surged to his feet, the harness digging into his body from the weight of the tanks and adding to his distress.

Fearlessly the shark came right up to the dive platform on the boat, that seemingly knowing gaze looking up as if analyzing him. Then she swam away, and he finally released the harness to remove the tanks. Relief swept through him as he slipped off the tanks and their weight no longer pulled against his damaged body.

He rubbed at his injured shoulder and arm, the scarred skin rough beneath his palm. Slowly his muscles relaxed, and he rotated his shoulder to work out the pain as he watched the shark swim away but then circle back once more.

He crouched, wanting to get a closer look.

Wanting to touch her again.

As she neared, he reached out and stroked the length of her from snout to dorsal fin, her flesh rasping along his fingertips. The power in those muscles was a reminder of the strength he had once possessed before his injuries.

With a sharp swipe of her tail, which banged against the boat with a loud thud, the shark rushed away this time and sank beneath the surface.

Victor eased himself onto the deck of the dive boat. Securing his tanks and other equipment, he started the engine for the short trip back to shore, but as he did so, he looked back and caught sight of her fin again, almost as if waving goodbye.

She who was called Nali by the local Kuna people listened to the vibrations of the engine carrying him away from her.

His touch still lingered on her body, a reminder of how long it had been since she'd been human. Since she'd experienced the pleasure of warm, soft skin and the rush of desire.

Too long, she thought, swimming along the surface for just a moment before diving down to rejoin her brethren along the edges of the reefs. Not that she was truly like them.

She was of a different kind, one of the last of her race in this area. Over the centuries the others had been taken by fishermen greedy either to claim so large a prize or to rid the ocean of a feared predator.

It was why she usually avoided contact with the humans, but this one had intrigued her over the last few weeks as she watched him from the deeper waters near the reef. He'd had no fear of her cousin sharks, swimming among them, taking pictures. Returning time and time again until she'd been drawn closer and had seen him. Seen the scars on his body that she recognized as burns.

More than once a sailor from a doomed ship had drifted down into her waters with wounds such as his, so she was familiar with them. Understood the pain like she'd seen today on his face as he'd left the waters. His ocean-blue eyes could not hide the distress as they'd met hers when she swam by and he'd touched her again.

A shiver of anticipation worked through her body. How she longed for that touch. For the feel of his nearly perfect body along hers. For the chance to wake to the sight of that masculine face and those intense eyes in the morning light.

She drove away those thoughts with a sharp swipe of her tail, which propelled her back to open ocean and safety. She'd risked too much to come see him. There were too many other humans who'd want to take her, out of fear or greed, and coming in this close to shore just tempted them to hunt for her.

Much like the beautiful man tempted her for other reasons.

As passion stirred within her again, she thought about the man and all that could not be.

She was nearly the last of her kind and maybe that was the way it was meant to be. The burden of not belonging in either world was an obligation she didn't wish to pass on.

Chapter 2

Thanks to a combination of a moonless night and a bit too much of the old man's homemade hooch, Victor stumbled up the steps. Not even the delicious meal that his landlord, Saila, had made for him had been enough to combat the effects of the alcohol.

Cursing as he banged his shin on the steps to his rented shack, he managed to stagger to the bed and plop facedown and fully clothed on the sheets. The dizzying circles in his head finally calmed after a few minutes and, because it was too hot and humid despite the faint sea breeze coming through the open windows, he reluctantly sat back up and dragged off his clothes.

Lying back down, he propped up the pillows to sleep upright enough to catch the breeze. It washed over him peacefully, like the soft caress of the ocean, and in his mind he pictured being beneath the waves once more. Floating free in the clear, cool liquid. It was so different from the heat and flames that had been his realm during his years as a firefighter. Heat and flames that had nearly stolen his life in more ways than one.

Dashing away those thoughts, he allowed the memories of the ocean to bring him peace by recollecting that day's encounter with the shark and the tales Saila had told him during their dinner.

The old man had been a wonderful storyteller, crafting believable and compelling stories of the shark people who lived in the Kuna Yala waters. People who lived and loved the ocean but were enticed by the allure of the land and the humans who were so different from them, so tempting.

He chuckled loudly, perplexed by that. If anything, he was the one who was tempted by the call of the sea, by the gift it gave him in its welcoming embrace.

Behind his closed eyelids, the image of the large shark filled his vision, intriguing him. Her formidable body circled, coming closer and closer. She drove him to shore with the bump of her snout until his feet brushed the silken sand and he rose in the water.

In his mind, he took a step back, watching as the fin dipped beneath the surface until all he could see in the daylight was a dark shadow. A shadow that slowly morphed, shrinking and changing as the fins became arms and legs and she rose up from beneath the sea.

The water sluiced down a body impossible to resist. Full, copper-tipped breasts. A narrow waist and generous hips that flowed into long, muscular legs.

He dragged his gaze back up to her face, and those dark charcoal eyes held him as she approached, the sunlight turning the drops of seawater on her body into glimmering liquid diamonds.

His cock jerked to life, hardening and tightening with need as she moved toward him, a sexy sway in her walk. A knowing, determined smile on her face, filled with promise.

Victor groaned aloud as the woman in his dream reached down and encircled him, her hand slick along his cock from the seawater. Sure and daring as she stroked him, she leaned forward to brush the tips of her breasts along his chest.

He fought wakefulness, wanting to savor the dream. Blaming Saila's stories and his moonshine for the need twisting his gut and the temptress filling his dreams.

Reaching down, he grabbed hold of his dick and stroked roughly, mimicking the actions of the beautiful woman in his fantasy, reaching for completion until he came with one powerful pull, shooting his seed all along his hand and abdomen, imagining driving himself into the intriguing woman.

Finally spent, he cursed beneath his breath at allowing himself the dreams that had seemed all too real.

Maybe it was because it had been way too long since he had let himself have a relationship with a woman. At first it had been his injuries and what it had taken to recover from them. Then it had been his determination to finally follow his heart. His single-minded focus was what had gotten him this research grant and to these islands.

But he was here now and fulfilling his dream. Somehow it hadn't occurred to him that doing so alone might dampen the joy of the accomplishment.

Maybe in time he could find someone with whom to share that joy. Someone who loved the ocean as much as he did and would be willing to share it with him.

Maybe, he thought as he pushed out of bed, opened the front door and strode across the sand to the ocean. He sank in the water to just beneath his chin to cool the heat of his spent passion.

The ocean was a midnight blue, devoid of moonlight, but even as dark as it was, he caught sight of the fin and the body moving toward him.

He froze, cursing himself for not remembering it was feeding time for sharks.

But as the fin came closer, he realized it was the large female shark from the reef. She circled around him with lazy, almost exploratory turns that made his head spin a bit thanks to Saila's home brew.

Nali had sensed him, smelled him, as soon as he stepped into the water, and she'd been unable to keep away.

Heat flared to life within her as she realized he was naked.

Beautifully naked. His cock hung halfway down a well-muscled thigh, but she dragged her gaze away from that and up his body to the sculpted muscles of his midsection and chest. His arms were floating wide and, despite herself, she swam until his palm brushed along her flank.

She imagined him doing that in her human form—a big mistake because, within her, the need to transform ate away at her control.

Unwilling to reveal herself, afraid of it and all the risk it would bring, she shot away from him like a bullet, finding the gap in the reefs that led to deeper water.

Only there would she be safe from him. Safe from herself.

The scrape of her skin along his palm surprised him for a moment. It was almost as if she needed his touch, but that was impossible, he knew.

A heartbeat later she raced away through a break in the reefs and then down beneath the surface, where he lost sight of her.

He wanted to follow but then reminded himself of the lunacy of being in the ocean alone at this time of night. Besides, she had been along the reef for days and would likely return again.

With that thought, he returned to shore, slightly more alert as he trudged up the steps and toweled down before dropping back into bed.

As he closed his eyes, she returned in his dreams and he welcomed her.

Chapter 3

Despite what he had hoped, the large female shark had not returned in the past few days.

Victor had spotted another boat in the area during that time. A duo of spear fishermen manned the vessel, and he worried that she might have had an encounter with them. Of course, he probably would have heard about that from someone in the nearby village. News of anyone bringing in as large a prize as that shark would certainly spread quickly through the area, especially in light of the ancient tales of the shark gods in these waters.

As he swam over and through the reef, searching for her, the anxiety of her absence tied his gut into a painful knot until he spotted a large dark shadow emerging from the open ocean.

Gracefully she moved onto the shallower floor of the reef bed, a dozen or more smaller sharks surrounding her like a cadre. He sank down to wait, watching her approach. Anxious to touch her once again. To see that almost-human gaze.

It was so peaceful there as he waited. The only sounds were those of his breath and his heart beating loudly, racing slightly with the anticipation of meeting her once more.

She drifted closer, circling him. Playing a coquette's game as she came close enough to touch but then raced away when he reached for her.

He smiled at the game against his mouthpiece and waited for her teasing play, but as he did so, a rough sound intruded. The thump-thump-thump of an engine approaching before it cut off. A short distance away, closer to the open ocean, the shadow of a boat darkened the ocean floor.

He looked up just as two men dropped into the water, spear guns in hand.

They moved quickly toward him. Toward her.

Victor realized then that during their little game, she had become trapped in a cul-de-sac of coral walls. The only way out was past him and the two spear fishermen.

Even as he thought that, a flash of silver sped past him in the water and skimmed close to the shark's body before smashing into the coral.

A second later, a second spear just missed the shark's dorsal fin as the great animal surged upward, trying to put distance between itself and the other divers.

Victor glanced toward her only to find that her way out was closed off there by one of the divers who swam close to the surface, training his weapon on the shark.

Pushing off the bottom at the same time as the animal dove downward, Victor placed himself in the line of fire and held his hands out, urging the fishermen to stop their assault.

A burble of air escaped the spear gun only a moment before agonizing heat tore through his side, stealing his breath. He looked down at the spear piercing him as dark circles danced before his eyes. Battling the pain, he maintained consciousness only long enough to register the blood oozing from his wound while below him the school of reef sharks moved as one, surging up in his direction.

The blood, he thought. They would begin a feeding frenzy at even the faintest trace of it, much less the steady stream coming from his side as he slowly drifted downward.

He was a dead man unless he could somehow get to the surface and away from them. He tried to swim with his one arm, but the movement brought debilitating agony through his side. Bracing his hand against the spear, he tried to stem the flow of blood as the sharks came ever closer, but he couldn't.

A bump came against his fins as one of the school swam past his feet, but, to his surprise, the sharks raced past him and toward the two other divers in the water. As one they rammed the men with their snouts as if they were dolphins, driving the men away from him and from the queen shark.

Over and over they attacked until the men had been pushed back to their boat, bruised and slightly bloodied from a bite or two. The swarm of sharks circling the hull of the boat obscured it for a moment, but then the engine kicked in and the boat sped away.

Safe. She was safe for now, he thought as he slowly sank to the bottom and prepared to die. Each time he tried to move, the pain immobilized him. He would never reach the surface without help and he doubted the two divers would be quick to put in a call to anyone.

But still he hoped, calming his breath to conserve oxygen. He kicked weakly to move closer to shore, but the reef he so loved was in the way of salvation.

A shadow fell across the pink–white sand only moments before she joined him on the ocean floor, circling around anxiously. He held out his hand and she swept past it before swimming away. The next time she came, she slipped beneath his outstretched arm and her fin caught against him, lifting him upward.

In his mind he heard, "Hold me." Or maybe he thought he did. His thoughts were scattered, his brain disoriented from the pain. But even with that, he did as she asked and circled her thick form with his good arm. Beneath it came the flex of muscle as the mighty shark moved him up and over the wall of reef and toward shore.

It was like flying. The reef below him rushed past in a blur of speed until the kaleidoscope of colors and marine life gave way to smooth sand.

He tried to rise as his fins scraped the shore, but his knees were rubbery. With a push, however, she was lifting him upward, above the ocean's surface.

He spit out the mouthpiece and groaned as the weight of the scuba gear and the spear in his side brought fresh rounds of pain.

"You're almost there," he heard in a soft voice—feminine and with the slightest trace of an accent.

He glanced over and forced his eyes to focus past the fog forming on the inside of his mask.

The woman from his dreams stood there, his arm draped over her bare shoulders. Dark-grey eyes filled with worry as she bore his weight and half-dragged him from the surf.

"Who are you?" Even speaking hurt as the breath necessary for words pulled at the spear through his side.

"Nali," she said as she continued plodding through the surf with him, her gait slightly unsteady. Like that of someone trying to find balance on a rolling ship or a little toddler learning to walk.

That unsteadiness combined with the ungainliness of his flippers sent them tumbling down into the calf-high water. As they fell, she tried to shield his body with hers but failed.

The end of the spear hit the soft sand, driving it deeper through his body in a blast of searing pain.

This time there was no holding back the darkness that clawed its way into his brain and he blessedly released himself to it, ending his agony.

Nali muttered a curse at his rough groan and the heavier weight of his body.

He had passed out for sure, and as strong as she was, he was bigger. His weight combined with that of his scuba gear was difficult to handle after so many months away from land. Still, she had to get him from the ocean and to somewhere she could tend to his wound.

With a mighty shove that had her feet sinking into the soft, wet sand, she pulled him upright. As she did so, she caught sight of her father rushing toward them from his home.

"Nali," he cried out, joy alive in his voice until his gaze settled on the man and the blood streaming down his side, turning the water at their feet a sickening pink.

Her father rushed forward through the surf and slipped the man's other arm around his shoulders. Together they dragged him out of the water and gently lay him down on the sand.

"What happened, daughter?" he asked while he worked at removing the man's gear.

"Spear fishermen. I came too close to the reef, and they were there, hunting for me. He tried to stop them," Nali answered, keeping to herself the reason why she had ventured into waters where she was no longer safe.

"The spear has not hit anything vital, but we must get it out to stop the bleeding."

Nali nodded and jerked her chin in the direction of her old shack. "Is he staying there?"

Her father nodded. "You have not used it in so long—"

"It's okay, father. I understand," she said and lay a gentling hand on his muscled forearm. The hairs there were growing silvery, a reminder of the immortality he had given up for a life on land.

"Let's get him inside then," her father said. Together they lifted Victor from the sand and dragged him to the thatch-roofed building just yards away from the water. His feet banged the steps with dull thuds as they carried him inside to the bed, where they gently placed him on his uninjured side.

Nali glanced around her old home. It was familiar but not. The man's belongings had cluttered up the once neat spaces around the single room. In deference to her father, she hurried to her closet, took out a robe and slipped it on before returning to the bedside. As she examined the man's wound, her father sprang into action, gathering towels and bandages for tending to the injury.

The spear had bit through muscle about an inch in from

his side. Deep enough to be painful but luckily not far enough inward to hit anything vital.

She worked quickly to unscrew the barbed head of the spear and placed her hand against his flesh to hold the shaft of the spear steady. His skin was warm with life but wet with his blood. She applied pressure there while drawing out the spear with a steady hand.

Even though he was unconscious, he groaned from the pain. For a moment his eyes flickered open, but then dropped closed once more. Marvelous blue eyes, like the ocean that was truly her home.

As she worked the spear out of his flesh, a sickening sucking sound turned her stomach as the spear came loose and blood flowed freely from the wound. Her father quickly joined her, packing gauze against the exit wound as she did the same to the front. Then they bandaged the injury tightly, using the pressure to stem the bleeding.

Satisfied with their handiwork, they gently lay him flat on the bed. Nali experienced relief at the gentle rise and fall of his chest and the steady beat beneath her fingers as she checked his pulse.

"Will he be all right?" she asked as her father brought over a basin with fresh water and a towel so they could wash his body clean of the ocean's salt and his blood.

"If infection doesn't set in."

Infection. She'd forgotten how fragile mortal bodies were but was reminded of it yet again as she passed the damp towel across the scars marring a large part of his left upper body. She ran her fingers along the rough skin, wondering how he had been hurt.

"Burns," her father said, in tune with her thoughts. Then he quickly added, "He was a firefighter."

She nodded and continued her chore. Seeing that she was apparently in no rush, her father pulled up a chair opposite her and sat.

"It's been too long, daughter."

"It has, and I'm sorry. But it's no longer safe for me to visit too close to shore. I wish I could visit and spend more time, but you know that after a week, each day that passes makes it harder to shift back." Holding the man's arm, she wiped it clean and tried to ignore the skitter of desire at the feel of his skin beneath her fingers. Tried to keep her gaze from wandering to the leanly muscled body whose beauty was not diminished by the scars. If anything, the scars were like a badge of courage from his past profession.

"What's his name?"

"Victor Edwards."

"Why is he here?"

"I rented him the shack because you were no longer visiting," her father answered obtusely, well aware that wasn't the answer she sought. Also obviously wanting to foment guilt at her absence, no matter how justified she'd been to stay away.

Playing his game, she looked around her old home and shrugged. "I don't see any fires here."

Her father chuckled and shook his head. "He's no longer a firefighter, Nali. He's got a research grant to study the reefs in this area. To study you."

Chapter 4

The kind of study she had in mind was far from scholarly, Nali thought as she washed Victor's body. As she pulled off his wet trunks to reveal his gorgeous cock, her insides clenched as she imagined him hard and filling her with his thick length.

Because she was too tempted to linger and explore, she quickly swiped the wet towel across him and then rushed to finish, heat flashing across her body. She swiftly turned away from her father to hide the way her nipples had tightened and hurried a few feet away to a small closet. Inside, several of her dresses still hung, and she quickly tossed one on to hide her want.

But she had not fooled her keen-eyed father. "I shall leave you now, Nali. If a fever should set in, call me."

As he rose, she rushed over and hugged him hard, missing him and the feel of his arms around her, the smell of him, so comforting.

"I won't go without coming by again," she promised.

He smiled, a tired smile, and caressed her cheek. "You are so like your mother. But both your memories fade with your absence."

She fought down the knot of anguish that tightened her throat and brushed a quick kiss along his cheek. "I will be by. I have some time before I must leave," she repeated and with a regal dip of his head, he left.

Nali returned to the man's side and covered his body with a clean sheet. No sense staring temptation in the face all the rest of the day. When she was done, she walked around the one-room shack, checking out the items she had noticed earlier. Maps, papers, photos and an assortment of equipment took up the hand-hewn table to one side of the space. She and her father had shared many a meal there before she had been exiled to the deep ocean by the actions of fishermen like those who had attacked them earlier.

A basket of fresh fruit sat on the kitchen counter along with a prescription bottle. Pain pills. A half-eaten loaf of bread was wrapped in plastic. Inside the tiny ice box beneath the counter were a variety of cheeses, a slab of a local cured ham, eggs and milk. The latter was probably for the battered stovetop coffeepot and tin mug that looked as if they had seen their share of use.

The closet where she had grabbed her dress held only a pair of faded jeans, a pair of khaki pants and some casual shirts. Leaning forward, she buried her nose in them to memorize his unique scent. After, she took a quick look through the old three-drawer chest and discovered only the very basics for dressing.

Except for all his fancy equipment, he was a simple man, she decided as she walked back and sat on the chair by the side of the bed. She hoped he would rouse soon so she could be on her way at nightfall. It would be safest for her to travel then, hidden in darkness.

But as dusk came and night fell, he was still unconscious, and as she leaned forward and ran her hand across his chest, the heat there warned that all was not well.

She checked his wounds and frowned at the hint of redness around the edges of the injury.

Not good.

She rose and went to one of the kitchen cabinets where she had stored a collection of remedies that her family would use when one of the villagers was hurt. Removing several of the bottles, she mixed up a paste to place on the wounds to try and control the spread of any infection.

Returning to the man, she gingerly spread on the paste, but he jumped and moaned. The paste was caustic. That was part of why it worked, but as she spread more on the exit wound, he finally roused.

"Who are you?" he asked as he watched her work and place clean gauze over his wounds.

"Nali. I am Saila's daughter."

Victor shook his head, fighting back the confusing images swirling through his brain. It was the woman in his dreams. The one with the charcoal-black eyes like the shark but with skin as rich as copper. Long, straight hair framed a determined chin, a sharp slash of a nose and a full, luscious mouth.

As she noticed his perusal of her, she smiled. Perfectly white human teeth.

But she hadn't been human before, he was almost certain of that. Even now he could recall the grate of shark skin against his side gradually softening as they had neared shore. And with that change, the muscled bulk of the shark had thinned and filled out into womanly curves.

Tempting curves, he realized even in his weakened condition as his gaze dipped across the dress that hugged her shapely body.

He shivered but not from passion. Inside, cold filled his gut even as burning heat spread from the wound in his side.

He gritted his teeth against that ache and reached up, gingerly running his hand across the bandages.

She covered his hand with hers, her skin so smooth and warm. So warm, he thought as another shiver racked his body and his lips began to tremble.

"Cold." He glanced up at her, and she offered a reassuring smile as she ran a damp cloth across his forehead, then down along his cheeks.

"You have a fever," she said and dampened the cloth again before passing it along his shoulders and his chest.

The wetness was welcome, but the heat of his body quickly burned off that relief and soon he was shaking, his teeth chattering as if he were freezing.

Nali ran the cloth across his flushed skin once again, trying to offer him comfort, but as the tremors in his body grew stronger and stronger, she knew it would take more to break the fever. When he glanced at her, those sea-colored eyes wide and pleading, she had to help him.

Chapter 5

Placing the basin with the water and washcloth within easy reach, she whipped off her dress and slipped beneath the sheets. Cuddling close to him, she offered up her body heat to quiet the tremors in his. His skin was hot and dry beside hers, and she took hold of the damp cloth, passing it along as much of his body as she could, trying to lower his body temperature.

As she passed the cloth along his forehead and cheeks—as red as if he'd run a race—a ghost of a smile passed across his hard, masculine lips before they trembled with imagined cold once more.

"Thank you," he said and placed his hand at her waist, urging her close. They were almost the same height, so every part of their bodies touched.

The tender act gripped her heart hard. It had been so long since she'd been touched like that. So long, and never by a man as handsome as this one. Not even the scars could diminish his beauty or the strength in the lean body tucked beneath hers.

She once again dipped the cloth in the basin, the action dragging the pebbled tips of her breasts along the wall of his chest. Against her thigh came the jump of his erection, responding to her even with his weakness.

Wetness erupted between her legs, but she fought the need.

"I'm sorry," he said and tried to move away, but she pressed him down to keep him still.

"You are a man. I'm a woman. It's to be expected," she said because that was the natural order of things. The logic of nature had guided her people. It was only with the advent of man into their area that things had gotten out of whack and her people had been virtually exterminated.

"You're a woman now, but you weren't before," he said, gently rubbing his hand up and down her side as she did the same with the damp cloth, cooling his heated flesh.

She could have denied it, passed it off to the effects of his wound, but something about him made it impossible for her to deceive him.

"Not before," she confessed but then urged him to rest.

With a nod, he closed his eyes while she continued caring for him. As the hours passed, she was pleased as the tremors in his body gradually abated and his skin cooled. Soon after, the slight sheen of sweat on his body confirmed that the fever had broken.

Tired from all that had happened and loathe to leave him, she tucked herself against his side to rest, but her inner spirit swam within her, alert and restless as was the way of the shark.

It was that spirit that detected the change in his body—the awareness of her and the arousal that rose up in him. The smell of it, so richly masculine, awakened her desire.

As he stirred and went to move away, she rose and lay a hand on his chest to keep him near.

"Why do you wish to go?"

She sat up slightly and her breasts brushed against him. The action tightened them immediately and, for a moment, his gaze dipped down, his look as powerful as a caress, before jerking back up to her face.

"I don't want to take advantage of your kindness." His voice was stronger, all traces of weakness gone. The flush on his skin now was from passion and not fever. Her one concern was that he might reopen the wound with anything too strenuous, but she relished the idea of his touch against her.

"I think I'm the one who owes you thanks for saving me."

With a shake of his head, he said, "Do you really want me to believe—"

"My name is Nali. You know what that means in Kuna," she said and for a moment he furrowed his brow, searching for the word. Recognition slammed into him.

"Shark. Nali means shark."

"When you are better, I will show you. It's the least I can do as thanks." After she finished, she trailed her hand up and across his shoulder and smoothed her palm over the rough scars there.

"How did this happen?"

"A fire. I went in to rescue a child, but part of the building collapsed on me." He said it nonchalantly as if it had been just a routine thing.

"You saved the child?" she asked, trailing her hand down his arm to his uninjured forearm. The hair there was soft beneath her palm.

"My team got her out."

"You like being a hero," she said and shifted her hand down the final few inches to cradle his hand in hers.

Victor didn't know what to make of her. She seemed almost innocent in some ways. Possibly crazy, he thought, although he couldn't deny his dreams and the vague recollections of what had happened in those moments after he'd been speared.

But there was one thing of which he was certain.

"You can keep the whole hero gig. I prefer being alive."

A knowing smile blossomed on her lips, and those almost-black eyes gleamed with an intriguing mix of amusement and passion. Taking his hand in hers, she guided it upward along her lean, curvy flank and to the swell of her breast.

"Then why are you afraid to live right now? To share yourself with me?" To prove her point, she pressed his hand to her breast and, beneath his palm, her nipple puckered into an even tighter nub. She shifted her thigh across his to cover the erection he had been fighting. The softness of her and the damp heat at her core made him groan with need.

"Let me love you, Victor. I will be careful," she said, smoothing her thigh across his erection before dancing her hand down his midsection to take his cock in her hand.

"Yes," exploded from his lips as she encircled him with her hand and stroked, her movements sure and determined.

She smiled then and bent her head to sample the shape of his lips with her mouth. Her touch was questioning and uncertain, unlike the sure caresses of her hand. Over and over again she drifted her mouth across his lips, avoiding a true kiss.

When he dug his fingers into the short, dark strands of her hair to urge her in for a deeper taste, she pulled away to instead drop a kiss on the underside of his jaw. Then she worked her way downward to his nipple where, with a little nibble, she flitted to her next stop: his navel.

He moaned and shifted his hips upward against her hand as he realized her intent.

She slipped her long, powerful body between his legs and guided his cock to her mouth. With a quick swipe of her tongue, she nearly had him coming, but he held back, needing her. Wanting to be buried inside her as he came. It had been so long since he'd allowed himself the pleasure of a woman's body.

But Nali had other plans for him.

She took him into her mouth, her tongue dancing all along his head and length. Her smooth hands worked his cock and balls until he had to close his eyes against the sight of her, the sensations were so intense.

"Nali, ride me," he pleaded and bent to urge her upward but groaned at the pain in his side from the movement.

"Soon, Victor. Soon," she promised and sucked him deep into her throat while caressing his balls. The pleasure of her mouth was so intense, he had to dig his hands into the mattress to keep control. He wanted to haul her down onto the bed and plow into her, bring her the kind of pleasure she was offering him.

"Nali," he said roughly, and against his cock came the coolness of the night air as she finally relented and moved up his body. She straddled his hips and held herself there, poised over his erection, the dark copper tips of her breasts tight. An almost sad smile appeared on her face before she reached down and guided him to her center.

The heat and wet of her bathed the sensitive head of his cock for only a second before she plunged down and took him into her body.

Nali gasped at the fullness of him. She held herself still against the sensation of being one with a man again. How long had it been, she wondered? So long that she was tight and the feeling had been slightly painful at first, but now pleasure slowly suffused her from the feel of him stretching her, filling her with the heat of his body.

Yet she still felt empty in some ways. Alone. She had spent so much of her life alone, she thought.

The gentle swipe of his thumb wiped away the tear as it ran down her cheek.

"Have I hurt you, Nali?" he asked and raised his other hand to rest along her shoulder, the touch filled with comfort.

She shook her head vehemently. "No, Victor."

He dropped his thumb to brush it across her lips, the touch as potent as any kiss. A kiss she had avoided before because it would be like giving her heart to him, a heart that would break as soon as she had to leave him to return to her true home.

"I will not hurt you. Ever," he reassured.

"I know," she said and meant it. He was a hero. His body and actions in the ocean had provided proof of that.

"Tell me what you want. Anything."

She met his gaze and his face shimmered in her sight

from the tears she battled. The one thing she wanted she could not have, but she would settle for this—for his body and his passion—until it was time to return home.

"Touch me, Victor. Love me."

His full lips, those lips she wanted to taste so badly, thinned into a tight slash of control. His eyes turned the color of the sea during a storm and were as turbulent. He sensed her pain and her need.

But there was only one thing he could provide her.

He moved his hands down to her breasts and tenderly cupped her, exploring the weight of them, strumming his thumbs across the taut tips and dragging a pleased sigh from her.

"You are beautiful, Nali. So strong," he said as he dipped his hand down for only a moment to rub the back of it against her muscled midsection and then back to her breasts.

He deepened his caress there, tweaking her nipples. Inside, her muscles jerked and stroked him.

Sucking in a breath, he said, "That feels good. Does it feel the same for you?"

"Yes-s-s," she replied on a long sigh, before she added, "But I want…I want your mouth on me."

He smiled then, the first real one she'd seen from him. In the ocean, only his eyes had smiled thanks to the mouthpiece, but now there was nothing to hold it back. To hide it.

It transformed his face, filling it with joy. Bringing out the deep dimples that made the years fall away from his features. She realized then that he was younger than she'd first thought. The weight of his pain, both past and present, had made him seem older.

"Lean forward so I can have my taste."

She shuddered in anticipation and did as he asked, aware

that his mobility was limited. But as she neared, he propped one elbow on the bed and rose up partway to drift a kiss against her nipple before licking and sucking it.

Moaning, she threaded her fingers into the thick strands of his dark hair and held him close, loving the feel of him against her breasts. Each tug and pull of his mouth brought more heat and dampness to her core, made her vagina jump and clench against him until just having him inside her wasn't enough.

She had to move, had to release the animal inside her restlessly searching for satisfaction.

She shifted her hips, riding him as he continued pleasuring her, as he offered words of encouragement, urging her to find her own. He stroked his hand along her hip and buttock to guide her until passion stole their breath and she had to see him. Had to watch his face as pleasure swamped them and pulled them deep.

He met her gaze, his eyes serious now. All traces of the boy gone as the man sought release, sought her pleasure with a forceful roll of his hips that buried him so deep it broke free the passion within her.

She came hard and fast, her breath exploding from her body. Trembling roughly above him, she jerked her hips along him one final time and he followed her down, calling out her name.

"Nali."

By small degrees she lowered her body until her breath fanned his face. He shifted up again, intent on kissing her, but she turned her head at the last minute and his mouth brushed her cheek.

With a wiggle, she made to move off him, but he eased his hand to the small of her back to keep her near.

"Don't leave me. Not yet."

She braced one hand against the mattress and glanced down at him, her eyes narrowed. Doubt was alive in the dark grey of her eyes.

"Why?" she asked with that trace of innocence—or maybe it was better to call it awkwardness, as if she was unused to the ways of men and women. Maybe she was. If he believed what she had told him, maybe she was not used to human ways.

He cradled her face and smiled, swiping his thumb across the stain of color on her cheek. "Has it been that long that you don't understand?"

A mischievous grin erupted on her full lips. "The wham bam thank you, ma'am?"

He chuckled and ruffled the spiky strands of her hair. "I don't want to feel used. I don't want you to feel used. So will you stay?"

Nali hesitated for a heartbeat, then nodded and rested her head on his chest while her lean length nestled on his, their bodies still joined. His arm wrapped around her loosely, as if he sensed that the wildness within her could not rest if captive.

Even as her human body accepted the comfort of his arms and allowed calm to wash over her, the shark spirit within her stayed alert, remaining active long after she had closed her eyes and surrendered to the fatigue brought on by assuming a mortal form and the events of the day and night.

It was that spirit that experienced the stirring of dawn as the first rays of the sun peeked above the horizon and pulled her from the first real sleep she'd had in months.

With that awakening came hunger gnawing in her belly, especially as the smell of food cooking from her father's home wafted in through the open windows of her shack.

She eased from Victor's side but sat on the edge of the bed, examining him. Skin tanned to a golden hue by the Caribbean sun showed no signs of fever and his breathing was deep and regular. As a soft snore escaped him, she smiled.

It was good to know he wasn't perfect, although most of him was. Including that magnificent cock, she thought as she lifted the sheets for another look at the length of him as it rested along his thigh. Her insides twisted again with need at the thought of the pleasure they had shared the night before, brief as it had been.

She had wanted for too long, and he had been too fragile to make it last.

Hopefully some rest and food could improve both of them.

With another hungry growl from deep in her belly, she rose and slipped on her dress. She was about to go in search of her father when he entered, bearing a tray with plates. The mouthwatering smells of fried empanadas and ripe fruits teased her nostrils.

She brought a finger to her lips to ask for his silence, then gestured in the direction of the steps to the shack.

He smiled in recognition of what she wanted. How many times had the two of them sat on those steps, sharing some moments or a meal? Enjoying a quiet night or sun-filled day?

It had been too long, but in the past year fishermen had grown too aggressive in their pursuit of her as game. It had driven her out to deeper ocean and kept her from visiting. Only the anxiety of her cousin sharks at Victor's presence had urged her to come in to see what had them so riled. Yesterday's attack only proved her foolishness in venturing close to shore, but now that she had, she was going to take advantage of it in any way she could for as long as she could.

So she sat on the step beside her father, the tray with the breakfast he had made balanced across their legs. They were silent as they ate and enjoyed the quick rise of the sun into a crisp blue sky. The morning air was cooler and slightly damp, bringing a nip to her bare arms.

She rubbed them before snatching up another empanada.

Her father laughed as she made short work of the meat-filled pastry. "I guess you were hungry."

With a nonchalant shrug, she said, "You get tired of eating fish all the time."

Her father shot a look back at where Victor slept in the large handmade bed. "From the looks of it, food wasn't the only human thing you craved."

They had never kept anything from each other before and she wasn't about to start now. "He is a handsome man. Strong. Caring." She knew that even though they had barely spent any time together.

"From what I can see he is a good man."

She arched a dark brow. "Playing matchmaker? You know how impossible that is."

Her father chuckled and shook his head. "If it were impossible, you would not be here today, daughter."

She couldn't deny the truth, so she wouldn't. But there was one thing about which she had to warn her father. "He knows what I am. He remembers how I changed."

"And if he repeats it they will think he's crazy."

Neither of them mentioned what would have happened ages ago, when their numbers were still large enough to protect. Now their people were too scattered and few to carry out a death sentence for such knowledge.

Especially when no one would believe him.

The rustle of sheets and a soft moan alerted them that Victor was awake.

"Take the rest to him. Feed him. Make him well," her father said as he rose and handed her the tray.

Although he hadn't said it, she knew what else he was thinking. Make him yours. Make him stay. Make lots of babies.

She would do none of those things in the week she had before she had to return to the sea. But she would satisfy those human needs gnawing at her gut much as the hunger for food had that morning.

Turning, she walked into the shack with the last of the empanadas and fruit.

Chapter 6

Sunlight pierced the handwoven fabric of her dress, silhouetting the lean, womanly shape of her as she stood at the door.

Even with the slight pain in his side, the sight stirred him.

She walked toward him, lush hips swaying from side-to-side, reminding him of how she had ridden him last night and brought him such pleasure.

A sexy smile pulled at the corners of her full lips and her dark eyes glittered with awareness of his attraction to her. Her gaze dipped down to the light sheet covering him, which failed miserably to hide his growing arousal.

"I see you're feeling better." She sat on the edge of the bed and placed the tray across his lap to offer him some privacy.

"I am." A rumble from low in his stomach followed his statement.

"Hungry, too, I see," she said with a chuckle.

"In more ways than one," he mumbled as she grabbed a piece of mango and brought it to his lips.

The fruit was ripe, lush and juicy but almost tasteless as he recalled the sweetness of her nipples. When she went to shift her hand away, he gently ensnared her wrist and, before she could protest, sucked one finger after another into his mouth, licking away the mango juice.

She shuddered and her eyes widened. Her voice had a needy quaver as she spoke. "There's plenty of fruit."

He grew even harder as he imagined those parts of her he had not tasted just yet. Picturing the flush on her nether lips and the juices he wanted to wring from her, he was thankful for the tray that hid the way his cock hardened and jerked at those thoughts.

But he didn't want to rush her. Not just yet, so he nodded and released her hand, picked up a piece of fruit and offered it to her. Like a wild animal unsure of who was feeding her, she stole it quickly from his hand.

They continued sharing bits of fruit and the empanada pastries until not a single thing remained on the tray.

Victor leaned back against the headboard and rubbed his belly. "That was tasty. Did you make them?"

She shook her head. "My father. My mother taught him well."

When she removed the tray and set it aside on the floor, her gaze dipped down to his lap and just that quick, needy look had him hungering for her touch and taste once more.

"Are you always this..."

"No," he admitted quickly. Since being injured during the fire, and after, when he'd decided to finally follow his dreams, he'd had little time for relationships.

"So why me?" she asked, but even as she did so, she slipped her hand beneath the sheet and covered his erection.

He jumped at her touch, surprised by the openness of it. By that hint of innocent wonder he'd sensed in her.

"I guess I could ask the same thing, Nali. Why me?"

"You saved my life." Her response was possibly too quick and she averted her gaze, looking down to where she moved her hand on him, stroking and exploring the length of him.

"As you did mine," he reminded her.

A shrug followed his comment, unsure and almost evasive.

Victor placed his thumb and forefinger on her chin and with gentle pressure urged her face upward to meet his gaze. "I like you touching me. I like touching you, but there's more going on here than just that."

He surprised himself by saying that, true as it was. She fascinated him, and it had little to do with her beauty or the fact that she maybe wasn't quite as human as she seemed right now.

"Nothing else is here. Nothing but man–woman things." Beneath her words there was pain and loneliness. Sadness gripped him hard with that realization.

He was a man who didn't like to see others suffer. It was what had driven him to be a firefighter. The realization of how he suffered was what had put him on the road that had led him here. Maybe that was fated to be. Maybe she also was fated, he thought and swiped his thumb along the line of her jaw.

"Maybe in time you'll see that it can be more, Nali."

She had been touching him the whole time, but now she stopped and tears shimmered in her gaze again, as they had last night. "There isn't enough time. I cannot stay for long."

He nodded. "Then let's make the most of the time we have."

He moved forward to kiss her once more, but yet again she demurred, looking away. So he took advantage and dropped a kiss on the sensitive skin just beneath the shell of her ear, continuing downward to the crook of her neck, where he inhaled deeply.

She smelled as clean and fresh as an ocean breeze.

He licked the soft skin there before closing his lips against her flesh and sucking gently. Her hand tightened on him and he smiled against her neck.

"Do you like that, Nali?" He licked and sucked her again and a soft sigh escaped her.

"Yes."

"What else do you like?" he asked and moved his head down the exposed line of her shoulder until he reached the edge of the dress she wore. He reached up and pulled the fabric downward, exposing the full swell of her breasts.

"I like when you kiss me there," she said and skimmed her gaze across her breasts for only the briefest moment before returning that gaze to his lap and the motion of her hand beneath the sheets.

He lifted her dress up and over her head, regretting even the short moment she left him to allow that before once again diving her hand beneath the sheet to touch him.

The soft daylight spilling in through the open windows bathed her body, bringing out the gorgeous golden color of her skin and the deep caramel of her nipples. They were already hard and he had to restrain himself from devouring her. He wanted to savor this gift from the sea and bring her not just pleasure, but joy.

His body tight with restraint, he bent and touched the tip of his tongue to her nipples, ignoring the pull in his side, which objected to the movement.

She jumped once again from that simple touch and then cupped the back of his head with her hand and pressed him close.

As Victor encircled her nipple with his lips, Nali closed her eyes against the sight of it. Against the pleasure that tender touch brought.

She didn't even realize she had moaned until he asked, "Did I hurt you?"

"No," she answered without hesitation and tightened her grasp on the back of his head, stroking him harder beneath the sheet.

A kaleidoscope of colors filled her vision as she took in all the sensations being with him brought. The heat and damp of his lips sucking and the gentle nibble of his teeth. The caress of his rough, calloused fingers—a man's touch—along her nipples and the sensitive skin of her breasts.

Beneath her hand his cock was hard and hot. So full and responsive. Her vagina clenched in emptiness, wanting to be filled by that length once more. At her core, her clitoris swelled and begged to be touched.

She dropped her hand downward and found that nub, caressing herself until he whispered, "Let me, Nali."

He slipped his hand between her legs and, with a man's sureness, exposed her clitoris to his touch. He stroked and pressed against it while he continued loving her breasts with his mouth and his other hand.

Wave after wave of pleasure swamped her and she clenched her hand around his cock. Stroking harder, faster, he brought her ever closer to a climax, and she pulled him along with her with the caress of her hand.

He grunted at one sharp pull of her hand and then said roughly, "I need to be in you, Nali. I want to be in you when you come."

She was almost there, and she didn't hesitate to yank away the sheet and straddle him. Sinking down on him hard, she shattered, her back bowing as the pressure of him filling her sent her over the edge.

His wild groan burst against her breasts as he joined her with his release, but he didn't stop loving her. His lips skimmed the tips of her nipples, kissing the fullness of her breasts before moving up to that sensitive spot just beneath her neck. As he had before, he opened his mouth on her and sucked. Between her legs, desire slammed into her again, dragging her upward.

She wrapped her arms around him and held him close, riding the ebbing hardness of his cock as with another bite on her neck she came once more.

Chapter 7

Victor cradled her in his arms as her body shook from the force of her climax. Her muscles milked the last of his release from him, the powerful undulations of her vagina caressing him. He maintained his erection long past the point he had thought possible from the failing strength of his body.

The spear through his side had not hit anything vital, but the wound and last night's fever had weakened him.

Even as he soothed her, running his hands up and down her back, kissing that sensitive spot on her neck where he had marked her with his loving, his mind and body were pulling him to rest and restore his strength.

He fought back the fatigue, understanding just how much she needed the connection, both physical and mental.

When some semblance of calm had returned to them, he shifted so they were lying down once more, facing each other. Their legs intertwined and his arms lay loosely around her waist.

"Will you stay?" he asked, risking a glance at her face

to judge her state of mind. He suspected Nali was much like the shark that had circled him warily in the water, approaching only to retreat once more.

She surprised him by meeting his gaze directly and cupping his jaw. She ran her thumb across his lips in a caress as intimate as any kiss. It made him wish that by the time she left him, she would find the courage to really kiss him.

"Why do you want me to stay?"

"Because I'm tired of being alone." An honest answer and one he hadn't thought to make. Since leaving the fire department, his single-minded goal of becoming a marine biologist had kept him apart from those around him. It was only once he'd come here, to complete the task he'd dreamed of, that he realized he had no one with whom to share the joy of that success.

Nali nodded and lay her hand along the swell of his chest, close to his heart. "Rest, Victor. I'll be here when you wake."

With a smile, he closed his eyes, an unexpected lightness in his heart that matched the freedom that came to him beneath the surface of the ocean.

Nali did not fail to miss the way the tension ebbed from his body. She waited until the slow, regular breath of sleep confirmed he was resting. Only then did she take a moment to explore him in ways she could not while he was awake, fearing they would reveal too much to him. Make her too vulnerable.

She glanced up at his face in rest. That boyish smile still graced his lips. Lips that were both tender and demanding. She touched the spot where he had marked her and it sent a zing of arousal through her. She had never considered herself so wanton, yet he brought out the desire to always be joined with him. Even now, despite the satisfaction he had brought her just moments earlier, her insides vibrated with need.

Tamping it down, she continued her visual exploration of his body, dipping her gaze to the damage along his shoulder, arm and upper chest. The flesh there was both shiny and rough, and she held back from touching it, afraid of waking him. But she had seen him grimace after he'd pulled himself from the water, and she suspected the wounds were more than surface deep.

Definitely more than just physical scars.

Tired of being alone, he had said and she understood. As one of the last of her kind, hunted as game, she spent far too much time in the solitude of the sea. Restlessly seeking that which she would never find there: love.

Her father had found it on shore with Nali's mother. He'd given up what he was, the leader of their diminishing group, to live on land with her.

Only her mother had died and left them both alone.

Just like Victor would one day leave, Nali told herself as she shut her eyes against the tears she had already shed far too often in his presence. They were a sign of weakness and she was far from weak.

She was Nali, the shark goddess. Goddesses did not cry. Nor did they sacrifice who they were for mere mortals. Her father had learned the painful reality of that choice.

Victor could only provide a respite from her loneliness. A week of loving before she returned to her home.

With that decision made, she allowed herself to enjoy the sensation of him surrounding her. The warmth of his skin was as delicious as that of the Caribbean waters. The rasp of his chest hairs against her breasts was a tease much like the softness of his dick along her belly. She itched to reach down and awaken his passion once more, but she knew he needed to rest.

Which reminded her that when he woke, she would need to check his bandages and feed him.

Mentally she made a list of the things she required to help him heal quickly, and once she was certain he was in a deep sleep, she eased from his side to gather them.

She intended to make the most of the time she had on land.

The enticing smells of something spicy woke him from sleep.

He reached out for Nali, but she was gone and that made him pop up in bed, straining his side.

She turned at the sound of his movement and smiled. She wore the dress made from the brightly colored molas the Kunas created and was busy working at the gas-powered stove at the far side of the room.

She stopped stirring, shut off the flame, then walked back to the bed and sat on the edge as he rose and leaned back against the pillows. With an ease that relaxed him, she brushed a kiss along his cheek and rubbed the back of her hand along his midsection.

"You slept the day away," she said.

He glanced toward the open windows and realized the sun was low in the horizon.

"You wore me out," he teased and stroked his hand down her arm.

Her smile brightened and a stain of pink erupted on her

cheeks. "You're just weak." Her smile turned awkward as she quickly added, "From your injury."

He grinned and shook his head. "Don't worry, Nali. My male pride is not that fragile."

"I have some fresh ointment and bandages. We should change your dressings."

Before he could say anything else, she sprang into action. She walked to the table and came back with a tray that held a basin of fresh water, clean towels, bandages and a small dish filled with something green and pasty-looking.

"What is that?" He pointed to the dish.

"It's more of the ointment I used last night."

He grimaced. "The one that stung like a bitch."

A mischievous grin returned to her features as she bent and unwrapped the bandage around his midsection. "Surely a big, strong man like you can handle a little sting."

"So much for my male pride," he teased back, liking the easy way they had together.

"It's healing nicely," she said, and he looked down at his side. The puncture wound had no traces of pink or anything else that warned of infection. Surprisingly, it even seemed to be knitting without the benefit of stitches.

"It is." He watched as Nali dampened the cloth and then gently cleaned both sides of the wound, exposing the small-ish area that had yet to close. That made her frown and scoop up a goodly amount of the paste with two fingers.

Her gaze flitted to his for a moment. "Brace yourself."

He did, dragging in a breath and gritting his teeth when she smoothed the paste over the area and the burn registered in those parts that were still raw. When he released his pent-up breath, she covered the areas with clean gauze.

A moment later, she wrapped the bandages around his mid-section again to keep them in place and apply pressure to help close the wounds.

As she worked, the smell of her tantalized him and the feel of her hands on him, even at the simplest task, renewed his desire. He covered his growing erection with his hand, but she brushed his fingers away and instead eased her hand over him. Only the thin fabric of the sheet separated the smooth flesh of her palm from his dick.

"Why do you wish to hide this?" she asked, her caresses exploring the hardening shape of him.

"I don't want you to think that's all I want from you," he admitted. He wanted to know Nali, the woman, and not just her body.

She shrugged and continued with her caress. "This is as natural as breath. As beautiful."

He reached down and stilled the motion of her hand. "I want to give you more than just this."

She pulled away from him and tilted her chin up at a de-termined angle. "What if this is all that I want?"

He arched a brow in challenge. "Then I'd say you're a liar."

In a burst of speed, she flounced away from him and back to the counter, where she tucked away the medical supplies in one of the cupboards. Then she started up the flame again and resumed her cooking. "You must be hun-gry. I know I am."

He was hungry, and not just for food or sex. He was hun-gry to know more about her and what made her tick. Maybe in time she would give him what he wanted.

He hated the thought of being stuck in the bed all day,

having had too much of that during his recovery from his burns. He scooted to the edge of the bed and applied pressure to his side for support as he forced himself to his feet. Dizziness made him waver for a moment before it passed, and he walked to the table she had already set for a meal.

He was pleased that he could manage more than just a shuffle. Despite his earlier complaint about the paste she had applied, the heat of it working through his side had cut down on the pain.

"What's in that green glop?" He sat down at the table.

"Some herbs and leaves the Kuna have used for centuries," she answered with a sharp shrug before dishing out whatever she had been cooking onto plates.

She walked over and placed the dishes on the table, her movements jerky. Clearly she was still annoyed with him, but he was not about to let her mood ruin the coming night.

"Thank you. This looks and smells delicious."

"It's a simple meal," she replied as she forked up some of the omelet she had made.

"Simple is always better." He took a big bite, enjoying the sweetness of the onions and the crispness of the potatoes enveloped in the fluffy egg mixture. Cutting off a piece of the chorizo sausage also on the plate, he found its spiciness contrasted pleasantly with the smoothness of the omelet.

Thick slices of rustic bread sat on a dish in the middle of the table and he grabbed a slice, buttered it and ate it, enjoying the yeastiness of the still-warm bread and the sweet cream of the butter.

"Delicious. Did you make the bread?"

Another shrug greeted him. "I had to do something while you were sleeping."

He chuckled at her seeming outrage. "Forgive me for being so weak. Not all of us are as strong as…" He paused then, reminded of the fact that she might be something other than mortal.

"Just what are you? What is your father?"

Another shift of her shoulders came, but she seemed slightly more uneasy. "We have been here far longer than when the Kunas came to these islands. Until then we were alone, surviving in the sea and coming to land for just brief moments."

"But when the Kuna arrived—"

"They were kind but fearful. We were intrigued by their worship, and more and more of us came to shore. Some forgot the ways of our people. Others lost their lives as more men came to hunt us for sport."

"Your father is like you?" he asked, intrigued to know more.

"My father *was* like me, but then he met my mother during a visit to shore."

And gave up what he was, Victor realized.

"Do you think that is what love is about? Giving up what you are for someone else?"

His question brought her up short, with her fork halfway to her mouth. After a pause, she set it down and nodded. "It's what happened to my father and so many others."

"And you do not wish for it to be that way with you?"

"No," she answered abruptly and far too testily.

Her hand rested on the table and he covered it, squeezing reassuringly. "Love is about sacrifice, but that doesn't mean you need to stop being who you are. What you are."

She withdrew her hand, picked up the fork and finished

eating silently. He did the same. He understood her a little better, but that did not make things any easier.

When they were done, she cleaned up quickly while he sat at the table, reluctant to return to bed. But she had something different in mind. That was clear as she stalked over to the bed, yanked off her dress and lay down, as if waiting for him.

His cock jerked and came to life at the sight of her, creamy copper skin dark against the sun-bleached whiteness of the sheets. But as he had told her earlier, he wanted more from her and no amount of anger on her part was going to change that.

"Are you not coming to bed?" she finally asked while staring up at the thatched roof of the shack.

"I'm not sleepy." He had to fight back his chuckle at her moue of annoyance.

"I'm not here to sleep. I want to make love," she announced in regal tones.

This time he could not contain his burst of amusement, which only earned him a nasty glare. "You may be waiting a long time."

With a huff, she said, "Then I'll just satisfy myself."

He stifled a groan as she reached up and cradled her breasts, tweaking the tips into tight peaks. Her first sigh escaped her lips. She closed her eyes then and shifted one hand between her legs, parting them as she dipped her fingers to her center and pressed while continuing to play with her nipples.

His balls tightened painfully and he couldn't just sit there, despite his earlier declarations.

Almost hobbling over from the pain of his erection, he sat beside her on the bed, his hip against hers.

Her eyes flew open then, but before she could say a word, he said, "Let me help you."

He lay his hand on hers as it rested between her legs and found her clitoris in the damp nest of her curls. He pressed against it, dragging a sharp gasp from her.

He smiled and bent, ignoring the pull in his side so he could wrap his lips around a tight nipple and suckle her while he worked her clit.

She moaned then and grabbed hold of his hand, urging it downward to her vagina and the wetness of it. He eased his fingers into her while she returned to touching her clitoris. Her juices dripped over his hand and hers.

He left her only long enough to stroke himself with her wetness and urge her hand to him.

With a rough exhale against her breast as she encircled him, stroking, he returned to loving her, driving his fingers in her over and over. He bit and sucked on her sensitive nipples until she was writhing against the sheets and her hand was urgent on his erection, moving on him roughly as they both reached for release.

But he was not a greedy man. As he had told her, it was not just about this and his own satisfaction.

He left her then, slipping to the floor to kneel while urging her to the side of the bed. The movement and position exposed her to him, rewarding him with the view of her glistening and flushed sex. He parted her lips with his hands, revealing the hard and swollen nub of her clitoris, and she moaned and shifted restlessly beneath his hands.

He didn't hesitate, bringing his mouth to that nub while he eased his fingers inside her once more.

Nali shook with his possession of her and nearly came against his lips and tongue, but it was too good to rush. Too pleasing as he used that gifted mouth on her and then reached up and played with one of her breasts while she caressed the other.

She keened with pleasure like the animal she was inside. The animal that wanted to taste and bite him. That reached down with both hands and clawed at his shoulders to hold him close until her body could no longer contain the pleasure and it spilled over her, bringing a release that had her screaming his name and arching her hips against his mouth and hands.

His caresses gentled as she came back to Earth, his hands soothing along her thighs. His kiss at her center was soft as he left her to rise, and her eyes shot open to watch him.

He guided his cock to her vagina and slowly pushed forward, stilling when he was buried deep within her and the soft hairs on his pubis brushed the still sensitized nub between her legs.

"Victor," she pleaded, wrapping her legs around him, needing a moment to catch up from the earlier pleasure.

He smiled, knowing her need. Bracing one hand beside her on the bed, he traced her lips with his index finger. She could smell herself on him, taste herself as she dipped her tongue out before he drew that hand down to the love bite on her neck that was still tender.

As he skipped his finger along that spot, she moaned and her vagina contracted against him with need. Still he did not move, his restraint far stronger than hers.

Her breath exploded from her body as he strummed her nipple with his fingers and then bent and tasted her again.

"You are so sweet. So lovely," he whispered and bent his head, bringing his lips close to hers.

She wanted to taste him, but she feared that intimacy. Feared that if she had that taste, she would forever hunger for it. And so she avoided him again, escaping his kiss as she said, "Make me come. Make me shatter again."

He grunted his response and answered her request, shifting his hips back to withdraw the thick length of his dick before driving into her. His movements were hard and rough, almost angry as he sought her release and his.

It came fast and powerfully, dragging them both over while he continued pumping his hips into her, extending the pleasure of the moment until his arms trembled and sweat dripped off him and onto her. Until they both could barely breathe from the shock of the passion still gripping their bodies in its aftermath.

Finally spent, he dropped down beside her, his body heavy and damp with sweat. The ends of his longish hair were wet with it as she wrapped her arms around him and soothed him. She kissed the side of his face and whispered, "Thank you."

Chapter 8

Victor wanted more than her thanks, but he couldn't say it, aware he would drive her away.

He understood now why she feared the intimacy. Why she had likely kept herself innocent of the demands of human passion and pleasure.

With passion such as this, it would be tough not to lose sight of who she was. Not to sacrifice herself the way her father had—giving up his life beneath the ocean for Nali's mother, an act that had brought him great joy but also immense sadness.

Victor had seen that melancholy in her father when he had first met him, and now he knew the reasons for it. Yet he had also seen the joy when Saila had spoken of both his wife and his daughter. He suspected the old man would not have given up that happiness for anything in the world.

That was a lesson Nali would one day have to learn.

He just hoped he would be the man she chose to teach her that joy.

He lay down beside her and splayed his hand across her sculpted midsection, which shivered beneath his touch as she recovered from the aftermath of their loving. Along the smooth skin of her hip, his cock grew flaccid, but even with that, the temptation of her still-puckered breasts was too much for him to resist.

He bent and kissed the tips, the touch of his lips reverent. His mind was absorbing every minute detail of her in case she might leave him only memories.

Nali sighed with pleasure at the tender caress of his mouth against her breasts. The tips were overly sensitive and even his most gentle actions awoke need deep between her legs.

She was sore there. She had never been sore before. Never allowed herself such multiple intimacies with any man or even any of her people on land or in their true form in the sea.

As she shifted her legs, trying to assuage the want to have his touch again, he raised his head and met her gaze. He let the hand that had been on her abdomen drift down until his fingers just brushed the nest of curls in her center.

Her breath soughed from her, faster and faster as he skimmed his fingers against her and she came from just that touch.

She knew then that she could not stay the week. She could not stay another second.

"I am lost in you," she said as she bolted from the bed and raced out the door of the shack.

Victor could not move as fast, hampered as he was by the wound in his side. But he chased after her as best he could, only to see her dive cleanly into the midnight blue of the ocean and disappear beneath the glass surface of the sea.

He cursed beneath his breath. He hadn't meant to drive her away, but he just couldn't keep his hands off of her.

He stood at the shore's edge, searching for any sign of Nali.

Only the silvery glitter of the moonlight greeted him, but he could not leave until he knew she was safely home.

Nali propelled herself through the water, her strong arms and legs pulling and kicking her forward and through the intricacies of the coral reef. It was harder to navigate at night in her human form, the darkness making it difficult to see beneath the surface. As she turned one corner, she nicked her arm on the coral and a ribbon of blood leaked from the scratch.

It would attract the sharks, especially at night, leaving her no choice but to morph back into her true form. Back into the predator that she was—the hunter and not the prey.

Pain radiated throughout her body as bone, muscle and skin transformed, legs joining together into the thick powerful tail of her shark form. Her face flattened into the broad snout and jaws as her shark spirit assumed control.

As the faint trace of her human blood brought a few inquisitive sharks closer, her change completed and she emitted an immense underwater roar, chasing away most nearby marine life.

But even in her natural state, a new sense of restlessness lay deep in her heart. One that she tried to drive away by racing through the sea, putting distance between herself and the shore, where she knew he waited.

She had seen him there for only a moment, but it was long enough to see the determination on his face. To see the yearning in his eyes for something that could never be.

Never ever, she said to herself as she reached the edge of the reef and the drop-off to open ocean—the route to safety.

Few of the local fishermen ventured this far out in search of her, and luckily, outsiders were still few in this part of the world.

For good measure, she dived down into the midnight inkiness, where even during daylight there was little light. In that murky darkness she swam, circling the ocean floor over and over. Hoping to drive away the sight of him, the feel and taste of his humanity, which had proved far more tempting than she had thought possible.

She understood her father better now, although it didn't make her situation any easier.

Over and over, round and round she went, but as the hours passed, she realized just how futile an exercise swimming away might be. Even with that insight she had to try to forget him. Forget that which she could not forget.

And so she swam, giving rein to the animal spirit within her. Protecting the unique gift the sea had given her people and which she could not reject for any reason.

Not even for love.

After an hour of standing, searching the ocean for the familiar sight of her fin cutting a swath through the water, Victor had plopped down on the sand to wait for her.

It wasn't much later that her father joined him, settling himself on the sand, a bottle of his homemade liquor in one hand and two glasses in the other.

Victor waved him off, recalling well the bite of the alcohol and the aftermath of its sting.

With a shrug, Saila poured himself a glass and sat there, sipping it for long minutes until he finally said, "You may have a very long wait, *mi'jo.*"

"I'm a patient man."

Saila chuckled. "The last time she ran off like this was when her mother died. I didn't see Nali for nearly a year."

He jerked his head around to stare at the old man. "A year? Didn't you worry something had happened?"

Saila nodded and then took another sip. "Every day. Every day I rode out into the deep ocean, slid into her embrace and called out for my daughter, but she didn't come."

Victor arched a brow. "You can call for her?"

With a shrug, Saila explained. "It's one of the few powers left from what I once was—a sonic cry if you wish."

Interesting, Victor thought. He had picked up a stray sound pattern or two from his monitoring stations and had thought they were from dolphins or a passing school of whales. Now he had another possibility.

"Why do you think she would not return?"

"Pain. Anger," Saila answered quickly. "There was nothing we could do when her mother got sick. Illness and that kind of death are hard for Nali to understand."

"Your people do not get sick or die?"

Saila shook his head. "Not like that. We are a strong race, so strong that even our hybrid children possess the full powers of our people."

He eyed Nali's father up and down. Roped muscles were evident on his wiry body and Victor had seen first-hand proof of his strength as he had worked beside the man on several occasions. But he was old. Human-old as far as he could tell.

"So you will not die?" he asked, seeking clarification.

"I will die just like any human. When I chose to stay on land, I gradually lost almost all the gifts of my people."

Nali would see that as both a betrayal and something to fear, for both her people and herself.

"I do not wish to change Nali. I only want time to explore what I feel for her."

Saila finished his drink and poured himself another. "It always begins that way, but then the time together is too short. The absences are felt more strongly. Some cannot handle the separation and part ways. Others sacrifice themselves and lose who they are. What they are."

Nali's parting words came back to him, jabbing at his heart as painfully as the spear that had pierced his side.

I am lost in you.

He didn't want her to be anything other than what she was, but the heartache he sensed in Saila was too keen not to ignore. The old man had lost both daughter and wife because of his decision.

A difficult and almost impossible choice. One that Nali obviously did not wish to consider.

"I think I'll take that drink now," he said, and the old man poured him a full glass.

He grimaced at the first bite of the alcohol, which deadened his taste buds and warmed him from his gullet to his stomach. With each sip the world became a little fuzzier and the ache in his heart dimmed. But only a little.

He was only about a quarter of the way done with the glass when he decided he'd had enough. He had never liked being drunk and it wouldn't solve anything. Plus he wanted to go into the water tomorrow in search of Nali. A wetsuit would protect his side and, although he couldn't manage the air tanks thanks to the injury, he could snorkel.

Pushing off from the wet sand, he stumbled on his feet, head dizzy from a combination of alcohol and fatigue.

Saila was immediately at his side, shaking his head and tsking. "Shame when a grown man can't handle his liquor," he teased.

"If you can call that rot gut liquor," Victor said as they walked together to the steps of Nali's shack. He paused at the base of the stoop, looking back out to sea. The surface was smooth as glass with not a break to be seen in the moonlight.

Saila tracked his gaze and then sighed. He understood what it was to wait for her and be disappointed.

"Rest, *mi' jo*. You'll need strength to be patient."

Victor nodded and hurried to bed. The sheets were in disarray from their lovemaking, and it took all his resolve to straighten them and climb back in.

They smelled like her, clean and sharp like a brisk ocean wind. The alcohol had loosened some of his control and he grew hard at her lingering fragrance and the memories of her. At the image of her playful grin and her tears.

He hated that he had brought her those tears.

Forcing Nali from his mind, he urged himself to rest. He needed to finish healing so he could go in search of her. So he could show her he was not a threat to what she was and what she wanted in her life.

Sleep claimed him with each breath until he was snoring softly and deep in dreams.

* * *

That sound sleep kept him from hearing her soft footfall at the threshold of the shack.

Nali braced her hand on the jamb and stared at his back. His muscles were relaxed, the skin tanned by the potent Caribbean sun. That golden expanse of skin was marred by the glaring white of the bandages around his midsection and the scars along his upper body.

The scars of a hero.

And like the hero he was, he had both saved her and doomed her.

No matter how hard she'd tried, she had not been able to stay away, even for a night. She itched to walk over and lay with him. Make love to him again.

But if she did, would it only entrap her more? Set the hook like a fish caught on a line? Or could she break free of the net in which he'd snared her?

With a hesitant step across the threshold, she walked toward him until she was at the bed. He was sprawled across it now, his big bulk taking up most of the space. She hadn't realized how immense he was and how much room he took, maybe because they'd been plastered together the entire time.

She eased beneath the sheets and, with a shove, woke him.

He jumped at the action, rolling to face her. Surprise gave way to joy on his face. "You came back."

"It's my house, remember?" she joked, unable to give the true reason for her return.

He grinned and nodded. "It is. Thanks for sharing."

As much as she wanted to make love to him again, she

needed rest also. The jumble of emotions and the energy needed for her to shapeshift had drained her.

He seemed to sense that as he hauled her near and whispered, "Let's get some rest."

With her head pillowed on his chest, she listened to the steady lub-dub of his heart and the sound of his breathing. Both had a peaceful rhythm now, unlike the frantic hammering and roughness after they'd made love. She matched her breath to his, allowing that calm cadence to lull her to sleep.

In the morning they would talk. And make love, she thought with a smile. That was the one thing of which she was sure.

In the morning they would make love.

Chapter 9

He smiled as the weight of her on his chest registered and her pleasant heat bathed his body.

He cracked one eye open and peered down, almost afraid that if he woke, she'd vanish before his eyes.

But she didn't. Instead she burrowed tighter and tossed her thigh over his, pinning him to the mattress, murmuring a protest when he dragged in a deep breath and stretched out a morning kink.

"Good morning," he said, skimming his fingers up and down her back.

She inched open an eye and stared up at him. "Hmm. Is it good?"

Because he was already hardening beneath the smooth heat of her thigh, it possibly was, but this morning he needed more than just her body.

"That all depends," he said and shifted from beneath her to lie on his side and gaze at her.

Nali seemed to understand what he wanted. She likewise

shifted to her side and faced him, lay her hand on his chest and tenderly stroked back and forth across the thick muscle there before settling her hand over his heart.

"You're asking me for more than I can give."

Victor smiled sadly and hooked his arm around her waist, fearing she would bolt again as she had last night.

"Is it so hard to consider loving me, Nali?"

An indignant laugh escaped her. "Love. My parents had that, and what did it get them? Death? Loneliness?"

"But you're alone now, aren't you? You've been alone for a long time, whereas they had years and years of happiness."

A rejoinder was impossible because in her heart Nali knew the truth of his words. But she wanted him to understand where she stood.

"I will not leave the ocean to live on land."

"I would never ask that of you. The ocean is the one place where I also feel free."

Nali narrowed her gaze. "Why? Why do you feel so trapped on land?"

He shrugged. "After the accident, the pain from the burns and broken bones was unbearable at times. Once I healed enough, the water was the one place where that pain would go away."

Nali moved her hand upward to trace the edge between smooth and scarred flesh. "Your life before was ruled by fire just as mine has always been controlled by water."

He shook his head. "Just elements, like air and earth. They might bind us physically, but what we feel in here," he said and tapped his chest, "is what truly sets us free."

Not understanding, she glanced up at him and begged him with her gaze to explain.

"It wasn't just that the weight on my physical body was gone in the water. It was the weight on my spirit. I finally recognized that being a firefighter wasn't really my dream, but my father's. That's when I decided to change my life and do what I always wanted to do."

Nali had never wanted anything other than the basics. That simplicity of life had been the way of her people forever. But some had grown to want more. Her father had wanted more, and up until Victor, she had not understood that want.

Now she did.

"I want you, but I also want my life in the sea."

"You can have both. I promise that."

"I want to seal that promise," she said and before he could respond, she surged up and covered his mouth with hers. She sealed the promise with a kiss from the heart he had awakened with his love.

Victor accepted her gift, letting her set the pace as she explored his mouth, her lips skimming lightly before she deepened the kiss, opening her mouth on his, accepting the slide of his tongue to taste her and dance in celebration.

Over and over they kissed, sharing breath and life through that simple connection until they were both breathing roughly and needing more.

He grazed the tips of her breasts with the back of his hand and they puckered instantly beneath his touch. Smiling against her lips, he said, "I love how sensitive your tits are. How they get tight for me."

She chuckled and unerringly found him with her hand, stroked him and said, "Your cock is just as responsive."

When she ran a finger along the sensitive head of him,

he jumped from the overwhelming sensation. He sucked in a breath and held it, reining in his need.

They had satisfied passion well in their short time together. This time he wanted it to be about more. He wanted it to be about the promise they had made to each other.

"Do you trust me, Nali?"

Wide-eyed, she nodded and he urged her to her back but gently eased her thigh over his hip, his front to her side. The position let him bend to kiss her mouth and her deliciously hard nipples. But it also let him slowly slide into her vagina from behind while dipping his hand down to part her center and find the nub buried there.

She gasped against his mouth at his possession, but he whispered, "I want to take it slow this time."

Nali heard his words through the haze of desire gripping her body. Her head rested on his arm and as he leaned over her to suckle her breasts, he rubbed her clit while filling her with his thick length. There wasn't an ion of her that wasn't aware of him and his possession.

Every part of her ached for the sensations he was creating to never end.

When he bit down gently on one hard nub, she called out his name and fisted her hand in his hair, dragged him forward so she could sample his mouth again, nip at his full lower lip and savor the spill of his warm breath.

"Nali, you are so lovely."

She yanked on his hair again, pulling him away so she could see his face and gauge the truth of it because she wasn't used to such man-woman things. All she saw was love and honesty.

Skimming her hand down his arm, she twined her fingers with his and said, "You're beautiful, too, Victor."

He smiled and it reached up into those sea-blue eyes that glittered as if kissed by the midday sun. "I'm glad I please you."

She dipped her gaze to where they were joined and playfully drew their hands there, a lighthearted laugh escaping her as she teased, "Then please me some more."

His broad, unrepentant grin filled her with warmth as he bent and whispered against her lips, "That will be my pleasure and yours."

With a sure hand and his gifted mouth, he proceeded to show her, bringing her to the peak and then dragging her over with the first powerful thrust of his hips. Her body trembled around him as her climax nearly swamped her, but then he kept up his kisses and caresses and started a steady, determined stroke of his hips that had her clinging to him. Her back arched away from him as her release became a long, never-ending stream of pleasure so intense that for a moment her eyesight wavered.

"Easy, love. Easy," he urged as she held onto him, her nails digging into his flesh as her world reeled.

Victor gritted his teeth at the force of her climax, which threatened to pull him under like a riptide. Her vagina caressed and held him, the friction of it almost unbearable at the shift of his hips at her center, at the musky smell of her rising up and the delicious salty-sweetness of her nipples beneath his lips.

At the bite of her sharp nails into his skin, he grunted as that pain melded with the pleasure, reminding him that would be his life with her. Pain at her absence and this rapturous love with her presence.

He could deal with it, he thought and, nearly light-headed from desire, he stroked harder into her, faster, until she bucked off the bed with a long powerful release that he could no longer battle.

With a harsh grunt, he came, spilling his seed into her. Savoring the way her muscles milked him and she rose up to kiss him again, the whisper of her lips a benediction.

Gently he lowered himself to her side and wrapped his arm around her waist. She shimmied near and lay a hand on his thigh possessively. Neither one of them was going anywhere, he thought as long minutes passed and their tender, soothing caresses restored some semblance of sanity and calm.

"Will it always be like this?" she asked, that touch of innocence he had sensed earlier back in her voice.

"I hope so," he answered honestly.

That earned a small smile from her as she closed her eyes and said, "I'm tired. I'd like to sleep now."

She didn't wait for him to do just that, dropping off almost immediately.

She was funny that way, so basic in her needs. Maybe because her life until now had been that straightforward. Food and rest. Night and day. Uncomplicated and simple.

Until he had interceded in her life and changed everything.

He grinned at that, not in the least bit upset with how he had shaken up her existence because she had done the same to his.

Lying there, he let his mind wander to what their life

together might be like. He considered what they would do next.

Besides eat, he thought as his stomach rumbled noisily.

Not wanting to wake her, he slipped from the bed and over to the long counter along the far wall of the shack. He busied himself with cutting up ripe fruit he had picked from the nearby trees and plants. Luscious mangos and papayas. Ripe bananas. Then he scrounged around in the icebox, which still had a small chunk of ice in it. He pulled out a hunk of a native white cheese and sliced it up for some protein. Maybe later he could visit Saila or the nearby village for something more substantial, he thought as he finished prepping the meal.

Nali woke to the sound of his moving about. As she opened her eyes, she noticed him standing naked by the counter, working on something.

He had a beautiful ass. She had noticed that about him one time when he had skinny-dipped while out by the reef. As he turned with the tray in hand, she appreciated the other side of him and the cock that hung down his thigh.

"Like what you see?" he teased and sauntered over, a brash swagger to his gait.

Chapter 10

Nali refused to let him get a swelled head. "The food looks great."

He chuckled, but instead of returning to the bed, he set the tray down on the hand-hewn table off to one side of the room. It sat beneath an open window, which faced the ocean, and he took a seat and gave her a come-over jerk of his head.

She supposed they couldn't spend all their time in bed, as pleasant as it might be. Rising, she grabbed hold of her dress from the chair where he must have neatly folded and placed it. She eased it on, hiding herself from him.

At the table, she took the spot adjacent to him. The table was so narrow their knees bumped beneath its surface.

Snagging a piece of mango, she was about to feed him but then remembered what that had led to last time. Popping the fruit into her mouth, she chewed on it thoughtfully before trailing her fingers along the bandage at his side.

"How is it feeling?"

He shrugged. "I barely notice it."

"I'll have a look at it and change your dressings after we eat."

"Thanks," he said and then fell silent while he ate the fruit and cheese.

Nali was not so inclined. "You said your father was a firefighter."

"My dad and his dad and every Edwards going back to the first one who set foot in New York. What about your family?"

"My father is—was—like me. My mother was Kuna. Her family came here when the Kuna fled the Spanish in Panama."

Victor treaded carefully because he knew of Nali's conflict with her parents and their relationship. "Your mother must have been very special."

A broad smile erupted across Nali's lips and remembered joy lit up the dark grey of her eyes. "She was. She was a wonderful cook and so funny. She could always make me laugh."

"So the way to your heart is with food and jokes?" he teased, trying to keep the conversation from getting too serious.

"Definitely food, as long as you don't feed me fish. I am so tired of eating fish," she said with a laugh and a shake of her head.

Victor joined in her laughter but murmured, "Damn, there go the dinner plans."

"Baba—"

"Baba?" he asked.

"My father. He usually goes to town for meat when I come to shore."

Victor nodded. "I'll go see him when we finish."

"No, I'll go. I need to spend some time with him, but first, let me check your side."

Without waiting for his reply, she popped out of her chair and back to the cupboards above the counter where she had stored the medical supplies. She removed them and then walked back.

He eased the chair away from the table and waited for her, moved by the sight of her, by the ease with which she moved, as comfortable on land now as in the sea.

It was impossible to fight his arousal nor did he wish to. She had told him it was as natural as breath and maybe it was, at least with her.

She said nothing about his state as she kneeled beside him to examine his side. With calm efficiency she removed the wrappings and gauze and examined the wounds.

"They are closed. It won't be long until they are completely healed."

She popped up again and returned to the counter to fill the basin with water and grab a clean towel. Once she was kneeling beside him again, she tenderly washed away the healing paste and he noticed the stellar-shaped wound where new skin was already knitting closed.

"Chicks dig scars," he said, recalling what one of his firefighter buddies had told him as he lay all bandaged up in the hospital.

One side of Nali's mouth tilted in a smile. She rose to her knees and brushed a kiss across his lips.

"Chicks dig heroes," she said and then returned to her task, cleaning and drying his side, then applying a different kind of ointment before binding him up once more.

She set the supplies on the table behind him, and as she did so, her breast grazed his arm. The touch, innocent as it was, tightened his balls and made him ache as his cock swelled.

As she stepped back from the table, she didn't fail to notice. But she didn't act on it either. Instead she surprised him by saying, "Are you up for a walk?"

He was up for something totally different, but he didn't want her to think all he wanted from her was to fuck.

"Let me just get some clothes." He began to rise, but she lay a tender hand on his shoulder.

"You're fine the way you are."

He skimmed his gaze up and down her loose, flowing dress and then arched a brow. "Seems kinda unfair, doesn't it?"

"It does." Grinning, she quickly ripped off her dress and tossed it on her chair.

The beauty of her slammed into his gut once more. He had never seen such a gorgeous woman, much less one who seemed to be so comfortable in her own skin.

Her human skin, he thought, although she had been just as sure, maybe more so, in the water.

Rising from the chair, he slipped his hand into hers, lacing his fingers with hers. Together they walked out of the shack and into the late morning sun, which was already strong enough to burn if you weren't careful. They kept to the shade provided by the palm trees and underbrush not far from the shore, strolling away from the shacks, talking once again about their lives and what had brought them here.

Nali listened, lightness in her heart and soul as he regaled her with a story from his days as a firefighter. When he finished, she said, "You loved your friends there."

Victor smiled and shook his head. "I did but not the job.

This is where I was meant to be," he said and opened his arms wide.

She stepped to him and tenderly ran her hand over his scarred shoulder and arm, her breasts barely grazing the hard wall of his chest. "I'm glad you're here."

He cradled her waist with his hands. They were so big they almost encircled her. Big, but gentle, she thought as he used tender pressure to draw her near.

"I'm glad, too," he said and brought his lips to hers, his kiss light at first as he traced the edges of her mouth and nipped at her lower lip with his teeth before opening his mouth on hers.

She sighed, her breath mingling with his as they kissed, but there was something different in this interlude. Something far more lasting than the spark of passion that flared so brightly before burning out. As the kiss went on and on, it kindled warmth deep in her heart. A heat far more enduring when love kept it banked.

Love.

She hadn't expected it. Didn't want it, but standing there beside him, experiencing emotions she never had before, she didn't think she could live without it now.

She didn't think she could live without him.

She pulled away from him then, knowing now why she had been so restless after her headlong rush back to the sea that was her home.

He was her home now.

And he had promised to let her be who and what she was. She had to believe in that promise; otherwise she was lost.

A gust of wind kicked up then, pulling her from her thoughts.

She glanced upward and noticed the roiling clouds,

smelled the storm that was about to strike. A second later the first fat raindrop plopped on her upturned face, but she didn't run. She stood there, arms outstretched, reveling in the sensation of the cool water sluicing down her body. The chill of it against her sun-warmed skin caused her nipples to pucker.

He was there suddenly, wrapping his arms around her body, laughing as he twirled her around in the rain until the storm had passed as quickly as it came.

But the storm inside them had only begun, she thought as he guided her to the shade beneath some palms and sat on the bank of low wild grasses. He pulled her down with him and she went willingly, straddling his legs. No hesitation in her as she guided his cock to her center and sank down on him.

Their satisfied sighs filled the air and they just sat there, joined, peaceful for long moments until he cupped her breasts, his hands slick from the rain. Leisurely, he caressed her tight nipples until she had to move on him to satisfy the ache caused by the tug and pull of his fingers.

Between her legs, his dick warmed and filled her. The friction of him and the length butting up into her had her dripping wet. Her movements on him grew faster, harder, as she sought release, and when he bit down on her taut nipples, she came in a long rush of pleasure.

He joined her, his breath rough against her breasts. His arms encircled her tightly as she rode him, drawing out the pleasure of their union until she could no longer move.

Cradled together, they lingered until some semblance of calm had returned and they ventured out into the sun to dry off.

Holding hands, they returned to the shack.

Saila must have stopped by in their absence. More fresh fruit filled the bowl on the counter, and when Nali peeked in their ice box, she saw a new chunk of ice and as an assortment of meats. Nali smiled at her father's thoughtfulness, and together she and Victor prepared a meal before falling into bed and into each other once again.

The next few days passed in that same pleasurable mix of passion and coming to understand one another. It was because of that understanding that he knew she had to leave. He walked to the water's edge with her.

"I will be waiting," he said as he kissed her, sealing the promise.

"I'll be back," she replied and then waded out into the deeper water, diving down and through the tangle of reef until she was safe to morph into her true form and disappear into the yawning waters.

As much as she wanted to come back in her shark form and play with him in the shallower areas in the reef, the incident a week earlier had shown her the insanity of it. She would not risk her life or his for those playful moments.

So she prowled the ocean depths, restless as always, only now she knew the reason for it. Knew there would be an end to it shortly.

The days passed, possibly too slowly, but she bided her time, aware that she had to be strong enough to morph and maintain her human form. That would only come with time or with sacrifice.

Like her father's sacrifice. He had used up all of his powers to become human, but she couldn't. As much as she was missing Victor, she would miss her life in the ocean possibly as much.

When the day finally came, she moved back toward the

reef, transforming as her sleek body reached the shallower waters. She rose from the surf to find him sitting at the water's edge, waiting.

His bright smile filled her with warmth greater than that of the sun's rays as they touched her body. He jumped up and strode into the water, unwilling to wait. He grabbed her in his arms and hugged her close.

He kissed her hard and with such longing her insides twisted with both guilt and want.

"I've missed you," he said between kisses.

"And I, you," she confessed.

He sank down with her in the waist-high water and reached between their bodies to cradle her breast. He swiped his thumb across her nipple, which was already tight with need.

"I can't wait," he said and to prove it, he used the buoyancy of the water to lift her and replace his hand with his mouth. He sucked on her nipple and she wrapped her hands around his head and held him to her.

She couldn't wait either.

She wrapped her legs around him and accepted the slide of his cock deep inside. He filled her, physically and emotionally, and she wasn't sure she could ever get enough of how he made her feel.

Victor groaned at the warmth of her surrounding him and the salty-sweet taste of her breasts against his mouth.

It had been a difficult week without her. Lonely and frustrating. When he had seen her rising from the surf, the real-life Venus from his dream, he hadn't been able to wait to have her.

He suckled her, loving her tits with his mouth, biting

and licking and savoring the response of her body, the soft cries and the way she clenched his cock with her pleasure.

He loved the way her body worked his dick, the way her vagina squeezed and caressed him. Her hot wetness was a temptation impossible to refuse.

But soon that wasn't enough and he had to move in her, had to take them higher, push them over the edge.

He rose with her, her strong legs still wrapped around his waist, his erection buried deep, and strode through the surf until they were almost out of the water. Almost, but not quite, he thought as he carried her down into the gentle wash of the sea.

The water caressed her body as the waves ebbed in and out gently. He moved in her, made love to her breasts and mouth, pulling her ever higher toward a release. He shifted his hips in and out of her until she cradled his hips and arched her back to deepen his penetration. Her body bowed tight with her passion as the wash of the ocean spilled around them.

He was on the edge, reaching for their completion. He found the mark with one powerful thrust that shifted them upward on the sand and had them both shouting out their pleasure.

He dropped down on her, spent, his cock jerking and spilling his seed as she drew him in with the final contractions of her climax.

She rubbed her hands up and down his back, soothing him. Her gentle touch was so welcome after their week of separation.

When some semblance of strength had returned to his legs, he swept her up into his arms, surged to his feet and hurried with her into the shack where he had prepped the makings of a steak dinner for her.

"How did you know I was on my way home?" she asked as she glanced at the counter and he let her slide down his body.

He shrugged. "I just knew."

She smiled and twined her fingers with his and rubbed her other hand up and down his forearm with gratefulness.

"Thank you," she said with such emotion that he glanced down at her, confused.

"It's just a steak."

But it wasn't. It was so much more.

"You understand me. That I need to leave you to be me."

He nodded, turned and took her into his arms again, cradling her head close to his chest, where the strong steady beat of his heart registered beneath her ear. Strong and steady, like he was.

"I understand, and as hard as it is for me to see you leave, the joy of having you back is that much greater."

She smiled, rose on tiptoe and kissed him again, grateful for that. She loved him even more for that sacrifice.

"I will always come back to you," she promised and opened her mouth on his, inviting him to love her yet again.

His smile was alive against her mouth as he gave himself to her once more, whispering his vow as he led her to their bed.

"And I will always be waiting."

* * * * *

THE DARKEST EMBRACE

MEGAN HART

Megan Hart began writing short fantasy, horror and science fiction before graduating to novel-length romances. In 1998, Megan took up writing in earnest, attending her first writing conference and getting her first request for a full manuscript. In 2002 she saw her first book in print, and she hasn't stopped since.

She's published in almost every genre of romantic fiction, including historical, contemporary, romantic suspense, romantic comedy, futuristic, fantasy and perhaps most notably, erotic. She also writes non-erotic fantasy and science fiction, as well as continuing to occasionally dabble in horror.

Megan's goal is to continue writing spicy, thrilling love stories with a twist. Her dream is to have a movie made of every one of her novels, starring herself as the heroine and Keanu Reeves as the hero. Megan lives in the deep, dark woods with her husband and two monsters…er…children.

To learn more about her, visit www.meganhart.com or find her MySpace page at http://www.myspace.com/author_m.

Chapter 1

The GPS's carefully modulated female voice had informed them it was "recalculating" twenty minutes ago, and so far the percentage bar at the top of the unit had remained at a solid, unyielding and entirely unhelpful eighty-eight percent. Jessie wasn't worried—they were on a major highway, the scenery was pretty and she was with Max. She didn't mind the drive.

Max, on the other hand, had already apologized several times, sheepishly admitting he hadn't bothered to print out directions or look at a map beforehand. Now he gave a frustrated sigh and reached to reset the device. "I'm sorry, Jessie. I really didn't think Karen would let me down."

Karen? Jessie kept her expression neutral. She'd known Max for nearly five months. They'd been dating seriously for three. He'd often referred to an "ex"—sometimes the "evil ex" and sometimes "that crazy woman I was with," and once, after a night of too many beers, he went so far as to say "that insane fucking bitch." It was the only time Jessie had ever heard him swear. It had been so sexy that she'd have pounced him right then and there if they'd been alone instead of in the middle of his best friend's living room at a party. He'd never said his ex's name.

"Recalculating," the GPS said.

"Shut up, Karen," Max said, visibly irritated, and shot Jessie another apologetic look. "Sorry."

Jessie burst into laughter. "Karen's the GPS?"

He nodded, watching the road as he fiddled with the unit. "Yeah, you can pick the voice for it. John, Alex, Lisa…"

"And you picked Karen." Jessie laughed again, wishing she could lean over to kiss his face right off but keeping herself in her seat instead. There'd be plenty of time for kissing when they got to the cabin—at least if she had anything to do with it.

"Yep." Max grinned.

Jessie melted.

They'd been introduced by Jessie's friend Kelly, who was dating Max's friend Len. Kelly had confided to Jessie that Max had had a spectacularly bad breakup that he wasn't really ready to date anyone, that he was a super-sweet and nice guy who wasn't going to expect a lot from her, but they really needed another couple to get this great deal on a night out at the local casino, and would Jessie please, please, please do Kelly this favor and agree to go out with him? Jessie, wary because Kelly had set her up with a couple of real douche bags in the past, had only agreed because Kelly promised to pay for her share of the night out. As far as Jessie was concerned, a steak dinner and a hundred bucks' credit for the slots was worth a night out even with a total jerk—though Max had turned out to be anything but. He was everything Kelly had promised, and more. They'd become an easy foursome after that for nights out, and after a few weeks, Max had hesitantly asked to exchange phone numbers "so we don't have to go through Kelly if we want to get together." Five months later, they were on their way for a weekend of camping in the remote wilds of northwestern Pennsylvania, and Jessie was determined that it was going to be a romantic weekend getaway.

Their first.

Five months since that first "not a date," three months since Max had asked her if it would be okay if they went to the movies without Kelly and Len. He'd taken her to see a truly awful superhero flick and left her on her doorstep with nothing but a kiss on the cheek. Since then, they'd graduated to casual hand-holding, a few make-out sessions that had always been inconveniently interrupted by one thing or another and a lot of increasingly suggestive text message exchanges. Max was a flirt, but he seemed more comfortable with innuendo over the phone or online than in person. He'd told her he thought people took things too fast, and while it had been refreshing at first to discover he was such a gentleman, Jessie was ready for more.

So funny, she thought, watching him as he concentrated on the road ahead, occasionally glancing at the GPS to confirm they were still on route. Five months of being together almost every day, if not in person, then on the phone or messaging, had taught her a lot about Max. Jessie knew his favorite color, his brand of cologne, that he hated raisins cooked in anything and called them "Satan's boogers." She knew the name of his first dog, where he'd grown up, his shoe size and that he loved pecan pie but hated lemon meringue. She knew so many bits and pieces of him that she didn't doubt she knew the whole…except for the parts about his ex. That was an open, blank space in the lexicon of Max.

They were both in the early thirties with several relationships under their belts. Jessie, in fact, had been married once already to her college sweetheart, Doug. He'd been vindictive and nasty, fought with her over money and levied accusations at her with such vehemence that Jessie had found it difficult to believe she'd ever once loved this guy enough to think she could spend the rest of her life with him. Yet, to her, Doug still had a name. He was an asshole, but she wouldn't have called him crazy. She wasn't afraid to talk about the mistakes she'd made with him, but she didn't feel like she had to go over them ad infinitum either. She understood Max's hesitance in moving forward, but not his completely closed-mouth attitude about it. Whatever had gone on with Max and his mysterious ex must have been horrifying to have affected him that way.

"In point two miles," Karen intoned, "take exit 4A on the left."

"We're almost there." Max tapped the steering wheel and gave Jessie another grin. "Just about another forty-five minutes or so once we get off the highway."

"Good." Jessie shifted in her seat. She needed to use the bathroom, stretch her legs, soothe the growing rumble in her stomach. They hadn't stopped since lunch, both of them eager to make the four-hour trip as fast and easy as possible.

"It's so beautiful here," she said a few minutes later when they'd taken the exit as Karen instructed and then another couple of side roads. Tall evergreens rose on both sides of the road, so thick she couldn't see more than a few feet beyond the twisting two-lane road. "How'd you find out about this place?"

Max shrugged. "Online. A buddy of mine told me about this site where you can book out-of-the-ordinary weekend getaways—stay in a castle or a tree house, things like that. I figured a cabin in the woods wasn't all that exotic, but I wasn't sure you'd be into something…weirder."

"So long as there's indoor plumbing and hot water, I'm good." She looked at him when he didn't answer. "There is indoor plumbing, right? And hot water?"

He burst into laughter, looking at her. "Yes, there's—"

"Look out!" Caught up in looking at him, Jessie hadn't been paying attention to the road in front of them. A dark flash of something big moving in front of them caught her gaze.

Max swerved. The Chevy Suburban shuddered as it crossed what would have been the center line on a bigger road. The tires dipped into the rut on the side of the road as Max yanked the wheel in the other direction, keeping the big vehicle from going into the ditch but sending them bouncing so hard that Jessie's seat belt locked against her shoulder and neck. The suitcases in the back rattled, the clink and clank of bottles in the boxes of food they'd brought along becoming the alarming crunch of broken glass. Jessie was sure the SUV was going to cross the road completely and hit the trees on the other side, but it came to a skewed stop with a squeal of brakes.

"Are you okay?" Max unbuckled his seat belt to lean across to her. "Jessie?"

Touched that his first thought was for her but a little too shaken to speak, she nodded. Something big and dark moved at the passenger side window, skittering around the back of the Suburban. With a gasp, she twisted in her seat to look out the back window.

"Something's back there," she said.

Max looked, too, but the road on both sides was still clear of anything but asphalt and shadows. "Did you see what it was?"

"No." Jessie took a few calming breaths. "It was fast whatever it was."

"Deer probably. They're all over up here. Glad we didn't hit them." Max shook his head. "Thank God you were paying attention. Hey, you sure you're okay?"

He scooted closer to twist a tendril of her hair away from her face. When he leaned in to kiss her, Jessie slipped a hand up to cup the back of his neck, holding him close. The kiss started off sweet but lingered, turning sexy. Max broke it, his lips still so close they brushed hers with every word.

"We stopped really suddenly. You might be a little sore," he whispered.

"Maybe you'll have to give me a massage," Jessie whispered back and kissed him again, her mouth open and waiting for his tongue.

He gave it to her in soft, slow strokes that got faster when she moved against him. His fingers wound in her hair, tugging a little to bring her closer. Everything inside her melted and turned liquid. Heat pooled low in her belly at the soft moan from the back of Max's throat. Her fingers found the seat belt buckle and unclicked it so she could slide across the bench seat toward him.

His mouth opened wider, their teeth clashing just a little as she moved. His hand in her hair pulled harder as she dug her fingers into his shoulders with one hand, the other high on his denim-clad thigh. She shivered at the bunch and shift of his muscles under her hand.

The rap of something hard on Max's window scared them both into breaking apart. Breathing hard, her heart already pounding from the taste of him, Jessie put a hand to the throbbing pulse at the base of her neck. Max had put out an arm to shield her, but relaxed a little at the sight of a black-and-red plaid shirt and a bearded face peering through the glass. The man on the other side of the window rapped again, a wide gold ring clinking on the glass.

"Sit back," Max murmured. He cracked the window a little, smart enough not to open it more than half an inch. "Hi."

"Youse okay?" The man leaned a little lower to stare across Max's shoulder at Jessie from under bushy eyebrows that raised a little when he saw her. "How 'bout you, ma'am? You all right?"

"Fine. We're both fine." Max cracked the window a little more. "Almost hit a deer."

"Yeah, they'll try to run you off the road around here, that's for damn sure." He nodded and took a step back from the Suburban as he tapped the roof, then bent again to look in the window. "Where you headed?"

"We're going…camping," Max said with a pause.

"Oh, up at Romero's, I bet?" The man's grin showed white, even teeth too large for his mouth. Jessie had thought him to be a lot older until she saw that grin—now she'd have put him in his late twenties instead of forties, and the change was startling.

Max glanced at her, then back at the stranger. "You know it?"

"Yeah, I know it. It's my brother's place. It's up the road

a ways. You'll have to take the next two lefts before you get to the lane. I can go ahead of you, if you want."

"That's okay," Max said evenly. "We have a GPS."

The man guffawed. "Good luck with that. We get shit service out here. Cell phones, too. Might as well use smoke signals for all the good they'll do. But, hey, if you just take the first two lefts, you'll get there. You can always stop in at Dave's Meats if you need more directions."

He thumped again on the roof and took another step back. He made a show of looking up and down the road, then at the SUV. "You didn't hit the deer, did you?"

"No, I don't think so." Max shook his head, already moving to put the SUV in gear.

"Good." The stranger's voice dipped so low for a second that it was almost impossible to hear him through the window. "Good you didn't hit it. Your tires, though. They look a little low."

"Yeah? Damn." Max craned his neck to look into the driver's side mirror as Jessie did the same on her side.

She couldn't see the tires, and she wasn't about to get out of the Suburban and look—or let Max. There was something creepy about that guy, something she couldn't put her finger on and was probably just her overactive imagination. Even so, there was going to be no getting out of the SUV.

Max must have had the same idea because he nodded at the guy through the window and put the truck in reverse, carefully executing a perfect three-point turn to get them back on the road in the right direction. As he pulled away, Jessie looked over her shoulder to watch the guy get smaller in the distance. That's when she realized what had been so strange. The man had needed to lean down to look in the Suburban's window, but the vehicle itself was huge.

"He must've been super-tall," she blurted, twisting again to look behind her, but the stranger had disappeared. "And where'd he come from anyway?"

"Hell if I know," Max answered as he took the first left. "But I sure hope he gave us good directions."

Max should have known better than to trust the GPS. Now he was going to look like an idiot to Jessie when they couldn't even make it to the cabin he'd spent so many hours carefully researching to find. He'd wanted this weekend to be perfect—romantic and sexy, just like Jessie herself—but it wasn't off to the greatest start.

"There," she said, pointing. "There's Garden Stop. Oh, and there's Dave's Meats."

It was a normal-looking gas station and convenience store with old-fashioned pumps out front but modern neon advertisements in the spotless plate glass window in the front. It also came complete with the obligatory sexless, ancient person in a rocking chair, smoking on a pipe. Max looked at the gas gauge and figured it was better to be safe than sorry. He pulled up to the pumps, but the sign said he had to prepay inside.

"No credit card payment," he said ruefully with a glance at Jessie who was peering around him at the front of the store. "We're really in the boonies."

She laughed and unbuckled her seat belt. The click of it reminded him of how she'd slid across the seat to him before, which reminded him of the way her mouth had felt on his and how she'd smelled and sounded, and then his dick

was starting to stir and he had to concentrate on something
else so he didn't embarrass himself.

"I hope they have a restroom," she said as she got out.
"And that it's not too gross."

They had more than a restroom—they had a full set of
showers, available for only five bucks, according to the sign.
HUNTERS WELCOME was hand-lettered on the faded
sign. Jessie looked at it, her mouth quirked in the half smile
that drove him a little too crazy for comfort.

"I'm sort of afraid to see what kind of shower they have
in there."

"I'll go inside, pay for the gas. You need anything else?"
he asked, thinking about the crash of glass from the back
of the truck. He should check it out, see what had broken
and what they might need to replace.

Ten minutes later, he'd paid for the gas inside. And while
it pumped, he'd opened up the truck's double back doors
to assess the damage. The plastic crate he'd packed with a
couple bottles of wine had tipped, and the rich earthy smell
of the good Bordeaux he'd picked because Jessie liked red
better than white hit him in a wave. Shit.

The damage got a little worse when he tried to pick up
the glass and promptly sliced his thumb at the base. Bright
blood welled to the surface, just a bead at first but then a
rapid gush as he cradled it to his chest. Jessie came around
the back of the truck just then, her mouth open to say something that she stifled at the sight.

"Max, what happened?"

"It's nothing. Just a flesh wound," he joked, knowing
she'd get the reference to Monty Python. They'd watched
it on one of their first dates.

She took his hand and looked at it, not even wincing at the sight of blood. She frowned. "No, it's not. That's pretty deep. What did you cut it on?"

"Wine bottle." He used his chin to show her the broken bottles inside, the dark wine splashed all over the rest of the groceries.

"Well," she said with a grin, "that's too bad, isn't it?"

A second later, though, she was frowning again in concern, his hand cupped in hers, her thumb pressing the wound to stanch the blood. "You need stitches. Or at least a bandage. C'mon, I'm sure they have something inside. Go wash your hands in the bathroom. I'll see what's in the store."

He wanted to protest, reassure her that he was fine. Manly enough to handle just a little flesh wound. The truth was, the cut was already throbbing, the blood flow slowing but caked into his skin, and the way the skin gaped was making his stomach hurt.

Jessie closed her hands over his, gently cupping his wounded thumb. "Go."

In the restroom, he used a paper towel to turn the hot water faucet until a trickle of first lukewarm, then scalding water shot out and splashed his front. Max did the best he could to clean it, but it was starting to hurt a lot more and he muttered a particularly creative string of curses.

Turning from the sink, he caught sight of the advertised shower, a narrow stall with a sagging, mildewed curtain shielding what looked like equally moldy tiles behind it and a steadily dripping showerhead. You'd have to pay him a helluva lot more than the five bucks they wanted to charge to get naked in that thing. On impulse, he twitched the curtain aside and stepped back at once with a stifled shout.

It looked like an abattoir.

Summers growing up as a kid, Max had spent a lot of time on his uncle's farm. Uncle Rick and Aunt Lori had raised a few dairy cows, kept a bull, a coop of chickens, one or two pigs. They kept animals for food, not profit, and definitely not for pets. Max had learned that the hard way after he'd adopted a spindle-legged calf named Doey. Years later, when he watched the film version of The Silence of the Lambs, the scene in which Clarice described the sound of the lambs screaming had sent him from the theater faster than any of Hannibal Lecter's tooth-sucking comments about fava beans. To this day, he couldn't eat veal.

The barn had looked like this shower stall the day he'd found them slaughtering Doey.

Max backed up so fast that the heel of his boot caught on a ridge of tile. To catch himself from falling, he flung out his injured hand. Fresh pain, bright and wide and thick, covered him, and he let out a yelp that echoed in the dimly lit room. He could smell it now, he thought. The stink of old, dried blood. And hear the soft buzz of flies battering themselves against the small window set high in the wall.

Shit and blood, that's what Uncle Rick had always said brought flies. Shit and blood.

Outside in the late-afternoon sunshine, the scene in the restroom seemed surreal. When he came around the corner, he found Jessie talking to the old woman/man sitting in the rocker on the front porch. Rather, the ancient lump of wrinkles and raggedy clothes was talking. Jessie seemed to be just listening.

"Stay out of the woods," the old person was saying.

Jessie glanced up at him, her expression so carefully neutral that he could tell she was trying hard not to laugh. "Thanks, Mrs. Romero."

"Who this?"

Jessie reached for Max's good hand to pull him closer. "This is Max, my boyfriend."

It wasn't the first time she'd called him that, but it was still so new the word tied knots in his gut. "Hi."

Mrs. Romero tipped her wizened face toward his, her eyes asquint, mouth still sucking greedily on the pipe. "You bleeding?"

"He cut his hand," Jessie explained, pulling out a package of gauze bandages and first aid supplies from a cheerfully bright yellow plastic bag. "I'm going to fix him up, though. He'll be okay."

This set Mrs. Romero cackling so much that she pulled the pipe from her lips to point it at Jessie. "Oh, I betcha. He'll be perfect."

Another burst of cackling laughter sent the old woman into a spate of thick, congested coughing that bent her forward so far that Max was sure she was going to tip right out of the rocker. The door behind Jessie opened and a blonde woman wearing jeans and a denim shirt came out to grab Mrs. Romero by the shoulders and keep her upright. It took Max a second or two to figure out what seemed so off about the woman: Just like the guy back on the road, the blonde woman was extremely tall.

She shot them both an apologetic look. "Sorry. Mom, Mom! Mom, you got to calm yourself."

Jessie backed up a few steps to get out of the way. "Sorry to upset her."

The blonde woman shrugged, patting Mrs. Romero on

the back until the coughing fit eased a little. Mrs. Romero fixed Max with a solid glare and pointed her pipe at him. "Perfect."

Somehow, the way she said it didn't make him feel perfect.

"Sorry," the blonde woman said again. "She's...old."

"We need to get going," Max said. "We're supposed to be getting to the cabin."

The blonde stood. "Oh, you're the renters? Freddy's been waiting for you so he can show you around, how to use the stove and stuff. You're late."

"We ran into a little trouble on the road," Max said. His hand gave a twinge.

She shielded her hand to look up at the sky. "You'd better get moving, then. It's getting dark and you don't want to try to unpack in the dark. Storm's coming."

"There aren't any lights?" Jessie asked with a quick glance his way.

"Gas lights," the woman said as she rubbed Mrs. Romero's back and the old woman turned her face to the side and spit on the porch floor. "Gas heat, stove, hot water. But you don't want to be out too long after dark, the bugs will eat you alive."

"Better bugs than Mrs. Romero," Jessie said with a soft giggle when they were back in the truck and she'd torn open the package of bandages to work on his hand.

An innuendo rose to his lips about being eaten by Jessie being better than anything, but he quashed it. What was so easy for him over text or instant message never came out right in person. Instead, he let her take his hand to clean it with the antiseptic wipes she'd bought. It stung, but that wasn't why he hissed in a breath. It was when Jessie took his hand and gently kissed the wound before pressing a gauze pad against it and wrapping it with a bandage that his heart skipped and thudded. Not to mention the rise in his pants.

Still cupping his hand in hers, she looked up at him from under her lashes. "This could make it hard for you to use your hand."

"Yeah…" Max croaked, throat suddenly dry.

"Well," Jessie said with a slowly spreading smile, "it's a good thing you can still use your mouth."

Chapter 2

The final trip to the cabin was as scenic and lovely as the first part of the journey, and thankfully much less eventful. Max eased the Suburban down increasingly narrow and isolated roads. Over a ravine, the wooden bridge little more than a series of heavy timbers. Past a few other cabins, some with lights or curious faces in the windows, but most dark. Then, finally, up a long, winding dirt track with the trees so close that they brushed the sides of the SUV, and...

"Wow," Jessie gasped at the sight of it.

The cabin featured two pretty gables and a covered wrap-around porch with carved columns and loads of intricately carved wooden gingerbread trim. Soft yellow light shone from the upper windows and from inside, but a brighter glow shone as they parked in front. At home there might still be light in the sky, but here in the forest, night was already close. The front door opened and a shadowy figure emerged holding a lantern. Jessie was already getting out of the truck, but paused at the sight. Surely the man wasn't ducking to get out through the door?

"Hi! Freddy Romero." The man held out his hand toward Max and gave Jessie a nod. "You're late. Got scared you weren't coming."

"Ran into a little trouble on the road," Max said.

Freddy gave a startlingly loud laugh, his teeth bright and shining in the growing dusk. "Deer."

"Yeah, how'd you know?"

"My brother Jason told me," Freddy said. "Said he came across you. Everything okay?"

Max nodded. "Yep."

Jessie moved closer to him to look around Freddy. "It's lovely here."

"Right, right. Let me show you around, get you settled. Get out of your way before the storm hits," Freddy said with a grin that was closer to a leer. "Give you your privacy."

The tour of the cabin took ten minutes, five minutes longer than necessary, as far as Jessie was concerned, because there wasn't really much to learn. Freddy paused in the doorway with his lantern, pointing out a list of places where they'd find instructions, if they needed them, for the hot water heater, the stove, the hot tub.

"Hot tub!" Jessie said happily with a grin at Max, who looked surprised. "Yay!"

"It's new," Freddy explained, and finally left them, closing the door behind him.

Jessie turned to Max, who was giving the cabin an appreciative looking-over. As soon as the door clicked shut, she was in his arms, her mouth on his. She wasn't sure at first if he'd catch her if she jumped, but when his fingers slid down her back to hook under the curves of her ass, she leaped. He caught. In just a few steps he'd carried her to the back of the couch facing the fireplace in the cabin's main living space—it was the perfect height for her to settle on with him standing between her legs.

They'd kissed before, lots of times, but this time there was a promise in the way his tongue moved against hers that hadn't been there before. Max reached up and tugged the elastic band from her ponytail and buried his fingers into the hair at the base of her neck, tipping her head back to he could get to her throat. His mouth moved over her tender skin. The press of his teeth made her gasp.

She wanted him like fire—had been wanting him for months. Jessie tugged Max's shirt from his jeans and ran her palm up his flat stomach. Warm skin. The tiny scruff of hair on his belly. A little higher, to the curve of his ribs, then down again to slip her fingers just inside his waistband. Not far…just…a little…

His cock, hard in his jeans, pressed her clit when he pushed his hips forward. Jessie spread her legs wider, hooking her ankles over the backs of his thighs. She leaned back a little, confident his hand between her shoulder blades would keep her from tumbling backward over the couch. Max mouthed her throat, nipping and sucking until she couldn't stop her moan. At the sound of it, he shuddered and opened a button on her blouse. Then another. One more, his mouth following the opening fabric, until he found the slopes of her breasts exposed by her demi-cup bra, so carefully chosen for just that reason. Her nipples were already tight and aching, jutting through the lace, and when Max found one with his lips, Jessie thought she might explode right then.

The heat that had been fluttering in her belly since the trip started had moved downward, centering in her clit, being teased so mercilessly by the pressure of Max's erection. She pulled him harder against her, and they rocked back together with such force that the couch creaked and the shade of the lamp on the end table rattled. Breathing hard, Max broke the kiss.

"Wait," he whispered.

Thunder rumbled outside, echoing her frustration. Jessie frowned. "Wait? No."

Max eased himself away, keeping a hand on her to help her off the back of the couch. "Just wait."

Disappointment edged its pinpricks all over her, but she tried valiantly to keep her voice calm. "Are you kidding me?"

Max laughed, and she couldn't lie, that laugh totally charmed her. Always. But right now, it sort of pissed her off, too. Rain spattered on the roof, and the windows lit with a flash of lightning. The storm Freddy Romero had promised was here.

"Girls have needs, too, you know," Jessie suddenly said. "I know it's only supposed to be the guys, but I'll tell you something, Max, I'm ready to eat you alive and I'm going to be pretty fucking disappointed if you tell me again that we should take our time."

The first time he'd said it, during a heated make-out session on her couch, she'd been unsure he meant it, or if it was just his way of politely disengaging from something he didn't want to be doing. But after that, gleaning bits and pieces of his past relationship with his crazy, unnamed ex, Jessie discovered Max's desire to take things slow, to wait, not to rush into the physical was genuine and incredibly sexy. Frustrating, but hot.

Now, though, she was done with waiting. Done with slow. She grabbed him by the front of his shirt and pulled his mouth toward hers, though she stopped just short of kissing him.

"Please," she said in a low voice, "don't tell me you brought me all the way out here for the weekend so we can play UNO."

"No." His hands settled on her hips, pulled her closer to rub his still-hard cock on her belly. His mouth found hers and teased it open. He sucked gently on her tongue before pulling away to look into her eyes. "I just didn't want the first time to be on a couch."

God, how could any man be so freaking perfect? Her irritation dissipated, especially when he brushed her hair out of her eyes and ran his finger along her jawline before slipping his hand into hers to squeeze her fingers. He backed up a few steps toward the wooden staircase, tugging her by the hand, gaze never leaving hers.

"First," he said, pulling her gently up step by step, "I want to lay you down on the bed and take off all your clothes, slowly, kissing every part of you I reveal."

The words sent more heat all through her. She stumbled a little on the stair. Max caught her. Kissed her while he led her up another step. They'd reached the landing, and he pushed her against the wall to kiss her breathless.

"Your mouth," he said, kissing the places he mentioned. "Your jaw, your throat."

His hand went between her legs, knuckles pressing the soft fabric of her leggings. Against her clit. Rubbing so slow and gentle it was about to make her lose her mind.

"And here," Max murmured against her skin as his hand moved on her.

Oh, yes. There. She'd dreamed of him touching her there, thought of it the countless times she'd given in to her frustration and imagined her hand was his. An incoherent noise slipped out of her.

Max eased her up another few steps to the bedroom, which took up the entire second floor. The sound of the rain was so much louder up here, like stones rattling on tin. He led her to the bed and covered her with his body as she lay back on the soft quilt. Then, he undressed her. Piece by piece, her unbuttoned blouse, the soft leggings, the lacy bra and panties she'd bought especially for this trip. All pulled off by his strong, long fingers, every inch of her revealed and worshipped with his lips and tongue, just as he'd promised.

Her mouth, where he urged her lips to part so his tongue could slip inside. Her throat, where he pressed his teeth to the beat of her pulse. Her nipples, one and the other, suckling each until she had to arch her back and shake from the sensation. Her ribs, her belly, her hips, her thighs all got their share of Max's devotion.

"So…fucking…perfect," Jessie said.

Max paused with his fingertips under her knees, his mouth teasing a particularly sensitive spot on the inside of her thigh. "Hmm?"

"You," Jessie said, glaze-eyed with pleasure, not close to

coming but feeling as though when she tipped over it was going to last forever. "You, Max. So perfect."

He laughed, self-conscious, and ducked his head. She pushed herself up on her elbow and tugged his hair until he looked at her. That was beauty, Jessie thought. This perfect man, still clothed, lying between her legs with his wet lips and flushed face. She touched his cheek, suddenly feeling close to tears and not wanting to cry, dammit, because she wasn't going to cock-block herself with emotion.

"I'm not," he said.

She pulled him to her mouth. "Shut up. You are, to me."

He propped himself up so that he wasn't crushing her, one hand resting lightly on her hip. His fingers twitched, tickling. "Perfect doesn't last."

More emotion closed her throat and stung her eyes. Jessie traced his lips with a fingertip before pulling him for a kiss.

"I know that," she whispered into his mouth. "But it can last long enough."

There was no way she was going to give him a chance to back out now. It took only a little effort to push him to the side and get him on his back, to straddle him and work the buckle of his belt. The button and zipper on his jeans— and finally, at last, to get him as naked as she was. Jessie didn't take her time the way Max had. She stripped him completely as fast as she could.

Then she began to devour him.

Kissing, stroking, licking, sucking. She left no scant inch of him uncovered with her mouth and hands, an echo of the time he'd spent exploring her body, but not soft and not slow, and sure as hell not sweet. There'd be time for that later, she thought when she took his cock in her mouth and drew him in as deep as she could. Second rounds were for slowing down.

When his hand tangled in her hair again, she tensed, working her tongue around the head of his prick. She half expected him to pull her away, but when he instead used his hold on her hair to move her a little faster, Jessie moaned. The taste of him had always driven her crazy, and it was amplified here. She let herself take him in a little farther down the back of her throat, then gripped the base of his cock and eased her mouth up, up and up while her hand followed. Slick from her spit, his cock pulsed on her tongue. She sucked gently at the head, then ran her tongue around the rim.

"Fuck," Max muttered. "Oh shit, that feels so good."

"I want you to feel good." She stroked her hand up and down, palming the head with a little twist of her wrist that made him shudder. Seeing him react that way turned her on even more, if that were possible, and she already thought she might just explode. Incinerate.

"I want you to feel good, too. C'mere." He let go of her hair to ease her upward on him, his cock rubbing her clit as she straddled him. Every thrust of his hips pressed his heat to her.

She was so wet that she slid against him, but when she moved to lift up so he could put himself inside her, Max again whispered, "Wait."

Jessie made a low mutter of frustration but paused. "What?"

They'd already had the discussion about birth control and STDs and condoms and responsibility. She knew it couldn't be that. She searched his face for some sign that he was going to tell her he'd changed his mind, that he wanted to go still slower than this. She'd die, she thought. No, she'd kill him.

Max gave her his charming grin, the one he knew would always appease her. He shifted so his prick pushed more easily between them, against her clit as he held her hips and moved his own. Just a little. Then, pause. A little more. Each small motion rubbed the head of him on her, until she could only let her head fall back, her mouth open and eyes heavy-lidded with the pleasure of letting him get her off with just this.

It wasn't enough and it was too much all at the same time. He sent her up and over into orgasm without ever moving faster or changing the pace. Climax rocked her, and Jessie shuddered. His name eased out of her on a long series of sighs she couldn't muffle and didn't want to. The world tipped and went unfocused. When she came back to it, she found him still looking at her, though the grin had faded and become a different sort of look, one she wasn't sure she could identify.

Before she could think to ask him what was wrong, Max had pulled her mouth to his. Their bodies moved naturally, his cock sliding inside her as easily as if he'd guided it with a hand, though all she'd done was lean forward for his kiss. She shuddered again at the way he filled her. Her fingers dug into his shoulders. The kiss deepened. Max gripped the back of her neck, holding her to him while he moved inside her hard enough to move her entire body.

The bed shook. Everything shook. Jessie came again when he muttered her name. A moment after that, Max cried out, low. Jessie forced her eyes to open, to focus, to pay attention. She wanted to watch his face when he spent himself inside her, and it was worth every effort, because Max was looking into her eyes until the very last second when pleasure overtook him. When he gave up to it, and her, at last.

Chapter 3

If heaven had a smell, Max thought, it was bacon and fresh coffee; if it had a feeling, it was the weight of warm, naked female flesh against his bare back. Turning, he arranged himself against Jessie, who snuggled sleepily against him with a sigh. Burying his face in her hair, he ran his hands down her back to cup her ass and pull her closer against him.

She murmured something that sounded like his name and wriggled. When she moved against him like that, he was rock-hard in half a second. Max couldn't stop himself from kissing her when Jessie blinked up at him with one of those sexy smiles that so slayed him.

She wriggled again, sort of like a protest. "Toothbrush!"

"Forget it." He slid a hand between them to stroke a finger through her curls and find her clit. Slow, steady circles, his gaze on hers to watch her pupils dilate. He dipped a finger lower to find her wetness, and when she shivered, decided to keep going. Max pushed a finger inside her. When she moaned, he went a little deeper.

Smiling, Jessie rolled onto her back with one arm flung over her eyes and lifted her hips to encourage him. Her mouth opened, tongue sliding along her lower lip. When Max bent to take one of her nipples between his lips, she threaded her fingers through his hair, tugging. God, he loved the way she responded to him, like everything he did was…

Perfect.

That's what she'd said last night.

Sometimes, Max was admittedly an idiot, but not about this. He knew perfection was a lie that twisted itself around people in the beginning and bit them in the ass when they got to know each other. It wasn't real or meant to last, and anyone who expected it to was more than dumb—they were crazy. But he didn't want to go there, so he pushed away thoughts of the past and crazy Patty, who'd tried her best to make his life hell, and he concentrated on the woman now shifting restlessly beneath his mouth and hands.

He'd thought about this since the first time he saw her, that strawberry blond hair pulled high on top of her head, her purple Converse sneakers paired with a long black skirt and a Metallica concert shirt he'd seen right away was genuine and not something she'd picked up at Hot Topic for kicks. Jessie's blue eyes, her smile and laugh, the way she shook his hand when she introduced herself, had heated him up from the start, but he'd been trying so hard to be careful that he'd sort of made an ass of himself. He knew it. Too much waiting. He was lucky she hadn't given up on him.

He'd make it up to her now, he thought, and ran his tongue around her sensitive areola until her nipples puckered even tighter. She was so wet for him he could easily slip a second finger inside her, his thumb still pressing her clit as he moved his hand. Her pussy clutched at his fingers, and she gasped, her hand gripping his wrist to slow him.

"Wait," she said with a laugh, not opening her eyes, her voice thick with arousal.

His own command, thrown back at him. Max waited. Her body pulsed around him. He wanted to be inside her so much that it took everything he had not to dive in. When she tipped her hips the tiniest bit, encouraging him, he moved his fingers again. She went tight around him, her pussy gripping, her clit jumping. Fuck, it made his cock jump, too. Her hoarse cry echoed around the loft. She covered her mouth as though she meant to hold it back.

"I want to hear you," Max said, surprised he could find his own voice.

"Oh, God. Max." She moaned. Then, louder. "Oh, yes."

He couldn't hold off any longer—he had to taste her. Max slid down the bed to center his mouth on her clit. He lapped at her sweetness, suckling gently while still moving in and out of her with his fingers. Shit, he wanted his cock inside her, but he had to make her come first. Had to make her lose her mind for him.

When she came, her taste flooded him. Her pussy clamped against him in slow rolling flutters that sent echoing shocks all through his dick. Pain in his scalp flared, just a little, and he realized she was pulling his hair to get him to move upward. He wasn't going to resist, not any longer. Max moved up Jessie's body to capture her mouth. She opened for him. Her fingers dug into his ass as he moved between her legs, guiding himself into her slick heat.

He wanted to make love to her for hours, but there was no way he was going to last that long. He was already shaking from how good it felt to be inside her, balls deep. At the scratch of her nails down his back, Max let out a low yell. Pleasure swept him. He was the one losing himself. He lost himself in her and didn't even care.

A few minutes later, Jessie kissed his shoulder, prompting him to roll to the side. "How's your hand, honey?"

Truthfully, he'd forgotten all about it. It stung a little when he poked at the bandages, but it wasn't bad at all. "You fixed it right up. It's okay."

She took a peek under the bandages, then kissed him again. "You must heal fast. God, breakfast smells amazing. I didn't even hear you get up."

"I didn't get up." Max looked at her. "I thought you made breakfast…."

Both of them were up and out of the bed, snatching up clothes, shoving legs into jeans and arms into shirts, in thirty seconds. At the top of the stairs, Max motioned for her to stand behind him. He listened, craning his neck to hear any movement from downstairs. At the clink of silverware on porcelain, he took one step down the stairs with Jessie close on his heels.

"You stay here."

Both her brows went up. "And let the serial killer get you? Um, no."

"I doubt a serial killer would be making us breakfast." Something like that would be reserved for crazy ex-girl-friends, he thought grimly, remembering the time Patty had let herself into his apartment and cooked him dinner, then thrown a pan of hot pasta at his face when he told her she needed to leave.

But downstairs, all they found was a breakfast table set with two plates, a pot of coffee perking merrily on the counter and eggs and bacon in a covered pan on the stove. Jessie looked at it, then him.

"Is this a bed and breakfast maybe?"

"It's not supposed to be." If anything, he'd picked this place because it was out of the way and they'd have plenty of time to be totally alone. "But it smells good."

Jessie went to the window to look out. She twitched the red checker curtain to one side and smiled bemusedly. "Someone's in the backyard. A woman."

Swiftly, Max crossed to the window and yanked at the curtain, a sour taste in his mouth, all ready to see Patty's signature cloud of pale hair. The woman by the shed was blonde, all right, but golden. She looked too much like Freddy Romero to be anything but a relative, from the plaid shirt to her towering height. The top of her head was even with the shed door, and that was with her shoulders hunched. She had her back to the cabin, her attention focused on something in front of her.

"You think she made us breakfast?" Jessie asked. "You think she was in here this morning…while we…"

Frowning, Max opened the back door. "Hi!"

The woman turned, and the shock was enough to make him step back. From behind, he'd guessed her to be in her late twenties by the length and style of her thick blond hair, and the curves of her body. Her face, on the other hand, belonged to a much-older woman. Fifty, at least, and that was being kind. Deep lines bracketed her mouth, which hung open to reveal yellowed teeth that were curved inward. Her hands, too, were ancient, gnarled and thick-knuckled, with long curved nails. Something moved and writhed in her hands, something black and white and gray, furry. It squealed, briefly.

The woman calmly wrenched its neck, and the thing went still.

"Coons," she said with a smile that would have been charming on a wolverine. "Baby coons in the shed, got to get rid of 'em or else they make a mess of the garbage."

Behind him, Jessie let out a low cry. Max backed up a step to keep himself between her and this weirdo with the dead raccoons, but the woman didn't try to run at them or anything. Instead, she casually tossed the tiny corpse into a burn barrel next to the shed. Wiping her hands on the hem of her shirt, she gestured at the house.

"Made breakfast for ya."

"Thanks," Jessie said from around his shoulder. She grabbed his hip.

The woman nodded and gave them both an assessing look before showing the entire crooked picket fence of her smile. "I'm Carrie."

"Freddy's…sister?" Max guessed.

Carrie made a one-two pow-pow with her fingers, like guns. "You got it! Youse need anything else while I'm here?"

Max glanced at Jessie, who shook her head. "No, thanks. We're good."

Carrie grinned again, inching closer. "If you do, just let me know. I'll be back later to check the traps."

"Traps?" Jessie squeezed his hip, then moved forward a little and rubbed her arms against the morning chill.

Max had thrown on a flannel shirt, but she wore only a thin tank top. Now he shrugged out of the shirt and slung it over her shoulders. She gave him a grateful smile.

"Oh, yeah." Carrie nodded, and then gave a long, lingering and totally creepy look toward the woods beyond the small patch of grass surrounding the cabin. "Got 'em all baited up."

Max, his arm around Jessie's shoulders, followed her gaze but could see only trees. Nothing even rustled there. "What are you trying to trap?"

"Whatever I can get," Carrie told them both without even a hint of a smile.

"I'm sorry," Max said for about the fifth time as he swiped at numbers on his cell phone—the one without even one bar of service.

Jessie took the phone from his hand and turned it off, then set it carefully on the kitchen table. She put her hands flat on his front and hooked her fingers into the front of his shirt to pull him closer for a kiss that she purposefully kept lingering long enough to border a little on ridiculous. Only when she felt him relax against her did she pull away just enough to nip at his lower lip, then brush another kiss over it.

"Shut. Up," she said. "I told you already, it's fine."

Max wanted to call Freddy and tell him not to have his sister hanging around the place. Jessie didn't disagree— she'd dumped the food, no matter how delicious it smelled, after watching Carrie strangle a raccoon and then wipe her hands on her shirt. But she also didn't want to spend their day worrying about it. Not when there were so many other ways to occupy their time.

"Oh, hey," Max said when she slipped her hand down the front of his jeans and gave him a careful squeeze. "Um, okay."

"I love the way you kiss me," Jessie told him matter-of-factly, pushing onto her toes so she could look into his eyes. "Love it."

Max laughed softly and pulled her closer. "Good, because I love kissing you."

She steadied herself with her hands on his shoulders, brushing another kiss against him but not letting it go deeper. Somehow, her face found a place in the hollow of his shoulder. His hands on the small of her back. They moved slowly together to inaudible music while she pressed her hand flat to the comforting beat of his heart beneath the flannel.

This, Jessie thought, felt like falling in love.

She could have stayed like that for a long time, but her stomach was growling. With another kiss, she nibbled gently at his jaw for a second before slapping him on the ass. "Breakfast," she said. "I hope you packed more bacon because it hurts my heart that we had to throw that all away."

An hour later they'd both eaten and showered in the charming claw-foot tub that wasn't big enough for two but managed to fit them both anyway. Max had packed a picnic basket. Bread, cheeses in a cooler bag, an unbroken bottle of wine and even glasses. Also, in a touch that made tears prickle in the back of her eyes, a bunch of flowers with a matching vase.

"Romantic," Jessie told him.

Max grinned. "There's a waterfall."

There certainly was. A small one that had been fed to greatness by last night's storm, set back a mile or so from the cabin at the end of a winding path that had turned to thick mud from the rain. It cut through the trees that got increasingly thicker the farther into the woods they got. A jutting wedge of rock made the water gush out far over the rest of the cliff, leaving plenty of room to walk beneath it to the other side, where they found a soft patch of still-damp grass and leaves and spread their blanket. Their morning lovemaking had eased some of the edge, but that didn't mean she didn't pounce him as soon as she could.

"You'll spill the wine!" Max protested, but held the glass away from him so she could straddle his lap.

Jessie took his face in her hands. "I am crazy about you, Max Arnec. You know that, right?"

For an embarrassing few seconds, she thought she'd gone too far. Said too much. It wasn't like her to be so open, but something about Max had always made her that way. Honest.

She stopped worrying when he inched her closer to kiss her mouth. "The feeling's mutual."

She'd just settled into a sweet, lingering kiss, when something flashed through the woods just out of sight behind them. Startled, Jessie pulled away to look over Max's shoulder. He frowned.

"What?"

"I saw something."

There it was again, the push and rustle of something in the leaves. Jessie squinted, trying to catch sight of it, but the shadows were too deep…and Max's mouth too delicious for her to worry herself too much about it. At least, not until the rustling got much, much closer.

"What the hell is that?" Jessie eased herself from Max's lap, the memory of yesterday's close call on the road still fresh.

Max stood, looking into the woods. Nothing happened

but the whisper of the wind through the branches, and he turned to look down at her with a bemused smile. "A deer maybe."

A chill skittered down Jessie's spine that had nothing to do with the sweet fall breeze. The scent of something sour and rotten tickled her nose and left a bad taste in her mouth. She covered them both, shaking her head as she stepped back.

"Let's go back to the cabin."

They hadn't done more than crack open the bottle of wine, but Max nodded right away with an uneasy look over his shoulder. "Yeah. Sure. Okay."

"We can hit the hot tub," she offered brightly, bending to pack up the basket even as she kept a wary eye on the trees all around them. Now she heard noises from the opposite side of the clearing. Then the other.

The thing was circling them.

Together, she and Max shoved everything into the basket and folded the blanket, which he slung over one arm. Jessie took his hand, the wine bottle in her other one. She meant to kiss him again, but before she could, something so big and loud crashed in the woods behind them that both of them jumped.

"Let's go," Max said.

But Jessie, mesmerized by the bending, breaking trees, didn't move. Something big moved in the shadows, and it wasn't a deer. Something with gangling limbs that stood upright, tall enough to push aside branches that would have been a good foot above Max's head. Something strong enough to snap the branches right off the trees instead of just pushing them out of the way.

"Jessie," Max said calmly, matter-of-factly, without a tremor in his voice, "run!"

They both launched themselves at the same time, dumping blanket, basket and bottle. The path that had seemed so charming before now tripped her up, though Jessie kept her feet and didn't fall. Max grabbed her by the elbow to help her and tripped over a root. He stumbled forward, but he didn't fall either. It slowed them, though, this clumsiness, and the waterfall was still burbling unseen in the distance.

Jessie risked a look behind them, expecting to see some shaggy, shambling thing on the path. All she saw was the tops of the trees around the bend shaking. The tops!

Around another bend, and the jutting outcrop of rock with water pouring over it was directly in front of them. Going beneath it had been fun and silly, slippery, a good excuse for her to cling to Max as they crossed it. There was no time for that now, and without talking about it, the two of them headed straight for the stream itself.

Max reached it first and turned at once to hold out a hand to Jessie. The bank wasn't high, but slick grass and mud made it impossible not to fall down unless she jumped. She didn't hesitate, just leaped. One foot hit the water first, the other a second later and connecting with a large boulder. Pain, instant and infuriating, knocked the breath out of her.

Max, soaked to the knees, had tight hold of her wrist, but her boot had become lodged in the space between the rock and one beside it. Her flesh scraped, her bones grinding, when he pulled her. Jessie let out a short scream. Max's grip slipped from her and he went into the water with a splash.

"I'm stuck!"

She could hear the thing now, whatever it was, and there

was more than the snap and crack of branches breaking. Now she could hear the whistling grunt of its breathing, too. The thump of something heavy in the dirt prompted her to look back again, but whatever chased them still hadn't made it around the bend.

Max knelt in the water, strong fingers working at her boot. He worked steadily, without looking up even as she urged him to hurry. With a sharp yank, Max pulled hard enough for Jessie to get her foot out. Then he had her by the wrist again, his other hand on the small of her back to help her along. And still, Jessie froze, unable to move.

There was something in the water. Red-and-black checked shirt, denim jeans. And there, deeper in the water, a hint of what might have been long blond hair, tangled in the underwater plants, waving gently in the current.

"Jessie, c'mon!"

On the other side of the boulder, Max couldn't see the horror in the water in front of her. Jessie could only point, shaking. He stopped only long enough to scoop a hand beneath her legs and carry her to the other side of the stream, where he staggered on the slippery bank.

Jessie's ankle exploded into fresh agony when she put her feet down to keep him from dropping her, but she bit back a scream. Grimly, she forced herself up the bank, Max at her side. Whatever was behind them must have killed Carrie, that was the only thought Jessie could form, and she wasn't about to end up like that.

She ran.

In another few minutes they reached the cabin's yard. She was flagging by then, but rallied at the sight of the porch and a door that locked. Max slammed it behind them, then leaned against it, panting, while Jessie stumbled to a kitchen chair and collapsed.

For a minute or so, she had no breath for words. They were both covered in mud from the knees down, with more splashed on their arms and faces. The ankle she'd caught in the rocks ached, her sock torn in several places. Her ankle was already swelling. The stitch in her side made her sit back and press a hand to it. When she thought about what she'd seen in the water, she wanted to throw up.

Max twitched aside the curtain on the door to look out. "Nothing's out there."

"What was it?"

"Not a deer," he said. "A bear maybe."

What she'd seen was nothing like a bear. Or a deer. Jessie hobbled to the sink to get a drink of water, dipping her head to pull it straight from the tap. Mouth dripping but nowhere near calmed, she looked at him.

"It wasn't a bear, Max."

He looked out the window again before crossing to her. He took her in his arms. She felt safe there, Jessie realized, which was nice but a little naive. He kissed the top of her head.

"It was Carrie," she told him. "In the water. Wasn't it? Something killed Carrie and dumped her there."

Max squeezed her and let her go. "It looked like her."

Jessie shuddered. "We need to call someone."

"No phone."

She'd forgotten. "Then we need to get out of here."

But when they got to the SUV, it was clear they wouldn't be going anywhere. All four tires had been slashed, the big vehicle itself settled into the mud left behind by the night's storm. It was such a cliché, such a scene from every horror movie she'd ever seen, that Jessie could only sag against the vehicle and hang her head.

"We can't be more than four miles from the store," Max said. "You stay here. I'll go—"

"No! Are you kidding me? You're not leaving me here, Max!"

"You'll be safe in the house, Jessie."

She barked laughter. "You think so? Have you ever watched a scary movie? Don't you know the first thing that happens when people split up?"

Incredibly and beautifully, he smiled at her. Then he kissed her, his hand cupping the back of her neck to hold her to him. "I know."

"We go together," she said, already wincing at the pain she anticipated in her ankle. "All the way."

Chapter 4

The storm that had passed long enough for them to enjoy their picnic—at least until they'd been attacked by whatever the hell had come after them from the woods—was back and with a vengeance. The midafternoon sky had gone to twilight, the thickness of the trees further masking any hint of sunlight. Back at the cabin, Max had bound Jessie's swollen ankle in a tight grip of bandages, but she was still limping. It would have been faster for him to do this alone, but she'd made a good point. He didn't want to risk anything happening to her if they split up.

"How much farther?" She wasn't even out of breath and hadn't complained, but her face was white with pain he hated himself for being unable to shield her from.

"Half a mile maybe?" Max paused to look upward at the canopy of leaves and branches overhead. He hefted the hand ax he'd grabbed from the woodpile out back. The weight of it pressed the still-sore wound in his hand, but it was bearable. Jessie carried a rusty rake doubling as a cane. Neither weapon was that great, but both were better than their bare hands in case that thing came after them again.

"Shit." Jessie wiped a grimy hand over her forehead, leaving a smear. She leaned on the rake, taking the weight off her foot, and grimaced.

"Is it bad?" Max indicated her ankle.

She smiled. "I'll be okay. Let's get to the convenience store before the storm hits, though. It looks like it's going to be worse than last night."

It was already worse, something they learned when they rounded the bend in the road and found what was left of the bridge ass-end-up in the ravine. The rickety timbers had cracked in half, dumping most of the bridge and leaving only scraps to show it had been there at all. Max muttered a curse as they eased up to the edge and looked down at the wreckage. The stream that had been little more than a trickle the day before was now a gushing, frothing river. As he watched, it tore away a hunk of the ravine and sent a mudslide skidding down to disappear into the angry water.

"Stay back," he warned Jessie, but a sudden clap of thunder stole his words.

She knew, though. Nodding, she hopped back. The rake dug into the soft earth, gouging holes. "Now what?"

Lightning lit the sky like an LED lantern, followed moments later by another bang of thunder louder than the first. The light was so bright that Max threw up a hand to cover his eyes, wincing at the afterimages imprinted on the insides of his lids. But only as an automatic response and only for a moment, because what he'd seen illuminated in that few seconds, formerly hidden in the shadows, sent his heart rocketing into his throat.

"It's here."

Jessie yelped, turning, almost losing her balance on her bad ankle before she caught herself with the rake. "Where?"

"I saw it in the tree line over there." Max pointed. Lightning blinded them both again; thunder drowned them out.

There it was, the thing that had come after them before. Easily seven-feet tall with broad shoulders and long, gangly arms and legs, the thing had a sloping head covered with long, matted hair. The rest of its body looked pale and mottled, with dirt or hair, he couldn't tell. But its eyes...

"Oh, God," Jessie cried. "What the hell's wrong with its face?"

The eyes, red and burning, were twice as large as seemed normal for the rest of the face. It was humanoid, but definitely not human. Definitely not a bear. Another crack of lightning turned the thing to blazing white before darkness obscured it once more. So far, it only watched, making no move toward them.

"What do we do?"

Max, keeping his gaze on the thing, took her hand. "Back to the cabin."

"I'm not sure I can run," Jessie told him. The wind whipped up her hair the way it was starting to slash the pine trees back and forth.

The first fat drops of icy rain spattered. In the next flash, the thing was gone. Max scanned the tree line but could see nothing.

"I can carry you if I have to," he said.

She laughed at that, and he loved that about her. That even in the midst of one of the most fucked-up situations Max had ever experienced, Jessie could laugh. She pulled him close for a kiss that should have been totally inappropriate but tasted so sweet it was worth every second.

"You don't have to carry me." She looked up at the sky, now completely black. Rain pattered on the trees and ground, and she swiped her face clear of it. "But I'll go as fast as I can."

Back at the cabin, a fire roaring in the fireplace, all the windows and doors locked, Jessie sipped a mug of hot cocoa and propped her ankle on a pillow. It wasn't broken, at least there was that. It just hurt like a son of a bitch and needed some ice, but there were no ice packs and the freezer had offered up only a few lame cubes.

Max looked out the front windows, though there was nothing to see but black and the storm. "You were right. It wasn't a bear."

"Bigfoot," Jessie said.

He looked over his shoulder at her. "The hell?"

Jessie couldn't help it; she busted into laughter at the sight of his affronted face. "You're not a believer?"

"No, hell no." Max vehemently shook his head and twitched the curtain closed. "Besides, aren't Bigfoots supposed to be hairy? That thing was...naked."

She laughed again at the way he shuddered saying the word. But he was right. The thing in the woods had been naked. Sexless, too. "And there was something wrong with its face."

"Red eyes."

"Yes, that. But its mouth, too." She used her hand to demonstrate, placing her fingers in a circle around her mouth and pulling her hand away, fingers closing, to indicate the way the tapering mouth had looked to her. Like a tube or a funnel. "A proboscis," she said.

Max's brows went up.

"Like…a butterfly," she explained.

"That thing was no butterfly."

Jessie patted the couch beside her until Max came over to sit. "No, but it looked like that, didn't it? Like a fleshy… tube. Thing."

Max made a disgusted noise. "I thought that was its tongue."

"Whatever it was," Jessie said, "it was big. And fast."

"It didn't attack us that second time." He turned toward her, his knee pressing hers. "It looked right at us, but it didn't come after us."

Jessie shifted, stretching her arm out along the back of the couch to toy with his sleeve. "Maybe it's territorial? And we were in its territory before. Maybe it has young or something that it was trying to protect."

"Like it's an animal."

She paused, thinking again of the way it had moved. How it had looked. "It's not human, Max. Unless it's some crazy sort of inbred monstrosity."

They looked at each other.

"Well," Max said.

"It was an animal," Jessie told him. "It had to be."

"Maybe it was an inbred monstrosity of an animal."

It should have been impossible for her to laugh right now—with her aching ankle and their disabled SUV, a washed-out bridge and some freakish thing stalking them from the woods—but she laughed anyway, because Max could always make her laugh. It was one of the things she loved so much about him....

Oh, shit, Jessie thought with something like wonder. She loved...

Something huge and loud clattered on the front porch, interrupting her thoughts and sending Max rocketing from the couch to grab up a poker from next to the fireplace. Jessie tensed, heart pounding, but relaxed a little when he turned from the window. In the firelight his hair looked very dark, his eyes very blue.

"The wind blew the swing over." He looked out the window again, up and down, before turning back to her. "There's a bunch of trees down in the yard, too, but nothing else."

She let out the breath she'd been holding, and it turned into an unexpected yawn. Max came back to the couch and set the poker close at hand when he settled in beside her. Jessie scooted closer.

His hand passed over her hair when she snuggled against him. "You should go to sleep. I'll stay up. Keep watch."

"No way. You think I could sleep up there by myself anyway?" She stifled another yawn and wriggled as close as she could, even if it meant suffering the ache in her ankle when she shifted.

Max kissed the top of her head. "In the morning, someone will come."

"You think so?"

"I only rented the cabin for the weekend," he reminded her. "I'm sure Freddy will be by to make sure we're all checked out."

"Unless he can't get across the river." Jessie breathed

Max's delicious, familiar scent. She'd have recognized him anywhere by the combination of fabric softener and soap, the musky hint of his cologne.

Max was quiet for a few seconds. "Then we'll hike our way out."

Jessie tipped her face to his, not laughing this time. "You know what?"

He looked down at her. "What?"

"If I had to be stranded in a cabin in horrible storm with some creepy monster thing outside terrorizing us, I'm glad it was with you."

He looked surprised, but only briefly. His mouth creased into a smile she could feel against her mouth when he kissed her. "Same here."

With a sigh, Jessie snuggled back against him. In silence, she watched the fire leap and crackle, and listened to the roar of the rain on the roof. The lightning and thunder had subsided, though every so often there was another far-off rumble. Sleep had seemed impossible just a short time before, but now her eyes started to get heavy and her tongue loose.

"Max..."

"Yeah, baby?"

The endearment warmed her. She snuggled closer, eyes closing, words slurring a little as she drifted. "Why don't you ever talk about your last girlfriend?"

"She tried to kill me."

Jessie blinked awake. "What? For real?"

"Yes. She tried to run me over with her car. She tried to hit me with a frying pan to the face. And she set my apartment on fire trying to burn all my clothes." Max cleared his throat, and she thought he was done, but he continued. "She also befriended my younger sister online under a man's name and posted nude pictures of her with links so that our friends and family would find out."

"Oh, God. Why would she do that?"

"Because she's crazy." Max's lips pressed her hair.

"I'm crazy," Jessie breathed, "about you."

This time, the low rumble was from Max's laughter and not from thunder. Helpless against her exhaustion, Jessie lost herself in disjointed but somehow comforting dreams, all featuring Max. Kissing her, dancing with her, making her laugh, making love to her.

Making her love him.

Jessie woke to the fire burned low, the storm still rushing outside, though now the rain sounded soothing and comforting, not so angry. Max had adjusted them on the couch so that he lay behind her, his face buried in her neck and one arm cradling her, his hand flat on her belly beneath her shirt. Waking just a little, Jessie murmured his name, but he didn't answer. She settled back against him, snugging her ass tight to his crotch.

Max's fingers twitched on her skin.

Jessie woke up a little more.

Another carefully orchestrated wiggle. Max sighed into her hair. She smiled, shifting her hips to press herself against his growing erection. She'd changed earlier into soft pajama pants. Max wore sweatpants, and there was no denying that the more she wiggled, the harder he got.

Her ankle had stopped hurting, or maybe it simply didn't matter anymore when his hand slipped into the front of her pants and his fingers brushed her clit through her lace panties. A moment later he pushed them inside the front of her panties to find her bare flesh. Jessie's back arched, and one hand went up to caress the back of Max's head, pulling his mouth closer to the curve of her shoulder, bared by the neckline of her T-shirt. He feasted there, each lick and nibble sending pleasure along every nerve and straight to her clit where his fingers still played. When she rocked back against him, grinding, his muttered "yes" almost tipped her over the edge right then.

Somehow, without falling off the couch or even twisting around, Jessie eased her pants down her hips until she could kick them off. The soft fleece of Max's sweatpants caressed her bare behind for a minute or so while he also maneuvered, getting himself naked, too.

It felt so good when he pushed inside her that she cried out, low and wordless. A voice full of need. His fingers tickled the underside of her knee, the couch rocked. If she'd opened her eyes, she might have been alarmed at how close to falling off she was, but all Jessie could think about or feel was the perfect, thick length of him fucking into her.

They'd been lovers for two days, but already he knew her body better than anyone else ever had. The pace, the rhythm, the perfect amount of pressure, exactly the right pattern of circles on her clit. Jessie was going up, up, up and over, but she wanted Max to go there with her.

"Come with me, Max," she murmured. "I'm so close."

"Close," he agreed, his voice muffled in her hair. His hot breath caressed her skin. His fingertips on her clit slowed, maddeningly, but his thrusts got deeper.

She cried out again, louder this time, and gave up to the pleasure overtaking her. She shook with it. Twisting, she found his mouth, the darting sweetness of his tongue. She breathed in as he breathed out, and she took him deep inside her in every place she could.

Sated and shivering with delicious aftershocks, Jessie became aware of the roughness of the couch cushions on her bare skin, how perilously close to the edge she was hovering, and worse, of a sudden chill that raised gooseflesh all over her. They were both a little clumsy in the aftermath, Max doing his best to make sure she didn't roll off and hit the floor, Jessie being careful not to nudge or knee him in soft places. What might have been awkward only made her laugh, though, because everything with Max always felt so natural, even this.

She stood to look for her pajama pants, which she must have kicked farther than she'd thought. Max rolled upright on the couch, his sweatpants tangled around his ankles. It was not an idyllic picture like in the movies, and no romance novel she'd ever read had ever described the postcoital dance of trying to get dressed and cleaned up at the same time. It was not a movie or a book, Jessie thought as she found her pants and started pulling them on, this was life. And it was better than fiction.

"It's so cold all of a sudden," she said, just as Max shot off the couch and pushed her to the side so fiercely that she stumbled.

The pain in her ankle flared again, another sharp pain from the edge of the coffee table biting into her calf compounding it. Jessie pinwheeled her arms, confused. As she caught her balance, she realized Max wasn't shoving her out of the way; he was pushing her behind him to protect her.

The front door was wide open, the cold night wind and rain blowing inside.

"Maybe the wind blew it open," Jessie said from behind him.

"It wasn't the wind. I saw her." Max checked the front door lock again, but couldn't shake the chill. "It was my ex, Jessie. I know it."

Jessie poured them both mugs of hot cocoa she'd made on the stove. She added a plate of cheese and crackers Max had imagined them eating on a picnic blanket with a bottle of wine, not at three in the morning off chipped plates while a storm raged outside. He wasn't hungry, but he sat when she gestured and sipped from the warm mug.

Jessie stood behind him, her arms around him and her cheek pressed to his. She said nothing, which he appreciated. He could feel the rise and fall of her breath against his back.

"All I wanted," Max said miserably, "was to have this great weekend away with you."

She nuzzled him. "Parts of this have been a great weekend, honey."

The pet name warmed him more than the hot cocoa. Jessie had always been affectionate with him. Kind since the beginning. Open, that's how he thought of her. A hugger, a kisser, the kind of woman who'd squeeze your shoulder if she thought you needed a little boost.

He turned his face to kiss her. "Stalked by some weird thing and my batshit crazy ex? Doesn't sound so great."

Jessie's low laugh tickled his ear. "How could it be her, all the way out here?"

"It's her," he said grimly. "And I wouldn't put it past her to have done all of it."

Jessie kissed his cheek and sat at the table, still close enough to nudge his knee with hers. "You think she's the one who slashed the tires?"

"She's done it before."

"Wow." Jessie frowned and pulled her mug closer, warming her hands on it.

Max swallowed the sour taste of memories. "Her name's Patrice. She was intense. I liked it at first, but after a while, she got out of hand. I know she had issues that had nothing to do with me, but I didn't when I got together with her. I shouldn't have slept with her because that escalated everything."

Jessie didn't make a joke of anything, didn't laugh. Her dark eyes wide with sympathy, she covered his hand with hers and linked fingers with him. She brought his hand to her lips and kissed the knuckles, one by one, before pressing his palm to her mouth. She closed his fingers over the kiss and smiled at him.

"You're so beautiful," Max blurted. "You know that?"

Jessie pretended to preen. "Oh, yeah, I know."

He kissed her mouth, holding her close, breathing in her scent and taking her warmth. He'd kept everything inside him locked up for so long he wasn't sure he could let go. But he knew that if he didn't tell Jessie everything about what had happened with Patty, he'd never be able to.

"It could've been worse," he said. "The thing with my sister. The pictures were blurry, and we found them and got them taken down really fast. What made it so bad wasn't that she'd conned Tina into taking pictures like that and sending them to a stranger, but that Patty had taken the pictures herself. She'd stalked her, peeking through the windows, following her into the changing room at the lake when Tina went swimming with her friends. That sort of thing. She tried to make my sister's life hell because I broke up with her."

Jessie's lip curled, but she kept her hand linked tight with his. "What a bitch."

"Yeah. I had no idea. I mean, I knew she was a little... off, but not like that."

"When did she try to run you over with her car?"

"The day I told her I didn't want to see her anymore. I didn't break up with her the best way, I know that." Max swallowed another rush of bitterness at the admission. "I could've been nicer about it."

"Oh, Max, there's no good way to break up with someone." Jessie kissed his hand again, pressing it to her smile as she shook her head. "And I can't imagine you ever being anything but nice."

"I told her I thought she needed to get help. And I did think that," Max added. "I mean, I really thought she needed like, serious psychiatric care. I should've helped her. Taken her to a doctor maybe...."

"Did she want to go?"

Startled by the question, he blinked. "What?"

"Did she want to go for help?"

"No. She said she was fine, that I was the crazy one. I hadn't called her crazy, not to her face," Max said. Shame heated him at the memory. "But she might've overheard me saying it about her."

Jessie nodded but said nothing.

"That's when she tried to run me over with the car. I

jumped out of the way in plenty of time. There wasn't a chance she could actually have hit me."

"But she tried."

He nodded. "Yeah, she tried."

"After I found out what she'd done to my sister, I went to her house to confront her. She lived in this big old place that had been her grandparents' house. Even when we were together, I never went over there. She always came to my place. Or—" he paused, remembering, feeling sick "—hotels. Places like that."

He sneaked a peek at Jessie's face, expecting her to look angry or annoyed or at the very least, carefully neutral in the way he'd learned over the years usually meant a woman was actually pissed-off. She only looked concerned. Still, he hated saying this to her. Hated having her know.

"I'd never been inside, but once I got in, I could see why she'd never invited me over. It was trashed on the inside. Papers and garbage everywhere, furniture overturned. It stunk like cat pee, though I didn't see any cats, and she'd never mentioned having any pets. I was pissed off, and I went into the kitchen, calling out her name, trying to get her to come out. That's when she hit me with the frying pan."

"Oh. Ouch. Oh, God, your poor face." She touched it gently as though that could take away the pain.

"She missed, mostly." Somehow, Max found a grin for her. "Glanced off my head and hit my shoulder and back. I was lucky. She definitely might've killed me. Good thing she had such bad aim."

"Good thing." Jessie kissed him softly. "No wonder you never wanted to talk about it."

But there was more, and even though he didn't want to share it, he had to.

"I was so mad at her when she hit me that I hit her back. Hard. I punched her in the face." Max forced himself to look into Jessie's eyes. "Broke her nose. She went down right there on the kitchen floor, blood gushing all over, and I just stood there. I couldn't believe I'd hit her. And then she got up and went for a kitchen knife."

In Jessie's face, Max saw no judgment. Only silent encouragement. He went on.

"She was so much smaller than me, there's no way she could've really hurt me. But she had a knife, and I just… reacted. I hit her again. When she ran away upstairs, I followed her. I swear, Jessie, I was just going after her to make sure she wasn't going to hurt herself. There was already so much blood. I couldn't tell if she was hurt worse than it seemed. I followed her up the stairs, and she attacked me again. We struggled. She managed to hit me in the face, this time with some piece of junk she grabbed from a pile on the stairs. I was woozy, couldn't tell what was going on. I pushed her away and she fell…on the knife. Then down the stairs."

Jessie's eyes went wide, her mouth slightly open. "Oh. God. She died?"

"When I managed to get myself together, I looked for her, but she was gone."

"The monster never dies the first time," Jessie said.

Max shook his head. "She wasn't…if I'd been a little nicer, if I'd helped her…"

"Hey—" Jessie took his face in her hands and centered his gaze on her "—you didn't know what would happen. You're not responsible for her issues. What happened to her?"

"The police found her wandering a few blocks away. She was detained for psychiatric evaluation. She got put on meds. We, um…we dropped the charges against her," Max said. "And she never raised any against me. The last time I saw her, she seemed much better. She'd put on some weight, looked healthier. She was with some guy in a diner. She didn't see me, and I didn't say anything to her."

"So what makes you think she's here now?"

It was a legitimate question, one unfortunately he had an answer for. "Because every year since we split up, she's sent me a birthday card. The same one. She must've bought a box of them or something. They all have a giant number one on the front."

"Like for a first birthday?"

"Like she's the only one for me," Max explained. "It's what she always used to say to me. 'I'm the only one you'll ever really love.' But I didn't love her, Jessie. I never even came close."

Jessie shuddered. "Creepy. Wow."

"You're the first girl I've dated since Patty. I thought enough time had passed. Last year, she didn't send a card. I figured maybe she was over it, but I guess not."

"You think she followed us all the way out here? Slashed our tires? You think she killed Carrie? You think she's the thing in the woods?"

He didn't want to think so, but… "Yeah. I think maybe."

Jessie shook her head. "Honey, there's no way. First of all, how would she even know about this trip? You kept it such a secret. Even Kelly didn't know. And you saw that thing. Whatever it was, it's not a person."

Something knocked on the front door.

Chapter 5

The sharp rap of knuckles on the front door startled Max so much that his hand jerked, knocking the mug of cooling cocoa to the floor, where it smashed. Jessie yelped, but he was already out of his seat and heading for the front door. Max yanked it open to the night outside. The rain had stopped, but chilly air swirled in, making Jessie shiver.

"Who is it?" she cried. It had to be a person, her rational mind insisted. A creature, a thing, a monster or even an inbred, freakish animal wouldn't knock like that. It had to be a person. "Is it Freddy?"

"Son of a bitch!"

Jessie, avoiding the shattered porcelain, went after him, but Max was already on the front porch. By the time she got to the door, he'd pulled on the boots he'd left there the night before. In another half minute he was off the porch and in the front yard, heading for the trees.

"You stay here!"

"Max, wait! Where are you going?"

He jerked a thumb behind him but didn't turn. "I saw her, Jessie. I told you I saw her! She ran off into the woods! You stay here."

Even with no shoes or coat, Jessie still considered running after him. She paused, though, watching him head for the tree line. It would be stupid of her to follow him without getting dressed and getting a weapon, because no matter what he'd seen, it was better to have protection. As she turned to head back into the house, she saw what had convinced him so strongly that he was running off after his ex.

On the front door, painted in thick mud, was a giant number one.

"Oh, shit." Jessie didn't waste another second. Inside the cabin she found socks, her still-wet and muddy boots, her jeans still damp from yesterday, but better than the soft pajama pants she wore. She pulled a heavy sweatshirt over her head, but when it came time to get her ankle into the boot, she was stumped.

It hurt. A lot. She did it anyway, with a low, gritting cry as she seated her foot into the boot and laced it tight.

She took the rake she'd used yesterday. Also a big kitchen knife from the block on the counter. The irony of that wasn't lost on her.

The sun had come up while she and Max slept. Even though the sky was still gray when he'd run off, by the time Jessie was finished getting ready to go after him, the sun had started to burn away the clouds. The air was still crisp, a perfect autumn day. It looked like the rain was going to hold off. With the knife strapped to her belt and the rake in one hand, her tightly laced boot providing sufficient support for her ankle, Jessie was ready to kick some ass.

No bitch, she thought, was going to get between her and Max.

In the front yard, she found the gouges his boots had left in the mud. But before she could follow them, the chugging, guttering mumble of an engine turned her toward the back of the house. Freddy came around the side on a battered four-wheeler, his wide grin totally out of place with everything else that had gone on over the past day.

"Hiya! Great day. Just coming to check on youse since the bridge washed out." He pronounced washed like it had a letter R in it. Freddy paused. "You okay?"

"No." Jessie pointed at the Suburban. "Something slashed our tires. And there's something in the woods. And… Freddy…"

She didn't know how to tell him right out that his sister might have been killed. No matter how creepy Carrie had been, Jessie was still hoping for the best, that she was okay. "We found something in the stream by the waterfall when the thing was coming after us. Carrie's clothes. Some of her hair. I think whatever attacked us might have hurt her. Or worse."

Freddy looked her over, his gaze taking in the knife and the rake, and maybe something in her face. His cheeks drained of color. "Carrie?"

"Your sister."

"Oh, shit. Shit, shit!" Freddy hopped off the four-wheeler and ran to her, grabbing her by the shoulders and shaking her. "What was it? What did you see?"

"Her clothes, for sure. Her hair," Jessie repeated, trying to think about what she'd seen in the stream. No blood, but…"

"It wasn't my sister. Carrie's been dead for years."

"No." Jessie shook her head. "She was here when we woke up yesterday. She made us breakfast, and it was pretty freaking creepy, let me tell you. She told us not to go in the woods, but we didn't listen. And then we went hiking to the waterfall and we were going to have a picnic, but this... thing, this huge thing came crashing out after us, and we ran—"

Freddy let go of her and started pacing. His boots squelched in the churned mud, obscuring Max's boot prints and anything else that might have left its mark. "I thought youse'd be okay. It's early yet, too early...but I guess if it really needed something...maybe I was wrong about the timing..."

"Freddy!" Jessie's shout turned him. "Calm down. What the hell are you talking about?"

Freddy's gaze was haunted. "What did you see?"

"I'm not sure." Jessie paused, trying to put all the pieces into place. "What did I see?"

Freddy paced again, pulling at his hair and muttering. It took Jessie grabbing his arm to get him to stop. "My grandma always called it the Greedy One."

"So...it's not a person?"

"Not anymore."

Jessie's stomach turned. "What is it, then?"

"Don't know. It lives in the woods all around here." Freddy looked shifty. He backed away, hands up when he saw her expression. "But it's not supposed to be hungry now! It's too soon!"

"Are you fucking kidding me?" Jessie's fingers gripped the rake handle so hard that her knuckles turned white.

"Seriously? You're trying to tell me there is really some…thing…in the woods and it eats people?"

"It doesn't eat them! Not like you think. I mean…it takes them. Yes, it does. It needs people. It's greedy for them, but it's not…it doesn't eat them. It just…takes what it needs from them."

"Which is what exactly?"

Freddy's eyes darted back and forth again, his mouth turning down. "Essence."

Jessie slumped, her knees weak and stomach still churning. "Like…a soul?"

"No. Real essence. Um…it's greedy, hungry for…" Freddy made a familiar, if off-color, gesture: a forefinger inserted into the hole made by his other fist, in and out.

"Sex? It wants sex?"

Freddy looked embarrassed.

Jessie's laughter was so far from humorous that she was surprised it didn't come out as a shriek. "It wants to what, fuck us?"

"It wants that feeling. The rush. An essence," Freddy quickly said. "It feeds on that. It seduces its prey and sucks it dry."

"It kills what it feeds on?"

"Eventually," Freddy said. "It can keep them alive for a really long time."

"Oh, God." Jessie started for the woods, ignoring Freddy and the mud and everything but following Max's boot prints. "Max!"

"What you saw wasn't my sister!" Freddy shouted after her, but Jessie had no more time for him. No time for this.

She needed to get to Max before whatever had led him into the woods did.

* * *

The fall of auburn hair was the same. The slight build, the freckled arms, hands with long fingers. The face, though, was only barely Patty. Unformed, the eyes the wrong shape but the right color, the mouth a lipless slash. The thing in front of him was a monster trying to wear Patty's face and body, and failing.

Every part of Max ached. He'd followed the monster straight into the woods and into a ditch lined with sharpened sticks and boulders. Nothing had punctured him too badly, thank God, but he was a mess of bruises and scrapes. He may have cracked a few ribs, too. Woozy from the pain, he'd been aware of something grabbing him by the back of the collar and dragging him through the woods to this slanting, ramshackle shelter built against the side of a cliff. It wasn't quite a cave, though much of it was set into a huge crack in the rock. The rest of it had been constructed of broken trees and woven vines.

Now he sat propped against the rock, his shirt opened to the waist. The thing had been kissing him all over, its wet, slurping mouth leaving a trail of slime along his bare skin. The thought of it made him heave, but he couldn't move even to turn his face and spit. Something in the saliva, Max thought blearily. Something like a venom that half paralyzed him and, disgustingly, acted as sort of an aphrodisiac as well. It burned, but there was no denying it also sent another sort of fire through him.

The Patty-thing shuffled in front of him, its hair obscuring that awful face. The body, from the back, bore no resemblance to Max's ex-girlfriend. Broad, bony shoulders, the spine clearly outlined, knob for knob. Jutting hip bones.

Sexless. The arms, too long and stretching longer. When the thing stood, its head brushed the makeshift roof.

It hadn't spoken a single word, but now it whispered, "Darling."

Max choked and tried to turn his head when the thing came close to his mouth and pried open his lips with its bony fingers to give him the darkest embrace. The long, slick stroke of its meaty tongue sent ripples of revulsion through him, but after a minute he found himself relaxing into it. Not accepting it, simply…unable to resist…

Jessie was no tracker. She'd gone hunting with her dad once in a while, more as an excuse for both of them to hike into the woods together and enjoy some one-on-one time rather than an actual hunt. She couldn't remember her dad ever coming home with anything he'd killed. Still, he'd taught her how to look for signs something had gone through the forest before them—rubbed bits of trees, crushed grass, gouged earth.

Following Max wasn't hard at all. He hadn't been trying to hide his tracks, had left huge patches of bent branches and footprints. At least for the first few hundred feet into the woods. Then the trail, such as it was, became harder to find. With the ground so soft from the storm, she'd thought it would be easier; but in the cover of the deep shadows, everything got harder to see.

She listened instead.

Head up, muffling the sound of her own panting breath as best she could, Jessie strained her ears for any sound. Max's voice, the crack and rustle of underbrush. Anything.

There was nothing but the far-off rush of water and the beat of her heart in her ears.

She stopped herself from running pell-mell through the woods, screaming his name. That wouldn't help, and might end up with her going in the wrong direction. The need to find him was staggering enough to knock her to her knees, but Jessie kept herself centered, focused.

The half-assed story Freddy had told her would have been completely unbelievable if Jessie hadn't always harbored a secret fascination with the strange and unknown—and if she hadn't seen at least part of the thing with her own eyes. Ultimately, it didn't matter what it was. Jessie was going to find Max.

She gave in, at last, to the need to scream his name. Once, then again, even louder. She put everything she had into it, let her voice rise up and up until it cracked.

"Jessie!"

She heard but didn't see him. "Max! Where are you?"

She turned at the sound of rustling brush, her rake raised and her hand on the knife. A moment later, a familiar black-and-blue plaid shirt emerged from the trees. Jessie let out a low cry and limped toward him. She was in his arms immediately, her face buried against his chest.

"Hey, now," Max said. "It's okay."

Jessie looked at him. "What happened?"

His mouth worked and brow furrowed, but it took him a while to find the words. Blood had crusted along his hairline and in one corner of his mouth, though she couldn't see any wounds. Max shook his head.

"It was Patty. I told you. I saw her, and I went after her."

"What did you do to her?" Jessie touched his scalp with gentle fingers, looking for the source of the blood.

Max ducked from her touch. "Nothing. She went into the woods. I couldn't see her. Let's go back to the cabin. Get something to eat. I'm starving."

"Wait a minute." Jessie pushed onto her tiptoes to get a better look, but again he ducked away from her. "Stay still. I want to see where you're hurt."

"I'm not hurt."

She hugged him again. "Thank God. Freddy had this crazy story about something in the woods, some sort of... thing..."

Max's arms went around her, squeezing. "Freddy."

"Yeah. I wouldn't have believed it except, you know...we saw something." A chill scratched at her when she thought of the monstrous, misshapen shadow. "I don't know what it was, but it was definitely weird."

"It was Patty," Max told her in a rough voice. "It was Patty."

Jessie looked at him again, uneasy. "Maybe you should sit down. You look pale."

Max kissed her. His mouth pried at hers, his hands roaming up and down her back until they settled on her hips and pulled her close. His grip was too tight, hurting. His tongue stabbed at her.

Heat spread through her; desire rose unexpectedly and fiercely. Burning. Crackling through her nerves like an electric shock, the sheer force of it weakened her knees so that she sagged against him.

Max's mouth moved from hers to her throat, nipping and licking. One hand went between her legs, pressing her through the denim. She went crazy for his touch, arching, an inarticulate moan escaping her.

The world swam.

Max's hands dug into her hair. He breathed hard into her ear, panting, his breath hot and somehow thick. He moved against her. The press of his teeth stung too much, too hard, and although Jessie sometimes didn't mind a little pain, this was too much. All of it was—What did he want to do—fuck her right here in the middle of the woods with monster and ex-girlfriend and Freddy as witnesses?

"Max…"

He pressed her harder, his mouth working on her neck. Sucking. She was drunk on the pleasure, head spinning and stomach churning like she might puke or pass out.

This was wrong.

Then she realized what it was. Max smelled of fabric softener and soap and cologne, but the man mauling her throat reeked like a wet basement. Jessie put her hands on his chest and pushed, but he clung to her like a burr.

What had Freddy said? It was hard to think, exactly like she was hammered, though Jessie hadn't been truly drunk since she was a freshman in college. She got a knee up between them, pressing his balls but not quite shoving hard enough to get him off her.

What you saw wasn't my sister.

That's what Freddy had said. The question was, if it wasn't his sister, what was it? And if this wasn't Max—

"Get the hell off me!" Jessie put all her weight behind the sharp, upward jerk of her knee into not-Max's crotch.

The blow would have felled a normal man, but the thing gobbling and grabbing at her only grunted and went back half a step. She caught sight of its face and screamed, a high whistling cry of disgust and terror. It had Max's eyes, but his mouth had turned into a long, fleshy tube capped with a contracting ring of muscle.

Jessie jerked her knee upward again, harder this time, as she shoved it. Simultaneously, she wrenched herself free of its grip. Its fingers had gone long and wiggly, its arms dangling far below its sleeves. Its head swooped loosely back and forth on its neck as it grabbed for her, but she stumbled back, out of reach. Her hand found the knife on her belt and she pulled it free.

This thing wasn't Max, and Jessie was going to make sure it didn't get her, too.

Chapter 6

Max came to shivering, curled on his side on a bed of damp leaves. He wore only his briefs. Every part of him ached, especially several raw spots on his neck and chest that came away sticky with blood and slime when he touched them.

"Jessie." He was on his feet in seconds, though he sagged against the stone cavern wall to steady himself.

Everything seemed far away, everything seemed muffled. Max shook his head, then again, hard enough to rattle his eyeballs. When that didn't work, he bit his tongue until the copper taste of blood squirted into his mouth. The pain was white and bright and knocked him down.

He got up.

He made it to the doorway before the earth came up and hit him in the face. Spitting dirt, Max rolled onto his back and found strength in the sight of the sky. Blue with white, fluffy clouds, just a glimpse of it visible through the canopy of trees, but it was enough.

His bare feet found every rock and thorn, but those pains

were nothing compared to the thought that Jessie might be in danger. Max pushed through tangled branches, fighting the slap of pine needles. From the clearing up ahead, he heard the sounds of struggle.

When he burst through the final, entangling embrace of the underbrush, Max was in full-on battle mode. Fists raised, heart pumping, he staggered toward Jessie who was on the ground, the thing ready to pounce her. It wore his clothes, the son of a bitch. His hair. Fuck, it probably wore his face, and the idea that it could have used it to try and seduce her vanquished any last trace of fuzzy head or weak limbs.

Max grabbed it by the back of the shirt and yanked. It stumbled back, gangly arms flailing. Crimson arced, spattering the ground and Max when the thing turned.

It didn't look like him anymore. It didn't even look human. Blood gushed from the slash in its throat, and even though the thing scrabbled helplessly at the wound, there was no stanching it.

Jessie sprang up, a carving knife in her hand, but she didn't use it to slash again. "Max!"

Together, they watched the thing go to its knees. Every part of it had distorted now, bulging and shuddering as it shifted rapidly through face after face. Hair in a rainbow of shades grew and shrank. It sprouted breasts that just as quickly disappeared. Its mouth contorted, the shriek coming from it like the sound of tires screeching, kettles whistling.

Incredibly, it looked at them. It saw them and it knew them. It wasn't human, but whatever it was, knowledge gleamed in its narrow-eyed gaze. Intelligence and something like hatred. It lurched upward, slashing at Jessie with fingertips suddenly transformed into claws.

Max didn't think, he moved. He pushed himself between the talons and Jessie, catching the brunt of the blow. Pain ripped up his side and across his chest. Behind him, Jessie cried out.

Then she was at his side, gripping the rake like a baseball bat. "Down!"

Again, no thought, just action. Max ducked as Jessie swung like a pro. The rake's tines connected with the thing's jaw, the sound thick and meaty as the blow rocked the monster's head back. Its wounded throat gaped and tore, more blood gushing.

Jessie swung again. This time, the thing's head completely came away, leaving a jutting, gore-spattered stump from which sudden writhing tendrils sprouted. Its entire body heaved and shuddered before slumping forward, finally still.

"Not so greedy now, are you?" Jessie said and spit on it.

That's when the monster started to change again.

The monster never dies the first time.

Jessie knew that from the movies, but this was no movie. This was real life, and apparently when you cut off something's head, it really did stay dead. The thing in front of them shook and shifted, melting. Flesh oozed and bubbled like it had been dunked in acid. The stench was horrific.

In moments only a puddle of Max's clothes remained. The dirt had soaked up whatever remained of the Greedy One. What had been green was now dead and brown. Jessie wondered if anything would ever grow there again.

"Jessie?"

She turned and gathered Max into her arms, not caring that he was covered in muck and blood. She kissed him hungrily. She breathed in deep, taking in his smell. Then she burst into exhausted, exhilarated tears.

Cleaned and bandaged, Max's wounds were far from superficial, but he'd live. Dressed in clean, dry clothes, the only indication that he wasn't his usual self was the stiff way he moved. Jessie had tried to get him to stay on the couch while Freddy changed all four of their tires with replacements he'd brought from the garage, but Max had insisted on overseeing the installation. He didn't trust Freddy, and Jessie didn't blame him.

"It was too early," Freddy said miserably. "I thought youse would be okay."

"How could you rent this place to anyone at all, knowing that thing was out there?" Jessie demanded.

Freddy shook his head, looking away, and Jessie caught a glimpse of something sly on his face before his expression became contrite. "Needed the money."

"And so long as it was taking us, it would leave you alone," Max said. He'd been quiet before this, but now his voice stabbed the air, harsh. "Right?"

Freddy stammered, twisting his hands together, around and around. Grime had sunk deep into his knuckles, but it was better than blood, Jessie thought. He shook his head again.

"No, no…"

"Bullshit," Max said evenly.

Jessie looked at him and took his hand. Their fingers linked, squeezing. "Max?"

"That thing," Max spat, "was inside me. In my head. You think I wasn't inside of it a little, too? I know what it wanted, and why you let us come here, knowing what would happen. If it took us, it would leave all of you alone."

Jessie's gut twisted, and looking at Freddy's guilty face, she knew what Max had said was true. "You son of a bitch!"

"What are you gonna do?" Freddy cried, making a fist that didn't look at all threatening. "You gonna go to the police? What will you tell 'em? Nobody will ever believe you!"

"How long?" Max demanded, advancing on him. "How many years?"

"Forever!" Freddy shouted. His voice softened and trembled. "It's been around here forever."

"Why didn't you just kill it?" Jessie asked. "I mean, it was strong and scary, but…it wasn't invincible. Why wouldn't you have hunted it down and killed it if it kept feeding off people?"

Freddy said nothing, and finally, Max answered for him.

"Because it was family," he said quietly. "Right, Freddy?"

Freddy got that sly look again, but just for a couple seconds before he completely broke down. "It didn't take anyone for a long, long time. Years. It took Carrie when she was twenty, that was twenty years ago…. We thought maybe it was satisfied. We figured maybe it had had enough! But then she started showing up, hanging around and it was Carrie, but it wasn't anymore. At first she was young, like she'd been. Young and pretty. But then she started getting old, her face was a mess. And we knew it would only be a matter of time. And I got kids!" he shouted. "I got kids."

"So you thought you'd sacrifice us?" Jessie spit away the sour taste. "Because it looked like your sister? It just looked like her, Freddy, don't you get it? It wasn't Carrie any more than it was Max!"

"But it was still family, wasn't it, Freddy? That thing belonged to you, and you all belonged to it. It had become part of all of you." Freddy said nothing. Max made a rude, dismissive gesture. "We're gone. C'mon, Jessie, let's get out of here."

The cell still didn't work and neither did the GPS, and the bridge wasn't repaired, but Freddy had sketched them an accurate map of how to use alternate roads to get back to the main highway. They spent the time in silence until they reached asphalt, and then Max pulled to the side of the road and turned off the ignition.

He turned to her. In an echo of that first day when they'd made out in the front seat after almost running off the road, Max and Jessie dived for each other. She clung to him, his hands in her hair, while she kissed the breath out of him.

"I was so scared," she said around the lump in her throat.

"I wanted to make sure it couldn't hurt you," Max answered.

They kissed again for what felt like a very long time, and even though there was need behind the embrace, it was more a comfort than anything else. When finally they broke apart to breathe, Jessie buried her face against him. She fought tears. Max held her close.

"I would never let anything hurt you," Max said. "I love you."

She already knew that, of course. She'd seen it in every

look he ever gave her. But Jessie lifted her face to his and kissed him with salt on her lips. "I love you, too."

More kissing, this time a little more heated, although she had to be careful because Max's wounds had to be sore beneath the bandages. Still, when he took her hand and put it on the bulge in his jeans, Jessie burst into breathless, ecstatic laughter. She cupped his face and looked deep into his eyes.

"Never take me camping again," she told him.

"Never," Max promised. "Never ever."

"Feel free to take me to the nearest hotel, though," she said, "and to make mad, passionate love to me until we both can't see straight."

"Gladly," Max said with another kiss that set her on fire. "Always."

Then he put the truck in drive and they left the horror behind them.

* * * * *

COUGAR'S CONQUEST

LINDA O. JOHNSTON

Linda O. Johnston is the author of more than fifteen romance novels, including paranormal romance and romantic suspense.

Armed with an undergraduate degree in journalism with an advertising emphasis from Pennsylvania State University, Linda began her versatile writing career running a small newspaper, then working in advertising and public relations, and later obtaining her JD degree from Duquesne University School of Law in Pittsburgh. In addition to her writing, she continues to practice law.

Linda lives in the Hollywood hills with her husband and Cavalier named Lexie, plus Lexie's younger Cavalier friend, Mystie.

Chapter 1

Brett?

No, that couldn't be Brett Sorrellson standing there at the edge of the crowded sidewalk still filled with students waiting for rides home after school.

Gwynn Macka's brain must be even more fried than she had thought to imagine that Brett might be here, at this small middle-school campus in the Rim of the World Unified school district, way up in the San Bernardino Mountains of Southern California. The area was so far from Denver in distance and attitude that it might as well be on the other side of the globe.

But Gwynn wasn't fooling herself. Though she hadn't seen Brett for more than a year, she would never forget his sharp-edged good looks, the way his astonishingly intelligent hazel eyes had bored into her as if she were a computer enigma to be studied and solved on the spot.

Or his buff masculine physique, very unexpected in a guy who pretended to be nothing but a computer nerd. A physique that he kept buff—and knew how to use to its full advantage.

Oh, yes, Gwynn had found that out. Enjoyed it.

Loved it.

Until what they'd had ended so abruptly. Until the brilliant, sexy, wonderful man she'd cared for so deeply had learned the secret she couldn't share with anyone outside her family, and she'd been forced to flee.

Even at this distance, while Gwynn stood at the top of the steps overlooking the pickup driveway, she couldn't doubt her eyes. And how appropriate it was to see him there at the end of this highly taxing school day and before she returned home to what she knew would be a typically stressful time with her parents and brother.

How had he found her? She'd been so careful. Hadn't even used her own name before, when they had known each other.

Well, no matter now. She couldn't just stand there pretending not to see him. Nor did she dare to confront him.

She needed time to think. She turned and hurried back into the building, using the crowd of teachers and students at the exit as her camouflage. She practically ran through the halls toward her classroom, ignoring curious glances of other teachers who conversed outside their own classrooms—none really her friend since she feared getting close to anyone. Not around here—and not ever again.

Inside, she barely glanced at the rows of tablet-armed students' chairs. She headed immediately to her large teacher's desk at the front where she secured her personal property. Pulling the key from her pocket, she unlocked the drawers and grabbed her purse. From a file cabinet to the side, she yanked out folders of biology homework that she'd planned to grade here later that afternoon for her students. Working at home was impossible, but she'd figure out something.

She locked her desk again, jammed her key in the pocket of her gray linen slacks, and dashed toward the door while clutching all she carried.

But her way out was blocked by a tall, looming, gorgeously handsome—and fully unnerving—form.

"Hello, Gwynn," said the deep voice that had always wrapped itself inside her and churned all sorts of lava-hot effects from her most vulnerable body parts. "Good to see you again."

Brett smiled as he regarded the shocked look on Gwynn's face. He tried to keep his expression friendly but knew it was sardonic. And maybe a bit triumphant.

"What are you doing here, Brett?" she demanded. She didn't sound defensive the way she used to, just angry.

Had she changed that much over the past year? Or did she just want him to think so?

"I'll bet you can guess," he responded lazily, leaning against the doorjamb. "It took me a while to get here after I located you. But I thought you knew me well enough to realize that I enjoy a challenge—especially one I can use as a puzzle over the internet."

She had remained in front of him, hugging files to her shapely chest as if using them as a shield against him. She needn't worry. As much as he had once loved caressing her curvaceous, full breasts, that wasn't why he had come.

Although given the opportunity...well, sure. He'd enjoy making love with her just once again. For old times' sake.

"No, actually, I can't," she said. "I don't know why you're here. I should think it would be pretty obvious that I didn't want to see you again after I left Denver."

"Ah, but I definitely wanted to see you again," he said, broadening his smile. Her eyes widened for an instant as if in utter terror.

Damn. He knew how vulnerable she had seemed before. But he had come to believe that was just part of her act. Her seduction of him. Her method of playing him as a fool.

But what if it was real? Had she genuinely felt vulnerable because of who she was, even when no one was aware of it?

Or was it all a pretense?

He would find out.

"Well, you've seen me," she said in a tone so icy that he felt transported for an instant to the cold Aspen mountain slope where they had skied together months before she had disappeared. "Now go back to Denver."

"I don't live in Denver anymore," he told her.

That appeared to shock her. "Really? I thought you loved it there."

"Too many memories," he said casually, although he felt anything but casual.

Her eyes closed for an instant before opening again. "I…I'm not sure what to say."

He regarded her for a minute, not saying anything, either.

She was as beautiful as ever. Her prominent cheekbones underscored deep chocolate eyes that looked even more haunted now, and perhaps afraid as she regarded him warily and, maybe, with a touch of regret—or was he only hoping for that? Her pink lips were less glowing and pouty today than in his memories of her, since she had initially drawn them into a taut line of displeasure while watching him. Now, they were slightly open, all alluring, suggesting silently that he kiss her. Or was that just another thing he wanted to read there?

Her tawny hair was rolled into a knot at the nape of her neck, which suggested it was still long and sexy. She wore a blue shirt and gray slacks, a nice outfit for a schoolteacher, he supposed. As before, she looked slender and sleek. And of course now he knew why.

Had known it for over a year.

Brett had watched Gwynn change, under a full moon, from this incredibly sensuous, attractive woman he had once loved into a wild, stalking cougar. Oh, and not the euphemistic term now used for an older woman who dated younger men.

No, Gwynn was an actual mountain lion. A shape-shifter.

And now he had come to see her for a reason other than seduction and self-satisfaction.

He had a proposition for her. One that would be of great value to her.

He just needed to get her to listen to it.

"You don't need to say anything," Brett told her. But she could see in the studiously bland way he looked at her that he blamed her. She'd known so many of his expressions, and blankness on his face was a way of hiding what he really felt.

She had thought she couldn't feel much worse after running away, knowing she had hurt him. Had hurt herself, too, of course, but that didn't matter.

The kind of hurt she'd evidently caused him, though—it

was more than simply disappearing and ending a relationship that should never have existed in the first place. From
what he'd said, she had caused repercussions in his life that
she hadn't anticipated at all.

She had somehow made him move away from the city,
and therefore the job, that he had loved.

"Brett, I'm so sorry," she breathed, wishing there was
some way she could make things better for him. She had
no illusions that she could ever have made them much better for herself, although she was still weighing options. "I
never meant to—"

"Of course you did," he said easily, as if they were talking
about the weather. "Or you wouldn't have gotten involved
at all, under the circumstances. But it's okay. I'm not here
to issue any blame. Or to make you feel bad."

She stared at his handsome, still-expressionless face once
more. She had the irresponsible and inappropriate urge to
reach out, touch his cheek where a hint of beard was beginning to grow.

She had done that so often, before. Had loved the raspy
feel on the sensitive palms of her hands.

It had always led to his touching her in return. Gently
and neutrally, at first. But then they'd stroked each other
more roughly. Torn at each other's clothes…

Why was she doing this to herself? To punish herself
even more than just seeing Brett again, knowing what they'd
meant to one another—and how she had been so wrong, so
cruel, to have gotten close to him?

Right now, she wanted to edge around him. Flee her
classroom.

Run away from him yet again.

But she knew that wasn't possible.

At least tonight was not a night of a full moon. Tomorrow was, though. He must know that and have planned his arrival here accordingly.

But she would have to make certain that he was nowhere near her then. Otherwise, the results would be even worse than the last time, when he'd seen her. Not just dangerous—for both of them—but potentially disastrous.

For now, she moved sideways and sat on one of her students' chairs. Put the files on its desk arm and lowered her purse to the floor. Sank there, feeling defeated, unsure what to do as her mind flailed for a solution.

"Then tell me," she nevertheless said calmly, "why are you here? And how did you find me?"

"I came here to change your life—again." His renewed smile was even more brittle this time. "The way you changed mine, but better."

"What do you mean?" Gwynn felt a gnawing anxiety inside. Now that he knew where she was, who she was, did he intend to tell the world? That had always been her fear.

That had also been one reason her family had been so furious when she had first made it clear years ago that she had no intention of staying in the San Bernardino Mountains with them. They'd done many terrible things to try to change her mind.

They had tried even harder to prevent her from leaving when she had finally gotten up the nerve and made plans she'd thought would work so she would never have to come back.

How they'd laughed when she had returned with her pro-

verbial tail between her legs. Made her pay for daring to
flee in the first place.

Made clear she would continue to pay for her lapse in
judgment over and over, for the rest of her life.

She was a shapeshifter, a cougar on each night of a full
moon, and so were they. They lived in a world where they
were outcasts, bonded uncomfortably together in an attempt
to shut out the rest of the world—even though their feline
instincts taught them to be loners. Regular humans didn't
believe in them, didn't understand.

Regular humans ridiculed—and killed—whatever they
failed to understand.

Was that why Brett was here?

Not that she expected him to pull a gun and shoot her.
But there were other, less direct ways to end a life.

"I mean I have a proposition for you," he said. "An offer
you can't refuse." He laughed as he used the old expression
that had come to mean that refusal meant death.

She shuddered, doubting she wanted to hear what he had
in mind. "How did you find me, Brett?" she asked sorrow-
fully, as if knowing would somehow make their confrontation easier to bear.

"I'll tell you that when I tell you the rest. I assume you
don't want to talk here, where your coworkers or some kids
could barge in?" He'd made it a question, though it was a
statement she agreed with.

"No," she said. "That would be a bad idea." So would
going anywhere with him, but what choice did she have?

"I thought that'd be the case when I drove up the mountains to this area. I looked around for somewhere we could
talk without anyone around—and you know what I found?"

She shook her head slowly, certain she wouldn't like whatever it was.

She was right.

"I discovered an overlook, a really nice, remote ledge with a guardrail around it, with a view of the mountainside and Lake Arrowhead below. We can go there."

Yes, they could. And it would remind her—and, undoubtedly, him—of a similar overlook they had adopted as their own in the Colorado mountains with a breathtaking view of a forest and a vast and scenic lake. A place that had come to symbolize their relationship, for every time they would go there it resulted in deep, heartfelt kisses that segued into nights in nearby hotels of endless, satisfying—completely wonderful—lovemaking.

"My car is nearby," Brett continued. "You can ride there with me." The unspoken threat, if she failed to agree? The challenge was in his eyes and became closer to being verbalized when he added, "I think you'll find it worthwhile in many ways to come along, Gwynn. We'll catch up on old times, then I'll tell you something that you've probably never even dreamed of. That's what my offer will be about."

"Okay." She tried to keep her sense of defeat out of her tone. "I'll go with you."

Chapter 2

The view was, in fact, spectacular.

Brett looked past the parking area where they stood, down toward the vista of thick green trees below, broken up by the brilliant blue of Lake Arrowhead, with its myriad fingerlike inlets surrounded by expensive homes. He made himself study it.

But his gaze kept returning to Gwynn. And that view definitely was even more than spectacular. It was breathtaking.

He was with her again after all this time.

Locating Gwynn Katian—no, Gwynn Macka—hadn't been easy initially, even for him. He knew his way in and out of, around and through the internet. Prided himself on his skills. Though he had suspected immediately after she'd disappeared that she had used a false name, even that hadn't made his quest much easier.

But he had dug in, given it his all, and found her—relatively fast, too, once she had settled into her job here.

His success had filled him with elation, and not just because he had proved his computer skills yet again.

And amazingly, Gwynn wasn't all he had found. He'd had to examine every aspect of his life-altering discoveries. Then, in fascination, he'd immersed himself in what he'd learned before coming for her.

Now Gwynn stood within arm's reach, almost exactly where he wanted her to be. Yet not close enough.

Not yet.

"Nice view, isn't it?" He spoke calmly, but even so she flinched at the sound of his voice.

"Yes, it is." She still didn't look at him. She seemed to attempt to avoid any kind of contact or even acknowledgment of his presence.

But he? He wanted her in his arms, beneath his caresses. And more.

Just one more time.

Gwynn, though, appeared to stay focused on the scenery below. She kept one hand on the wooden guardrail facing away from him. He doubted that she was enjoying what she saw since her posture was rigid, and not even her head turned to indicate that she was doing more than staring in one direction.

Not looking at him, avoiding him as much as possible in this small but far from intimate area.

He had no doubt, though, that her thoughts, like his, were on the past, when they had visited a similar vista in the mountains near Denver, where they had met.

When they had been anything but remote toward each other.

When their initial sightseeing had led to hugs, touches

and, ultimately, a rushed journey to the nearest hotel where they had made love for the first time.

It hadn't been the last.

So what if she now pretended to ignore him? That caused him no pain. He was in charge here. It was time to remind her.

"Ready for that proposition I mentioned?" He spoke in a friendly yet remote tone. If he allowed triumph to sound in his voice, he knew what her answer would be.

What he would tell her actually would be of more benefit to her in many ways than to him. But it would be good for him, too. She had no idea yet that he had joined the military. He was now recruiting, and the more successful he was, the faster he could be promoted to higher ranks with greater responsibility and prestige.

Not bad, for someone who hadn't the unusual background of those who rose most quickly in the unit he had joined and now revered.

Alpha Force.

"Sure, I'll listen," she eventually said, sounding as if she didn't care in the least what he had to say. "What is it?"

In the past, she had always looked him in the eye, smiling, soaking in his words. Not now. She kept staring into the distance, her expression guarded.

"Let me give you a little background first." He took a few steps forward to join her at the rail, ignoring that she moved sideways to avoid him. "You know, you didn't hang around long enough to find out what I thought about the fact that you were a shapeshifter."

He heard her draw in her breath, and from the corner of his eye he saw her cringe, as if he had struck her.

He forced himself not to move, not to take her into his arms for reassurance. She would only recoil even more.

But it was damned hard being this near without touching her, even knowing she had fled from him before and probably hated seeing him now.

At her silence, he continued, "I'd never heard even fictional stories of a shapeshifting cougar before. Wolves, sure. Even birds, from that classic movie *Ladyhawke*. But a mountain lion? At first, I was shocked that my lover changed shape under a full moon." He purposely refrained from saying "the woman I loved." He had told her that before he'd realized she had kept something so vital from him—and before she ran away. "But after you were gone and I had an opportunity to think, I realized how fascinated I was by it. Too bad you didn't hang around long enough for me to tell you."

He did pause then, staring at her still-averted face. Waiting for some reaction.

She turned then to look at him. The expression in her dark eyes was skeptical. "Fascinated how? Like you'd just seen a carnival freak show? Or some crazy sci-fi thriller come to life? Or—"

"You're the one calling yourself a freak or unreal creature," he reminded her. "Not me."

He again wanted to touch her as she winced, but refrained. What was it about this woman that brought out all his protective instincts? He'd wanted to take care of her from the first, but that was because she had always seemed so vulnerable—before he knew why.

Even now, after she had accidentally revealed the truth about herself and fled—leaving him in bewilderment and

pain that continued to haunt him in unguarded moments—
her reactions still caused him to want to fix things for her.

Well, he would do that, but not in any way she might
anticipate.

"Fair enough," she admitted. "And, well, for whatever
it's worth, I do apologize, Brett. I never intended to get so
close to any man—anyone at all—and yet with you..." Her
voice trailed off, and he saw tears in her eyes before she
again turned away.

"Don't worry about it," he said. "I was upset when you
left. But after thinking about it, I understood why you left,
even if I didn't like it. And my amazement and fascination—
well, it did turn my life in a different direction. I don't suppose you've ever heard of Alpha Force, have you?"

Her puzzled expression was his answer.

"I didn't think so. They work extremely hard to keep it
secret. I work hard at that now, too. Believe it or not, I've en-
listed in the military, Gwynn. And I'm going to tell you some
pretty incredible stuff. First, though, you have to promise to
keep it as much of a secret as your shapeshifting."

"You're in the military? That's so unlike you—well, it's
unlike how you used to be."

He swallowed his annoyance that she didn't answer his
question. "You weren't who I'd thought you were, Gwynn,
so why do you think you know who I am?"

Her smile was wan. "You're right about that."

"So, do you promise not to reveal to anyone what I'm
about to tell you?"

She shook her head, not necessarily in denial but in apparent puzzlement. "How can I promise to keep a secret
when I don't know what you're talking about?"

"It'll be to your benefit," he promised. "But I can't tell you more without your commitment. I can't walk you through getting a highest level government clearance, especially not this fast, so I'll just have to trust you. But before I can, I'll ask you again. Will you keep what I tell you to yourself?"

She glared at him in apparent exasperation. "Okay, since you said it'll be to my advantage, but—"

"No buts. Just yes or no. Will you keep it secret?"

"Yes," she spit.

"Good. Now, just listen to this. I'm sure you'll find it hard to believe, but I'm not just in the military. I'm part of the outfit I just mentioned—Alpha Force. It's a highly covert special ops unit. And wait till I tell you what you have in common with many of its members."

Her eyes widened as he paused. "You're not about to tell me, are you, that some of the members are—"

"That's right," he said with a broad grin. "Shapeshifters."

Gwynn couldn't help it. She shook her head vehemently in denial. "You're just joking, trying to get back at me for not telling you everything about myself. But it won't work, Brett. I'm not that gullible. You've found me. You've shown what a great investigator you are. But—"

"I figured you'd react like this. I got permission to show you a video depiction on my smartphone. And, yes, I know pictures like that can be fudged by digital animation, like in commercial movies. But what I'm about to show you is something used by Alpha Force for recruitment. It's real, and if you get interested enough to come with me to the headquarters I'll prove it. Watch this."

He'd already pulled his phone from his pocket. Brett

pushed the screen for a very special app, and in moments there was a depiction of a man shifting from human form into a wolf beneath a three-quarter moon.

"That's one of the first and most senior officers of Alpha Force, Lieutenant Patrick Worley."

Gwynn watched the phone's screen in fascination—and incredulity. When the shifting was done, she looked at Brett. "It's real?" she whispered, knowing how unsteady her voice sounded. "There are more shifters in that unit, and, well, they work together?"

The only shifters she knew were her family members. They hated her. They hated one another. Talk about dysfunctional, and yet, they had to work together, like it or not, to keep the world from finding out about them.

That was why she had left home as soon as she'd been old enough, defying them. Surely, she'd believed, there were others out there. Even if she couldn't find them, she still needed to get away from the horror that constituted her relatives.

She had managed to go to college, get a job at the company where she had met Brett, all without being detected.

But she'd had nowhere else to go after she had inadvertently allowed Brett to watch her shift. She couldn't stay there, in Denver, after that.

She had come home and regretted it sorely ever since, yet she had not yet devised a better alternative, though she was working on it. Constantly. So far, though, her research had yielded nothing that made it worth trying to flee from here again.

But Brett had mentioned recruitment by this military

group Alpha Force. A military group of shapeshifters? Was he trying to recruit her?

What did that mean?

She wanted to know more. She also had to fight with herself not to throw herself into Brett's arms. She remembered only too well how much they once had meant to each other.

She had loved his hard, irresistible body and all it had done to hers. He had been her first lover. Her only lover. She had missed that when she had fled back here.

She had missed him.

But she wasn't foolish. Despite what he had said, what she had seen on his phone, he might be here to exact a particularly painful kind of revenge on her.

To tempt her with salvation—and present her instead with even more devastation than she had experienced before, when she'd had to leave him.

"Shifters who work together?" he asked, repeating her question with a smile that suggested she was naive for even asking. "Oh, yeah. And more. Tell me, Gwynn. Have you ever shifted when there wasn't a full moon?"

"No," she retorted. She had her answer. He was just attempting to play her. Shifting outside a full moon? Despite the film clip she had just seen, it was impossible.

"Alpha Force members can shift anytime they want," he told her. "The commanding officer, Major Drew Connell, is a medical doctor. So is Lieutenant Worley, whom you just saw. Drew has developed a really special form of medicine, an elixir, he calls it. When a shifter drinks it and has a certain kind of light reflected on him or her, shifting can occur anytime. I'm told it's unusual for most shifters to retain their full human awareness while in animal form, but Alpha Force members who take the elixir do."

"Really?" She couldn't help her amazed and incredulous tone. It sounded so wonderful.

It sounded much too good to be true.

"Really," he said with a nod.

The smile on his face was a challenge. She knew that expression, boyish yet all man. She had seen him wear it when he'd dared her to come along with him to hike up that mountain near Denver on their first outing.

To enjoy the view that had been so similar to this.

To kiss him when they'd reached the summit.

And to join him in bed.

She couldn't help it. She took a step toward him. Ran her fingers through the dark brown hair that was now so much shorter than when she'd known him.

A military cut?

He closed his eyes. "Don't do that, Gwynn." His tone rasped, as if she was torturing him.

She was torturing herself, too.

But so what? Would touching him tell her whether he was lying or telling the truth about his new purported military affiliation? This Alpha Force group? The astounding elixir he had described, and its effects?

Of course not.

And yet she didn't release him. Instead, she threw her arms around him. Pressed her body against his, feeling his hard, muscular frame.

Feeling, down below, another kind of hardness, one she had never anticipated feeling again—at least not with Brett.

"Oh, Brett," she whispered.

And then, suddenly yet as if it was the most natural thing in the world, as if there had never been any secrets between them, any gaps of time, his mouth lowered onto hers in a kiss that made her gasp in recollection and pleasure.

Chapter 3

Her mouth was every bit as sweet, as tantalizing, as he remembered. She played the same games with him, too, as if they had shared their last kiss only yesterday—the way her tongue teased and toyed with his. Her lips were both firm and inquisitive, challenging him to kiss her harder, deeper. Which he did.

As they kissed, he pressed himself against her. Wanting to touch her everywhere—and more. A lot more. And not via mere memories. Once again. Just once again.

Carefully, not wanting to frighten her off, he let his hands roam along her soft and sensuous body, over her back and down to her tight buttocks. He wanted to caress her, stroke her, above her clothes, beneath them, the way he had done so often before. She felt so much the same, and yet different. Slighter. Her sleekness was more angular now, as if she had lost weight. Was it because of what had happened between them?

He still found her sexy. Oh, yes. Even so, he pulled back

just a little, worried about hurting her in her unexpected fragility.

That brief movement was enough to make her stop. To back away. She seemed breathless. Her dark eyes were luminous as she looked at him. She straightened her blue blouse as if she were a schoolmarm. Hell, she *was* a schoolmarm now.

Not the brilliant pharmaceutical lab technician he had known. He understood that, since she was hiding here, she'd had to change the entire focus of her career, her life, in a relatively short time. Well, he'd done so, too. The changes had been monumental for both of them. He loved what he was doing now. Did she?

"Guess we're letting our memories get the better of us," she said quietly, her smile tremulous.

But what he remembered most warmly now wasn't just the first kiss they had shared at that similar overlook in the mountains. No, it was afterward, at the hotel, when they had been unable to resist…and the rest, then, had been history.

That was irrelevant now.

"Not really," he said, attempting to sound indifferent. He had no intention of asking more about why she really hadn't stayed around to talk to him, or what life had been like after she'd run away; what had made her lose weight; why she'd become even more defensive and delicate than she had been back then.

And she had been both.

But his goals now were too important to risk scaring her off. His hopes and desires had to be sublimated to needs much more critical than his—those of his new employer, Uncle Sam, and all the military stood for.

Hell, back then he'd never have anticipated where he'd now landed, thanks to Gwynn. And how much it would mean to him. But he had become so involved in research into shapeshifters—leading to his amazing discovery of the existence of the highly covert Alpha Force—that he had delayed coming for Gwynn until he had looked deeper into the secret unit and, fascinated, joined it.

"I admit, though, that kissing you again was fun," he added when she said nothing. He smiled in a bland, nonconfrontational, not especially amused way. "So what do you think? Will you come with me to check out Alpha Force?"

"I...I'm not sure. I just don't believe—"

"That I'm on the level? That the film I showed you is real?"

"That you're actually in the military, for one thing," she shot at him, looking him up and down.

He was wearing military camos of sorts, though far from official—a sleeveless muscle shirt and jeans, not fatigues. He'd worn his hair longer when they'd known each other, too, but those things clearly weren't enough to convince her.

Which wasn't surprising.

He had another method he'd intended to try, but if she didn't believe him now, simply talking to his commanding officer wasn't likely to do it for her, either; still, it might help.

And doing that would also have another benefit. Thinking about his new job, his fellow military members, his commanding officer and all of that certainly wouldn't keep his sex drive revved up, not the way being in Gwynn's presence again did.

"Oh, yeah," he said. "I'm in the military, all right. You

of all people should recognize that." He glanced down toward his jeans zipper, then back into her face. "Didn't you notice how much I stood at attention just now, when we were close together?"

He'd wanted to shock her, amuse her, something. And he did get a reaction. One that really pleased him.

She looked at him with her dark, dark eyes clouded over with what appeared to be lust. She stared first at his face, and then downward enough that the body part he'd referred to was back at full attention again immediately.

He took a step toward her, ready to take her back into his arms, to see what happened next without exactly planning it.

He held out his arms, and she smiled.

Gwynn definitely wanted to hold Brett again. Tightly and immediately. That kiss—it had been so wonderful. So spectacular.

And feeling him against her a minute earlier had been incredible. Addictive. She wanted it again.

But before she got that close to him once more a couple of cars roared onto the blacktop paving and stopped near them. In moments, some kids darted from the cars toward the overlook railing, screaming and followed by two shouting women, probably their mothers.

As a schoolteacher, even of students a bit older, Gwynn knew she could handle this situation and make sure the kids came out of it safely, but she didn't want to. Instead, she decided to let the stampeding parents take charge, which they did. The kids were herded to safety almost immediately.

When Brett shrugged then walked around to open the

car door for her, she slid into the passenger seat without a word to the intruders.

"Let's get out of here," Brett said as he slipped into the driver's side. His expression suggested as much frustration as she felt, but she found herself silently thanking the families for showing up just then. The situation before their arrival had been too much like the past. She wasn't ready to relive it, no matter how tempting that might feel.

"Let's go grab an early dinner," Brett continued, shoving the key into the ignition. "Before we do, though, I want you to talk to my superior officer, Major Drew Connell. Maybe he'll convince you to come see what Alpha Force is all about. He's at the headquarters in Maryland so I don't want to wait till too late to call although he's expecting to hear from me."

It was now almost eight o'clock in the East, since it was nearly five o'clock here in Southern California. Not too late after a day on which she'd taught school. She usually stayed for a while to grade papers or work on lesson plans. But an early dinner sounded good to Gwynn. Getting home later than anticipated always required an explanation to her family.

And no explanation ever satisfied them.

She shuddered at the thought of her useless attempts to apologize and explain herself when she had returned home last year after fleeing and staying away for a long time— yet not long enough…. She was still paying for that. Would be forever unless she developed a reasonable and permanent way to leave.

Gwynn said little as Brett drove along the winding mountain roads, forcing her thoughts away from the upcoming, inevitable confrontation if she dared to return home late.

She inhaled, enjoying Brett's scent even more now, after their kiss. Her senses were those of a feline, not just a human, and she could tell that his sexual interest had been roused by their embrace.

She made no comment at all when he drove into the parking lot of the ritzy Lake Arrowhead Mountain Inn.

It did, after all, have a well-regarded restaurant.

The fact that it again triggered those memories she was working so hard to ignore… She cast them aside as best she could.

Brett pulled into a tight parking space, then grabbed a strange-looking phone out of the console between them. "This is a government-issue satellite phone," he said. "It's more secure than a regular cell."

Which suggested again that what he was saying was real, not just an attempt to make up nonsensical stories to get back at her for fleeing.

He pressed a button, then spoke into the receiver. "Hi, Major. Yes, I'm with Gwynn…Macka." She heard his hesitation over her name.

It wasn't the one he'd known her under, and she suspected he was trying to rub that in. Or maybe not. Maybe it was truly an effort for him to remember what her name really was.

He talked for a few minutes, then handed the phone to her. "Here," he said.

"Gwynn?" said a voice. It could have been anyone, not necessarily the military officer Brett had mentioned. Even recognizing that, she decided to act as if she believed all

Brett had said, at least for now. The voice continued. "I'm Major Drew Connell, the commanding officer of Alpha Force. Brett told me he's briefed you a bit about who we are and what we do."

"That's right," she said noncommittally.

"He also said he has invited you to come and visit. Check out Alpha Force. Did he mention that one of our members is a shape-shifting lynx? Her name is Lieutenant Nella Reyes, and if you come here I'll make sure she's around for you to meet. We'll also let you try out our elixir that permits shifting at times other than the full moon. Then we'll see if it makes sense for you to enlist and join us. We could use a cougar in our group. You'd be the only one."

A shapeshifting lynx? Gwynn had never met any shapeshifters besides her family. And to know of another feline. To actually meet her. Gwynn felt almost overwhelmed with excitement over the idea.

And to be able to test the elixir. To be able to change outside a full moon. Even keep more human awareness than usual while she shifted.

Excitement? Hell, she was suddenly ecstatic about the idea.

And yet she'd already been so worried even about coming home late tonight, dealing with her family over that.

To go away, even for a few days, over a weekend, to test whether Brett and this Drew Connell were for real. Not to mention Lieutenant Reyes—was that her name?—and the elixir.

How could she do that? And when?

Was Brett aware that tomorrow night was a full moon?

Surely he was. What did he plan to do then, now that he had found her? Watch her shift?

She wasn't about to allow that. Not again.

Chapter 4

After talking just a short while longer, Gwynn handed Brett the phone. She looked both bemused and excited, an attractive and appealing combination.

"So...I know it wasn't a real commitment to the major," he said, "but you sounded fairly positive about going there and checking things out."

"Yes," she said. "I did." She shook her head slightly, causing the knot of tawny hair at her neck to move sideways and back.

Was that a negative reaction, or just a touch of indecision? He decided to assume it was the latter and pretend he hadn't noticed. While pondering, Brett fought the urge to reach over and pull out the pins that held her hair in place. To run his fingers through her soft, straight locks the way he used to.

Back then, the shade of her hair hadn't reminded him of a gorgeous, sleek mountain lion. But then, he hadn't known she was capable of shifting into one.

And why did a hint of her possible negativity turn him on so much now?

Or would anything Gwynn did now, positive or negative, turn him on, feed his desire to get her into bed again?

He wanted her. Badly. Shapeshifting cougar or not. Or maybe that knowledge even added to her appeal now.

But as great as the sex between them had been before, it wasn't appropriate now—not even that one final time he now craved. He forcibly squashed all desire down inside him and tried to pretend it wasn't there.

"I can start making arrangements for you right away," he said instead, glad how neutral his tone sounded. "Can you do it this weekend?" Today was Wednesday. That should give him enough time to arrange a flight for both of them on an air force transport from one of the nearest bases, like Edwards just north of L.A.

He'd accompany her to Ft. Lukman, introduce her around, do what was necessary to give her a taste of Alpha Force. Then he would back off. At that point, he'd have accomplished all he intended to. It would remain up to his commanding officers to convince Gwynn to join, and for her to agree.

And if—when—she did, he would remain far away from her. He had other duties in Alpha Force besides recruitment, mostly making use of his information technology skills. He occasionally acted as an aide to some of the male shifters, since the process required that the shifter be naked at the time of the change, and then when he or she returned from animal form it was always initially in the nude, too.

Sometimes expediency required that the nearest or most

available aide be the one to help out, but policy encouraged assistance by an aide of the same sex whenever possible.

That meant he'd never be there for Gwynn, even if she decided to enlist. A very good thing. But he had to get her into a position to join in the first place.

"What do you think, Gwynn?" he prompted.

"Let me think about it." Her tone sounded so strained that he went against his best judgment and turned in the car seat to face her.

Oh, yes. No matter how much he argued with himself, he still wanted her. Bad idea.

He tamped the feeling down once more, even as his eyes moved over her body, from her gorgeous, clearly worried face to her breasts hidden by her shirt.

"You've got to at least try," he insisted, knowing that coming off as demanding wasn't likely to convince her. "You've got nothing to lose and a whole lot to gain. I've heard the shifters in Alpha Force remark over and over about how great their elixir and its benefits are. Plus, they seem to get along so well together. Camaraderie and all that. And they do so much for our country—covertly, of course."

Damn. He sounded just like a recruiter. And why not? That was what he was.

"I understand," she said. "And I'm definitely interested in finding out more. But…well, there are other factors I need to consider."

Once again the vulnerability that had always attracted him, brought out his protective instinct, showed in her wide-eyed expression.

Made him want to fix things for her, whatever they were.

"What factors?" he asked, knowing from her sorrowful

yet secretive gaze that she was as unlikely to explain today as before. At least now he had a hint, but her shifting clearly wasn't all of it.

"Never mind," she whispered. Her eyes remained on his like a deer's caught in headlights. Only it wasn't just vulnerability he saw there now.

No, there was something more. Was he reading her correctly?

Time to find out. He reached across the seat, leaning so he could place his hand at the back of her long, lovely neck. As he did so, he felt the knot of her hair. Gently, he removed some of the pins holding it there, all the while staring into her eyes.

She didn't object. In fact, whatever he had seen there before seemed to melt into an expression a lot more heated, more suggestive.

More of what he remembered from their prior time together.

"Gwynn," he breathed, then moved enough to cover her mouth with his once more.

So foolish. She was being so foolish to allow herself to be seduced by his suggestions of how her future could be improved.

Even worse, she was allowing herself to be seduced by Brett's very presence.

But his kiss…again. How could she resist it?

His taste was so familiar yet so rare. So different. It made her want to cast all sense aside and tear off his clothes. Her own, too.

But they were in a car. And…

"My room isn't far," Brett said as if he read her mind. His voice was husky. His hands remained in motion, stroking her back outside her shirt.

Moving downward, caressing just the top of her buttocks over her pants.

"Show me," she breathed.

In moments, they were outside the car, walking hand in hand into the hotel lobby. It was crowded but Gwynn was barely aware of the people at the desk, near the bar, even with them in the elevator.

She was only conscious of Brett, close at her side. Holding on as if he were worried she'd slip away and disappear. Again.

But that was not about to happen, at least not at this moment. And if she shoved him away from her once more, she would at least tell him about it this time.

If? No, *when.*

And then, there they were. Exiting the elevator. Hurrying down the wide hotel hall nearly to the end.

The delay felt excruciating. And exciting.

Brett used his card key to open the door. He held it open and she entered.

Before she could do more than inhale, the door was closed behind them. She was once more in Brett's arms.

His mouth again met hers, and his tongue entered her mouth, teasing and exploring and igniting her so much that her knees nearly buckled.

He expertly lifted her into his arms and deposited her on the fancy gold-and-brown coverlet of the bed. Almost immediately, he was on top of her. His body was rock hard and enticing. She was the one to grip his buttocks now, but his clothes were still on.

She moaned as he moved off her, but only for a moment as she felt his hand slide beneath her shirt, moving upward to gently grasp one breast. He moved his thumb over her bra, stroking her nipple. "Brett," she moaned, letting go of him just long enough to start unbuttoning her blouse.

"Let me," he said. She felt his hands replace hers, then move downward and around until, after moving and gyrating in assistance, she was naked.

But he wasn't. Not yet. She edged sideways on the bed just enough to make it clear he had to stay away, yet not long.

Only long enough for her to help him off with his shirt and jeans.

And then for her to look at him all over.

He was every bit as gorgeously masculine as she remembered. His maleness thrust toward her, hard and so alluring that she moved downward and took him into her mouth. He groaned as she teased and sucked…and grew even more aroused.

Again he seemed to read her mind. He moved her gently away from him and once more she lay on her back on the bed, completely nude. Fully wanting him as, this time, he was the one to play, first with her breasts and then lower, touching her first, then following his hands downward with his mouth while she cried out in her need for him.

He let go of her for a moment, making her nearly weep from the sudden abandonment. But then she heard the sound of plastic being ripped, knew he was protecting her, protecting them.

He was quickly back on top of her again. And then, inside her. His thrusts were soft at first but sure. She moved her hips to meet and encourage him.

As his strength and speed increased, so did her motions in response—mindless, needful, inevitable.

She cried out as her pleasure reached a crescendo. At the same time, Brett moaned, and Gwynn soared into complete fulfillment.

Chapter 5

Brett lay on top of Gwynn for several long minutes after reaching an orgasm that had rocked him everywhere, from his sated body to his wild but exhausted mind.

"Wow," she finally said from beneath him, her skin hot and smooth and still highly enticing to his touch. She wasn't moving either, though he worried that his weight was too much for her slender body.

"Yeah, wow," he echoed.

"That was even better than…" She didn't finish. Didn't have to. But she stirred and added, "Not that things weren't wonderful before, of course. But this was…"

"Yeah," he said again. "It was."

Her laugh bounced him slightly, and he rolled over carefully to lie beside her, keeping one arm over her.

She moved so she was facing him, her head tucked under his chin. Her breathing began to slow, and he let his hand move down her back so he could stroke her buttocks.

He couldn't help himself. Even now, when he felt so good,

he knew he hadn't had enough of her, notwithstanding his vow to himself to indulge in sex with her just one more time.

He might never feel that he'd had enough of her, but he would have to deal with that. He'd found her. Was doing what he had to for his own sake, which happened to coincide with hers despite her not understanding that yet.

But he wouldn't let himself get so involved with her again. Maybe, truthfully, it was a touch of revenge he'd had in mind, or maybe it was clear self-preservation, but he would get her to join Alpha Force, then ease himself away from her once more.

Permanently.

He was fascinated by shapeshifters. Definitely. But having an ongoing relationship with one? Especially this one, with whom he'd already had a relationship that she had fled from?

Not on his agenda.

For now, though, well, another bout of lovemaking could fit onto that amorphous agenda of his if he let it. It was still just one night, even if he indulged multiple times. Maybe he'd indulge even more than one night, too, till they got to Ft. Lukman. And then...

Gwynn moved away from his exploratory caresses. "I—I've got to leave," she said.

"We haven't had dinner yet," he reminded her, speaking softly against her lemon-scented hair. "And maybe we could have some more dessert, both before and after."

"No," she said so firmly that it jarred him. "This was—well, you know I enjoyed it. But I have to run."

Why? Did she have another guy in her life, one his research hadn't discovered?

"After dinner," he commanded. Then, because she froze, then started to move farther away, he said more softly, "I want to tell you more about Alpha Force. You haven't said for sure that you're coming to Ft. Lukman, and I need to convince you."

He didn't like her hesitation. But before he determined what to say next to ensure her cooperation, she said in a tone he couldn't interpret, "Okay. Dinner. But let's eat now."

It wouldn't be easy to get her family off her back that night, but she'd think of something, Gwynn told herself as she showered in the hotel bathroom before leaving for dinner. She had to, no matter how difficult they made it.

They couldn't hurt her any more than they already had. She knew the ugliness she had to expect after disobeying their directives. She could deal with it.

She showered alone under the softly pelting water that touched parts of her that Brett had so recently stroked... and more. Of course she also remembered the times before when Brett and she had showered together....

But not now.

Now, she had to think of what to say when she got home that night. An excuse for being late, something related to her job and teaching and the school. Her family despised that she'd entered into a new career around here, but they hadn't balked at her contributing her salary toward their comfort.

Not that she gave all of it to her parents and brother. She had a secret bank account where she saved as much as she could. She'd doubted at first that she would ever get up the nerve to leave here again, and the longer she stayed, the more remote the possibility seemed. But she had a nest egg, just in case.

And now...

Now, thanks to Brett, she just might, in fact, get up the nerve to do something positive with her life once more.

Do something that would make her proud to be a shapeshifter, instead of ashamed and terrified about it.

And with Brett remaining in her life?

Was that possible?

They'd just made love. And so far, since he'd found her, she had seen no reason not to trust him, except for his possibly crazy story about this Alpha Force.

Well, she'd see about that. Maybe.

If she dared to break away.

Dinner with Gwynn at the gourmet hotel restaurant was both enjoyable and frustrating.

She seemed remote now to Brett. Interested in Alpha Force. But she still didn't commit to visiting Ft. Lukman with him.

She asked a lot of questions, though. Like how he had found her.

Hell, why not. He told her.

Facing her across the table as she nibbled on a serving of fish—her lack of interest in the food making it seem obvious why she'd lost weight—he said quietly, so no people sitting around them in the crowded room could hear, "After I saw you...you know, and you disappeared, I did a lot of online research trying to find you, and also to learn about what I'd seen."

He'd found an amazing array of material on shapeshifting, ranging from pseudo-fiction to that which purported to be real but was available only to those with special on-line skills like his. Aka hacking, though he never admitted to that.

"Really?" she said, pausing. "I've looked, too, but haven't found much—a good thing, I thought. What did you see?"

"Well," he said in an even softer voice, "I learned that real, nonfictional shifters aren't common, though they're not extremely rare, either. But those who can control when they shift and who can maintain human awareness—they're almost unheard-of. Except for those in Alpha Force."

She blinked those gorgeous dark eyes, as if she still didn't believe what he was saying.

He continued, "That's why I sought it out after discovering that such a military unit existed. You got me so fascinated that I had to learn more, so I wound up enlisting." Which took a lot of time to work out, time in which he had delayed coming here to confront Gwynn. He had located her not long after beginning his search, as soon as she had secured her teaching job. "Good thing I'm a computer geek."

He could smile about that now, but he'd been highly conscious of it when in college and at his first job in the pharmaceutical company where he'd met Gwynn. He'd been all information technology nerd then, and she'd been a skilled lab technician. The differences and his consciousness of geekiness hadn't stopped him from pursuing Gwynn and believing she'd cared for him back.

Of course he'd also fought it by building up his body to the max, too. Real geeks didn't do that.

But not even that had been enough for Gwynn to tell him all there was to know about herself.

Or to keep her from running away after he found out.

Well, he'd do what he needed to for his newfound career, which would help her, too. And then he'd back off.

For revenge? He'd considered that before, still pondered it. But he thought of it more as self-preservation. She'd been the one to leave before. And now, he would be the one to show her that things could change and people didn't have to hang around any longer than they chose to.

She was fascinated—not only by Brett's description of how he had found this Alpha Force, but also by the fact that he'd changed his whole life as a result of seeing her shift.

Because he'd liked it? Or because of his keen intellectual curiosity, which had attracted her in the first place?

It didn't really matter. As much as she cared about him, as wonderful as it was to make love with him, they were much too different to stay together even if she dared to leave again and follow him. She was a loner. She had to be.

Her family had taught her that. The hard way.

Her family. As she'd listened to Brett, a major part of her mind remained churning about how she was going to handle tonight. A lapse of a mere hour or two? They'd jump on her as if it had been another year.

When fleeing from Brett because he had seen her shift, Gwynn had considered alternatives besides returning to her childhood home. Nothing had seemed any better—not when she knew she had to hide that she was a shapeshifter, and her family, as difficult as they were, had been good at keeping that secret about all of them.

Now, she was under her family's control, despite her quest for where she could go next, what she could do.

How on earth would she approach leaving long enough to go visit Alpha Force?

She would do it, though. She had to. In case it was real, she had to check it out.

"Isn't that fish any good?" Brett asked. When she glanced at him, startled at his question, she noticed that his plate was empty while hers was still practically full of food. "I thought felines liked fish," he said more quietly.

She forced a smile. He didn't need to know all that was on her mind. He had been so protectively male before that she knew he would try to interfere, which could be a horrendous mistake.

"I do like fish," she said. "And you obviously like pot roast. Now, tell me again about how we can travel most easily to Ft. Lukman this weekend."

"You've decided to go?" His handsome face looked so pleased that she wished they weren't in public. She wanted to lean over and kiss him.

What the hell? She leaned across the table and placed her lips on his. She'd planned on it being just a quick kiss, but it went on for longer than she'd anticipated.

When she finally pulled away, she sat back down and nodded, knowing her face was flushed and her hands were shaking.

"I've decided to go," she confirmed.

Chapter 6

"Where the hell were you?" demanded George Macka, Gwynn's father.

Filled with misgivings yet having no choice, she had finally returned home. It was nearly nine o'clock that night. Not very late in the scheme of things, but later than her controlling family permitted.

They'd all been waiting for her in the tiny, drab kitchen of their wooden cabin secluded deep in the mountainous woods near Big Bear Lake. Ready to pounce, figuratively, at least, on this night when the moon was not yet full.

"I'd say that my dear little sister was out screwing some guy," said her brother Eddy. "But no one sane would screw around with a bitch like her. Besides, she wouldn't dare. She knows what we'd do to a fool human who touched her."

As always, her mother, Genevieve, stayed quiet, watching Gwynn with anger and accusation written all over her face.

The two men in her family resembled each other, from their short, pale brown hair and portly builds to their choice in clothing—fraying jeans beneath plaid shirts that were too tight. Her father was clearly the patriarch, though, with heavy jowls and deep wrinkles in his forehead and at the edges of his eyes.

Their mother, less wrinkled yet with deep, disapproving grooves beside her mouth, preferred shirt dresses in solid colors. Her hair was as light as theirs and much shorter than Gwynn's.

Gwynn didn't feel as if she were part of them, despite the one incontrovertibly distinguishing characteristic that they all shared.

They were all shifters. Cougars. Wild and angry and dangerous once a month beneath the full moon, they were each a loner then, like real mountain lions.

If only Gwynn didn't have to get past that hurdle tomorrow night. At least she would be able to take off with Brett for the weekend, after her school day on Friday. Maybe he'd been lying through his teeth to her. But in case it was real, she owed it to herself to check it out.

"Good thing it isn't tomorrow," Eddy said, startling Gwynn with his words that partly paralleled her thoughts. He stomped out of the kitchen, followed by their father.

George turned back at the door, though. "I'll let you go to that damned school tomorrow," he said. "But you'd better be here before five o'clock or else."

She knew what "or else" meant. He'd confine her during the time of their shift, as punishment. Not allow her to participate in the only good thing about their shifting routine each month: prowling wildly, alone, through the mountains, enjoying the rare sense of freedom.

When the men had left, Gwynn prepared to hurry off

to her bedroom down the hall. To spend the night thinking about everything that was to occur in the next few days.

But before she did, her mother's voice sounded tiredly from behind her, where she sat at the small kitchen table. "I don't know what you may have been up to tonight, but your brother got back here only a little while before you did."

Gwynn turned. Her mother looked exhausted rather than angry. Sometimes she acted as if she was on Gwynn's side, but rarely. Mostly, she didn't counter the men who controlled them.

"What do you mean, Mother?" Gwynn was afraid to hear the answer.

"The way they were talking—well, I hope that whatever your reason was for getting back here late it wasn't anything they shouldn't know about. I got the impression that Eddy was following you. Which might be a good thing, if you're pressing your luck around here again. I'm tired of having to act like you're part of this family."

With that, she stood and stomped out of the room.

Gwynn couldn't sleep that night. She pretended nothing was wrong in the morning when she drove back to school in her car, which she'd picked up in the same parking lot last night after Brett dropped her off and waited till she was safely inside. She wasn't sure whether he'd tried to follow her home, but she'd gone by a circuitous route until she'd reached the narrow road that led to her family's house.

Knowing where she lived would not be a good thing for Brett. Especially that night.

Before classes started that morning, she tried calling the cell phone number he'd given her but he didn't answer. Because of her family's reaction last night—and the possibility that Eddy had been following her—she intended to tell Brett to get lost. That she was dumping him again.

Anything to make him leave before tonight, when the moon would be full.

Anxious since she hadn't been able to speak with him directly, she left him a voice mail and sent a couple of text messages asserting that, though she'd had fun with him yesterday, she never wanted to see him again. That it was time for him to get out of her life for good. Leave this area immediately.

Tomorrow, once the shift was behind her—and the shifts of the rest of her unpredictable yet ferocious family—she'd contact Brett again. Apologize without explanation and tell him that she was ready to go with him to Ft. Lukman, or even just meet him there if he'd tell her where it was.

But for now, she was worried about Brett. If Eddy had in fact seen him with her last night...well, the only way to fix that would be to ensure he wasn't around for her family to deal with in their own destructive way tonight.

But students were streaming into her classroom. She had to get to work.

This school day was much like every other, except in her mind. She diligently worked with her students, explaining fundamentals of biology as accepted by regular humans, answering questions and doing everything else that she usually did.

But her thoughts were on Brett. She hadn't gotten a return phone message or text from him by lunchtime, or even by the time school ended for the day.

Maybe that was a good thing. Maybe his being here had

been just to let her know he'd found her, to torment her with the sad joke of bedding her once more and being the one to leave.

Or perhaps he'd bought into her nasty messages and had already left town.

As devastating as that all sounded to her, she hoped, for his sake, that it was so.

The school day was over. As she had between classes and at lunchtime, Gwynn pulled her cell phone from her purse as she sat at her desk in her empty classroom and looked at it.

No missed messages or texts. Brett hadn't called back or otherwise attempted to get in touch.

It was better that way, she told herself as she started gathering her things to head home, in plenty of time not to incur her family's wrath. Not tonight, of all nights, with the full moon about to rise.

But she couldn't help thinking that, as determined and obstinate as Brett usually was—at least used to be—she'd assumed he would at least call back to let her know he had given up on her.

Even though, on some level, she'd hoped he hadn't.

Her purse strap over her shoulder, she locked her desk and stood.

"Hello, Gwynn."

Startled, yet not entirely surprised, she looked up to see Brett in the doorway. He wore jeans again, and a black T-shirt that hugged his muscles.

"I thought I told you—" she began, ignoring the flutter of relief and even happiness that let loose inside her.

"Never mind what you told me. I want to know what's going on."

He had walked inside the room, and she hurried to confront him. Voice low, she hissed, "You know exactly what's going on."

"The full moon tonight, you mean?" His tone was muted, too, fortunately.

"Yes. I've got to go. And you need to leave this area. I'll talk to you tomorrow." She tried to edge by him, but he grabbed her arm over the sleeve of her cotton blouse.

"What's really on your mind, Gwynn? You know I'm aware of what's going to happen tonight, so it can't be that. Is there something else I should know?"

She couldn't help looking into his troubled yet curious hazel eyes. She shook her head. "No. Please—"

"If you want me to stay away, you need to tell me why—and it's not just because you don't want me to see you shift. What is it?"

She gnawed on her bottom lip, her mind racing to decide how to play this. "If I tell you, will you promise not to try to watch me? That you'll hang out in your hotel room tonight?"

"Sure."

Could she believe him? She doubted it, but she had to try. It was the only way she could protect him, knowing that her family was apparently aware of her having been with him yesterday and might do something this night to harm him if they happened to see him.

"I mean it. You need to stay far away tonight. My family…well, I never told you about them, but when I left for Denver, it was mostly to escape them. I had to come back, though, when…when I had no place else to go. I can deal with them. But I have reason to believe they'll be watching for you if you're around tonight. They can be vicious even when they're not shifted. And when they are, like tonight, vicious doesn't even begin to cover it. So please, please, keep your promise and stay away." She searched the planes of his face, the stony look in his eyes, for some kind of guarantee.

She saw none.

"Please," she said again, and reached up to kiss him.

"Okay," he said, sounding reluctant as she finally broke away. His gaze was searching but not readable.

She only hoped he was telling the truth.

Brett never liked lying. But he did so easily when he had a good reason.

He had one now.

As nighttime approached, he left his hotel room carrying full nighttime camouflage gear to don later in his rental car. Though Gwynn hadn't appeared to want him to know where she lived, he'd already found out. Checked out her family—two parents and a brother and her, living in a house in the woods that Google Earth had located via satellite and shown to be a small, run-down shack.

Before dark, he drove to a gas station with a convenience store that appeared to be the closest retail facility and parked there.

Then, changing clothes out of the sight of any store employees, he slipped into the forest and hiked until he located the house.

He had purposely chosen this timing to confront Gwynn here, where she had fled into the mountains. He had also known her family was here.

He hadn't realized, before this afternoon, though, that she

was afraid of them. She'd obviously wanted to protect him, whatever the problem was. But did she need protection, too?

He was damned well going to find out.

She'd already said that her family members were shifters, too. He'd come with photographic equipment to record how things went. He would figure out later if, and how, he could use the evidence.

He had talked to Major Connell several times during the day. He'd listened to Gwynn's messages, read her texts, and chosen not to respond until he'd confronted her in her classroom.

Tonight would mostly be observation, unless her family in some way attempted to harm Gwynn.

Then, it would be time for action.

In any event, tomorrow would be one for activity—to gather her up and get her out of here over the weekend.

And then...well, he'd have to see about the future and how Gwynn fit into Alpha Force.

Or not.

And how his own life would be affected by her decision. Probably very little, once he'd recruited her and he backed off. It was one thing working with shifters, and something else to get more involved, something he doubted he wanted to do.

Night was falling. He now moved around through the trees until he was able to watch for the moon to emerge over the horizon.

The full moon.

As promised, Gwynn had come home right after school, as soon as her confrontation with Brett was over. The energy in the household was almost palpable early that evening.

Her family was jazzed. Ready to change and to roam.

And her? She was even more ambivalent than usual.

Oh, yes, she loved how it felt to be shifted, a feline in the wild. She always had.

But being alone, as she'd been in Colorado, was preferable to knowing that her family members were nearby and treated her like the lowliest form of dirt imaginable.

"Come out here, Gwynn. Now." That was her father. He was on the back porch of their house. She felt certain that the rest of the family, except for her, were there, too.

She felt especially uneasy this night. Could she trust Brett to stay away?

He might not know exactly where she was, but he had traced her to this area. He was smart, innovative, and in some ways unstoppable.

Even though she was inside and not directly in the glare of the full moon, she felt the initial tugging beneath her skin that told her that her shift was beginning.

Sighing, she did as she was told and headed to the back porch to be with her family.

Her parents, her brother, were all illuminated somewhat by the light of the moon, barely visible near the horizon beyond the stand of nearby trees. They appeared to be in varied degrees of discomfort, limbs twisted, the beginning of their cougar pelts erupting from beneath their skin.

None wore any clothing, of course. The change took place whether a shifter was dressed or not, but its discomfort was somewhat lessened by nudity.

Gwynn stood just outside the doorway, undressing quickly. A good thing, since her own change had begun. She writhed, staring at her arms as they lengthened and she sat back on her haunches, fur growing quickly on her limbs, her body.

She heard a roar deep in the throat of her father, followed by answering growls of her brother.

They were staring into the woods beyond the clearing around their home.

Her gasp sounded almost human to her as she realized what they were growling about.

There, only partially hidden behind the trees, was Brett, dressed in black, but still visible.

An intruder.

A human.

One who was very much in danger.

Chapter 7

Fascinating.

Brett was shooting a video on his special camera, watching as the four people on the back porch of that small, decrepit cabin morphed from human form into cougars.

Just like he had seen one of them do so many months ago: Gwynn.

He'd been amazed, horrified, almost sickened then, until he'd had time to think about it.

Now, he was still amazed but fascinated. Excited. Drawn to them.

Maybe the entire family could be encouraged to join Alpha Force.

On the other hand, if his impressions about Gwynn's fear this afternoon were real, Alpha Force would not want her possibly out of control family members.

Back when he had known her before, she'd never answered any questions about her origins or her family. He had the sense that something was wrong there, although he didn't know what.

He'd developed some theories, though. After seeing her change, his huge amount of research had included not only shapeshifters but cougars, too.

Like all felines, they tended to be solitary hunters. Staying in family groups was not natural when they were fully grown. Not while they were in feline form.

Having the group together like this as humans—did that lead to problems, too?

He'd watch them now. Follow Gwynn to memorialize with his camera how a changed cougar with only limited human awareness, if any at all, acted during a shift.

And to make sure she remained safe. That took precedence over his promise to stay away from her tonight.

He hadn't had a camera with him the last time he had seen her change. Not even a smartphone.

Of course then he hadn't been anticipating what he'd seen.

As he watched under the brightness of the full moon, two of the creatures—now all cougar—leaped almost in unison from the porch, then stalked in his direction.

Not good, he realized, stiffening in place as his self-protective instincts hollered at him to run. They had no pack mentality as werewolf shifters did, or at least they shouldn't. But they did appear to have one common goal.

One that was not good for him.

Still, their following him would keep Gwynn safe.

He carefully began walking backward through the darkening forest, glancing behind himself often to avoid tripping over piles of leaves or backing into trees.

But the two mountain lions kept getting closer.

Good—but how could he lure them away without harming them or allowing them to hurt him?

He had brought a weapon, of course. He was in the military. But using it on these cougars was definitely not a good idea. They were unusual creatures that deserved to live, as long as they didn't harm him.

Plus, they were Gwynn's relatives.

He began to withdraw from the area more quickly.

That was when the cougar in the lead sprang toward him.

Brett had no choice. He reached beneath his shirt for his holstered pistol.

But before he could aim it, a third cougar reached them— a female that had to be Gwynn, since the fourth remained near the house. This one placed herself between the males and him, blocking them. Baring her fangs and making deep, roaring growls.

The others immediately stopped and stared, as if they didn't believe what they saw.

And then their fury and feral nature were focused entirely on her. Both crouched as if preparing to spring on her.

Shooting was even less of an option now. He might hit Gwynn. He nevertheless had to do something to help her. To keep her safe.

Since he'd joined the military, he'd intensified his own rigorous workout regimen and added to it official fighting and self-defense techniques that were mandatory for all soldiers. Would any work on a wild cougar?

As the two advanced on a snarling Gwynn, now crouched and ready to spring back at them, Brett shouted to get their attention. If they attacked him, he would use all his resources—his wits and his training—to fight back, using his gun only as a last resort.

He would not let them harm Gwynn.

They hesitated at the noise, and that was enough for Gwynn to leap off the ground, landing on the head and shoulders of the larger, older-appearing cat. She used her claws to remain on top, and Brett saw blood appear on the other animal's pelt.

The attack lasted only moments, and then Gwynn was off the cougar and back on the ground facing both of them and warning them with a low feline roar.

Instead of joining together and attacking her in return, the other two cougars remained still, bending their heads as if in submission. As if they acknowledged she was in charge. They bared their fangs, yet they quickly slunk away in different directions.

The cougar that was Gwynn looked him straight in the face with her gleaming, dark eyes, perhaps in challenge, or maybe just in acknowledgment of his presence.

"Thanks," he told her. Then, very carefully, he backed into the woods.

He knew she continued to follow him until he reached the parking lot where he'd left his car and got into it. He didn't always see her, but he heard the soft rustling of the underbrush in areas he had just vacated.

She was chasing him.

And still protecting him.

He wanted to be in a position to protect her instead. But he knew when to back off and accede to circumstances.

He would protect her in other ways. That was why he was here.

In the driver's seat of the car, he put the key in the ignition and turned it. The engine grumbled to life, and the headlights switched on automatically.

There, standing before him, was a gorgeous, sleekly tan cougar with her erect, rounded ears perked high, her mouth open to reveal her teeth yet again. This time, she looked triumphant.

The moon had disappeared below the horizon.

Gwynn's shifting back to human form was finally over.

She was near her family home, in the parking lot where she had last seen Brett drive off. Nude, of course. The chill mountain wind of morning reminded her of that as it circled her, stirring the leaves on the trees surrounding the clearing.

Standing still, she listened for a moment to ensure she heard no indication that there were other shifters near enough to sense. She also listened for Brett and his car.

No, he had left. As he should have.

As always, she retained memories of all that happened when she was shifted, recollections of what her senses had experienced, not the rest of her brain, since she was all cougar during her change.

Last night she had definitely added to those sensory recollections.

She recalled that Brett had tried to intervene when the cougars that were her father and brother had attempted to attack him and she had confronted them. They had turned on her, and Brett had attempted to protect her. But she instead attacked them and, in their surprise, they had been the ones to surrender and run.

Or so she believed, if the memory visions in her head were accurate.

At least she hadn't seen them again all night, although she had stayed in the trees and followed Brett's car for a while to make sure he remained safe.

What if Brett had been right? That under other circumstances she would have had more complete, comprehensive, memories.

That Alpha Force military unit members had a way of retaining their human awareness and cognitive abilities while shifted. That they could rationally determine what to do while in animal form.

Could use the ability to shift in ways she could only imagine.

Not the way her family did.

Despite living together in so dysfunctional a way, her family members usually separated immediately after shifting on the night of a full moon. But last night the men had apparently decided to attack Brett together.

Her family had known about Brett's presence in the area and around her. They had determined to attack him in unison, as rare as working together while shifted was for them.

They probably hadn't imagined she would dare to intervene.

Well, neither had she—before. But she couldn't allow them to harm Brett.

And he had attempted to protect her, too.

Even in shifted form, her mind fully engaged as a cougar, she had known what she had to do. That made her proud.

Her family was not used to Gwynn taking a stand of any kind. No, they had learned, by her behavior all these years—including returning home believing she had no other choice—to mean that she was as submissive as her mother was, willing to obey the men in the family.

And now?

It was time for her to go back to her house and get ready for this day of school teaching.

And to see how her family reacted to her this morning.

"Everything okay?" Brett knew that Gwynn had been aware of his presence from the moment he walked into her classroom that Friday afternoon. He was dressed in nice civilian clothes that went well with her professional outfit of blouse and skirt.

He wished he could pull all attire off both of them.

He hadn't realized what a turn-on her shapeshifting could be, until what had happened last night.

"It's fine." Her smile appeared almost radiant, the most genuine smile he had seen on her since he had shown up around her home.

Except for those smiles, of course, that had resulted from their lovemaking...

But he realized only too well that this wasn't the time to focus on that. He needed answers from her.

"I'm glad," he said. "So, I've arranged a military transport for us first thing tomorrow morning. Will that work for you?"

Before she could answer, a student came in carrying some paperwork that she clearly needed to deal with. Brett faded to the side of the classroom to watch her.

He had purposely stayed far away from Gwynn all day,

knowing she would be teaching and wouldn't appreciate his interference.

But early that morning, when the moon was no longer in the sky, he had sneaked back to her house to watch her leave for the day—and to satisfy his concerns that she was okay, that her family hadn't harmed her over what had transpired the night before.

He'd hated that, although he'd tried, he hadn't found her again last night or been able to follow her to ensure her safety. But he believed that she was in charge after her confrontation with her family.

He also believed that the usual wild feline mentality would keep her safely solitary for the rest of that night.

And now? Now, he was happy to be back with her. To reassure himself that she was, indeed, okay.

And to torment himself with wanting her. She seemed so relaxed. So...well, hot.

He knew now that his intention of having sex with her only one more time had been a joke. Given a choice, he'd want her in his bed every night from now on.

But it was premature to even hope that. Especially without knowing how she felt about leaving here and checking out Alpha Force.

The student finally left. Gwynn walked over to the side of the room where he stood.

"You asked about this weekend."

He nodded.

"Last night—actually, this morning—I had a real confrontation, a human one, with my family."

"I'm sorry," he said, reaching out and taking her slim hands into his larger ones. "Because of your saving me?"

He kept his voice low, not that there was anyone around who could hear them."

"Exactly. And because they dared to attack you. But even then—well, thanks for coming to my defense when they turned on me. But I could have handled it."

"You did handle it," he acknowledged lightly, even as his heart sank. Would she tell him now to get lost, that she didn't want any further disputes with her parents and brother?

"Yes, I did. Then and later." She was smiling now. "I have a lot more to tell you about how I get along with my family, but you've seen some of it firsthand. The only time I've ever gone against them before was when I left home, and then I wound up coming back. They were sure that I would remain subservient to them forever."

She looked so excited that he wanted to kiss her. It took a lot of effort to keep reminding himself that they were still in a middle-school classroom and kids could pop in at any moment.

"But you're not." He didn't make that a question. "Does that mean…?"

"It means I'm going with you tomorrow. I want to learn all about your Alpha Force. And the idea that you have a way for me to control my shifts and how I react then."

He couldn't help it. He glanced around momentarily, then leaned toward her and kissed her smiling lips.

Only briefly. For now.

But he could finally believe that there might be a later.

Chapter 8

*T*he woods at the edges of Ft. Lukman, Maryland, were not as dense as those in California's San Bernardino Mountains.

Gwynn was delighted to recognize this while stalking along the forest floor. The leaves were moist against her paws. It had rained here yesterday.

She was aware of the weather. She was aware that the full moon had been two nights earlier. This night's moon had slivers shaved off its appearance.

Not that she would ever have thought of any of that before while in cougar form.

Now, though, she had shifted at a time of her choosing—with help.

After drinking the special elixir of Alpha Force and having an artificial light resembling moonlight shined on her naked body.

By Brett Sorrellson.

He had told her the truth. There was an Alpha Force, a covert military unit whose members included shapeshifters.

Most were men, most shifted into werewolves, but she had met Lieutenant Nella Reyes, the woman who shifted into a lynx, whom the major had mentioned on the phone. Plus, there was a shifting hawk.

She felt free, despite knowing that military restrictions and orders would be imposed on her if she chose to enlist in the military and join this secret group.

She knew what her decision would be.

There. She had been told that her shift would be short for this, her test, her first time. The twisting and pulling of her limbs, her insides, her skin, had begun.

Knowing she would soon be back in human form, she bounded back toward the clearing where her shift this time had started.

Toward the place where Brett waited for her.

He was there, as she'd known he would be.

She was naked now as she shifted back from cougar form. He had her clothes waiting for her, and he draped a long shirt over her immediately and fastened a couple of buttons in the front.

She reveled in the feel of his strong hands as he touched her. His eyes were glazed with heat and desire, but he did nothing out of line, nothing suggestive of sex as he asked, "How did it go?"

"Fantastic!" She couldn't keep her excitement from bubbling over into her response. "Everything you said it would be."

She was aware even more now of how she had gotten here—thanks to Brett and his fascination with her shapeshifting from the moment he had discovered it.

She had fled in fear, when what she should have done was given him a chance.

He, instead, had given her a chance, changed his entire life because of what he had seen that fateful night.

Now he was about to change her life, too.

"Thank you so much, Brett." She didn't even try to hide the hoarseness in her voice, the result of emotion—and more—as she pressed her body, still barely dressed, against his.

She felt how much he, too, was attracted to her. Wanted her.

"If I join Alpha Force," she said, her tone still raspy as she wrapped her arms around him and drew even closer still, "is it possible for two members to fraternize?"

"Yes, ma'am," he responded in an irregular whisper of his own. "Especially when one has saved the other from great bodily harm."

"No problem," she said, "when the one in danger has such a great body."

He laughed. "I was amazed yet again that night, Gwynn. And I'd no idea that seeing you get so ferocious yet protective would make me want you all the more...later."

Her turn to laugh. "Well, then," she said, "why don't we adjourn to your quarters for the rest of tonight. Tomorrow, I'll start signing whatever I need to, to become a member of Alpha Force. Especially if that means we'll get to spend more time together afterward. Does that work for you?"

"Oh, yeah," he said emphatically, "that works." He lowered his lips to hers.

* * * * *

NIGHT OF THE TIGER

DORANNA DURGIN

Doranna Durgin spent her childhood filling notebooks first with stories and art, then with novels. After obtaining a degree in wildlife illustration and environmental education, she spent a number of years deep in the Appalachian Mountains. When she emerged, it was as a writer who found herself irrevocably tied to the natural world and its creatures—and with a new touchstone to the rugged spirit that helped settle the area, which she instills in her characters.

Dun Lady's Jess was Doranna's first published fantasy novel and she now has fifteen novels of eclectic genres on the shelves and more on the way. Most recently, she's leaped gleefully into the world of action-romance. When she's not writing, Doranna builds author websites, wanders around outside with a camera and works with horses and dogs—currently, she's teaching agility classes. There's a Lipizzan in her backyard, a mountain looming outside her office window, a pack of agility dogs romping in the house and a laptop sitting on her desk—and that's just the way she likes it. You can find a complete list of books at www.doranna.net along with scoops about new projects and lots of silly photos.

Chapter 1

Coyote!

Marlee knew it the moment she saw him, human form or not. The man coming down the Sentinel headquarters hallway was a full-blooded shape-shifter—his eyes sharp, his presence full of strength and purpose and charismatic intensity. He stalked directly toward her, clearly on his way from the tactical dispensary, a heavy gear bag over his shoulder and a frown forming at the sight of her.

Marlee ducked hastily into the employee gym—the room where she'd been headed in the first place, here in the sleek, clandestine subfloor levels of Sentinel Brevis Southwest, regional operations for the desert climes. She didn't want to deal with the coyote's sharp gaze, his questing nature—the sudden bloom of awareness as he realized who she was.

And he would, because of *what* he was. What they all were, the full-bloods. Not that it ever showed on the outside, but Marlee Abril Cerrosa knew it in her heart: this man was coyote.

The gym door closed gently behind her, enclosing her in that familiar cool space—weight machines lining the wall, free weights in an extruded corner nook, and a row of cardio options. Brevis took the fitness of its field and support agents seriously.

Of course, Marlee was neither. Not any longer.

Metal crashed from the free-weight nook; a muttered curse followed.

Marlee found him in an instant, sitting on a weight bench in cutoff sweats and no shirt, the smattering of hair on his chest a dark rusty blond to match unruly hair above. Tiger. Bengal tiger.

Irritation tightened her mouth. She'd come here in midmorning because so few others ever worked out at this time; she could count on a solitude free of knowing looks and silent accusations.

And then he stretched, his private disgruntlement turning to a wince as he worked his arm and shoulder, twisting his torso…revealing a splash of scarring.

Marlee's irritation gave way to guilt. She'd learned to judge the age of such things—to recognize those injuries from the Core D'oìche attack.

The injuries she'd caused.

Arrogance. As if she had such power. As if she'd done more than feed minor pieces of information to the former Atrum Core Prince, Fabron Gausto, or plant a computer virus or two, thinking them to be insignificant and low-level tinkerings.

No, she hadn't even known. She'd been taken in by the Atrum Core; she'd been used.

Sometimes Marlee thought her ignorance made it even worse.

Oh, hell—the Sentinel had seen her. He didn't quite release the stretch as he gave her a distracted nod—and then he looked again, sat up a little straighter, seemed a little larger.

And there it was. That which had always terrified her: the tiger, looking back at her.

How the field Sentinels ever blended into outside society at all, she didn't know. How this man could even try amazed her. The gleam of *wild* in pale hazel eyes, the subdued brown streaks in rusty blond hair tapered short at his nape to obscure them, the barely quiescent aura of power—it all shouted of his otherness. It was an alluring strength, a charismatic strength...but never a comfortable strength. Not for a moment.

Especially not with his obvious flare of interest.

Heat prickled on Marlee's cheeks and neck, tingling down her spine; she had a sudden, uncomfortable awareness of every sensitive spot on her body.

"I'm sorry," she finally managed to say. And then, before he could ask why—before he could figure *out* why—she gave him a reason...if not the true reason. "I didn't mean to interrupt you."

"It's a big room," he said, and he was still eyeing her. "Until now, not one of my favorite rooms."

Hell, he *was* interested.

And Marlee's body was as treacherous as the rest of her—shifting uncomfortably, so aware of her isolation and her loneliness. Aching to leave before he understood who she was, aching to stay just a moment longer...

"You must be staff?" he said, finally releasing his stretch—only to reveal another slashing scar across one broad pectoral.

"Between assignments," she managed to respond, understanding now why he was here, and how that was her fault, too. She'd seen it before—that first wave of healing field agents sent out too soon after Core D'oìche—so desperate was the situation here at Southwest Brevis, so thin were their agents on the ground. And so great was the need in the field, where the Atrum Core had wasted no time taking advantage, wreaking subtle chaos in their centuries-long quest for power and pushing all the ancient boundaries of their ageless cold-war battlefield with brevis regions around the world. Core D'oìche had merely been another of that power-hungry faction's strikes against the shape-shifting Sentinels and their mandate to protect the earth and its people.

And, not ready, the Sentinel field agents had been vulnerable, and so many of them had simply come right back again, newly hurt.

"Hey," he said, tipping his head just a little, "don't worry about it. We'll come back from this—and we'll beat the bastards while we're at it. We always have."

Not always. Marlee panicked then, understanding that he'd misread her—he'd thought that she, too, had somehow been displaced by Core D'oìche. He didn't realize she had instead been one of *the bastards*.

But she managed to say, "I'm counting on it," and didn't have to fake that truth. It was her only possible redemption, whatever became of her life here. She faced years more of haunting these hallways—simply because she wasn't someone they would ever dispose of, and she wasn't someone they trusted to go free.

She could blame her sudden chill on that thought, or she could blame it on this man's unwavering attention. Either way, she didn't think when she crossed her arms beneath her breasts, warming herself.

The bracelet slipped along her wrist—the fine metal bracelet that might have been unimaginative jewelry…or might have been just what it was: a monitor. It kept her out of certain areas; it recorded her entry into other areas. It keyed to an alarm that would sound if she put so much as a foot out of this building to breath fresh air. *Real* air.

His gaze flickered to the bracelet. She knew the exact moment he realized who she was.

Marlee Cerrosa, the traitor. The lightly blooded Sentinel working Southwest Brevis IT support, who had nearly gotten their consul killed, who had helped the hostile Atrum Core prepare for the recent and devastating attack during the night of Core D'oiche.

Marlee Cerrosa, permanent prisoner—no escaping brevis and no escaping herself. No matter that she'd cut her dark hair boy-short to match features gone delicate with strain, or that she'd spent endless hours in the gym, watching her olive complexion turn pale with the lack of sunlight and trying to feel strong and safe amidst a people whose unrelentingly untamed nature turned their lives into secrets.

The Sentinel came to his feet in a surge of energy, hands fisted at his sides, his intensity all turned to anger. Startled, Marlee took a step backward; her heel stubbed over a the leg of a weight machine. She caught the metal frame, steadying herself—lifting her chin as if she could convince either of them that she wasn't frightened.

It didn't stop him from coming closer, three long strides that proved there wasn't a thing wrong with those long legs. "You *should* be afraid," he said. "What the hell are you even doing here?"

"Living," she snapped. "As best I can. Until I can prove myself again."

He didn't back down for a moment, standing right there within reach, the recent scars livid and the Core D'oìche scars only minimally less so, these several months later. "What makes you think you can ever do that? After the price we've all paid because of you?"

She knew her chin trembled; she hated it. "It wasn't just me," she whispered. She wanted to say *I never understood. They used me, they made me, they broke me.* "I did what I could to fix it."

"Too late," he told her, inexorable, and never mind that she'd ultimately saved the life of their consul. *"Too damned late."*

Her fingers tightened around the steel frame, but she didn't take another step back. *Wouldn't.* Her newly honed muscles gave way to watery knees—at his nearness, at his presence. The scent of him surrounded her, a combination of sweat and the faintest hint of something woodsy she couldn't swear wasn't simply part of the tiger. She made her voice come out, no matter that it lacked strength. "What do you want from me?"

That stopped him—if not in the way she expected. He didn't step back—not physically, not emotionally. But he took a breath, narrowing his eyes. "You want redemption?" he said, his voice hard with scorn. "Then prove it. Put yourself on the line for it. *Earn* it." And then he smiled, ever so slightly, nothing of humor in it at all. "Help me find the mole who's still setting us up."

Chapter 2

This is a mistake.

Scott should have known better than to relax, to let himself *feel*…to respond to the woman now beside him when he'd first spotted her in the gym.

Because nothing was normal these days, and nothing was right. Not with brevis—infiltrated by moles and traitors—and not with Scott O'Brien himself.

It certainly wasn't right to discover this woman had been the cause of all the things wrong with him now. The badly healing muscle of his shoulder, the freshly scored muscle of his chest…

The way he'd lost his tiger.

Marlee Abril Cerrosa. He'd heard of her, the mixed-blood tech who'd betrayed them all; he'd known she was here, under house arrest within brevis HQ. He hadn't expected her to be small, or wickedly fit beneath those Latina curves, or delicate of feature beneath that dramatically short hair.

He hadn't expected her to be vulnerable.

He sure as hell hadn't expected to feel like an ass for bringing her down here to brevis medical—mostly as an excuse to get her down onto this floor, but, yeah…to face what she'd done, too.

Her toasty complexion had gone pale; her face strained. Her chin trembled now and then, as if she barely managed her game face at all.

Here, where so many of the victims of Core D'oìche lingered.

They didn't know who she was. They thought she was *Abril*—they thought she'd come down from tech support to dispense a fresh batch of games, DVDs and e-reading devices loaded with books. And still, after she waved an ostensibly cheerful goodbye to those scarred and haunted Sentinels, she came out of the lounge to close her eyes and lean flat against the hallway wall, as if it might even hold her up.

Scott did that instead, closing a hand around her arm; he regretted it when she flinched—and then felt a swell of anger, hard and pounding in his chest. "You needed to see that."

She made a visible effort to relax in his grip—to not care about his proximity—and probably didn't know that the flutter of the pulse in her throat gave her completely away.

A tiger noticed such things. Along with her scent, and the small details of her posture. *This one wants to run.*

But he was surprised when she said, "I probably did need to see it." She took a deep breath. "Until now, I've only seen pictures. Or…like you. In the gym." She opened her eyes—a rich shade of brown, sad and worried. "I've never understood…the injuries…"

He knew that one without thinking. "Core workings, released through amulets. Energy with claws." And he understood the faint puzzlement on her expression, too, because Core amulets and Core workings emitted an ugly taste of corrupted energy readily discernible to most Sentinels. It shouldn't have been possible to take them by surprise at all. "Half of them were those new silent amulets, but either way...full-bloods aren't clones. Not all of us can track amulets. So we never saw it coming." The anger beat at him from inside. "Tell me you know at least that much about the agents you were working against."

Her quick resentment surprised him—the way her mouth firmed as she seemed to grow just a little taller. She shook off his arm. "Maybe *you* don't know as much as you think you know. Maybe the way you are *right now* is one of the reasons the Core was able to work me."

"What the—" Scott stopped, waiting for the physician and healer team to pass by and garnering only scant glances; he knew from the tone of the conversation that they were at odds over someone's treatment—and he knew from experience that such arguments happened all too often in the aftermath of Core D'oìche. He moved closer to Marlee, one arm thrust against the wall. The bad arm, and it let him know it; he pushed back at it—felt what was left of the tiger snarl at it. But when he spoke again, he kept his voice low—remembering that they were in public, here on the medical floor. "What the hell," he said, "are you talking about?"

"That," she said, scorn lacing her voice. "You and your tiger—and the wolf and the bobcat and the jackal we just left. Instead of taking responsibility for your strength, you use it to get what you want—you don't even know it. The rest of us are just here to disregard, or to bully if we get in your way—or even sometimes when we don't. The Core is

treacherous, but they aren't *wrong*—if you didn't have someone looking over your shoulder, who knows what you'd have
done with the rest of us by now."

Scott glowered at her, not even hearing the words at
first—knowing only that this woman who had done so much
harm thought she could justify herself. "You don't know
what you're talking about."

"Don't I?" she snapped, bitterness lacing those words.
"What happened to *me* when I was young and bullied?
Months in a cast, that's what. Months of rehab. What happened to the young full-blood who tried his claws out on
me? A slap on the paw, *that's* what. A few days of restrictions and a few visits to a counselor. His life went on...mine
didn't. Not for a long time. And by then, the Core had found
me, and started whispering in my ear."

Disbelief joined with anger. "An *accident?*" he said, and
he didn't back off one bit—because if he did, he would be
acceding her point. The one about how he was using his very
presence to ram home his anger. "You did all this because
of some childhood *accident?*"

But Marlee Abril Cerrosa had apparently had enough of
full-bloods, regardless of their strength. She stiff-armed him
in the chest with enough force to gain herself some space,
following it up with another shove as she stepped away from
the wall. "You jerk," she said. "Looming over me like that,
and then dismissing the moment that changed my life just
like *that*. Well, you know what? *You* asked for answers. It
wasn't an *accident*. And it wasn't right that it was treated
like one. That has to be part of the deal, if you don't want the
rest of us to look for ways to feel safe. You have to be *more*
careful, you have to be *more* thoughtful, and you damned
well have to keep your hands to yourself!"

He hadn't touched her. He hadn't come close. But he felt the first stirrings of guilt.

No, not just guilt. Admiration. She was terrified—of that he had no doubt. And her words stung. "We put ourselves on the line," he said, his voice low and ragged. "Every day, we're out in that field, taking the hits—from the Core, and from the rest of the world. *Sentinels*. We protect this earth, and we protect the rest of you along the way."

She produced the world's smallest violin with her thumb and forefinger. "Hooray for you," she said. "Do you think we'd need it, if the Core hadn't once been so alarmed by the very nature of what you are?"

"And you," he shot back at her. "You're one of us, whether you like it or not. But you still could have opted out—lived outside brevis activity altogether. Light-bloods have that choice. The rest of us don't." The rest of them were, by default, regional field agents in the age-old conflict with the Atrum Core.

"I told you," she said, her voice brittle and tight. "The Core got hold of me early. Between your kind and their kind, I wasn't left with any choices at all."

He snorted. "You had your choices. You're a grown woman."

"I was a *child*," she said, and now she stalked him, stepping forward so he had to move back. "I was a *little girl*, and the Core filled my head with fear and whispers. Where was brevis then, tiger? Who protected me from the bully, and who protected me from the Core? Don't you talk to me about *choices*. I'm doing the best I can."

He found himself without a response. He found her words landing hard...and sticking. She had been a little girl....

And she had been unprotected.

And that wasn't right.

Not that she was done. "I'm not one of *them*," she said. "I never meant to do anything but balance the scales. I never knew anything about Core D'oìche and I never knew about the silent amulets. I'm just a damned good systems tech who probably won't ever have a normal life. But at least I take responsibility for my screwup. I deserve to be here, no matter how little choice I had along the way."

"You—" he said, and then stopped, facing too many choices—and too many questions. And then her words finally hit him—the significance of what she'd said earlier. His anger gave way to a keen curiosity. "How did you know?"

The question took her by surprise—and, denied his angry response, she eased back into a perplexed frown. "How did I...what?"

"You knew," he said. "I didn't introduce those agents in the lounge as wolf or bobcat or jackal. I gave you their names."

She stepped back, crossing her arms beneath her breasts, a move that only served to highlight fit curves. "It was obvious."

He shook his head. "Not everyone *knows*, Marlee. Not even the full-bloods. Maybe you're more one of us than you think."

She shook her head. "Don't exaggerate. I'm observant, not Sentinel. Besides, you said you wanted my help." The bitter edge came back. "To redeem myself, as if that's ever going to happen. So what is it, exactly, you think I can do down here?"

"Be someone other than me," he told her, and watched her eyes widen. He grinned, and made no attempt to keep it nice. "Be *not Sentinel*."

Chapter 3

Marlee closed her hands into fists. Not from any great emotion, as much as it lingered—but because her fingers and palms still tingled with the sensation of the solid muscle with which they'd just made contact.

Maybe she was lonelier than she'd thought.

Lonely didn't mean losing her head. Any more than *frightened* had once meant losing her perspective.

I was a little girl.

How could she have known to ignore the whispers of her nurse, her physical therapist...the subtle string of adults who came through her life until the time the Core finally contacted her directly?

She eyed Scott O'Brien with wary curiosity, taking in, again, those pale hazel eyes, that rusty blond hair tamed only by its cut and length—just enough left to offset the intensity of his features—and his strapping build. Leaner than a tiger might be, but all tiger nonetheless.

At least to her eyes.

He stared right back at her. Waiting. She had no idea what he saw in her—and she didn't want to know. She said, "What then, am I supposed to do?"

He held out his hand. "Come with me."

The gesture so surprised her that she almost didn't move. Not until he turned his hand over, palm up in a repeated invitation, did she put her hand in his.

A big hand, warm and comfortable, his fingers curling around hers. "There are too many little things going wrong here," he said, keeping his voice low as they passed the healers' station and moved toward the stairs. "*Here*, on this floor. Everyone knows it, and everyone blames it on—"

"Me," she suggested.

He glanced at her as if he wasn't sure whether it was a joke or not, and she shrugged.

"I was going to say they blame it on being overworked," he responded. "Never mind the number of agents that poured in here—the injuries just aren't responding as they should. There are these lingering effects...." He trailed off, going somewhere inside himself. Remembering, maybe, what they had just seen—agents haunted by fluctuating energies, lingering sensations, ruined coordination... Scott shook his head. "So nothing's normal around here, and no one seems to be surprised at all the other stupid things going on."

She followed him into a quiet hallway of imposingly closed doors, most of them with red lights overhead: surgery rooms. Procedure rooms. She took the quiet as a good sign, and she asked Scott, "Like what?"

He waved a hand down the hallway. "CT scanners with wiped programming, digital radiology with artifacts all over the images, autoclaves breaking down, contaminated specimens..."

A whole lot of stupid. But she cast him a curious look, forgetting to be wary. "And you know all this because…?"

For some reason it made him retreat, to stiffen as though she'd slapped him. "Because," he said, and looked away, his teeth gritting more noticeably with each word, "this is my floor. I'm one of them. The agents they don't know how to fix."

She tried to absorb that information, looking at the hale nature of him, the obvious physical confidence…the tiger brimming out. "Surely your shoulder isn't enough to—"

"It's not," he said, hard words that cut her off. He took a breath, and added, "I went out in the field. It was the wrong choice. Now they're starting over again."

It explained little, but it was clearly as far as he was prepared to go. "So," she said. "You hang around here and while they're poking and prodding, you look for trouble."

"Guy's gotta have something to do," he grumbled, as though she'd caught him out.

"I still don't understand what you want *me* to do."

At that, he looked downright uncomfortable. "This is the work of someone on the inside, no question. Someone doing their bit by making it harder for us to get over Core D'oíche. I need you—*Abril*—to volunteer down here, just like you did today. You might see something I won't be privy to— because the mole won't consider you a threat."

No matter that Scott was messed up by the Core workings. He was a field Sentinel; he was a threat.

"Doesn't answer my question," she told him, looking down the hall to the stairs. "Why *me?*"

"Because," he said, his words simple and his gaze anything but, locking on to hers, holding her there. "You're the one person in this building I know *isn't* the mole."

Marlee looked at him, stunned, her emotions roiling. She whirled away—hiding herself, breathing deeply...walking away down the hall.

It didn't matter that he just wanted to use her. The feeling of being trusted, utterly trusted—

She couldn't even remember what that felt like. She could barely recognize it now. She only knew the relief of it swept through her with an intensity that left her reeling.

She stopped at the exit to the stairwell, trying to regain her composure. Scott gave her a few moments, and then came up behind her. Silent, of course, because what was a Sentinel if not full of natural prowl? But he made a noise in his throat from a few strides away, and she wasn't surprised when he moved up behind her, close enough to share his warmth and definitely close enough to share his very physical presence.

He didn't make the mistake of offering sympathy or understanding. He gave her a moment longer, and then cleared his throat. "I've laid wards around the hallway, the stairs... nothing anyone will notice. But if anyone puts any tiny workings into play—even stealth workings—I'll know about it."

Marlee murmured, "No working belongs in brevis, no matter how innocuous."

He shifted, putting his back to the wall, stretching his bad shoulder with a tug from his good arm, as if it had become such a habit he didn't even realize it. "You know, most people are surprised that I do wards."

She looked at him askance. "And shields, and a little bit of healing, right? It's a good skill set for a field agent. Why am I supposed to be surprised?"

He looked at her a long moment, and then shook his head. "I don't know about you, Marlee Cerrosa. But for now, let's just say that *most* people don't see that. Most people assume a tiger shifter is all muscle."

"You tempt me to get out my little violin again," she told him—although in truth, he tempted her to put her hands back on his chest, feeling that which had left such an impression the first time.

His expression had gone distracted, his mouth turning wry. "Timing," he said, after he shook himself back to attention, "is everything. That was one of my wards pinging off. Want to go hunting?"

Hunting. It was a far cry from hanging out with her eyes open, and she wasn't even certain of doing that much. But Scott's eyes sparkled with new life, and he held out his hand again—and that became enough. She found herself heading for the stairwell—not running, as she'd supposed they might, but stalking.

It didn't matter that she was the petite one, the lightweight one…Scott was the one who defined stalking grace, moving with powerful stealth, each step a perfect balance in motion.

Marlee simply tried not to get in the way.

They slipped through the door and into the stairwell, and Scott knew just where he was going—down, to the next level. Down, where the critical care patients had a suite of rooms and their own staff, their own dedicated, instant response procedures.

A faint noise whispered up the utilitarian stairwell, concrete and steel carrying the sound. Scott hesitated in midstep—frozen, his head at an inquisitive angle, his posture full of the hunt…his expression patient. Marlee could all but see a tiger's tail, the faint twitch of the white tip; the swivel of a white-spotted ear. She thought he'd forgotten her—but he gave her hand a squeeze as she froze into place beside him, so aware of her human awkwardness, her human failings.

She heard another noise, louder this time, followed by a faint tapping.

Scott lifted his head slightly; his quiet smile seemed predatory. He looked back at Marlee, meeting her gaze with meaningful purpose. It only took an instant for her to realize he'd tried to reach her, silently, as so many of the Sentinels could do. But even as the knowledge of it twisted inside her, reminding her anew that she was in fact not truly Sentinel, he merely pointed first at her and then at the midstory landing.

She got that message clearly enough. She was to remain at the landing when they reached it.

And then Scott took on a distant expression—one that instantly panicked her, the face of a full-blooded Sentinel reaching inward to take his tiger.

Before she could do so much as recoil, everything changed. Scott made a sound of surprise—a wordless thing that echoed in the stairwell. His eyes widened with it, even as he stumbled back against the painted cinder-block wall and sagging downward, arms wrapped around some immense, buried pain.

The person below made a sound of alarm; footsteps clattered down the stairs below them, heading deeper into the structure's clandestine subfloors. A door push bar sounded loud, and the door closed again with a clang of metal.

Marlee only stood frozen, helpless, watching Scott O'Brien slowly crumpling to the cement floor. Finally, she crouched to put a hesitant hand on his shoulder—only then realizing, as he rolled bonelessly toward her in response to her touch, that he'd passed out altogether.

Chapter 4

Everything inside Scott ached.

His bad side and shoulder ached from hitting the concrete floor; his soul ached, bereft for his tiger.

He should have known better than to try to take the change, of course. It had been an instinctive thing. But if the instinct had persistently failed since his injuries of Core D'oìche, never had it backlashed on him that way.

Oh, yes. He ached.

"You can't tell anyone." He turned his gaze on Marlee, who stood in the greenhouse balcony of this small but beautifully appointed apartment. This entire top floor of brevis HQ, rising out of and blending into Old Town Tucson, was comprised of such apartments—a little oasis of guest rooms for visiting Sentinels, recuperating agents and agents between assignments.

And now, Marlee's jail cell.

Her hand jerked slightly at his words and so did her watering can, splashing a stream of liquid onto the tile. She set the can aside. "Interesting, that you think you're the boss of me."

He closed his eyes. "What I mean to say," he told her, through somewhat gritted teeth, "is please. *Please* don't tell anyone."

Her response was a stillness that made him open his eyes; he found her watching him, her expression troubled. Before he could say anything, she said, "You scared the hell out of me. What would I have done if you hadn't gotten up on your own? You want to risk that it'll happen again, whatever the hell it was?"

He knew what it was. And he was pretty sure it would happen again. But if he told the healers, they'd want to cage him in—keep track of him. Probably try to reproduce what happened—probably talk endlessly about it.

He didn't want to think about it at all.

To his surprise, she took a step closer, crossing into the small main room of the apartment. To his complete amazement, she narrowed her eyes in perceptive accusation. "You know, don't you? You know exactly what happened. You just haven't told me."

Right. Because if he didn't want to think about it, he sure as hell didn't want to *talk* about it.

"It's okay," she said, surprising him yet again as she turned away, heading for the tiny kitchenette to pull out ice cubes and plastic tumblers and a pitcher of chilling water. "It's not like you owe me anything. Besides, I already know it has something to do with your tiger."

With a few quick steps, he reached the kitchenette, pushing right into her space. "How—"

"Stop it," she said, and absently pushed him back. The

feel of her hands against his chest put his entire body on alert—even if she'd only meant to put him in his place. "You were about to take the change," she said, answering his question as she held out a full tumbler. "You *were* taking the change. That's when it happened."

He narrowed his eyes, his hand closing tightly around the cool plastic, feeling it flex before he backed off. "You're guessing."

She lifted her gaze as she closed the refrigerator door. "Why would I?"

Marlee Abril Cerrosa. The light-blooded Sentinel who considered herself less than, but who could discern the forms their agents took, who saw beneath his tiger to his other field skills—who could tell when he reached for the change. And who didn't seem to realize that not everyone could do the same.

How would that feel, growing up bullied and frightened, and always seeing, exactly, the predators around her?

"I won't tell," she added, as if she could sense the unease of his thoughts and misattributed them. "Not yet, anyway."

"Not yet," he murmured. Well, that was fine. By the time it came to *yet*, he wanted to have this thing figured out.

It left silence between them; Scott found he'd moved closer again. Her glance said she'd noticed, but instead of reclaiming her space, she looked troubled. "What now?"

Scott swallowed a quick sting of regret. "Nothing's changed—except now I know it for sure. Someone's using Core workings in medical."

"Tell someone, then."

The sensible thing to do. Scott left the tumbler sitting on the little counter extension and prowled the length of the room. "If I do, they'll lock me up."

Marlee sent him a justifiable look of scorn. "Scott," she said, holding up her locator bracelet, "*this* is locked up. What they'll do to *you* is put someone else on the situation while they try to fix you."

Frustration bubbled up; he spun away to prowl the short distance to the main room wall. "They don't have anyone to spare for *the situation*." Dammit, he wanted to hit something. He wanted to take the tiger and bound through open spaces, sprinting to the end of the hunt and the takedown. He wanted to feel the stretch and coil of limber muscle; he wanted to give voice in a roar, not a rough baritone. "I can do this," he said. "I can spare them this."

"And prove yourself?"

He turned on her, but by the time he found her gaze, he'd registered the understanding in her tone. Understanding, and a startling empathy and—

"I can only imagine what it must be like to be used to being *you* and then to find yourself like me."

He released a harsh breath and moved closer. This time, she didn't push him back—she didn't flinch or stiffen. She only looked at him, a hint of sadness in her expression and her gaze steady on his.

His hand twitched on an impulse to reach for her. "Marlee—"

The tiger in him should have heard footsteps approaching her door—should have been prepared. But the man in him was all tangled up in Marlee, and so they both jumped at the sharp rap of knuckle against wood.

"Security, Miss Cerrosa." Short and hard, words that meant *open this door quickly or we're coming in.*

Marlee cast him a frown and would have reached for

the door, but Scott beat her to it, sending a glance that was partly proprietary and partly apologetic for usurping her authority, here in the one place that she might have any. "Hey, fellas," he said, facing the two men on the other side with a relaxed congeniality. They weren't as tall as he was, not as substantial, but their blood shone true enough—if they weren't shifters, they were close to it. Something canid in nature, and partnered for their similarities in style.

One of them pushed the door farther open; the other walked in past Scott. "Miss Cerrosa, you'll have to come with us."

"What?" She cast Scott a startled glance. "No. No, I don't. I haven't done anything."

"You entered a restricted area." The man reached for her arm.

Marlee neatly sidestepped him, her expression one of utter confusion—albeit confusion that quite abruptly cleared. "The medical floor? Do you mean the medical floor? I just took down some entertainment disks. Ask at the healers' station—they okayed it."

"You'll have to come with us," the man repeated, and Scott knew that tone. Authority figure, not listening. Not caring, either.

Marlee's mouth set; she grew a scant half-inch taller. "I'm not going anywhere. Not unless I hear from Nick Carter. My arrangement is with him, not with you."

"The consul has all of brevis to run. He doesn't have time for you." The second man hadn't come past Scott—not quite. Now he gave Scott an assessing glance as he considered it.

Scott found himself shifting to block the way. "Gentlemen," he said, "you're scaring her. That's not the way we do things here."

Or was it? Had it always been? Marlee's startled glance told him she hadn't expected him to stand up for her. That she hadn't truly known what that was even like.

"Things change," said the man who stood too close to Marlee. "She ought to know. She helped change them."

"The stairwell," Marlee said suddenly. "It was the stairwell."

Scott snorted. "Good, because we can take care of this right now. She was with me in that stairwell. And what we were doing is none of your business."

Marlee's jaw dropped just a little bit more—but it didn't stop her from taking advantage of the moment, moving back just a little bit more.

"Go ahead," Scott said. "Write that down in whatever notes you're keeping, and then think hard about how to improve your manners for the next time you'd like to speak with Miss Cerrosa." He, too, knew how to make himself bigger, how to draw on the tiger's nature. He knew how to hide it, too, when even that little bit of a connection brought out a spike of driving pain.

He knew how to use human wiles, as well. "You can be certain that *I'll* be thinking about how you can improve your manners. And so will my buddy Maks—and, if comes to that, Nick Carter."

"Hell," one of the men blurted out. "That means Jet would be in on it, too."

Jet was Nick Carter's deeply bonded life mate—wolves, both of them, except that Nick took the wolf as his other form, while Jet had been born wolf and twisted into human shape by Core workings. And while Nick might indeed be stretched thin with a wounded Southwest Brevis, Jet wouldn't hesitate to take two canids to task if she heard they'd acted with disrespect.

Scott's grin was as predatory as his stance. "I imagine she would."

The man stepped back, held up his hands. "Okay," he said. "Okay. I guess if I have to worry about Jet's reaction, then I must be crossing a line." He looked back at Marlee. "Stay out of the stairwell, okay? Too many vulnerable people down there."

"Yes," Marlee murmured, exchanging a glance with Scott. *That's exactly it.* Exactly why they'd been there in the first place. "I understand."

The two left with a haste that spoke of previous encounters with Jet. Marlee reached for the back of the little couch, feeling just a little bit bereft. One more illusion of freedom, stripped.

"I'm sorry," Scott said, shifting awkwardly where he stood, his expression full of new understanding. "I don't even think they see what they do. I guess I didn't."

"You know Maks," she said, by way of reply. Maks, who took a Siberian tiger as his other—mysterious background, silent by nature—and the Sentinel who, with Marlee and a small group of others, had ultimately invaded Fabron Gausto's operations to bring him down, saving Nick Carter in the process. Just not soon enough to stop Core D'oìche.

"It's a tiger thing," Scott said of Maks, and shrugged. "We spar. He doesn't say anything, he whips my ass, and then when the time comes, he covers my back."

"I liked Maks," she said unexpectedly, her voice a little wobbly in the wake of the confrontation. "He made me feel safe."

That, somehow, didn't surprise Scott at all. The deep stab of jealousy, filling in where the pain of the missing tiger now faded, did. He took one step forward—just one. "What about me, Marlee? Do I make you feel safe?"

Her startled gaze met his, and for a moment he saw that which might have been her *other*—something small and fleet of foot, gentle of nature and vulnerable for it. And, apparently, honest. "You make me *feel*," she said. "Maybe that's even better."

Chapter 5

After a week during which Marlee played the role of Abril, the medical floor patients and personnel became used to seeing her; she became used to seeing them.

She became used to seeing Scott, too.

Now she ducked out of the patient lounge to a chorus of goodbyes, and found herself grinning.

Big, brave Marlee. Not afraid of the sick people.

She ignored her little voice. Not being afraid of the sick people was a fine place to start. And in the past week, she had learned a thing or two about them.

Such as the fact they had no idea, most of them, of how much presence they projected. They had no idea what it was like to be fully human and facing a Sentinel of great strength and speed—someone who could see in the dark, manipulate energies into wards and shields and sometimes even exude pure power…someone who could take an alternate shape of lethal grace.

At least, not until they'd had to face their own mortality

with these Core-driven injuries. Until they'd learned what it was like, in some small sense, to be human in a Sentinel world.

It gave her some emotional room to step into—to explore. It also gave her the chance to learn that the medical floors weren't warded in general because such things turned tricky for the healers—and right now, the healers needed all the help they could get. They counted, instead, on the layers of security between here and the upper levels; on the restricted access and heightened vigilance.

Marlee didn't go back into the stairwell. But she did walk the halls—sometimes alone and sometimes with Scott. She marveled at the casual way he would take her hand, or drape his arm over her shoulder…or the whisper of his hand against her back. He had no problem with touching, this tiger didn't. Or with looking. For if half the time she found him scowling, his anger directed at his injuries and failings, the rest of the time she found him watching her. Simply watching—and almost, but not quite, saying something. Almost, but not quite, reaching for her. As if the touch that was often so casual, in that moment might mean more.

Then again, what did she know? She was a woman who once thought she'd known herself, but no longer. Everything was up for doubt.

The elevator glided to a smooth stop, made a self-important *ding* of arrival, and the doors opened. Marlee headed for the gym—and stopped short a moment, suddenly aware of the smile tugging at the corner of her mouth, the lightness in her steps. She put fingers to her mouth…confirming it. Believing it.

Surely, getting caught as a mole wasn't the best thing that could have happened to her, after all. Surely not.

But she was still lighthearted as she grabbed her bag from the workout room and ducked into the bathroom to change, and lighthearted as she started her workout, waiting for Scott to finish his physical therapy session and join her.

But after she'd finished her workout and toweled herself down, she glanced at the clock. This time she wasn't smiling.

She was worried.

Or maybe she was just annoyed at being stood up. She jammed hastily folded clothes into her bag and headed out into the hall...only to do an automatic about-face at the sight of the same coyote who'd driven her into the gym a week earlier, and then startle back when she nearly ran into someone new. *Bear.*

Marlee fought the initial panic at being trapped between them—and by then the coyote had passed her by, and by then she'd seen that this was not a Sentinel who shone with his otherness, but merely a shaggy-haired person of a somewhat shambling nature with a long fluorescent light bulb in hand. She made herself stop and draw a breath...and to pretend she was speaking to the men and women she knew on the medical floor. *Practice, practice, practice.* "Excuse me," she said. "I don't suppose you've seen Scott O'Brien around here? We were supposed to meet..."

He looked her up and down and offered a noncommittal grunt. "See him sometimes, but not today." Then his gaze sharpened. "You're that Cerrosa woman, aren't you?"

"Abril," she said, making it sound like a correction when

it was nothing but confirmation. "My name is Abril. Like the month."

The man merely grunted again, and nodded at the elevator. "Try the primary medical floor. Seen him there, sometimes."

"Thanks." She offered him a brief smile and headed to the elevator, and despite her concern, her chest felt lighter... her confidence kicked up a notch higher.

One of the healer assistants nodded a greeting when she arrived on the floor. "Haven't seen him," the woman offered, as if Marlee could be coming back down again only for one thing. "He had physical therapy a little while ago—maybe they wore him out." She smiled, a little ruefully. "They do have enthusiasm."

Except Scott had gone in to PT for ultrasonic phonophoresis, working on the lingering inflammation in the strong curve of muscle just beneath and over his shoulder blade. She'd seen those scars more closely in the past several days; they were nothing a non-Sentinel would have healed from at all. But Scott drove himself toward perfection—even as Marlee grew ever more certain the shoulder wasn't the reason he was here at all.

"I'm just going to check his room, okay?"

The woman grinned. "Have at it."

Marlee gave her a double take, tried to hide it, and suddenly found herself aware of and startled by the assumption she saw there.

Scott's hand at her back, Scott's arm around her shoulders, Scott's grin, breaking free of his constantly simmering anger to respond to some acerbic thing she'd said.

Hmm.

She tapped lightly on his door, alert for the sounds of the little flatscreen within—or for the sounds that he was, as sometimes happened, employing the furniture for push-ups or handstands or free weights, their workout date forgotten.

Silence.

Surely he hadn't gone off on his hunt without her—or without telling her.

At that spike of alarm, she tried the door—waiting, for decency's sake, for any sound of protest at the intrusion.

What she heard was a sound of distress.

Remembering his fierce privacy, she bit her tongue on an exclamation of dismay and shoved into the room, dropping her bag, kicking the door closed and finding him huddled in the corner.

The look he turned on her was purely feral. Purely tiger. Purely warning.

But his bare torso quivered with pain, and his muscles stood out in clenched relief, and this was one tiger who wasn't going anywhere. Marlee looked into that feral gaze— that *other*—and took a deep breath as she went down to her knees beside him. "Scott," she said, with a calmness she didn't feel. "Come out of there and talk to me."

His eyes widened slightly—not panicked, but wild, and not able to understand. *Trying.*

"Scott," she said gently, and ran the back of her fingers along the skin of his upper arm—a gentle, caressing touch that left a shiver in its wake. "I see you in there. Now come back and talk to me."

The tiger snarled, shining out from within him, clamping down on her wrist with a strong hand.

She should have been terrified—of what he was, of what

he could become, of what he could do to her. Instead, her fear rode high—but it was only for Scott, and for not what he might do to her. It was for what he might do to himself.

There was no point in fighting that grip, and she didn't. She leaned in close, feeling the wild gust of his breath against her cheek, the bruising grind of the bones in her wrist. "Scott," she said. "I *see* you."

He pulled away from her with a gasp—a final jerk of resistance. And then the strength drained from him, and he was only a man, the tiger in retreat as he lay panting. She stroked him—a long, reassuring pass over his shoulder and arm, a gentle scrape of fingers through disheveled hair. And she startled when he moved again—faster than she'd expected, fiercer than she'd expected, and she found herself caught up in a tight embrace.

A needy embrace. Just like any man in extremes, hunting comfort—clutching to it.

She hugged him back, tears stinging her eyes as the impact of it hit her—this strong man, this *Sentinel*, reaching out to her. Relying on her. She rested her cheek against the damp skin beside his neck and held him.

After a moment, the desperate nature of the embrace changed. He disengaged slightly, enough to look her in the eye—his own expression still a little bewildered, but ruefulness creeping in. "Yeah," he said, searching her gaze—sparing a thumb to brush across her wet lashes. "I see you, too."

"What happened?" Marlee asked him. "Did you try to take the tiger again?"

Scott couldn't hide his surprise, or—when she laughed shortly to see it—the face he made at her. "How did you—"

She laughed again, this time without humor. "I've spent my whole life trying to make myself feel safe. That means watching the ones you're afraid of—knowing them." She cocked her head at him. "Or maybe you Sentinels just aren't as inscrutable as you think."

At that he scowled, but it was for the sake of form and quickly passed; she didn't even flinch when he closed the distance between them to kiss her forehead, but she did when he froze in an abrupt aftershock of pain, his breath briefly caught in his chest.

"Dammit," he said, once he was breathing again. "I guess it's not going to let go so quickly. Time to get out of here." He climbed to his feet, tugging her up along with him. The sheet fell away; he caught it, wadded it up and tossed it on the bed.

"Get out of here?" she said, looking wary. "You need to tell the healers what's going on, not run away from it."

This time his scowl was real. "I don't run from anything, Marlee. I run *toward.*"

It didn't seem to impress her. "Great," she said, her hands going to her hips and her mouth quirked in disapproval. "Where angels fear to tread…"

"Hey," he told her. "I know how that phrase starts. And I'm no fool. I just need to do this my way. And I don't need a room full of—"

Observers. Healers, watching him. Doctors, taking notes about him. Interfering with him…stopping him.

That, she seemed to understand; she relaxed her confrontational stance. And then, when another aftershock shot through him, sucking away his breath, she threw her hands up in exasperation. *"Fine,"* she said, grabbing the dark blue

T-shirt hanging over the impersonal hospital bed and shoving it at him. "Let's go, then. Exactly where are we headed? And why am I coming with you again?"

"For one thing, we're going to your place," he told her, ignoring her scowl as he pushed his head through the shirt's neck opening and jammed a hand toward one sleeve. "For another..." He took a deep breath. "For another, I need you."

He watched as the words reached her—the slightly widened eyes, the quick drop of her mouth. And then she pulled herself back into *irascible*. "Dammit," she said, and grabbed her gym bag. "Let's go."

Chapter 6

"There," Marlee said, pushing the door closed with her foot and tossing her bag onto the small couch. She headed right for the kitchen to pull out the ice water. "We're here. Now exactly what did you need from me?"

"Maybe," Scott said, casting around for his own answers, "just a place where I don't feel like a lab rat. For a little while."

She added an energy powder to the pitcher, poured, then shoved a second tumbler across the counter at him without even hesitating this time. Bossy, in fact. "I'm not even sure you'll fit on the couch. Try again. Because that's not needing *me*. So either you were playing me when you said that, or—"

"No!" He took a quick step toward her, only to be brought up short when she stabbed a finger at the tumbler. And then, since she was right—he probably needed this energy drink and more—he grabbed the thing and gulped it down.

By then she'd slipped out into the main area, yanking her things from the gym bag and tossing them into the hamper tucked away in the small shower stall. She threw the bag into the tiny entry area closet…and stood there with her hands again on her hips.

He wiped his mouth with the back of his wrist, but that, too, was only buying time. "Marlee," he said, riding a surge of frustration, "you see things. There's more Sentinel to you than—"

She cut him off with a derisive sound, moving to the edge of the enclosed greenhouse of a balcony—giving herself room.

"Listen to me!" He crossed that space in two long strides, grabbed her shoulders, clamped down tight. "It's more than just *paying attention*. You can see what we are—all of us. The wolf, the bobcat, the jackal—"

"The bear," she muttered, nonsensically. "As if *anyone* couldn't tell that man is a bear."

What the hell…bear?

"Not everyone *can*," he insisted. "Do you really think we could mingle with the rest of the world if it was so obvious? Do you think we'd have stayed hidden for thousands of years? I sure as hell know better. It's *you*, Marlee. And if you can see them…if you can see me…maybe…" *Maybe you can help me find the rest of myself.*

"You're wrong," she said, and spat the words. "I'm nothing more than anyone else. I never have been, I never will be."

Frustration grew to anger. What was he doing, asking for help from the woman who had been behind his injuries in the first place? Had he really thought she'd *want* to? That she'd step out of her little safe place, just for him?

Unthinking, he gave her a little shake—and all hell broke

loose, Marlee right along with it. She twisted free of his grip, coming back at him with a sudden rain of blows. "No more!" she cried, her face gone as fierce as any agent tapping the other. "None of you! You don't get to make me feel small anymore!"

In that instant of astonishment, he could do nothing but block her—small as she was, quick as she was, strong as she was—restraining her fury with the press of his entire body.

She glared at him, her cheeks flushed, her expression beyond defiance. "I'm not afraid of you! I *won't* be afraid of you! Any of you!"

Scott shouted right back. "I'm not trying to *frighten* you!" He released her wrists, ignoring her hands at his sides, gripping his T-shirt—not quite shoving, but controlling…claiming space. His hands cradled her face—careful with those delicate features, careful with the fury he held, and completely overcome by his own confusion, by his body's sudden surge of response to her. "God, Marlee, I'm not trying to…I'm not—"

Her fury faded to a confusion that mirrored his own.

"Gonna kiss you," he muttered.

"Yes," she breathed, and beat him to it. Her hands, pushing, suddenly tugged him in. Her knee, futilely trying to jam up to his groin, instead moved to wrap her leg around his. Her mouth found his—responded to his, with kisses as fierce as her anger, kisses along his jaw, kisses hot against his neck, *teeth* against his neck, until the heat flooded through his body and his hips jerked in primal, undeniable response.

She buried her hand under his shirt, her body arching against his with a small and needy cry. The stretchy sports-top zipper defied him only for a moment and then he had his hands on her…rubbing his thumbs over the exquisite handful of her breasts, letting his head fall back as she scraped her teeth over his chest in response, her breath hot on his skin, her body moving against his until damn, there were entirely too many clothes involved.

"Marlee," he said, "I'm gonna—"

"Yes," she said, and this time it was a demand. They separated just long enough to zip and tug, and if her panties came down with the shorts, his pants fell away to bare skin. She crouched—quickly, gracefully, freeing herself of the shorts and then pulling his pants away.

On the way back up, she didn't move nearly as quickly. He sucked in air, caught in dizzying sensation…quick fingers, hot tongue, the brush of her breast against his leg, the streaking tug of rising pleasure. His chest vibrated in a deep and helpless groan; his legs quivered and she cupped him, lightly scratching, tugging—

No warning this time. He pulled her to her feet, found her waist, hoisted her up until her legs wrapped around him, and still she hadn't let up, her mouth on his skin, her body moving against his. He steadied her, hands curving around the tightly toned muscle of her bottom as he stepped back… stepped back again, hunting the vaguely remembered chair. It bumped the back of his legs and he sat hard; Marlee rode him down. "I'm gonna—" she said, rising slightly, reaching between them.

"Hell, yes," he said, surprised he had the breath for it, and then losing that breath entirely as she brought herself down around him and now he trembled from restraint, wanting to take her and—

Marlee took *him*. She took him deep and then, while his hands closed helplessly at her waist, she straddled both him and the chair to move over him. Hot pleasure rose and his skin started to tingle, his body tightened, his breath came ragged. He clutched at her—at her thighs, at her waist, hands seeking, sensations clutching right back at him, her sob of pleasure twisting them together in one interlocking, building—

"I'm gonna—" he blurted.

"Hell, *yes*," she said, as breathless as he, her eyes bright and then closing, her spine arching, her hips jerking and her body closing around him. Scott closed his eyes and lost himself to sensation, crying out as he rose…and rose…reaching so hard—

And then he lost himself to Marlee.

Chapter 7

Marlee wasn't certain when or how they'd made it to the bedroom, falling down on the haphazardly made bed to tangle the covers even further. She wasn't sure when it had become late evening, the long desert twilight still washing the room with gentle light.

She remembered clearly the moments she'd stretched out in the bed alongside Scott, her bare leg over his; she savored the clear tactile memories of their intimacy of her hand wandering the planes of his chest, across the muscle strapping his ribs, down the faint hollow of his abdomen and over the gentle rise of his hipbone.

She certainly remembered being lured to explore him more intimately—seeing what made him twitch, what made him quiver, what made him groan…what made his fingers clench down into the covers and his head tip back with that sometimes startled, sometimes fierce, always exquisite expression of pure, responsive pleasure.

She remembered very clearly indeed that he seemed to understand her own body quite well.

"Hmm?" he said, stirring sleepily, his hand skimming her body from her shoulder down through the dip of her waist.

She somehow understood it to be a question. "You *were* trying to take the tiger again, weren't you? And you can't. That's why you got hurt again. That's why you're still here at brevis."

His fingers on her waist stilled, utterly; his body under her hand stilled, not even, for that moment, breathing. And then his chest rose and fell in a silent sigh. "It's got to go both ways, Marlee."

She understood that, too. "Yes," she said quietly. "I think see things I shouldn't. Things that mean I'm more Sentinel than I realized, even if I don't want to be."

His arm tightened around her, squeezing briefly. "You're strong," he said. "You're quick. You've lived your whole life with your fears right there in your face, and no one know-ing…no one understanding. It'll be easier, now that you realize."

Two could play that game. "And *you* still have your tiger."

"I—" He stopped his protest, then shook his head. "You really see it?"

"Bengal tiger," she said promptly. "It shines from you."

He was quiet another long moment, his stomach gently rising and falling with each breath—and totally giving the lie to his pounding heart, the beat kicked up strong and fast. "I believe *you*," he said finally, a curious vulnerability laced with anger. "I'll work on believing *me*, too."

It took only a turn of her head to nip him, not quite gently. He yelped dramatically and pulled her close in a long, tight hug before they lay in silence another moment.

"I never thought that it would feel good to be held with such strength," Marlee finally said. The way he'd hoisted her up to him, the way he'd held her…the way he'd carried her here and then held his weight off her as he covered her, moving inside her…protecting her. "I never thought it would make me feel *safe*."

To judge by his reaction, there was no better thing to say to a Sentinel with a lover in his arms.

Marlee brushed a hand over the weeping branches of the balcony's potted paloverde tree and looked out into the Tucson night, savoring the sated feel of her body…that sensation of not being *alone*.

Scott clattered around in the kitchen, hunting red meat and finding only what she knew he'd find—a few frozen burgers in her careful three-ounce portions. "No wonder you're so small," he muttered.

She wasn't. Or she hadn't been. Not until she'd learned to take her frustrations out in exercise. As a systems support tech and Atrum Core mole, she'd been soft and heading toward plump, her posterior more of an ass than an asset— her emotions turned inward.

Scott came up behind her, crunching a carrot stick, and made himself at home up against that asset. "Bare?" he said, and offered her the carrot.

She took an absent bite and he popped the remainder in his mouth, crunching companionably as she chewed and pondered and gave up. "Bare, what?"

"What you said earlier. Wolf, bobcat, jackal, bear. The

first three hang out in the medical lounge, but there's no bear there. Ruger never did hang out there, and he's out in the field again anyway. More or less."

Oh, the *bear.* "I was thinking of the guy who works repairs in the sublevels."

Scott shifted to face her, reaching out to smooth some imaginary stray piece of her short-cropped hair. He was like that, she'd discovered. Always touching, always a little bit possessive.

She found she didn't mind as much as she thought she might.

He said, "There aren't any bears in custodials. No one there takes anything but the human."

"Sure there is. The sloth bear. Big guy with shaggy black hair and a...well, a *nose.*" She spread her fingers over her own nose to indicate the broadness of the man's features. "I talked to him just today, when I was looking for you at the gym."

Scott's hands stilled; he stopped looking as though he was pondering the chance to slip his hands beneath the soft drape of the short-sleeved peasant top she'd pulled on over her cutoffs. "I know him," he said, and shook his head. "He doesn't take the bear—he never has. He's just not strong enough."

Marlee crossed her arms; she raised a brow at him.

Scott closed his eyes. "Oh, hell," he said. *"Hell."* Right there before her eyes, the man who had just loved her body into satiation turned into the man of seething anger she'd first met in the gym. He stalked away from her and into the bedroom, and returned tugging his shirt over his head, struggling briefly with the injured arm before getting it lined up just right.

Marlee looked into the brimming fury of pale hazel eyes and something within her shrunk with the loss of what she'd so briefly had.

Except Scott tugged the shirt straight—and then he held out his hand. "Coming?"

"What do you mean, *coming?*" But even as she asked it, she reached for his hand. "To do what about *what?* You know there's been someone using Core workings on the medical floor—I know that the custodian takes the bear when he lets everyone think he can't. It doesn't add up to—"

"He's got no reason to lie about not taking the change," Scott growled. "A lifelong lie, at that. It's him, you *know* it's him—"

"I know he needs to answer some questions," she said. "But aren't you going to call someone? How about those two guys who came up here to—" But she saw the look on his face, and she stopped short, understanding. "It's because it's me. They'll never believe me, and even if they did, they wouldn't believe it means anything."

"Drake has been working those floors as long as anyone can remember," Scott said, not even trying to deny her words. "He's a nice guy—people like him."

"*I'm* nice," Marlee said pointedly. "People liked me, too."

"Yeah," he said, and couldn't hide a lingering hint of betrayal in his voice. "I bet they did."

She narrowed her eyes at him. "Is it going to be like this?"

The flat, implacable strength in her voice made him blink—it made her blink, too. But she held his gaze, and she held her determination. Because she deserved better than what he'd just given her—and thanks to him, she knew it.

Scott took a deep breath and let it out slowly. He let go

of his urgency, too, stepping back to her. "No," he said, and cupped her head to tip her face up, taking a kiss—hard and long—with the same possessiveness with which he'd touched her earlier. "It isn't."

She heard the unspoken words still lingering; she waited. He gave her regret, and shook his head. "For me, it isn't. For the others…it is. Maybe it always will be. So for this, we're on our own. Or I can go by myself if you—"

"No!" The force of her reaction startled them both; she hunted composure. "No, I'm not going to sit here wondering and worrying and waiting. Let's go." She jammed bare feet into her cross-trainers and tucked the apartment key into her front pocket, giving the tracking bracelet a nervous twist. "Not that I have any idea what you think we can do about it."

Scott's grin was nowhere near reassuring. "We'll see what happens when we poke the bear."

Chapter 8

After so much time on the medical floor, Scott knew exactly where to find Drake Williams at this time of night: at home.

That the man was still here meant nothing good.

That he lingered in the diagnostics and surgery area, a screwdriver and an outlet plate in his hands and a suspicious, tidy little package waiting on the empty gurney beside him, meant nothing good at *all*.

The hell of it was, Scott would have passed him right by if Marlee hadn't stopped short. Scott saw nothing but empty bed stations, clips and cords neatly tucked away, privacy curtains drawn back. It was only at second glance that he saw Williams, and stiffened with surprise.

No wonder the man had never been seen at his sabotage. No wonder he had triggered Scott's warding in the stairwell, but nowhere else. He had Core workings to obscure his presence, amulets he could trigger in privacy so he could approach in safety. No doubt they were the new silent amulets…no doubt they were smuggled into the building long before the Sentinels knew they'd have to be on guard for such things.

The stairwell had probably been private enough, until Scott had warded it. Their failed attempt to stop the man hadn't deterred him…only driven him to seek more secure privacy for the moment in which he invoked the amulets.

But Marlee had seen Williams' bear, she'd seen Scott's tiger—and she'd seen past this working. Scott squeezed her hand, with no time for words—

Because, of course, Drake Williams had no problem seeing *them*—or perceiving that his working had failed him. He stood in awkward hesitation, clearly considering a bluff—a hearty good-evening, and he'd be on his way.

Scott didn't think so. "Drake," he said. "I think we need to talk."

Williams took another moment to process the situation, and shook his shaggy head. "That's not going to happen."

"Mr. Williams," Marlee said, "please listen to me. I know what you're feeling, but this doesn't have to go badly for you." No doubt she did understand how this man could be manipulated. He was a Sentinel without grace, without intensity, without the quickness or personal presence. He'd come late to the change, or he wouldn't have been able to hide it at all. Like Marlee, he'd probably spent his life feeling *less than*.

The Core had given him a way to feel *more than*.

Williams snorted, dropping the screwdriver beside what were almost certainly plastic explosives. "*You* got caught."

Marlee's voice stayed quiet. "So are you."

"By you?" He snorted again. "By the man who can't even take his tiger any longer?"

Scott took a sharp breath. *Direct hit.* And no one was supposed to know that, much less one of the custodians. The familiar anger crept in, a hot throb in his chest, up the back of his neck.

Marlee touched his arm. She said, "Yes. By us." And she reached past Scott to pick up the desk phone at the healer's station.

Williams shoved the gurney aside and lumbered forward, and Scott didn't need Marlee to warn him about the man's imminent transition to his bear, not with the energies already flowing a swirling snap of light around him. Williams reared up as the bear, just shy of Scott's height, a third again heavier, mouth opened wide to brandish both teeth and slobber. Scott pushed Marlee back—out of the way, out of danger—and reached for his tiger, unthinking.

Hot fire flooded his body, raking out from the center of him, taking his legs out from beneath him as if he'd never been strong enough to stand in the first place. He cried out, as much frustration as pain—shoving the tiger away, lifting his head...staggering back to his feet.

He looked up just in time to take the mighty backhanded swipe of the enraged bear. He slammed against the healer's station, ribs giving way—hearing the crack of it but not quite feeling the pain yet, seeing nothing but a blur of black fur, the flick of a massive paw as he took another hit. Marlee cried out with rage, far too close; Scott blinked hard to clear his vision, and looked down to see himself on hands and knees and poised to take another blow. But the bear grunted only in surprise, its squalled protests mixing with a series of strange hollow impacts.

Marlee. Marlee, leaping upon the bear's shoulders to cling tight, slamming the animal's shaggy head with a thick metal clipboard, jabbing at its eyes. "Believe, dammit!" she shouted, and only belatedly did Scott realize she spoke to him.

Believe!

She'd been right about Williams's bear. She'd seen right through the Core working to find him here. She'd been *seeing* all her life.

I believe you, he'd told her. *I just don't believe me.*

Once he had. Once he'd reached for the tiger and felt nothing—there, in those days immediately after Core D'oìche, when everyone had been so stunned, when he'd still been so sorely wounded. It hadn't hurt to try the change, then. Only later, when he'd been bitter and angry and…

Disbelieving.

The tiger, called upon and then disbelieved. The tiger, striking back.

Marlee lost her grip on the bear and tumbled to the floor, awkward and desperately trying to roll away. The bear turned for her, shaking its head and clawing air in a temper taken over by the beast.

No one had ever known Williams could take the bear. No one had ever trained him to deal with the surge of power, the purity of instinct and reaction.

Marlee scrambled away—the bear thumped down to all fours with a ponderous leap, catching Marlee up in one extended paw and flicking her aside…flicking her against the wall, where she crumpled, still and silent as the bear gathered itself again.

I believe you. Scott launched himself at the bear, *reaching—*

Finding. Flashing through the pain to exultation, the tiger's roar filling his head, the coiled explosion of strength filling his body. He slammed into the bear, digging claws in long enough for a quick grab-hold and two wicked blows from his hind legs before he sprang aside, putting himself between Marlee and the bear.

"Scott!" Marlee gasped, and he found her tugging futilely at the tough plastic around her wrist. She thrust the arm at him, her gaze on the bear—and Scott had no time for it, turning instead to rise up against the bear, slipping backward as the bear raked him hard, leaving torn flesh in his wake.

"Scott!" Marlee said, demanding now—she'd made it to her knees, her wrist held out to him. "No one's coming, Scott—they can't *hear.*"

The Core working, obscuring as much sound as sight—leaving them battling in isolation.

Scott whirled on her, jaws open, diving for her wrist. She flinched—hell, who wouldn't flinch?—but held steady, and he hooked a canine through the plastic and flicked his head aside.

Marlee cried out at the forces wrenching her arm—and then, once the bracelet had been removed, scrambled away. Scott paid for that instant of inattention, claws raking his flank, the raw scent of blood in the air. He spun, a single flowing motion, and clamped down on the bear's splayed paw, biting hard, releasing, springing aside.

And then his snarl was for Marlee, darting back in with fire extinguisher in hand, using it to bludgeon the bear from behind—once, twice—before the bear slapped her aside.

This time when she landed, she didn't move again.

The tiger took over, tipping over the edge to fury; quick slapping paws brought him face-to-face with the bear's open jaws. He tumbled away in a twisting dodge and launched back again, in spite of the new background shouting, the demands to stand down—the sudden baffled look on the bear's face, the sudden insulting sting of a dart in Scott's flank.

The strength drained from his legs as the bear fell away. His vision tunneled in and he folded down, just enough left in him to stagger over to where Marlee lay, so still, and rest his heavy head beside her hand before the tranquilizer took full effect and his eyes drifted closed.

Chapter 9

Scott opened his eyes to white acoustic ceiling tiles, one of which was painted with a big classic yellow smiley face. He closed his eyes and groaned, fully prepared to again give way to the lassitude in his body.

"Hey."

His eyes popped wide open again; he turned his head to find Marlee curled up beside him, her lower arm, hand and wrist encased in a cast and bruises mottling one side of her face. Her short hair was scruffed every which way, and her eyes were rimmed with red. Somewhere along the way, her clothes had been replaced with dark blue scrubs.

Somewhere along the way, Scott's clothes had simply disappeared.

"—The hell—!" he said, not understanding any of it.

"It's okay," she told him. "We're okay."

"The hell—!" he said again, remembering her hands on him, remembering his hands on her, squinting to remember—

The bear. The tiger. Marlee, swatted across the room to land in a heap. He jerked upright, learned instantly what a terrible mistake that had been, and fell back to the firm surface with enough force to jar every aching bone into complaint.

"Well," Marlee said, and she still hadn't moved. She was curled up on a gurney close to his, cozied up to a pillow and looking sleepy and most likely medicated. "We *were* all right."

"The hell," he muttered, just to say it again. He moved more carefully this time, propping up on his elbows to survey the parts of him that were visible above the sheet in the cool room. Bruises bloomed dark over his ribs, claw marks healing with Sentinel speed over top them. He lifted the sheet, found more signs of healing, ugly wounds already cleaned and medicated. And he remembered the sting of that dart with annoying clarity. "Dammit, they tranked me!"

"And him." Marlee nodded to the other side of him, and he found Drake Williams—still sedated, as naked as Scott but far, far hairier. He, too, bore healing wounds. Scott couldn't help his satisfaction to see that Drake had gotten the worst of it.

He settled back down to the gurney, wishing for a pillow. Hell, wishing for a set of his own scrubs. "Your bracelet," he said. "They were already on alert for you. When the bracelet came off..."

"They came running," she agreed.

"And took me down," he grumbled—and then shot a quick glance over to Marlee, realizing how bad it would have been for her to be caught in the middle of this mess, her guilt predetermined. He glanced at her wrists, half-afraid he'd find handcuffs.

He didn't. But she already wore, on her uninjured wrist, another locater bracelet.

She shrugged, somehow hardly moving at all. "I'm still a traitor. Nothing will change that."

He swore again, this time more sharply. "They understand that you helped *catch* our furry friend? That you were working *with* me?"

"It was pretty clear he wasn't any friend of mine." When Scott just looked at her, she said dryly, "If a Sentinel healer can't tell the difference between bear and tiger claw marks, she's got no business being here."

"Claw marks?" he said, and felt the anger start to build again—a different kind of anger than before. Not bitter, but inescapably protective.

"Oh, stop," she said. "It's over. We got the bad guy, Scott—they found Core amulets in Williams's toolbox."

"We got the bad guy," he said, absorbing that. No more little *accidents* in brevis medical; no more lurking threat.

"And you found your tiger."

"You *saw* me," he said, grateful at that—knowing it had taken her belief in order to awaken his own. She said nothing, only watched him, and he extended a hand to touch the tips of her fingers where they emerged from her cast. "As it happens, Marlee Cerrosa, I see you, too."

"I guess I'll just have to get used to that." She sounded rueful, as if she hadn't expected anyone to ever see beyond what she'd done to who she really was. She hesitated, then voiced her thought anyway. "I think things will be a little better for me, now. Anyway, you and your tiger…you've shown me what it's like to be safe."

Maybe Scott was still dopey—or maybe he saw what he thought he did in her eyes, in her expression. What he *hoped* he did. "I'll always do that," he told her. "Always, Marlee."

She watched him with an expression that looked as hopeful as he felt—and seeing something there that made her relax, a little smile at the corners of her mouth. "Good," she murmured. "Now reach over here and pull me closer."

His hope turned into a rakish grin. "Always," he told her, and did just that.

* * * * *

TEMPTING THE JAGUAR

KATIE REUS

Katie Reus has been reading romance for as long as she can remember, but she didn't always know she wanted to be a writer. After graduating summa cum laude with a degree in psychology and working too many jobs she hated, she finally figured things out. She currently lives in the South with her own real-life hero. When she's not busy with her family, she spends her days writing dark paranormal romance and sexy romantic suspense.

Chapter 1

Estrella Rios smoothed a hand back over her hair, hoping her unruly curls stayed in place. At least for the next three hours. As a favor to her former college roommate, who was also her best friend, she was filling in for one of the hired servers at Sabrina's first professional art show. It was at a well-known studio and drew serious buyers. Estrella understood her friend's neurotic need to control every little detail tonight.

Since Estrella had waited tables during college, carrying a tray around all night was a piece of cake. Or it would be if a certain tall, extremely sexy man would stop staring at her—and following her around. It was unsettling. Well, she couldn't prove he was following her, but everywhere she turned, there he was.

Watching her with pale green eyes that were damn unnerving, he moved with a liquid, almost supernatural grace.

Almost as if the man knew she was thinking about him, he appeared in her line of sight again. Even with the throng of people between them she could feel the heat of his gaze, as if he was actually touching her. He stared at her with laser-like focus. Then he blinked and she sucked in a deep breath. *Oh crap.* He was like her. She could see the animal lurking in his gaze. It had only been a brief flash but she'd recognized the animal peering back at her.

He was a shifter—a human who could turn into an animal. The few male shifters she'd met in college were jerks who thought they could dominate and tell her what to do just because she was packless. That was another term she'd learned while in college. Apparently packless translated to unprotected in the shifter world. Whatever. She wasn't concerned with learning anything about packs or other shifters. She'd grown up in the human world. Luckily, all of her friends were human and she'd blended into their world almost perfectly from the time she was five years old and abandoned to the foster system. She knew how to blend in and hide from those who thought their strength gave them a free pass to treat her however they wanted.

Swallowing hard at the thought that the hot stranger could be just like some of the other shifters she'd known, she took a step back and collided with a wall of muscle. The tray in her hand dipped, the champagne glasses sloshing and threatening to fall, but two strong hands encircled her from behind. One steadied the tray and the other clutched possessively around her hip.

She knew it was him before she even turned around. He had an earthy scent that reminded her of the forest after a fresh spring rain. No matter how good he smelled, she did not appreciate the way he was holding on to her. As if he knew her and had the right to touch her.

Firmly clasping the tray, she stepped away from him and was careful to keep the drinks balanced as she turned. When her eyes clashed with his pale ones, a shot of pure warmth and adrenaline punched through her. The man was certainly attractive in an edgy, dangerous sort of way. With dark hair just a little too long and sharply defined cheekbones, he looked as if he'd been cut from stone. He'd triggered her fight-or-flight response, but not necessarily in a bad way. Her inner jaguar told her to run fast and far from this man who was clearly a predator. She could see it in his gaze. No one in their right mind would mess with this guy.

Even though her jaguar was spooked, her purely female human side was very interested. Estrella was glad her dress wrapped around her like a second skin.

"Your name," he said, his voice raspy and sexy as it twined around her.

She blinked as his words jerked her out of her stupor. "Excuse me?"

"What. Is. Your. Name." All right, he was definitely ordering her to tell him.

And she did *not* like his demanding tone. "Think you can ask like a normal person?"

He blinked and she realized she'd taken him off guard. Clearing his throat, he took a step closer, and she was very thankful to have the flutes of champagne as a barrier. "You're in my Alpha's territory but you haven't announced your presence or asked for permission to be here. I want your name."

Uh-oh. So there was no doubt he knew she was a shifter too. Maybe she'd broken some unwritten rule. Estrella ignored the sliver of fear that trailed down her spine. "I don't know what an Alpha is and I don't really care." Though she could guess what it was. "I don't have to ask *anyone* for permission to be *anywhere*. And if you even think about touching me again, you'll lose your hand."

He blinked again and this time she knew she'd surprised him. Something told her that didn't happen very often. Before he could respond, she swiveled and moved to mingle with other art patrons. She used her supernatural grace to weave through the crowd of well-dressed people as she offered them drinks.

When she finally turned back toward the trio of black-and-white oil paintings of the Everglades, Estrella felt a mix of relief and disappointment that the mystery man was no longer hovering there. For a moment her gaze lingered on the paintings, each one depicting the moon in various phases. In the third one, Sabrina had added a stark orange moon—the only splash of color in the darker scenes. Forcing her gaze away, Estrella quickly scanned the rest of the first floor before doing an actual physical walk through.

He was gone. And she had a job to do.

Ignoring the disturbing disappointment that welled up inside her at his absence, she pasted on a smile and returned to the kitchen to refill her tray. The way customers were drinking, she hoped it would make them loosen up and help her friend's sales.

Three-and-a-half hours later Estrella's feet ached—thanks to her four-inch heels—but at least the crowd was gone and the studio was closed. The servers from the catering company were loading up their van, but that didn't fall into her realm of duties. She'd just done them a favor by picking up some of the slack and now she was sitting on one of the cleared off food tables and munching on petit fours. After demolishing five, she was thinking about eating a sixth when Sabrina strode out of the manager's office, a giant grin on her face.

Her friend had flatironed her hair for the event and had pulled it back into a tight ponytail, showing off her sharp cheekbones and gorgeous café au lait skin. Sabrina's dark eyes narrowed slightly. "How many of those things have you eaten?"

Estrella shrugged and returned her friend's grin.

"I don't know how you eat all that processed crap or where you put it all." Sabrina mock-shuddered and grabbed a strawberry off her plate.

Estrella just shook her head. "You don't know what you're missing." She popped another of the mini cakes into her mouth, savoring the sweetness. Thanks to being a shifter her metabolism was high, which meant she had to eat a lot more than most people. Of course her friend didn't know she was a shifter. It was the only secret Estrella had ever kept from her. "So, how was the show?"

"A lot better than expected. I'll be able to cover rent for at least the next six months if I budget right, which means I can officially quit my waitressing job." Sabrina picked up her purse off the table so Estrella stood and snagged her own clutch, leaving her plate behind.

Estrella had just done the same after selling a few of her sculptures. Of course money was definitely tight, but she'd decided to take the plunge and throw herself into her work full-time. At least until her money ran out or she sold more pieces. Hopefully the latter would happen instead. "Do you realize this means we're both full-time artists? Both doing exactly what everyone said we were crazy to even think about trying?"

Sabrina's megawatt smile was blinding. "I'm scared to quit my job, but...I'm more scared not to."

"I totally understand." Estrella and Sabrina had met as freshmen in college and had been inseparable ever since. No one else she knew understood what it was like trying to make it as an artist more than her best friend.

"I'm tempted to go out and celebrate but I'm so tired." Sabrina stopped in front of their vehicles as she fished her keys out of her purse.

Estrella did the same and stifled a yawn. "Go home and get some sleep because tomorrow you're giving your notice at work."

"You just don't want to go out—but you're right, I do need sleep. Thanks again for tonight." Sabrina gave her a quick hug and a kiss on the cheek before pressing her key fob.

Following suit, Estrella got into her Jeep and steered out of the nearly deserted parking lot. Instead of heading east like Sabrina she turned west in the direction of the new place she'd recently rented on the outskirts of Huntsville, Alabama. The cottage-style house in the middle of the woods had been perfectly priced and allowed her to shift and run free in privacy. Plus it had a small air-conditioned studio attached to the house where she was able to work. It was like the place had been custom-made for her.

As she turned off onto the two-lane road that led to her place, she was surprised when headlights appeared in her rearview mirror. The road was a dead end and there was only one more—*unoccupied*—house about two miles down from hers. Slowing her vehicle, she started to pull off onto the side of the road when she spotted another set of head-lights behind the first vehicle. *What the heck was going on?*

She stopped so that whoever was behind her could pass. When the vehicle behind her also pulled off, panic jumped inside her.

The headlights directly behind her shut off and she real-ized it was a truck. It was too dark to see who was inside other than to make out a big, broad-shouldered silhouette. Definitely male. Estrella quickly debated her options. She could try to turn around and outrun the man in her Jeep but he could easily block her with his vehicle. No, she'd be better off if she jumped out, shifted and made a run for it. If this was a group of shifters who wanted her for nefari-ous purposes she'd have a much better chance in her ani-mal form. As a jaguar she was powerful and could run at incredible bursts of speed. Considering the way that shifter had been eyeing her at the party tonight, she couldn't dis-count anything.

The moment her fingers touched the door handle, a tear-ing sound made her jerk around. Claws sliced through the plastic window of her Jeep. There was no way the silhouette she'd seen in the truck behind her could have moved so fast.

Before she could move, the figure was jerked away by someone else. Whoever it was moved in a quiet, fast blur. Scrambling, she leaped from her vehicle. Someone let out a strangled cry but the sound was cut off abruptly. Hurrying away from her Jeep, she froze as she rounded it and saw a giant black wolf use his freaking *claws* to rip the head off a man. The wolf snarled angrily, its white teeth dripping blood as it tossed the head to the side.

Estrella's mouth almost fell open as the decapitated man shriveled to ash right in front of her. *What the hell?*

She stumbled back into a wall of muscle. Turning, she nearly shrieked as a man with fangs and claws protruding from his hands grasped her by the shoulders. At least he wasn't slicing her up with his claws.

"Don't worry about the wolf, you're coming with me, *bonita*," he purred. His amber eyes were definitely not human.

Ohmygodohmygodohmygod! This guy was a vampire. Her brain rejected it, not wanting to believe the creatures were even real. But this guy was so a vampire. And he thought he could take her?

Instinctively, she shoved at his chest before undergoing the change into animal. She'd seen a wolf change once and his shift had been brutal and had taken precious moments. Hers was seamless as her jaguar form took over. Her clothes shredded as her bones quickly realigned and her much stronger and bigger animal side took over.

She lunged at the vampire, going for the throat as she knocked him to the ground. That wolf shifter might not be an ally but she'd seen the way he'd taken down that man—vampire. She'd been forced to kill a wolf shifter in the past and it looked like these other creatures had the same weakness. Decapitation probably killed everything.

The vampire with an olive complexion similar to her own held up his arms defensively as he cried out. "I don't want to hurt you!"

If she'd been in her human form, she'd have snorted. *Yeah right.* She bit into his forearm, surprised by the taste of his blood. It was sweeter, not as coppery as animal and human blood.

The dark-haired vampire slashed at her, raking those claws down her left side as he tried to dislodge her. Behind her she heard more snarling. Afraid of a sneak attack, she let go and risked a quick glance over her shoulder. The black wolf was sparring with two more vampires.

She didn't know why he was putting himself in danger for her, but if he could take on two, she could take on this one. The vampire struggling underneath her hold was keeping his throat and face protected so she went for one of his biceps, keeping him pinned to the ground with her weight and strength.

He cried out in pain as she tore through tendons and muscles. A hard fist slammed into her head, loosening her jaw. Letting go, she rolled over onto her paws and jumped back, putting a few feet of distance between them.

"We don't want to hurt you!" he shouted, palms raised.

She snarled and started for him again. He sprinted away from her. The vampire shouted something and she saw a blur of movement as one of the others who'd been sparring with the black wolf ran back to the SUV parked behind the truck. They dove into it and seconds later tires squealed as they tore back the way they'd come.

Still panting, she took a cautious step toward the limp wolf on the ground. Even though it was dark, thanks to the stars, moon and her extrasensory abilities, she could see a pool of crimson spreading onto the road underneath the other shifter.

Though she didn't know the wolf, he'd still been fighting the vampires. For her? Maybe. She didn't know what to make of this guy.

She knew she should probably be more focused on the fact that vampires were real and she'd just been attacked by one, but she had to help the wolf. As she neared the animal it let out a soft moan. Nudging his jaw with her nose, she froze when its eyes blinked open. They were the exact pale shade of green as the man from the art studio.

Chapter 2

Rainer stared into the eyes of the beautiful female jaguar shifter. She was a sleek orange feline with dark black spots. Jagged pain lanced down his left side. One of the vamps had sliced into him, breaking a rib and piercing him with a silver dagger. The rib was already healing and the silver hadn't gotten into his blood stream so while he hurt, he was almost four hundred and fifty years old and more than capable of compartmentalizing his pain.

For a brief moment he tensed, wondering if the female planned to attack him too. The thought of sparring with this woman, even in self-defense, made something painful well up inside him. Some primal part of him just couldn't do it. But then she let out a soft whine and nudged him with her nose and he realized she was worried. Or at least concerned about him.

He tried to move then realized he must have been injured worse than he originally thought. More pain ripped through his right shoulder like tiny daggers digging into him. Damn vampire had sliced through him with his claws. Rainer let his head fall back against the pavement. He'd heal soon enough and if those vamps didn't come back and the woman didn't try to attack him, he'd be fine.

But she clearly had other ideas. After whining and nudging him again, she turned tail and disappeared around her Jeep. Less than a minute later she came back around in her human form wearing a form-fitting T-shirt and shorts. All shifters he knew carried around multiple changes of clothes so it made sense she had something extra to put on. It was a shame she'd had to destroy that skimpy black dress though. He'd had some wicked fantasies earlier tonight of slowly peeling it off her. Watching her carefully, he relaxed slightly when she opened the back door of her Jeep.

"Come on, big fella. You're coming home with me so you can heal. Do not make me regret this," she murmured as she bent down and picked him up.

Rainer was huge and if she'd been human she wouldn't have been able to lift him. As it was, the petite woman strained and grunted as she slid her arms under his big wolf body and lifted him up. Though it would have hurt like hell, he could have jumped into the back on his own, but he was afraid any sudden movements would scare her.

And he wasn't above playing the sympathy card if it got her to take him back to her place. She was living in Huntsville, which was his Alpha's territory and she hadn't made her presence known to anyone that he knew of. Considering that his oldest brother Alaric was second-in-command to Knox, his Alpha, Rainer would have known if a jaguar shifter had been living in their territory. Then she'd acted as if she didn't know what an Alpha was. Whatever was going on with this woman and whoever she was, he was damn sure going to find out.

Because those vampires tonight had been hunting *her*.

After gently sliding him onto a thick quilt, she shut the back door while she muttered to herself about how she was definitely going to regret letting a wolf into her home. If he'd been in human form he would have smiled. Inhaling deeply, he scented her on the quilt and the smell soothed him on a primal level. Most shifters carried quilts or blankets around in their vehicles in case they decided to stop somewhere and sleep out in the woods, on the beach, or wherever.

He didn't like leaving his truck but there was no identifying information inside and the license plate wasn't linked to his pack. If someone stole it, well, he'd take care of that later. The gentle hum of her engine would have lulled him to sleep but after only a minute of driving the vehicle shut off again and she got out.

Making a split second decision, he shifted back to his human form. His bones cracked, broke and realigned and skin quickly replaced fur. Rainer wanted to be able to talk to her and he wanted to know why they'd stopped when they were in the middle of nowhere. She definitely hadn't gone far.

Seconds later the back door opened. The woman's dark eyes widened and she took a step back. She seemed almost frozen to the spot as her gaze raked over him. He was turned on his side, still covered in blood and aching, but the way she stared at him made another part of his body react. When her eyes landed on his groin area, her olive-hued cheeks tinged bright pink and she quickly averted her gaze.

Looking at a spot over his shoulder, she cleared her throat. "Do you need help getting out?"

No. "Yes." Yeah, he definitely wasn't above playing the sympathy card if it got her to touch him. Rainer sat up and winced when he saw the blood he'd left behind. "Sorry about your quilt," he muttered.

"It's fine. We need to get you cleaned off." Still keeping her gaze not quite on his face, she slid an arm under his shoulder and helped him slide out. Her body was stiff and tense as she held on to him, making it clear she didn't like touching him.

He inhaled deeply, memorizing her jasmine scent. It was so pure and classic he wanted to bury his face against her neck and just breathe her in. "My name's Rainer," he said as his feet touched the paved driveway that led to a cottage style one-story home in the middle of the woods. Perfect for privacy, but not for a single female shifter who clearly had no pack for protection. He frowned at the thought of her out here all alone. His inner wolf flexed its claws, wanting to protect her.

She paused for a moment. "I'm Estrella. Now come on. I want to get you inside before those...*things* come back."

He let her name roll around in his head as he savored it. But the uncertain way she said "things" made him curious. "You've never seen a vampire before?"

Her grip around him tightened as she hissed in a breath. "Those men really *were* vampires? I'd thought so but I still wasn't sure if I was right or if they were even real..." She trailed off and put a key in the front door.

The second they stepped inside she let her arm drop, leaving him standing naked and dripping blood in her foyer. He started to call out but she returned a moment later carrying a towel covered in old paint splatters. Keeping her dark brown eyes on his she held the towel out, effectively blocking his lower body from her line of vision. "This is so you can cover yourself." Her cheeks had turned that delicious shade of pink again.

Despite the residual pain pulsing through him, Rainer wondered what it would be like to nip and kiss her very full lips. "Does my nudity bother you?" Most shifters were immune to nudity, but he still wrapped the towel around his waist.

"Uh, *yeah.*" She said it as if he was stupid. Her gaze trailed to his shoulder and to his surprise she took a step closer and ran a gentle finger over his almost healed wounds. "You're almost healed so if you want to take a shower and clean off the blood I think I can find a clean set of clothes that fit. Then I'll take you back to your truck."

And get him the hell out of her house, was her unspoken message. That wasn't happening anytime soon. Not until he got his answers and not until he was certain she wasn't under threat from those vamps. Eyeing her, he let his gaze trail down her lithe, lean body for the second time that night. Even though she wasn't wearing that tight dress, her top and shorts showed enough that he could fantasize about running his hands and mouth over all her smooth, olive skin. Her body practically glowed.

She'd had her hair pulled back at the art studio but after her shift to animal then back to human it was free and her tight corkscrew curls framed her face, giving her an almost innocent quality. He couldn't be sure but he guessed she had some Mediterranean and possibly Hispanic heritage. Wherever she was from, the woman was gorgeous. For the first time in over four hundred years he felt absolutely tongue-tied as he stared at her. As he brought his gaze back up though, something else struck him. "That vampire clawed you, too."

She shrugged. "Yeah, so?"

"How did you heal before you even put on your clothes?"

"The same way you're healing now," she snapped, annoyance and some other foreign note in her voice that he couldn't define.. Fear, maybe?

That's when he realized how tired she was. Dark circles ringed under her eyes and she'd just admitted she'd never seen vamps before so he knew she had to be reeling somewhat from the shock of that revelation. "Ah, sorry. Thank you for bringing me back here. I know it wasn't easy to bring a strange shifter into your home, especially a male of a different species. I'd appreciate a shower but then I'd like to talk to you about some things, namely those vampires."

She blinked, looking stunned for a moment. Oh yeah, he'd get a lot further with this sexy woman with a bit of politeness. For a fraction of a second her eyes strayed to his bare chest and lust flared in their depths so bright it stunned him. But then it was gone and she nodded sharply at him, her face a mask of confusion. "This way." She led him down a short hallway and motioned inside the first door on the left. "Since you can stand I'm sure you can take care of…everything else. I'll see what I can find for you to wear," she murmured, careful not to touch him as she skirted past him and disappeared down the hallway and into another room.

He wondered if she'd gone into her bedroom. That thought brought up visions of her splayed naked on a giant bed as she waited for him. Rainer scrubbed a hand over his face. What the hell was wrong with him? He was reacting to this female like a randy cub.

During a very quick and cold shower, he washed all the blood and grime off his body and was pleased to see all his skin had knitted back together. After he was done he found a pair of large sweatpants and a T-shirt folded neatly outside the door. They were definitely a man's because they were too big for her and that thought made an unwanted emotion ripple through him. *Jealousy.*

By nature he was territorial but he hadn't felt jealous over a female in centuries.

The shirt was snug but it was dry so once he was dressed he headed back the way she'd led him to find her walking in the front door carrying the bloody quilt. He cringed inwardly at the mess he'd made, but she didn't seem concerned.

"Are you ready for me to take you back to your truck?" she asked as she dropped the quilt into a bundle next to the door.

"Eager to get rid of me?" When she didn't respond he continued. "I told you we need to talk about those vamps."

She shrugged and wrapped her arms around herself as she leaned against the closed front door. "So talk."

Okay, she wasn't going to make this easy on him. "Whose clothes am I wearing? Boyfriend's?" He hoped the question would take her off guard.

She blinked those big dark eyes in confusion, then snorted. But she still didn't give him an answer.

Damn if that only rankled him even more. "Can we sit somewhere and talk?"

After a pause she said "sure," and nodded to her right and stepped into a cozy room with a couch, loveseat and giant pillows tossed around an intricate teak coffee table. The bright reds and oranges should have been garish but the splashes of color in the room complimented the many sculptures. Rainer had followed Estrella from the art show and realized she was friends with the artist when he'd seen her in the parking lot. Now he wondered…"Are you an artist?" He sat at one of the couches while she dropped down onto one of the overstuffed pillows.

"I'm a sculptor but I don't want to talk about that. Were you following me? And what's the deal with those…vampires?" She still seemed to struggle with the concept.

"You tell me. I've been hunting them and they were most definitely hunting *you*."

She actually laughed, the sound so rich and vibrant it was like a punch to his senses.

"I'm serious," he said quietly, injecting the truth into his words.

She froze, her darker skin paling to the point he felt guilty for being the one to scare her. "What?" It was a whisper.

Rainer made a split second decision to tell her everything he knew. There was no point in lying and something told him he'd get a lot further with this woman by being truthful from the start. "My Alpha and oldest brother are away because of the peace treaty being signed between shifters and vampires."

Estrella stared at him blankly. Either she was the best actress on the planet or she really had no clue what he was talking about.

He continued. "On orders from my Alpha, I'm part of

the team patrolling Huntsville and the surrounding area because of issues with a group of vampires who recently descended on the city. I've been tracking them and they've been tracking you."

She shook her head, those gorgeous curls swaying around her face. "That's insane. Why would vampires give a crap about me?"

"Exactly. *Why* would they care about you? Who are you and where are you from?"

Estrella's jaw tightened and he didn't blame her. He was a strange male in her home demanding answers.

But whatever was going on, they needed to figure it out before those vampires came back for her. And he knew they would. They would probably get reinforcements then come back tomorrow night. It was standard operating procedure. "I've been honest with you but if you need more, I have three brothers: Alaric, Conrad and Hardwin. We've all been part of Knox's pack for close to three hundred years and—"

Her eyes widened. "Three hundred…. Are shifters immortal?"

Oh, shit. "How old are you?" he asked.

"Twenty-six."

"Do you not know anything about your kind?"

She visibly bristled at the question. "I'm an artist and a human. That's all I need to know," she snapped as a tremor rolled over her.

"You're not completely human and you know it. Earlier you said you didn't know what an Alpha was so here's a quick lesson. Knox recently expanded his territory and now rules all of Alabama. When you crossed into this state you should have told him you were here and by the looks of it, you're living here on a semipermanent basis."

She swallowed hard and a wave of fear rolled off her. He could scent it, so potent, and he realized it was because of him. He was leaning forward, his hands on his knees, staring at her hard. He probably looked like an asshole. But he'd wanted to get some things straight with her. Easing back in his seat, he forced himself to relax.

Estrella pulled her knees up to her chest and wrapped her arms around them as she began to talk. "My parents died when I was five. I got put into the foster system and was eventually adopted by a very nice older human couple who couldn't have kids. They never knew anything about my shifter abilities. I grew up in Miami, went to college there, and only recently moved here with my best friend. Living here is a lot cheaper, there's a growing art market and I have no one to return to in Florida anyway. My adoptive father died of a heart attack about two years ago and my adoptive mother died six months later of heart problems. I don't think she was able to live without him."

"Miami," he murmured, her lack of knowledge making sense now. There were no packs living in central or south Florida and vampires never made their homes in the state. Not even day walkers. Living in a place called the Sunshine State just went against their nature. "Have you ever met any of your own kind before?"

She shrugged, the action jerky. "I met a couple wolves in college." Something else rolled off her then that made his inner wolf still.

"Did someone hurt you?" He knew too well what could happen to an unprotected female shifter in this world. It wasn't as bad in modern times but centuries ago, you either lived with a pack or you didn't survive for long.

Her spine straightened. "They tried." There was a snap of anger in her words that made him smile, even while the thought of anyone attempting to hurt this beautiful woman made him see red.

He started to respond when his senses went on high alert. Without thinking, he turned off the lamp, sending the room into darkness. Light from the moon streamed in through the sheer curtains and with their extrasensory abilities they could see fine.

"What's going on?" she asked quietly. Estrella had dropped her arms from around her knees and was tense with anticipation.

He held up a finger to his mouth as he listened carefully. With his hearing, he had no problem picking up outside sounds. Normally he tuned everything out but it had suddenly hit him that he didn't hear *anything* outside. This time of year crickets in Alabama were bad and he'd heard them when they arrived.

Now, silence.

Which meant there was a predator—or more likely predators—outside. It was a few hours from dawn. The vampires shouldn't have had time to regroup. Rainer had been battling them long enough to know how they operated. They'd never have a base of operations so close to someone they were targeting. Not to mention if they'd set up shop in the state, he'd know about it. So if they planned to take Estrella—and that would happen over his dead body—they'd be cutting it down to the wire trying to get her back to wherever their base was over the state line.

"Our *friends* are back," he murmured.

Fear and anger pulsed off her in equal waves as she silently stood with a lethal, beautiful grace that made him forget to breathe for a moment.

"Do you trust me?" he asked.

She paused, then shrugged.

That would have to do. He could stay and fight them but decided against it. If these vamps were desperate enough to come back for her now, there was no telling how many numbers they'd brought. Nope. He and Estrella were going to run.

It was just a matter of getting out of here first.

Chapter 3

Estrella knew she was probably crazy to trust this wolf, but so far he'd been up front about who he was. Lies had a very distinctive metallic scent and Rainer was telling her the truth. Of course he could be holding something back, but right now she knew they needed to get the heck out of her house.

Something was wrong. There was an eerie silence surrounding them and her innate animal sense that she never ignored had her inner jaguar going nuts. She was clawing at Estrella's insides, begging to be set free. And Estrella was about to let her out when Rainer took her hand in his. His very big, callused hand. Just that small connection soothed her inner jaguar and increased her physical awareness of this very powerful wolf. Didn't matter if they were surrounded by enemies, her growing attraction to him wouldn't be denied.

He held on to her as he crept to one of her front windows. Carefully, he peered outside then stiffened before pulling her close.

She swallowed hard as his head bent to hers. That distinctive sandalwood scent twined around her. His breath was warm against her skin. "I see at least three but there will be more. We need to escape out the back and shift. Then we run fast. Stay in front of me, I'll make sure none of them hurt you. Once we get far enough away, we'll have backup." She barely heard him and he was millimeters from her ear, his tongue practically caressing her lobe.

Nodding, she inhaled deeply, hating the strange effect he was having on her. She knew they were in all sorts of danger if there were more of those scary vampires outside her house and she was touched that he promised to have her back. But part of her couldn't shake the strong magnetic pull she felt for him. It was getting stronger now that they were touching.

Her face was still pressed into his neck as his free hand cupped her cheek. Rainer drew back a fraction and lightly brushed his lips over hers. The action was sweet and she might have mistaken it for chaste if not for the way his hips jerked against hers. She figured he was trying to distract her from the threat outside and she appreciated it.

Grabbing her hand tighter, he stepped away and nodded toward the back of her house. "Lead the way."

Her house wasn't big and he probably could have found the way on his own but she quickly moved through her house. Estrella was relieved that he didn't let go of her hand. He was clearly protective and the knowledge warmed her entire body. It had been a long time since a male had wanted to look out for her.

Once they reached the back door he expertly maneuvered so that he was in front of her and barely moved the curtain covering the small window to check outside. After a moment he said, "I see four more."

Her heart rate accelerated. So there were at least seven of those creatures outside waiting for them. But why?

Rainer stripped off his shirt then turned to her. He motioned with his hands that he was going to crack the door open, then they'd shift and bolt through the door. His hand charades might have amused her had the timing not been so wildly inappropriate.

"Send the female out unharmed and we won't hurt you, wolf!" A loud, male voice boomed from outside, cutting down any of her humorous thoughts.

Her skin chilled. It suddenly hit her that these vampires actually wanted *her*. This wasn't a case of Rainer being mistaken about their intentions. He'd told her they'd been hunting her but she hadn't wanted to believe him. And that vampire from earlier had said he didn't want to hurt her even though he'd told her she was coming with him. She couldn't deny the facts in front of her even though she wanted to.

Rainer growled low in his throat, anger practically sparking off him as he eased the lock open and barely pulled the door back an inch. He looked at her and nodded once as he stripped off his pants. His ripped body would put pro football players to shame. And what was between his legs...she shuddered again as warmth spread throughout her. Now was definitely not the time to be noticing that.

Knowing it was silly to feel self-conscious especially considering the circumstances, she stripped off her own clothes and underwent the change at the same time Rainer did.

He nudged the door open with his nose, and they both sprinted out onto her back porch. Using all her strength and supernatural speed she flew across her open backyard, which led directly into the thick forest.

A shot rang out and dirt flew up a foot from Rainer. Straining, she urged her body onward, glad Rainer was just as fast as she was.

"No! Don't hurt the princess!" that same male voice shouted, though he sounded a lot farther away than before.

Princess? What the hell? Once Estrella and Rainer breached the thick trees, they moved even faster. Wind rolled over her fur as her paws pounded the hard, crunchy earth. There was shouting behind them, but she managed to tune it out the farther they ran.

The trees around them grew thicker, the forest blanketing them in protection. Since there was no way to tell Rainer, she did what came natural to her beast. She took to the trees, jumping from branch to branch, tree to tree, as they raced. It gave her a much better vantage point to spot any possible dangers and she always kept Rainer in her line of sight.

Some primal part of her wouldn't let him get away from her. The need to see that he was okay and yes, protect him, was like a living thing inside her. She didn't understand it and she wasn't sure she liked it. But it was there nonetheless.

The voices and shouts had long since faded in the background and once the trees started to thin again she jumped back to earth and fell right in line with Rainer. She wasn't sure how far they'd gone but it had to be at least eight miles, maybe more. He let out a low yip that sounded almost like a greeting. Maybe he was glad she was running next to him again.

When he slowed she followed suit. By the way he was moving it was obvious he was somewhat familiar with this territory. Since she was an orange jaguar and therefore stood out in the forests of Alabama, she tended to stay within a two-mile range of her home so she'd never been this far out before. He clearly had.

Once they'd slowed to a complete walk, she nudged him in the side with her nose. He yipped at her and actually snapped his jaws. It wasn't in anger, but almost playful. The action took her off guard. She'd never had anyone to run with. Not since she was a cub—and those memories were fuzzy. Her father was the only one she even remembered running with. Never her mom.

They reached a clearing, but she froze when she saw a man standing near the opening of a cave. He was tall with dark hair and had a similar build to Rainer, but she didn't plan to cover the rest of the thirty yards to find out who he was. She growled, drawing Rainer to a sudden stop.

He looked at her, then back at the man and barked. As if she should understand what he meant. Estrella went down on her belly, ears back, and he flopped next to her. He nudged her side with his nose, trying to get her to stand.

She knew she was being stupid and maybe a little irrational, but she was terrified. The reality of what had just happened was slowly sinking in. Freaking vampires had chased them down and she was on the run with a very sexy wolf shifter. A shifter she knew next to nothing about. She didn't think he'd lured her into a trap or anything, but fear clawed through her as past experiences raced through her mind.

Rainer let out what she thought sounded like a frustrated bark then shifted to his human form. He crouched down in front of her and she tried to ignore the fact that he was naked. "That's one of my brothers," he said quietly, reaching out and stroking a hand over her head.

How could he have known they'd be there? Alarm surged through her and she started to back away but Rainer shook his head, as if he understood exactly what she was thinking.

"My brothers and I communicate telepathically. When the rest of my family was alive, we all did. Some blood relatives are like that. Do you remember being able to do that with your parents?"

She shook her head, though an elusive memory tickled her thoughts. Did she?

Rainer sighed. "My brother brought us clothes. I'd like to take you back to my pack's land. You'll be safe there. The sun will be up in a few hours and we can check on your house then."

She shook her head again. She wasn't going anywhere.

Sighing once more, he stood. "Leave the clothes!" he called out to his brother, which she figured was for her benefit since they could apparently communicate telepathically.

The man by the cave opening paused and Estrella was under the distinct impression that he and Rainer were having a conversation. Finally the man tossed the clothes down and stalked off into the forest.

"Come on," Rainer murmured.

As they moved she tried to ignore the fact that he was naked but it was pretty hard considering the man was walking, talking sex appeal. All those hard muscles and sharp, flat planes made him an artist's dream. Of course she wasn't thinking about actually sculpting him because she didn't want anyone else to see him naked. But she wouldn't mind running her hands all over him. Then following up with her mouth and tongue.

When they reached the pile of clothes he turned around to give her privacy as she shifted back to her human form. She didn't sense anyone else in the immediate vicinity so she didn't mind being naked. The change was fast and part of her didn't want to put clothes on. Especially as she stared at his sculpted backside. She inwardly chastised herself. He was being perfectly polite and giving her privacy and she was ogling him like some lovesick teenager. Being naked around him sounded like a lot more fun than being clothed, but she tugged on the plain green T-shirt that left a good three inches of her stomach bare and a pair of drawstring lounge pants.

Rainer turned just as she put on her pants. Those startling green eyes of his seemed to practically glimmer as he raked them over her in a very appreciative sweep. When his gaze landed on her face, the look in his eyes scorched her. Her nipples instinctively reacted, pulling into hard buds.

Despite the cool April breeze whistling around them she felt as if she could combust on the spot. She wrapped her arms around herself, feeling nervous. "Do you think the vampires followed us this far?"

He shook his head. "They won't venture into my pack's territory. Besides, two of my brothers and a few more pack mates are out patrolling."

"Oh." She had a lot more questions but couldn't formulate a single one into an actual sentence.

"I want you so bad I can't think straight," he practically growled, the bewilderment on his face and in his voice mirroring her own insides.

Her eyes widened at his bluntness, especially since he seemed almost surprised he'd admitted it. She felt the same way. She hadn't taken a lover in years so this searing need for Rainer had taken her by surprise. "I want you, too," she finally whispered.

She *did* want him. Bad. After what they'd just run from she was pumped up on adrenaline and the thought of losing herself with the sexiest man she'd ever met felt like the best decision in the world.

Too many emotions twirled through her and when his gaze landed on her lips, she knew she was about to do something she might regret. She didn't care though. In a flash of movement she started to cover the distance but he was faster.

Rainer's hands settled on her hips as he tugged her close. His mouth landed on hers, his tongue immediately invading her mouth. His kisses weren't gentle or sweet. Nothing like the tender brush of his lips from earlier.

Right now he was taking and claiming.

The thought of being claimed by this male made the warmth between her legs spark into full-blown heat. The last man she'd been with had been in college years ago and he'd been human and fragile. Nothing like Rainer.

She wanted to let loose. To be free. To be herself for once.

Grabbing her hips, Rainer hoisted her up so that she had to wrap her legs around his waist. His erection pressed against her core and she couldn't help but rub against him. Even though he was wearing thin pants, the friction against her clit made her buck harder against him.

He chuckled against her mouth and pulled back slightly as he strode into the cave. "I've wanted to do this from the moment I saw you wearing that black dress and those fuck-me heels. I wanted to take you right on the floor of the art show and I didn't care who was watching."

The image that evoked made her face flame. Since she didn't trust her voice, she grappled with his shirt and tugged upward. Raising his arms, he let her take it off. Her throat tightened as she got to see his body up close and know she was about to put her hands all over him.

All those defined lines and striations. Unable to stop herself she leaned forward and nipped his hard skin. She kissed a path across his chest until she reached one nipple. Drawing it between her teeth she pressed down until he shuddered.

Her legs were still wrapped around him and she was vaguely aware of him moving them, then kneeling on something soft.

She looked up for a brief moment and realized they were on a quilt—no, sleeping bag. Whatever it was, she didn't care. She just wanted more of this mysterious man. And she desperately wanted to feel him inside her.

Pushing up on her knees, she straddled him, sinking deeper against his body and he practically tore her shirt off. A shiver stole through her as his hungry gaze landed on her breasts.

Before she realized his intent, she was flat on her back and his mouth was on her breast. He sucked, hard. Her back arched off the ground as he tugged her already hard nipple between his teeth.

A rush of warmth flooded between her legs as he cupped her other breast. He tenderly caressed it while he ran his thumb over her nipple in teasing flicks. The simultaneous yet opposite actions of his gentle hand and rougher mouth against her breasts made her moan in pleasure.

She clutched his head as she squeezed her legs around his waist. Feeling his hard length pressing against her lower abdomen wasn't enough. She wanted all of him.

Despite having a human best friend and her deceased adoptive parents, she'd felt isolated for so long. Having to pretend her entire life she wasn't a shifter had been difficult. Not around Rainer. She could completely be herself with him and it was refreshing. Her inner walls clenched with the need to be filled by him.

As if he read her mind, he slid his hand down the front of her pants. There was no teasing. He cupped her mound and slid two fingers inside her wet sheath. The abrupt action had her rolling her hips against him.

She let out a strangled sound as he dragged his fingers against her inner wall. Surprising her, he kept his strokes gentle and slow. Almost too slow.

When he raised his head to look at her, she tunneled her fingers farther back through his hair, loving the silky feel. "Tell me something about yourself," he demanded in a low voice.

She blinked, unsure she'd heard right. Her inner walls clenched around his fingers in desperation as he slowed even more. She needed him to move faster. "Now?" she rasped out.

He buried his fingers completely inside her and rested his thumb right on her clit, but then stilled his movements.

"I hate avocados," she blurted, feeling silly but so turned on with no release that she wanted to scream.

Rainer grinned and it completely softened his face. A tiny dimple appeared on his left cheek, giving him a boyish quality. Looking supremely satisfied with himself, he resumed stroking his fingers inside her, this time with urgency.

She let her head fall back and when he began rubbing his thumb over her clit she lost it.

Growling low in his throat, he sucked her breast into his mouth again and tugged her nipple in that almost-but-not-quite painful way. She let out a silent scream as her orgasm surged through her.

It was sharp and fast and had her grasping on to his shoulders in a fruitless effort to ground herself. The orgasm just kept going, punching through her and stealing her breath until she limply fell against the sleeping bag.

As her orgasm faded, Rainer finally withdrew his hand and tugged her pants off. "You're so fucking beautiful," he growled in that deep, intoxicating voice she craved. "And your scent—it's like you've drugged me with it."

Something warm blossomed inside her at his words. Estrella reached for him, eager to take his pants off too, but he beat her to it.

Her eyes widened when she finally saw his cock. And not just a glimpse of it like earlier. Seeing it up close and personal made her shudder in primal awareness. The man was certainly proportional everywhere. Then she remembered…"Condom?"

He froze, looking at her in curiosity. "You're not in heat."

She blinked, uncertain of his meaning. Since she'd turned sixteen, she went through an unbelievably painful week twice a year where she was sexually frustrated and almost nothing could ease her. "You mean those are the only times I can get pregnant?"

He nodded, his frown increasing, probably because he

was surprised she didn't know more about shifters. "And we can't get diseases," he said quietly.

Clearly she had a lot more to learn about shifter life but right now she knew all she needed to. Sitting up, she reached for him but he grabbed her wrists and pinned them above her head as they tumbled back onto the softness. She squirmed, trying to get him to push inside her but he remained firm.

Those pale green eyes had turned dark and smoky as he watched her. Under his gaze her breathing increased, her chest rising and falling rapidly. "Why aren't you moving?" she whispered, suddenly feeling self-conscious.

"I don't take lovers lightly." His voice was raspy, almost edgy.

"Me neither." It had been almost five years for her, but she didn't plan to tell him that.

"Good." There he went again with that growl. The sound was so sexy her inner walls clenched.

"And…I've never been with a shifter before." She felt like she needed to tell him something more about herself. Something personal.

His eyes flashed darker for a moment, then a purely masculine smile covered his face as he captured her mouth again.

Still keeping her wrists captive, Rainer reversed their bodies, moving so that Estrella was on top. He wanted to see every inch of her as she rode him. The most primitive part of him scoffed, wanting to ride her hard and claim her. But not this first time.

She needed to feel as safe as possible with him. Though it killed him, he could give up control. Hell, he could do anything for this woman.

Something inside him had flared to life the moment he'd met her. Deep down he knew it was the mating call. He didn't want to believe it, but his inner wolf wanted her and would accept no other. Ever. Considering they still needed to learn a lot about each other, he planned to make sure this first time together was done right. He wanted to give her so much pleasure she'd never want to be without him.

"Ride me, sweetheart." He let her wrists drop and was thankful when she immediately pushed up on his chest and straddled his waist.

Her lips were glossy and slightly swollen as she watched him. Keeping her eyes on him, she raised up and lowered herself over his cock. She let out a long, satisfied breath as she sat fully on him.

Unable to control himself, he thrust inside her. She was so tight, it would take all his self-control not to come before she climaxed again. And he'd make damn sure she did. He wanted to see that blissful expression on her face again.

Her entire body was that beautiful olive color and her nipples were a slightly darker shade of brown. Right now they were rock hard and as she rose up on her knees, her breasts slightly swayed, driving him insane.

He clenched her hips tight as she moved up and down, over and over. There was no way he could take his eyes off her. It humbled him that she was here with him now. She clearly knew nothing about shifter life, but she'd made the decision to let him into her body and they hadn't known each other that long. She was so beautiful it almost hurt him to watch her. Those dark corkscrew curls bounced with her every graceful movement. They were riotous and so at odds with the way her body seemed to flow over him.

He was so close to losing it but he refused to embarrass himself. Somehow he pulled one of his hands off her hip. Reaching between their bodies, he teased her clit. Unlike earlier, this time he used more pressure, rubbing her harder.

She let out a gasp and he felt her inner walls tighten around him each time he rubbed. Oh yeah, it wouldn't be long before she came again.

She still watched him with those big brown eyes as she rode him. It didn't matter that both their movements were becoming jerkier and less restrained, she never took her eyes off him. It was the hottest thing he'd ever experienced.

When her climax finally hit, he realized it was coming a split second before it happened. Her inner walls clenched convulsively around him and a rush of warmth spread over his cock as she threw her head back.

With that, he let go. Unable to restrain himself anymore, his hips pumped frantically as he thrust inside her. He felt almost possessed as he emptied himself inside her in hard, long thrusts until finally she collapsed on top of him.

Her curls spread over his chest as she laid her head on him. Stroking a hand down her spine, he rubbed her in a gentle, soothing rhythm until he realized she'd fallen asleep. The steady beat of her heart and soft breathing made him smile.

Wrapping his arms around her, he slowly turned their bodies and pulled out of her as he turned on his side. He kept her tucked close to his chest and shut his own eyes. He hadn't been sleeping much the past week and he remembered how tired she'd looked earlier back at her house. Right now he felt so utterly content and peaceful and he knew it had everything to do with the woman in his arms.

Under normal circumstances he'd be out there hunting down those vampires but there was no way he was leaving this woman to anyone else's care. Since he knew his pack mates were patrolling and he trusted his own senses to detect an intruder, he let sleep overtake him, too. Tomorrow he could worry about introducing her to pack life in general. Not to mention he planned to start his goal of convincing her they were mates. Considering she had almost zero background about their world he had a feeling he had his work cut out for him. Luckily, he was more than up to the task. Anything for Estrella.

Chapter 4

Estrella stirred as she felt warmth embracing her entire body. She moved and realized there was a big, callused hand draped across her stomach. The hold was light, but she knew Rainer wasn't asleep. She could feel his heartbeat where his chest pressed against her back and his breathing wasn't steady enough for slumber.

"You're finally awake," he murmured, his mouth right next to her ear. He gently nipped her earlobe, pulling it between his teeth. Shivers of pleasure danced across her skin.

He was definitely awake. His erection pressed insistently against her back, making her smile. Sunlight streamed in from the mouth of the cave, telling her it was still early morning. Stretching, she rubbed her butt against his hard cock. She giggled when he groaned in frustration.

Rainer rolled her so that she was on her back and he was propped up on one elbow looking down at her. He had what looked like a day's worth of beard growth though he'd been fairly clean-shaven the night before. She bet he had to shave twice a day. Reaching up, she cupped his cheek and smiled. "You get to tell me something about yourself now. I should be mean and wait until you're about to come and then force you, but I'm nicer than that."

He grinned again and that boyish charm was back. Her heart rate tripled when he smiled like that. "Well, I hate avocados, too. I have three older brothers, I'm part of Knox's pack—which you already know—and my parents died about three hundred years ago." He swallowed hard, his grin dying. "They were murdered."

"I'm sorry. I…understand what that's like." She hated that she did. "Do you mind if I ask what happened?" It was too personal and she knew she should be pulling back from him out of self-preservation—what chance did a wolf and jaguar have at a relationship?—but she wanted to know everything about Rainer.

His jaw ticked once but his pale gaze never strayed from hers. "They were killed by vampires because someone betrayed them."

The way he said "someone" was odd, but she didn't comment. His hand, which still rested on her belly, flexed once. "Tell me what happened to yours."

She should have expected it since she'd asked him. The only person she'd ever told about that night was Sabrina. "I was five so it's all a little fuzzy, but men broke into our house really early one morning." Estrella shut her eyes, trying to banish the images but that only made it worse. "They must have been shifters, or maybe vampires—I didn't know they even existed until now but I guess it's possible—because they were so strong." Her voice cracked on the last word as flashes of the blood soaked bedroom swam in her mind.

"Look at me," Rainer said softly. When she opened her eyes, his expression was soft. "You don't have to tell me the rest of it."

She wanted to, though she wasn't quite sure why. She needed someone else to know about that night. That she wasn't crazy, despite what the cops had said. "My mom got me to safety. She broke a window and basically threw me outside. Told me to run. Screamed it at me actually." Saying the words out loud felt so freeing. She'd never been able to tell her friend the rest of this story but she was going to tell Rainer. "My mom told me to run and hide in the human world. I knew I was different, I could turn into an animal after all, but I didn't really comprehend what she meant. I knew what she meant by run, though. So I did. I shifted forms and then ran until...I heard my father scream. The sound was horrific so I turned back. When I got back to my house I looked in the living room window and saw my father dead on the floor." He'd been decapitated, but Estrella couldn't force herself to say the words. "I watched as one of them killed my mom with a long sword. Later the cops said only my father was dead and my mom was missing, but I know what I saw." The damn memories were burned into her brain. She didn't care what anyone said. Her mother hadn't just disappeared. Maybe her killers had taken her body but she'd seen what they'd done to her.

She'd run until she'd felt as if her legs would fall off. Then she'd shifted back to her human form once she'd reached the heart of Miami. A police officer had found her wandering the streets naked and helped her.

Rainer tunneled his hands through her hair and pulled her so that her face was against his chest. He murmured soothing sounds as he stroked her back and told her not to cry. That's when she realized she was. The last time she'd cried had been the night her parents died.

She swiped away the wetness on her cheeks, hating the way her chest ached and throat burned as she held back even more tears. What she'd just told him was definitely bad first-date etiquette. She'd pretty much broken every rule, but it was hard to care. Even if she'd admitted way too much about herself, she was glad he knew this about her. Finally, someone knew the truth. And not just someone, but Rainer. She could be herself in the bedroom with him so she might as well just put it all out there right now. He'd protected her last night and now he was comforting her.

"I'll fucking kill them," he murmured so low she almost didn't hear him.

Startled, she pulled her head back to look at him. "What?"

"Whoever killed your parents, I'll—"

She pressed a finger to his lips and shook her head. She'd buried her ghosts a long time ago and the thought of him putting himself in danger made her ache inside. "Rainer, no. I don't know who they were. The cops had no leads and it happened over two decades ago. Just…no."

He didn't respond for a long moment. Instead he leaned forward and tentatively touched his lips to hers. His kisses were soft, exploratory and incredibly sweet.

She felt more raw and vulnerable than she ever had before and he was being perfect. As his tongue stroked against hers that same need she'd experienced last night was back but with more urgency. She felt so drawn to him on a primal level it scared her a little. Okay, a lot.

He rolled over so that his body covered hers. She loved the feel of all that muscle and strength over her. Spreading her hands along both his shoulders and arms, she dug her fingers into his biceps as he pushed up, slightly separating their bodies.

Instinctively, she arched her back, wanting to feel his chest brushing against her nipples. But he was just moving so she could fully wrap her legs around him. They hadn't bothered getting dressed during the last few hours so there were no barriers between them.

As she spread her legs to accommodate him, he settled his cock right against her opening. But he didn't enter her like she expected and needed.

Estrella tightened her legs around him, digging her heels into his butt as she tried to urge him forward, but he remained immobile, poised above her. She was wet and aching for him and he was clearly trying to drive her insane.

"There's something you should know, Estrella." She loved it when he said her name all deep and sexy like that. Before she could savor it, he continued. "I'm territorial, possessive and where you're concerned I know I'll be jealous. When I said I didn't take lovers easily I meant it. I haven't been with anyone in decades."

Oh. She supposed for someone over four centuries old that probably wasn't that long, but he was still a male. It was a freaking long time. Her eyes widened slightly in surprise. "Is talking right before sex or right before I orgasm going to be a thing with you?" she asked, her voice teasing.

Chuckling, he pushed into her in a long, hard thrust that sent a jolt of awareness through her entire body.

"I rarely talk during sex, but you seem to bring it out in me," he murmured as he began moving inside her in slow strokes.

His thickness filled her completely and she lost the ability to speak. She definitely didn't need words during sex. Her body could talk for her. Right now it was screaming for release.

Instead of watching each other like they'd done last night, he cupped the back of her head and drew her up until their mouths meshed. Their tongues danced an erotic rhythm as he pumped into her.

She wrapped her arms around him, digging her fingers into his back way harder than she'd have done had he been human. It was almost as if she needed to mark him, to claim him somehow. Part of her even wanted to bite him a little, but she held back. She might have let go last night, but they were still learning about each other and she didn't want to freak him out.

When he reached between their bodies and began rubbing her clit, her inner walls clenched out of control. He knew how to exert the exact amount of pressure on her sensitive bundle of nerves to drive her absolutely insane with pleasure.

Drawing back, she began nibbling kisses along his jaw as he continued thrusting inside her in even strokes. Unable to help herself, she nipped his earlobe between her teeth. When he sucked in a breath and his strokes became jerkier, the most feminine part of her smiled.

What she wouldn't give to make this man lose absolute control. Arching up, she rubbed her breasts against his chest, savoring the feel of her nipples brushing against the hard planes of his body.

"Mine," he growled next to her ear as one of his hands cupped her breast in a dominating grip. He squeezed a little roughly before tweaking her nipple between his thumb and forefinger.

The abrupt action made her gasp then moan. As he pinched the hard nub, it bordered on pain but quickly morphed into pure pleasure. Her inner walls tightened even more around his cock.

"Mine," he said again, this time even more demanding.

Oh yeah, she could definitely get behind that. Her body could be his if he kept playing it so expertly. It was as if all her nerves were on edge, tingling and ready for release. She was so close, it practically hurt. The ache inside her grew until he cupped her other breast. Part of her wondered if there was more to his 'mine' declaration, but she refused to allow her thoughts to go there. Not now. She just wanted to enjoy herself and not get tangled up in her own thoughts.

As he rolled both her nipples in tune with his thrusting, she finally let go. Her climax slammed into her like a freight train, running her right over so that she could barely catch her breath.

She grabbed his head, tugging his mouth to hers as her orgasm exploded, shattering through all her nerve endings. Hungrily and almost out of control, she kissed him, needing that extra connection as she found her release.

His own release wasn't far behind. Tearing away from her mouth, he let out a shout as he came inside her. Unlike their first time, his shout was so primitive it rocked her to her core. The sound echoed off the cave, reverberating and wrapping around them until she was aware of nothing else but him.

She wrapped her legs tightly around him, staying locked in place even after he'd settled on top of her and their breathing had evened out.

Eventually he lifted his head and pinned her with a stare so molten hot she was surprised she didn't catch on fire. It was like she was caught up in a storm and couldn't look away. Hell, she didn't want to. She'd gladly be caught by this sexy man.

"You're mine, Estrella."

Her insides practically quivered. She wanted to demand he say it again, even if the statement itself scared her. Those three words sounded a lot more intense than she figured he meant and she didn't want to read into anything. She'd been alone for so long, reaching out only to a few humans. The thought of letting someone into her heart and then having it shattered when things didn't work out—yeah, she couldn't go there right now.

She cupped his cheek, gently rubbing her thumb against his smattering of facial hair. "Rainer—"

She was cut off by an unfamiliar male voice. "Holy shit, Rainer. The entire forest can probably hear you."

Anxiety threatened to take over as it registered that they weren't alone anymore and she was very naked. Normally she could scent intruders, but she'd been so wrapped up in Rainer she hadn't noticed. She guessed it was the same for him because he seemed surprised. Rainer didn't seem to care about nudity but she'd grown up in the human world and it mattered to her. She turned her head toward the opening of the cave's mouth at the same time Rainer did to see the same male from the night before entering. It was one of his brothers.

Embarrassed, she tried to cover up but Rainer beat her to it. "What the hell!" he shouted, moving off her and blocking her so that his entire body shielded hers.

She didn't like to cower behind anyone but she huddled against Rainer, not wanting anyone, especially Rainer's brother, to see her. She was already embarrassed enough by what he'd just said about the forest hearing them. It wasn't something she'd even thought about but if his pack mates had heard them...her face flamed and she buried it against Rainer's muscular back.

"What's your problem?" his brother asked, his voice surly.

"I don't know. Maybe you barging in here while my female is naked," Rainer snapped, sounding furious. The scent that permeated off him was so sharp she could practically taste his anger.

Wait a minute. *His female?* She wondered if that was just a shifter term for lovers or if he meant something more by it.

There was a long pause and she realized they were talking telepathically. Popping her head up, she glared at his brother and pinched Rainer's side. "It's rude to do that when there are other people in the room." Or cave.

Rainer looked over his shoulder at her and actually looked sheepish. "Sorry. My brother was telling me your house is clear. We've got two of my pack mates standing guard, but there are no vampires anywhere near there."

"It's daytime anyway, right? I thought they couldn't walk around in the day." Or at least he'd insinuated it when he'd said they could return to her house the next morning.

"Day walkers are rare, though my Alpha is mated to one."

Her eyes widened. "Your Alpha is mated to a vampire?"

She'd assumed that would be impossible. But here she was sleeping with a wolf, so what did she know.

Rainer nodded and opened his mouth to say something, but the man at the cave opening cut him off. "So exactly where are you from? And why are you living so close to our pack land without having introduced yourself? There's a reason those vamps were after you and I want to know why." His brother's voice was almost hostile, his questions close to shouting.

Estrella felt her throat close up at the accusatory way he spoke to her. And the dark look in his eyes made her extremely uncomfortable.

"Damn it, Conrad. Enough with the third degree," Rainer snapped, his own anger almost palpable.

"I have a right to know. The entire pack does. Alaric and Knox are going to be pissed," he snarled.

Feeling nauseous, Estrella laid back down and used Rainer's body as cover while she snagged the clothes they'd discarded the night before. Somehow she managed to shimmy into them while Rainer and his brother continued to argue. She'd heard enough. Once she was dressed, she sat up and placed her hand on Rainer's side. When he saw her dressed he reached for his own clothes.

"Listen, I appreciate your help last night," she said to Conrad—who rudely hadn't bothered to introduce himself before tossing questions at her, "but I'm going to get off your land right now. I'll talk to your Alpha or whatever it is I need to do but it's early and I don't need some rude jerk shouting at me."

Rainer's brother rubbed a hand over his face and when his gaze connected with hers again, he looked slightly apologetic. "I'm sorry. With the vampire-shifter treaty taking place right now we can't afford any incidents."

She shrugged, unsure how to respond. Suddenly she felt very uncomfortable now that it was daylight. She'd just spent a night in a cave with a wolf shifter she was only just getting to know and he was involved with this big pack and a world she knew nothing about. Estrella wrapped her arms around herself, wishing she was back in her home. Rainer's arm landed around her shoulders as he pulled her close. His embrace was comforting, but she knew she couldn't get used to it.

Looking down at her, his expression was gentle, but also tense. "Before we go to your place, let's go back with my brother. You can meet some of my pack mates and my other brother who's still in town—he's much nicer than Conrad," he murmured jokingly.

Estrella shook her head and looked down, feeling totally out of place. "I just want to go home."

Rainer's grip on her tightened. "Don't pull away from me," he said quietly, almost desperately.

How did he read her so well? Instead of responding, she took a step out of his embrace. There was no way she was having this conversation with his brother and who only knew how many of his pack mates nearby. "Can we just go?"

Growling low in his throat, Rainer shot his brother a dirty look before nodding at her. "Yeah."

Relief swelled up inside her. Last night with Rainer had been amazing, but clearly she'd jumped into whatever this was too soon. She just wanted to get back to her quiet, uncomplicated life.

Chapter 5

Rainer wanted to pummel his brother for the rude way he'd behaved to Estrella. They'd driven back to her place instead of shifting and running and she'd been quiet the entire time. Not that he could blame her. In addition to Conrad, another pack mate had come with them, which had probably only compounded her nervousness. Rainer wasn't positive, but considering his history with females—or one treacherous female in particular—he knew his brother was just concerned about him.

But he didn't need a babysitter and he sure as hell didn't need someone making his female so uncomfortable. It was like she'd completely withdrawn into herself and he hated it.

Staring out the window, her dark hair covered most of her face so he couldn't even look at her profile. He ached to reach out and run his fingers through her hair, to pull her close. But he figured she wouldn't welcome his touch and he didn't know her well enough to know the right thing to do.

As they pulled down her driveway, her hand was already

on the door handle. The second his brother parked, she was out of the car and striding toward the side of her house, clearly heading to the back where the door should still be unlocked. Cursing under his breath he hurried after her.

"Estrella." She stopped only when she reached the back door. She opened it, but didn't step inside.

"What?" Nervousness rolled off her in potent waves. She placed a hand on the frame, almost like she was steadying herself. Either that or trying to block him from entering.

"Are you going to talk to me?"

"I just…" Her voice cracked and it ripped open his heart. When her eyes welled up with tears, it was like a double whammy. She might as well have punched him in the gut.

Gathering her into his arms, he nudged the door farther open with his foot and guided them inside. He then picked her up and didn't stop until they were in her kitchen. So far it didn't look like there had been any damage to her home. The two pack mates he'd seen near the edge of her property line watching it had already done a sweep so he knew it was clear of danger. The vamps had probably been too busy chasing after them then getting back to safety to stick around and tear apart her home.

Though he didn't want to let her go, he set her down on one of the chairs at what looked like a custom-made oak kitchen table. He took a step back then nodded at the coffeemaker sitting next to her refrigerator. "Coffee?"

She nodded gratefully so after searching the cabinet above the pot, he started making it and let her get herself together. "I don't know why I was crying," she said softly.

"Vampires that you didn't even know existed chased you down, you were forced to go on the run with a strange shifter, and last night between us was intense and unexpected. At least it was for me. I've never experienced *that* with a female before. Then you got yelled at by my own freaking brother." He couldn't even put into words what "that" was, but he hoped she felt the same.

She chuckled softly and when he looked over from where he stood at the counter, he relaxed. Her arms were wrapped defensively around herself like before yet she seemed more at ease. "I guess you're right. Last night was pretty insane. And what we shared...yeah, intense seems like the right word." Her cheeks flushed crimson and he was relieved she was clearly still affected by him.

After pulling two mugs down from one of the cabinets, he leaned against the counter and watched her carefully. The percolating coffeemaker was the only sound in the otherwise quiet kitchen. When it became obvious she didn't plan to continue, he said, "One of those vampires called you princess last night."

Her eyebrows furrowed as she nodded. "I know. It was weird, right? At first I thought maybe it was an insult but that doesn't really make sense, does it? And why didn't they want me hurt?"

He'd wondered the same thing. The confusion rolling off her at the moment was so real, he had no doubt of her sincerity. Rainer had already told his brothers all of this and he knew Alaric had definitely relayed the message to their Alpha, but Knox and Alaric had more important things to worry about at the moment. And nothing was more important to Rainer than Estrella. Whatever was going on with the vampires, he'd be taking care of her.

Covering the distance between them, he sat tentatively

next to her. Her legs were crossed and that shirt his brother had brought for her showed way too much skin. Not that he was complaining, but it was hard to concentrate on talking when all he wanted to do was strip her again and bury himself inside her. "Why did you pull away from me in the cave?"

She shrugged, the action jerky. "I was overwhelmed with everything and your..." She trailed off.

"And my brother didn't help things any."

Estrella shook her head. "It's obvious he's concerned about you. I shouldn't have called him a jerk."

Rainer's jaw clenched once. "You were right, he was being a jerk. But he's not normally." In fact, Conrad was usually the charming one of them. "When I told you my parents were murdered because someone betrayed them— it was my fault."

Estrella's dark eyes widened. "What?"

He'd held back last night but if he wanted to take this relationship with her in the right direction, he had to be honest. No matter how much it pained him. Opening up to people who weren't his brothers was a foreign experience. "It was about three hundred years ago." But even thinking about it still killed him inside. "I was involved with a wolf shifter from a neighboring pack. Things were different back then between supernatural beings. We fought for land, even the right to choose a mate. Life was definitely less civilized."

Surprise rolled off her and he knew he'd be explaining a lot about their different species in the future. Not that he minded. She deserved to know everything about supernatural history and he wanted to be the one to teach her. "This female," he spat the word, unable to even say her name, "that I thought I loved—" He froze when he realized Estrella was growling.

She stopped abruptly as if she'd surprised herself. Blinking, she blushed again. "Sorry. Please continue."

He held back a smile. Right now nothing should be easing his internal pain, but her reaction touched something inside him he was glad hadn't died. "Long story short, a female shifter led my parents into a vampire trap. My brothers and I were also supposed to be there, but it didn't work out that way." And for decades after he'd wished he'd died with his parents. The shame and guilt of knowing he'd been responsible for their deaths had been almost too much to bear. "Once we realized what had happened, my brothers and I and a few other pack members killed them all. Her pack, the vampires. Everyone who didn't flee."

She sucked in a quick breath and it hit him that if she'd grown up in the human world this would all be new to her, even if her parents had been killed.

Rainer hadn't killed his former lover. Conrad had unfortunately had to do that. She'd come at Rainer, ready to kill him and he'd been unable to strike back no matter how evil she'd shown herself to be. It was probably why Conrad was so leery of Estrella. "Our world is different than what you're used to."

She nodded slowly and he could practically see the wheels turning in her head. Finally she spoke. "Why did she betray you?"

"Land." It was a simple answer for an act that had nearly destroyed him.

Rage surged off Estrella, the bitter scent unmistakable. "Is she dead?"

Rainer nodded.

"Good." Her one word response surprised him.

Before he could say anything, he scented his brother's presence nearby at the same time Estrella did. She stiffened in her seat and glanced at the entryway of the kitchen. Moments later when Conrad stepped inside wearing cargo pants and a simple black T-shirt, Rainer tried to see him the way she did. His brother was just as big as Rainer and his expression was fierce and deadly. No wonder she'd been nervous back in the cave. Hell, it was a surprise she'd trusted Rainer as much as she had.

Conrad looked between the two of them, then focused on him. Rainer stood, partially blocking Estrella because he wanted her to know he'd protect her. Even from his own brother's hostility.

Conrad lifted an eyebrow at him, but didn't send a telepathic message. He just said, "We're leaving. Brought your truck to her driveway. Looks like someone went through the glove box, no doubt the vamps. You need to have her pack a bag and bring her back to the compound as soon as possible."

Rainer closed his eyes for a brief moment, resisting the urge to massage his temple. He'd wanted to ask Estrella first—or subtly insist. With his brother ordering her, he knew she was going to resist out of pure instinct. He knew because he'd do the same if some stranger tried to give him orders.

He felt Estrella move before he actually heard her jump up from her seat. "I'm not going anywhere. This is my home. And if I decide to leave, it won't be because you ordered me to," she snapped at Conrad.

This was just perfect. Rainer turned to face her, completely blocking Conrad from her view. *Leave now,* he mentally ordered his brother. Though he didn't hear him go, his brother's scent faded instantly and Rainer knew they were alone. When he reached out to cup her face he breathed a silent sigh of relief that she didn't pull away.

She actually leaned her cheek into his hand as she silently watched him. Good. It was obvious she needed his touch as much as he seemed to need hers. That extra contact went a long way in soothing his inner wolf and he could only hope he had the same effect on her. He'd always assumed his true mate would be a wolf, but he had no doubt that Estrella was it for him. They had a lot to learn about each other, but the heat and desire between them was undeniable and scorching. Not to mention his wolf had already accepted her jaguar. "I would appreciate it if you would pack a bag and come back to my place. At least for a week while we try to figure out who is after you and why." They might know it was vampires but they didn't know what coven they were from and they definitely didn't know what their ultimate purpose was.

She bit her bottom lip, her expression unsure. "A week?"

"Is the thought of spending a week with me really such a bad thing?" he asked jokingly, even if it sliced him that she was unsure when all he wanted to do was go on lockdown with her and only come out for meals.

"No, it's just that I have to work. I have a few commissions that I need to finish and—"

"Whatever you need for your work, we'll transport to the pack's compound. And if you need money I'll—"

Now she cut him off as she held up a hand. "Don't even go there."

Okay. He could respect that even if he did want to take care of her in every way. "We could stay here if you wanted, but it's not smart." There was no way he'd actually let her stay here. Not without an army surrounding them, but he was trying to be diplomatic.

"I know. I just don't like anyone ordering me around. Actually, I had just planned to stay with my friend, Sabrina. What does a compound mean? It sounds scary." A thread of fear twined off her.

He chuckled. "It's what we call the mansion my pack lives in. It's huge enough that we all have a lot of space. Everyone has their own rooms, which are basically apartments. We all take care of each other and Knox is a fair Alpha."

"But I'm a jaguar." Her lips pulled into a thin line.

"So?"

She swallowed audibly. "Other than you, the only wolves I've come in contact with before haven't been exactly... nice."

There was something about her tone that made his inner wolf go on red alert. "What does that mean?"

"I don't know all these rules and regulations you guys seem to have so if I tell you something you have to promise me it stays between us."

"You think I'd betray or hurt you?"

"No. I just don't know if I can be punished for what I did. What I *had* to do." Her body had gone completely stiff as she watched him warily.

"What happened?" His inner wolf was clawing at him as scenarios raced through his mind.

"In college I met a few wolf shifters. I'd guessed there had to be other shifters out in the world, but none lived in

Miami that I knew of. And I still haven't met any jaguar shifters." There was a note of sadness in her voice that he might have missed if he hadn't been listening so intently. "Anyway, they were all dominant and arrogant and one of them pushed me too far. He tried to rape me and told me it was *my* fault because I was stupid enough to be packless." She gave a derisive snort, but the pain etched on her face was deep.

Rainer's inner wolf flexed its claws, death and rage the only thing it saw for one brief moment. Rape? He wanted to respond, but his throat tightened almost painfully. No words would come out as he imagined her at the mercy of some asshole.

She continued. "That was my first lesson on what pack-less meant and why I've avoided shifters ever since. I... was forced to kill him." She stumbled over the words then stopped talking and just stared at Rainer, clearly waiting for his response.

It took a long moment for him to get his inner wolf under control. The thought of her being targeted because she didn't belong to a pack had his claws aching to unleash and lash out at anyone who'd ever tried to hurt her. He'd never been so grateful that someone—a stranger—was dead. Whoever that wolf was, he was damn lucky he wasn't alive.

"Rainer?" Estrella's soft voice brought him back to reality. Her eyes were wide as she stared at him.

His breathing was erratic and he had to force his inner wolf back down. Though he couldn't see himself, he figured his eyes had likely changed to a darker shade of green, revealing his wolf—which explained the way she was watching him.

"You were more than justified in killing him," he finally said. "Whoever he was, he was likely packless or a lone wolf by choice. Shifter violence against females is rare among all the different species. I'm sorry you ever had to deal with any of that. I wish we'd met years ago. Hell, I wish you'd had your parents or someone nonhuman to watch out for you growing up." Being a lone female shifter was hard and he hated that she'd been by herself for so long. No wonder she'd been so wary of him when they'd first met. And he hadn't helped things by being so arrogant.

A small smile touched her lips. "Everyone has crap to deal with and even though I miss my parents every day, I've had a good life. Trust me, it could have been a lot worse. I've seen what happened to some of the kids in the foster system and it's not pretty."

Wrapping his arms around her waist, he pulled her close, savoring the feel of her lush body pressed against his. She wasn't alone anymore and he desperately wanted to be the one to protect her. Even if things didn't work out between them—that thought killed him and he knew without a doubt it would be because she pushed him out of her life—he didn't want her alone anymore. He might be a wolf, but she was now under his pack's protection. There was no doubt his Alpha would welcome her. Right now, Rainer just needed to convince her to stay with him and not go to her friend. "Come with me?" he asked before dropping a light kiss on her forehead.

Estrella sighed and nuzzled her face against his chest. "You'll fight dirty if I say no, won't you?"

He smiled as he rested his chin on top of her head, inhaling her sweet scent. "I can think of plenty of dirty things I'd like to do right now."

She chuckled, the sound wrapping around him and squeezing tight. "Fine, I—"

They both froze as a high-pitched ringing cut through the air. Estrella glanced over her shoulder toward the direction of her living room. "That's Sabrina's ringtone."

Estrella's friend. "Grab it."

She hurried to the other room and even though he couldn't scent or hear anyone else in the house and his pack mates had already swept it earlier, he did his own sweep while she took her friend's phone call. Plus he wanted to give her privacy.

When he returned to the living room he found her sitting on the edge of one of her couches, a brittle smile on her unusually pale face. "Rainer, I'm going to stay with my friend instead. I appreciate the offer, but I'm just not ready to live with a bunch of strangers, even temporarily. There's no reason I can't help you find out what's going on from someplace else."

Rainer's blood chilled at whatever she wasn't saying. He could have easily listened to her conversation but he'd tuned her out, needing to give her the privacy she deserved. Now he wished he'd paid attention because whatever had happened in the last sixty seconds was very bad. He could see it in her body language and scent the fear pulsing off her in angry waves. And he'd be damned if he let her push him out now. Whatever was going on, he was sticking by her side.

Chapter 6

Estrella watched Rainer as she tried to keep her breathing steady. His expression was dark, angry and a little confused. Unfortunately she felt as if her insides might unravel at any moment. Sabrina hadn't been on the phone, but that same male from the other night had. The one Estrella had clawed and the same one she'd heard shout in the woods not to hurt her. Terror latched its claws deep into her chest as she replayed the man's words in her head. *Meet me alone at dusk or your friend dies.*

"What the hell are you talking about?" Rainer snarled, his expression darkening. "You were just about to come with me."

She stood, phone still clutched in her hand as she tried to drag in a breath, desperately needing to pump some oxygen into her lungs. Estrella couldn't let Sabrina die and these creatures wanted her, not her friend. "I have the right to change my mind. Unless you plan on *forcing* me to go with you?" It took every ounce of her willpower to keep her tone sharp.

He jerked back, almost as if she'd slapped him and guilt blew up inside her. She ruthlessly shoved it away. No time for stupid emotions right now.

She hated hurting Rainer, but she had to save Sabrina. "I'll give you my cell number so you can contact me, but I'm going to leave now. I just need to pack a small bag." Avoiding his gaze, she tried to skirt past him, but he grasped her upper arm.

Not hard enough to bruise, but he wasn't letting her go anywhere. "Who was on the phone?" There was a dark edge to his voice and his pale eyes had darkened to a stormy green that sent a chill down her spine.

"I told you—"

"Don't lie to me. Who. Was. It." His fingers slightly flexed and for a moment she could see his wolf lurking beneath the surface.

Estrella wanted to kick him out of her home, but she knew he wouldn't go easily. And if she left on her own, deep down she knew this man would follow her. Not to mention, no matter how strong she was physically, she knew so little about vampires and their weaknesses. She could use the backup and Rainer had already proved how strong he was. Taking care of things on her own was instinctual and was why she'd lied, but damn...she could use the help. "I don't know his name, but he has my friend." Her voice cracked on the last word.

Rainer's expression softened slightly, but not much. "What did he say?"

"Just that he has my friend and I have to meet him at the

art studio right after sunset or they'll kill her. I don't know what they want—other than me. They want to trade her freedom for me and I have to go. Sabrina has been my best friend since I was eighteen and I love her more than..." Her voice broke again and hot tears welled up. What the hell? She never cried but in the last twenty-four hours she was like a leaky faucet.

Rainer let out a string of creative curses and he still hadn't let her arm go. "You're not going anywhere alone."

"She's my—"

"I didn't say we weren't going to get her back. I just said you're not going alone. How could you..." He trailed off and turned away from her. Rubbing a hand over his face, he told her to hold on and then was silent for a long minute.

She figured he was talking to one of his brothers. Or maybe all of them. The way he'd said "we" made a foreign sensation ignite inside her. She'd never had many people to depend on before and the thought that she did now was almost too much to fathom.

When Rainer turned back to her, his expression was blank. "Pack a bag, we're headed to the compound. When it's near dusk, my brothers and a few pack mates will head to the studio. We'll get your friend back."

She frowned. So "we" didn't mean him and her. "I'm going with you."

He let out a harsh laugh. "The hell you are."

"Unless you plan to kidnap or restrain me, I'm going. That guy told me to come *alone*. If I don't do what he says, I have no doubt they'll kill her. I'm not some weak female you need to protect," she growled low in her throat. Estrella healed fast—faster than him, as she'd seen last night—

and she'd killed before. She could do it again. Anything for Sabrina.

Rainer growled back at her, his frustration clear in every line of his strong body. Finally he nodded. "Fine. I'll wait outside for you." He turned on his heel and stalked from the room, the tension practically rolling off him in visible waves.

Estrella hurried to her room and packed a small bag. There were hours to kill before the meet and she wanted her own stuff at Rainer's. As soon as the sun set, she was getting her friend back. No matter what Rainer thought, she was going and there was no way she was letting those vamps see that he was with her.

She was starting to care for Rainer in a way she hadn't thought would be possible, but she couldn't let him have his way in this. She had to be there to help her friend. If those vampires didn't see her at the studio, for all she knew they'd kill Sabrina. Estrella wasn't going to let that happen.

Hours later, Estrella tapped her finger against her knee compulsively—as if she could somehow make time go by faster—and stared out the window of Rainer's SUV where they sat across the street from the art studio. Five of Rainer's pack mates, including his brother Conrad who had been giving her the cold shoulder all day, had gone into the art studio about an hour ago. They were supposedly going to hide inside and had wanted to get set up before the meeting. Since she hadn't heard an alarm or seen any cops drive by, it was safe to assume that they hadn't tripped any alarms. She was grateful for the backup because in reality, there was no way she could take on a bunch of vampires by herself. She knew that. Still, a huge part of her worried their presence might get Sabrina killed.

After the big show last night, Estrella knew the owner hadn't planned to open up his place for the next three days so as things went, it was a decent place to stage a meeting with no outsiders. She wondered how the vampires had known it would be unoccupied. Maybe Sabrina had told them.

God, Sabrina. Estrella couldn't stop the worry spinning out of control inside her as she thought about her friend. It was like a tornado assaulting her insides.

Rainer's hand on her knee stilled her movements, causing her to look at him.

"We're going to get her back." He watched her with wary green eyes.

All day he'd been distant, even though he'd been physically present. He'd taken her to his pack's compound and he hadn't been kidding about the place being a mansion. She'd been introduced to a lot of wolf shifters and even a vampire who was mated to one of the warriors. Everyone had been friendly enough. She'd seen a lot of surprise and some jealousy on some of the females' faces, though she knew that had everything to do with Rainer being suddenly unavailable and nothing to do with actual jealousy of her. She couldn't blame them. Rainer was definitely a catch, even if he was acting distant from her right now. She didn't think he was angry, but he was holding back.

Nodding, she looked away from him, hating that there was a wall between them now. It was her own fault, but she didn't know how to tear it down. She didn't know enough about him and pushing him away to handle things on her own had been her instinctive response after receiving that phone call. If she had to go back, she'd do the same thing again.

"Damn it," Rainer cursed.

She swiveled back to him again. Before she could ask him what was wrong, other than the obvious, his mouth was on hers, claiming and taking. His tongue invaded her mouth with no hesitancy, as if he had every right to kiss her. He stroked against her in a frantic dance while one of his hands cupped her cheek, holding her possessively.

When she'd allowed him into her bed, she'd let him into her life. All day, even with the walls between them, he'd been like her shadow, silently making a claim on her for everyone to see. His hand had never left the small of her back when they'd been outside his room.

Eventually he pulled back and she was pleased to see he was breathing just as hard as she was. "Whatever happens after tonight, you're still mine," he growled, a possessive note in his voice.

She blinked, surprised by his statement. He'd been the one to pull away from her, even if she had helped mix the mortar to build the brick wall between them. "I know." She wasn't walking away from him, even if her original instincts had told her to run far and fast. She *had* to see where this thing between them went even if her heart was shredded in the end.

Now it was his turn to look surprised. Those gorgeous eyes of his widened for a moment before a harsh smile settled on his face. "Good." He looked like he wanted to say more, but the sound of her phone buzzing in her pocket made them both freeze.

She'd turned it to vibrate earlier and now felt frantic as she struggled to fish it out of her jacket pocket. When she saw Sabrina's number again, her blood chilled. "Hello?"

"Hello again—"

"I want to talk to Sabrina, now! How do I know you haven't hurt her?" This wasn't part of their plan, but Estrella didn't care. She wanted to hear her friend's voice.

"Your friend is fine and we would never hurt her without a reason, so don't give us one." His voice was razor sharp.

Steeling herself, she said, "I talk to her now or I'm not meeting you."

He sighed and as she heard a rustling in the background, she watched as an SUV with unusually dark tinted windows pulled into the parking lot of the art studio across the street. The vehicle drove through it, then around the corner toward the back of the building. Next to her, Rainer straightened and she was under the impression he was having a telepathic conversation with Conrad.

"Estrella?" Sabrina's voice was slurred.

Estrella's heart soared. "Sabrina, are you okay?"

"Fine...jush really tired. Dunno whash going on." Oh yeah, she had to be drugged.

Before Estrella could respond, the same male came back on the line. "See? Your friend is fine. I gave her a little sedative to keep her compliant."

It was more than a "little" for her friend to be so out of it, but she was alive and seemed relatively unharmed. Though Estrella wouldn't know for sure until she saw her. "Okay. So what do you want?"

"You." A simple, one-word answer.

"Why?"

He paused long enough that even more panic took root inside her, clawing its way through her like out of control vines. "You really don't know?"

"I wouldn't be asking now, would I?" she snapped, angry and confused.

"Meet me in the studio we discussed. The back door will be open." He disconnected before she could respond.

"They're already inside," Rainer murmured, drawing her attention to him.

"What did your brother say? Has he seen Sabrina?"

Rainer nodded, a frown marring his face. "She's unhurt, though clearly drugged. From the way they're talking, the vamps truly don't plan to hurt her. They plan to free her."

"Why is that a bad thing?" His expression confused her.

"It's not. We just don't know what their end game is and their behavior isn't what I'd originally expected. They didn't want to hurt you the other night, though they didn't care about my well-being," he muttered, his own confusion seeming to grow.

"How many are there?"

"Five."

"And there are seven of us so we can take them. I can't believe the vampires haven't seen your pack mates yet." Estrella had hated this part of their plan, but Rainer had been unwilling to allow her to walk in there alone and now she was actually grateful to have backup so close.

"They're in the rafters and have masked their scents—though that will only last so long."

She pushed out a sigh of relief as she wrapped her fingers around the door handle. "I'm ready then." She planned to use the shadows to get across the street unseen.

Rainer brushed his knuckles down her cheek, hating to let her get out of this vehicle. But the most primal part of him knew that if he tried to stop her, she'd never forgive him. While he told himself he could live with her hate and rejection, he couldn't. So now he had to shove his protective, possessive wolf side down and let his mate walk into a room of vampires.

The only real reason he was doing it was because his pack mates were already there as backup and he'd seen how fast she healed. She was only twenty-six compared to his four hundred-and-fifty, yet she'd healed with the speed of his thousand-year-old Alpha. Rainer still didn't know what to think of that, but it soothed his inner animal that she could take care of herself.

Cupping his cheeks, Estrella leaned closer, brushing her lips against his softly before pulling back. She tasted as sweet as the subtle jasmine scent of hers. "Thank you for helping me and my friend." Then she was gone. Like a shadow, she slid from the vehicle and disappeared into the darkness.

And he wasn't far behind. It didn't matter that she had protection inside, Rainer planned to be a scant step behind her, guarding her with his life if necessary.

The two-lane street wasn't well lit and even though it was a nice part of town, this strip of shops closed down early, which meant there were no random humans strolling down the street. There weren't any restaurants nearby and most of the shops were wholesale places that did a lot of business over the internet. It was probably one of the reasons the vamps had chosen it.

Using his supernatural speed he raced down the street,

heading east before crossing over to the other side. Even though Estrella was momentarily out of his line of sight, he knew where she'd be entering the building and he planned to meet her there. Not to mention they had other scouts out on the street watching her that he hadn't even told her about. He'd brought the full force of his pack here for her.

Ducking behind a building that sold wood flooring and carpet, he raced behind the few buildings until he reached the art studio. The black SUV with tinted windows was the only vehicle in the paved parking lot. It was too dark for him to see inside and there were too many heartbeats in the near vicinity for him to distinguish who was where.

As he decided on his next move, Estrella appeared from around the corner of the art building and strode toward the back door cautiously. As she moved, one of the side doors to the SUV opened and Rainer didn't think. He just jumped into action.

Using his stealth and natural animal-hunting abilities, he hurtled himself at the tall male in a leather jacket and jeans who had stepped out and tackled him so that they fell back into the vehicle. Rainer quickly assessed that no one else was inside as he grabbed the vampire by the back of the neck then slammed his face into the window. It shattered under the impact. As they struggled, two of his pack mates who'd been lookouts appeared from almost out of thin air.

Releasing the guy, he shoved him at his friends. "Don't kill him...*yet*," he murmured, as his pack mates restrained the vamp who was still recovering from the bash to the head.

The vamp might be supernatural but Rainer guessed he was young considering how easy he'd subdued him.

He had complete faith in his pack mates' abilities so he

didn't glance over his shoulder as he hurried toward the back door where Estrella stood. She'd seen him take down the vampire and now watched him in confusion.

He couldn't do it. Just couldn't let her walk in there and offer herself up like bait. *Take out the vamps, but try not to kill them. Just make sure Estrella's friend isn't hurt,* Rainer ordered Conrad telepathically and prayed the woman came out of this unscathed. If she didn't, Estrella would never forgive him.

As Estrella's eyes locked with his, it was like she could see what he'd just done. Her eyes widened in horror as she jerked the door open and raced inside.

Chapter 7

Estrella's heart pounded wildly against her chest as her inner jaguar took over out of sheer panic. The guilt she'd seen in Rainer's eyes had slammed into her chest with the intensity of a semitruck. In that instant she'd known what he'd done and panic had seared her with the knowledge that Sabrina might be hurt or worse.

Letting her beast take over, Estrella ignored the shredding of her clothes and shoes as she transformed. Her bones quickly realigned and fur now replaced skin as she sprinted down a short hallway. The sound of angry shouts and grunts had her terror growing.

She followed Sabrina's scent to the door that opened up into a giant storage area that took up almost the entire back half of the building. She used her weight and strength and launched herself at it. Her paws hit the door and a loud crack split through the air as it broke underneath her.

She tumbled into the storage area to find Rainer's pack mates still in their human forms fighting with the vampires.

They were all spaced out in pairs fighting in the middle of the room. The overhead track lighting was dim, creating an eerie atmosphere draped in shadows. Blades and claws slashed at each other as blood and angry cries filled the air. A few of them looked at her and she knew the rest of them were acutely aware of her presence, but none of them could tear themselves away from fighting without getting killed.

Sabrina sat huddled in a corner, her eyes glassy with fear and probably a whole lot of shock. When she spotted Estrella, she let out a strangled sound. Estrella didn't blame her. A giant freaking jaguar in an art studio would scare the crap out of her, too.

But her friend was alive. That was what mattered.

Quickly assessing the situation, she snarled and crouched low. All the males seemed evenly matched and the vampire she'd attacked the other night was fighting with Conrad. Too bad that vamp was hers. He'd taken her friend and he'd pay.

Ready to strike, she searched for an opening when a roar that made her entire body quiver filled the air. She'd known Rainer was seconds behind her but when she turned to see him in his giant wolf form hurtling through the door, she froze and stared at his magnificence. His black coat gleamed beautifully and his pale green eyes glowed. He growled at her, and even though she knew it was borne out of fear, the sound was angry and terrifying .

"No!" The vampire shouted, momentarily drawing her attention away from Rainer. The vamp used the opportunity to punch Conrad in the face so hard he flew back into a case of storage tubes with a loud crash. Knife raised, he raced at Rainer.

Estrella couldn't attack the vamp in time, but she could

do the next best thing. The thought had barely processed in her brain as she threw herself at Rainer's body. She might be smaller as a human but in her jaguar form she was lethal and strong. Shouldering him, she shoved him to the ground, wrapping her forearms and paws around him. She braced for the impact of the blade slicing into her skin.

At the sound of the blade slamming into the floor next to her, she rolled and realized the vamp had intentionally shoved the blade there. He truly hadn't wanted to hurt her so she used that knowledge to her advantage as she tried to keep Rainer's body beneath her, to protect him.

But he was having none of that. Rolling them, he quickly pinned her beneath him and snapped and snarled at the vamp with the discarded knife.

The room around them went eerily quiet as the vamp held up his hands. "Don't hurt the princess, please." A quiet, desperate plea.

Rainer's head tilted slightly to the side and if he'd been in human form, she'd have said he looked confused. Well, she felt the same. What was up with this guy calling her princess?

Hating that she couldn't talk, she shifted back to her human form and tried to ignore the fact that she was naked in a room full of men and her shocked best friend who Estrella was purposely ignoring. She couldn't deal with seeing Sabrina's fear right now even if she could scent the sharp, almost acidic aroma.

Rainer still didn't move or make an attempt to shift back to his human form. He just stayed hovering over her protectively, ready to strike anyone who came too close.

"Why are you calling me princess and why are you acting all concerned?"

The vampire who was clearly the spokesperson, went down on one knee and gave her a slight bow. *What the hell?* "I tracked this beast the other night following you. My own people have been after you, trying to bring you home, but when we thought the wolves wished to harm you—"

Anger slammed into her. "Hold the freak up! First, these wolves have done nothing but protect me. Second, I'm not a princess *or* a vampire. Hello? Did you not just see me turn into a jaguar?"

"You truly don't know your heritage? I thought you were being evasive because the wolves were listening or coercing you. We needed to know before we took more drastic actions against them." He shot a glare at Conrad who was a few feet away, carefully watching him.

She blinked and shook her head as she tried to wrap her mind around what he was saying. Yeah, she could feel a serious migraine coming on. She was going to go back to that heritage bit, but first, "Why were you all 'you're coming with me *bonita*' all scary like if you're so freaking concerned about me?"

He blinked at her, utter confusion in his expression. "I told you I didn't wish to hurt you. We thought the wolf was following you, but couldn't be sure. Then you attacked *me* that night. I only defended myself, but made no killing blows. And you are *muy bonita*. Pretty, beautiful—it's not an insult."

Rainer growled but the vampire and Estrella ignored him. He definitely didn't like the vamp calling her pretty but that was the least of her worries right now.

The vamp continued. "I thought you would understand Spanish. Your mother spoke five languages, you grew up in Miami, and you are Hispanic."

Estrella's entire body went cold as she focused on one thing. This guy had known her mother? Had he been one of the men who killed her?

Rainer, seeming to understand the changes going on with her let out a soft growl then shifted back to his human form. His shift was brutal and he let out a groan as his bones shifted back into place. Still crouching over her, he gave his brother a sharp look. "Give her your shirt," he snapped.

Conrad quickly stripped and tossed it to them. It was ripped down the side, but the black T-shirt would be better than her naked state. Estrella still had her arms crossed over her breasts as she glanced around the room. Luckily no one was watching her. The other pairs of vamps and shifters were definitely aware of what was going on, but they were all in staring contests with one another, ready to attack at any second. The only person staring at her in not exactly horror, but definite confusion, was Sabrina.

Her friend was in a slight state of shock. Her dark eyes were wide and her arms were wrapped around knees that she'd pulled up to her chest. As Rainer slipped the shirt over Estrella's head, she slid her arms into the armholes but didn't take her eyes off her friend. "I'm so sorry," she murmured. "Did they hurt you?" If they did, Estrella would kill them.

Sabrina shook her head and opened her mouth to speak, but no sound came out. So she just shook her head again.

Guilt punched through Estrella. She needed to deal with these lunatic vamps, then get her friend out of here. "We'll be leaving soon, I promise," she said before turning back to the vamp. As she stood, she was thankful the T-shirt fell almost to her knees. Rainer stood half in front of her, his entire *naked* body tense as he blocked her from the lead vampire.

"Tell me why I shouldn't kill you right now." Rainer's voice was almost pure animal in that moment.

Estrella swallowed hard. Holy crap. He could totally do it, too. She could feel the rage and energy pulsing off him in terrifying waves. It was almost like he was another person. She'd known he was deadly before, but what he was exuding now was lethal. Everyone in the room seemed aware of it too.

The vamp looked at Rainer and took a slight step back as he held up his hands in a passive gesture. "We do not wish to harm the princess and we never would have hurt her friend. As you can see." He motioned with his hand toward Sabrina but didn't take his eyes off Rainer. "We just wanted to get a take on the situation and figure out whether she was truly captive or had the ability to leave of her own free will. If she hadn't met us, we would have known she was captive then we would have launched an assault to free her from you. And we only shot tranqs at you the other night, wolf."

Estrella narrowed her eyes at him. "That's some seriously messed-up logic. But I don't even care about your bullshit. I want to know how you knew my mother. Did you have something to do with her death?" Her claws ached to unsheathe and she was barely restraining her inner jaguar at that thought.

Shock rippled off the vamp that was so pure she had no doubt of his sincerity when he said, "I loved your mother like a sister. She mated with a jaguar and left our coven to be with him. I respected her decision—even though I thought it was stupid to abandon her people."

Her immediate reaction was to deny this vampire's words as pure insanity, but some vague memory played in her mind. "Let's say I believe that my mother was a vampire. What do you mean, *her people*?" Estrella couldn't remember once going running with her mother, only her father. In fact she'd never once seen her mother shift forms, but Estrella had been five. It wasn't something she'd thought much about after their deaths. She'd just assumed both her parents had been jaguars because *she* was a jaguar.

"Amira Villanueva was the daughter of my coven leader, Amir Villanueva. She was slated to take over should Amir ever die. She was considered a princess to our coven as are you—now that we know of your existence."

Estrella placed a hand on Rainer's forearm, needing his support. Rainer immediately wrapped an arm around her shoulders and held her close. She savored his strength.

The vampire watched the interaction between the two of them. Surprise flared in his eyes briefly before his blank mask fell back into place. What? Had he not actually realized she and Rainer were together?

She wasn't sure she believed any of this, but needed to ask more questions. "So why come after me now? And what the hell is your name?"

He blinked in surprise. "My name is Taran. We didn't even know you existed until recently. Didn't know a jaguar-vampire mating could produce a child, but when I killed…" His jaw clenched and he took a deep breath. "I was recently forced to kill a member of our coven in self-defense and when he died, I took his memories through his blood. He'd been plotting to take over the coven and I wanted to see who his companions were, if any."

Estrella looked up at Rainer, her eyes wide. "Can vampires really do that?"

Rainer nodded, his expression grim. "It's rare, but yes. Some can."

She looked back at the vampire. "So what does that have to do with how you found out about me?"

The vampire looked almost apologetic. "The man I killed was one of the vampires who killed your parents. He wanted your mother dead should he ever decide to attempt to dethrone Amir. I've already killed the others who were there that night, too. I saw you in his memories and I also saw his intentions from that night. He'd planned to kill you, but you were too fast. Even as a child, you ran too fast for him. Then you disappeared into the human world so he made the decision to let you go. He'd decided you weren't worth the trouble since no one knew of your existence. He hadn't even known about you until that night he came after your parents."

Estrella's chest tightened as she struggled to breathe. She so badly wanted to deny his words, but she couldn't scent any lies from him. Lies had a particular metallic stench and this guy gave off nothing but pure honesty. It would also make a lot of sense as to why her mother had disappeared. If vampires turned to ash like the one she'd seen the other night, then that's why her mother's body had never been found. She glanced over her shoulder at Sabrina and was thankful to see her friend didn't look quite as in shock as earlier. And she couldn't scent as much fear off her either, just curiosity. But Estrella still wanted to get her out of here and she desperately needed to digest all this information alone.

She turned back to the vampire and tightened her grip around Rainer. "I don't know if I even believe you—"

Taran held out a cell phone to her. Everyone in the room tensed as Rainer let out a low growl. Conrad took a step forward and grabbed the phone then covered the distance to Rainer. Then he stood half in front of Estrella, taking the opportunity to block her even further from the vampires. She would have smiled at his show of protection if she had the energy. Rainer looked at the phone, then handed it to her. The vampire had taken snapshots of framed pictures—mostly of her mother and a man who was older than her—that spanned different decades. It could be a hoax, but Estrella couldn't imagine why the vampires would bother.

"You might not exhibit any of our vampire qualities, but you must carry the gene and are considered a blood born despite your jaguar body. We think you can theoretically have a blood born if you mated with a vamp—"

Rainer's low growl filled the air once again. "Estrella isn't mating with anyone except *me*."

Taran nodded slowly as he looked between them. "I see that. I was just making a statement. I—we," he held out a hand, motioning to the other vampires still locked in staring contests with Rainer's pack mates, "would like to welcome you back into our coven. You have a home, a family. Your grandfather desperately wants to meet you. When your mother left, they said many angry things to each other and he wants another chance. He would have been here, but he is at the treaty signing and could not leave."

Estrella still had a billion questions for this guy, but now wasn't the time. "My friends and I are leaving. You will not follow and you will never harass, touch or even look at any of my friends again. If I find out you actually did hurt Sabrina, I'll cut off your head." When he went to argue, she shook her head. "I want to sit down and talk with you and if what you're saying is true, I want to meet my grandfather, but I will not be bullied or forced into anything. You have my phone number so text me your number and I'll be in touch. Take my offer or leave it because I'm leaving *now*."

The vamp nodded, though his jaw was clenched tight. It was clear he wanted to argue, but knew he'd lose. Looking at his men, he nodded again and they all carefully left the storage room.

"Call the boys, tell them to let the vamp outside go," Rainer said to Conrad who immediately pulled out his phone.

Estrella turned at the sound of Sabrina standing up. Her friend's dark eyes were wide but at least not glassy anymore. She swayed on her feet and Estrella immediately covered the distance to support her—even though she was terrified of her friend's rejection and probable horror at the knowledge of what Estrella was.

"You can seriously turn into a jaguar?" were Sabrina's first words.

Estrella nodded, unable to find her voice.

"Holy crap, that's kind of insane—and pretty cool. I'll probably freak out once these drugs wear off, but..." Sabrina lunged at her then, throwing her arms around her neck. "Thank you for coming for me. I knew you would," she whispered, her voice thick with tears.

Estrella hugged her back, then glanced at Rainer. The rest

of his pack mates were cleaning up the storage room, but he was still standing there in all his naked glory watching her with a curious but guarded look.

Did he not want her now? Not only was she a jaguar, but chances were she was also part vampire. How freaky was that? Why would he want her when he could have a normal wolf shifter to warm his bed? Shuddering, she looked away and moved to slip an arm under Sabrina's shoulders. She just wanted to get her friend out of here for now. Everything else could wait.

Chapter 8

Rainer paced along the length of the tiled foyer in his pack's mansion. He'd barely seen Estrella the past three days because she'd spent them holed up with her best friend. Not that he blamed her. Her friend needed her and he would never take that away from either of them. The human, Sabrina, had taken the knowledge that there were supernatural creatures alive and living side by side with her in stride. Conrad was currently keeping an eye on her to make sure she didn't panic and tell other humans about them. Most people probably wouldn't believe her anyway, but until the shock of her newfound knowledge wore off, they were being cautious.

Right now, however, Rainer just wanted to hold Estrella in his arms to convince himself that what they'd shared was real and she hadn't changed her mind about them. They'd talked on the phone a few times but the conversations had been brief. It had been obvious she wanted time alone to digest what she'd learned about herself as well and he hadn't wanted to smother her. In a few hours his Alpha, oldest brother and Estrella's vampire grandfather would be returning to the compound and he'd never been more nervous in his life.

"You all right?"

Rainer turned at the sound of Angela's, Knox's mate's, soft voice. Wearing black leather pants, a black T-shirt and black boots she'd paused at the bottom of the winding staircase, her dark eyebrows raised in concern. She'd arrived back in Huntsville a day before her mate to get the house ready for their guests' arrival.

Rainer shook his head. No, he wasn't all right. "I miss her." The words were out before he could contemplate censoring himself. Who cared anyway if Angela knew how he felt? Hell, the entire pack knew by now. He'd been biting off the heads of anyone who even looked at him wrong the past couple days.

Angela's gaze softened, which made him feel pathetic. Before she could respond, his handheld radio beeped.

"Rainer, your female is on the property. I'm escorting her to the front door." It was King's voice, one of his pack mates.

Rainer's heart rate tripled and he jerked open the front door and strode outside. A nearly full moon hung low in the sky and the crickets were out in full force tonight, creating a symphony of noise. He barely heard them over the blood rushing in his ears. Their property was surrounded by the forest and thick foliage and the only way on to it by vehicle was a small two-lane road. Though he'd wanted to escort Estrella he'd known he wouldn't have been able to keep his hands off her if he'd picked her up. They'd have never made it out of her house if she still accepted his touch.

And his Alpha had been very insistent that she be at the mansion when he and their guests arrived.

He watched as one of their SUVs pulled up and parked in front of the mansion. When Estrella stepped out of the passenger side, his eyes widened. She wore a knee-length simple black halter style dress with strappy heels and her dark curly hair was wild around her face. She looked sexy as sin and all he wanted to do was strip her and bury himself inside her tight body.

Nervously, she smoothed her hands down the front of her dress, looked down then back up at him. He quickly covered the distance between them and tugged her hands, pulling her tight against him. The moment he did, some of the fear left her face.

"Do I look all right?" she whispered as she slid her hands up to his shoulders.

He nodded and forced himself to speak. "You look gorgeous. Your family won't be here for a few hours though."

"I know. I came early because I wanted to see you." Her dark eyes were wide as she watched him. Almost as if she was nervous about his reaction.

Rainer decided to lay everything out there. She might stomp on his heart, but hell, the woman had thrown herself in front of him to take a knife for him. She was worth it. "I've missed you so much, Estrella. I can't do anything without remembering what you taste like, what you feel like. I swore I'd give you time before I told you, but you're my mate. I knew it the moment we met. There's a lot you still need to learn about pack life and your history and hell, everything, but I want you forever."

She sucked in a deep breath and instead of responding, lifted up on her heels and crushed her mouth to his. Her kisses were needy and frantic and nearly bowled him over. Rainer was vaguely aware of King clearing his throat and saying something about Estrella's bags, but he didn't care.

Lifting her up, he hurried toward the house and practically flew up the stairs. They passed a few of his pack mates, but he ignored them all. Getting Estrella to his room and naked was all he could focus on.

He felt practically possessed until he slammed his door shut with a booted foot. After locking his door, something he rarely did, he let out a long sigh of relief. "I've been waiting forever to get you alone," he growled as he set her on her feet.

Hope flared in Estrella's eyes. "Really?"

His head cocked slightly to the side. "Are you kidding me? It's taken all my restraint to give you space the past three days."

She looked surprised before frowning. "You don't care that I'm also part vampire? Or at least have vamp blood in my veins?"

Rainer let out a harsh laugh as he started taking off his boots. "I don't care about any of that." His own Alpha was mated to a vampire, but that wasn't the reason he truly didn't care. She was sweet, sensual, caring and she'd been willing to take a blade for him. She'd thrown her own body over his when that vampire had tried to attack him.

Estrella wrapped her arms around herself as a new thread of nervousness rolled off her. "You've been really short with me on the phone the past couple days."

He paused as his second boot hit the hardwood floor. "I didn't know what to say and I didn't want to scare you by telling you I want you as my mate."

Her arms fell. "You were serious then? I know you said

it to Taran, but I thought you were just being territorial or something when you didn't bring it up again."

He growled again, unable to stop himself. "Of course I'm serious. I'd never joke about something like that. No shifter would." Panic slammed into his chest as he realized she'd never actually responded. She'd just kissed him and that could mean any number of things. "Do you not..." He couldn't get the words out. Fearful that if he said the words, they'd become a reality, they stuck in his throat.

"I want to mate with you too!" Her heated declaration soothed him immensely. "You're the only thing in my life that makes sense. The past few days without you only made it that much clearer and I don't want to even imagine a world without you. I...I'd like to take some more time to get to know one another before we actually mate, but I thought maybe you could move in with me or—"

"Yes." Rainer had already talked to his Alpha about that very thing. He wanted to teach Estrella about her history and get to know her *away* from the pack. He'd just thought it might take a little more convincing. While he had no doubt of his own feelings, he hadn't realized she felt the same.

She took a tentative seat on the edge of his bed and his gaze followed the delicate line of her neck down to her cleavage. It remained there until she cleared her throat, drawing his eyes back to hers. Her full lips curved up slightly as she said, "You don't mind living away from your pack?"

"Not as long as I'm with you." He was already in love with her and his wolf side was completely in sync with her jaguar side. "Now take off your dress, sweetheart." His hands were shaking and he didn't trust himself not to rip it off.

A burst of lust rolled off her so potent he couldn't help but smile. "You're very demanding," she murmured.

"In the bedroom, yes I am." When she went to take off her shoes first, he shook his head. "Leave them." The thought of making love to her with those on—his brain short-circuited as she untied the halter at her neck and the straps fell to reveal her breasts. She reached behind herself and he heard the soft sound of her zipper being pulled down.

Then her dress pooled around her feet leaving her standing there wearing a scrap of lace and straps that barely covered the juncture between her thighs.

He swallowed hard before tugging his shirt and pants off. Rainer told himself to go slower, but the thought of getting inside her nearly consumed him.

Foreplay.

The word sounded so loudly in his head, he paused before scooping her up and laying her out on his bed.

As she spread her legs, he slid her panties down her smooth, toned legs. The sweet scent of her arousal intensified as he blindly tossed the material aside. "Foreplay," he muttered.

She giggled, the sound wrapping around him like a siren's song. "Are you telling yourself that or me?"

"Myself." He looked up at her, stretched out on his giant bed as if she were an offering. Her olive skin seemed luminescent under the dim light of the moon streaming through his open drapes. "I would have killed all of them for you." He didn't need to expand, knowing she'd understand. Before they'd realized who those vampires were he'd been ready to bring the entire building down around their heads.

"I know."

"Does that scare you?"

She shook her head sending her curls bouncing. "No."

That was all he needed to know because if the time ever arose that he had to defend her again, he wouldn't pause to kill for her. Estrella was his.

Dipping his head between her legs, he licked the length of her wet pussy and couldn't bite back a satisfied groan when she gasped at his sudden onslaught.

He wanted to make her scream his name. As he teased her, his entire body shuddered at her taste. She was sweet perfection.

Her legs trembled around his head, squeezing him with each stroke of his tongue. He kept his teasing light and playful.

When she tunneled her fingers through his hair and gripped his head, he grinned against her compliant body. Her breathing had turned erratic and the scent of lust that rolled off her nearly drowned him.

"Skip foreplay," she demanded.

Grinning, he shook his head as he zeroed in on her clit. Pressing his tongue against the bundle of nerves, he exerted more pressure than he had so far. Her hips rolled against his face as she let out a yelp of surprise and pleasure.

Since it was clear she was ready for him, he slid two fingers inside her without warning.

"Rainer," she moaned his name as she tore her hands from his head and clutched the bedding underneath her.

Her inner walls clenched convulsively around his fingers so he slowed his movements. The first time she came tonight would be when he was inside her. And there would definitely be more than one time. He'd make sure of it.

Slowly, he dragged his fingers along her inner walls and savored the desperate sounds she made. Though he hated to tear his mouth away from her, he lifted his head. "What did you say? I didn't quite hear that," he murmured.

"Make love to me now," she demanded, her voice full of desperation. As she spoke, her inner walls tightened around him even more.

Those words had an immediate effect on him. Unwilling—and unable—to tease her any longer, he withdrew his fingers and covered her body with his. The heels from her shoes dug into his ass as she wrapped her legs around him.

The slight pain gave way to pleasure as he rocked into her. When she let out a sigh of relief, it nearly unraveled him. Knowing she was just as desperate to be with him as he was with her soothed the most primal part of him while it simultaneously unleashed him.

Palming her breasts, he tweaked and teased her hard nipples. The tiny buds had drawn tight and each time he rubbed one, her inner walls tightened even more around his cock.

Burying his face against her neck, he nipped and kissed her, savoring her natural jasmine scent. She was so close he could feel it with each stroke.

Thank God because he was close to coming, too. As he continued to pump into her, they found a frantic rhythm until finally he reached between them and rubbed her clit, hoping to push her over the edge.

With a cry, she dug her fingers into his back and let out a moan that pierced him soul deep. He'd given her that pleasure. No one else. And no one else would ever touch what was his.

It was too soon, but he couldn't stop himself from saying the words "I love you," as he climaxed. His orgasm was harsh and anything but graceful. His entire body shook as he emptied himself inside her.

Rainer wasn't sure how much time passed as they lay wrapped in each other's arms, but eventually Estrella toed her shoes off and wrapped her legs completely around him. She gently nuzzled his neck, nipping at him with her teeth and then following up with soft kisses. Feeling too raw and open to look her in the eye, he kept his face buried against her neck.

Finally, she dug her fingers into his back, pinching him. "Look at me," she demanded. When he lifted his head, all he saw was love and lust in her hot gaze. "I love you, too."

He blinked once, unsure he'd heard right.

She cupped his cheek, pulling him so his face was an inch from hers. "When we met, it's like a missing piece of a puzzle fell into place inside me. I know we have a hell of a lot to learn about each other, but what I know so far is enough for me. You're mine and I'm not letting go."

His inner wolf howled in satisfaction. He wasn't letting her go either. No matter what. They belonged together and that was that. He breathed out a sigh of relief he hadn't even realized he'd been holding on to at her words. Covering her mouth with his again, he rolled so that she was straddling him. It didn't matter that soon people would be arriving to meet Estrella, he wasn't letting her out of his bed for a good, long time.

* * * * *

A sneaky peek at next month…

NOCTURNE™

AN EXHILARATING UNDERWORLD OF DARK DESIRES

My wish list for next month's titles…

In stores from 20th June 2014:

❑ The Resurrectionist — Sierra Woods

❑ The Vampire's Wolf — Jenna Kernan

In stores from 4th July 2014:

❑ Vampire Kiss — Michele Hauf, Lisa Childs, Lauren Hawkeye, Laura Kaye & Linda Thomas-Sundstrom

Includes 5 stories!

Available at WHSmith, Tesco, Asda, Eason, Amazon and Apple

Just can't wait?

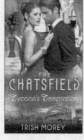

THE CHATSFIELD®

Enter the intriguing online world of
The Chatsfield and discover secret
stories behind closed doors...

www.thechatsfield.com

Check in online now for your exclusive
welcome pack!

Join the Mills & Boon Book Club

Want to read more **Nocturne**™ books?
We're offering you **1** more absolutely **FREE!**

We'll also treat you to these fabulous extras:

- 🌹 **Exclusive offers and much more!**
- 🌹 **FREE home delivery**
- 🌹 **FREE books and gifts with our special rewards scheme**

Get your free books now!

visit www.millsandboon.co.uk/bookclub
or call Customer Relations on 020 8288 2888

Kamehameha the Great, Kohala, Hawaii

Opaekaa Falls, Kauai

Hawaii

Hawaii

Little Hills Press

First Edition 1990, Second edition 1994

This edition, January 1998
(c) Maps - Little Hills Press
(c) Photographs - Hawaii Visitors Bureau, Sydney

Little Hills Press Pty Ltd
Regent House, 37-43 Alexander Street
Crows Nest, NSW, 2065, Australia

ISBN 1 86315 120 6

DISCLAIMER

Whilst all care has been taken by the editorial team to ensure that the information is accurate and up to date, the publisher does not take responsibility for the information published herein. As things get better or worse, places close and others open, some elements in the book may be inaccurate when you get there. Please write and tell us about it so we can update in subsequent editions.

Contents

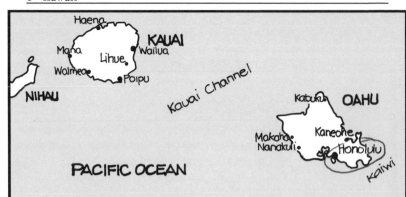

PACIFIC OCEAN

HAWAIIAN ISLANDS

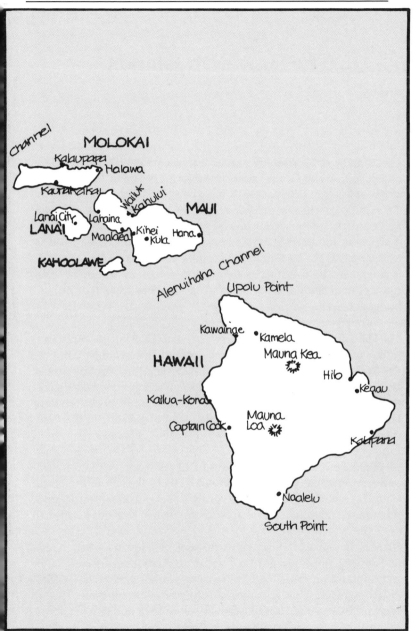

The Hawaiian Islands

The Islands of Hawaii are situated approximately 3870km (2400 miles) south-west of the coast of California, 4485km (2781 miles) south of Alaska, 6205km (3847 miles) east of Tokyo, and 8065km (5000 miles) north-east of Sydney, Australia. The eight islands that make up the main group are the result of underwater volcanic cataclysms hundreds of thousands of years ago in the 3226km (2000 miles) fault at the bottom of the Pacific Ocean. Even today, Hawaii is a land in the making. Its two active volcanoes are among the most spectacular in eruption, and among the least harmful to human life in the world.

The Hawaiian archipelago stretches 2451km (1523 miles) south-east to the north-west from Cape Kumukahi, the easternmost point of the Island of Hawaii (known as the Big Island), to the tiny speck known as Kure Atoll. Seven of the eight most southerly islands are the inhabited portions of the State. Three of the north-western Hawaiian Islands had a total population of 31 persons in the 1980 census.

The Big Island has a total land area of 10,407 sq km (4034 sq miles) and a population of 120,317. It is almost twice the size of the other islands combined. The island grows sugar, coffee, cattle and macadamia nuts, and has two volcanoes, Mauna Loa and Kilauea.

Maui is the second largest with an area of 1881 sq km (729 sq miles) and 91,361 inhabitants. The Valley Isle produces sugar and pineapple, and cattle and horses are reared there. The 3045m (10,023 ft) Haleakala is the largest dormant volcano crater in the world. Lahaina was Hawaii's capital before 1845, and still has some of the atmosphere of an old whaling town.

Next in size is Oahu, 1533 sq km (594 sq miles), the most populated island with 836,207 people. Home to the capital city of Honolulu, the principal port, the major airport, the business and financial centre, and the educational heart of the State, Oahu is probably best known for the famous Waikiki Beach, Diamond Head and Pearl Harbour.

Kauai, the Garden Island (1416 sq km - 549 sq miles) with 50,947 inhabitants, offers magnificent scenery and lush vegetation, waterfalls, the spectacular Waimea Canyon, the 'hidden' valley of Kalalau, and colourful tropical plants and flowers.

Next comes Molokai with an area of 673 sq km (261 sq miles) and a population of 6717. Known as the Friendly Isle, Molokai has pineapple plantations, ranches, and some spectacular cliffs along its northern Pali Coast. On a 34 sq km (13 sq mile) peninsula below high cliffs is Kalaupapa, the Hansen's Disease settlement, officially called Kalawao County.

Almost the entire island of Lanai, 361 sq km (140 sq miles) with 2426 inhabitants, was a Dole Company pineapple plantation, until the recent advent of tourism.

Niihau is a privately owned island, with livestock raising as its principle industry. Legend says it was the original home of the goddess Pele. The area of the island is 181 sq km (70 sq miles) and the population, 230.

Kahoolawe is an uninhabited island that was used for target practice by the US Navy and Air Force. The 116 sq km (45 sq miles) is littered with unexploded shells, and no one is allowed to go ashore without permission.

There have been various explanations of the name 'Hawaii'. It is said to have been named by Hawaii Loa, traditional discoverer of the islands, after himself. Hawaii or Hawaiki, traditional home of the Polynesians, is also given as the origin. This is a compound word, hawa, the name of the traditional place of residence, and -ii, or -iki, meaning little or small, thus, a smaller or new homeland.

Since -ii also means raging or furious, the name is sometimes explained as referring to the volcanoes. It is often written with the glottal-stop mark: Hawai'i.

History

It was long believed that the Polynesians first arrived in Hawaii from Tahiti around 1000 AD, but new discoveries have suggested that the true date may be closer to the 6th century AD or even earlier.Researchers believe that the Polynesians who conquered the Pacific in their double-hulled canoes came originally from South-East Asia. Tahiti is thought to be one centre of Polynesian development, but there is evidence indicating that Hawaii was first settled from the Marquesas. Regardless, to those familiar with the vast reaches of the Pacific Ocean, the seamanship of the Polynesians is a feat of staggering proportions.

The intrepid British explorer, Captain James Cook, is accredited with discovering Hawaii in 1788, when he sighted Oahu and landed on Kauai. Cook named the archipelago the Sandwich Islands, after his patron the Earl of Sandwich, and for many years the islands were so known to the western world. On Sunday, February 14, 1779, Cook was slain in a fight with eh Hawaiians at Kealakekua on the Island of Hawaii. Previously the islanders had thought Cook was the god Lono, who had vowed to return to his people, but they changed their minds, and proved just how mortal he was.

At the time of Cook's arrival each island was ruled as an independent kingdom by hereditary chiefs. Around 1790, one of these chiefs, Kamehameha, consolidated his power on the island of Hawaii in a series of battles, and then conquered Maui and Oahu. By the time of his death in 1819, Kamehameha I had united the islands under his rule. He established the Kingdom of Hawaii which survived until 1893.

In 1820, the first American missionaries arrived from New England. Not only did they bring Christianity to a people becoming disillusioned with their ancient gods, but they represented the first of several migrations that led to the cosmopolitan character of

Hawaii's people today. With the arrival of people from distant lands, new diseases were introduced, to which the natives had no immunity. They also had no immunity to the alcohol brought by these new arrivals, and a state of chaos was soon reached. The missionaries gained great success because they aligned themselves with the chiefs against some of these evils.

Kamehameha's eldest son, Liholiho, took the title of Kamehameha II. His short reign was noted for the official demise of the old religion and the breakdown of ancient taboos. Liholiho and his queen, Kmamalu, both died of measles within a few days of each other while visiting London in 1824.

Another son of Kamehameha, Kauikeaouli, was proclaimed King with the title of Kamehameha III. During his 30 year reign many hazards to the little kingdom were surmounted, and its independence recognised by the great powers - France, Britain and the United States. A semi-feudal inheritance was gradually transformed into a constitutional monarchy.

Among notable events during the reign were the opening of Lahainaluna School on Maui in 1831, the oldest high school west of the Rocky Mountains; the establishment on Kauai of the first permanent sugar plantation in 1835; the publication of the first newspaper in the Pacific area (1834); the proclamation of the Constitution (1840); the publication of the first school laws (1841); changes in land ownership concepts through the Great Mahele (1848); and the updating, through a new Constitution, of the structures of government (1852).

In February 1843, Lord George Paulet forced cession of the Hawaiian Kingdom to Great Britain, as the result of a dispute between the two countries, but the action was repudiated by Rear Admiral Richard Thomas in July of the same year, and Hawaii's independence was officially recognised. Honolulu's Thomas Square honours his memory.

Honolulu becomes the Capital

In 1845 King Kamehameha III and the Legislature moved to Honolulu from the capital at Lahaina, on Maui. On August 31,

1850, he declared Honolulu officially the capital of the Kingdom.

During the middle of the 19th century, Hawaii was a centre of whaling activity. An infant sugar industry had found a shortage of plantation labour, and in 1852 chinese were brought to the kingdom by contract. Thus began the stream of imported labour which lasted until 1946. The first Japanese came in 1868, while Filipinos started arriving at a much later date. Koreans, Portuguese and Puerto Ricans are among the other national groups brought to the islands.

The growing importance of sugar was reflected in Hawaii's political picture during the next few decades. The sugar planters favoured annexation of Hawaii by the United States to establish a firm market for the product. The Hawaiian monarchs, on the other hand, intermittently attempted to establish and implement a policy of Hawaii for the Hawaiians.

During the reigns of Kamehameha's grandson, Alexander Liholiho, who ruled as Kamehameha IV (1855-1863), and his brother, Lot Kamehameha, Kamehameha V (1863-1872), there was a succession of inconclusive wrangles over the constitution between those insistent on limiting suffrage and strengthening the power of the throne, and those wishing to extend the franchise and limit the powers of the monarch.

With the death of Kamehameha V, the line of direct descendants of Kamehameha ended, and the legislature, following the plebiscite, elected Prince William C. Lunalilo as King. He died a year later, and David Kalakaua was elected his successor. Disorders sparked by adherents of his rival contender, Dowager Queen Emma, widow of Kamahameha IV, broke out in Honolulu when the results became known, and the government was forced to call upon American and British marines to restore order.

Kalakaua brought to fruition negotiations with the United States which were initiated by Lunalilo, and in 1875 a treaty of reciprocity was signed between the two nations. By its terms, Hawaii assured itself of a market for sugar in the United States, and upon its renewal in 1887 the US secured the exclusive use of Pearl Harbour as a coaling station.

Despite his being known as the Merry Monarch, (he wrote the State Song Hawaii Ponoi) Kalakaua's reign (1874-1891) was a stormy one. He was continually battling for an increase in his personal authority. He dreamed of a Polynesian empire. He made a trip around the world and while in Japan proposed a marriage alliance with the Emperor's family. His efforts, however, were unsuccessful, and under pressure he signed a new constitution in 1887 which further curbed his power, and set up a cabinet-type government responsible to the Legislature. This led, in 1889, to an unsuccessful insurrection by those opposed to the new constitution and its reform measures.

Kalakaua died in 1891 during a visit to San Francisco, and was succeeded by his sister, Liliuokalani, the last Hawaiian monarch, who reigned less than two years. Her policy was to eliminate the restrictions which had been placed on the monarchy, and to this end she attempted to proclaim still another constitution. This led in 1893 to a bloodless 'revolution', her deposition as Queen, and the formation of a provisional government under the leadership of Sanford Ballard Dole.

The provisional government requested annexation by the United States, but President Grover Cleveland was not in sympathy with the provisional government or with the revolution and refused. The Provisional Government then converted Hawaii into a Republic and Dole was proclaimed president in 1984.

Annexation

President William McKinley had a more sympathetic attitude regarding annexation, and the outbreak of the Spanish-American War in 1898 brought matters to a head. Hawaii's strategic military importance in the Pacific was recognised, particularly its potential threat to the United States were another great power to occupy the islands. By Joint Resolution of Congress, the islands were officially annexed, and formal transfer of sovereignty was made on August 12, 1898. The new possession was then organised as a Territory and Dole was appointed its first Governor, taking office on June 14,

1900. The first Territorial Legislature convened on February 20, 1901.

During this period, a young cousin of S.B. Dole who had come to Hawaii from New England to seek his fortune, established a second major industry. James D. Dole, continuing experiments with pineapple which had been made by others, finally found a variety that would grow successfully, and he made his first canned pineapple pack in 1903, producing 1,893 cases. From this beginning came Hawaii's great pineapple industry of today.

Hawaii's people participated in World War I, but Hawaii was actually a backwash of that great struggle. During the 1920s increased efforts to promote Hawaii for tourists were initiated.

In 1927, army lieutenants Lester Maitland and Albert Hegenberger made the first successful non-stop flight from the Mainland, marking the arrival of the trans-Pacific air age in Hawaii. A commercial inter-island air service began two years later. Radio-telephone service among the islands and to the Mainland was established in 1931, and extended to Europe and South America in 1932. (A telephone system had first been established in Hawaii in 1878.)

The effects of the Great Depression in the 1930s were not as serious in Hawaii as they were in more industrialised areas. With growing international tensions, and particularly the aggressions of Japan in the Far East, the 30s saw a build-up of American military power in Hawaii. They also saw the binding of Hawaii closer to the Mainland by Pan American World Airways' inauguration of regular commercial passenger flights in 1936.

International tensions burst into flame at 7.55am on the morning of December 7, 1941, when the first Japanese bombs fell on Pearl Harbour, causing nearly 4000 casualties, and seriously crippling the great American fleet berthed there. Hawaii quickly mushroomed into an armed camp, and was the nerve centre of America's whole Pacific war effort. The joyous celebration of V-J Day on August 14, 1945, was heartfelt.

The Japanese population of Hawaii was the object of some suspicion at the beginning of World War II. This was completely eliminated by the 442nd Regimental Combat Team, composed largely of Nisei (second generation American of Japanese ancestry) from Hawaii, which became the most decorated outfit of the war.

Hawaii spent the greater part of the war under martial law, or a modified concept of it with blackouts, curfews and similar regulations.

A law permitting organisation of agricultural workers, passed by the Territorial Legislature in 1945, brought major labour organisations to the islands within a year.

The late 40s were marred by a series of labour-management conflicts including the very serious waterfront strike of 1949 which lasted six months.

With the outbreak of the Korean conflict in 1950, Hawaii was again called upon. The unpreparedness of the nation as a whole led to a particularly heavy demand on Hawaii, closest to the conflict, and Hawaii's people suffered more military casualties per capita than any other state.

Statehood

From the 1930s through the 50s the dominant political theme in Hawaii was Statehood. First proposed during the reign of Kamehameha III, it became a more defined goal shortly after World War I, when Hawaii's Delegate to Congress, Prince Jonah Kuhio Kalanianaole, introduced a bill to that effect. More strenuous efforts were made in the 1930s, when the late Samuel Wilder King was Delegate, and this effort was continued after World War II by Delegate Joseph Rider Farrington, and after his death, by his widow, Delegate Elizabeth Farrington. A plebiscite showing a 2-to-1 vote in favour of Statehood was conducted in 1940. A Constitutional Convention which wrote Hawaii's modern constitution was held in 1950.

All these efforts finally culminated in 1959, when John A. Burns

All these efforts finally culminated in 1959, when John A. Burns was Delegate, and both Houses of Congress passed the necessary legislation, the Senate on March 11, and the House on March 12. Hawaii officially entered the American Union as the 50th State on Admission Day, August 21, 1959.

William F. Quinn was Hawaii's first elected Governor. The second was John A. Burns, who served 12 years. He died on April 5, 1975. Third was George R. Ariyoshi, elected to his third and final term in 1982. John Waihee is the fourth.

On April 23, 1959, the last Territorial Legislature officially designated The Aloha State as the official 'popular' name for the State of Hawaii.

The State's motto is "Ua mau ke ea o ka aina i ka pono" which means "The life of the land is perpetuated in righteousness." The saying is attributed to King Kamehameha III as of July 31, 1843, when the Hawaiian flag once more was raised after a brief period of unauthorised usurpation of authority by a British admiral.

The State flag has eight stripes (representing the eight major islands), of white, red and blue. The field closely resembles the Union Jack of Great Britain, from which the original flag was designed.

Official Emblems

For its official flower the State of Hawaii has chosen the yellow hibiscus grown throughout the islands. More than five thousand types of hibiscus hybrids have been identified.

Hawaii's State tree is the indigenous kukui, better known as the candlenut. The nuts of this tree provided the ancient Hawaiians with light, oil, relishes, and medicines. By joint resolution, the Legislature of Hawaii also established official flowers and colours for each island, as follows:

Hawaii Island	Red Lehua (Ohia)	Red
Maui	Lokelani	

Canoe racing, 4th July, Oahu

Waikiki at dusk

Kalakaua Avenue, Honolulu

Molokai	White Kukui Blossom	Green
Kahoolawe	Hinahina	
	(Beach Heliotrope)	Grey
Lanai	Kaunaoa	
	(Yellow & Orange Air Plant)	Yellow
Oahu	Ilima	Yellow
Kauai	Mokihana (Green Berry)	Purple
Niihau	White Pupu Shell	White

The Nene (pronounced 'nay-nay'), a variety of goose, is the State bird. The largest land bird, it has adapted itself to live in harsh lava country, by transforming webbed feet to a claw-like shape, and modifying wing structure for shorter flights.

A century ago nene were abundant on the islands of Maui and Hawaii. Hunting and wild animals all but destroyed the species until they were protected by law and a restoration project established in 1949. Today there are a few hundred wild nene and they are on the increase. Birds raised in captivity are released to join them. In 1985 State Legislature designated the small, colourful humuhumunukunuku-a-pua'a, or rectangular triggerfish, as the official fish of the State. The 1979 Legislature designated the humpback whale, an annual visitor to Hawaiian waters, as the State's official marine mammal.

Climate

Hawaii's climate pattern is a combination of cooling trade winds and equable temperatures throughout the year. Rarely are there severe storms of any kind.

The north-easterly trade winds bring the rain-bearing clouds, which are caught by the mountains. Thus, there is an enormous range of rainfall, with the windward sides of the islands being generally wetter than the leeward.

Waialeale on the Island of Kauai has an average annual rainfall of 11,455mm (451 ins), and is one of the two wettest spots on earth although there are areas on the same island, only a few kilometres away, which have a rainfall of less than 508mm (20 ins) a year. The driest spot recorded is Puako, on the Big Island, with an average annual rainfall of 240mm (9.47 ins).

The highest official temperature recorded at Honolulu International Airport between 1980 and 1990 was 34 C (94 F); the lowest was 11 C (53 F). The average temperature is 25 C (78 F). Snow is found during winter months on the summit of Mauna Kea and Mauna Loa. The highest temperature ever recorded in the State was 38C (100F), in 1931. During the day it is hottest between 11am and 2pm.

Population

The total population of the island group is approximately 1,134,800 with about half under the age of 30.

Everyone in Hawaii is a member of an ethnic minority. No single racial group constitutes more than about one-third of the population.

In an American context, the various peoples of Asia have followed a pattern similar to that set by European immigrants to other areas of the United States - the second and third generations have become thoroughly Americanised.

Languages

While ancestral languages are still heard in Hawaii, English is universally used. The native Hawaiian language is also an official State language, and it is often used on emblems and symbols representative of the State. This language is gradually disappearing though, being rarely spoken at home, and taught in only a few schools and at the University of Hawaii.

However, most of the place names and street names are in Hawaiian, so a few words, and a guide to pronunciation, will at least make you sound like a native.

The Hawaiian alphabet consists of seven consonants (h, k, l, m, n, p and w) and the five vowels (a, e, i, o, u). All the vowels in a word are pronounced, and some words contain a glottal stop (') instead of a written consonant.

The consonants are pronounced the same as in English, except that 'w' when it follows 'e' or 'i', is pronounced as a 'v'.

The vowels are pronounced as follows:

a as in tar
e as in red
i as in bee
o as in old
u as in rude

'ae	yes
aikane	friend
ala	road, path
alii	chief, royalty
aloha	welcome, greetings, love, farewell
'a'ole	no
haole	Caucasian
hapa	part, half
hele mai	come here
holoku	fitted ankle-length dress with train
holomu'u	fitted andle-length dress
huhu	angry
hula	Hawaiian dance
iki	small, little
ipo	sweetheart, lover
kahili	feather standard
kahuna	priest, expert
kai	sea
kala	money
kamaaina	native, local resident
kane	mael, husband
kapu	forbidden, keep out
keiki	child
kokua	help
lei	garland, wreath
lua	toilet
mahalo	thanks
maika'i	good, fine
malo	loin cloth
manu	bird
manuahi	free, gratis
mauna	mountain
mele	song

moana	ocean
mu'umu'u	loose-fitting dress
nani	beautiful
ne'i	this place
nui	big, large
'ono	tasty, delicious
pa'u	wrap around skirt
pehea'oe	how are you?
poi	cooked taro corn pounded into paste
pua	flower, blossom
pua'a	pork, pig
pupu	shell
tutu	grandmother
wahine	female, wife
wai	fresh water
wikiwiki	hurry, fast

Religion

Hawaii's religions are as diverse as its cultural heritage. The missionaries who arrived in 1820 were mostly Congregationalists, followed in 1827 by Roman Catholics. In the Constitution of 1840, freedom of worship was guaranteed for all religions.

Later arrivals of thousands of Portuguese and Filipino immigrants greatly increased Catholic numbers in the islands.

The Latter-Day Saints (Mormon) began work in 1850, and the Methodists arrived in 1854. In 1862 Kamehameha IV invited the Anglican Church to establish itself in Hawaii.

Meanwhile, the arrival of the first Chinese contract labourers in 1852 saw the establishment of Chinese temples, some Confucianists, some Taoist, and some Buddhist.

Similarly, Japanese forms of religion followed in 1885. Five of the main forms of Mahayana Buddhism were established in Hawaii: Shingon, Jodo, Jodo Shin (Hongwanji), Zen (Soto) and Nichiren. The Japanese also brought Shinto shrines of many varieties.

Lutherans were established in 1883, Seventh-day Adventists in 1885, the Salvation Army in 1894, Christian Scientists in 1902, Northern Baptists in 1930, Southern Baptists in 1940, Unitarians in 1953, and Presbyterians in 1959. The Religious Society of Friends (Quakers) also have an establishment. The first Jewish synagogue was established in 1950.

Hawaii's many beautiful church buildings include the Mormon Temple at Laie, Our Lady of Peace Cathedral, St Andrew's Cathedral, Central Union Church, The First Church of Christ Scientist, and Kawaiahao Church on Oahu; Kaahumanu Church, Maui, St Benedict's, Hawaii; and Wailoi Church, Kauai. There are many contemporary-styled churches as well as Buddhist temples and ancient Hawaiian heiaus.

Festivals

In January or early February, Hawaii celebrates the Narcissus Festival, for the Chinese New Year, and selects a Narcissus Queen to reign for the year.

In late March or April comes the Cherry Blossom Festival, with its Cherry Blossom Queen, inspired by the cherry blossom season in Japan. A St Patrick's Day parade is held March 17. Prince Kuhio Day on March 26 is a State holiday.

Also held in the spring is Hilo's Merrie Monarch Festival featuring competitions between Hawaii's best hula halau (schools).

Lei Day is celebrated on May 1, with gorgeous displays of flower leis.

Kamehameha Day on June 11 is a State holiday, with parades and pageants.

Fiesta Filipina is an annual festival sponsored by the United Filipino Council of Hawaii, and is usually held in June.

During July and August the Bon Odori, a Buddhist festival with dances, is staged. Summer also sees a 50th State Fair. Aloha Week Festivals, filled with Hawaiian pageantry and music, come in September. Festivities are held throughout the State featuring dances and craft demonstrations. Admission Day, another State holiday, is the third Friday in August.

Okinawans, Portuguese, Samoans, Koreans and others have festivals and commemorations at various times.

Despite the warmer weather, Christmas is celebrated in Hawaii in the same way as on the Mainland. Large shipments of Christmas trees are brought in from the Pacific Northwest every year.

Such national holidays as President's Day, Memorial Day, Independence Day, Labor Day, Veterans' Day and Thanksgiving are also celebrated. Several of these have been converted into three-day weekend holidays by State law. New Year's Day, and Martin Luther King Day, January 16, are also observed.

Entry Regulations

Valid passports are required by all except Canadian nationals with an ID card, and British subjects holding a valid British passport and proof of their status as a 'landed immigrant' in Canada.

Visas are required by all except Canadians and British subjects who comply with the passport conditions. Visas are available from US embassies and consulates, and are valid for five years.

The following goods may be imported without incurring customs duty: **200 cigarettes, or 50 cigars, or 3lb of tobacco, or proportionate amounts of each.**

1 litre of alcoholic beverage (age 21 or over).

Gifts or articles up to a value of US$400.

Health Regulations

No vaccination certificates are required, except for yellow fever if arriving from an infected or endemic area.

Currency Restrictions

All import and export of currency transactions of over US$5,000 must be reported to US Customs. All gold coins and any quantity of gold must be declared before export. Otherwise there are no restrictions on the import and export of either local or foreign currency.

Embassies

Australia: Australian Consulate-General, 1000 Bishop Street, Honolulu, ph 524 5050.

New Zealand: No resident representative. Refer to NZ Consulate-General, Tishman Building, 10960 Wilshire Boulevard, Los Angeles, ph (213) 477 8241.

Canada: No resident representative. Refer to Consulate-General of Canada, 1 Maritime Plaza, Golden Gateway Center, San Francisco, ph (415) 981 2670.

Singapore: No resident representative. Refer Washington DC

UK: No resident representative. Refer to British Consulate-General, 3701 Wilshire Boulevard, Los Angeles, ph (213) 385 7381.

Money

Currency is the United States Dollar (US$) which equals 100 cents. Notes are in denominations of $1, $2, $5, $10, $20, $50 and $100. Coins are in denominations of 1c, 5c (nickel), 10c (dime), 25c (quarter) and 50c.

Approximate exchange rates are:

AUS$	= US$0.69
NZ$	= US$0.54
Can$	= US$0.76
Sing$	= US$0.58
UK £	= US $1.55

Communications

The telephone service throughout Hawaii is provided by GTE Hawaiian Telephone Co. The Country Code is 1, and the Area Code is 808. A local call from a public phone costs 25c, calls from hotels attract a service charge.

Hawaii is served by nine daily newspapers, several weekly and semi-weekly papers and numerous magazines, as well as The Associated Press, United Press International and their affiliates. The two major daily newspapers are the afternoon Honolulu Star-Bulletin and the morning Honolulu Advertiser.

There are nineteen commercial and two public television stations, and eight cable television companies. There are also 56 commercial and public radio stations, 28 of them FM.

Miscellaneous

Local time is GMT - 10. There is no daylight saving in Hawaii.

Opening Hours

Banks: 8.30am-3pm Mon-Thurs, 8.30am-6pm Fri.

Businesses: 8am-5pm Mon-Fri.

Shops: 9am-9pm Mon-Sat. Some shops open Sunday.

Credit Cards are widely accepted.

There is a departure tax of US$20.00, but it is included in the price of your airline ticket so is relatively painless.

Electricity supply is 120 volts AC.

Health

The local tap water is considered safe to drink. Milk is pasteurised and dairy products are safe. Local meat, poultry, seafood, fruit and vegetables are generally considered safe to eat.

Hawaii has high health standards. Life expectancy at birth in 1979-1981 was 77.02 years, the highest of any of the 50 states. In 1992 there were 2726 physicians and surgeons, 906 dentists, 8552 registered nurses, and 606 pharmacists licensed and residing in Hawaii. In 1986 there were 25 acute care hospitals, 40 long term care and eleven specialty care facilities.

It must be remembered however, that all the above are expensive, so it is imperative for travellers to ensure that they have adequate medical insurance before heading Stateside. This can be organised through your private health insurance company, or by your travel agent.

Tipping

Hawaii is part of the United States, and so tipping is the order of the day. Although 4% sales tax is added to bills, 5% to accommodation, and most everything else has some type of addition, you are expected to tip as follows:

Restaurant - 15%

Taxi Drivers - 10%

Porters - 50c per bag

Room service waiters, barbers/hairdressers - 10% to 15%.

Travel Information

How to Get There

By Air

The international airport is Honolulu, about 6km (4 miles) north-west of Honolulu, and 10km (6 miles) north-west of Waikiki.

Direct flights from the West Coast of America also land at Keahole Airport in Kona on Hawaii Island, and others fly to Kahului Airport on Maui after a brief stop in Honolulu.

By Sea

The main ports are Honolulu and Lahaina. The following cruise lines run services to Hawaii - P&O/Princess Cruises, Royal Viking, Cunard/NAC Line and Royal Cruises.

Accommodation

Finding accommodation in Hawaii is definitely not a problem. There are modern hotels, from the most luxurious to very modest, on all the islands.

Apartments and condominiums are also there in abundance.

Local Transport

Air

Aloha Airlines, Hawaiian Airlines and Island Air have frequent inter-island services.

Taxi

Taxis are plentiful on all islands, and have meters.

Car Hire

There are international and local agencies providing this service.

Technically, an international drivers licence is required, but some offices still accept current foreign licences. As with any other place in the world, it is best to compare rates and to read the small print of rental agreements. Traffic drives on the right. The speed limit is 88km/h (60 mph).

Food

The great variety of food reflects the multi-racial atmoshpere in Hawaii. Immigrants from different parts of the world have brought with them recipes from their homelands, and added them to the traditional Hawaiian fare. As a result, no matter whether you want to dine on Asian, European or Hawaiian, there will still be a large selection to choose from.

The classic Hawaiian luau features a whole pig, skinned and rubbed with rock salt and soya sauce, placed on chicken wire and filled with hot stones from the imu fire. It is cooked along with sweet potatoes, plantains and sometimes laulaus (butterfish and taro shoots wrapped in banana leaves and steamed). The pig is traditionally eaten with the fingers, accompanied by poi (thick paste made from ground taro - which we are not going to guaranteee you'll like, but you should try it), opihi (a black, salty, clam-like mollusc) and lomi lomi salmon (salmon rubbed with an onion and tomato marinade).

Chicken luau is another variety, with the chicken cooked with taro tops and coconut cream. This is served mostly with limu (dried seaweed), chopped roasted kukui nusts and paakai rock salt.

Hawaiian breakfasts are enormous, even by American standards, and the fresh fruit is delicious.

Note: In the "Eating Out" sections of the following chapters the eateries are rated according to the price of a main course, as follows:

$21 and over	expensive
$16 - $20 -	moderate
$11 - $15 -	inexpensive
$10 and under	budget

Shopping

Hawaii is truly a shopper's paradise. Being the 'crossroads of the Pacific', the islands offer an astonishing variety of shops and goods. Fashions from Europe, apparel from the Far Eat and of course, the ever-present, ever-colourful Aloha attire of Hawaii itself can be purchased. Shops feature artwork from among some of the most talented artists in the world, and sell fine hand-crafted koa wood figuringes carved by local artisans.

If jewellery is on your shopping list, you have come to the right place - from inexpensive rings and brooches featuring parsley dipped in gold and decorated with coral, to jade and precious stones either loose or in unique settings.

And, of course, there is the widest range of swimwear available, for all tastes and sizes.

Sport and Recreation

Water sports head the list since Hawaii has marvellous swimming beaches. Surfing, so popular these days, was the ancient Hawaiian sport of kings. The annual Triple Crown of Surfing attracts participants from all over the world.

Reefs and offshore areas present unmatached opportunities for scuba and snorkelling enthusiasts.

Other beach sports include outrigger canoe rides and catamaran cruises.

Sailing is also very popular. The biennial Transpacific Yacht Race from California to Honolulu, the Kenwood Cup, is a yachting classic. There is an annual Molokai-to-Oahu canoe race.

There is good deep-sea fishing in Hawaiian waters. Some of the largest marlin in the world have been hooked in island waters.

An International Billfish Tournament is held annually in Kona, and the Hawaii Big Game Fishing Club holds two statewide gamefish tournaments each year.

Surfcasting and shore fishing are also popular island pastimes, and there is even freshwater trout fishing on Kauai.

Hiking and hunting trails are found in the islands' green mountains. Cabins are available in some state or national park areas, and most islands offer camping sites. Pack trips can also be arranged.

For the golfer, there are many courses on six islands. Also available are many public tennis courts.

Hawaii offers college baseball; a full season of football culminating in the Hula Bowl, Pro Bowl and Aloha Bowl; college basketball; an annual PGA Golf Tournament; and a polo season. Hawaii boasts of the 50,000-seat Aloha Stadium.

Hawaii is also proud of her tradition of Olympic champions... Duke Kahanamoku held the Olympic 100m sprint championship for nearly 20 years starting in 1912, and created a tradition of champion island swimmers. Keala O'Sullivan won a bronze medal in the 1968 Olympic diving competition. David McFaull and Michael Rothwell won silver medals in the 1976 Olympic Tornado Class boat racing finals.

In December, the annual Honolulu Marathon is held. It is one of the most popular in the US. The Ironman Triathlon on the Big Island also attracts national attention.

Oahu

Known as "The Gathering Place", Oahu was once the common meeting ground for Hawaii's island kings. It is probably the best known of the Hawaiian Islands, because it is hom to Honolulu, Waikiki, Diamond Head and Pearl Harbour.

Oahu is the third largest island in the group, with a population of 836,207. The only royal palace in the United States is found on this island.

It is estimated that around 4,000,000 people a year visit Oahu, mainly staying in the Honolulu-Waikiki area.

Honolulu is a modern city, with tall buildings, broad streets and bright lights. It has been the capital of the State since February 1845, when King Kamehameha III took up residence in the city.

How to get there

Hawaiian Airlines (Ph: 838-1555) fly to Honolulu from:
Seattle -daily
San Francisco - daily
Los Angeles -daily
Las Vegas -daily
Qantas (Ph: 800-367-5320) has flights to Honolulu from:
Sydney -daily
Melbourne -daily
Vancouver -daily
Los Angeles - Mon, Wed, Thurs, Sat.
United Airlines (Ph: 800-241-6522) fly to Honolulu from:
Los Angeles -daily
San Francisco - daily
Chicago - daily
New York -daily
Canadian Airlines (Ph: 426 7000) flies to Honolulu from:
Montreal -daily

Toronto - daily
Vancouver -Friday
Air New Zealand (Ph: 262 1234) flies to Honolulu from:
Los Angeles -Monday, Wednesday, Thursday
Saturday, Sunday
Vancouver -daily except Monday
Auckland -daily
Christchurch -daily

Tourist Information

Hawaii Visitors' Bureau, Suite 801, Waikiki Business Plaza, 2270 Kalakaua Avenue, Honolulu, Ph 923 1811, Fax 922 8991.

'**Guide to Oahu'** is a free magazine, published every Friday, which has a wealth of information, special offers and coupons.

Accommodation

It is estimated tha there are 36,000 accommodation units in the 5 sq km of coastline that inlcudes Waikiki Beach, so it is logical to assume that the number of units on the whole island should be able to accommodate every visitor at any time. Amazingly, it is still a wise move to book your accommodation before you leave home.

Here we offer a selection of hotels with prices in $US for a standard double room per night, which should be used as a guide only.

Waikiki area

Halekulani, 2199 Kalia Road, ph 923 2311, fax 926 8004 - 456 units, restaurants, cocktail lounge, swimming pool - from $265.
Diamond Head Beach Hotel, 2947 Kalakaua Avenue, ph 922 3861, fax 924 1982 - 56 units - $190-210.
Hyatt Regency Waikiki, 2424 Kalakaua Ave, ph 923-1234, fax 923-7839 - 1230 units, restaurant, lounge, pool - $180-210.
Hilton Hawaiian Village, 2005 Kalia Road, ph 949 4321, fax 947 7898 - 2543 units, restaurants, cocktail lounge, swimming pool - $155-240.
Hawaiian Regent, 2552 Kalakaua Avenue, ph 922 6611, fax 921 5222 - 1346 units, restaurants, cocktail lounge, swimming pools - $185-$260.

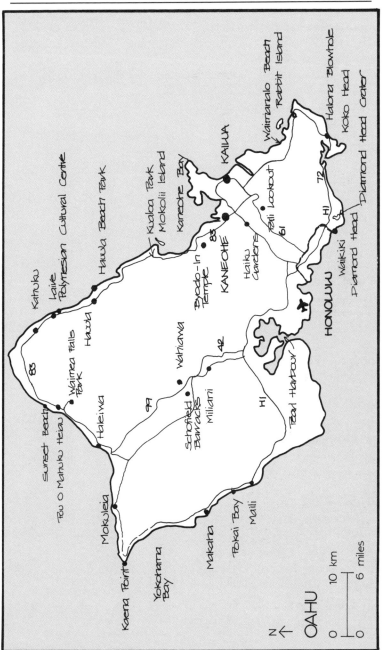

OAHU

N ←

0 ___ 10 km
0 ___ 6 miles

Kaena Point
Mokuleia
Yokohama Bay
Makaha
Pokai Bay
Maili
Pearl Harbour
H1
Schofield Barracks
Mililani
Wahiawa
42
99
Haleiwa
Waimea Falls Park
Haleiwa
85
Sunset Beach
Pu O Mahuka Heiau
Kahuku
Laie
Polynesian Cultural Centre
Hauula Beach Park
Hauula
Kualoa Park
Mokolii Island
Kaneohe Bay
Byodo-In Temple
83
KANEOHE
Haiku Gardens
Pali Lookout
61
KAILUA
Waimanalo Beach
Rabbit Island
Halona Blowhole
Koko Head
Diamond Head Crater
Diamond Head
Waikiki
HONOLULU
H1
72

Hawaiian Waikiki Beach Hotel, 2570 Kalakaua Avenue, ph 922 2511, fax 923 2656 - 715 units, restaurants, cocktail lounge, swimming pool - $138-$212.

Coconut Plaza Hotel, 450 Lewers Street, ph 923 8828, fax 923 3473 - 80 units, restaurant, cocktail lounge - $95.

The Breakers Hotel, 250 Beachwalk, ph 923 3181, fax 923 7174 - 64 units, swimming pool - $91-$97.

Royal Garden Hotel, 440 Olohana Street, ph 943 0202, fax 946 8777 - 230 units, restaurant, cocktail lounge, swimming pool - $130-$180.

Aloha Surf Hotel, 444 Kanekapolei Street, ph 923 5532, fax 924 7160 - 9 units, restaurant, swimming pool - $80-$89.

Ilima Hotel, 445 Nohonani Street, ph 923 1877, fax 924 8371 - 99 units, restaurant, cocktail lounge, swimming pool - $85-154

Hawaiian Monarch Hotel, 444 Niu Street, ph 922 9700, fax 922 2421 - 439 units, restaurant, swimming pool - $98-119.

Hawaii Polo Inn, 1696 Ala Moana Boulevard, ph 949 0061, fax 949 4906 - 57 units, snack shop, swimming pool - $65-95.

Royal Grove Hotel, 151 Uluniu Avenue, 923 7691, fax 922 7508 - 85 units, swimming pool - $43-85.

Outrigger Hobron, 343 Hobron Lane, Honolulu, ph 688 7444, Cocktail lounge, swimming pool - $65-85.

Outrigger Waikiki Surf, 2200 Kuhio Ave, Honolulu, ph 688 7444, - cocktail lounge, swimming pool - $65-85.

Honolulu area

Executive Centre Hotel, 1088 Bishop Street, ph 539 3000, fax 523 1088 - 106 units, restaurant, swimming pool - $125-$165.

Pagoda Hotel, 1525 Rycroft Street, ph 941 6611, fax 955 5067 - 362 units, restaurant, cocktail lounge, swimming pool - $85.

Airport area

Best Western The Plaza Hotel, 3253 N. Nimitz Highway, Honolulu, ph 836 3636, fax 834 7406 - 274 units, restaurant, cocktail lounge, swimming pool - $96-$108.

Pacific Marina Inn, 2628 Waiwai Lp, Honolulu, ph 836 1131, fax 833 0851 - 117 units, restaurant, cocktail lounge, - $74.

North Shore

Rodeway Inn Hukilau Resort, 55-109 Laniloa Street, Laie, ph 293

9282, fax 293 8115 - 48 units, swimming pool - $74-84.

Turtle Bay Hilton Golf & Tennis Resort, Kahuku (PO Box 187), ph 293 8811, fax 293 9147 - 485 units, restaurant, cocktail lounge, swimming pool, golf course, tennis courts - $210-$250.

Hostels

Backpackers Vacation Inn & Plantation Village, 59-788 Kamehameha Highway, Haleiwa, ph 638 7838, fax 638 7515 - 20 units - dormitory room $12-$16 per person.

Honolulu International AYH Hostel, 2323A Seaview Avenue, Honolulu, ph 946 0591, fax 946 5904 - 40 beds - $12 for AYH and IYHF members, $15 for non-members.

Package Tours

Package tours are an economical way of visiting Hawaii, or anywhere else for that matter. The tour companies, because of their buying power, can arrange special prices with airlines, hotel chains, hire car outles, shuttle services, etc. They also have local representatives, which is an asset if you find yourself in need of a helping hand.

Packages to Hawaii can involve spending all the available time on one island, usually Oahu, or you can be a bit more adventurous and arrange a few days on two or three of the other islands. Ask your travel agent for advice, or read the holiday and travel sections in the newspapers. Make sure you shop around to get the best value for your holiday dollar.

Hawaii is also a good place to break the long flight from the US to Australia/New Zealand, or vice versa, and three to five day stopovers can be arranged whichever airline you are using, including inexpensive accommodation and transfers from the airport.

Local Transport

The Honolulu International Airport is located 13km (8 miles) from Waikiki, about 30 minutes by taxi. If you are an independent traveller, taxi is one way to get to your hotel, but it's expensive, the ride to Waikiki averaging abot US$20, with a 30c charge per suitcase, plus a tip. For pick-up ring 836 0011.

Other choices are:

* Terminal Transportation, ph 836 0317, have a service from the airport to Waikiki for $7.

* Gray Line. The most obvious buses at the airport, because of their large 'Airporter' signs, and their 40ft length, Gray Line buses run from the Airport to Waikiki every 20 minutes from the main terminal. The service to the Airport is every hour.

* The city bus for only $1.00, but you are only allowed one case, which must fit on your lap.

* A pick-up service organised by your hotel. Check to see if you are entitled to this service.

City Buses

Simply called The Bus, this is the best way for getting around. The fare is $1.00 per adult, 50c per youth, and no charge for children 5 or under when accompanied by an adult, from anywhere to anywhere, as long as you keep going in the same direction. Request a free transfer when boarding the bus for each fare paid if more than one bus is to be used during one continuous trip.

The buses display route numbers and destinations above the driver. You enter through the front door and deposit the exact fare, in coins, in the box. The driver does not carry change.

When you wish to alight, signal the driver to stop by pulling the cord along the windows, or by pushing the yellow strip. Exit is through the centre door after the green light appears.

For bus information ph 848 5555, between 5.30am - 10pm.

Waikiki Trolley

An open trolley leaves from the Royal Hawaiian Shopping Centre every thirty minutes for a ninety minute ride through Waikiki, the Ala Moana area and downtown. The conductor doubles as the narrator, and points out places of interest, shops, restaurants and entertainment spots along the way. The trolley operates daily 8am-4.30pm, and an all day pass costs $17 adults, $5 children under 12, ph 596-2199.

Car Rental

If you are travelling in the peak holiday seasons (August, Christmas/New Year, February) it is wise to pre-book a hire car, because although there are plenty to choose from, there are plenty of visitors as well. Here are some names and addresses.

Alamo Rent A Car (reservations 800-327-9633), 3049 Ualena Street, Honolulu, ph 836 6000, fax 833 7897; 3055 N. Nimitz Highway, Honolulu, ph 833 4585, fax 834 0031; 142 Uluniu Street, Honolulu, ph 924 444; 2164 Kalia Road, Honolulu, ph 923 3337.

Avis Rent-A-Car (reservations 800-331-1212), Outrigger East Hotel, 148 Kaiulani Avenue, ph 917 3700; Honolulu International Airport, ph 834 5564; 2002 Kalakaua Avenue, Honolulu, ph 973 2610; Hilton Hawaiian Village, 2005 Kalia Road, Honolulu, ph 973-2624.

Budget Rent-A-Car (reservations 800-527-0700), Honolulu International Airport; Waikiki - 1837 Ala Moana Boulevard; 2379 Khuio Avenue; 2301 Kalakaua Avenue; 2424 Kalakaua Avenue; 2169 Kalia Road.

Dollar Rent-A-Car (reservations 944 1544), 1600 Kapiolani Boulevard, Suite 825, ph 926 4242; Honolulu International Airport, ph 831 2331; 1958 Kalakaua Avenue, Waikiki, ph 926 4264.

Hertz Rent-A-Car (reservations), 233 Kaewe Street, Suite 625, ph 523 5181; 2424 Kalakaua Avenue, Honolulu, ph 971 3535; Honolulu International Airport, ph 831 3500.

Aloha Funway Rentals, ph 946 2766, have mopeds and motorcycles for hire, and Island Scooters, ph 924 9331 have bicycles.

Distance and Driving Time from Waikiki to:

Downtown Honolulu -	6km (4 miles), 15 minutes.
Pali Lookout -	14km (9 miles), 20 minutes.
Laie (via Pali) -	61km (38 miles), 1 hour 15 minutes.
Pearl Harbour -	18km (11 miles), 25 minutes
Makaha -	58km (36 miles), 1 hour.
Hanauma Bay (via Kalanianaole Highway) -	
	13km (8 miles), 20 minutes.
Makapuu Point -	19km (12 miles), 30 minutes.

Kailua Junction (via Kalanianaole Highway) -
                    34km (21 miles), 50 minutes.
Circle Trip from Waikiki around Koko Head and return by Pali
                    56km (35 miles), 1 hour 15 minutes.
Circle Trip from Waikiki via Pali and return by Laie and Wahiawa
                    135km (84 miles), 3 hours 30 minutes.

Eating Out

There are over 1,000 restaurants on Oahu, and probably one or two in your hotel, but following are a few recommendations, rated by the price of a main course: expensive - $21 and over, moderate - $16-$20, inexpensive - $11-$15, budget - $10 and under.

American

Perry's Smorgy Restaurants, Outrigger Coral Seas Hotel, 250 Lewers St. Honolulu, ph 923 3881 - open for breakfast, brunch, lunch and dinner - buffets and salads - inexpensive.

Tapa Cafe, Hilton Hawaiian Village, Tapa Tower, 2005 Kalia Road, Honolulu, ph 949 4321 - indoor/outdoor dining for breakfast, lunch, dinner, cocktails - moderate.

Orchids, Halekulani, 2199 Kalia Road, Honolulu, ph 923 2311 - great food and spectacular views - open for breakfast, brunch, lunch, dinner, cocktails - expensive, all major cards.

Mezzanine Restaurant, Waikiki Terrace Hotel, 2045 Kalakaua Avenue, ph 951 2511 - a range of pastas with unique sauces - open for breakfast, lunch, dinner, cocktails - moderate.

Hard Rock Cafe, 1837 Kapiolani Boulevard, Honolulu, ph 955 7383 - open for lunch, dinner and cocktails - inexpensive.

Oriental

Wo Fat Restaurant (Hawaii's oldest restaurant, opened in 1882), 115 North Hotel Street, ph 537 6260 - good food plus souvenir T-shirts and chopsticks - open for lunch and dinner - budget.

Hee Hing Restaurant, Hee Hing Plaza, 449 Kapahulu Avenue, Waikiki, ph 735 5544 - Hong Kong style cuisine - open for Dim Sum, lunch and dinner - budget. Major credit cards accepted, large open style.

Dynasty II Restaurant, Ward Warehouse, 2nd floor, 1050 Ala

Moana Boulevard, Honolulu, ph 596 0208 - award-winning cuisine - picturesque sunset view over Kewalo basin - open for lunch and dinner - moderate.

Golden Dragon, Hilton Hawaiian Village, Rainbow Tower, 2005 Kalia Road, Honolulu, ph 946-5336 - award winning Cantonese cuisine overlooking Hilton Lagoon - open for dinner and cocktails - moderate.

Italian

Pasta Festival, Hilton Hawaiian Village, 2005 Kalia Road, Honolulu, ph 949 4321 - casual indoor/outdoor dining - open for dinner and cocktails - inexpensive.

Salerno Italian Restaurant, McCully Shopping Centre, 1960 Kapiolani Boulevard #204, Honolulu, ph 942 5273 - food recommended- open for lunch and dinner - moderate.

Ciao! An Italian Restaurant, Sheraton Waikiki, 2255 Kalakaua Avenue, Honolulu, ph 922 4422 - excellent food and decor - open for dinner - moderate.

Sergio's, Ilima Hotel, 445 Nohonan Street, Honolulu, ph 926 3388, seafood specialty, open for dinner.

Luaus

Polynesian Cultural Centre, 55-370 Kamehameha Highway, Laie, ph 367-7060 - buffet dinner with dishes from seven different Polynesian Nations - expensive.

Paradise Cove Luau, Ko Olina Resort at West Beach, ph 973-5828 - authentic Hawaiian foods - expensive.

Sheraton's Spectacular Polynesian Revue, Sheraton Princess Kaiulani Hotel, 120 Kaiulani Avenue, Honolulu, ph 971 5305 - two dinner/cocktail shows nightly - expensive.

International

Hula Hut Showroom, 286 Beachwalk, Honolulu, ph 923 8411 - reat international buffet with live entertainment - open dinner and cocktails - expensive.

Maile Room, Kahala Hilton, 500 Kahala Avenue, ph 734 2211 - evening entertainment by well-known Hawaiian Danny Kaleikini - open for breakfast, brunch, lunch, dinner, cocktails - expensive.

Ship's Tavern, Sheraton Moana Surfrider, 2365 Kalakaua

Avenue, Honolulu, ph 922 3111 - excellent food, magnificent setting - open dinner, cocktails - expensive.

Cascada, Royal Garden at Waikiki, 440 Olohana Street, Honolulu, ph 943 0202 - popular restaurant with creative cuisine - open lunch, dinner and cocktails - moderate.

Ocean Terrace, Sheraton Waikiki Hotel, 2255 Kalakaua Avenue, Honolulu, ph 922 4422 - arguably the best buffet in town - a la carte menu as well - open breakfast, lunch, dinner and cocktails - expensive.

Mala Restaurant, Ocean Resort Hotel, Waikiki, 175 Paoakalani Avenue, Honolulu, ph 922 3861 - good selection of hot and cold dishes, plus sandwiches, etc - open breakfasts, lunch, dinner and cocktails - budget.

Steak & Seafood

Duke's Canoe Club - Waikiki, Outrigger Waikiki Hotel, 2335 Kalakaua Avenue, Honolulu - open-air beachside setting featuring great seafood - open for breakfast, lunch, dinner, late supper and cocktails - moderate.

Monetary Bay Canners Fresh Seafood Restaurant & Oyster Bar, Outrigger Waikiki Hotel, 2nd Floor, Oceanview, 2335 Kalakaua Avenue, Honolulu, ph 922 5761 - fresh seafood specials daily - open for breakfast 7.00-11.30am; lunch 11.30am-4.30pm; dinner 5.00-10.00pm; cocktail lounge 7am-1am - moderate.

The Village Steak & Seafood, Hilton Hawaiian Village, Tapa Tower, 2005 Kalia Road, Honolulu, ph 949 4321 - grill room to tempt tastebuds - open for dinner and cocktails - inexpensive.

Sizzler Restaurants, 1945 Kalakaua Avenue, Honolulu (and 12 others state-wide), ph 955 4069 - open for breakfast, lunch and dinner - budget.

Fast Food

McDonald's, Burger King and Domino's Pizza are well represented, and Pizza Hut can be found in Waikiki Shopping Plaza and at 2301 Kuhio Avenue, Honolulu. I that that is enough in this category.

Entertainment

There is plenty to do in Downtown Honolulu when the sun goes down.

Bars, Discos

Waikiki/Honolulu

Bobby McGee's, 2885 Kalakaua Avenue, ph 922 1282 - disco for rages 21-30 nightly 7pm-2am.

Esprit, Sheraton Waikiki Hotel, 2255 Kalakaua Avenue, ph 922 4422 - nightly live entertainment and dancing.

Jazz Cellar, 205 Lewers Street, ph 923 9952 - cheap drinks on Monday and live rock every night - music from 9pm-4am, happy hour 2-4am!

Maile Lounge, Kahala Hilton, 5000 Kahala Avenue, ph 734 2211 - the same band has been playing here for over 15 years, so they must be doing something right - open Tues-Sat 8pm-1am.

Rumours, Ala Moana Hotel, 410 Atkinson Street, ph 955 4811 - video and disco dancing Wed-Fri 5pm-2am, Sat 8pm-4am. Sun has ballroom dancing 5-9pm.

Wave Waikiki, 1877 Kalakaua Avenue, ph 941 0424 - live dance music 9pm - 1.30am, then recorded music until 4am - for the young.

Honolulu

Studebaker's, 500 Ala Moana Boulevard, Honolulu, ph 531 8444. Has complimentary Happy Hour Buffet, and features 50s and 60s music with entertainment. Open Mon-Sat 11am-2am, Sun noon-2am.

Dinner/Cocktail Shows

If you are interested in seeing a show, but not interested in having dinner at the same place (which is generally in the 'expensive' range), you can book for a cocktail show. These usually costs slightly more than half the price of the dinner show, and include one cocktail, tax and gratuity. Bookings are essential for both options.

Brothers Cazimero, Monarch Room, Royal Hawaiian Hotel, 2259 Kalakaua Avenue, ph 923 7311 - traditional and modern Hawaiian music with hula dancers - dinner show Tues-Sat 8.30pm, cocktail show Fri-Sat 10.30pm.

Charo, Tropics Surf Club, Hilton Hawaiian Village, 2005 Kalia Road, ph 949 4321 - a mixture of Latin and Hawaiian music - dinner 6.30pm, cocktails 7.30pm, show 8.00pm.

Don Ho, Hula Hut Theatre Restaurant, 286 Beachwalk, ph 923 8411 - South Pacific show featuring the "King of Hawaiian Entertainment" - dinner Sun-Fri 8pm, cocktails 8.30pm, show 9.00pm.

The Krush, Polynesian Palace, Outrigger Hotel, 247 Lewers Street, ph 924 8844 - Broadway show songs, jazz and pop Tues-Sat 10.30pm and midnight.

Polynesian Cultural Centre, 55-370 Kamehameha highway, Laie, ph 293 3333 - an entertaining display featuring students from the Brigham Young University's Hawaii campus - dinner served from 4.30pm for the show at 7.30pm - Jan-March and June-August ther are two shows, 6.00pm and 7.45pm.

Society of Seven, Main Showroom of the OUtigger Waikiki Hotel, 2335 Kalakaua Avenue, ph 923 7311 - one of the best known happenings in Honolulu - showtimes are 8.30pm and 10.30pm Mon-Sat, with Wed 8.30pm only.

Dinner Cruises

I think everyone will agree that dinner cruises the world over fall into the 'expensive' category, but some of the following would be more in the 'super-expensive' category if we had one. Make sure you enquire about the costs when making the booking.

Aikane Catamarans, 677 Ala Moana Boulevard, ph 522 1533 - dinner cruises depart 5.15pm, moonlight sails 7.45pm

Alii Kai Catamarans, Peir 8, street level, Honolulu, ph 524 6694 - departs nightly at 5.30pm

Hawaiian Cruises, ph 852 4183 - departs nightly at 5.30pm

Star of Honolulu, 350 Ward Avenue, ph 334 6191 - different prices on different decks.

Windjammer Cruises, 2222 Kalakaua Avenue, ph 922 1200 - buffet or deluxe dining - entertainment and dancing.

Shopping

People have been known to visit Honolulu simply to shop, and while I don't fall into this category, I have to admit that it would be possible to spend a few days in this occupation. All the big hotels have groups of shops, and it is worthwhile checking these out.

A must is the Aloha Flea Market at the Aloha Stadium carpark on weekends from 7.30am-3.00pm. You can drive to the market, or travel by the Aloha Flea Market Shuttle, whose coaches have large baggage compartments to take your purchases on the return trip.

For information on boarding and schedules, ph 955 4050.

There are several large shopping complexes in Honolulu:

The Royal Hawaiian Shoping Center, 2201 Kalakaua Avenue, Waikiki, ph 922 0588 - open Mon-Sat 9am-10pm, Sun 9am-9pm. This centre has over 150 stores and services on three levels. Shops range from up-market fashion, such as Chanel and Louis Vuitton, to local outlets like Little Hawaiian Craft Shop and Royal Hawaiian Gems.

The Waikiki Shopping Plaza, 2270 Kalakaua Avenue, ph 923 1191, opposite the Royal Hawaiian, has some good clothing shops.

International Market Place, 2330 Kalakaua Avenue, ph 923 9871, is open daily 9am-11pm and has a plethora of souvenir stalls.

Ala Moana Shopping Center, 1450 ala Moana Boulevard, Honolulu, ph 946 2811 - ope 9.30am-9pm. This is one of the largest outdoor shopping malls in the US, and indeed, in the world. Department stores include Americans Sears and J.C. Penney, with Neiman-Marcus on the drawing board, and the Japanese Shirokiya that is an experience in itself.

Liberty House, ph 941 2345, very popular fro stylish Hawaiian wear, is represented in the centre as are Hawaiian Island Creations, ph 941 4491, and Irene's Hawaiian Gifts, ph 946 6818. In all there are over 200 stores, and the largest international food court.

Ward Warehouse, 1050 Ala Moana Boulevard, ph 591-8411, Honolulu, 531 6411, has 60 specialty shops and 8 restaurants, many with boat harbour views. If you are after casual shoes, try Thongs 'N Things while you are here.

Pearl Ridge Shopping Center, 98-211 Pali Momi, ph Honolulu, is open daily 10am-9pm, and has a monorail between buildings.

Kahala Mall, 4211 Waiwlae Avenue, ph 732 7736, near the slopes of Diamond Head, is in the residential area of Kahala. It has branches of good clothing stores, such as Liberty House and Reyn's. The mall also has eight cinema's.

Following are a few old favourite haunts.

Clothing

Hilo Hattie, 700 Nimitz Highway, advertise they are open 8.30am-5pm, 365 days a year. You can watch skilled workers turn tropical print fabrics into quality aloha wear for the entire family. They also sell souvenirs, Hawaii videos and books, floral perfumes, tropical jams and candies, jewellery, purss and hats. There is a free Hilo Hattie Bus to and from Waikiki. Ph 524 3966 for information.

Liberty House has many shops on Oahu and on the other islands as well. They offer Aloha Shirts and Muumuus as well as high fashion items and resort wear.

Leather Goods

Leather of the Sea, 2275 Kalakaua Avenue, Suite 1007, ph 971 1300, are the "World's Largest Wholesaler of Eel Skin Products." Their showroom has golfbags, wallets, shoes, puses, briefcases, portfolios and other eel, snake and lizard skin products. Open Mon-Sat.

Chinatown

Unlike the Chinatowns in other American cities, this section of downtown Honolulu is a blend of shops, restaurants and market displaying not only Chinese goods, but wares and foods typical of the countries of origin of Hawaii's early-day immigrants.

Bounded by Ala Moana Boulevard/N. Nimitz Highway, Nuuanu Avenue, Vineyard Boulevard and the Kapalama Canal, Chinatown's 15-block area is packed with places of interest. It is 10 minutes from Waikiki by City Bus No. 2, or take the Waikiki Trolley to Stop No. 14. If you drive yourself, there is plenty of parking.

Sightseeing

Downtown Honolulu

Unlike any other city in the United States, Honolulu has a history of kings, queens and a palace, and all the associated intrigue. Some of the history can be explored on a walking tour of this area.

Iolani Palace

Completed in 1882, the building is the only royal palace on American soil, and was home and seat for the last two monarchs. It has been entirely renovated, displaying a magnificent interior. Palace tours are conducted Wed-Sat, 9am-2.15pm, and cost $4.00 adults, $1.00 children. For reservations, ph 522 0832.

Iolani Barracks

Originally situated on Hotel Street, the barracks were moved brick by brick in 1965 to its present position in the palace grounds. It was here that the Royal Guards had its headquarters and home from 1871 to 1893.

Coronation Pavilion

The Royal Hawaiian Band plays each Friday at 12.15pm in this small round bandstand. It was originally built in 1883.

King Kamehameha Statue

Located on the ocean side of the Palace, the statue of Hawaii's most loved king, who unified the Hawaiian kingdom, shows him holding a barbed spear in his left hand as a symbol of peace. His right arm is outstretched in a gesture of 'aloha'.

Kawaiahao Church

Dedicated in 1842, the 'Westminster Abbey' of Hawaii offers Sunday services in Hawaiian and English. The church is on S. King Street.

Mission Houses Museum

The oldest existing buildings erected by the first missionary contingent to Honolulu are in the civic centre area. Open to the public daily except Monday. Admission is $5.00 adults, $1 children.

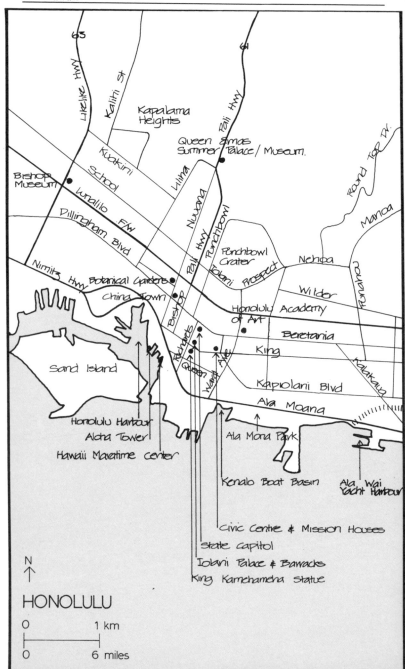

HONOLULU

0 — 1 km

0 — 6 miles

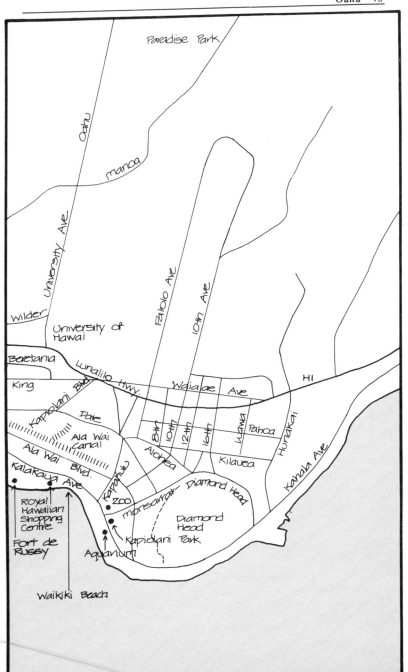

State Capitol

Located directly behind the Iolani Palace, this $24.5m building is the centre of Hawaii's political power. The architectural design shows the state's volcanic and oceanic origins.

Washington Place

The residence of Queen Liliuokalani until her death in 1917, the building is now the hom of Hawaii's governors. It is the oldest continuously occupied house on Oahu, having been built in 1846.

St Andrew's Cathedral

Situated on Queen Emma Street, the Cathedral is an English-Norman styled church that was built in 1867 largely due to the conversion and support of Queen Emma and King Kamehameha IV.

Aloha Tower

Built in 1926, this 10-storey tower was once Hawaii's tallest building. It is still the official maritime signal point and the state's harbour headquarters. The tower is open to visitors and offers an excellent view of the harbour area.

Hawaii Maritime Center

Situated at Honolulu's Pier 7, the complex includes the $6m Kalakaua Boathouse, a two-storey exhibition of shipping, fishing, surfing, whales, and other marine objects. The center also has two museum ships: the Hokule'a, a performance-accurate Polynesian voyaging canoe that serves as the flagship for a canoe display; and the Falls of Clyde, one of the world's last four masted, full-rigged sailing vessels. Open daily 9am-5pm. Admission is $7 adults, $4 children, ph 536 6373.

Foster Botanic Garden

On the corner of Vineyard Boulevard and Nuuanu Avenue, in a 8ha (20 acre) setting, the garden features an orchid section, prehistoric plant area and a special collection of palms. Admission is $1.00 adults.

Midtown Honolulu

Midtown is bounded by the ocean, Ward Avenue, Beretania Avenue and Kalakaua Avenue and the Ala Wai Canal. it is the centre of communications and shopping.

In this area are the Ala Moana Shopping Center and teh Ward Warehouse Shopping Center, and The Bus terminal at Ala Moana is the busiest on Oahu.

Ala Moana Park
Ala Moana is the most popular city beach of Honolulu because of its safe swimming areas, but the sand is very coarse. It is a man-made beach. In the total area of 31ha (76 acres) there are jogging paths, picnic tables, tennis courts, a bowling green and softball fields. Nearby are the Aina Moana Park, also known as Magic Island, and the Ala Wai Yacht Harbour.

Honolulu Academy of Arts
Built in 1927 and accredited by the American Association of Museums, the Academy is internationally renowned for its extensive collection of Asian and Western Art, and the beauty of its grounds and buildings. It is a registered national and state historic place. Located at 900 South Beretania Street, the Academy is open Tues-Sat, 10am-4pm, Sun 1-5pm. There are free tours Tues, Wed, Fri, Sat at 11am, Thurs 2pm and Sun 1pm, and there is no entrance fee. For information ph 538 1006/3693.

Kewalo Boat Basin
It is from here that the tour boats set off for cruises to Diamond Head and Pearl Harbour. Nearby are the John Dominis and Fisherman's Wharg restaurants.

Waikiki
Although we think of Waikiki Beach, it is actually a series of beaches, stretching from Duke Kahanamoku Beach in the west to Sans Souci Beach at the Diamond Head end of Kalakaua Avenue. Swimming is good for almost the entire length of the beach, except near the Kapahulu Wall. Keep in mind, though, that these are not the great surfing beaches of Hawaii, there were no waves when I was there.

Waikiki Aquarium

At 2777 Kalakaua Avenue across from Kapiolani Park. A top attraction for visitors, the Aquarium contains a world famous collection of tropical fish. Open daily 9am-5pm, admission is $6.00 adults, children under 15 free, ph 923 9741.

Kapiolani Park

The 88ha (220 acre) park separates Waikiki from the residential area on the south-west of Diamond Head. The Kodak Hula Show, which has been entertaining visitors since 1937, is presented here Tues-Thurs at 10am. There is no admission fee.

Honolulu Zoo

The zoo is at 151 Kapahulu Avenue and is open daily 8.30am-4.30pm. Entry is $3.00 adults, children free ph 971 7174, or 971 7171 (recording). Along with the usual lions, elephants, etc. there are some rare creatures, native to Hawaii, whose ancestors greeted the first settlers.

Fort DeRussy Army Museum

The US Army Museum at Fort DeRussy has ancient Hawaiian weapons as well as weapons and uniforms used by the US forces in campaigns from the Spanish-American War to the Korean War. There are also enlargements of the Honolulu newspapers from the early days of the US involvement in World War II after the invasion of Pearl Harbour. The museum is open Tues-Sun, 10am-4.30pm, and there is no entry fee. Tours by appointment, ph 438 2819/2821.

In the Regional Visitor Center, Fort DeRussy, there is a free exhibition/media show of Pacific life - Tues-Sun, 10am-4.30pm, ph 438 2815.

Diamond Head

Christened by British sailors who mistook the calcite crystals they discovered for diamonds, Diamond Head is one of the most recognisable characteristics of Hawaii. The Hawaiian name for this ancient volcano was Leahi, 'brow of an ahi' probably because its silhouette resembles the profile of the ahi (tuna). Whichever you like to call it, in the sunlight it does seem to sparkle with diamonds.

Diamond Head is a National Natural Landmark and a state

monument. Within its crater is a park and a one-mile hiking trail, which leads to a spectacular 232m (760 ft) summit view of Honolulu and the ocean. From Waikiki take the Beach bus east to the corner of Kahala Avenue and Diamond Head Road, and follow the sign posts.

Since 1982, the Clean Air Team has conducted excursions to the summit of Diamond Head. You can meet the team's volunteer leaders at the entrance to Honolulu Zoo every Saturday at 9am. A small flashlight is recommended for the tunnel along the ascent. Adults are asked to make a $3 donation.

Honolulu

Greater Honolulu and Pearl Harbour

Pearl Harbour

Pearl Harbour and the USS Arizona Memorial are among the most visited attractions in Hawaii. The local Department of Business and Economic development states that over 1.8 million people visit this historic site yearly.

Even if you are not old enough to remember the horrific attack on Pearl Harbour by the Japanese on December 7, 1941, bringing the United States into World War II, you will still be impressed with the Arizona Memorial, which is built over the ship's hull. To stand on the memorial and watch the fish swim around the rusting hill, knowing that the bodies of many sailors were never recovered, despite several attempts,cannot fail to move even the 'been there, done that' type of visitor.

A visit includes an historical film and shuttle trip to the Memorial and tickets are available on a first-come, first-served basis from 8.00am-3pm. The visitor centre is open 7.30am-5pm, closed Thanksgiving, Christmas and New Year's Day. Admission if free, ph 422 0561. Please note that, for reasons of safety children under 114cm (45 in) are not allowed on the shuttle or the Memorial.

There are also many cruises available to Pearl Harbour and the *Arizona*, but these, while extremely comfortable and offering cocktails and snacks on board, do not allow you to board the Memorial, they sail around it.

Moored near the Memorial ground facility and open for inspection, is the preserved USS *Bowfin*, the WWII submarine credited with sinking 44 enemy ships. The Pearl Harbour Submarine Museum is open for visitors daily 8am-5pm, and the tour costs $10 adults, $5 children.

For information on USS *Bowfin* and the Submarine Base Museum, ph 423 1341.

Bishop Museum and Planetarium

At 12525 Bernice Street, the museum houses the world's foremost collection of Hawaiiana and Polynesian antiquities. It was founded in 1889 by Charles R. Bishop, husband of Princess Bernice Pauaki, to house the royal possessions of the last direct descendent of King

Kamehameha the Great. The collection has been added to over the years and is very well respected. Open daily 9am-5pm, and entry is $7.95 adult, $6.95 children 6-17, ph 847 3511. Take Bus 2 from Waikiki, alight at the Kamehameha Shopping Centre, and Bernice Street is one block towards the ocean.

Queen Emma's Summer Palace
Situated at 2913 Pali Highway in the Nuuana Valley, the palace was built for Queen Emma, wife of Kamehameha IV, as a cool retreat in the late 1800s. Now it is a museum displaying period artefacts. Admission is $4.00 adults, and for information ph 595 3167

Nuuanu Pali Lookout
The Lookout is the site of King Kamehameha's rout of his enemies in the battle that established him as ruler of all the islands. From Waikiki take the H-1 West Freeway, then take the Pali Highway turn off (Exit 21B). A few kilometres further on, turn right just before the Pali tunnel.

The Punchbowl (The National Memorial Cemetery of the Pacific)
Located at 2177 Puowaina Drive, know to the ancient Hawaiians as Puowaina (Hill of Sacrifice) the cemetery is located in the Punchbowl Crater. Over 26,000 American servicemen and women from four wars are buried here, and the names of 26,280 others missing in action are listed on marble walls called the Court of the Missing. There are special ceremonies held here on Memorial Day and Veterans' Day, and a dawn service is held on Easter Sunday.

There is a very good views from the Punchbowl of Pearl Harbour, Honolulu and Waikiki.The cemetery is open daily 8am-6.30pm. For information ph 546 3190.

Manoa Valley and Paradise Park
Manoa Road runs the entire length of Manoa Valley. At its south end is the Punahou School, built in 1841 for the children of the missionaries. Further up the valley, a left side road leads to the Waioli Tea Room, which is run by the Salvation Army, and was the model for Robert Louis Stevenson's 'Little Grass Shack'.

At the northern end of Manoa Road is Paradise Park, a 6ha (15 acre) garden set in a rainforest. Visitors can explore ancient Hau and bamboo trails and ethnic gardens. There are also hundreds of tropical flowers and birds. The internationally famous \Dancing Waters and the entertaining Animal Quackers Duck Show are held here. Open daily from 10am-5pm, entry fee is $7.50 adults, $6.50 juniors (13-17) and $3.75 children (4-12).

For information ph 988 2141.

South-East Oahu

Hanauma Bay

Located in Koko Head Park, the Bay is an extinct volcano crater which has been flooded by the ocean. Legend says the volcanic action 10,000 years ago was caused when Pele, the Fire Goddess, made her last attempt to find a home on Oahu. The bay is a state marine conservation area. Consequently, no fishing is allowed, which make for very friendly fish and excellent snorkelling. Elvis Presley fans will recognise the scenery from the movie *Blue Hawaii*.

Halona Blowhole

Best viewed from the lookout on Kalanianaole Highway near Koko Head Crater. Miniature geysers are formed by the ocean forcing though a tiny hole in the lava edge. Near here is the small beach where Deborah Kerr and Burt Lancaster frolicked(?) in From *Here to Eternity*.

Makapuu Beach

The most popular body-surfing beach on Oahu, Makapuu is out of bounds for surf boards. The huge waves, however, can be deadly in winter, and it is recommended that only experienced surfers tackle them even in summer.

Sea Life Park Hawaii

Located at Makapuu Point, Sea Life Park is Hawaii's premier marine park. It has more than 4000 forms of marine life, and features water shows with dolphins, penguins and seals; the Hawaii Ocean Theatre, whalers Cove, Hawaiian Reef Tank; Rock Shores Exhibit; Sea Bird Sanctuary; Turtle Lagoon; Sea Lion feeding pool and show; Hawaiian monk seal care centre; Penguin habitat; touch pool; Pacific Whaling Museum; gift shops; and the Sea Lion

Cafe. Open daily 9.30am-5pm (Fri open until 10pm with a Kamaaina Night of music), admission is around $25.00 adults, $10.00 juniors (6-12), $5.00 children (4-5). For information ph 800 767 8046, ph 259 7933.

Waimanalo Beach

The longest continuous beach on Oahu (5km - 3miles), Waimanalo has good surf for beginners in the arts of body and board surfing. The northern end of the bay is part of the Bellows Field United States Air Force Base, and is know as Bellows Beach. This part is only open to the publish on weekends and certain holidays.

Rabbit Island

Near Waimanalo, this is one of the many interesting islets that border Oahu. The islands looks like the head of a rabbit, and was once overrun by the them.

Windward Oahu

Windward Oahu faces the trade winds, and heavy rainfall throughout the year produces forests and jungles.

Kailua

The beach here is good for swimming and windsurfing. The beach park is divided into two by the Kaelepulu Canal.

Kaneohe

There are outstanding coral gardens in Kaneohe Bay, and glass-bottom boat tours leave from Heeia-kea Pier on Kamehameha Highway north of Kaneohe several times daily, ph 247 0375.

Haiku Gardens

This area was once a favourite haunt of the ancient Hawaiians, but now it is a jungle park with a restaurant overlooking grass houses, lily and tropical fish pons and bamboo groves, ph 247 6671.

Byodo-In Temple

Japan's 900-year-old architectural treasure is duplicated in detail at the Valley of the Temples Memorial Park, beneath the cliffs of the Koolau mountains. The oriental garden setting also has a carp pool, a 3m (9 ft) Buddha statue and a tea house. Open 9am-5pm, entry is $2.00 adult, $1 children, ph 239 8811.

Kualoa Regional Park

The beach here is narrow but long and sandy, and is a favourite picnic and swimming spot. From here there is a good view of the mountains and Kaneohe Bay. A few hundred metres offshore is the little island known to Hawaiians as Mokoli'i, but to others as Chinaman's Hat. Legends says that the goddess Hiiaka destroyed Mokoli'i (little lizard) and what can be seen today is all that remains of him. At low tide it is possible to walk out and explore the island.

Sacred Falls

Off the highway near Hauula is a clear stream falling from sheer cliffs to the pool below. Lower falls drop over 27m (87 ft) cliff. Legend has it that the falls are sacred to Kamapuuam, the god of swine, who could change into a pig or man at will.

Hauula Beach Park

There is a large walled-in swimming area here, but the main attraction, for photographers especially, is the beach hibiscus trees. During July and August the trees have yellow blossoms in the morning which gradually turn during the day to russet, then bright red, then they fall. Best seen in the morning, when there is a carpet of red flowers and trees covered in yellow.

Laie

Laie is a settlement of mainly Hawaiian and Samoan Mormons. About 2,400ha (6,000 acres) in this area have been a church project since 1864. They include the town of Laie, the Polynesian Cultural Center, a lodge and restaurant, a branch campus of Brigham Young University, and the Mormon Temple. This temple, built in 1920 was the first Mormon Temple to be constructed outside of Salt Lake City.

Polynesian Cultural Center

The Center is made up of native villages representative of those in Fiji, Tonga, New Zealand, Tahiti, Samoa, Marquesas and Hawaii.

The 17ha (42 acres) complex advertises that it has been the number one visitor attraction for over 25 years. (I think that may be true if you do not count Pearl Harbour.) There are lagoons, waterfalls and lush tropical flora,and when the sun goes down there are Polynesian buffets and revues on an open air stage replete with a cliff backdrop and fountains for curtains.

General admission is $25 adults, $13 children; admission dinner 'mana' evening show package with Laie tour, walking, tram shuttle and canoe tours, band concert - $45 adults, $25 children; Alii Luau Package, including admission, luau, IMAX movie and evening show (instead of Buffet) is around $60 adults, $40 children. For information and reservation, ph 923 2911, 800 367 7060.

North Shore

The North Shore is the area between Kahuku Point, in the north-east corner of the island, and Kaena Point, a rocky cape in the north-west. This is the part of Oahu that is famous for its surfing beaches, and where the championship surf meets are held.

Kahuku

The kahuku Sugar Mill was in operation from 1890 until 1972, and although it no longer processes sugar can it is the main feature of the village. It is now a complex of shops, a museum and displays, with a 'World of Sugar' tour.

Sunset Beach

A 3km sandy beach, averaging 60m (66 yds) wide, is one of the most famous and dangerous on Oahu, and the home of The Pipeline and Banzai Beach. Swimming in the summer away from the lave rock outcrops is quite safe. But in winter it is definitely inviting disaster.

Pupukea Beach Park

Here the coral reef causes a marvellous display of pounding surf in the winter, and forms the walls of tidal pools in the summer. A photographer's dream.

Puu o Mahuka Heiau

On the spur off Pupukea Road is this large ancient temple, which is a national historic landmark and state monument. The walls are up to 158m (520ft) long, and human sacrifices were made here. Legend says that a famous priest forecast that the islands would be overrun by strangers from distant lands. From the temple there is a good view of Waimea Bay, inlet and beach park, and of the square stone belfry of St Peter's and St Paul's Catholic Mission Church.

Waimea Falls Park

A Narrow Canyon extending into the Koolau mountains, this was once a heavily populated hawaiian village. Today, the 727ha (1,800 acres) site between Haleiwa and Kahuku is an unspoiled environment of tropical plant life, roaming animals, hiking trails and 14m (45ft) falls. The park is open daily 10am-5.30pm and entry is $19.95 adults, $9.95 children. There are picnic grounds, a restaurant, diving shows and Hawaiian games and dances.

Twice each month during the full moon, the Park open its gates free to the public for 'Moonwalks', one-hour guided treks to the waterfall and back, offering an opportunity to experience life in an ancient hawaiian valley at night.

Each year during the first weekend in October, the Makahiki Festival is held. This is a two-day celebration with dancing, games and arts and crafts.

For information ph 638 8511 or 923 8448. Take the No.8,9 or 20 bus from Waikiki and transfer to the No.52 Circle Island bus at Ala Moana Shopping Center.

Waimea Bay

The original town of Waimea was destroyed by a flood in 1894, and now there are always more visitors than locals. The falls and park are the main attractions for most, but for experienced surfers the December and January tides with their 9 and 10m waves are the magnets. The official brochures say that swimming when surf is six feet or more is dangerous, which ensures that when the surfers are catching the waves there will be plenty of spectators.

Haleiwa

A mixture of old plantation and fishing village, Haleiwa was invaded by hippies in the late 60s and early 70s, but their arrival has not destroyed the charm as a pleasant village. Haleiwa Beach

Park is one of the few beaches on the North Shore where swimming is safe all year round.

Liliuokalani Church

Also known as Waialua Protestant Church, the fifth sanctuary built on the old mission site. In the church is an ancient bell, a memorial archway, and a clock presented by Queen Liliuokalani in 1890, on which the letters of her names are used instead of numbers. The clock also has seven dials and seven hands indicating the months, days of the week, the weeks of the year, the days of the month, and phases of the moon.

Mokuleia

Once the site of a family ranch, this corner of Oahu was the home of the Dilingham Air Force Base, now called the Dilingham Air Field Glider Porter. You can take time out to watch the gliders, or if you are feeling adventurous, you can try gliding yourself. Original Glider Rides - Mr Bill - conduct the sessions. Reservations are not necessary you can just turn up, but if he knows you are coming then you can be assured of getting a ride and of being well looked after. Times are from 10.30am-5.00pm daily, flights leave every twenty minutes. They also last twenty minutes and prices are from $100 for one passenger, $120 total for two passengers. They have been operating for 28 years.

In addition to the Original Glider Rides have a 1941 Vintage Stearman with an open cockpit. The charge is $125 for a 20 minute North Shore run, $175.00 for a 40 minute run into Pearl Harbour. The other plane is a Pitts S-2B with a closed cockpit. It is a sport aerobatic biplane and for $150.00 you can have your own rollercoaster performance for 15 minutes. Watch your breakfast! These guys operate year round and to go on any of these you need to make a reservation. If you want any more information, ph 677 3404.

There are polo fields near here which have enjoyed royal patronage over the years.

Western Oahu

There are not a lot of tourist amenities on this side of the island, and the locals like it that way. Apart from the resorts of Maskaha Valley, restaurants are scarce, and shopping centres specialise in food more than anything else.

If you want to visit Kaena Point, the most westerly point of Oahu, 4WD or sturdy hiking boots are essential as the Farrington Highway ends at Yokahama Bay and the track beyond goes through jagged wasteland.

Yokohama Bay Beach

A favourite surfing spot, the bay takes its name from the Japanese fishermen who tried their luck here.

Kaneana cave

Near Makua just before the end of the Farrington Highway, is the Kaneana Cave, named after the sharkman deity, who is supposed to have made his home in the cave.

Makaha

The Makaha Valley has the most developed resort area outside Waikiki, with hotel rooms, units, two 18-hole gold courses, tennis courts, manicured lawns and a heliport.

If you are just passing by, pop into the Resort and ask at the front desk fro permission to visit the Kaneaki Heiau, an 18th century war temple that has been restored by the Resort and the Bishop Museum. The temple was dedicated to Lona, the god of agriculture, and was a place of prayer and barbaric human sacrifices.

Makaha Beach is the most famous on this coastline, and the International Surfing Championships have been held here since 1952.

Pokai Bay Beach Park

One of the few beaches where it is safe to swim all year, Pokai Bay is also one of the few safe places to anchor when the heavy surf is running. There is a good lookout point on the Barbers Point side of the bay, Ku'ilio'loa. It has views of the coast from Makaha to Maili and of the Waianae Mountains.

Central Oahu

If you are coming from the north, first it's sugar-cane fields, then it's pineapples and more pineapples.

James Dole opened the first pineapple cannery in 1899, and today Hawaii produces about 45% of the world crop. On Kamehameha Highway is the Dole Pineapple Pavilion, where you can try the fresh fruit. They also have other snacks, souvenirs and gifts, and are open daily 9am-5pm. Ph 621 8408 for information.

Wahiawa

At the northern side of Whitmore Avenue, just before the town of Wahiawa, is a dirt track leading through field to the Kukaniloko Birth Stones. It was here that the wives of the ancient chieftains gave birth to their children, to the accompaniment of chanting and beating drums.

In the centre of Wahiawa (108 California Avenue) are the Healing Stones, which some folk still believe have healing powers. They are in a rough concrete shelter that could hardly be called a temple.

The Hongwanji Mission, 1067 California Avenue, has a Buddhist temple which has been carved from Japanese cypress and painted with gold leaf. A side entrance is usually open.

The Wahiawa Botanic Gardens, at 1396 California Avenue, has 4ha (9 acres) of plants that thrive in the cool wet regions. Open daily 9am-4pm.

Schofield Barracks

When visiting the barracks you may have a feeling of deja vu, but relax, you probably have seen it before. It was here that From Here to Eternity and Tora!Tora!Tora! were filmed. Nearby is Kolekole Pass in the Waianaes, through which the Japanese flew to bomb Schofield and Wheeler Air Force Base.

The Tropic Lightning Museum in the grounds of the barracks has weapons and artefacts from several wars. Open Wed-Sun, 10am-4pm, enter by the Macomb Gate on Wilikina Drive.

Mililani

The Catholic Church of St John, 95-370 Kuahelani, is worth a visit for its cement walls, granite altar, and sculptures depicting the Stations of the Cross. There are also bronze statues of the Virgin Mary and St John.

Tours

E Noa Corporation, 1141 Waimanu Street, Honolulu, ph 593 8073, 800 992 7498 have a variety of tours on offer:

Circle Island Beach and Waterfall Adventure Tour
Includes snorkelling at Hanauma Bay, with equipment and instruction provided, and lunch. Hotel pick-up 7.30-7.45am return 5.30pm - Over $60 adult, $50 children 6-12, $40 children 5 and under.

Royal Circle Island Tour
Full day 193km (120 miles) tour with hotel pick-up at 8.45-9.00am return 5.30pm. Visits Diamond Head, Hanauma Bay, Blow Hole and Sandy Beach, Makapuu Lookout, Windward Oahu Coastline, Pali Lookout, Byodo-In Temple, Sunset Beach/North Shore beaches, Waimea Valley, and pineapple and sugar cane fields - $50+ adults, $40+ children 6-12, $31 children 5 and under.

Pearl Harbour and Polynesian Cultural Centre
Circle Island Tour
Escorted tour of the daytime activities at the Cultural Center. Hotel pick-up 12.30-12.45pm return 10.30pm - $75+ adults, $50+ children 5-11, free children 4 and under.

Deluxe Little Circle Island Tour
Half-day 97km (60 miles) tour, including Pali lookout. Hotel pick-up 9-9.15am and 2-2.15pm return 1pm and 6pm - $30 adults, $25 children 11 and under.

Honolulu City Tour and Historic Waterfront
Narrated, informative tour of the city including a magnificent view from atop Mt Tantalus. Hotel pick-up 2.30-2.45pm returning 5.45pm - $20 adults, $14 children 11 and under.

Arizona Memorial Excursion
Narrated 56km (35 miles) tour to Pearl Harbour including boarding the Memorial. Hotel pick-up at 6.45-7am and 8.45-9am returning

10.30am and 12.30pm - $20 adult, $17 children over 115cm (45").

Pearl Harbour and Honolulu City Tour

Morning or afternoon 80km (50 miles) tour with pick-up at 6.45-7am and 11-11.15am returning 11.45am and 4pm - $30 adults, $25 children over 115cm (45").

North Shore and Waimea Falls Park Tour

Half-day excursion along Oahu's north shore and a tour of Waimea Falls park. Pick-up at 8.15-8.30am and 12-12.15pm returning 1.30pm and 5pm - $40 adults, $35.00 children 7-12, $23 children 6 and under.

The Old Town Honolulu Trolley Tour is a nostalgic trip into Honolulu's past. The two-hour narrated tour includes unlimited on and off privileges for the day. Sign-posted stops/pick-ups are: Iolani Palace; Chinatown/Wo Fat; Academy of Arts; King Kamehameha Statue; Mission Houses Museum; State Capital; Hilton Hawaiian Village; Hawaiian Maritime Center, Aloha Tower; Ward Center; Royal Hawaiian Shopping Center; Restaurant Row - $15 all day pass.

There are also daily tours to Dole Cannery Square, Ala Moana Center, Ward Warehouse and Hil Hattie.

Other companies offer similar tours at competitive prices.

Gray Line Hawaii, 435 Kalewa Street, Honolulu, ph 836 1883.

Ilima Tours and Transportation, 2819 Mokumoa Street, Honolulu, ph 833 3000.

Polynesian Hospitality, 330 Pacific Street, Honolulu, ph 526 3565.

Roberts Hawaii Tours, 680 Iwilei Road, Suite 700, Honolulu, ph 523 8860.

Soltours & Travel, 1833 Kalakaua Avenue, Suite 710, Honolulu, ph 944 4015.

Trans Hawaiian Services, 3111 Castle Street, Honolulu, ph 735 6467.

For a different type of touring contact Rainbow pacific Helicopters, 110 Kapalulu Pl, Honolulu, ph 834 1111, 800 289 6412.

Sport and Recreation

Cruising and Sailing

All Hawaii Cruises Capt Bob's Picnic Sail, Ala Moana Boulevard (Suite 414), Honolulu, ph 942 5077 - 42ft glass-bottom catamaran and 28ft catamaran - 4 hour picnic and snorkel sails on the Windward coast.

Honolulu Sailing Company, 47-335 Lulani, Kaneohe, ph 239 3900. Charters start at $50 per person. $150 per day for lessons.

Tradewind Charters, 1833 Kalakaua Avenue (suite 612), Honolulu, ph 973 0211 - private and shared sailing with hand-on participation. Have half day, full day and sunset sails, boats up to 70 ft. Group charter $65 per person, private charter $375.

Nautilus Waikiki, 1085 Ala Moana Boulevard (Suite 101), Honolulu, ph 591 9199 - 60ft semi-submersible vessel with topside viewing deck and underwater viewing compartment - hourly cruises from Kewalo basin - private charters available.
Phone for a price.

Windjammer Cruises, 181 Ala Moana Boulevard, Pier 7-A, Honolulu, ph 531 0286 ext.310, 800 367 5000. They do quite good dinner cruises.

Fishing

To fish privately it is important that you contact the Aquatic Resources Division, Recreational Fisheries Office, 1151 Punchbowl Street, Honolulu, open 9am-4.30pm, ph 587 0110. They can advise on how to go about getting a license and where you can fish.

Interisland Sport Fishing, 864 Papalalo Pl, Honolulu, ph 591 8888. Private and shared sports fishing charters aboard one of three vessels for marlin, tuna, mahi and wahoo.

Tradewind Charters, Deep sea/bottom dishing. Marlin, ahi, mahimahi and ono can be caught all year round. Shared and exclusive charters available, ph 973 0311. Prices from $65 depending on your plans.

Sport Fishing, Kewalo Basin Slip J, Honolulu, ph 596 2998. Well equipped boats available for charter.

Golf

It is not advisable to just turn up for a game. make a booking beforehand to ensure you get on a course.

Kato's Golf Tours, 239 Kamani Street, Suite 202, Honolulu. Oahu's courses are often crowded. Kato's can guarantee a good day on the course of your choice. Package includes free transportation, green fees, cart, free use of golf clubs and shoes, ph 947 3010.

Del Mar Golf College, 84-626 Makaja Valley Road, Waianae, [ph 695 5561. Open daily 9am-5pm.

Some Courses

Honolulu

Ala Wai Golf Couse, 404 Kapahulu Avenue, ph 296 4653, 296 2000 for reservations. Green fees $40, buggy rental $14, club rental $20. Close to Honolulu and run by the county. Very crowded. (Par 70) Can make a reservation up to 3 days prior.

Hawaii Kai Golf Course, 8902 Kalanianole Highway, Honolulu, ph 395 2358. Green fees $85 including buggy. (Par 72) Near Makapuu Point with great views.

Kaneohe

Koolau Golf Course, 45-550 Kionaole Road, Kaneohe, ph 236 4653 for reservations. Green fees $100 including buggy, club rentals $50. A challenging course.

Pali Golf Course, 45-050 Kamehameha Highway, Kaneohe, ph 266 7610, 298 2000 for reservations. Green fees $40, buggy rental $14. Maintained by the county and crowded.

Kahuku

Turtle Bay Hilton Golf and Tennis Club, 57-091 Kamehameha Highway, Kahuku, ph 293-8574. It has two courses - 9 hole - $25 for 18 holes; 18 hole course at Kuilima $125 including buggy.

Kahuku Golf Course, Kahuku, ph 293 5842, 296 2000 for reservation and ask for directions where to find it along Oahu's northern most part. Nine holes and a 'roughy', Green fees $20 for nine holes.

Check out whether they have buggies (carts). Mostly on a first come, first serve basis.

Sheraton Makaha Golf Club, 84-626 Makaha Valley Road, Makaha, ph 695 9544. Green fees $160 including buggy. Little less in the afternoon during the week.

Hiking

Contact the Department of Parks and Recreation for starters, there address is 650 S. King Street, Honolulu 96813, ph 527 6343. They have hiking trail maps and would be the best to get you started. The University of Hawaii puts out a very good book The Hiker's Guide to Oahu which covers all the trails and the access points.

Scuba Diving, Snorkelling

The best thing is to shop around certainly among the companies we mention here to get an idea of the price for what you want to do. Be very direct about your capabilities and experience otherwise you can find you are wasting money on a course that does not suit. Water sports are demanding.

Aaron's Dive Shops, 602 Kailua Road, Kailua, ph 262 2333; and 98-406 Kamehameha Highway, Pearl City, ph 487 5533. Equipment rental, sales, services, PADI instructor. Give courses - Introductory dive $90, Scuba certification classes from $130.

Aloha Dive Shop, Koko Marina Shopping Centre, 7192 Kalanianaole Highway, Honolulu, ph 392 5922 - no experience necessary. Half day dive $75, there prices are reasonable. Give courses. Three day certification course - $375-$400.

Dan's Dive Shop, 660 Ala Moana Boulevard, Honolulu, ph 536 6181 - dives for beginners and experienced.

Waikiki Diving Centre, 1734 Kalakaua Avenue, ph 955 5151. One of the biggest diving shops on Oahu, specialising in private dives.

Skydiving

Skydive Hawaii, 68-760 Farrington Highway, Mokulela, ph 637

The 'Arizona's' rusting ventilator and turret, Pearl Harbour

Young hula dancers

Haleakala Crater, Maui

Iolani Palace, Oahu

9700, fax 637 5498 - located at Dillingham Airfield - tandem or single jumps available. Tandem jumps about $195 per person. This is how first time jumpers do it.

Tennis

Diamond Head Tennis Centre, 3908 Paki Avenue, ph 971 7150 - nine courts.

Ala Moana Park, ph 522 7031 - ten courts

Kapiolani Tennis Courts, 2748 Kalakaua Avenue, Waikiki, ph 971 2525 - four courts.

Hawaii Price Golf Club, 91-1200 Fort Weaver Road, Ewa Beach, ph 944 4567 - two courts.

Turtle Bay Hilton Golf and Tennis Club - See golf.

Windsurfing/Sailboarding

You can just hire boards - Boogie boards $10 per day, surfboards from anything from $20-25 per day, Windsurfing equipment anything from $30-$40 per day. Many companies combine charges with lessons which start from $25.00 per session. For hiring it is advisable to take along the credit card for the security for the rental.

Kailua Sailboard Co, 130 Kailua Road, Kailua Beach Centre, ph 262 2555. Beginners and experts on Kailua's safe beach, with all-day equipment rental plus transportation and lessons.

Local Motion, 1714 Kapiolani Boulevard, Honolulu, ph 955 7873. Has five shops which rent out gear. Not sure if they teach but certainly can put you in contact with a comp[any that does.

Other shops: Koko Marina Shopping Centre, 7192 Kalanianaole Highway, Honolulu, ph 396 7873. Windward Mall, 46-056 Kamehameha Highway, Kaneohe, ph 263 7873. 2164 Kalakaua Avenue, Honolulu, ph 926 7873. Waikele Shopping Center, 94-792 Lumiaina Street, Suite 209, Waipahu, ph 668-7873.

Naish Hawaii, 156-C Hamakua Drive, Kailua, ph 261 6067, 261 3539 - pro shop, services, standard and custom rentals, group and private lessons, new and used equipment.

North Shore Windsurfing School, 59-452 Makana Road, Haleiwa, ph 638 8198 - Oahu's oldest windsurfing school.

Kapaau
Mahukona
Waipia Bay
Hamakua Coast.
Kohala Mtns.
Honokaa
Lapakahi State Historical Park. 250
Kawaihae
Waipia Valley
14
Poauiolo
Laupahoehoe Point
Puukohola & Mailekini Heiaus
Waimea
Kalopa State Park
Kolekole Beach Park
Puako
Waimea Plateau
Hakalau
Tropical Botanical Gardens
Petroglyphs
Mauna Kea
Onamea Bay
Scenic Dr
270
190
Akaka Falls State Park.
HILO
20
Keaau
130
Keahole Airport
Kailua-Kona
Disappearing Sands Beach.
Mauna Loa
Cape Kumukahi Lighthouse
Pahoa
11
Puna District.
Captain Cook Monument.
Hikiau Heiau
Honaunau
St. Benedicts.
Kealakekua Bay
Kilauea Caldera
Kaimu
Kalapana
Hawaii Volcanoes National Park.
Wahaula Visitor Centre
Hookena
Milolii
Naalehu
Punalu'u Black Sands Beach.
11
Waiohinu
Whittington Beach Park.

N
↑

Heiau
South Point

HAWAII

0   10   km

0   6   miles

Hawaii- The Big Island

The youngest island in the hawaiian group, the Big Island is a land of contrast. larger in area than all the other islands combined, Hawaii has active volcanoes, snowcapped peaks, lush rainforests, monolithic cliffs and beaches of many colours.

It lies 193km (120 miles) south-east of Oahu, and is nicknamed 'The Orchid Isle' due to the profusion of these blooms, especially in the Hilo area.

The Big Island was the first to be settled by the Polynesians, and the first to greet the missionaries. Kamehameha the Great was born ion Kohala (c1753) and ruled from Kailua, where he died in 1819. It was on this island that Captain James Cook was killed, at Kealakekua Bay.

How to get there

The Big Island is the closest gateway to Polynesia from mainland United States, and has two major airports, at Hilo and Keahole-Kona. Both these airports are capable of accommodating wide-bodied jets.

Aloha and Hawaiian Airlines offer frequent daily inter-island flights. The flight from Honolulu to Hilo takes approximately 40 minutes, and that to Keahole-Kone, 30 minutes. The island of Maui is only a few minutes away by air.

There are also scheduled commuter and other taxi services operating between the islands.

Tourist Information

Information Office are located at 250 Keawe Street, Hilo, ph 961 5797, fax 961 2126; and at 75-5719 W. Alii Street, Kona Plaza Shopping Arcade, Kailua-Kona, ph 329 7787, fax 326 7563.

There is a 24-hour, 7 day a week recorded message service called Volcano update

Accommodation

The following prices are for a standard double room per night in US$, and should be used as a guide only.

Hilo

Hilo Hawaiian Hotel, 71 banyan Drive, ph 591 2235, fax 596 0158 - 284 units, restaurant, cocktail lounge, swimming pool - $104.

Hawaii Naniloa Resort Hotel, 93 Banyan Drive, ph 969 3333, fax 969 6622 - 325 units, restaurant, cocktail lounge, swimming pool - $100-$120.

Hilo Bay Hotel, 87 Banyan Drive, ph 961 5818, fax 935 7903 - 145 units, restaurant, cocktail lounge, swimming pool - $65.

Dolphin Bay Hotel, 333 Iliahi Street, ph 935 1466 - 18 units - $60.

South Kohala

Mauna Lani Bay Hotel, 68-1400 mauna Lani Drive, Kohala Coast, HI 96743, ph 885 6622 - 350 units, restaurants, cocktail lounge, swimming pool, golf course, tennis court - $285-495.

Hapuna Beach Prince Hotel, 623-100 Kauna'oa Drive, Kohala Coast, HI 96743, ph 880 1111, fax 880 3112 - 350 units, restaurant, cocktail lounge, swimming pool, golf course, tennis court - $325.

Mauna Kea Beach Hotel, 62-100 Mauna Key Beach, Kohala Coast, ph 882 7222 - restaurants, cocktail lounge, swimming pool, golf course, tennis courts - $280-$420.

Kemuela Inn, PO Box 1994, Kamuela, ph 885 4243, fax 885 8857 - 31 unites - $60-80.

Parker Ranch Lodge, Highway 19,(PO Box 458), Kamuela, ph 885 4100, fax 885 6711 - 21 unites - $75.

North Kona

Kona by the Sea, 75-6106 Alii Drive, ph 327 2300, fax 922 8785 - 78 condominium apartments, swimming pool - $140-160.

Royal Kona Resort, 75-5852 Alii Drive, ph 329 3111, fax 329 9532 - 444 units, restaurants, cocktail lounge, swimming pool - $130.

Aston Royal Seacliff Resort, 75-6040 Alii Drive, ph 329 8021 - 148 condominium apartments, tennis court - $145-160.

Kona Islander Inn, 75-5776 Kuakini Highway, ph 329 3181, fax 922 8785 - 51 units, swimming pool - $100-110.

Kona Seaside Hotel, 75-5646 Palani Road, Kailua-Kona, HI 96740, ph 329 2455, fax 922 0052 - 122 units, cocktail lounge, swimming pool - $60-90.

Keauhou Beach Hotel, 78-6740 Alii Drive, ph 322 3441, fax 322 6586 - 300 unites, restaurants, cocktail lounge, swimming pool, tennis courts - $100-110.

Kona Bay Hotel, 75-5739 Alii Drive, ph 961 5818, fax 935 7903 - 145 unites, restaurant, cocktail lounge, swimming pool -$70.

Koan Tiki Hotel, 75-5968 Alii Drive, ph 329 1425, fax 327 9402 - 15 units, swimming pool - $65.

Volcano

Kilauea Lodge, Old Volcano Road, Volcano Village, ph 967 7366, fax 967 7367 - 12 units restaurant - $105-135.

Volcano House, Hawaii Volcanoes National Park, HI 96718, ph 967 7321 - 42 units, cocktail lounge - $79-131.

Ka'u

Colony One at Sea Mountain, PO Box 460, Pahala, ph 928 6200, fax 928 8075 - 75 condominium apartments [27 rental units], restaurant, golf course, swimming pool, tennis court - $75-100.

Shirikawa Motel, on Highway 11, Waiohinu, ph 929 7462 - 12 units - $30-55.

Local Transport

Hilo International Airport is only 3km· from the hotel area of Banyan Drive, and the Keahole-Kona Airport is 11km from Kailua. But no bus services operate from either airport. Many hotels have shuttle services for their guests, but if you hotel does not, then your only choice is a taxi.

Bus

Mass Transportation Agency, ph 935 8241, operate buses on a fixed schedule over much of the island. The fares range from between $1.00 and $8.00 depending on the distance travelled. There is also an extra charge or luggage that will not fit under the seat. Timetables are available at 25 Aupuni Street, Hilo.

Hilo has a city bus service that runs between the shopping malls and downtown, and the fare is 75c (exact money needed).

A shuttle bus runs continuously from Lanihau Centre in Kailua-Kona to the Kona Surf Hotel, seven days a week 8am-10pm, ph 884 2883. Another shuttle plies the Keauhou-Kona area daily 8am-4pm, and this is a free service, ph 322 3500.

Car

If you intend getting close to Mauna Loa, a 4WD is mandatory, so if you do not want to join any of the tours on offer, you will need to hire a vehicle.

There are many car rental companies operating on Hawaii.

Avis Rent-A-Car (Reservations 800 831 8000), General Lyman Field, Hilo, ph 935 1290; Kona Keahole Airport, Kailua-Kona, ph 329 1745; Hilton Waikoloa Village, ph 885 2821; King Kamehameha Hotel, ph 329 1191.

Budget Rent-A-Car (Reservations 935 7293), Kona-Keahole Airport, ph 329 8511; General Lyman Field, Hilo, ph 961 0661; Mauna Kea Beach Hotel; Mauna Lani Bay Hotel.

Dollar Rent-A-Car of Hawaii, general Lyman Field, Hilo, ph 961 2101; Kona Airport, Kona, ph 329 2744.

Harper Car & Truck Rentals, 1690 kamehameha Avenue, Hilo, ph 969 1478

Hertz Rent-A-Car, Hilo Airport, Hilo, ph 935 2896; Kona Airport, Kailua-Kona, ph 329 3566; Ritz-Carlton Mauna Lani.

Distance and Driving Times

From Hilo to

Kamuela -	88km (55miles) -	1 hour 5 minutes
Hapuna -	117km (73miles) -	1 hour 45 minutes
Kailua-Kona -	154km (96 miles) -	2 hours 15 minutes
Volcanoes National Park -	48km (30miles) -	45 minutes
Kaimu Black Sand Beach -	48km (30miles) -	45 minutes

From Keahole-Kona Airport to

Place of refuge -	48km (30miles) -	45 minutes
Kealakekua Bay -	42km (26miles) -	1 hour
Kamiela/Waimea -	61km (38miles) -	55 minutes
Hapuna beach -	40km (25miles) -	30 minutes

Taxis

Readily available at the airport in Hilo, or phone from your hotel. Most taxis can be hired for touring, and have fixed rates for different areas, but it is still a very expensive option.

Eating Out and Entertainment

No one should ever go hungry on the Big Island, where there are plenty of restaurants offering every type of food imaginable. Again we have rated them according to the price of the main course.

Expensive - $21 and over

Moderate - $16-20

Inexpensive - $11-15

Budget - $10 and under.

Many of these places have live entertainment and you should check when making your reservations.

Hilo

Sandlwood Room, Hawaii Naniloa Hotel, 93 Banyan Drive, ph 969 333 - international cuisine - open for breakfast, lunch, dinner and cocktails - moderate.

Queen's Court Restaurant, Hilo Hawaiian Hotel, 71 Banyan Drive, ph 935 9361 - specialties from around the world plus great views - open for breakfast, brunch, lunch, dinner, cocktails - moderate.

Nihon Restaurant, 123 Lihiwai Street, ph 969 1133 - Japanese culture and cuisine - open for lunch, dinner and cocktails - inexpensive.

Uncle Billy's Fish & Steak Restaurant, Hilo Bay Hotel at 87 Banyan Drive, ph 961 5818 - breakfast 7-9am, dinner 6.30am-8.30pm - hula show at 6pm every night - inexpensive.

Soontaree's Thai Restaurant, Hilo Shopping Centre. cnr Kilauea & Kekuanaoa, ph 934 7426 - traditional and modern dishes (no MSG) - open for lunch and dinner - moderate.

Ken's House of Pancakes, cnr Banyan Drive and Kamehameha, ph 935 8711 - open 24 hours a day, 365 days a year - popular for over twenty years- budget.

McDonald's, 177 Ululani Street, ph 935 9092; Waiakea Kai

Komohana

Amakahi

Aloe

Alanuku

Kimana

Ponahawai St

Haili

Waianuenue

Kaiulani St

Wailuku St

Amacui Rd

Wailuku

Wailuku River

Wailuku

m

Keawe St

Munro

Kapiolani St

Ululani St

Kinoole St

Aala

Kilauea Ave

Kamehameha

Rt. 19 Bayfront Hwy.

Huglabi

Wailoa

Manono St

Lanihuli

HILO BAY

Kaiko'o Mall

Wailoa Visitors Centre

Hilo Shopping Centre.

← To University of Hawaii & Hilo Golf Course

↑ To Wainako Town Centre

Kohala

National Park.

Kekuanaoa St

Mililani St

Piilani

Manono St

Hinano St

Laukapu St

Civic Auditorium

Tennis Stadium & Pool

Golf Course

Kalanikoa

Waiakea Square

m

Banyan Drive

Kanoelehua Ave.

← To Volcanoes

↓ N

HILO

Reeds Bay

General Lyman Airport

Shopping Plaza, 88 Kanoelehua Avenue, ph 955 5745; and 2100 Kanoelehua Avenue, ph 959 6462 - budget.

Waimea/Kohala Coast

Mauna Kea Resort Clambake, One Mauna Kea Beach Drive, Kamuela, ph 882 7222 - traditional feast with show - expensive.

Royal Terrace, Royal Waikoloan Resort, ph 885 6789 - views over lagoon and beach - open for breakfast, brunch, lunch, dinner, cocktails, with nightly entertainment - inexpensive.

Merriman's, Opelo Plaza, Box 2349, Highway 19 and Opelo Road, Kamuela, ph 885 6822 - nationally acclaimed contemporary Hawaiian restaurant - open for lunch, dinner and
cocktails - expensive.

Donatoni's, Hilton Waikoloa Village, ph 885 1234 - lavish breakfasts and theme dinner buffets - northern italian
cuisine - expensive.

Coast Grille, Hapuna Beach Prince Hotel, One Mauna Kea Beach Drive, ph 882 1111 - open for dinner only - moderate.

Kona Coast

Fisherman's Landing, Kona Inn Shopping Village, ph 326 2555 - lunch 11.30am-2.30pm, dinner 5.30pm-10pm, to 10.30pm Fri and Sat - moderate.

Ocean Bar and Grill, Mauna Lani Bay Hotel and Bungalows, Mauna Lani, One North Kaniku Drive, Kohala Coast, ph 885 6622 - American cuisine - expensive.

Manago Hotel Restaurant, Highway 11, Captain Cook, ph 323 2642 - breakfast 7-9am, lku lunch 11am-2pm Tues-Sun, dinner 5-7.30pm Tues-Thurs, 5-7pm Fri-Sun - budget.

Hale Ho'okipa - Friday Night Kuau, Kona Village Resort, ph 325 5555 - traditional luau and imu ceremony, plus tour of the village beforehand - expensive.

Banana Bay Restaurant & Buffet, Kona Bay Hotel, 75-5739 Alii Drive, ph 329 1393 - all-you-can-eat buffet for breakfast, brunch and dinner - inexpensive.

Kuakini Terrace, Keauhou Beach Hotel, 78-6740 Alii Drive, ph 322 3441 - extensive buffet and a la carte menu with hawaiian entertainment - open for breakfast, brunch, lunch, dinner, late supper and cocktails - moderate.

Pele's Court restaurant, Kona Surf Resort, 78-128 Ehukai Street, ph 322 3411 - open air dining room, prime rib and seafood buffet Tues & Fri - open daily for breakfast, lunch, dinner, cocktails - moderate.

Island Breeze Luau, Kongh Kamehameha's Kona Beach Hotel, ph 326 4969 - Kona's only beachfront luau - expensive.

Poquito Mas, Kona Coast Shopping Center, 74-5588 C Palamo Road, ph 329 3528 - quick baja-style Mexican food - open for lunch, dinner and late supper - budget.

Pizza Hut, 74-5620 Palani Road, North Kona, ph 329 1698 - open for lunch, dinner and late supper - budget.

McDonald's, 75-5729 Kuakini Highway, ph 329 7178, and 81-6655 Mamalahoa Highway, ph 322 3364 - budget.

Volcano National Park/South Point Area

Kilauea Lodge, Volcano Village, ph 967 7366 - continental cuisine - open for dinner, cocktails - expensive.

Shopping

Hilo/Hamakua Coast

Hilo Shopping Center, cnr. Kilauea Avenue and Kekuanaoa Street, ph 935 6499, has over 40 air-conditioned shops and restaurants. There is plenty of parking.

Longs Drugstore has two locations - 555 Kilauea Avenue, ph 935 3358, and the Prince Kuhio Plaza, ph 959 5881. The stores are open daily, and there is ample free parking.

Woolworth in Prince Kuhio Plaza, Hilo, ph 959 4555, has literally everything for the shopping tourist. They also have a snack bar.

Liberty House has a branch in the Prince Kuhio Plaza in Hilo, and also in the Hotel King Kamehameha in Kona. The Penthouse is the Keauhou Beach Hotel is also one of theirs.

Hilo Hattie, Prince Kuhio Plaza, 111 E. Puainako Street, Hilo, ph 961 3077, have a large collection fo swimwear, T-shirts, and gifts. They also offer free guided tours of the establishment.

The Keawe Collection is a group of shops in Kaewa Street, that is well worth a visit, particularly the Potters gallery, cnr Keawe Street and Waianuenue Avenue, ph 935 4069, which has jewellery, raku, and pit-fired pottery, paintings, woodwork and other local handicrafts. Open 9am-5pm Mon-Sat.

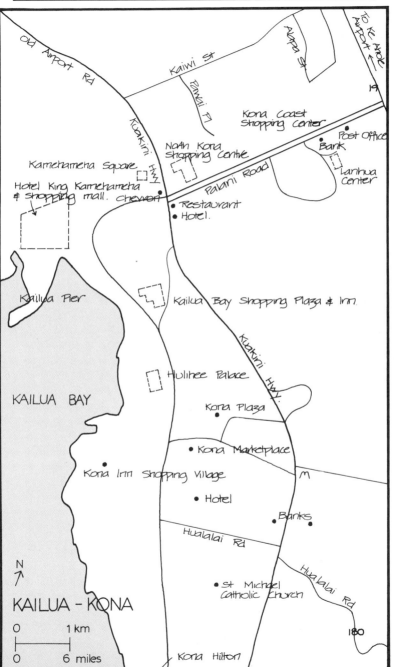

KAILUA - KONA

Honomu

The Crystal Grotto, Honomu Village, on the way to Akaka Falls, ph 963 6195, has a variety of quartz crystals and stones, island made wooden items, paintings and jewellery. Open daily 10am-5pm. Akaka Falls Flea Market is next to Ishigo's General Store in Honomu. It specialises in everything Hawaiian, open daily 9am-5pm.

Waimea/Kohala

Parker Ranch Shopping Center, near the junction of Highways 19 and 190, has over 35 shops and restaurants and ample free parking.

Ackerman Galleries, Kapa'au (opposite the King Kamehameha statue) ph 889 5971, are open daily 9.30am-5.30pm. They have fine arts with a blend of original works of island artists, boutiques, oriental antiques and primitive artefacts.

Parker Square, Highway 19, Waimea/Kamuela, has 25 specialty shops and services, and ample parking.

Gallery of Great Things, Parker Square, Highway 19, Kamuela, ph 885 7706, is open daily 9am-5pm and has works by Island artisans from small koa boxes to koa furniture.

Kona Coast

Hilo Hattie, 75-5597A Palani Road, ph 329 7200, is open 7 days a week 8.30am-5pm, and offers the same range of clothing, gifts and tours as their other stores in Hawaii.

Kona Discount Mart 1 and 2. These two everything-under-one-roof shops are at 75 5691 Alii Drive, ph 329 6366, and 75 5663 Palani Road, ph 329 8314. They will also arrange to pack and mail your purchases for you.

Holliday Galleries, Kona Plaza Shopping Arcade, ph 329 0046, have original paintings by local artists, and limited edition bronze sculptures. They also stock collections of well-known artists, such as Frederick Remington. Open Mon-Sat 9am-5pm.

Lanihau Center, on Palani Road, Kailua-Kona, has 22 shops and is a delight to visit for its scenic layout. There is unlimited free parking.

Kona Inn Shopping Village, 75-5744 Alii Drive , has over 50

specialty shops, restaurants and services. The Village is open daily 9am-9pm.

Keauhou Shopping Village, 78-6831 Alii Drive, on the corner of Kamehameha III Road, has 37 shops and services, and offers free shuttle service from Keauhou Hotels and Condo, ph 322 3500. The Village is open 7 days a week, Mon-Thurs, 9am-9pm, Fri 9am-7pm, Sat 9am-6pm and Sun 10am-5pm.

Lee Sands Wholesale Eelskin, Kona Marketplace, Shop 1210, ph 329 2285 has one of the largest selections of exotic leathers and skins, such as sea snake, salmon and mink.

Sightseeing

Hilo
The second largest city on the island and capital, Hilo, while not really a resort town, does have its own charm, albeit often in need of a freshen-up. The waterfront has been hit twice by tidal waves, in 1946 and 1960, and in Laupahoehoe there is a monument to those killed in the 1946 disaster.

Banyan Drive
Most of the city's hotels are one Banyan Drive, which is lined with rows of these enormous tress planted in the 1930s by visiting celebrities from all over the world.

Lihiuokalani Gardens Park
Names after the last hawaiian queen, the Park is 12ha (30 acres) of elaborate, authentic Japanese formal gardens. Situated on Banyan Drive.

Coconut Island
Quite close to the shore, Coconut Island was used by early Hawaiians for sacred birth and religious rituals.

Suisan Fish Auction
You have to be up early in the morning to catch this auction at the corner of Banyan Drive and Lihiwai Street, when the fishermen sell their catch.

Wailoa River and State Park

Off Kamehameha Avenue there are picnic areas surrounding Waiakea Fishpond, and the Wailoa Culture and Visitor Center, ph 961 7360. The park area was a busy business centre, but was destroyed by tidal waves.

Lyman House Memorial Museum
To learn about the history and different cultures of the Big Island, and the early missionary days, a visit to Lyman House is a must. The house was built in 1839 and is at 276 Haili Street, ph 935 5021.

Naha Stone
On Waianuenue Avenue, which turns of Highway 19 (Kamehameha Avenue) is famous Baha Stone which Kamehameha overturned, fulfilling an ancient prophesy that whoever could do this would be king of the islands - shades of King Arthur!

Rainbow Falls
One of the most impressive falls in Hawaii, the Rainbow Falls are in Wailuku River State Park. Nearby are the Boiling Pots, a series of cascades falling from Mauna Kea into lava pools.

Kaumana Caves
8km (5miles) from Hilo on Kaumana Drive are the Kaumana Caves, lava tubes formed during the eruption of Mauna Loa in 1881. Take care here as the terrain can be dangerous. From the area there are marvellous views of Hilo.

Hamakua Coast
Scenic Drive
11km (7 miles) north of Hilo on Highway 19 is the commencement of the 6km (4 miles) scenic drive leading to Hawaii Tropical Botanical Gardens at Onomea Bay. The 7ha (17 acres) gardens are a nature preserve and a sanctuary. Definitely a photographer's delight.

Alaka Falls State Park
Further along Highway 19 is the turn-off to Alaka Falls State Park, which has bamboo groves, ferns and orchids and the well-known Alaka Falls. These tumble 128m (420 ft) down a cliff face to the

Kolekole Stream below. On the way to the Alaka Falls are the Kapuna Falls (122m - 400ft) which are almost as dramatic.The area has plenty of hiking trails, and there are rest-rooms and drinking fountains.

Beach Parks
There are several beach parks along the coast, including Kolekole, Waikaumalo and Laupahoehoe.

Laupahoehoe Point
Situated between the 21 and 22-mile markers, in Laupahoehoe, the point is the site of an elementary school and old settlement which were destroyed by the 1946 tidal wave. A monument has been erected here in memory of the 24 students and teachers who lost their lives in the disaster.

Paauilo
An old plantation town on a side road off the highway, Paauilo affords the visitor scenes from old Hawaii. There are a rusted, tumble-down sugar mill, tin roofed cottages and decrepit store-fronts.

Kalopa State Park
On another side road to the west, the park is a lush forest and has camping grounds, cabins, picnic tables and restrooms. A good place to stop for lunch.

Honokaa
The macadamia nut capital of the world, Honaokaa is home to the Hawaiian Holiday Macadamia Nut Factory, and the largest sugar mill in the world. The mill can process 4,000 tons of sugar can a day. It uses cane waste as fuel thereby being almost totally self-sufficient in its operation.

The Hawaiian Holiday Macadamia Nut Co offer tours of their complex, and free samples in the retail store, ph 775 7743.

Honokaa is also an old plantation town, and many of the original buildings have been restored.

Waipi'o Valley

On Highway 240 is Waipi'o Valley, the Valley of the Kings. Historically and culturally important, it is 9km (6 miles) long and 1.6km (1 miles) wide, and is bounded on either side by lush, green cliffs 610m (2,000 ft) high. A favoured place of Hawaiian royalty, the once inaccessible valley can now be explored being part of a guided tour. The Waipio Valley Shuttle, ph 775 7121 is a 1.5 hours jeep tour which includes great views of Hiilawe Falls.

Waimea/Kohala Coast

Waimea

Waimea, also called Kamuela, is cowboy country, and home to what are claimed to be the world's largest independently owned cattle ranches. The famous Parker Ranch runs about 50,000 cattle on its 101,000ha (250,000 acres). The ranch was founded by John Parker, a sailor who jumped ship in 1809. It has a Visitor Center and a Museum, ph 885 7655. The museum includes a Duke Kahanamoku Room which will be of interest to sports fans.

In the town there are several historic churches, the Imiola Congregational Church, with its fine koa woodwork. It was built in 1857. There are also a few shopping centres, and at the corner of Highways 19 and 250 there is the Kamuela Museum, ph 885 4724, which has a fine collection of artefacts, though somewhat in disarray.

Kohala Mountains

Not far from the Kamuela Museum, Highway 250 heads north through the Kohala Mountains. Here the landscape changes as thew road goes higher, with cactus, eucalyptus and lantana taking over the landscape. There are fantastic views down to the dry, black lava Kohala coastline.

Kapaau

Situated on Highway 270, Kapaau is the site of the original King Kamehameha I statue. Made in Florence in about 1879, this statue was lost at sea on the way to Hawaii, and found after a replica has already been installed in Honolulu. The original was refurbished and sent to this area, the birthplace of the king.

Rodeo at Makawao, Maui

Township of Wailuku, Maui

Seven pools, Maui

Mookini Heiau

Off Highway 270, on the turn-off to the airport, is tone of the island's most historically important temples, Mookini Heiau, believed to have been built about 480AD. King Kamehameha's birthplace is further west along the same road.

Lapakahi State Historical Park

On Highway 270, south of Mahukona, the Park was once an ancient Hawaiian fishing village, which has been reconstructed, giving an insight into ancient Hawaii. Open daily 8am-4pm, no admission fee, ph 889 5566.

Puukohola Heiau

The temple, on Highway 19 near the end of Highway 270, was built by Kamehameha I in 1791 because a prophet said this would ensure his victory over the other island kings. He dedicated the temple to his war god by killing the last remaining rival chief, probably ensuring the prophesy would come true.

Puako Petroglyphs

There are three sets of rock carvings here, and a well sign-posted route along the trail at the end of the road. These carvings are among the best in all the islands.

The country between Puako and Kailua-Kona is lava crusted. There are views of Hualalai to the south, Mauna Kea to the east and Maui to the north. There are modern-day rock adornments along the way, where people have written their names among the black lava and the white coral.

Kailua

Originally a fishing village and first capital of the islands, Kailua in now jam-packed with hotels, restaurants and shopping malls.
Mokuaikaua Church

Situated on Alii Drive in the centre of town, the church is the oldest Christian place of worship on the islands. The first missionaries landed in 1820 and built this lava and coral building in 1836. The 34m (112ft) steeple is a landmark and symbol for Kailua town.

Hulihee Palace and Museum

Situated across the street from the Mokiaikaua Church is the Hulihee Palace, which is now a museum, ph 329 1877. The two-storey building was the royal holiday home. Open daily 9am-4pm, admission is $4 adults, $1 children 12-18, 50c children under 12, ph 329 1877.

Alii Drive

Alii Drive is the main street of Kailua-Kona and just about everything in the town is on this Drive. It then continues south from the town for about 8km (5miles), passing Disappearing sands Beach, also known as Magic Sands Beach, because the sand is seasonally washed out to sea leaving only black lava rocks, then it 'magically' returns.

St Peter's Catholic Church

On the rocky shore of Kahaluu Bay, St Peter's was built by the missionaries on the site of a Hawaiian Heiau. It is very small but the locals claim it is only the world's second smallest church (We do not know where the smallest is.).

Keauhou Bay

At the end of Alii Drive, the beautiful bay has plenty of resorts and several interesting historical sites. The Keauhou Beach Hotel will provide a map of the area showing the points of interest.

South Kona

Highway 11 crosses the slopes of Mauna Loa along the coffee belt, then passes through the small towns of Hanalo and Kainaliu, with their friendly island inhabitants, arriving at Kealakekua, with its famous 'Little Grass Shack'.

Kona Historical Society Museum

Close to the Grass Shack, the museum is filled with fascinating artefacts and memorabilia from the days of 'old' Hawaii. Nearby are Mrs. Field Macadamia Nut Factory, the Honwanji Buddhist Temple, the Central Kona Union Church and the Lanakila and Christ Churches.

Captain Cook Memorial

A white obelisk has been erected near the spot where Captain James Cook was killed in 1779. To get there go through the village of Napoopoo to Kealakekua Bay, and the monument stands on a distant shore. The best way to see it is to take one of the many boat cruises on offer that tour the bay. The cliffs behind the obelisk are riddled with Hawaiian burial caves.

Hikiau Heiau

A large lava structure on the shore nearby is the Hikiau Heiau, where hawaiians once worshiped Cook as the god of Lono - one of the four major gods from Tahiti. Just before he was killed Cook performed a Christian burial service for one of his crewmen in the temple.

Pu'uhonua O Honaunau

Translates as Place of Refuge, and was once a sacred sanctuary for defeated warriors or kapu breakers. It is now a national historic park and well worth visiting. There are free booklets for independent touring of the palace, heiaus and wooden idols found here. There are two ways to get to the park - either by the unimproved road south from Kealakekua Bay, or via the main highway to the route 160 turn-off.

Wakefield Botanical Gardens

On the way from the Place of Refuge, the Gardens have spectacular tropical flowers and plants.

St Benedictine's Church

Situated up the hill from the Place of refuge is St Benedictine's 'painted church'. The church's interior is a beautiful work of art by a Belgian priest who transformed the wooden chapel with murals of religious scenes. The grounds of the church have been the location for several Christmas television specials.

Highway 11 continues south past Hookena, passing over the 1919, 126 and 1950 lava flows. About 48km (30miles) from Kailua, there is a turn-off to Milolii, a vintage South Seas fishing village, with fascinating tide pools.

South Point

Ka Lae (South Point) is the southernmost point of the United States. To get there follow Highway 11 to the South Point turn-off, then follow the narrow road about 19km (12miles) to land's end and the lighthouse, where there are the remains of the oldest Hawaiian settlement in the Islands. Archaeological findings dating back to 750AD include ancient canoe moorings set in solid rock.

Ka Lae has the island's only green sand beach, made of volcanic olivine particles.

Kalalea Heiau

The temple stands on the tip of South Point, and offerings are still made here. The heiau is believed to hold a shark or other gods over which prayers are offered.

Palahemo Well

Situated inland form the Kalalea Heiau is this well which was used by the early settlers. Fresh water floats atop the salt water in a tidal pool. There are ancient petroglyphs (rock drawings) on the rim of the well.

Green Sand Beach

For the adventurous, or those with 4WD, there is a track along the shore for about 5km (3miles) to Green Sand Beach.

Waiohinu

A small town on Highway 11 where there are the keikis (offshoots) of the monkeypod tree planted by Mark Twain in 1866. The original tress was felled by high winds. Nearby is the beautiful Kauaha'ao Church.

Naalehu

A small town, renowned for being the southernmost community in the United States.

Whittington Beach Park and Punalu'u Black Sand Beach

Both parks have camping and picnicking facilities. At Punalu'u archaeologists found ancient canoe moorings. The Ka'u Cultural Center, which is near the Black Sands Restaurant, has displays on the birth of the macadamia industry, and also a spectacular mural painted by Herb Kane, a well-respected kamaaina artist.

The Punalu'u Bakeshop, source of the famous Punalu'u sweetbread, is also the Visitor Center. It is open daily 8.30am-5pm, ph 929 7343.

Volcanoes National park

The most active volcanoes in hawaii, Mauna Loa and Kilauea, are linked directly to the Pacific Plate's source of magma. A visit to the Kilauea Visitor Center, ph 967 7311, will give all the information and tips on viewing times, etc. that you need to fully appreciate the splendour of the park. Crater Rim Road features 18km (11miles) of spectacular scenery, passing lava flows and steam vents in its circuit of Kilauea Crater.

Kilauea Iki Trail

Crater Rim Road takes the visitor to the Thurston Lava Tube, a 137m (450ft) tunnel surrounded by ferns. The Kilauea Iki trail begins from the Thurston lava Tube's parking area. The two hour hike offers views of Byron;s Ledge, Kilauea Caldera, Halemaumau fire pit and Puu Puai vent, before descending into the crater. Please take notice of the warning signs, and follow the path of piled lava pieces that mark the trail.

Devastation Trail
A half-mile walk in an area devastated by a 1959 cinder fallout. The pumice-covered landscape is covered with flowering plants, which makes an interesting contrast.

Halemaumau Crater
The firepit last erupted ion 1982, and is the legendary home of Pele, the goddess of volcanoes. It is really a crater within a crater, being entirely contained within Kilauea.

Other attractions in the park include the Jaggar Museum, the Sandalwood Trail, and the scenic Chain of Craters Road.

Wahau'la Park Visitor Center
The centre, on the ocean side of the Chain of Craters Road about 45km (28miles) from the Kilauea Visitor Center, was demolished by lava in June 1989. The ocean end of the road is now closed to traffic, and enquiries should be made at the Kilauea Center as to the possibility of viewing the lava flows.

In this area is Wahau'la Heiau, a temple built about 1250 AD. This is thought to be the last place where priests practised human sacrifice to appease the gods, and these days the temple is in danger of being covered with lava.

Puna
Volcano Village
Situated on the Old Volcano Highway, the village has small shops, snack bars and overnight accommodation in a rural setting.

Highway 11 passes through the townships of Glenwood, Mountain view and Kurtistown, with their many orchid nurseries. At Keaau, Highway 120 branches off to the east, and the Puna district. It links up with Highways 132 and 137 for a circuit route.

Kalapana
This is a black sand beach studded with palm trees. The black sand is caused when the molten lava reaches the sea a fragments. The ocean then grinds the black glass-like pieces into fine sand.

Star of the Sea Painted Church
Built in 1931 near Kalapana, it was moved in 1990 when lava

inundated the town. It has not yet found a permanent home but is on blocks near the end of Highway 130.

Cape Kumukahi Lighthouse

The lighthouse is situated on the state's easternmost point, and is reached by a gravel road from the intersection of Highways 137 and 132. This entire area, apart from the lighthouse, was destroyed in 1960 when a lava flow swept through on its way to the sea. To give an idea of the size and strength of the flow, it actually added about 455m (500yards) of land to the island. Next to the lighthouse stands an ancient hawaiian Heiau.

Tours

'Io Aviation, Hilo International Airport, ph 935 3031 are open 9am-6pm daily. They have narrated scenic tours in helicopters and airplanes. They have a combined Hilo/Volcano tour at competitive rates, and also offer big game hunting helicopter tours.

Big Island Air have the only two-hour island flight seeing tour with commentary by the pilot. For reservations phone their 24 hour line at Kona Airport, ph 329 4868. They also have a jet charter service.

Blue Hawaiian Helicopters, Hilo International Airport, ph 961 5600 - 7am-10pm, Complete island tour with landing almost 2 hours - $220 per person.

Kenai Helicopters, have trips to Mauna Loa, the Hamakua Coast, Kilauea Crater, or a Mauna Loa/Kilauea combination. For reservation ph hawaii 245 8591, Kauai ph 329 7424.

Papillon Helicopters, ph 885 5995 have personalised tours that take you anywhere you want to go on the Big Island, including the Captain Cook monument, and the City of Refuge.

Volcano Heli-tours, Hawaii Volcanoes National Park, ph 800 967 7578.

Atlantis Submarines, ph 329 6626 or 667 2224, 8am-3pm. Kona based, the submarine tour lasts one hour and goes to depths of up to 100 feet. This is a unique way to see the coral reefs and marine life. Children under 4 not permitted on this tour.

Parker Ranch Tours, ph 885 7655 for information and reservations. They have Paniolo No.1 Country tour daily from 9am-1pm and noon-4pm, and Paniolo No.2 Shuttle Tour every 20 minutes for 1.5 hour tour.

Ski Guides Hawaii, PO Box 1954, Kamuela - guided snow skiing and ski rentals on Mauna Kea, Thanksgiving through to June.

Whalewatching

Dab McSweeney's Whale Watching Adventures, Inc. PO Box 139, Holualoa, ph 322 0028, around $45 for a session.

Red Sail Sports, 1 Waikoloa Beach Drive, Waikoloa, ph 885 2876. These people are into everything related to the water, sailing scuba diving, whale watching. Best to phone and tell them what you would like to do.

Sport and Recreation

Golf

Kona Country Club, 9.5km (6miles) south of Kailua-Kona on Alii Drive, ph 322 2595. Open daily, starting times required. 27-hole course, 18 holes par 72, 9 holes par 36. Green fees - 18 holes - $100.

Waikoloa Village Golf Club, midway between Highways 19 and 190, ph 883 9621. The course was designed by Robert Trent Jones Jr and is challenge to the serious golfer. 18 holes par 72. Call for tee times and green fees.

Waikoloa Beach Resort Golf Course, near the Royal Waikoloan Hotel on the Kohala Coast, ph 885 6060. 18-hole course, par 70. Call for tee times. Green fees generally $100.

Mauna Lani Resort's Francis H. I'i Brown Golf Course, South Kohala, ph 885 6655. Green fees - 18 holes, par 72 - guest $85, non-guest $175.

Mauna Kea Gold Course, Mauna Kea Beach Hotel, Kawaihae, ph 885 5400, 18 holes, apr 72. Starting times required one day in advance - $135.

Volcano Golf and Country Club, Hawaii Volcanoes National Park, ph 967 7331. A unique course in a volcano. Green fees - 18 holes, par 72 - $60.

Sea Mountain Golf Course, Punalu'u, ph 928 6222. A championship course. Green fees - 18 holes, par 72 - $55.

Discovery Harbour Golf and Country Club, Waiohinu, ph 929 7353. A very scenic course. Call for green fees. 18 holes, par 72.

Tennis

Department of Parks and Recreation, 25 Aupuni Street, Hilo 96720, ph 961 8720 will be able to tell you availability and prices. Normally the hotels restrict availability of their courts to their guests. There are some who allow others to play.

Hotel King Kamehameha, Kona, ph 329 2911 - 4 courts - $10 per day. Keauhou Beach Hotel, Kailua-Kona, ph 322 4237 - 6 courts - $10 per day. Royal Kona Resort, Kona , ph 329 3111 (formerly the Hilton Beach and Tennis Resort) - 4 courts - $10/day.

Horseback Riding

King's Trail Rides o"kona, ph 323 2388. Leave from Kealakekua Ranch Center, near Captain Cook. Experienced guides will assign you to appropriate tour and horse. Must have ridden a horse before to go on these tours. 7.30am-5pm about $75-1$150 depending on the ride. Camping trips are available.

Waipo Naalapa Trail Rides, Honokaa, 775 0419, two hour rides - $75.

Fishing Charters

A-1 Black Bart Sportfishing, PO Box 692, Kailua-Kona, ph 329 300.

Aerial Sportfishing Kona, PO Box 4059, Kailua-Kona, ph 329 5603.

Blue Hawaii, 78-6645 Alli Drive, Kailua-Kona, ph 332 3210.

Hua Pala Charters, 73-1089 Ahulani Street, Kailua-Kona, ph 325 3277.

Jack's Kona Charters, PO Box 1018, Kealakekua, ph 325 7558.

Kona Sportfishing Centre, 75-381 Kealakehe Parkway, Kailua-Kona, ph 326 1559, fax 326 2244.

Scuba Diving and Snorkelling

Big Island Divers, 74-425 Kealakehe Parkway, Kailua-Kona, ph 329 6068. Fair Wind Sailing & Diving Adventures, 78-7128 Kaleopapa Road, Kailua-Kona, ph 322 2788.

Gold Coast Divers, 75-5744 Alii Drive, Kailua-Kona, ph 329 1328.

Red Sail Sports, 1 Waikoloa Beach Drive, Waikoloa, ph 885 2876, fax 885 4169; also at the Hilton Waikola Village, Kohala Coast, ph 885 1235 ext 1200; Hapuna Beach Hotel, ph 880 111 ext 3690.

You will need to phone for prices and do a comparison.

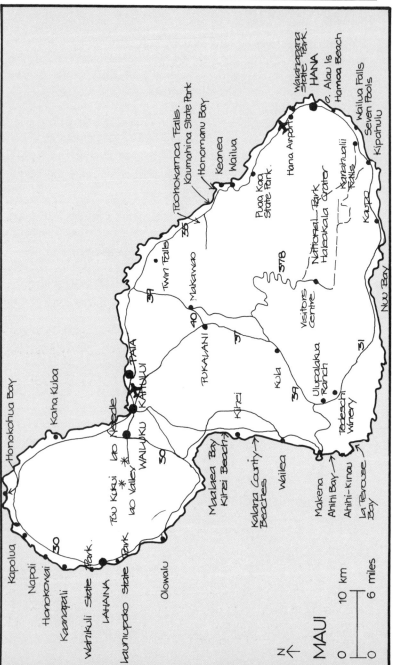

MAUI

N

0 ___ 10 km
0 ___ 6 miles

Kapalua
Napili
Honokowai
Kaanapali
Wahikuli State Park
LAHAINA
Launiupoko State Park
Olowalu

Honokohua Bay
Koha Kuba

Iao Needle
Puu Kukui
Iao Valley
WAILUKU
WAILUKU
KAHULUI
PAIA

50

Maalaea Bay
Kihei Beach
Kalana County
Beaches
Wailea

Makena
Ahihi Bay
Ahihi-Kinau
La Perouse
Bay

Twin Falls
Makawao
PUKALANI
Kihei

37
40
37

Honomanu Bay
Keanea
Wailua
Puaa Kaa
State Park
Kaumahina State Park
Hoohokamoa Falls

35

Hana Airport
National Park
Haleakala Crater
Visitors
Centre
378
Ulupalakua
Ranch
Kula
Tedeschi
Winery

37
31

Waianapara
State Park
HANA
o. Alau Is
Hamoa Beach
Wailua Falls
Seven Pools
Kipahulu
Kaupo
Kaeahualii
Falls

Nuu Bay

Maui

Geologist say that the island of Maui was formed by volcanic eruptions beneath the sea over long periods of time, the islands have a different idea of its formation.

Legend says that the demi-god Maui created all the islands when one day his fishhook caught up the ocean bottom. It was Maui who snared the sun and forced it to slow its passage, allowing the hawaiians more time to fish and grow taro.

Whichever theory you wish to believe, Maui , or the Valley Isale as it is called, is a splendid island in the pacific, with blue-green mountains, sun-drenched beaches, hidden coves and many waterfalls.

Maui was the site of the great victory in battle by King Kamehameha I, and the south-west coast was the playground of the Alii, the Hawaiian royalty.

The second largest of the Hawaiian Islands, Maui has an area of 1,880 sq km (729 sq miles) and is 113km (70miles) south-east of Oahu.

How to Get There

Aloha Airlines and Hawaiian Air offer frequent daily flights from Honolulu (25 minutes), and there are scheduled commuter and other air taxi services operating between the islands.

Maui is also served directly from mainland USA by United Airlines and American Airlines, and charter flights of trans-Pacific air carriers.

There are three airports on Maui.

The main one at Kahului has been renovated to the tune of $100 million, but it is still in the same place making it inconvenient f you are staying in the main resorts of West Maui and Wailea. However, there is not much you can do about it because this is the only airport on Maui with direct services from mainland USA.

The new Kapalua-West Maui Airport is only serviced by inter-island flights due to its short runway. There are shuttle services between the airport and the Kaanapali and Kapalua resorts. The other airport is at Hana and it is only services by commuter flights run by Aloha Island Air.

Tourist Information

The Maui office of the Hawaii Visitors' Bureau is at 1727 Wili Pa Loop, Wailuki, HI 96793, ph (808) 244 35030, fax (808) 244 1337.

Accommodation

Finding somewhere to stay in Maui is not a problem, but it is always wise to book ahead. The following prices are for a standard double room per night in US$.
They should be used as a guide only.

Lahaina

Mahana At Kaanapali, 110 Kaanapali Shores Place, ph 661 8751, fax 922 8785 - 140 units, swimming pool, tennis courts - $155-225.
Lahaina Shores Beach Resort, 465 Front Street, ph 661 4835, fax 661 48335 - 157 condominium apartments, swimming pool - $120-$130.
Maui Kaanapali Villas, 45 Kai Ala Drive, ph 667 7791, fax 922 8785 - 167 condominium apartments, restaurant, swimming pool, golf course, tennis court - $130-$150.
Maui Park, 35\626 L. Honoapiilani Highway, ph 669 6622, fax 922 8785 - 205 condominium apartments, swimming pool - $100-$110.
Kulakane Condominiums, 3741 L. Honoapiilani Road, ph 669 6119, fax 669 9694 - 31 units, swimming pool - $90.
Maui Islander Hotel, 660 Wainee Street, ph 667 9766, fax 661 3733 - 350 units, swimming pool, tennis court - $70-$90.

Kaanapali

Hyatt Regency Maui, 200 Nohea Kai Drive, Lahaina, ph 661 1234, fax 667 4498 - 815 units, restaurants, cocktail lounge, swimming pool, golf course, tennis court - $260.
Kaanapali Alii, 50 Nohea Kai Drive, ph 667 1400, fax 661 0147 - 210 condominium apartments - swimming pool, golf course, tennis court - $195-$295.
The Whaler On Kaanapali Beach, 2481 Kaanapali Parkway, ph 661

4861, fax (510) 939 6644 - 161 condominium apartments - swimming pool, golf course, tennis court - $95-$170.

Kaanapali Beach Hotel, 2525 Kaanapali Parkway, ph 661 0011, fax 667 5978 - restaurants, cocktail lounge, swimming pool - $150.

Mahana At Kaanapali, 110 Kaanapali Shores Place, ph 661 8751, fax 922 8785 - 140 units, swimming pool, tennis courts - $155-225.

Kapalua

Kapalua Bay Hotel and Villas, One Bay Drive, ph 669 5656, fax 669 4694 - 194 hotel units, 125 villas - restaurant, cocktail lounge, swimming pool, golf course, tennis court - $260.

Kapalua Ridge, 100 Ridge Road, ph 669 9696, fax 669 4411 - 60 rental units, restaurant, cocktail lounge, swimming pool, golf course, tennis court - $110.

Napili

Napili Shores Resort, 5315 L. Honoapiilani Highway, ph 669 8061, fax (402) 498 9166 - 114 condominium apartments, restaurant, swimming pool - $165-$195.

Napili Point Resort, 50 Napili Place, ph 669 8002, fax 669 8004 - 53 condominium apartments, swimming pool - $115-$155.

Napili Sunset, 46 Hui Drive, ph 669 8083, fax 669 2730 - 41 condominium apartments, swimming pool - $100.

Napili Village, 5425 L. Honoapililani Highway, ph 669 6228, fax 669 6229 - 25 units, swimming pool - $80-$100.

Kihei

Maui Price Hotel at Makena Resort, 5400 Makena Alanu Road, ph 874 1111, fax 879 8763 - 319 units, restaurants, cocktail lounge, swimming pools, golf course, tennis court - $270.

Mana Kai-Maui Resort, 2960 S. Kihei Road, ph 879 1561, fax 874 5042 - 667 unites (hotel/condominium), restaurants, cocktail lounge, swimming pool - $95-$195.

Hale Pau Hana, 2480S. Kihei Road, ph 879 2715, fax 875 0238 - 51 apartments, swimming pool - $110-155.

Luana Kai Resort, 940 S. Kihei Road, ph 879 1268, fax 879 1455 - 75 condominium apartments, swimming pool, tennis court - $105-$130.

Kihei Beach Resort, 36 S. Kihei Road, ph 879 2744, fax 875 0306 - 35 condominium apartments, swimming pool - $110.

Aston Maui Lu Resort, 575 S. Kihei Road, ph 879 5881, fax 922 8785 - 120 units, restaurant,. cocktail lounge, swimming pool, tennis court - $110-120.

Kihei Surfside Resort, 2936 S. Kihei Road, ph 879 1488, fax 874 3731 - 70 condominium apartments, swimming pool - $80-125.

Shores of Maui, 2075 S. Kihei Road, ph 879 9140, fax 879 6221 - 38 condominium apartments, swimming pool, tennis court - $65-90.

Maalaea

Hona Kai Resort, R.R. Box 389, Wailuku, ph 244 7012, fax 242 7476 - 30 condominium apartments, swimming pool - $77-115.

Wailea

Renaissance Wailea Beach Resort, 3550 Wailea Alanui Drive, ph 879 4900, fax 874 5370 - 345 unites, restaurant, cocktail lounge, swimming pool golf course, tennis court - $290.

Aston Waliea Resort, 3700 Wailea Alanui Drive, Wailea, ph 879 1922, fax 874 4878 - 516 units, restaurant, cocktail lounge, swimming pool, golf course, tennis court - $245-405.

Waliea Ekahi Village, 3300 Wailea Alanui, ph 879 9272, fax 874 0094 - swimming pool, golf course, tennis court - $135.

Kahului

Maui Beach Hotel, 170 Kaahumanu Avenue, [h 877 0051, fax 596 0158 - 148 units, restaurant, cocktail lounge, swimming pool - $$80.

Banana Bungalow Maui, 310 N. Market Street, Wailuku, ph 244 5090, fax 243 2219 - hotel/international hostel - 27 units, restaurant - $20 per person (3 or 4 per room), double $40 per room.

Hana

Hana Bay Vacation Rentals, P.O. Box 318, Hana, ph 248 7727 - private homes and cottages - $70-90.

Hana Kai-Maui Resort, P.O. Box 38, Hana, ph 248 8426, fax 248 7482 - 23 units (on Hana Bay), swimming pool - $110-360 (full board).

Local Transport

Bus

Bus services on Maui are limited. There is a service from Wailea to Kapalua, stopping in Malaea, Lahaina and Kaanapali, seven days a week. There is also a shuttle service between the hotels and Whaler's Village at Kaanapali Beach.

Car

There are plenty of car rental companies on Maui, the better known ones having offices at the airport. Others who have their offices in the towns will sometimes arrange for pick-up at the airport, but you pay for the privilege. Be sure to check your insurance cover, and beware that some companies do not allows their cars on the road around West Maui Mountains, or on the road around the south-east side of the island from Hana.

Distances and Driving Times

From Kahului Airport to:

Kahului -	5km (3 miles) -	5 minutes
Wailuku -	10km (6 miles) -	10 minutes
Kihei (Post Office) -	14km (9 miles) -	20 minutes
Lahaina -	43 km (27 miles) -	45 minutes
Kaanapali -	48km (30 miles) -	50 minutes
Haleakali (summit) -	60km (37 miles) -	1 hour 30 minutes
Hana -	84km (52 miles) -	2 hours 30 minutes
Kapalua -	58km (36 miles) -	1 hour
Wailea -	29km (18 miles) -	35 minutes

Here are a few names and addresses:

Alamo Rent A Car, 905 Mokuea Place, Kahului, ph 871 6235; Kaanapali Transportation, Building 30-C Halawai Drive, Honoapiilani, Kaanapali, ph 661 7181.

Avis Rent A Car, Kahului Airport, 884 W. Mokuea St, Kahului, ph 871 7575.

Budget Rent A Car, Kahului Airport, ph 871 8811 (toll free reservations ph 800 244 4721).

Dollar Rent A Car of Hawaii, Kahului Airport, ph 877, 2731.

Hertz Rent A Car, Kahului Airport, ph 877 5167.

Eating Out

Lahaina

Swan Court, Hyatt Regency Maui, 200 Nohea Kai Drive, ph 667 4420 - open-air dining room in romantic setting - continental cuisine - expensive.

The Moana Terrace Restaurant, Maui Marriott Resort, 100 Nohea Kai Drive, ph 667 1200, ext 365 - coffee shop with extensive menu - kids under 6 eat free - moderate.

Old Lahaina Cafe, 505 Front Street, ph 661 3303 - beachfront eatery specialising in grills and seafood - open for breakfast, brunch, lunch, dinner, cocktails - moderate.

The Beach Club, Aston Kaanapali Shores, L. Honoapiilani, ph 667 2211 - oceanfront setting, international cuisine, plus live Hawaiian music nightly - open breakfast, lunch, dinner, cocktails - inexpensive.

Longhi's, The Longhi Building, 888 Front Street, ph 667 2286 - great international food, an award-winning wine list plus entertainment - open for breakfast, lunch, dinner, cocktails - moderate.

Spats, Hyatt Regency Maui, 200 Nohea Kai Drive, ph 667 4420 - Italian cuisine in candlelight setting - open for dinner and cocktails - expensive.

Chart House (Lahaina, 1450 Front Street, ph 661 0937 - seafood/steaks with views of Lanai and Molokai - open for dinner, cocktails - expensive.

Hard Rock Cafe, Lahaina Centre, 900 Front Street, Lahaina,ph 667 7400 - same set-up as all the others - open for lunch and dinner - budget.

Golden Palace, Lahaina Center, ph 661 3126 - Cantonese and Szechuan cuisine - open for lunch, dinner, cocktails - budget.

McDonald's, 885 Wainee Street, ph 667 2681; and 4403 Honoapiilani Highway, ph 669 0032.

Pizza Hut, 127 Hinau Street, ph 661 3696; and 3600A L. Honoapiilani Highway, ph 669 6996
(takeaway & home delivery only).

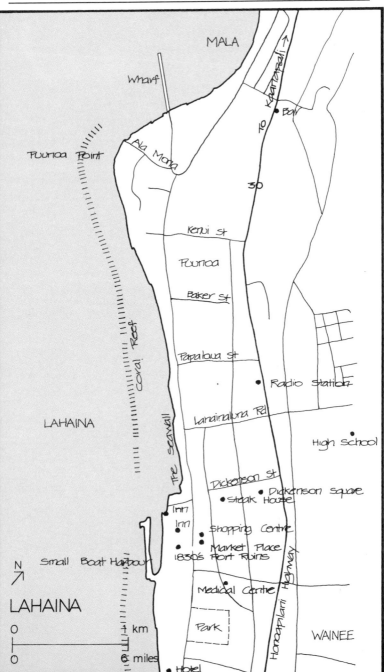

MALA

Wharf

To Kaanapali →

Buoy

Puunoa Point

30

Ala Moana

Kenui St

Puunoa

Baker St

Papalaua St

Coral Reef

Radio Station

Lahainaluna Rd

LAHAINA

High School

The Seawall

Dickenson St

Dickenson Square

Steak House

Inn

Inn

Shopping Centre

Market Place

1830's Fort Ruins

Small Boat Harbour

N

Medical Centre

Honoapiilani Highway

LAHAINA

Park

WAINEE

0   1 km

0   6 miles

Hotel

Kaanapali

Sheraton Maui Luau, Kaanapali Beach Resort, 2605 Kanapali Parkway, ph 661 3500 - good atmosphere - expensive.

Chico's Cantina & Cafe, Whalers Village, 2435 Kaanapali Parkway, Building G, ph 667 2777 - Mexican and American cuisine - open for lunch, dinner, late supper, cocktails - inexpensive.

Sound of the Falls, Westin Maui, 2365 Kaanapali Parkway, ph 667 2525 - Pacific bistro - open for brunch (Sunday) and dinner - expensive.

Leilani's On The Beach, Whaler's Village, 2435 Kaanapali Parkway, Building J, ph 661 4495 - open-air dining, seafood/steak - open for lunch, dinner, late supper, cocktails - expensive.

Tiki Grill, 2525 Kaanapali Parkway, ph 661 0011 - good fast food at poolside grill - moderate.

Kapalua

The Grill, The Ritz-Carlton Kapalua, One Ritz-Carlton Drive, ph 669 6200 - continental and Hawaiian cuisine - open nightly for dinner with entertainment and dancing - open on Sunday for brunch - moderate.

Papillon, Kapalua Bay Hotel & Villas, One Bay Drive - open-air restaurant with great views - international cuisine - open for dinner, cocktails Tues-Sat with seafood buffet on Friday, Sunday for brunch, and daily for breakfast - expensive.

The Grill & Bar At Kapalua, 200 Kapalua Drive, ph 669 5653 - world class dining at Kapalua Bay golf course - extensive menu - open for lunch, dinner, cocktails - moderate.

Beach Pavilion, The Ritz-Carlton Kapalua, One Ritz-Carlton Drive, ph 669 6200 - oceanfront dining, American cuisine - open for lunch - budget.

Kihei

Frangipani, Maui Sun Hotel, 175 E. Lipoa Street, ph 875 900 - outside seating, continental cuisine - open for breakfast, lunch, dinner, cocktails - inexpensive.

Kamaole Bar & Grill, Maui Coast Hotel, 2259 S. Kihei Road, ph 874 6284 - casual all day family dining - budget.

Prince Court, Maui Prince Hotel, 5400 Makena Alanui, ph 874

1111 - Hawaiian cuisine with entertainment - open for dinner, cocktails Wed-Sun, brunch Sun - moderate.

Maui Lu Longhous, Maui Lu Resort, 575 S. Kilei Road, ph 879 5881 - casual - open from breakfast, lunch, dinner, cocktails - inexpensive.

Pizza Hut, 2395 Kihei Road, Dolphin Plaza, ph 875 4881 - takeaway and home delivery only - budget.

McDonald's, 1214 S. Kihei Road, ph 879 0627 - budget.

Makena/Wailea

Cabana Cafe, Four Seasons Resort Wailea, ph 874 8000 - American cuisine and Hawaiian entertainment - open for lunch and dinner - moderate.

Seasons, Four Seasons Resort Wailea, 3900 Wailea Alanui, ph 874 8000 - elegant oceanfront dining - international menu plus entertainment and dancing - open dinner only - expensive.

Humuhumunukumukuapua'a, Grand Wailea Resort, Hotel & Spa, 3850 Wailea Alanui Drive, ph 875 1234 - thatched roof Polynesian style restaurant set on salt water lagoon - specialises in local seafood - open for dinner only - moderate.

Le Gunji, Diamond Resort Hawaii, 555 Kaukahi Street, Wailea, ph 874 0500 - French style, Teppanyaki - intimate fine dining - open for dinner and cocktails - expensive.

Lanai Terrace, Maui Aston Resort, 3700 Wailea Alanui Drive, ph 879 1922 - ocean views and varied menu plus specials - open breakfast and dinner - inexpensive.

Cafe Ciao, Kea Lani Hotel, 4100 Wailea Alanui, ph 875 4100 - informal Italian, deli/bakery - breakfast, lunch dinner and takeaway - budget.

Volcano Bar, Grand Wailea Resort, Hotel & Spa, 3850 Wailea Alanui Drive, ph 875 1234 - poolside bar and grill with casual menu and entertainment - open for lunch, late supper, cocktails - budget.

Maui Onion, Renaissance Wailea Beach Resort, 3550 Wailea Alanui Drive, ph 879 4900 - famous onion rings and smoothies - fashion show Wed, artists display work Fri - open for lunch and cocktails - budget.

Kahului/Wailuku

Rainbow Dining Room, Maui Beach Hotel, 1700 Kaahumanu

Avenue, Kahului, ph 877 0051 - American - open breakfast, lunch and dinner - budget.

East West Room, Maui Palms Hotel, 150 Kaahumanu Avenue, Kahului, ph 877 0071 - Japanese, plus dancing and entertainment - open lunch, dinner, cocktails - inexpensive.

Red Dragon Chinese Restaurant, Maui Beach Hotel, 170 Kaahumanu Avenue, Kahului, ph 877 0051 - 10 course Cantonese menu, plus entertainment and dancing - open dinner, cocktails - moderate.

Chart House (Kahului), 500 North Puuene, Kahului, ph 877 2476 - Aloha atmosphere, steak/seafood - open lunch dinner, cocktails - moderate.

Tropical Restaurant, Maui Tropical Plantation, RR1 Box 60, Wailuku, ph 242 8605 - overlooking lagoon and scenic Waikapu Valley - buffet and a la carte menu - open breakfast, lunch, dinner, cocktails - inexpensive.

McDonald's, 2138 Main Street, Wailuku, ph 244 8211 - Budget.

Entertainment

Most of the hotels have a luau at least once a week, others have them more often. For example, The Hyatt Regency on Kaanapali Beach has its "Drums of the Pacific" revue Mon, Tues, Wed, Fri and Sat in their outdoor theatre. The Luau show begins at 5.30pm - adults $42, children (6-12) $34, infants (5 and under) free.

We will presume you have tried a Mai Tai in Honolulu, after all it's almost obligatory, so now you can experience a Maui Tai. Blackie's Bar have dreamt up this one, but beware, it may be even more lethal than the original. Blackie's is on Highway 30 between Lahaina and Kaanapali, ph 667 7979, and they advertise they have the coldest beer on Maui. You can also get tacos, burritos, enchiladas, nachos and burgers, and they have live jazz Mon, Wed, Fri and Sun, 5.30-8.30pm.

Shopping

West Maui

Shopping Centres

Lahaina Center, cnr Front & Papalaua Streets, is the newest of the major shopping centres. It is home to the local Hard Rock Cafe, and several small retail outlets.

505 Front Street, next to the Lathaina Shores Hotel, has over 45 shops, including art galleries, boutiques, and beach-front restaurants. The centre is open seven days a week 9am-9pm (6pm Sun) and has plenty of free parking. Ph 667 2514 for information.

Lahaina Cannery Shopping Center, between Lahaina and kaanapali Beach, is built on the site of the original pineapple cannery, and has over 50 shops and restaurants. Open daily 9.30am-9.30pm, the centre has free parking.

Whalers Village, Kaanapali Beach, also has over 50 shops and restaurants, with a free trolley service daily from 9am-11pm with departures every thirty minutes.

Lahina Galleries has three locations - 728 Front Street, ph 667 2152; the Kapalua Gallery at Kapalua Bay Resort, ph 669 0202; and Gallery Kaanapali in Whalers Village, ph 661 5571. The galleries feature the works of artists Robert Lyn Nelson, Guy Buffet, Americo Makk and Hisashi Otsuka, and others.

Open 9am-9pm daily.

Central Maui

Kaahumanu Centre, 275 Kaahumanu Avenue, ph 877 3369, occupies a whole block in the heart of Kahului. There are over 60 shops and restaurants, and the centre has free parking.

Maui Mall Shopping Centre, cnr Kaahumanu and Puunene Avenues, ph 877 5523, has over 30 shops, etc.

East Maui

Azeka Place Shopping Centre, 1280 S.Kihei Road, Kihei, ph 879 4449.

Kamaole Shopping Centre, 2463 S. Kihei Road, Kihei, ph 879 5233.

Rainbow Mall, 2439 S.Kihei Road, Kihei, ph 879 6144.

Wailea Shopping Village in the Wailea Resort, ph 879 4474, has 25 shops and restaurants.

Sightseeing

West Maui

Olowahu Beaches

On route 30, 10km (6 miles) south of Lahaina, there are beaches north and south of Olowalu General Store. The surfing is good about half a mile north of the store.

Launiupoko State Park

5km (3 miles) south of Lahaina, near the West Maui Mountains, is Launiupoko State Park. The beach is good for fishing, but not for swimming.

Puamana Park

A good place for a picnic with excellent views, about 3km (2 miles) south of Lahaina.

Lahaina

Kamehameha the Great made this his capital in 1795, after conquering Oahu. Kamehameha III had his capital here, and it remained the capital of the Islands until 1845.

When the missionaries arrived in 1823, they were shocked at the attitudes and carryings-on of the natives and the sailors who visited their whaling ships. The Congregationalists put a stop to the licentious behaviour, but not before there was a battle royal with the sailors, in which the mission homes were attacked with cannons. The Lahaina of today is an interesting town, filled with sites and scenes of great interest to students of Hawaiian history and legend.

Carthaginian II, a steel hulled schooner docked in the harbour, is a modern version of the type of ship that carried the missionaries to Hawaii in the 1800s. It now houses a museum of the old whaling days and is open daily 9am-4.30pm. Entry is $3.00

The Pioneer Inn on Wharf Street was built in 1901, and just north of this is the Hauola Stone, a chair-shaped stone which the ancient Hawaiians believed had healing powers.

The Banyan Tree in front of the courthouse was planted in 1873 and is said to be the largest in all Hawaii.

The Courthouse was originally built as a palace for King Kamehameha III, and relocated here in 1859. There is an art gallery in the basement. On either side of the courthouse are the ruins of the old fort, built in the 1830s.

The Baldwin Home, the oldest building in Maui, is at 696 Front Street. Built out of coral and stone in the early 1830s for the Rev Dwight Baldwin, a medical missionary, the house is now a museum, ph 661 3262. Open daily 9am-4.30pm - entry $2.

Waiola Cemetery and Church are both on Wainee Street. The cemetery has graves dating back to 1823, and the church was the site of the first Christian services held on Maui.

Hale Paahao, is also on Wainee Street, and is an old gaol built for the drunken and disorderly members of the whaling crews in 1854.

Lahainaluna School, up the hill on Lahainaluna Road, was established by missionaries in 1831, and is the oldest school west of the Rocky Mountains. The first building of poles and grass was replaced by a stone building which still stands. From the school there is a superb view of Lahaina.

Hale Pa'i, Lahainaluna Road, is a printing house which still has the quaint old press on which Hawaii's first newspaper was printed in 1834.

Lahaina Jodo Mission, about half a mile north of Lahaina on Ala Moana Street, is a Buddhist complex with a temple and pagoda. Here is the largest ceremonial bell in Hawaii, and a giant bronze Buddha.

Maluulu o Lele Park is a good swimming beach on Front Street, near Whalers Market.

Lahaina Beach is north of Lahaina town on Puunoa Place, and is the best beach in Lahaina.

Wahikuli State Park

Located on Route 30 between Lahaina and Kaanapali, the park has picnic areas and restrooms, and there are tennis courts opposite. The swimming is very good, but surfing is poor.

Kaanapali

North of Lahaina, on Route 30, Kaanapali is a town full of hotels and condominiums. Hanakaoo Beach Park has good swimming on both sides of Hanakaoo Point. The white sandy Kaanapali Resort Beaches are all along Route 30. They have good views to Molokai and Lanai, and although often very crowded, are well worth a visit. Around Black Rock at the Sheraton Maui Hotel, there is very good swimming, body-surfing and skin diving.

Napili
Napili also has its share of hotels and condos, but it also has Napili Bay Beach with excellent swimming and snorkelling. Be warned that the currents can become hazardous when the surf is high.

Kapalua Beach (Fleming Beach)
One of the most picturesque and safest swimming beaches on Maui also has great snorkelling. It's about 11 km (7 miles) north of Kaanapali, off Highway 30.

Honokohau Bay
Near here Highway 30 becomes Highway 34, and the road hugs the coastline high above the ocean in between sandstone cliffs. A little further along the road is not sealed and becomes a mass of potholes and ridges, but for the stout-hearted the scenery is very picturesque.

Kahakuloa
Visiting this village, in a valley beside a deep bay, is like stepping back in time. The little wooden houses are protected from the wind by the headland rising from the sea, and the people live, and raise their cattle, much the same as their ancestors did.

Puu Kukui
After Kahakuloa, the 1,764m (5,788 ft) Puu Kukui dominates the scenery.

Halekii Heiau
North of the town of Kahului on a side road, are the remains of ancient temples of worship, sacrifice and refuge, ordered to be destroyed by King Kamehameha II in 1819. Heiau has now been partially restored.

South Maui

The coastline from Maalaea Bay to Makena is one beautiful beach after another, making this area a favourite holiday destination. The road follows the coast from Kihei to La Perouse Bay, but the last stretch from the 1790 lava flow to the Bay is 4WD territory.

Maalaea Bay

It is from Maalaea Bay that the Pacific Whale Foundation have cruises to 'spot the whales'. Every year North Pacific humpback whales journey south from Alaska to breed in the warm waters of Hawaii. They usually arrive around November and stay until June. The largest of these giants feed only in the polar regions, building up an extremely thick coat of blubber, off which they live during their time in Hawaii. A point of interest - the whales don't have teeth, but rather horny bone plates that hang from the upper jaw and form a sieve-like mat, netting small animals. More information on the cruises is found under the section 'Tours'.

Kihei Beach

Stretching from Maalaea Bay to Kihei, the beach is accessible from the highway along its entire length. It is not really a swimming beach, but good for jogging. There are picnic tables and rest-rooms at Kihei Memorial Park, near the centre along the beach. As with all the beaches in this area, afternoon winds can be a real problem.

Kalama County Beach Park

Situated on South Kihei Road across from Kihei town, Kalama is not a very good swimming beach, and the outlying reefs cause shallows. There are picnic facilities.

Kamaole Beach Parks

Three parks in all, with lovely green lawns, trees and best of all, they're good for swimming. Same problem as all the others with the afternoon winds.

Wailea

A deluxe 606ha (1500 acres) beachfront resort, owned by Alexander & Baldwin, one of the original giant sugar companies. The complex includes two hotels, condominiums, restaurants, two championship 18-hole golf courses, a tennis club, and five excellent beaches with views of neighbouring islands. The resort is three times the size of Waikiki.

Makena
One of Maui's best and most beautiful beaches, and not as commercially developed as some. Once it was a haven for hippies, but the Seibu Corporation of Japan has built a 404 ha (1,000 acres) resort and the area has gone up-market.

Ahihi-Kinau Reserve
A fascinating land and ocean reserve of over 808ha (2,000 acres), with lava flows, tidepools, and coral reefs that protect numerous species of fish and coral.

La Perouse Bay
La Perouse Bay and Ahihi Bay were once one and the same. Then Haleakala erupted in 1790 and the lava flow formed Cape Kinau, dividing the bay into two. La Perouse Bay takes its name from the French explorer who anchored here in 1786, prior to his last fatal trip.

Central Maui
The commercial and civic centres of Maui are in the adjoining towns of Kahului and Wailuku.

Kahului
A busy harbour town, Kahului has plenty to offer the shopper, but not much for the sightseer. There's nothing to entice the surfer either, as the beaches in this area have extremely strong currents and are definitely not for the faint-hearted.

Kanaha Pond Wildlife Sanctuary
Situated on Highway 32, the Sanctuary was once a royal fishpond, but now it is a bird refuge, with particular emphasis on the rare Hawaiian stilt.

Wailuku

The county seat of Maui, Wailuku is at the foothills of the West Maui Mountains, and is an interesting old town. It has a woodfront section, off Market Street, called Happy Valley - so named because it was once the red-light district, not because of the disposition of its inhabitants.

Kaahumanu Church is the oldest church on Maui, having been built in 1837, and was named for Maui-born Queen Kaahumanu who attended services on the site in 1832. The only way to see the inside of this church is to attend the 9am service on Sundays, which is conducted in Hawaiian. The church is in High Street.

Hale Hoikeike is the Maui Historical Society museum, in the Bailey Mission Home, built in 1841. It has an interesting display of early missionary items and Hawaiian artefacts, ph 244 3326. Open Mon-Sat 10am-4.30pm, and admission is $2 adults, 50c children.

About 2km down the road is Kepaniwai Heritage Gardens, a country park with Chinese and Japanese pavilions, a taro patch and thatched hut, several arched bridges, a swimming pool and an oriental garden.

Iao Valley State Park

The valley is a tranquil park now, but it was the site of a bloody battle in 1790 when Kamehameha conquered Maui in the famed Battle of Kepaniwai.

Iao Needle

After Haleakala Crater, the Iao Needle in Iao Valley State Park is probably Maui's most famous landmark. The mountain is a 686m (2,250 ft) high cinder cone, and Maui's most-visited attraction. The park is open daily 7am-7pm.

East Maui

The Hana Highway (36) between Kahului and Hana, is one of the most scenic drives in Hawaii. The road is very windy, and although it is only about 84km (52 miles) between the two places, the drive will take from 2.5 to 3 hours.

Paia

Only 11km (7 miles) east of Kahului is the quaint little town of Paia, and this is where the twists and turns in the road commence, as it winds past sugar cane fields, across gorges, through valleys and along fern covered hillsides.

Paia was originally a sugar town that really took off during World War II when a Marine camp was established nearby. After the war the rot set in when Alexander & Baldwin shut down its Paia operation and most of the residents moved on. Paia became a hippy town in the 1960s, but in the late 70s windsurfers found nearby Hookipa Beach and the town became the windsurfing capital of the world. Consequently, Paia has more than its share of budget accommodation.

Twin Falls

Just off the main road about 32km (20 miles) from Kahului, Twin Falls has a swimming hole which is a welcome visiting place if the weather is hot.

Puohokamoa Falls

There is a picnic area here, beside a large pool - a perfect spot for a picnic lunch.

Honomanu Bay

On a dirt road east of Kaumahina State Park, about 48km (30 miles) from Kahului, is a beautiful black sand beach. Unfortunately, there are no facilities here, but it's a great spot for surfing, though often too rough for swimming.

Keanae Arboretum

It's worth a stop here to walk through the beautiful tropical gardens, and just past this spot there is a left turn onto the road to the peninsula. From the point there are great views of Haleakala. On the way there are rustic houses and a coral-and-stone church, which is not open to visitors.

Wailua

A lush agricultural and fishing village with a lookout that has a choice view of the entire Keanae peninsula and the coastline.

Puaa Kaa State Park
The name means "the place of the rolling pigs", which dates from the days when pigs were said to have rolled down the hills in this area. The park has a picnic area and waterfall.

There are a lot of side roads leading to lookouts with spectacular views of the coastline - if you have time, why not try them all?

Waianapanapa State Park
Here there is a lava tube that you can walk through to the edge of a black sand beach. Nearby there is a blowhole, and off the shore are several arches. Strong swimmers and scuba divers, by diving into a pool and swimming underwater, can reach a big inner cave, a legendary trysting place for lovers of old.

Hana Bay
Affectionately known as "Heavenly Hana", the town looks out over the bay. Because of the high rainfall in this area the countryside is lush and green with developed agriculture. In the town there is a plaque commemorating the birthplace of Kaahumanu, King Kamehameha I's favourite wife, who had a lot to do with the overthrow of the ancestral Hawaiian religious system.

The best view of the town is from Mount Lyons, the camel shaped hill with the cross.

Hana Cultural Centre, on Uakea Road, has an interesting display of Hawaiian artefacts and antique photographs.

Hamoa Beach
Reached by a side road several kilometres south of Hana, Hamoa is a privately owned beach. The uninhabited island just off shore is called Alau Island.

Wailua
At Wailua Gulch there are two large falls, Kanahualii and Wailua Falls, which cascade down the cliff faces. Ohe'o Stream, not far away, is better known as Seven Pools, because a series of falls tumbles into seven large pools that are rock-bound, and some provide good swimming holes. From here there is an extremely good view of the surrounding rugged coastline.

Charles Lindbergh's Grave

2km (1.2 miles) past Seven Pools there is the Palapala Hoomau church, and in the yard is the grave of Charles Lindbergh, the famous aviator. Lindbergh spent his last days in the area, and chose to be buried in this quiet, serene place.

Kaupo

There is not much to this little town of tin-roofed dwellings, but just above the town is Kaupo Gap. Through the Gap billowing clouds pour into Haleakala Crater.

Nuu Landing

There are ancient village ruins here among a laa and scrub landscape. Further along the road, which veers away from the coast are ancient petroglyphs.

Ulupalakua Ranch

Now we are back into the country of lush vegetation, and the nearby Tedeschi Winery, the only winery in Hawaii, gently beckons. It is well known for its light pineapple wine, a forerunner to the production of grape wine from vineyards on the slopes of Haleakala. The winery was originally an old gaol, built in 1857.

Also nearby are the ruins of the Makee Sugar Mill which dates back to 1878.

The Gardens are on Route 377 which branches off Highway 37 just before the octagonal church called the Church of the Holy Ghost (built in 1897). They have an aviary, pond, a Taboo Garden of poisonous plants, and many different species of protea. The gardens are open daily 9am-4pm and admission is $3 adults, 50c children, ph 878 1715.

Makawao

A small town that will you make you feel you are in the middle of the wild, wild west of the United States of a bygone era. They even hold a rodeo every July 4.

The town is the starting point for two tours. The first follows Olinda Road (Highway 39) past Pookela Church, built in the 1850s, through the Tree Growth Research Area, on past Olinda Nursery and the University of Hawaii Agricultural Station back to Makawao.

The second takes Highway 40 to the Hana Highway, through the town Haiku, then circles back to Makawao.

Haleakala National Park
It was here, according to Polynesian legend, that the demigod Maui captured the sun and held it to give his people more daylight hours. And it is here that you can stand and capture an unforgettable scenic memory. From the crater's top-most rim to its floor is a drop of 914m (3,000 ft). The floor measures 65 sq km (25 sq miles), a fascinating area of richly coloured cinder cones. Haleakala's last eruption was more than 200 years ago. A public observatory stands on the rim of the volcano's crater. The outer wall of the volcano, cut by ravines and gullies, slopes down tot he shore of the island.

The Park visitor centre is on Haleakala Highway at the 7,000 ft mark, ph 572 9306, and is open daily 7.30am-4pm. Entry to the park is $3 per car, $1 per hiker.

Tours

Air
Hawaii Helicopters, Kahului Airport (commuter terminal), ph 877 3900.

Maui Helicopters, Maui Inter-Continental Hotel, Wailea, ph 879 1601 or 877 4333.

Roberts hawaii, Kaonowai Street, Kahului, ph 871 6226.

Papillon Hawaiian Helicopters, PO Box 1478, Kahului, ph 669 4884 or 367 7095.

Coach
Various tour companies offer much the same tours - Island Circle, Haleakala Sunrise, Hana, etc - so it is a matter of choosing the one that appeals to you. Here are a few:

Gray Line Hawaii, 273 Dairy Road, Kahului, ph 877 5507.

No Ka Oi Scenic Tours, PO Box 1827, Kahului, ph 871 9008.

Polynesian Adventure Tours, 536 Keolani Place, Kahului, ph 877 4242.

Bicycle

Cruiser Bob's Legendary Haleakala Downhill is one of Maui's best known adventures. There are daily sunrise and picnic rides on custom-built bikes with mega-brakes. Rental bikes are also available. Call in at 99 Hana Highway, Paia, or ph 579 8444.

Maui Mountain Cruisers also bike down the slopes of haleakala on their competitively priced tours. They have a sunrise cruise which includes continental breakfast at the summit, and a champagne brunch at Koho's Restaurant. The midday cruise includes a fresh pineapple/pastries breakfast at the Sunrise Country Market and a delicious lunch. They use individually adjusted mountain cruiser bikes with ultrabrakes, safety apparel and transportation.
Ph 572 0195.

Maui Downhill Bicycle Safaris, Dairy Road, Kahului, ph 871 2155, offer much the same as the above companies.

Car

If you intend to drive the 84 km (52 miles) Highway 36 to Hana, a good tip is to get in touch with Hana Cassette Guides, ph 572 0550. They are located at the Shell Service Station on Route 380, just before Highway 36, Kahalui. The package includes a cassette player, photo album to help you identify Maui's exotic flowers, a comprehensive map and other useful information.

Sport & Recreation

Sailing & Diving

Captain Nemo's Ocean Emporium, 150 Dickenson Street, Lahaina, ph 661 5555 - 58' catamaran Seasmoke and custom dive boats - morning snorkel/scuba sails including breakfast and lunch; afternoon sunset sails; whalewatching in season; private charters.

Friendly Charters, PO Box 245, Kahului, ph 871 0985 - 44' trimaran Maalaea Kai 11 - 5-hour morning snorkel cruise including instruction, breakfast, lunch; whalewatching in season;
private charters.

Captain Steve's Rafting Excursions, PO Box 12492, Lahaina,

ph 667 5565 - 22′ Avon high-tech sea rider raft, 10-12 passengers, 13 for whalewatchers - full day Lanai tour including meals; whalewatching in season.

Gemini Charters, PO Box 10846, Lahaina, ph 661 2591 - 64′ Searunner catamaran Gemini - half-day snorkel whale watch in season; seasonal Lanai Adventure tour; seasonal Sunset Sail; seasonal Teen Sail.

Lahaina-Lanai Passenger Shuttle, PO Box 1763, Lahaina, ph 661 3756 - 40′ passenger shuttle Expeditions, 36 people; 50′ passenger ferry Expeditions 11, 64 people - service between Maui and Lanai 4 times daily, 40 minutes one-way.

Nautilus Maui, PO Box 86, Lahaina, ph 667 2133 - 60; semi-submersible Nautilis 1, with topside viewing deck and underwater viewing compartment - 5 daily 1-hour cruises from Lania Harbour; private charters.

Pacific Whale Foundation, 101 N. Kihei Road, (Suite 21) Kihei, ph 879 8811 - 53; power boat Whale One, 49 people; 50′ Gulfstar sailing ketch Whale 11, 26 people - wide variety of tours available and all profits benefit marine conservation.

Fishing

Aerial Sportfishing Charters, PO Box 831, Lahaina, ph 667 9089.

Finest Kind Sportfishing, PO Box 10481, Lahaina, ph 661 0338.

Rascal Sportfishing Charters, PO Box 1047, Kihei, ph 874 8633.

Golf

Maui Parbusters Golf Schools, Pukalani Country Club and Range, have lessons and clinics. Open 7am-9pm, ph 572 8062 - Green fees - 18 holes - $50.

Waiehu Municipal Golf Course, Waiehu, ph 244 5433 - Green fees - 18 holes - $25.

Kapalua Golf Course, Kapalua, ph 669 8044 - Green fees - 18 holes - guest $55, non-guest $85.

Royal Kaanapali Golf Course, Kaanapali, ph 661 3691 - Green fees - 18 holes - $85 daily.

Horseriding

Rainbow Ranch, at mile marker no. 29 in Napili, 10 minutes north of Kaanapali, ph 669 4991.

Pony Express Tours, Makawao, ph 667 2202.

Makena Stables, 7299 - A South Makena Road, Kihei, ph 879 0244.

The Maui Mule Ride, PO Box 265, Kula, ph 878 1743 - mule rides from the summit of Haleakala into the crater.

Tennis

Lahaina Civic Centre, 1840 Honoapiilani Highway, Lahaina, ph 661 4685 - five courts.

Wailea Tennis Club, 131 Wailea Ike Place, Kihei, ph 879 1958 - eleven courts.

Makena Tennis Club, 5415 Makena Alanui Road, Kihei, ph 879 8777 - six courts.

Royal Lahaina Tennis Ranch, 2780 Kekaa Drive, ph 661 3611 - eleven courts.

Hyatt Regency Maui, 200 Nohea Kai Drive, Kaanapali, ph 661 1234 - five courts.

Kapalua Tennis Garden, 100 Kapalua Drive, Kapalua, ph 669 5677 - ten courts.

Molokai

Molokai is the fifth largest island of the Hawaiian group, with an area of 676 sq km (261 sq miles). and was formed by two major volcanic domes thousands of years ago.

It is now called the Friendly Isle, but was known in ancient times as the Lonely Isle because the powers of its priests were feared throughout the islands. Warring chiefs ignored Molokai, while persecuted natives sought refuge there.

King Kamehameha I took over the island in 1795 when he was on his way to conquer Oahu.

During the next century, leprosy (Hansen's Disease) struck the islands and the Kalaupapa Peninsula became the place of exile for the disease's victims. From 19\866, lepers were forced to leave their families and live on this shore. The settlement was made famous by Father Damien, a Belgian priest who arrived in Kalaupapa in 1873 to serve as a pastor among the lepers. He stayed until his death from the disease in 1889, and in a sense his spirit pervades the island. He was made a Blessed (a preliminary to sainthood) by the Catholic Church in 1993.

Today Molokai is just the place to 'get away from it all'. It is closest to the spirit of Old Hawaii, has no traffic lights, and a local newspaper comes out every two weeks. Fences are often made from fallen trees to keep grazing cattle and horses off the roads, but remember that the occasional deer, pheasant or family of quail may claim right of way.

How to Get There

Molokai is 42km (26 miles) east of Oahu - approximately 20 minutes by air from Honolulu to Molokai Airport. *Hawaiian Air*, ph 553 93644, 800 867 5320, offers daily flights to Molokai, and there are a number of scheduled commuter and air taxi services providing frequent flights, eg *Island Air*, ph 800652 6541; *Molokai Air*

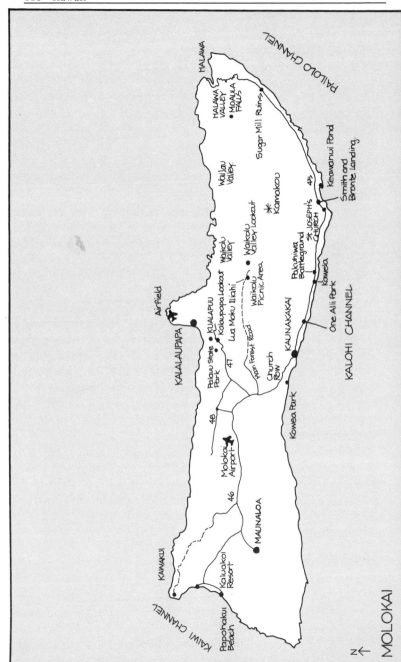

Shuttle, ph 567 6847 (Oahu ph 545 4988).

Tourist Information

The Hawaii Visitors' Bureau does not have an office on Molokai, but local businesses have established the Molokai Visitors' Association, PO Box 960, Kaunakakai, ph 553 3867 (8am-5pm).

Accommodation

There is not a great deal of accommodation on the island, but here we have listed a few examples, with prices for a double room per night in US$. These prices should be used as a guide only.

Colony's Kaluakoi Hotel and Golf Club, Kepuhi Beach, Maunaloa, ph 552 2555, fax (402) 498 9166 - 111 units, restaurant, cocktail lounge, swimming pool, golf course, tennis court - $95-115.

Ke Nani Kai, PO Box 289, Maunaloa, ph 552 2761, fax 552 0045 - condominium apartments on oceanfront, swimming pool, golf course, tennis court - $125-135.

Molokai Shores Suites, Star Route, Kamehameha Highway, Kaunakakai, ph 553 5954 - 26 rental units, condominium apartments on beach, swimming pool - $129.

Kaluakoi Villas, 1131 Kaluakoi Road, Maunaloa, ph 552 2721 - 78 units, cocktail lounge, golf course, swimming pool - $900-150.

Local Transport

The choice here is between walking and hitching, or driving. Actually hitchhiking is illegal, but the police aren't very strict in this regard.

There are a few car rental companies:

Avis Rent A Car, Hoolehua Airport, Kaunakakai, ph 567 6814; *Dollar Rent A Car of Hawaii*, Molokai Airport, ph 567 6156, fax 567 9012; *Budget Rent A Car*, Hoolehua Airport, ph 567 6877.

There are no 4WD rental agencies on the island.

Distance and Driving Times

From Molokai Airport to:

Kaunakakai -	13km (8 miles) -	10 minutes
Palaau Park -	14km (9 miles) -	15 minutes
Kamalo -	23km (14 miles) -	30 minutes
Halawa Valley -	58km (36 miles) -	2 hours

Kepuhi Beach -   24km (15 miles) -   25 minutes.

Eating Out

Molokai is not a gourmet's paradise, but you won't starve. Along Ala Malama Street in Kaunakakai   there are several budget restaurants. And at the other end of the scale, the Kaluakoi Resort has the Ohia Lodge, ph 552 2555, the most up-market restaurant on Molokai (open breakfast, lunch and dinner). The Hotel also has a snack bar that serves sandwiches, etc.

Kanemitsu's Bakery, Ala Malama Street, ph 553 5855, is great for an economical but tasty breakfast.

In the Hotel Molokai, 3km east of Kaunakakai, is the *Holo Kai Dining Room*, ph 553 5347, which has a steak/seafood menu - expensive.

The Pau Hana Inn, ph 553 5342, has moderately priced lunch and dinner menus, and a very Hawaiian atmosphere.

Oviedo's, Ala Malama Street, ph 553 5014, specialises in Filipino food at very reasonable prices.

Entertainment

Again, there is not much doing in the way of nightlife. The Kaluakoi Resort's *Ohia Lounge*, ph 552 2555, has live music each night 8-10.30pm

The *Pau Hana Inn*, ph 553 5342, has live entertainment and is very popular with the local people. Happy hour 4-6pm, dancing Fri-Sat 9pm-1am.

Hotel Molokai, ph 553 5347, has live music nightly 6.30-9pm

Shopping

Molokai is paradise for those poor men who have been dragged into every shop since they left home by their better-halves, and have to carry the ever-increasing luggage. **The shopping on the island is zilch, with a capital Z.**

Sightseeing

Kaunakakai and South Shore

Kaunakakai Town

The town is much the same as it was in the 1920s, and is the hub of the island - all roads lead to Kaunakakai. At the end of the town, barges load and unload their cargoes at the wharf of the deep-water harbour, alongside local fishing boats.

Nearby are the remains of the home of King Kamehameha V, and down the street is the extensive Kapuaiwa Coconut Grove planted by the king, bordering a beach park The beach offers safe swimming, but not much in the way of surfing.

West of the town there is a row of small, quaint churches of nearly every denomination.

On Hotel Lane is the *Guze Ji Soto Mission* (1927), the only Buddhist mission on Molokai. It is open only for services.

Kaunakakai to Halawa

One Alii Park

The park is just east of Kaunakakai and is a pleasant spot for a picnic, with views of Lanai. There are rest-rooms, a pavilion, drinking water and camping facilities. An offshore reef makes the water very shallow and protected.

Kawela

Several kilometres from Kaunakakai there is a signposted route to Kawela and the nearby Pakuhiwa Battleground. It was from here that Kamehameha I launched an armada of canoes supposedly 4 miles wide.

Kamakou

The volcanic dome is the highest point on Molokai - 1515m (4970 ft). This is the site of the Nature Conservancy's 1094ha (2700 acres) Kamakou Preserve with its rare plants and birds. Regular hikes are held by the Conservancy, with hikers picked up at Hoolehua Airport at 9am and returned by 4pm. Reservations should be made in writing and well in advance. Contact Ed Misaki, Box 220 Kualapuu 96757, ph 553 5236. The hikes cost $25 for non-members of the Conservancy.

St Joseph's Church

Built in 1876 by Father Damien, the church was restored in 1971, but is no longer used for services.

Smith and Bronte Landing

On the ocean side, a monument and plaque have been erected where Ernest Smith and Emory Bronte safely crashlanded their plane on June 14, 1927. The landing ended the first civilian trans-Pacific flight of 25 hours and 2 minutes.

Keawenui and Ualapue Fishponds

These two fishponds have been made a part of a national Historic Landmark. Keawenui Pond covers 22ha (54.5 acres) and is surrounded by a 610m (2000 ft) wall.

The ancient people depended on fish for their very existence, and fishing was also enjoyed as a sport by royalty and commoner alike.

Fish were caught with nets, hooks and lines, spears, traps and poisons, as well as by hand. They were also captured in hundreds of fishponds that at one time dotted the coastlines of all the islands. The ponds belonged exclusively to the kings and chiefs. The commoners, though they built, maintained and stocked the ponds, could fish the sea only beyond the ponds.

They were constructed by building stone walls in shallow offshore areas and at the mouth of natural inlets. A type of sluice gate (makaha) was used to allow small fish to enter, and to stop large fish from leaving. The ponds were usually no deeper than three or four feet, allowing sunlight to shine through the water and encourage the growth of foods for the fish to feed upon.

The ruins of fishponds can be found throughout the Hawaiian Islands, but there are more on Molokai than the others. At one time where were 58 along this island's coast.

Kaluaaha Church

The first missionary, Rev H.R. Hitchcock, built this first Christian church on Molokai in 1844.

Our Lady of Sorrows Catholic Church

Built by Father Damien in 1874, this is the second Catholic church to be built on the island. Next to the church is a pavilion containing a life-sized statue of Father Damien which was carved by a local resident, John Kadowaki.

Octopus Stone

Opposite Kupeke Fishpond, there is a white-painted stone at the edge of the highway where the road turns sharply inland. Legend says that the stone is the remainder of a cave where a supernatural octopus lived, and some believe the stone still has special powers.

Wailau Trail

The trail is on private property and is the only access to the largest of the north coast valleys, once a population centre of ancient Hawaii. The trail is very difficult.

Iliiliopae Heiau

Again, this heiau is on private property, but may be visited with permission. It is on the National Register of Historic Places, and is one of the largest heiaus in Hawaii, being 98m (320 ft) long and 37m (120 ft) wide. The heiau was a site of human sacrifice.

Puu Mano

The focus of many legends about the Shark God.

Wailua

Kamehameha Nui was raised here solely on taro leaves so that fishbones could not choke him. His giant awa cup is found near the stream. A rock by the road is said to have had an ear that could hear an enemy approaching, and the taro patch is just off the road.

Moanui Sugar Mill

The ruins and the stock are all that remain of a sugar mill that operated between 1870 and 1900. It was built and managed by Eugene Bal.

Puu O Hoku Ranch

"Hill of the Stars" is lush green ranchland with a magnificent view of the seascape. A working ranch with plenty of cattle and horses.

Lanikaula Grove

Just beyond the ranch building, between the road and the sea, is a sacred grove of kukui trees that is the burial place of Lanikaula, a Molokai prophet. The grove is on private land, but can easily be seen from the road.

Halawa Valley

The road zigzags down the ridge into the valley. There is good swimming in the bay and the mouth of the stream that divides the area. There is also a hiking track of 4km to Moaula Falls, which takes about an hour, but can be difficult if there has been rain.

Upper Molokai from Kaunakakai to Kalaupapa Lookout

Sandalwood Pit

Approximately 14km (9 miles) along the Main Forest Road, which is strictly 4WD or hiking, there is the Lua Moku Iliahi (Sandalwood Pit). The pit was dug the size of the hold of a ship, and the sandalwood placed inside. When it was full the wood was transferred to the harbour and loaded aboard a waiting ship.

Waikolu Valley

Along the Main Forest Road, just past the Sandalwood Pit is a lovely picnic area with views into the inaccessible valley that opens to the north side of the island.

Kualapuu (on route 48)

A former pineapple plantation town and the site of the world's largest rubber-lined reservoir.

Kauluwai

From here Oahu can be seen on a clear day. King Kamehameha I camped for a year in this area to train and condition his troops before attacking Oahu.

Kaiae

Now a residential area, Kaiae was the former dwelling place of chiefs. It was here that Rudolph W. Meyer, a German who married High Chieftainess Kalama, built a home in 1851. It now houses the R.W. Meyer Sugar Mill/Molokai Museum and Cultural Centre, ph 567 6436, admission $3.

Palaau Park

At the end of the road on route 47 is a wilderness of koa, paperback, ironwood and cypress trees. There is also a small arboretum with 40 species of trees labelled, and a camping ground with a pavilion and picnic area.

Kalaupapa Lookout

From the lookout there is a spectacular view of Kalaupapa, the wharf, churches, lighthouse, landing field, and crater, 488m (1600 ft) below.

Phallic Rock

About 180m (200 yards) through the woods is a 180cm (6 ft) rock to which local women made offerings for fertility.

Kalaupapa

A visit to Kalaupapa is a definite must, but remember that children under 16 are not admitted. The leper colony still exists, but the few remaining inhabitants are free to come and go, as the disease has been controlled with sulphone drugs since 1946. The only reason the patients still stay is that they are elderly, and having lived most of their lives at the settlement, they have nowhere else to go.

It was in 1866 that the Hawaiian government commenced exiling lepers to this lonely spot. Kalaupapa was then a fishing village, so lepers were sent to the old settlement at Kalawao on the eastern side of the peninsula. The boats they came in anchored off the coast, and the lepers were forced overboard and had to make their own way to the inhospitable land.

The terrible conditions continued until the arrival in 1873 of Joseph Damien de Veuster, Father Damien. Although he only intended to stay for a short time, the plight of the people changed his mind, and he stayed until his death from the disease in 1889. He built a simple wooden church, St Philomena's, in 1871, and in the nearby cemetery there is a monument to Father Damien. He was originally buried here, but his remains were returned to Belgium in the 1930s. Services are still held in the church.

Now designated a National Historic Park, Kalaupapa can be reached by air (Island Air, ph 323 3345), by mule (Molokai Mule Ride, ph 567 6088) or by foot (Damien Tour, ph 567 6171). The mule train trip takes 90 minutes to wind its way down the 610m (2000 ft) trail from the Kalaupapa Lookout. Although it may look a bit dicey, it is actually a very safe trip, and many say the experience of a lifetime.

Pali Coastline
The highlights of this coastline are the world's highest sea cliffs, and waterfalls plunging thousands of metres into the ocean. Air sightseeing tours and boats from Kaunakakai are available.

West Molokai from Kaunakakai
Molokai Ranch Wildlife Park
Here is an adventure of a different kind - an 'African' safari. The 324ha (800 acres) park is an animal preserve for rare and endangered hoofed animals, the terrain the vegetation are similar to that of the plains of Kenya and Tanzania. Living in the wild are Barbary sheep, eland, Indian black buck, sable antelope, impala, oryx, ibex, greater kudu, giraffe, ostrich, rhea, sika and axis deer - more than 400 animals in all for you to 'shoot', with a camera of course, ph 552 2681.

Kaluakoi Resort
The Resort stretches 4km (2.5 miles) along Papohaku, Hawaii's largest white sand beach. The complex includes a luxury hotel and resort condominiums with approximately 500 units in one and two storey Polynesian-style buildings, an 18-hole championship golf course, tennis courts, a shopping arcade and first class restaurants, ph 552 2555, fax 552 2821 - $95-200.

Maunaloa
Formerly a Dole plantation town, Manualoa is now virtually a ghost town with quaint buildings, but there are some shops selling works by Molokai artists and craftsmen.

Tours
Apart from the Kalaupapa tours already mentioned, *Gray Line Molokai*, ph 567 6177, and *Roberts Hawaii*, ph 552 2751, have general full-day and half-day tours that include the points of interest, such as the Halawa Valley, Kaunakakai and the Kalaupapa lookout.

Prices, of course, depend on the length of the tour.

The Nature Conservancy of Hawaii has tours of the rainforests and mountains of all the islands, so on this isle they have tours to Kamakou Preserve and Moomomi Dunes, ph 553 5236.

Molokai Ranch Wildlife Conservation Park, Molokai Ranch Outfitter's Centre, PO Box 259, Maunaloa, ph 552 2767, has a park tour that includes feeding the animals. Tours are conducted Fri-Mon, and the costs are $40 adults, $25 5-18 years, $10 under 5.

Molokai Action Adventure (Ma'a), PO Box 1269, K'kai, ph 558 8184, offer guided hunting tours with rifle or bow on the private ranchlands of Molokai.

Game includes deer, wild boar and Spanish goats.

Damien Tours, PO Box 1, Kalaupapa, 96742, ph 567 6171, have a tour of the former leper colony on Kalaupapa Peninsula.

Molokai Mule Ride, PO Box 200, Molokai, 95757, ph 567 6088, fax 567 6244, ties in with the Damien Tour. Must be 16 years and over - $120 for an 8 hour trip.

Sport and Recreation

Golf

Ironwood Hills Golf Course, Kalae, ph 567 6000. Green fees - 9 hole course - $20 daily for 18 holes.

Kaluakoi Golf Course (Kaluakoi Resort), ph 552 2739. Green fees - 18 holes - guest $55, non-guest $75.

Horse Riding

Molokai Horse & Wagon Ride, PO Box 56, Hoolehua, ph 567 6773. Wagon rides $37 adults, $18.40 children 12 and under; trail rides 1 1/2 hours $44 per person for up to eight people.

Molokai Ranch Trail Rides, ph 552 2767. Ninety minute morning ride $35, 4.5 hour lunch ride $75, including lunch.

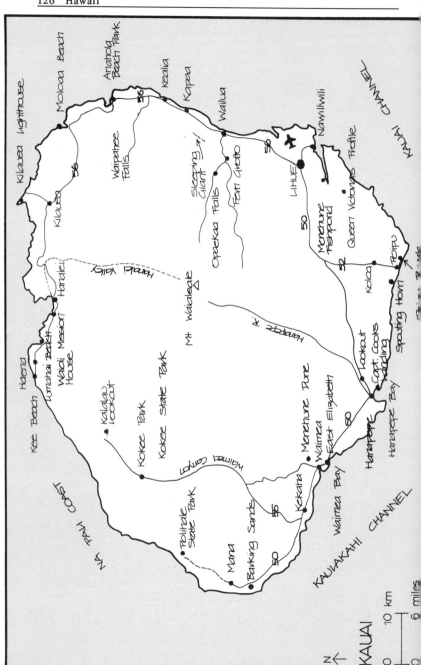

KAUAI

Kauai

Kauai is the oldest of the Hawaiian chain, both geographically and historically. It is nearly circular in shape, and is arguably the most beautiful of the islands. It was on the Garden Isle that the movies South Pacific and King Kong were filmed, but even these did not do justice to the natural scenery of the island.

Kauai was the first of the islands to be visited by Captain Cook in 1778, and it was the last to be an independent kingdom. It was the only island not conquered by Kamehameha the Great in his battles to be the king of a united Hawaii, and it was only by diplomacy that he arranged a treaty with King Kaumaulii of Kauai.

The first successful sugar plantation was established here, and it is the only island where the fragrant mokihana berry grows. The island is very rich in folklore, and the islanders are very proud of their heritage and history. The legendary race of little people, the Menehune, were very active on Kauai. Believed to be about 61cm (2 ft) tall, with ugly red faces and big eyes, they were nocturnal workers who in one night achieved the construction of the Alekoko fish pond at Niumalu, and the Menehune watercourse of Waimea Valley. There are some people today on Kauai who claim Menehune ancestry, and who say that the little people are still on the island, hiding in the dense forests.

Kauai is 153km (95 miles) north-west of Oahu, and has an area of 1432 sq km (553 sq miles).

How to Get There

Hawaiian Airlines and Aloha Airlines have frequent daily flights to Lihue Airport. There are also scheduled commuter and other air taxi services operating between the Islands.

Island Air, formerly Princeville Airways, offers flights to/from Princeville Airport.

Tourist Information

The Hawaii Visitor's Bureau has an office in the Lihue Plaza Building, 3016 Umi Street, ph 245 3971, fax 246 9235.

Accommodation

No shortages in this area on Kauai. The accommodation listed here is for a double room per night in US$, and should be used as a guide only.

Lihue/Nawiliwili

Outrigger Kauai Beach, 4331 Kauai Beach Drive, Lihue, ph 245 1955, fax (303) 369 9403 - 346 units, restaurant, cocktail lounge, swimming pool, tennis court - $130-210.

Banyan Harbor Resort, 3411 Wilcox Road, Lihue, ph 2145 7333 - 16 condominium units, swimming pool, tennis court - $95-105.

Aston Kauai Beach Villas, 4330 Kauai Beach Drive, Lihue, ph 245 7711, fax 922 8785 - condominiums - 118 units, swimming pool, tennis court - $160-199.

Garden Island Inn, 3445 Wilcox Road, Kalapaki Beach, Lihue, ph/fax 245 7227 - 21 units - $55-85.

Tip Top Motel, 3173 Akahi Street, Lihue, ph 245 2333, fax 246 8988 - restaurant, cocktail lounge - $60.

Waipouli

Aston Kauai Beachboy Hotel, 4-484 Kuhio Highway, #100, Kapaa, ph 822 3441 - 243 units, restaurant, swimming pools - $95-130.

Coco Palms Resort, 4-241 Kuhio Highway, Wailua, ph 822 4921, fax 822 7189 - restaurant, cocktail lounge, swimming pool, tennis court - $115-120.

Islander on the Beach, 484 Kuhio Highway, Kapaa, ph 822 7417, fax 822 1947 - restaurant, swimming pool - $100-120.

Kauai Coconut Beach Resort, Coconut Plantation (PO Box 830, Kapaa), ph 822 3455, fax 822 0035 - 300 units, restaurant, cocktail lounge, swimming pool, tennis court - $125.

Kapaa Sands, 380 Papaloa Road, Kapaa, ph 822 4901 - 21 apartments, swimming pool - $85-120.

Hotel Coral Reef, 1516 Kuhio Highway, Kapaa, ph 822 4481, fax 822 7705 - 26 units - $60-90.

Hanalei/Princeville

Pu'u Po'a, 5454 Kahaku Road, Princeville, ph 826 6585, fax 826 6478 - 50 condominium apartments, swimming pool, golf course, tennis court - $125-195.

Pali Ke Kusa, 5300 Kahaku Road, Princeville, ph 826 9066, fax 922 2421 - 98 condominium apartments, restaurant, cocktail lounge, swimming pool - $160-210.

Ali'i Kaii, 3830 Edwards Road, Princeville, ph 826 7444, fax 826 7673 - 35 condominium apartments, swimming pool, golf course, tennis court - $110-150.

Hanalei Bay Resort, 5380 Honoiki Road, Princeville, ph 826 6522, fax 826 6680 - 230 units, restaurant, cocktail lounge, swimming pools, tennis courts - $150-230.

Sandpiper Village, 4770 Pepelani Loop, Princeville, ph 826 6585, fax 826 6478 - 6 condominium units, swimming pool, golf course - $90-120.

Poipu/Kokee

Kiahuna Plantation, 2253 Poipu Road, Koloa, ph 742 6411, fax (510) 939 6644 - 333 condominium apartments, restaurant, cocktail lounge, swimming pool, golf course, tennis court - $175-400.

Poipu Kai, 1941 Poipu Road, Koloa, ph 742 6464 - 115 units, restaurant, cocktail lounge, swimming pool, tennis court - $85-165.

Nih Kai Villas, 1870 Hoone Road, Poipu, ph 742 1412, fax 742 9001 - 40 condominium apartments, swimming pool, tennis court - $140.

Poipu Bed and Breakfast Inn, 2720 Hoonani Road, Koloa, ph 742 1146, fax 742 6843 - 9 condominium apartments, swimming pool, tennis court - $120-135.

Sheraton Kauai Garden Hotel, 2440 Hoonani Road, Koloa, ph 742 1661, fax 742 9777 - 230 units, restaurant, cocktail lounge, swimming pool, - $95-125.

Waimea Plantation Cottages, 9400 Kaumualii Highway, #367 Waimea, ph 338 1625, fax 338 1619 - 44 units, swimming pool, tennis court - $160-210.

Garden Isle Cottages, 2666 Puuholo Road, Koloa, ph 742 6717 - 12 units - $70-95.

Prince Kuhio Resort, 5061 Lawai Road, Koloa, ph 245 4711, fax 245 8115 - 15 condominium apartments, swimming pool - $60.

Local Transport

There is no local bus service, so renting a car is the only way to go. Here are a few names and addresses:

Avis Rent A Car, Lihue Airport, ph 245 3512; Hyatt Poipu Kauai, ph 742 1527; Princeville Airport, ph 826 9773.

Budget Rent A Car, Lihue Airport, ph 245 9031.

Dollar Rent-a-Car of Hawaii, Lihue Airport, ph 245 3651.

Hertz Rent A Car, Lihue Airport, ph 245 3356.

National Car Rental, Lihue Airport, ph 245 5637.

Most of the roads on Kauai are accessible by car, but if you would still like to get around in a jeep, there's Rent-A-Jeep, 3137A Kuhio Highway, Lihue, ph 245 9622.

Distance and Driving Times

From Lihue to:

Poipu -	23km (14 miles) -	40 minutes
Waimea -	40km (25 miles) -	1 hour
Kekaha -	47km (29 miles) -	1 hour 5 minutes
Waimea Canyon -	64km (40 Miles) -	2 hours
Kalalau Lookout -	80km (50 Miles -	2 hours 10 minutes
Waiolua River -	11km (7 miles) -	20 minutes
Hanalei -	56km (35 miles) -	1 hour 15 minutes
Haena -	66km (41 miles) -	1 hour 30 minutes.

Eating Out

Most of the hotels have excellent dining rooms and restaurants, but if you occasionally feel like something different, here are a few names and addresses.

Lihue Area

Tip Top Cafe and Bakery, Tip Top Motel, 3173 Akahi Street, ph 245 2333 - offers local favourites and exotic pancakes - open for breakfast and lunch - budget.

Jacaranda Terrace, Outrigger Kauai Beach, 4331 Kauai Beach Drive, ph 245 1955 - excellent food in a great setting, buffet Friday night - open for breakfast, lunch and dinner - inexpensive.

Lihue Barbecue Inn, 2982 Kress Street, ph 245 2921 - home-style food in friendly atmosphere - open for breakfast, lunch, dinner, cocktails - budget.

The Terrace Restaurant, Golf & Racquet Club, Kalapaki Beach, ph 241 6080 - open-air restaurant serving American/Japanese cuisine - open for lunch and cocktails - inexpensive.

Gaylord's At Kilohana, 3-2087 Kaumualii Highway, ph 245 9593 - courtyard setting, continental cuisine - open for brunch, lunch, dinner, cocktails - moderate.

Dani's Restaurant, 4201 Rice Street, ph 245 4991 - Hawaiian fare - open for breakfast and lunch - budget.

Cafe Portofino, Pacific Ocean Plaza, 3501 Rice Street, #208, ph 245 2121 - Italian cuisine, great view of Kalapaki Beach - open for lunch, dinner, cocktails - moderate.

McDonald's, 3113 Kuhio Highway, ph 245 6123 - budget.

Pizza Hut, 3-3171 Kuhio Highway, ph 245 9531 - budget.

Poipu/Kokee

Brennecke's Beach Broiler, 2100 Hoone Road, ph 742 7588 - casual family dining - open for lunch (and brunch Sunday), dinner, cocktails - moderate.

Green Garden Restaurant, 13749 Kaumualii Highway, Hanapepe, ph 335 5422 - continental cuisine - open for breakfast, lunch, dinner, late supper, cocktails (closed Tuesday) - inexpensive.

Ilima Terrace Restaurant, Hyatt Regency Kauai, 1571 Poipu Road, Koloa, ph 742 1234 - continental cuisine - open for breakfast, lunch, dinner - moderate.

Dondero's, Hyatt Regency Kauai, 1571 Poipu Road, Koloa, ph 742 1234 - Italian cuisine - open for dinner only - expensive.

The Grove, Waimea Plantation Cottages, 9400 Kaumualii Highway, #367, Waimea, ph 338 1625 - Hawaiian cuisine - open for breakfast, brunch, lunch, dinner, cocktails - inexpensive.

Brick Oven Pizza, 2-2555 Kaumualii Highway, Kalaheo, ph 332 8561 - open for dinner - budget.

Tidepools Restaurant, Hyatt Regency Kauai, 1571 Poipu Road, Koloa, ph 742 1234 - seafood/steak and Japanese - open for dinner, cocktails - expensive.

Waipouli

Al & Don's Restaurant, Kauai Sands Hotel, 420 Papaloa Road, Wailua Beach, Kapaa, ph 822 4221 - casual dining, American cuisine - open for lunch and dinner - budget.

Lagoon Dining Room, Coco Palms Resort, 4-241 Kuhio Highway, Wailua, ph 245 3931 - open-air dining, American cuisine, entertainment - open for breakfast, lunch, dinner, cocktails - inexpensive.

Queen's Pool Bar & Broiler, Coco Palms Resort, 4-241 Kuhio Highway, Wailua, ph 882 4921 - casual poolside, light meals - open for lunch, cocktails - budget.

Wailua Marina Restaurant, 5971 Kuhio Highway, Kapaa, ph 822 4211 - international cuisine - open for lunch, dinner, cocktails - moderate.

Smith's Tropical Paradise Luau, Wailua Marina, Kapaa, ph 822 4654 - garden luau with an international flavour - expensive.

The Flying Lobster, Kauai Coconut Beach Resort, Coconut Plantation, Kuhio Highway, ph 822 3455 - great seafood selections, entertainment and dancing - open dinner, cocktails - moderate.

Pacific Dining Room, Kauai Resort Hotel, 3-5920 Kuhio Highway, Wailua, ph 245 3931 - casual dining with good ocean views - steak/seafood - open for breakfast, lunch, dinner, cocktails - moderate.

McDonald's, 4-0771 Kuhio Highway, Kapaa, ph 822 7290 - budget.

Pizza Hut, Waipouli Town Centre, 4-771 Kuhio Highway, Kapaa, ph 822 7433 - budget.

Hanalei Area

Beach Restaurant & Bar, Princeville Hotel, 5520 Kahaku Road, ph 826 2762 - great view of Hanalei Bay, swim-up bar - international cuisine - open for lunch and cocktails - inexpensive.

La Cascata, Princeville Hotel, 5520 Kahaku Road, ph 826 2761 - Italian/French cuisine - open for dinner, cocktails - expensive.

Charo's, 5-7132 Kuhio Highway, Haena, ph 826 6422 - Mexican cuisine, romantic atmosphere - open for lunch and dinner - moderate.

Bali Hai Restaurant, Hanalei Bay Resort, ph 826 6522 - island cuisine, entertainment - open for breakfast, brunch, lunch, dinner - expensive.

Chuck's Steak House, Princeville Shopping Centre, Kuhio Highway, Handle - steak/seafood - open for lunch, dinner, cocktails - moderate.

Entertainment

Kauai could never be called the nightlife capital of anywhere, but there is usually something happening in the large hotels, and there are a few bars and lounges you could try.

For what's on where it's best to pick up a copy of one of the free magazines from the visitors centre and Lihue Airport - Kauai Beach Press, This Week on Kauai and Spotlight Kauai.

Following are a few dance venues:

Club Jetty Restaurant and Cabaret, Nawiliwili Harbour, Nawiliwili, ph 245 4970 - Wed-Sat 10pm-3.30am.

Legends Nightclub, Harbor Village Shopping Centre, 3501 Rice Street, Nawiliwili, ph 245 5775 - music nightly 9.30pm-4am.

Paddling Club, Westin Kauai, Kalapaki Beach, Nawiliwili, ph 246 5048 - nightly 9pm-1am. Features five levels of up-market entertainment.

Kuhio's Nightclub, Hyatt Regency Kauai, 1571 Poipu Road, Koloa, ph 742 1234 - nightly 9pm-2am.

Buzz's Steak & Lobster, Coconut Plantation Market Place, Kapaa, ph 822 7491 - nightly 8.30-11.30pm.

Shopping

Kukui Grove Center, Kaumualii Highway, 1km from Lihue, is the island's largest shopping centre with department stores - Sears, JC Penney, Woolworths and Liberty House - bookshops and specialty stores. For the free shuttle service ph 245 7784.

Kilohana, Kaumualii Highway about 2km west of Lihue, is set in an old plantation house in 14ha (35 acres) of well-kept grounds. If you can't see anything you fancy to buy, at least the surroundings are beautiful.

Kauai Village, 4-831 Kuhio Highway, Kapaa, ph 822 4904, is one of the latest shopping venues on the island and is in the style of a plantation town.

Old Koloa Town, on Koloa Road on the way to Poipu, has several small shops.

The Spouting Horn in the car park at the blowhole, is a fascinating place. Local merchants set up stalls and sell their wares. If you are interested in local jewellery, here you can watch it being made, then barter for it.

Kiahuna Shopping Village on Poipu Road has a range of up-market shops.

The Coconut Market Place, Route 56, Wailua, is arguably the best shopping centre on Kauai. The little wooden stores are designed as plantation houses, and you will be able to find anything you are looking for.

The Coco Palms Hotel has several rather expensive shops selling handicrafts. Incidentally this is where Blue Hawaii, with Elvis Presley, was filmed.

Rehabilitation Unlimited of Kauai, 4531 Kuamoo Road, ph 822 4975, has on offer bamboo and coconut wares made by local disabled folk.

Princeville Center, off Route 56, is a good place for window-shopping unless you have a large budget.

Ching Young Village in Hanalei, is home to Village Variety Store, ph 826 6077, where it is always possible to pick up a bargain.

Sightseeing

Lihue

The colourful town of Lihue, Kauai's commercial centre, is the starting point for a tour of either half of the Garden Isle.

Sugar cane was first planted here around 1835, making it one of the oldest plantation towns in the Islands. The town houses the state and county offices, and has a regional library and convention centre.

Places of interest include:

The Kauai Museum, 4428 Rice Street, ph 245 6931, presents a factual history of the Garden Isle, using artefacts and photographs. Open Mon-Fri 9am-4.30pm, Sat 9am-1pm, admission is $5 adults, children free.

Follow Rice Street to Nawiliwili, turn onto Route 58, then on to Niumalu Road, then Hulemalu Road, and you will come to the Menehune Fish Pond. The pond is spread across a valley floor, and is believed by some to have been built in one night by the Menehunes.

The Grove Farm Homestead, just south of Lihue, was founded in 1864 by George Wilcox, and is now a museum complex that includes the old family plantation home, wash house, tea house, guest cottage and other amenities. The homestead is typical of the old Hawaiian plantation experience and tradition. Guided tours are available Mon, Wed and Thurs at 10am and 1pm, but advance reservations are required, ph 245 3202. Admission is $5.

On the Kaumualii Highway, about 3km west from the intersection of Nawiliwili Road is Kilohana, the site of the Wilcox sugar plantation. It is now a 15ha (35 acres) visitor attraction with horse and carriage rides, agricultural displays, local arts and crafts, and specialty shops. The estate is open daily 9am-5pm and admission is free, ph 245 5608. It is a good place for a picnic, or you can dine at Gaylord's restaurant in the courtyard.

South Shore Area

Queen Victoria's Profile

Along Route 50 on the left-hand side when you are heading for Poipu, there is a Hawaii VisitorsÆ Bureau sign pointing out the profile of Queen Victoria carved in the Hoary Head Range. You have to use your imagination for these sorts of things.

Koloa

The first sugar mill in Hawaii commenced operations here in 1835, and the remains of that mill are on the right side of the road. Nearby is a memorial to the various ethnic groups that contributed to the sugar industry on Kauai. The main street of the town has been restored and has some rather expensive boutiques, an old general store, and quite a few restaurants.

Poipu Beach

The park here has picnic facilities, rest rooms, showers, volleyball, playground, lifeguards, and excellent swimming. The entire area around here has some of the best diving spots on the island.

Spouting Horn

At high tide the waves force water through lava tubes and out a hole in the rocks to form a really spectacular fountain of spray and foam. Not your ordinary blowhole.

Hanapepe

An old village complete with wooden sidewalks and weather-beaten houses and shops. There was a bit of trouble here in the sugar strike of 1924, with sixteen workers being killed, and the town still retains the same spirit of independence. It's worth a detour to have a look-see. Parts of the mini-series The Thorn Birds were filmed in this town. From the Hanapepe Valley and Canyon Lookout there is a good view of native flora set in a gorge surrounded by eroded cliffs. This is also an historic canyon for it is the site of Kauai's last battle, in 1824.

Salt Pond Beach Park

From Hanapepe, take Lele Road to Lolokai Road, then follow that to the park and discover how the Hawaiians have made salt for the last couple of hundred years. They collect sea water in mud-lined drying beds, then leave the sun to do the rest.

Nearby is Burns Field, the island's first airfield but now home to several helicopter outfits.

Fort Elizabeth

An old Russian fort built by an employee of the Russian Fur Company of Alaska in 1817, who had high hopes of seizing Kauai for the Car. The fort was near the mouth of the Waimea River, but all that remains of the Russian dream are a few rocky ruins.

Captain Cook's Landing

I wonder if anyone has ever counted how many monuments to Cook's landing there are in the Pacific region. Anyway, hereÆs another. This commemorates the first place he landed in Hawaii in January 1778. Just follow the sign-posts to the lava monolith. Waimea Bay was for many years a favourite provisioning port with Pacific traders and whalers.

Menehune Ditch

Only small portions remain of what was once a great water course. Archaeologists say it was built before Hawaiians came to Kauai, and the method of construction is unlike any other in the islands. Therefore, as far as the locals are concerned, the ditch was built by the Menehune, but no claims are made that it was built in one night. It's just outside Waimea, on Menehune Road.

Mana

A dilapidated town on the way to Polihale State Park, from where there is an excellent view of Niihau, the westernmost inhabited island of Hawaii. Niihau is privately-owned and several hundred natives live there with a lifestyle similar to that of 19th century Hawaii. Unfortunately, it is off limits to visitors, except for aerial sightseeing (see Tours).

Waimea Canyon

The 1097m (3600 ft) deep canyon, sometimes called 'The Grand Canyon of the Pacific' is reached by taking Route 55 from Waimea. There are fantastic views along the way, but especially at the Puu Ka Ple and Puu Hina Hina lookouts.

Kokee State Park

Adjacent to Waimea Canyon, Kokee State Park (ph 335 5871) has picnic grounds, cabins and a wide variety of outdoor activities including hunting, trout fishing and hiking. The NASA Kokee Tracking Station is nearby.

Kalakau Lookout

The lookout is at the end of Waimea Canyon Drive, at 1456m (4120 ft) above sea level, and is the beginning of an incredibly scenic hiking trail. Once peacocks preened their plumage in this tropic Eden., and natives cultivated terraces of taro. No one lives here now, but it is arguably one of the most beautiful views on earth.

North Shore Area

Ke'e Beach

At the beginning (or end) of Route 56, where the Kalalau trail to the Na Pali Cliffs begins, is the reef-shrouded Ke'e Beach. It is a good swimming beach in the summer only, and has good facilities, including showers and rest rooms.

Wet and Dry Caves of Haena

Geologists say that the Maniniholo Dry Cave is a lava tube, but the natives 'know' it was dug by the Menehunes when they were looking for an evil spirit. The Waikapalae and Waikanaloa Wet Caves nearby are also 'known' to be the creation of Pele, the fire goddess, who was looking for fire, but found water. The water is stagnant now, but the caves make a good photographic study.

Lumahai Beach
Near the 33-mile market on Route 56, a path leads to the partly reef-protected beach. Probably best known as the Nurses' Beach in the movie South Pacific, the swimming is generally pretty good, but still take care. Fishing is pretty good here too.

Waioli Mission House
Visitors are most welcome at this quaint house built in 1834, and restored by the descendants of the first missionaries. It was the home of missionary teachers Lucy and Abner Wilcox, who originally came from New England. The house is open Tues, Thurs and Sat 9am-3pm, and entry is free but donations are accepted, ph 245 3202.

Hanalei Valley
Another name for Hanalei is Hanohano, meaning 'glorious' and that just about sums up the view gained from the Hanalei Valley Lookout on Route 56, opposite Princeville Shopping centre. The lower 365ha (900 acres) comprise a national wildlife refuge under the auspices of the US Fish and Wildlife Service to protect Hawaii's four endangered water birds - Hawaiian Stilt, Hawaiian Coot, Hawaiian Gallinule and Hawaiian Duck (or Koloa). In, and near, the town of Hanalei there are incredible mountain views, tumble-down buildings and crescent beaches - altogether glorious.

Kilauea Lighthouse
Situated on the northernmost point of the principal islands of Hawaii, the lighthouse was the first beacon seen by sailors venturing east from Asia, and had the world's largest clamshell lens. It is now part of the Kilauea Wildlife Refuge and is open to visitors Mon-Fri, 10am-4pm, ph 828 1413. When you are there, look closely at the nearby cliffs - you might be lucky enough to see albatross nesting.

Moloaa Beach
A secluded beach divided into two by a stream. It has good fishing

and skin diving. Swim with care. ItÆs on a side road off Route 56.

Anahola Beach
The park has a picnic area, rest rooms, showers and is less than 2km from the town of Anahole. There is a very strong current here so swimmers should be careful. The fishing is good.

Kealia Beach
There are no picnic areas, rest rooms or showers, just a great beach opposite the 'one-horse' town of Kealia. The swimming is good (again with caution) and people fish here for ulua, papio and threadfin.

Kapaa Beach
A pretty little beach with the normal facilities, not far off Route 56 and Kapaa town. The swimming and fishing are okay.

The Sleeping Giant
The outline of a mountain ridge shows a striking resemblance to a reclining giant. It is supposed to be Puni, a friend of the Menehune.

Opaekaa Falls
Opaekaa means 'rolling shrimp' and dates from the days when swarms of shrimp were seen rolling in turbulent waters at the base of the falls. The scenery near the falls is worth a visit.

Royal Birth Stones, Wailua
On Route 580 the Visitors' Bureau has signs posts to the Holo'Holo'Ku Heiau, a very old temple and place of refuge and sacrifice, and to Pohaku Ho'Ohanau, a sacred place in Hawaiian history. The women of Hawaiian nobility always tried to reach these sacred stones in time to give birth, to ensure the royal status of their children. Nearby are the remains of the king's house and the Bell Stone, which signalled the birth of a royal infant. This ancient noble place has been restored by the Bishop Museum and the Kauai Historical Society.

Smith's Tropical Paradise
A 9ha (23 acres) park with gardens, lagoons, exotic birds and a

unique narrated train ride that wanders through a rain forest, a Polynesian village, a Japanese island, a Filipino village and other interesting areas. Kauai's ethnic heritage is reflected nightly in a 75 minute musical production in the lagoon theatre.

Fern Grotto
Reached by ferry from the Wailua Marina, the grotto is a cave framed by ferns with a waterfall cascading to the rocks below. It's a popular place for wedding ceremonies.

Kamokila Hawaiian Village
Above the bend of the Wailua River, where war canoes of the King of Kauai, Kamualii once assembled, lies a restored old Hawaiian village. The village is open for visitors Mon-Sat 9am-4pm, and has daily craft demonstrations and guided tours. Admission is $8 adults, $5 children.

Tours

Air
There are many flightseeing tours on offer, with flights averaging around $130-135 per person per hour.
Papillon Hawaiian Helicopters, Princeville Airport, ph 826 6591.
Will Squyres Helicopter Tours, Box 1770, Lihue, ph 245 8881.
'Ohana Helicopters, Kuhio Highway, Lihue, ph 2226989.
Bali Hai Helicopter Tours, Box 1052, Kalaheo, ph 335 3166.

Tour to Niihau
Niihau Helicopters, Box 370, Makaweli, ph 335 3500, is owned by the Robinson family, as is the island of Niihau. There is only one tour, four times a day Mon-Fri, and it makes two stops - one near the sunken crater of Lehua, the other on a cliff overlooking the beaches of Keanahaki Bay. There is no ground transport at either stop. Cost for the three hour tour is $200 per person, and advance reservations are required.

Land
Robert's Hawaii, Box 3389, Lihue, ph 241 7255.
Polynesian Adventure Tours, 3563 Ahukini Road, Lihue, ph 2436 -122.

Grey Line Hawaii, PO Box 1551, Lihue, ph 833 8000.
Kauai Island Tours, Ahukini Road, Lihue Airport, ph 245 4777.

Water

Captain Zodiac Raft Expeditions, PO Box 456, Hanalei, ph 826 9371, have tours along the Na Pali Coast, except in heavy surf. Whalewatching in season.

Blue Water Sailing, PO Box 1316, Hanalei, ph 822 0525, offer tours and custom and inter-island charters on request.

Smith's Motor Boat Service, 174 Wailua Road, Kapaa, ph 822 4111, have tours up the Wailua River to Fern Grotto for $10. If you decide to 'go Hawaiian' and have your wedding there, they can make all the arrangements.

Sport and Recreation

Golf

Wailua Municipal Golf Course, 3-5351 Kuhio Highway, Lihue, ph 245 2163. Green fees - 18 holes - $25 weekdays, $35 weekends.

Kiahuna Golf Club, 2545 Kiahuna Plantation Drive, Koloa, ph 742 9595. Green fees - 18 holes - $75 non-guests, $68 guests,
$45 after 2pm.

Kukuiolono Golf Course, Kalaheo, ph 332 9940. Green fees - 9 holes - $10 daily.

Princeville Makai Golf Course, PO Box 3040, Princeville,
ph 826 3580. Green fees - 18 holes - $95 guests, $115 non-guests.

Princeville Prince Golf Course, PO Box 3040, Princeville,
ph 826 5000. Green fees - 18 holes - $95 guests, $125 non-guests.

Horse Riding

Po'oku Stables, PO Box 888, Hanalei, ph 826 6777 - Princeville area - valley rides $55; beach rides $95; waterfall rides (3-hour including lunch) $105.

South Sea Tours at Kauai Lagoons, 3901 Mokulele Loop, Box 32, Lihue, ph 245 2222 - trail rides through tropical landscape, adults $49 per hour, children $29 per hour.

Snorkelling/Diving

Capt Andy's Scuba Cat Divers, PO Box 1291, Koloa, Ph 822 8933 - 60' custom catamaran Spirit of Kauai - 4 hour snorkelling tour of south shore, including lunch, gear and lesson - $65.

Dive Kauai Scuba Centre, 976 Kuhio Highway, Kapaa, ph 822 0452 - custom dive boat, 12 passenger - introductory dive $80.

Fathom Five Divers, PO Box 907, Koloa, ph 742 6991 - boat dive 2-tank, certified divers $75 with own gear, $100 including gear.

Sea Fun Kauai, PO Box 3002, Lihue, ph 245 6400 - shore-based snorkel tours, 4-5 hour tour $55 adults, $37.50 children including transportation, equipment and instruction, wetsuit, guided tour of the reef.

Freshwater Fishing

The rainbow trout season opens on the first Saturday in August for 16 days, after that fishing is permitted only on weekends and holidays until the end of September. Other freshwater fish may be caught daily all year round. A freshwater fishing licence is required and can be obtained from the Department of Land and Natural Resources, PO Box 1671, Lihue, ph 245 4433. A 30-day licence for visitors is $3.75.

Bass Guides of Kauai, PO Box 3525, Lihue, ph 826 2566 - half-day trip, $110 for 1 person, $165 for 2.

Deep-sea Fishing

Gent-Lee Fishing & Sightseeing Charters, PO Box 1691, Lihue, ph 245 7504 - share 3/4 day $120, half day $90 - exclusive tour rates available.

Robert McReynolds' Sportfishing Charters, PO Box 767, Kilauea, ph 828 1379 - exclusive full day $500, half day $450 - shared $130 full day, $85 half day.

True Blue Charters, 3500 Rice Street, Lihue, ph 246 6333 - from Nawiliwili Harbour - full day exclusive $600, 3/4 day $500, half day $400 - shared 3/4 day $120, half day $90.

Tennis

Over 70 of the hotels and resorts have their own tennis courts, which are free for gusts but cost about $15 per hour per person for non-guests. There are roughly 20 public courts, and you should contact the Visitors' Bureau or the Country Department of Parks and Recreation, ph 245 8821, for information on bookings.

Lanai

Lanai, the Pineapple Isle, is 77km (48 miles) south-east of Ohau, 13km (8 miles) west of Maui, and 11km (7 miles) south of Molokai. The island has an area of 363 sq km (140 sq miles), being 29km (18 miles) long and 21km (13 miles) wide. It is, like all the other islands in the Hawaiian group, of volcanic origin.

The island was discovered by that intrepid Englishman, Captain James Cook, in 1779, but because of its reef-shrouded shores and dry, barren-looking landscape, nobody bothered much about it. The ancient Hawaiians had not been to keen on Lanai either, because they believed it was inhabited by evil spirits, until the Maui chief Kakaalaneo banished his errant son, Kaululaau, to the island because of his atrocious behaviour on Maui. Whilst on Lanai, the wild young man took a change for the better and drove out all the evil spirits. Lanai was then settled by Hawaiians and controlled by Maui chiefs.

The first missionaries, Dwight Baldwin and William Richards, arrived in 1835, and by the 1850s the Mormons had established a City of Joseph in central Lanai. This venture only lasted about three years because the drought and insect plagues convinced the missionaries this was no Eden.

Then in 1922, Jim Dole's Hawaiian Pineapple Company bought a major portion of the island from Harry and Frank Baldwin, descendants of the early missionary, for about $1.1m (proving there is more money in land than in missionary work).

Another man who changed the face of Lanai was George Munro, a New Zealand naturalist, who arrived in 1911. He is responsible for the Norfolk pines which surround Lanai City, and carried out much restoration work in the highlands, planting trees to protect the eroded hillsides.

Today, only about one-eighth of the island is under pineapple cultivation, but Lanai City, the commercial hub of the island, remains a plantation town. There are only about 40km (25 miles) of sealed roads on Lanai, but there are plenty of hiking trails to take you to remote beaches and incredible mountain scenery.

Lanai is privately owned and those owners provide the major accommodation on the island.

How to Get There

Hawaiian Airlines and *Aloha Island Air* have daily flights to and from Honolulu, and *Aloha Airlines* has two flights on Sat, Sun and Mon. The flight takes about 25 minutes.

Air Molokai also has frequent daily flights, as does *Aloha Airlines* from the other islands.

Tourist Information

The Hawaii Visitors' Bureau does not have an office on Lanai.

Accommodation

There are two resorts on Lanai:

The Lodge at Koele, a baronial manor with Hawaiian overtones on the edge of Lanai City; and *The Manele Bay Hotel*, an oceanfront resort. Both have restaurants, cocktail lounges, swimming pools, golf courses and tennis courts, and the reservation numbers for both are ph 565 7300, fax 565 3868. Room rates start from $315 (Hotel) and $365 (Lodge).

The Hotel Lanai, PO Box A-119, Lanai, ph 565 7211, the original hotel on the island, is still operating and its rates start at $95.

Bed and Breakfast Hawaii, PO Box 449, Kapaa, Kauai, ph 822 7771, fax 822 2723, can arrange this type of accommodation for $50-60 a double.

There is a small *camping group* at Hulopoe Beach, and for information on this write to the owners, Koele Company, PO Box L, Lanai.

Local Transport

None at all.

The only taxi company on the island is *Lanai City Service*, ph 565 7227, and transfers to and from the airport cost $7. To get around by cab, on the paved roads only, will cost about $10 from Lanai City to anywhere.

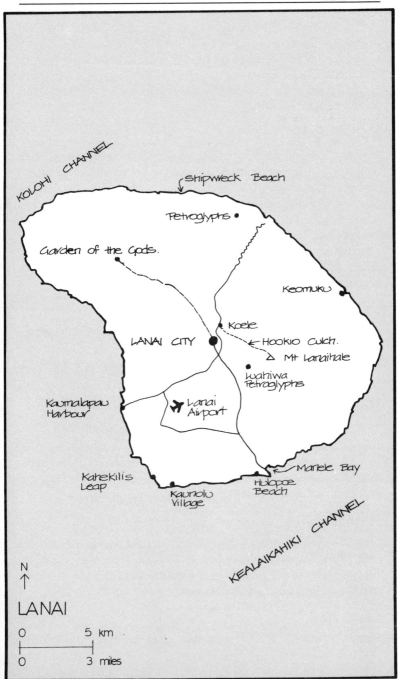

KOLOHI CHANNEL

Shipwreck Beach

Petroglyphs

Garden of the Gods.

Keomuku

Koele

LANAI CITY

Hookio Gulch.

△ Mt Lanaihale

Luahiwa
Petroglyphs

Kaumalapau
Harbour

Lanai
Airport

Manele Bay

Kahekili's
Leap

Kaunolu
Village

Holopoe
Beach

KEALAIKAHIKI CHANNEL

N

LANAI

0   5 km

0   3 miles

The only car rental companies are *Lanai City Service*, the local branch of *Dollar Rent A Car*, ph 565 7227, and *Oshiro Tour & U-Drive*, ph 565 6952. The best type of vehicle for Lanai's roads, or lack thereof, is a 4WD.

To find out about road conditions, contact Lanai City Service Inc, ph 565 7227.

Eating Out

Hulopo'e Court, Manele Bay Hotel, ph 565 7700 - main dining room featuring contemporary Hawaiian cuisine - open for breakfast and dinner - expensive.

The Pool Grille, Manele Bay Hotel, ph 565 7700 - sandwiches and snacks - moderate.

The Terrace, Lodge at Koele, ph 565 7300 - Hawaiian cuisine - expensive.

Ihilani, Manele Bay Hotel, ph 565 7700 - French cuisine - open for dinner - expensive.

Dining Room, Lodge at Koele, ph 565 7300 - French and Asian cuisine - open for dinner - expensive.

Hotel Lanai, 828 Lanai Avenue, ph 565 7211 - American cuisine - breakfast, lunch and dinner - inexpensive.

Blue Ginger Cafe, 409 7th Avenue, ph 565 6363 - hamburgers/pizzas - open for breakfast and lunch - budget.

Shopping

Richard's Shopping Centre, 434 8th Avenue, ph 565 6047.

International Food and Clothing Center, 833 Ilima Avenue, ph 565 7\6433, and *Pine Isle Market*, 356 8th Avenue, ph 565 6488, will be able to supply you with souvenirs and anything you have forgotten in the way of food or toiletries, but not much else.

Sightseeing

One thing to remember when you set out for a trip is that this is a very dry island. The rainfall is only 1066mm (42 ins) a year in the central plain, and the water on the trails is not drinkable, so make sure you take bottled water with you.

Lanai City

City by name, but really a plantation town built by Dole to house immigrant labour. It could never be described as a picturesque village, but it is where all roads on the island lead from (or to). The town is situated on a level plateau 488m (1600 ft) above sea level, below the slope of Lanaihale Mountain (1027m - 3370 ft).

Route 44 travels north from Lanai City through arid country, with scrub growth and red soil, but with sweeping views of Maui and Molokai.

North-east Area

Shipwreck Beach

The strong trade winds between Maui and Molokai have driven many ships onto Lanai's reefs, and the wreck on the beach is a World War II Liberty Ship. There are no facilities on the beach, but swimming is protected by the reef 200m off shore. To get to the beach take a left turn off Route 44 just before the tar ends, and follow this past squatters' shacks.

There are ancient petroglyphs of simple island scenes at the end of the track, and if you are interested, it is possible to hike from here to Polihua Beach along the shoreline.

Keomuku

Situated on the north-east shore, Keomuku is a ghost town 29km (18 miles) from Lanai City. The town was deserted when the Maunalei Sugar Company failed in 1901. The Kahea Heiau is 2.4km (1.5 miles) further on. It appears that stones from this temple were used in the construction of the sugar plantation, and the Hawaiians were convinced this was the reason for the sugar company's collapse.

The Munro Trail

The Trail, which it must be said is only for the adventurous, begins in Koele off Route 44, about 1.6km (1 mile) north of Lanai City. It is named after George Munro, the New Zealand naturalist, and follows an 11km (7 miles) jeep trail to Lanaihale (1027m - 3370 ft), the highest point on Lanai, from where there are views of every Hawaiian island except Kauai.

Hookio Gulch is roughly 3km (2 miles) up the trail, and the ridge beyond is scarred with notches made in 1778 by defending warriors in a futile attempt to defend Lanai against invaders from the Big

Island. Close by, a path leads to a lookout over Hauola Gulch, the deepest canyon on Lanai (610m - 2000 ft). The return journey from Lanaihale is either by a descent to Hoike Road, linking up with Route 441, or by retracing the outward route.

South-east Area

Luahiwa Petroglyphs

These are not easy to find, but as they are probably the finest rock carvings in Hawaii, they are worth the trouble. They are about 2km (1 mile) from Lanai City off Route 411, through a pineapple field and up a steep cliff, so as you can see it's better to get explicit directions from your hotel.

The clusters of rocks are like a picture gallery, and tell interesting tales of the ancient islanders.

Manele Bay

A small boat harbour containing ruins of old Hawaiian houses, and a park for picnics. There are usually a few sailboats in the bay, and plenty of people around. It is also possible to get a good view of Haleakala on Maui.

Hulopoe Beach

The best beach on Lanai, with a picnic area, showers, rest-rooms, camping facilities, and great swimming, surfing and snorkelling. It's about 13km (8 miles) from Lanai City.

South-west Area

Kaumalapau Harbour

Route 44 from Lanai City to Kaumalapau Harbour has the most traffic of any road on the island, for it is from this harbour that the pineapples are shipped to Honolulu.

Kaunolu Village

A national landmark, the area was a favourite summer residence of Kamehameha the Great, and his house, which was on the eastern ridge, had views of Halulu Heiau on the opposite side of Kaunolu Bay. This is regarded as the most complete archaeological site in Hawaii, and still has ruins of over 80 houses, stone shelters and graves.

Kahekili's Leap

Quite close to the village is the point from where Kamehameha's warriors tested their strength and courage by diving over 18m (60 ft) to the 4m (12 ft) deep water below, avoiding a 4.5m (15 ft) ledge on the way down. Those who survived were considered fit to be soldiers of such a great king.

North-west Area

Garden of the Gods

On the Awalua Highway, 11km (7 miles) from Lanai City, is the site of unusual lava formations and boulders which change colour at different times of the day. They look as if they have been placed there by a powerful deity.

Although this is one of the most visited sites on the island, it is still hard to find. Make sure you get directions from your hotel.

Tours

Lanai City Service, PO Box N, Lanai City, ph 565 7227, offers tours in 14-seat vans.

Oshiro Tour & U-Drive, PO Box 516, Lanai City, ph 565 6952, has guided tours ranging from 2 to 4 hours, for a minimum of 2 people.

Sport and Recreation

Golf

The Experience at Koele. Greg Norman designed this 18-hole par 72 course, the only one in Hawaii with Bent grass greens - open 8am-6pm - $150 non-guests, $100 guests.

Tennis

Manele Bay Hotel and the *Lodge at Koele* each have 3 tennis courts.

Horse Riding

Lodge at Koele, PO Box 774, Lanai City, ph 565 4561, offers guided trail rides on Lanai through pastureland and ironwood forest, with scenic views.

Hunting

The season for axis deer is from March to May and a licence is required, ph 548 8850.

Niihau

Niihau, the Forbidden Isle, is 27km (17 miles) west of Kauai, and has an area of 186 sq km (72 sq miles). It might just as well be thousands of miles away, because it is privately owned, and until recently visitors were not encouraged. Now the Niihau Ranch has helicopter tours to the island with stops at two remote beaches away from the main town, so are they really worth the effort?

Niihau had its first taste of the western world in 1778, when Captain Cook was anchored off Kauai and his boats were blown over to the shores of Niihau. When he went over to retrieve them he bartered some goats, pigs and seeds for salt and vegetables, and so introduced some western animals to the island.

Kamehameha I took control of Kauai in 1810, and Niihau was part of the package. He apparently didn't think much of it because he sold it to Mrs Elizabeth Sinclair, a Scottish widow from New Zealand, for $10,000. Now the island is owned by her great-great-grandsons, Bruce and Keith Robinson.

Niihau has its own dialect of Hawaiian, which is the main language, with English being taught as a second language in the school. There is no police force, no cinemas, no telephones, no hospital, no doctor or dentist, no electricity, no water system, and no alcohol. In fact, life is much as it was in the early 1900s, and the islanders want it to stay that way, so in the 1959 vote on Hawaii's statehood, Niihau was the only district to vote against it.

The Robinson Ranch raises cattle and sheep, the sheep coming from the herd that Mrs Sinclair originally brought to the island. They also keep bees, which is proving a money-spinner, producing about 27,2167kg (60,000 lbs) per year of kiawe blossom honey. Then there is the Niihau Sunset Brand Charcoal which is also proving a success, with half of its output being shipped to Mainland USA. But with the short, wet winters and long hot summers, the Robinson family is always facing one challenge or another to keep their tiny island solvent, hence the helicopter tours.

About the only thing Niihau is known for, apart from its isolation from the outside world, is its shell jewellery.

Niihau shells are found on the other islands, but not in such large numbers, and every day people sift the sands and sort out the burgundy, brown, blue and speckled shells. Leis made from these shells have been known to fetch thousands of dollars.

Residents of the island are free to leave, to further their education or whatever, but the majority return.

How to Get There

Niihau Helicopters, Box 370, Makaweli, ph 335 3500 - 4 flights per day - 3 hour tour with 2 landings - $200 per person.

Index to Maps

Index

General

Places & Attractions